# Wild and Free

Kristen Ashley

First ebook edition: December 29, 2014
First print edition: April 26, 2016

ISBN-10: 0692703233
ISBN-13: 9780692703236

Discover other titles by Kristen Ashley at:
www.kristenashley.net

Commune with Kristen at:
www.facebook.com/kristenashleybooks
Twitter: @KristenAshley68
Instagram: KristenAshleyBooks
Pinterest: kashley0155

# Prologue
# Mine

*Delilah*

Oh my God, they were hunting me.

*Hunting me!*

I ran, my breath ragged, a stitch cutting agony through my side as I heard them getting closer. Closer.

Fast.

Too fast.

I was a girl and maybe not Jackie Joyner-Kersee, but I wasn't out of shape. They'd gain but not that fast.

No way.

That didn't mean they weren't gaining that fast.

They were.

And I was terrified.

I turned into an alley, hoping in the darkness to lose them, and ran with everything I had left.

Straight to a dead end.

"Shit," I breathed, panting, turning, feeling them closing in on me.

Then there they were, on me as in *on me*. In the blink of an eye I was on my back, one of them pinning my body down with his on mine, one holding my arms down over my head, one holding my legs at my ankles while, I stared to the side in disbelief, two humongous, terrifying *dogs* circled, snarling and snapping their sharp, alarming teeth in my direction.

"Rip her throat out and have done with it," a voice coming from over my head bit out, and my attention went back to the enormous man who was lying full on top of me, pressing the breath out of me, and staring down at me in a way I did...not...*like*.

I tried to struggle, but the hands at my wrists and ankles held so strong, it was preternatural how strong they were. I wasn't pinned. I was completely immobilized.

"In a minute," he grunted, his eyes not leaving mine. "Christ, smell her. Divine. Fuck me, absolutely fucking divine." His face changed to a look I liked even less and he finished, "First I'm going to feed."

He was going to feed?

Oh man. What did *that* mean?

I didn't know. What I knew was, it was not good.

"Are you insane?" a voice coming from my feet asked like he thought the dude holding me was, indeed, insane. In fact, *very* insane. At the same time, ugly-scary growls came from both of the dogs.

It seemed to me these were warnings, but the guy on top of me was apparently insane because he ignored the warnings of the huge, vicious, snarling dogs. His head dipped toward me, slanted, then his mouth was at my neck.

Oh shit. Oh *shit*!

This was *definitely* not good.

I belatedly opened my mouth to scream.

Not that first sound came out because suddenly I wasn't immobilized. Nothing was on me, nothing holding me down.

I still didn't move.

This was because something I couldn't see, and not only because it was dark, but because it was happening so...damned...*fast*, was whirling around me.

I would know what that was when sickening, warm gushes of blood spurted across my chest and neck about a half a second before I saw a canine head (with no body, mind) roll across the asphalt in front of me. More blood splashed the pavement beside me in a hideous surge and I heard the heinous noises of body after lifeless body thudding to the ground.

Then I was up, my own body swinging like it was flying through the air, but I felt hands on me. A breeze was blowing through my hair, I was moving so fast, and then my back slammed against the brick wall of the building at the side of the alley.

I blinked, not feeling the wall at my back but the intense hard-muscled warmth of a body pressed to my front and before my eyes. A man.

A shock of black hair.

An intriguingly tilted set of eyes, the hue I couldn't make out in the dark, but shockingly, I could see one was a color that was light, the other a color that was definitely dark.

Strong jutting jaw, sharp cheekbones, heavy brow.

The slash of an angry scar that went across his forehead, through his left eyebrow, disconnected then rejoined on his cheekbone to slide all the way down his face, curling around his jaw and disappearing.

I panted in his blood-stained face.

He stared, intense and frightening, into mine, his gaze, honest to *God,* like a touch.

I stopped panting because I stopped breathing.

His face came closer and my stomach clenched, my muscles tensed near to snapping, my chest burned, but his head veered and he touched his temple to mine, slid it back, rubbing it through my hair.

I sucked in breath only to hold it again when his hands left my armpits. One traveled down my side and then curved to become an arm around my back, holding me so strong, I was plastered to his front. The other went up, over my shoulder and in to curl tight and freakishly warm around the side of my neck.

His chin dipped and I felt his lips at my ear.

*"Mine,"* he growled in a deep, guttural, forceful way that even I, who had no clue what was happening, I just knew I didn't like it one...single...bit, agreed.

When he said "mine," he meant *me*.

Uh-oh.

# I
# It's Only Just Begun

*Delilah*

He tossed me on the bed.

I bounced, staring at him as he prowled away from me and across the room.

I should have fought. I should have tried to run. I should have done anything but let him take my hand and drag me to his bike.

I didn't.

When we got there, he didn't let me go even as he swung astride it. Then he pulled me on *in front of him,* started up the bike, and we took off.

My dad was a biker. I'd been on a bike so often, if I had a nickel for each time, I'd be a millionaire. Hell, I even had my motorcycle license and my own bike at home in Dad's garage.

But I'd never ridden up front while someone else was driving.

If I didn't struggle and run when he took me to his bike, I should have done it when he stopped us in another alley, this one dark, dank, and not smelling all that great, located behind a Chinese restaurant.

And if I hadn't done it then, I should have done it when he shoved a big Dumpster out of the way like it weighed no more than a shoebox, lifted the grate under it, and dragged me down a flight of stairs into a dark hall, to a steel door, and through, to this room.

No one lived in a scary basement room off an alley under a Dumpster.

At least no one I wanted to know.

Vaguely, as I sat on that bed, it came to me that I hurt. My shoulders had scraped against the pavement when that guy took me down. But I ignored the ping of pain, seeing as I was clearly *In Trouble*, capitalized in a way that shit should be in neon. Blinking neon. In huge letters.

My mother's voice all of a sudden came into my head. "You're nuts. You've always been nuts."

This is what she'd said when I'd told her what I was doing during my vacation days.

She believed this and I knew she did because she said it to me more than once, starting from when I was about four.

It was safe to say I wasn't real tight with my mother.

"My little girl goin' on a quest," Dad had said when I'd told him. He'd also had a big grin of pride and approval on his face and he'd given me a tender cuff up the side of my head. "Good for you, Lilah. 'Bout time you took off and found what you needed to fill that hole in your gut."

Dad understood.

Dad always understood.

I didn't.

And now I understood it less.

My mind came back into the room when the guy walked toward me carrying some material in his hand. When he did, I couldn't believe I'd let my mind wander.

I watched him warily as he moved.

He was tall. Tall and lean. His shoulders were broad, his hips narrow, his legs long.

He had bulk, but it was spare. Regardless, even if I hadn't experienced what I'd experienced not thirty minutes ago, one look at him and you knew he had power. That scar. The way he held himself. The economical way he moved. He was not a guy who went to the gym to hone his body because he was into fitness or wanted attention. He was a guy who, if he went to the gym rather than drinking raw eggs and doing one-armed pushups on the asphalt of the alley where he'd parked his bike, he did it as a statement that no one should mess with him, because if they did, he'd fuck them up.

He had that scar and it was nasty.

But I'd put money down that the other guy got worse.

"Shower," he grunted as he tossed the material on the bed beside me and I continued to stare at him. "You reek of them."

"I...uh," was the only thing I could get out, seeing as there was *no way in hell* I was going to shower in this weird basement room with a guy in attendance who I did not know, who also terrified me.

And this was saying something, considering I was covered in blood and I'd never wanted a shower more in my life.

"Now," he growled.

"Who are you?" I whispered.

He didn't reply.

It was then I saw his eyes, and in the light of the room I could make out the colors.

One was a startling light blue. The other was a deep, rich brown.

I'd never seen eyes like that. Not in my life.

They were enthralling.

"*What* are you?" I asked, still in a whisper, this one breathless.

"Shower," he repeated.

I blinked, pulled myself together, and leaned a bit back. Even though he wasn't close, just standing beside the bed, that was close enough. "I want you to let me go."

"Case you hadn't noticed, not safe for you out there."

Uh.

What?

"I was…they were—" I began on a stammer, wanting to believe they were just bad guys out to do bad things and I'd gotten in their sights, but knowing in my gut it was something different.

Very different.

*Freaky* different.

"Hunting you," he finished for me.

How'd he know that?

"They were just—" I tried again but cut myself off this time when he leaned slightly toward me.

"*Hunting you,*" he bit out.

"That's what it felt like," I said quietly.

"'Cause that's what it was," he replied, straightening.

"Why?"

He lifted his shoulders in a shrug. "No fuckin' clue."

"You…you," I scooted back several inches on the bed, "just killed three men and two dogs."

He shook his head. "Not dogs. Wolves."

*What?*

"Wolves?" I asked, my voice pitched high. "What are wolves doing in a city?"

"Hunting you," he replied, losing patience. I heard it in his tone, saw it in his face, even in the lines of his body, and actually felt it in the room. "Now shower."

"You killed them," I reiterated.

"I did," he agreed nonchalantly, like he did that crap every day.

And he could.

He probably did.

Yes, neon, blinking, huge letters *In Trouble.*

"Why did you do that?" I pushed. "*How* did you do that? There was only one of you and five of them."

"Jesus, you need to shower," he clipped.

"I'm not going to shower!" I cried. The terrifying insanity of the situation finally crashing down on me, I lost it—justifiably, to my way of thinking. "You just killed three men and two wolves!

You're covered in blood. *I'm* covered in blood and in a crazy basement room under a Dumpster where I do...not...want...*to be*!"

"Would you rather be dead?" he returned.

"No," I snapped, then went on sarcastically, "but, you know, phoning the police rather than ripping five beings apart might have been a better option."

"Yeah, good idea," he retorted, matching my sarcasm. "I call the cops, they come in, and then those boys in blue are all dead because those things, they were not gonna stop until they took you out. They'd destroy anything that got in the way of them doin' that. You want that on your conscience? Because I sure as fuck don't."

"Cops have guns," I pointed out.

"And those things can take a bullet to the heart and survive it."

Was he insane?

"That's crazy," I scoffed.

Suddenly, his face was an inch from mine.

But he didn't move.

Or I didn't see him move.

Even so, there he was.

*Right* there.

I sucked in a breath.

He spoke.

"You need to take a breath. That doesn't work, you need to take another one. Then you need to feel it. *Feel it.* And you know *exactly* what I'm talkin' about. When you feel it, you'll know this shit isn't crazy. This shit is something else. I don't know what the fuck it is. I just know you're not gonna get dead because of it, seein' as I've waited three lifetimes for you, and now that I've got you, I'm keepin' you."

I stared into his eyes, unblinking, not speaking, my heart racing, his words freaking...me...*out*.

"I'm gonna go," he finished. "You shower. I want their stench gone by the time I get back."

Then he did just that. He went, pulling the big steel door open like it was made of flimsy plywood and slamming it behind him.

I stared at the door.

*I've waited three lifetimes for you.*

What did that mean?

*I'm keepin' you.*

I knew what that meant and I didn't like it one bit.

Then it hit me that I was sitting on an unmade bed in the basement room occupied by a crazy, murderous man who could move as fast as lightning and tear apart humans and animals in the blink of an eye.

That was when I burst from the bed and ran to the door.

I pulled on it, putting all my weight into it, but it didn't budge.

"Shit," I hissed and tried again.

No go.

"*Goddamn it!*" I yelled and whirled, taking in the room.

It was not small, not large. It had cement floors. Down one wall, in the far corner, I could see a shower cordoned off by glass block. No shower curtain. Next to that, a swaybacked, claw-foot tub, which, if I wasn't in my current circumstances, I would have thought was pretty cool. On either side of that, against the wall, narrow wire shelves holding towels and toiletries, not many of either, most of the shelves bare. A sink next to that, exposed piping under it, a utilitarian medicine cabinet over it. Next to that, glass block walls on both sides of a toilet. No door. No privacy. He either lived alone or his company didn't mind sharing a variety of intimacies.

I turned and saw stacked milk crates lining another wall, most of them with the openings pointed out, the top ones with the openings facing the ceiling. Jeans, sweaters, tees, boots, running shoes, henleys, thermals, all stuffed into the ones on their sides, a passing try at folding them—a poor passing try. Belts, socks, underwear shoved into the ones on top.

I looked across the way and saw a small kitchenette against the wall opposite the bathroom area. Not much counter space and what there was was taken up with a coffeemaker, a toaster, a microwave, and a dish drainer. Clean dishes in the drainer. Shelves over the sink with food and a variety of mismatched tableware. An old, bulbous-fronted, white fridge to one side, a narrow stove to the other.

Beyond that, two wooden hutches, their front door handles linked with chain and locked with padlocks. Secrets behind those doors, and in my current situation, I wasn't a big fan of secrets.

On the opposite wall to the milk crates, the bed I was on, shoved against the wall. Iron. Old. Unattractive. Though, the mattresses were good. The sheets light blue. The comforter rust colored. Lots of pillows. A standing lamp at the headboard, a nightstand beside it.

By the kitchenette, an ugly, old, round metal table with three chairs, none of them matching.

Rounding this out, a comfortable-looking-but-nevertheless-ratty armchair, a small round table beside it, a standing lamp next to the table, and sitting dead center in the room, the lamp's plug attached to an extension cord that snaked to the wall. A trip hazard if there ever was one.

But whatever. I wasn't going to be around long enough to trip.

I scanned the space and noted there were no rock concert posters on the walls. No calendars depicting Camaros or scantily-clad babes draped over Porsches. No racks filled with weapons. No insane manifestos written in precise, tiny handwriting on every inch of wall. All of this how I would guess that guy would decorate.

There also weren't any books. No stereo. No CDs. Not even a TV.

But there were two long, narrow garden-level windows, bars on the inside, blacked out.

If I was correct, these windows faced the street.

It was late; it had to be after one in the morning.

But I had to try.

I ran to the kitchenette, heaved myself up to my knees on the counter, and reached to the window.

I tried to find a latch to open it, but there wasn't one. I looked to the other and saw it didn't have one either.

Foiled again!

Not giving up, I commenced pounding on it and shouting, "*Help! Help! I'm held captive in here! Basement room off the alley under the Dumpster! If you can hear me, please help me! Call the police! My name is Delilah Johnson! Help me! Please!*"

I kept pounding and shouting and heard nothing. I did this for a while, until my voice started to get scratchy and my hand began to hurt.

I kept doing it until I heard the door behind me start to scrape open.

I stopped pounding and shouting, jumped from the countertop, and frantically searched around me. I pulled open a drawer in one of the two cabinets on either side of the sink and grabbed a steak knife.

It wasn't much, but it was something.

I whirled toward the door and froze when I saw who was walking in.

A petite, elderly Chinese lady and, with her, a very not elderly, not petite, very good-looking Chinese guy.

The woman came to a halt four feet in. The guy closed the door and moved in, looking around.

Then he muttered, "Jeez, what is it with Abel? This place looks like a safe house for terrorists."

I couldn't agree more.

"And would it kill him to put a door on the toilet?" he carried on.

"Chen, quiet," the woman admonished.

He shut his mouth, stopped staring at the toilet area with amused disgust, and turned his gaze to me. His eyes dropped to the knife I held out in front of me. He grinned, settled in, and crossed his arms on his chest.

The woman took a step forward and I kept the knife where it was but moved it toward her an inch.

She stopped.

"I'm Jian-Li, niece, sister, mother to Abel," she announced bizarrely, then motioned to the guy behind her. "And this is my son, Chen, nephew, then brother to Abel."

Well wasn't that just brilliant? I had hoped with the Chinese guy's opening remarks that these two were sane and might help me escape.

But from her introductions, which made no sense, I was thinking not.

"And you are…?" she prompted.

"Wanting to leave," I replied. "Like, *right now*."

She tipped her head to the side and her lips curved up in a soft smile. "Abel came to us and shared you were distressed about this evening's events. He's asked me to come down and explain a few things to you, thinking perhaps you might find me a little less… *imposing*."

She was right.

But seeing as she was crazy, she was also wrong.

"And since Ma can't open the door, I'm here," the son put in. I looked to him and he was still grinning. "Another thing I don't get about our boy, why he has steel doors installed in every pit he occupies. It's whacked."

I blinked.

*Every pit he occupies?*

"Chen, your opinions are not needed at this juncture," the woman noted.

"Ma, look at her." He swung an arm out toward me. "She's freaked."

"I can see that, and if you'll be quiet, I'll do something about it," she shot back.

He again settled in with his arms on his chest, mumbling, "This oughta be good."

"Chen!" she snapped.

"Ma, no joke, what you're about to say is gonna freak her more," Chen retorted.

Excellent.

"Uh, if I could butt in here," I butted in there, "your *boy* kidnapped me after committing five serious felonies, so I'm not sure I can *get* more freaked."

I didn't know if it was a felony to kill a wolf with your bare hands, but if I were a lawmaker, it would be.

After I said this, something changed in the woman's face that made me brace, and considering I was already alert and ready for attack, this meant every muscle in my body strung tight.

"*QĐn ài de*," she said quietly. "Perhaps you should sit down."

"I don't want to sit down," I returned. "I want *to leave*."

"That cannot happen and I think you know why," she replied gently.

"All I know is," I retorted, "I'm in a basement room that *does* look like a safe house for terrorists. I'm here not of my own accord. I'm covered in blood. And I watched one guy murder three men and two wolves not an hour ago. I should be at a police station. I shouldn't be talking to two Chinese folks who seem nice, but who are somehow connected with *that man*, and *that man* scares the absolute *pants* off me."

"Abel would never hurt you," the woman stated.

"Maybe not," I replied, "but he has no problem hurting other people...like *a lot*. Like until they're *dead*."

"Those other people were vampires," she announced and I stared, feeling my mouth drop open. "And, of course, werewolves."

Slowly I closed my mouth and whispered, still staring at her, "Brilliant. Awesome. Fucking *fabulous*. You're crazier than he is."

"I know it's hard to believe, but she's telling the truth," Chen put in.

"Great, and you're crazy too," I muttered, turning my stare to him.

He grinned again, shook his head, and declared, "Abel will just have to transform in front of you."

Transform?

"What?" I asked.

"He's a werewolf too," Chen told me.

I blinked.

"And a vampire," Chen finished.

I said nothing.

They didn't either, both watching me, assessing my reaction.

Eventually, I gave it to them.

"You're both totally insane."

"We're not, we're—" the woman started but stopped when it happened to me.

She didn't miss it, but then again, it would've been impossible to miss. As the agony sliced through my innards, I sucked my cheeks in, lurched back, bent double, and dropped the knife so I could wrap my arms around my stomach in a futile effort to contain the pain.

"What is it?" Jian-Li asked the same time Chen asked, "Hey, you okay?"

My mouth filled with saliva and the pain twisted, taking me down to a knee.

Chen was close in a flash, kneeling next to me, hand to my back. "Hey, hey, hey," he crooned. "What's going on? Are you all right?"

My head jerked back. *It* did it. I didn't make it.

And then my mouth moved.

"He's in danger."

Chen swore under his breath.

"Where?" Jian-Li demanded, also now close.

"I don't know, I don't know, I don't know," I chanted, feeling the pain at the same time feeling a panic that was so extreme, it was nearly consuming. I reached out a hand and clasped it on Chen's biceps, curling it tight and yanking him to me even as I leaned his way. "We have to get to him."

"You'll guide me?" he asked.

"Yes," I answered.

"Let's go," he said, straightening and pulling me with him. We were both racing to the door when he called back to his mother. "Call Xun and Wei."

"Of course," she replied, her tone urgent, and we were out the door, up the stairs, and down the alley where he stopped me by a motorcycle.

The man they called Abel had a Harley Sportster.

Chen had a crotch rocket.

My father rode a Harley. My father had ridden a Harley since before I was born. My father got a job at thirteen and worked it, saving every penny to buy his first broken-down Harley at the age of fifteen. And my father would disown me if he knew I did what I did next, that being jumping right on behind Chen after he mounted it and turned the ignition.

I wrapped my arms around his flat stomach and leaned deep, lips to his ear. "Left out of the alley, right at the next street. Hurry!"

We shot out of the alley and Chen turned left, then right at the next street.

The wind whipping my hair, Chen wasting no time, impossibly, since I didn't know how I knew, I just knew that I knew, I said into his ear, "Right at the light."

We hit the light and slung low, our bodies straining to the heavens, our knees nearly grazing the blacktop as he took the turn at the light.

"Alley, alley, alley!" I cried when he'd made the turn and righted us and the bike, then, "Left!"

He took us left and I nearly flew off the back of the bike and over his head when he braked so fast, the rear wheel came off the tarmac.

I looked around him and got what made him stop so fast.

Abel was fighting three men. Three huge men.

Three huge men with *swords*.

"Okay, my night just officially went off the charts, batshit crazy," I breathed.

I nearly fell off the bike as Chen dismounted swiftly, a phone at his ear and him talking into it. "Alley behind Guzman's. *Hurry*."

I heard the loud clang when one of the guy's swords crashed against the long length of pipe Abel was using to defend himself. I looked that way as Chen dashed toward the fray.

Unarmed.

"*Chen!*" I shrieked.

And I shrieked this just as a huge wolf came flying out of the shadows.

It was heading toward Chen.

It didn't make it to him.

This was because Chen leaped incredibly high at the last second and grabbed hold of a pipe sticking straight out of the brick of the building. He did a loop-di-loop like he was a male gymnast on the horizontal bar, flew off, then fell, aiming and connecting a vicious kick into the wolf's jaw before he landed. The wolf let out a canine howl and scuttled back three feet.

Chen didn't waste even a second in recovery. Having landed in a deep squat with one leg out, both hands to the tarmac, he whirled in a flash to standing. Using his legs and clearly martial arts moves, he beat the wolf back with brutal kicks, even turning full around to get his momentum going, connecting, and the wolf flew to his side, cheek-first in the asphalt, and skidded away.

"Holy shitoly," I whispered.

"Chen!" Abel bellowed, still defending himself and scarily retreating under the onslaught of three swords. "Get her to safety!"

"Kinda busy here, brother," Chen replied, still kicking at the wolf.

*"Get her..."* Abel roared, rounding his pipe and connecting savagely up the side of one of his attacker's heads, blood flowing out in a spray. The man fell down on a knee with one hand to the ground. *"To safety!"*

It occurred to me I was standing there, staring at this lunacy, and not doing anything.

So I did something.

But that something was not running away.

No.

That something was looking around for a weapon so I could help.

I hadn't found anything when Abel thundered, *"Move!"*

Instinctively, I sensed he was talking to me and leaped out of the way, toward the wall of a building.

I did it in the nick of time. Two crotch rockets rounded into the alley and they did it fast.

And they did not stop.

One fell to its side, the rider rolling off, the motorcycle skidding uncontrollably, bowling over two of Abel's attackers.

The other one stopped on a rear-end-whipping-around brake. The guy on it pulled out one of the two swords crisscrossed in a scabbard at his back, whipped it around, and lopped off the third attacker's head, the one who was still knee to the ground.

I pressed into the wall.

The guy who did the skid was running toward Chen. He leaped, going high, hitch-kicking in the air like a long jumper, landed on top of the wolf, and started raining what could only be described as karate chops all over the wolf's head and neck as Chen kept kicking the beast.

I heard a grunt of effort and looked back to Abel and the other guy. The other guy had unsheathed his second sword and was whipping them around his body so fast I could hear the blades slicing through the air. This was good, considering one of Abel's attackers was flashing around him at inhuman speed, stopping, carving his sword toward his target only for it to glance off those whipping blades. Then he'd flash somewhere else and try again.

Through this, I saw that Abel somehow had the dead guy's sword, and when he got his opening, he drove it into the other guy's stomach. While the guy was bending over his injury, Abel let the sword go, lifted his hands to the guy's head, twisted, and tore it clean from his body.

Oh my *God.*

"This isn't happening," I whispered, pressing deeper into the wall.

*"Off!"* I heard on a growled roar. My eyes darted back to Chen and his friend with the wolf only to see the wolf mid-transformation, turning into a dark-headed, seriously built, naked, humongous *man.*

"No," I breathed. "*That* didn't happen."

Hand-to-hand combat commenced and I instantly saw how a martial arts champion could kick the ass of a heavyweight boxing champion because that shit was happening *right before my eyes.*

Another almighty roar came and I looked back to Abel to see him appear, then disappear, appear, then disappear, again and again as he flashed around the alley in a swordfight to the death with his last armed attacker.

I held my breath just as Abel disappeared and reappeared by his friend. The attacker appeared and started to aim his blow, but Abel's friend stuck the guy in the back with both of his swords, whereupon Abel instantly swung high and took off his head.

My ass dropped to my ankles.

I caught a blaze out of the side of my eye. I looked back to Chen and his friend and saw the man was back to wolf and he was racing out of the alley.

"*We need him!*" Abel bellowed.

"On it," Chen shouted, running toward his bike.

"Not you," Abel stated, stalking toward Chen, still carrying his bloody sword. "Xun and Wei go."

"My bike may be outta commission, brother," one of the other dudes stated.

Abel turned his head to the man. "Take Chen's."

"We're wasting time," the other, *other* dude pointed out on a rev of his crotch rocket.

Then he decided not to waste one second more and tore out of the alley after the wolf.

Xun, or Wei, ran to Chen's bike, hopped on, started it up, and turned it around in the narrow alley at freakadelic speed, zipping by me and, not joking even a little bit, flashing me a grin as he went.

I stared after him for a nanosecond before I was hauled up with a hand clamped on my upper arm.

"You brought her to danger?" Abel bit out toward Chen, manhandling me until I was in position for him to let my arm go, but he then locked his arm around me so my front was plastered to his side.

"She felt you were in danger and knew how to get to you," Chen explained.

I felt Abel's eyes on me. Slowly and cautiously, I tipped my head back.

Yep, he was looking at me.

"You felt I was in danger?" he asked in a calmer voice, and if I was myself, which I was *not*, I would have noted the incredulous vein that threaded his tone intermingled with one that was undeniably tender.

But I was not myself.

I was a quivering mess.

Therefore, as a response, I demanded, "Okay, priority one, find me a place where I can have a total mental collapse."

"We need—" he started.

*"Now!"* I screeched, my body calcifying, cutting him off.

He might be a murderous badass, but he was not a stupid one. I knew this to be true when he looked into the eyes of a hysterical woman and hesitated not a second longer before he let my shoulders go, grabbed my hand, and dragged me to his Sportster.

"Xun's bike and the weapons," he stated simply as we went, throwing his sword to the side.

"Gotcha," Chen replied.

He got on the Sportster, which was parked at the side of the alley.

Instead of running for the hills, for some lunatic reason, I got on behind him and away we went.

Again, I did not run or fight or even say a word when he took us back to the alley behind the Chinese restaurant. I continued to do none of these things as he got off the bike, grabbed my hand when I alighted, and he took me to the still-opened grate, down the stairs, and back to the basement room.

However, I did yank my hand from his and advanced swiftly into the room when we got there, whirling and demanding to know, "There are werewolves?"

He studied me closely but did it replying immediately. "Yes."

"Are you a werewolf?" I asked.

His answer came slower, his body tightening visibly as he took his time doing it, but he eventually said, "Yes."

"The ones whose heads you cut off," I stated, but it was a question.

"I don't know," he answered, and kept the impossible, unhinged, but apparently true information coming. "But they move like me and have my strength, though they can't transform. So my guess... vampires."

"So you're a vampire too."

Another hesitation before he stated, "Yes."

"That's impossible," I declared.

He opened his mouth, bared his teeth, and I jumped back a foot when two razor-sharp fangs snapped over his eyeteeth.

"Holy fuck," I whispered, my hand snaking up to curl around my throat.

The fangs retracted before he said, "Nothing to worry about. I've already fed."

"On," I gulped, "*blood*?"

He shook his head but said, "Yes, now—"

"*Human* blood?" I asked.

"Yes," he clipped and moved toward me. I moved back as he kept speaking. "Now—"

"You feed on human blood?" My voice was rising.

"Fuck," he hissed. He stopped moving toward me but went on talking, and he did it sharply. "Yeah. I do. I'm a werewolf vampire. I transform to wolf and I feed on human blood. The bitch I had earlier didn't feel a thing, got off while I was doin' it to her, just like they all do. I've had her before, though I 'spect, you in the picture, I won't have her again. And I didn't harm her."

"So that's not another one to add to your body count for the night?" I asked.

"Nope," he answered casually.

I felt my brows go up. "She got off on it?"

"Helped I was fuckin' her at the time, but yeah, she did. Bitch begs me to bite her. Seein' as I need the blood, it works for me."

More of what he said hit me.

"*Me* in the picture?"

"You might have missed it with all that's gone down, but told you straight up you were mine."

He did.

He did do that.

It was uh-oh before.

Now it's a big, steaming pile of smelly *uh-oh*.

I looked side to side, still backing up, now whispering, "This shit is crazy."

"It is. Absolutely," he agreed, and him doing that made me stop and look back at him. When I did, he continued, "Until tonight, I didn't know there were others like me. Obviously, there are. And obviously something's up, because I never saw another like me, not in all the years I've been on this earth. You hit town and they're everywhere."

"Me?"

"You."

"Why?"

"You felt I was in danger?"

I shook my head but admitted, "Yeah."

"Knife through the gut, pain so extreme you're sure you'll bleed out in a second?" he pushed.

Oh God, how did he know?

"Yeah," I whispered.

"Felt that too, earlier tonight, when those guys were chasing you. Never felt that before in my life. Knew exactly where you were and had no idea how I knew. Knew exactly what you were the minute I laid eyes on you. You calm down, take a breath like I told you to do, I figure you'll know it too."

I was taking no breath and trying to feel *anything*, so I shook my head. "I just want to get out of here. Get out of here and go home."

That not being home to my apartment, but home to my dad's compound.

Though, it wasn't a compound, exactly. But considering the amount of guns he owned, the tall fence he'd built around the place so "no motherfucking asshole can be in my business," and the land he had (because when he said he didn't want anyone in his business, he meant it), I teased him by calling it his compound.

I didn't know if he could protect me from vampires and werewolves.

I just knew he'd die trying. And he had enough ammo to make that fight last awhile.

"What's your name?" Abel asked.

I blinked out of my thoughts and focused on him.

"Please take me to my hotel room so I can—"

He interrupted me again, "After I set those vampires on fire, seein' as I'm not takin' any chances, that's where I went so I could get your shit. They were crawlin' all over it, got a whiff of me, came after me. That ended swords against pipe in an alley. So you aren't goin' to your hotel room."

Shit!

"How did you know which hotel I'm staying at?"

His gaze traveled over me, then back to my face. "You a biker bitch?"

This correct assumption did not prove he also had clairvoyant powers, just deductive ones. I was wearing a leather choker, feather earrings, leather wristlet on one arm, abundant silver bangles on the other wrist, a Harley tee, faded jeans, and motorcycle boots—my uniform when I wasn't at work (though, I didn't always wear feather earrings...or bangles).

And, incidentally, he was in much the same outfit. His jeans more beat up, his tee older, faded, and totally kickass, and obviously he wasn't wearing a choker, earrings, or bracelets. Though he did have a chain wallet attached to his belt and a number of rings on his fingers.

"I would use the term 'motorcycle aficionado,'" I snapped. "But yes."

"Bikers stay at one place in Serpentine Bay."

He was right. I'd been there before with my father. It was a biker mecca. Every biker worth being called a biker went to Serpentine Bay at least once before they died. Dad had taken me on my eighteenth birthday, but he'd been here five times.

And when in Serpentine Bay, bikers stayed at one of two places: the campgrounds north of town or the biker-friendly hotel on the water called The Chain, also north of town.

I gave up on that and asked, "What do they want with me?"

"What's your name?" he asked back.

I shook my head.

"Could do this all night, and will, you don't tell me your name," he warned.

"Lilah," I gave in. "Uh...Delilah Johnson."

He stared at me a second before he lifted a hand, ran it through his dark hair, and looked to the floor, muttering, "Terrific. I'm named after the brother who was murdered and you're named after the bitch who stole her man's strength and betrayed him to his enemies. Fuck." His eyes came back to mine and he dropped his hand. "We're screwed."

"I would never do that," I hissed.

"Good to know," he kept muttering.

Our conversation was *way* off target so I commenced in getting us back on track.

"Seriously, honestly, please listen to me." I leaned toward him. "I *want to leave.*"

Suddenly, I wasn't ten feet away from him.

Suddenly, I was pressed to the wall and held there by his body.

"Searchin'," he whispered, his different colored eyes burning into mine. "My whole life, searchin' for something, missing something, something I did not know. Until I found you. And my whole life is a long fuckin' life to be needing something I could not find."

A long fucking life?

He looked in his early thirties.

"So Delilah," he went on, "you aren't leavin'. You aren't getting your ass killed. You're stayin' right here where I can keep you safe. And the first thing you're doin' is takin' a goddamned shower so you stop reekin' like those fuckers who laid their hands on you and tried to take you from me before I even gave you our first kiss."

*Our first kiss?*

Yep.

A big, fat, steaming pile of *uh-oh.*

"You scare me," I shared.

"I'll stop doing that, you get used to me," he replied.

This was doubtful.

I lifted my hands out to the sides (the only place I could move them) and dropped them. "This whole thing terrifies me, everything about it, and there are lots of everything about it, including the fact you took seven lives *in one night* all *in front of me*."

"You said you didn't want to die. Do you want me to die?"

At his words, that pain sliced through me again, gutting me in a way I could not hold back my wince.

"Yeah," he whispered, his quiet word eradicating the pain like that simple piece of proof of him alive, breathing, and talking had that power. Something, by the way, that freaked my shit *way* out. "They wanted you dead," he continued. "They wanted *me* dead. But *they* got dead. And hopefully Wei and Xun will get that wolf so maybe we can get some answers. Now I need to get out there and help them so you need to take a shower, put on my tee, and get some rest, because whatever shit is happening, I know one thing...it's only just begun."

I stared up at him knowing I should do everything I could to get the hell away, get to my dad, my dad being the person who would make me safe in a way that was safe *for me*, just as I knew I wasn't going to do that.

I was going to take a shower, put on his tee, and try to get some rest.

Because I had a feeling he was not wrong.

And there was the not-so-insignificant part of the whole night where I knew he was in danger, reacted to it violently, and led Chen to him without knowing how I did it.

I'd come to Serpentine Bay on a quest and I had a feeling I'd found my Holy Grail.

It was just that my Grail was scary as shit.

"I need to call my dad," I said quietly.

He moved away three inches, reaching in his back jeans pocket and pulling out his phone.

He handed it to me.

I took it, tipping my head down to stare at it in my hand because this surprised me and made me feel a lot more protected and a whole lot less of a kidnap victim.

"It's after two in the morning," he stated, and I looked up at him.

"Right," I whispered.

"You call him, you're gonna freak him. You two close?"

"Very."

"Can he take care of himself?"

"Absolutely," I answered firmly.

"You want reinforcements." Although a statement, it was also a guess.

I nodded.

"I hear that," he said. "But I'll ask you to give me the rest of the night, see if the boys got that wolf, see if we can get anything out of him, this meaning you'll have more information to give your dad so he knows what he's getting into."

The idea of telling my father I'd hooked up with a werewolf vampire and was unexpectedly under attack during my vacation quest to Serpentine Bay was not one I relished.

The good part of this was that Dad would totally believe me. I knew that sounded screwy, but he would. He was just that kind of guy.

And he loved me that much.

The bad part of this was that Dad would totally lose his mind, rally his brothers, and ride on Serpentine Bay ready for a fight and willing to go down in order to take out any being, natural or supernatural, who was a threat to me.

"I'll wait until morning," I said.

"Good," he murmured. "You keep that phone. It's good you have one, just in case. I'll get Jian-Li's before I find the boys."

I nodded, though I did this ignoring his "just in case" comment.

"Where'd you leave your purse?" he asked.

"I, uh..." I thought about that evening's events, remembering I had my purse when I went to the bathroom in that bar. I also had it when I left the bathroom and saw the men at the mouth of the hall and instinctively knew they were after me (another thing that freaked me, and not just that they were after me, but that I knew with one look they were). I still had it when I turned the other way and ran out the back exit.

I threw it aside somewhere in my dash.

"It's somewhere between the Mad Helmet and where you found me," I told him.

He nodded. "I'll see if we can find it."

"Thanks," I said softly.

"Shower."

It was me nodding that time.

"Rest," he went on.

That would be impossible.

I nodded again anyway.

He held my gaze before he said, "You're safe, Delilah."

I took in a deep breath.

He watched me do it, looked back into my eyes, stepped away, then, in a blur, he was at the steel door, opening it.

He went through and didn't look back when he pulled the door closed behind him.

# 2
# Torture

*Abel*

Abel walked through the back door of the restaurant. He smelled her and looked left.

Jian-Li was sitting in her armchair in her office drinking tea, the standing lamp arched over the chair giving off soft light that barely cut the dark.

Waiting up for her sons.

Waiting up for him.

He turned that way, stopped in the door, and leaned against its frame.

"Everyone is safe?" she asked.

"So far," he answered quietly.

She took a moment to let that sink in.

"There are others," she said softly.

"Yeah," he confirmed.

She drew in breath through her nose, took a sip of tea, then stated, "And they're evil."

He felt his jaw get hard, but he made no reply.

He didn't need to. She knew what had happened to Delilah and she could guess where her sons were now.

"We knew this," she continued.

"Guess my instincts were right. Just took two hundred years for that shit to come about."

She nodded once and said, "Then it's good we're prepared."

Abel said nothing. They'd be talking about this, just not now. He had a wolf to hunt and, if he found him, hopefully successfully interrogate.

"We're prepared, Abel," she said again.

"Yeah," he replied but went no further with that. Instead, he told her, "Gave my phone to Delilah. Need to borrow yours."

Her brows went up. "Her name is Delilah?"

He nodded.

"That's lovely," she said.

It was. It was also apropos. She was a temptress.

But he knew that. He'd been dreaming of her for over a hundred years.

The reality was better.

Even stuck in his thoughts, Abel still saw it shift over Jian-Li's face and felt his stomach tighten when he did.

"You're full?" she asked.

"I am, sweetheart," he answered gently.

She took another sip of tea, but she did it knowing she couldn't hide behind that cup.

She knew the hole he had inside, a hole that had never been filled. He'd shared it with her, his Jian-Li—his baby girl, his sister—the last in six women of her line that grew to be his confidant.

She knew he was searching for something, knowing for years it was not there to find.

Until thirty years ago, when the empty feeling became something else. A clawing in his gut that got stronger and stronger, year after year, until it got to a point it couldn't be ignored. It took an extreme effort of will to live day to day without jumping on his bike and riding the roads until he found whatever it was that would make the pain stop.

That night, the pain had stopped.

And Abel knew that, forty-five years ago, Jian-Li would have given anything to be the one who filled that hole. From birth, she'd grown up with him in her life. She'd loved him since she knew what that feeling meant. He'd loved her since before she was born.

But she'd fallen in love with him when she was in her twenties.

She was not the one who would fill the hole, and he'd helped raise her and knew he'd watch her grow, turn beautiful, age, and die. He'd done that before, too often. So he couldn't give her that, even in the lesser way he might have been able to give it to her.

"I'm happy for you, Abel," she said.

He straightened from the jamb. "Jian-Li—"

She lifted a hand and waved it, interrupting him. "I had that."

He felt the squeeze in his chest. "I know."

"I wanted it from you, but that was long ago," she continued. "But you know I found it elsewhere. It's just that he wasn't long for this world." Her next words were said with her eyes still kind but sharp on him, communicating more than what she was saying. "It takes time, but you come to terms with the fact that you were blessed, having once had it at all."

She'd found a good man, Ming. He'd made her happy. He'd given her three strong, smart, loyal sons. He'd accepted all that was Abel into their family as Jian-Li's mother's husband had done, and her mother's husband before him, and the mother before that, all the way back to the first who had found him and raised him from a pup.

But Ming had died twenty years ago, leaving Jian-Li broken in a way no one could fix, the second time she'd had to experience that, the first being with Abel and living day to day knowing she'd never have him, until she met Ming.

It was the measure of the man, and of his wife, that their three sons stood by her side, strong and stalwart, living their lives but keeping the family together to make certain their mother never endured another painful break that wouldn't heal.

"I'm glad you have that now," she went on.

Abel captured her eyes and whispered, "You know I've always loved you. From the moment you were placed in my arms, *tian xin*, I've loved you. And you know, no matter how long I have on this earth, that will never die."

Her smile was sad when she replied, "I know. As you loved and mourned my mother. And my grandmother. I know, Abel."

It had to be said, sometimes immortality sucked. In fact, immortality pretty much always sucked. It was just that some times were worse than others.

This was one of those times.

"I need to go help the boys," he told her in order to move them both out of the sadness.

She nodded again. "My phone is on the desk."

He went that way, snagged it, and shoved it in his back pocket.

Then he walked to her, bent low, and slid his temple along hers. "Go to bed," he said in her ear. "I'll see you tomorrow."

He pulled away but not far, just enough to catch her gaze as she said, "I will. Be safe. Take care of my sons."

"Always."

She gave him another soft smile.

He lifted a finger and touched it to her chin. Her eyes went tender but forlorn. They always did these days when he touched her that way. When she was younger, a toddler, a little girl, a teen, they lit with pleasure.

But now, knowing she was lost to him, had always been lost to him, then Ming was lost to her, and now that Abel was finally found, the melancholy was difficult to behold.

Nevertheless, he couldn't stop himself from doing it. That was hers, but more, he knew from experience it made it worse to try and take it away.

"Rest well, *tian xin*," he murmured.

"I will."

He smiled into her eyes, straightened, and moved away.

He was at his bike in the alley when Xun and Wei rode in.

They stopped close to him and he saw they had no wolf.

When their engines died, Xun announced, "We lost him. We need you to track."

He swung astride his bike as he replied, "Let's go."

They started up their bikes again as Abel did the same and they took off, Abel leading.

So he could catch the scent, they went back to the alley where the fight had happened, but he stopped well short of it, Xun and Wei stopping behind him.

Cop cars with flashing lights were blocking the alley, yellow police tape cordoning it off. There was a flash, black SUV parked on the street close to the police vehicles as well as a black Porsche. There were also a meager number of onlookers, meager as it was late and this was a business district. And the fire Abel had lit to be certain the vampires were disposed of had been put out.

They had no other choice but to drive by so he could catch the scent.

Abel turned his head to his brothers, jerked up his chin, got two return gestures, then he gave his bike gas, gliding by the scene, Abel hoping that no one looked their way. The bloodstains on their dark clothes had dried and darkened, imperceptible in the night (unless you were vampire or wolf and could smell it), but he and his two brothers still had stains on their skin.

He looked down the alley as he went by, seeing two dark-haired, well-dressed men who were not cops standing on the sidewalk outside the alley.

One was speaking to a police officer.

The other was on his phone.

But his eyes followed Abel.

Abel smelled them both and knew they were what he'd learned from their scent that night.

Vampires.

Since they were, they would no doubt smell him.

And the blood he and his brothers had all over them.

Fuck.

He buried the urge to put on more gas until they were well away from the scene.

But he'd picked up the scent and followed it, straight to the bay. They made it there without cop cars chasing them or gaining any company. He didn't know what that meant, but he didn't trust it and he didn't let his guard down.

He stopped his bike in the deserted parking lot by the rocky beach, swung off, and moved over the rocks toward the water, feeling Xun and Wei following him.

He stopped at the edge where the gentle waves were lapping the shore, this also being where the scent died.

"Gone swimming?" Wei asked.

"Yep," Abel answered.

"So we lost him," Xun stated, frustration in his tone.

"Yep," Abel repeated, also feeling frustration along with the disquiet gnawing at his throat.

"You have any dreams, premonitions, or freaking anything about the shit that went down tonight?" Wei asked.

This was a pertinent question.

Abel dreamed. He did it every night and had done it for as long as he could remember.

They were vivid dreams, most of them recurring. The last hundred years the majority of them were about Delilah, fucking her, eating her, her blowing him, him feeding as he finger fucked or banged her to orgasm, wild, unrestrained, like he sensed she was, like he sensed was how she lived her life.

He'd also dreamed of her laughing, burying her face in his chest, her dark hair all around, her mirth vibrating through his skin, his flesh, straight into his heart. And he'd dreamed of her behind him on his bike, her tits pressed deep into his back, her hair flying around, whipping his face, her cheek resting on his shoulder blade. And of her sitting back, feet up on the table, ankles crossed, chopsticks in her hand, white carton held up before her, noodles dangling from her mouth as she grinned at him, his brothers, and Jian-Li.

And last, he'd dream of watching her die on a street somewhere he did not know, drained by vampires and then torn apart by wolves.

In his two hundred and five years, he'd never sensed or even smelled another being like him.

But he'd dreamed of them. Dreamed of the danger they represented. Dreamed of them harming his family. Dreamed of them taking Delilah. Dreamed of them ripping her throat out, just like what had nearly happened that night.

Now they were there.

"Nope," he answered.

"Great," Xun muttered.

He turned to his brothers, who were once like his sons, who would become his fathers, the never-ending cycle of life that ended in sorrow. A cycle that went on without relief. Would go on without relief, but now would include Delilah.

He would have her.

He would love her.

Then he would lose her.

*It takes time, but you come to terms with the fact that you were blessed, having once had it at all.*

He hoped like fuck Jian-Li was right.

"I need to get back to Delilah," he declared.

Xun's brows went up as did the corners of his lips. "Delilah?"

"Don't let her near a pair of scissors," Wei advised, eyes to Abel's overlong hair, lips also grinning.

"Her namesake was not the one who used the shears," Abel educated him.

Wei looked to his brother, mumbling, "Whatever."

Abel took in two men he'd watched grow in their mother's womb. He'd watched them learn to crawl, to walk, to speak. Men he'd started to train the minute they could coordinate their limbs. Men who showed him the blind devotion they showed their mother, tonight not the first time they'd demonstrated it, though it was the first time their lives were in peril when they did.

And he knew his next play.

He'd already known it. He'd known it for decades.

He'd never liked it.

But now that it was upon him, he fucking detested it.

"There were vampires at the scene with the cops," he told them.

"Fantastic," Xun said through a sigh.

"Tell Chen and sleep with an eye open," Abel ordered.

He got nods before they turned back to their bikes, mounted them, and headed back to the city. But instead of going straight home, Abel led them to where he'd first picked up Delilah's scent outside the Mad Helmet.

He followed her fading scent, along with the now-dead creatures that had hunted her, and pulled over when he saw it on the sidewalk by some trash cans. Xun and Wei stopped with him and waited as he climbed off his bike, walked to the purse, and retrieved it.

He swung the long strap of the black suede bag, with its minimal studs and maximum fringe, over his head, smiling for the first time that night.

Delilah Johnson.

Total biker bitch.

Seeing as he bought his first Harley in 1922 and had never been without one since, he was getting the impression Delilah Johnson was made for him.

He swung his leg over his bike, ignoring the grins he was getting from his brothers, and headed them toward home.

They all parked in the alley, Wei moving directly to the back door of the restaurant where he'd find the stairs and go to the apartment above, where his mother lived.

His brothers all lived elsewhere. Tonight, they'd see to their mother.

And Abel.

Xun followed Abel to the grate.

Abel stopped and turned to him. "That bitch you're bangin' who works at The Chain?"

Xun nodded.

"Need you to connect with her. See if she can get into Delilah's room, pack up her shit, and get it out, all without anyone who might be watching noticing. The maid's cart or something. She needs incentive to do it right, there's five hundred dollars in it for her."

Xun smiled. "Probably she'd take a different incentive."

Abel shook his head before replying, "Then give her that. I really don't give a fuck what you give her. Just get Delilah's shit. Last name's Johnson. The sooner she gets it, the happier I'll be."

"I'm on it."

Abel lifted his hand and Xun clasped it, they thumped forearms and disconnected.

Abel moved to the stairs and descended them. When his head cleared the top, Xun dropped the grate and rolled the Dumpster over it.

Chen gave him shit for the precautions he took, city after city, everywhere they moved, doing it frequently so no one would notice the family getting older but Abel not.

But Chen didn't have his dreams.

And probably, after that night, Chen's shit about what he called Abel's "dungeons" would end.

He walked to the door, pulled it open, and moved into his room.

The light by the chair was shining, the rest of the space dark.

The first thing he did was move with human speed to the pile of her clothes on the floor by the bed. He moved slowly because he wanted to be quiet and not cause a breeze or give Delilah anything to sense that might wake her.

He didn't look at her as he gathered them up, went back to the door, opened it, and tossed them out. He stood in its frame, taking off his own bloodstained clothes and boots and tossing them out with Delilah's.

He closed the door, closing away the scent that gave him the near-irresistible urge to become wolf or bare his fangs and sink them into something with no intent to feed.

That done, he went to the table and dumped her purse there. Then he moved to the sink and quietly cleaned the rest of the blood from his skin, going back to the door to toss the bloodstained washcloth with the clothes.

Back inside, behind closed doors, he put on another tee and jeans and moved again to the bed.

He stood beside it, looking down at Delilah Johnson.

She was asleep on her side, hair still wet and spread across the pillow. One hand under her cheek, cheek in her palm. The other hand was curled into the covers, in her sleep, holding them tight to her chest as if protecting herself.

Her milky-green eyes, with their fans of dark lashes, were closed, but even in the dark, with his preternatural vision, he could see the rose in her cheeks against the flawless pale of her skin.

She was wearing his tee. Wearing his tee against that pale skin, using it to cover her abundant tits, the swells of her generous hips, that round ass.

His cock started to harden.

A century of her in his dreams, he would have assumed, finally having her, it would be difficult to move slowly with her.

He would never have guessed that every moment in her presence where he couldn't take her mouth, thrust his cock in her cunt, would be torture.

One side of him—wolf, vampire, or possibly both—was urging him to connect with her, claim her, fuck her savagely and pour his seed inside her, then pull out and coat her with it. He could smell her laying there, sleeping. He could taste the wild tang of her he knew from his dreams. And he knew down to his balls that his cum and her juices mingled would be the most beautiful essence he'd ever smelled in his life—or ever would.

He needed it. His body demanded it. The animal in him strained to it just as the monster in him craved her blood on his tongue.

He moved to the armchair, folded into it, and reached out to turn off the light.

He straightened his legs in front of him, crossing them at the ankles. He rested his hands loosely on his upper thighs. He dropped his head to rest against the back of the chair.

And he forced his eyes to close.

# 3
# Cocky

*Delilah*

I was on my back in the leaves, the stars overhead, Abel's hands curved around my ribs, yanking me down, his face between my legs.

He was sucking, deep and hungry, at my clit.

*Glorious.*

He stopped and buried his tongue inside.

My lips parted and my back arched. His fingers tightened and he drove me down harder on his mouth.

*Yes.*

His mouth opened on my clit again, tongue lapping, then came the suction.

I dug my heels in his back, feeling it coming, knowing it was going to be sublime.

He stopped, surged over me, his tongue bathing my neck, his cock ramming inside.

I felt his teeth tear through, my blood surging into his mouth, and my climax was on me.

*"Abel, baby,"* I moaned.

"What?"

My eyes opened and I immediately blinked at the unknown pillowcase my head was resting on.

"What?"

The question came again. I looked beyond the pillowcase and saw him sitting back in the armchair, the light next to him on, his legs straight, ankles crossed, head up, eyes open and on me.

And it hit my foggy mind for the first time that he was beautiful, every lean, scarred, amazing inch of him.

"What?" I parroted sleepily.

He lifted up and forward, bending his knees and putting his elbows to them, his gaze never leaving me.

"You called my name," he told me.

"I did?" I asked.

"Yeah."

"I was asleep."

He studied me with a look in my still-hazy-with-sleep mind that seemed a mingling of intent, amused and pained.

But all he said was "Yeah."

I pushed up to a forearm, lifting my hand to pull the hair away from my face, watching him watch my hand do this and also seeing the pain intensify on his features.

Weird.

I dropped my hand and his eyes followed it before they moved back to my face.

When they did, I asked, "I was talking in my sleep?"

"You said, 'Abel, baby.'"

Oh shit.

His head tipped to the side. "Good dream?"

"I...I don't remember." And I didn't, for which I was glad, but also kinda not.

"Too bad," he muttered, pushing to his feet and moving toward the bathroom area.

I shifted up to a hand in the bed, pulling the covers to my chest as I did so even though I was in his shirt, which was way big on me and provided excellent coverage.

In this position, I watched him go to the medicine cabinet, open it, and take something out, then turn and walk back to me, all the while talking.

"Didn't get the wolf. Lost his scent at the bay. You talk to your dad this morning, got nothin' else to give him."

"That's not good news," I replied.

"No." He stopped by the bed and tossed something on it. My eyes went to it as he finished, "It's not."

But I was staring at the new toothbrush in its wrapping sitting on the bed, my mind blank of everything. Absolutely everything. Everything but that *fucking* toothbrush.

"Givin' you ten minutes," he stated.

My head snapped up, the talons suddenly gripping my throat from the inside strangling me as I watched him start to turn.

Thus I had to force out my "A new toothbrush?"

He stopped turning and looked back down at me.

"Yeah, unless you wanna use mine, which I prefer you didn't."

I snatched it up in a grip so tight, the plastic buckled in my palm.

"*A new toothbrush?*" I demanded, my voice vibrating with extreme pissed-offedness.

His expression cleared, but his attention increased as he slowly and cautiously said, "Uh...yeah."

It was then his words from the night before blasted through my head.

*Helped I was fuckin' her at the time, but yeah, she did. Bitch begs me to bite her. Seein' as I need the blood, it works for me.*

"You get a lot of company?" I asked in a way his only choice of answer was a firm, unwavering "Fuck no."

Unfortunately, he didn't answer that way.

I watched his body brace as I heard his lips say "Shit."

I threw the covers back and jumped out of bed, leaning toward him, shouting, "Wrong answer!"

"Delilah—"

I interrupted whatever he was going to say by raising my arm and throwing the toothbrush at him. It bounced off his chest and landed on the floor as I started yelling.

"You fed from someone you fucked and you did that *yesterday*! The day you met *me*!" He lifted his hands like he was going to touch me, so I threw one of mine out, batting his away, shouting, "Don't touch me!"

"I didn't know you yesterday," he pointed out.

"So?" I snapped.

"Take a breath, Delilah," he ordered.

"Fuck that," I retorted, then demanded, "Why do you have an extra toothbrush?"

"You don't want the answer to that," he answered.

"Ding, ding, ding!" I yelled. "Wrong answer again!" Then I kept going. "Did I sleep in a bed last night where you *fucked other women*?"

"It won't happen again," he stated.

Oh my God!

"Damn straight it won't!" I shot back loudly.

"Even if it's to my peril, I think it's pertinent to point out at this juncture that you're in a serious fucking jealous rage and I haven't even kissed you yet."

I snapped my mouth shut.

He watched me do this before he grinned.

My stomach flipped over.

Oh yeah, he was beautiful.

"You wake up in a bad mood all the time or just when you think of me bangin' another bitch?" he asked.

Needles pierced through my brain at his last four words, the pain so severe, I flinched and felt nausea roil up my throat.

"Hey," his voice came soft at me. Soft and close.

I opened my eyes and saw him in my space, his face dipped to mine.

"What's the matter with me?" I whispered, my recent uncontrollable and totally irrational behavior filtering through my conscious, freaking me out.

"You get you're mine?" he asked back instead of giving me an answer.

I was not ready to commit to that verbally so I just stared at him.

He let that go but kept talking.

"If you're mine, I'm yours. Not even gonna think of another man's hands on you, much less anything else." His jaw tensed even as he continued, talking mostly between his teeth. "Tear the room apart if I did."

"This is freakadelic, Abel, and not in the good way freakadelic can be."

His head twitched as his brows drew together.

"Freakadelic?" he asked.

I nodded once. "And not in a good way."

He shook his head, but his features softened, most specifically his mouth.

Oh man.

Definitely.

Unbelievably.

*Beautiful.*

Uh-oh.

"I'm here," he stated.

"I can see that," I replied.

"And you're here."

"That I am," I confirmed unnecessarily.

His face dipped closer. "We're together, Delilah, nothin' else matters."

At that, I pulled in a soft breath, and as I did, his eyes dropped to my mouth as if he could hear it even though it was silent.

They moved back to mine. "Now you got ten minutes. I get time today, I'll put up a curtain or somethin', give you some privacy while we're here. But until then, I'll give you the room."

After saying that, he turned, moved to the kitchen, flipped on the light switch that illuminated that space, then he went to the door and out of it, giving me the room.

It was then I realized he was talking about the bathroom area.

I bent to retrieve the toothbrush that caused my first-thing-in-the-morning psycho behavior and hurried to the bathroom area, not about to waste my opportunity for some privacy for my morning business.

I took care of it, including washing my hands, brushing my teeth, and splashing water on my face, before I turned to the room, still drying my face with a clean hand towel I'd grabbed from the shelves.

It was then I spied my purse and my body grew solid.

I stared at my purse over the hand towel I had pressed to my face as all the events of last night washed over me, every freaking whacked-out, impossible-but-they-still-happened one.

He'd saved my life. He might have saved me from getting raped, but he'd definitely saved my life.

He'd protected me, and of an instinct I didn't know I had, I did what I could to protect him.

We'd both nearly died last night, and the last thing I knew before showering and hitting the sack was that he was out with his friends hunting a fucking werewolf.

But before he came home, he found my purse.

*He found my purse.*

Something I hadn't noticed, even if I couldn't believe for an instant I didn't, came clear in that moment. It was so enormous, I dropped the towel and stumbled to the armchair, leaning a hand heavily into it, taking my weight in my arm, holding myself up, my eyes never leaving my purse.

It was gone.

"Holy shitoly, it's gone," I whispered.

I'd lived with it since I could remember. "It" being what my mother was convinced made me nuts. It convinced her enough to make me go see psychologists, three of them, all of them declaring

I was attention seeking and, due to that, had an eating disorder and needed long-term psychological care and medication.

I was of a healthy weight. I didn't starve myself, didn't binge, didn't purge. I also was a good kid. I could be sassy. I could get in trouble, but nothing bad.

I just constantly felt "it," but didn't know what "it" was.

When Mom tried to force therapy and drugs on me when I was eleven, Dad stepped in, doing the impossible—an antisocial, antiestablishment biker winning custody of his daughter.

It took him four years and three appeals, but he did it. And while he was doing it, he'd managed to put up court-ordered obstructions to Mom medicating me (but, alas, I was forced into therapy; however, this was an hour a week I didn't have to put up with my mother, and my therapist was an all right guy, so it didn't scar me).

"That hunger inside you, little girl, you'll quench it," Dad had told me when I'd shared it with him. The gnawing pain, the desperation to get it gone, the lifelong struggle to learn to live day to day with it, like someone with a chronic illness learning how to cope and live life even though the debilitating symptoms never went away. "You'll know it when you find it and I know my Lilah. You'll get it, fight for it, earn it, beg for it, but in the end, you'll win it and you'll be whole."

Dad had been wrong.

I hadn't known it when I found it.

Looking at my purse, I knew.

The pain was gone.

I'd found it.

My God, *I'd found it.*

Moving from the chair to the table, I snatched up my purse, digging inside even as I aimed my ass to a chair and collapsed into it.

I pulled out my phone, activated it, hit the buttons, and made the call.

I put it to my ear.

"Yo, little girl, how's tricks in the Promised Land?" Dad's gravelly, slightly sleepy (no doubt I woke him, he usually didn't get up before ten), two-pack-a-day voice came at me.

"Daddy," I whispered.

His tone was alert when he instantly responded, "Where are you? I'll be on my bike in five minutes. Do I need the boys?"

Tears gathered in my eyes and I sucked in breath to control them.

"It's gone," I told him.

"What?" he asked sharply.

"The pain."

He was silent.

I felt a tear slide down my cheek as I slid an arm around my belly, holding myself close, holding the fullness tight to me. "I'm whole, Daddy," I whispered.

"What's his name?" Dad asked gruffly.

I closed my eyes and another tear fell.

Dad so totally got it.

"Abel."

"Kickass name," Dad muttered.

I smiled and opened my eyes. "He's got a Sportster."

"I already like him."

I felt a giggle slide up my throat but swallowed it down.

"There's more," I told him.

"Fuck. The asshole's married, I'm gonna rip his dick off."

"He's not married."

Well, at least all indications pointed to that fact. That said, I knew absolutely nothing about Abel except he was a heretofore fictional creature walking the earth.

I decided not to share that with Dad just yet.

But I did share, "I...I actually kind of do think I need you to call the boys and come out."

His gruff was back to sharp when he asked, "Why?"

"Abel kind of saved my life last night."

"What the fuck?" he bit out, and I could actually feel his movement through his words, either getting out of his recliner, where he'd fallen asleep watching something badass on TV (or porn), or rolling out of bed, leaving one of his bitches in it if he'd had company.

It was usually option two. As much as Dad was antisocial (this didn't include "the boys"), he liked to get himself some enough that he'd put up with a woman, at least long enough for her to take care of his needs and make him breakfast before he got her ass out of his house.

At this point, I heard the door scraping open behind me and I looked that way.

Abel caught my eyes, and half a second later he was bending over me, his face an inch away.

"Why are you crying?" he demanded to know, then didn't wait for my answer. He ripped the phone out of my hand, straightened, put it to his ear, and clipped, "You made her cry." There was a pause before, "Yeah, I'm him." Another pause before his eyes dropped to me and he muttered, "Right. Didn't know. Just got in, saw tears on her face. Here she is."

He then offered the phone to me.

I took it, my lips parted, my gaze never leaving him, and put it to my ear.

When I did, Dad must have sensed it with Dad Perception for he declared, "Already fuckin' love that guy."

Abel moved toward the kitchen as I said, "I...well, that's good."

"Fucker handed off the phone before I could have a word. Give it back to him. Wanna know what's goin' down with you and want that from him."

"We don't actually know," I told him. "He and his buds went after one of the, uh...guys who got away, but they didn't get him. So we're at a loss."

"*He* went after him?" Dad asked.

"Yeah," I confirmed.

"No cops?"

Oh man.

"Dad—"

"He an outlaw like your old man?"

I didn't know for sure, but I had a feeling he was.

Or he'd turned into one last night, for certain.

"We'll just say that the proper authorities were not notified," I stated, then stared as I watched Abel come out from behind the door of the fridge with one thing in each hand.

The first was a packet of bacon.

The second was a plastic bag filled with blood.

I swallowed.

He tossed the bacon on the counter, opened the microwave, and shoved the bag of blood in.

*Gluk.*

Through this, Dad hooted.

Then he asked, "You okay?"

"Freaked out but healthy," I answered.

"Am I gonna lose my motherfucking mind at what happened to you?"

"It wasn't that bad, Dad. Or, at least, Abel stopped it before it could get that way."

"Thank fuck," he muttered, then louder, "You still at the Bay?"

"Yeah."

"Right. To gather the boys and be there, take at least two days. He got you covered for that?"

Abel was beeping buttons on the microwave as I said, "Yeah. He's pretty, um...*capable.*"

"Ha!" Dad snorted. "Good to know. But you tell him one beautiful, shiny hair on my little girl's head is fucked, I'll have his throat."

Dad was forty-eight years old and spent his time taking odd jobs that paid cash so he could avoid paying more taxes than he had to in order to keep his house and land. He drank. He caroused. He rode his bike. He got laid. He communed with his brethren. He frequently did things I never knew about because they'd scare me. And he loved me.

He also worked out. Sure, he sometimes lifted weights with a cigarette hanging out of his mouth, but he did it.

Abel could still tear him limb from limb.

"That won't be a problem. I haven't known him very long, but so far he's been pretty good at taking care of me."

Abel turned and aimed his eyes my way.

I felt the look in them in my nipples, at my clit, and curving around my heart.

When Dad spoke again, I tore my eyes away and looked at my lap.

"All right, precious girl, gotta kick Charlene's ass out, rally the boys, and get on the road. Hang tight. I'll call you tonight and let you know when to expect us tomorrow."

"Okay, Daddy."

"Love you, Lilah."

"Love you more."

"Love you most, baby."

He did.

I tried, I tried hard, but he definitely loved me most.

"'Bye."

"Later," he replied and I heard him hang up.

The microwave sounded and I looked that way.

"You drink bagged blood?" I asked.

Abel pulled out the bag and turned to me. "You gonna be squeamish?"

"I, um...well, probably."

I mean, it was *blood.*

"Can drink it in the hall," he offered.

"It's your house, Abel," I pointed out, though it wasn't a house so much as a room.

"Can drink it in the hall, Delilah," he repeated.

I didn't repeat like he did. Instead, I told him, "People I care about call me Lilah."

He gave me that look again that I felt at certain very good parts of me.

"Drink your blood," I said, wondering how on earth I was saying that in a serious way when it was total insanity. "I'll start the bacon."

I pushed up from the chair, avoiding looking at him and moving to the kitchenette.

I found a frying pan in the cupboard and I already knew where the knives were, so I nabbed one and sawed open the package.

I was laying the strips in when I felt him move, so I looked to the side and watched him use the toe of his boot to open a trash can I hadn't noticed on the other side of the oven. He dropped the empty bag in.

That didn't take long.

A shiver slid up my spine.

"Blue is blood, Lilah," he said quietly, and I focused again on him. "White is regular trash. Yeah?"

I leaned back and saw there were two trash bins, one blue, one white. I righted myself, pressed my lips together, and nodded.

He moved my way and stopped close, looking down at the skillet.

"More," he declared.

"What?" I asked.

He looked to me. "More bacon. You've only got four strips in there and I'll eat four at least."

I felt my brows shoot up. "You eat human food?"

He stared into my eyes, then reached to me, took the bacon out of my hand, and tugged more out, placing the strips in the pan, all while talking. "Right. Quick education. I day walk. Got no problem with the sun. Sleep at night, though I'm a night person, not a morning person, but that only means I like to sleep in and stay up late, not that I need the night. And when I sleep, I don't do it in a coffin."

"Okay," I said when he stopped, thinking all that was good news, the coffin part especially, because, well...*euw*.

He tossed the package on the counter and reached for the drawer by my hip. I slid out of the way as he opened it.

He grabbed a fork, closed the drawer, and looked at me.

"No problem with silver. No problem with holy water. No problem with garlic. Ditto crosses. Don't need to be invited into anyone's house. In fact, outside of needing blood to survive, nothin' you think you might know about vampires or werewolves is true. This includes me not transformin' to wolf at the full moon. I can do it whenever I want and never do it unless I want to. I also can't turn people. Not that I've tried, but as far as I know, I was born this way."

"As far as you know?" I asked as he started moving bacon around in the skillet, which was now sizzling.

"Was found in an alley. I was a pup. Had transformed, did it then whenever because I hadn't learned control. Woman who found me took me in, thinking I was a stray puppy or dumped. Told me later I freaked her shit when I turned into a toddler, though she didn't use those words."

At this exceedingly sad story, I felt my insides freeze even as my lips whispered, "Oh my God."

He stopped scooting bacon around and looked at me. "Yeah."

"What did she do?" I asked.

He shrugged. "She tried to find my folks, and when that failed, she raised me."

"Just like that?" I pressed.

"Don't know her thought process. She didn't share that with me. All I know is all I knew was her. Her love. Her kindness. Her understanding. Her protection. I have no memories of before her. She figured out all I was before I could form a coherent thought, seeing as I'd catch rats and suck them dry and try to latch on to her whenever I got the chance, baring my fangs. She brought me animals to keep me alive until I learned to do what I needed to do, and only then did she let me go out and find humans."

I could not believe I was hearing this.

But I was hearing it, and I had to admit, it was utterly fascinating and extraordinary even if it was tremendously sad.

I mean, what kind of person would take into their home and then raise a werewolf vampire?

No other answer to that except a *really* good one.

"Was she Jian-Li?" I asked.

Something profoundly sad moved over his features as he looked back down to the bacon saying, "No."

Okay, it was not the time to dig deeper with that.

"Learned to do what you needed to do?" I prompted as he flipped bacon.

He looked to me. "Teeth are sharp, Lilah. Fuck you up. Pain, and that pain is bad. But I got it in me to protect against that. Figured it out on a fluke. Somethin' happens if I lick the skin before I bite. Means no pain to who I'm drawin' from."

"Well, that's good," I muttered.

"Yeah." He grinned. "And I hesitate to wake the wildcat in you that tells her tale through your green eyes, but it's also bad. Somethin' happens in my mouth when I feed, so if I'm doin' something else at the same time, means I can numb things."

I was confused. "Numb things?"

"Numb..." He paused and leaned slightly into me. "*Things*. Things you don't want numbed say I take a break from drawing to do other shit with my mouth."

I felt my eyes get big as I whispered, "Oh."

"Yeah." His eyes went to my mouth. "Oh."

I swallowed.

He lifted his gaze to mine.

"I eat real food," he stated, kindly taking the conversation out of the hot zone. "I do not fly. Nothing like that. Don't turn into a bat, just a wolf. But as you know, I'm a fuckuva lot faster and stronger than your average man. I hear better, see better, smell better, all that shit."

"That's cool, you know," I told him softly, mostly because, it not being fresh and flipping me out, it absolutely was.

He was back to the bacon. "It's a burden and a boon."

I was again confused. "How is it a burden?"

He looked back to me and I held my breath at what was in his eyes.

"You live your whole life being different from everyone, Lilah, things can get shitty. They can also get ugly. People are assholes. The good ones are hard to find. There's no one who knows what I am except Jian-Li, Xun, Wei, Chen, and now you."

"But...what about the women you...well, *used to* feed from?"

His lips quirked at my emphasis on "used to" before he turned away and lifted a hand to grab a plate off the shelf. I lifted my own to grab the roll of paper towels and pulled some off to line the plate.

All this was done while he spoke.

He just didn't say enough.

"I take care of that."

I finished lining the plate and looked to him. "How?"

He flipped the bacon again, he just didn't speak.

Uh-oh.

"How, Abel?" I pressed.

I should have known it was coming when he turned off the burner.

Then again, I hadn't known him for even a day so I really couldn't have known.

But one thing I could say for him, he gave it to me straight.

"I can control minds."

I blinked, stared, then took a step away.

Only then did I breathe, "*What?*"

"I can control minds," he repeated.

"Oh my God."

"Don't do it to Jian-Li or my brothers. Never. And won't do it to you."

"But you can...you can...*glamor people*?"

His brows shot together. "What?"

"Glamor," I snapped. "Like, you know, on *True Blood*."

His jaw got tight before he relaxed it and replied, "Told you, Lilah, nothin' you think you know about vampires or werewolves is true."

"But you said you can control minds," I shot back, sounding like I was getting panicked, probably because I was.

"What's this thing from this show?"

That surprised me. "You haven't seen *True Blood*?"

"Fuck no."

"Why not?" I asked. "I mean, if I were you, I'd at least be curious."

"Lilah, focus. What's this thing you're talkin' about from this show?"

I nodded, took in a breath, and explained, "See, the vamps look into their vic...um...well, the person's eyes, kinda mesmerize them, and tell them what to think or say or do, or maybe tell them to forget something. Then they think or say or do that, or, you know," I threw out a hand, "forget it."

He looked unsettled when his gaze went back to the bacon and he muttered, "Fuck."

"Oh my God, you can do that," I whispered.

He looked back to me. "No and yes. I can do that, all of that, but I don't have to be lookin' in their eyes. Don't even have to be in the same room with them. Just gotta have laid eyes on them at one point, be able to remember what they look like, and I have to be relatively close. Then I can do it."

"Oh my God!" I cried, not knowing if this was awesome or terrifying. "How close do you have to be?"

"Within a block."

My mouth dropped open.

He looked to my mouth, then back to my eyes. "It will never happen with you," he stated.

I closed my mouth only to open it to ask, "Would I know if it did?"

There was a brief hesitation before his "Not really, no."

*Not really, no?*

I did not like that.

I took another step back.

He turned fully to me and his face got hard. "You have my word."

Suddenly, I glanced around frantically. "Could this...is all of this...?"

I snapped my mouth shut and took two more steps back.

"Fuck, Lilah," he bit out. "I did not control your mind to be here."

"Dude, this, all of it..." I waved both of my hands in the air. "It's super-sized weird."

"It's also real."

"How do I know that?"

"You trust me."

My voice pitched higher. "How do I do *that*?"

"What would you never do?" he asked suddenly.

"What?"

"What would you never do?"

I took another step back, fairly shouting, "I'm not going to tell you that!"

Then, suddenly, I started barking like a dog.

I got three barks out before I heard his voice in my head saying, *Stop.*

I stopped, lifted my hands, and clamped them over my mouth, retreating three more steps.

"That's what it feels like," he said carefully, moving slowly my way. "I had to do it once, just this once, so you'd know how it felt and you'd know what's happening right now isn't that."

I took my hands away from my mouth and said, "But I didn't feel anything."

I started barking like a dog again, two barks this time before his voice was again in my head, telling me to stop.

"Again?" he asked.

Was he sadistic?

"No!" I shouted.

Then barked.

Then stopped.

"Do you feel it, Lilah?"

I hit bed, stopped moving, and lifted my hand his way. "Stay away from me."

"Pay attention, close attention, to *everything*," he ordered.

"Please stay away from me," I whispered.

Then I barked.

And stopped.

But I heard it then. Felt it. His voice in my head, whispering what to do, and the barely perceptible frisson it sent along the back of my neck, both of these beginning and ending in less than a heartbeat.

He stopped two feet in front of me and spoke quietly. "The women I fed from, they know me, they remember me, they remember what we do together. They remember everything except me feeding. I free them from that block when it happens so they'll want it, ask for it, get into it, but I put that block back up when I'm done with them. When I was younger, I did shit all the time, stupid shit, and I'll admit, sometimes mean shit. But I learned from that. It can bite you in the ass and it isn't nearly as satisfying as you'd think it'd be, even if they deserve it."

He took a step closer.

I leaned back over the bed.

He stopped moving but kept at me.

"The stupid shit I did, the people I did it to, they didn't know why they were doing what they were doing, or that I did it to them. They knew it wasn't them, but they still did it. It was fucked what I made them do, but it was *more* fucked watching them react to doin' something they knew wasn't in them to do. The women, I erase my bite from their minds. They know they miss it, and when they get it back they think they forgot it, want it, have it, before I take it away again. They just don't know I'm the one doing it."

"Right, well, don't ever do *it* to me again," I hissed.

"You were freaking and needed to understand," he explained.

"You made me bark like a dog!" I shouted.

He lifted his hands in the air and flicked them out impatiently. "Delilah, serious as fuck, would I tell you I could control minds if I intended to control *your* mind?"

That made sense.

Which sucked.

"Don't get rational with me when you just made me bark like a dog," I snapped.

"I didn't harm you," he returned, dropping his hands.

"That doesn't matter."

"I'd *never* harm you."

My back shot straight at his tone, a tone that made the words he said burrow inside like they were writing themselves on my soul as a never-ending vow.

"You need to know me," he said, his voice gentling. "You need to understand what I am, what I can do, *who* I am. I'm giving that to you. I'm doing it honestly. Nothing held back. You need that. *We* need that."

He was right.

That sucked too.

"I think you might get all this is gonna take some getting used to," I noted in my defense.

"Yeah, I get that," he replied.

"It'd be freaking awesome if it wasn't so fucking weird and didn't come with people trying to kill us."

I saw his body relax and his mouth get soft before he agreed quietly, "Yeah."

"You want honesty, I'll give it back to you," I began. "All if this is totally flipping me out and I'm hanging on by a thread here."

"How can I help that?"

He asked the question straight out and instantly, and after he did, my eyes fell on my purse on the table.

Shit.

I looked back to him. "We're connected, aren't we?"

"Yes."

"How?"

"No clue."

"Doesn't it freak you?"

"No, 'cause for the first time in my life, with you finally in it, I feel whole."

Oh my God, he felt like me.

*He felt like me.*

I closed my eyes and let myself feel it, something I'd never felt in my life until him.

Whole.

Even in all the crazy, it felt *marvelous.*

I opened them again.

"Is there more about the world I don't know? Like, does Superman exist?" I asked.

"Vampires and werewolves roam the earth. It's a possibility," he answered.

I smiled as I asked, "Could you kick his ass?"

"Absolutely," he replied.

"Cocky," I muttered.

He tipped his head to the side. "You want bacon and eggs?"

"Do I have to drink the eggs raw?"

His brows shot together. "Fuck no."

"Then yes."

His mouth still soft, he shook his head and reached his hand out to me. "You get the bacon, I'll get the eggs. We'll make breakfast, eat it, and you can tell me about your dad."

I looked into his eyes.

Then I looked to his hand.

Finally, I reached out my own.

His closed around mine and he gently pulled me to the kitchen.

He let me go to get the eggs.

I took care of the bacon and commenced in telling him about my dad.

# 4
# Bigger than Anything You'll Know

*Delilah*

After breakfast, Abel washed the dishes, I dried.

I was putting the last dish away as he was walking to the milk cartons, talking.

"I'll go upstairs, shower at Jian-Li's, then go out and get something to—"

He stopped speaking and I turned to him to see his eyes to the door. He moved that way, opening it and standing in it. A couple of seconds later, his brothers, all of them, came through, one of them miraculously carrying my bags.

Hallelujah.

"For a biker babe, your woman does *not* pack light," one of the brothers said as he came in and dumped my bags. He had blond-tipped spikes on top of his short, cropped hair, and he was wearing jeans and a tee that said, *Wake up. Kick ass. Repeat.* He was shorter than Abel (though, it would be difficult not to be, seeing as I reckoned Abel was at least six foot four). He was taller than Chen, but his other brother was taller than him. He was also taller than me. They all were, seeing as I was five-six.

And he was the one who had chopped the dude's head off last night.

His eyes came to me. "Yo, I'm Xun."

"Uh, hey, Xun," I replied.

"I'm Wei." I heard and my eyes went to the last one I hadn't met. The one who might have sacrificed his bike to take out two vampires to save his brother.

He had a faux-hawk, which looked awesome on him. He also had on jeans, but his tee indicated he liked the band Korn.

"Hey there, Wei."

"Hey, Delilah," Chen called, and I looked to him.

Chen had a spiky 'do too, but his included ragged bangs that cut across his forehead. This morning he was in a skintight, red Under Armour shirt and black track pants.

If I had to choose, I would pick Xun's shirt as my favorite, though Chen's was the hottest.

As for the rest, they all had cut cheekbones that they definitely got from their mom. They also had downward-angled jaws that they didn't get from Jian-Li, so I guessed they came from their dad. Xun and Chen had sharp, straight noses with flaring nostrils, which, if I was ever asked to tell you what a hot-as-shit nose looked like, it would be theirs. Wei's was more rounded without the flare, but although his brothers' noses were awesome, his was far from unattractive.

"Hey, Chen," I called back.

"Right, the lowdown," Abel stated, and I looked to him. "Xun's the oldest. He's also cocky and arrogant. Further, he's in your face pretty much all the time, and by 'in your face,' I mean he's in *everyone's* face."

I felt my lips curve and looked to Xun, who lifted a hand to his forehead in order to salute me, apparently unoffended by these remarks.

"Wei is number two," Abel went on. "He's cocky and arrogant and a daredevil in a way it's a miracle he's still alive."

I got that with the bike maneuver.

I looked to Wei and he gave me a formal bow when I did, one arm out, the other hand to his chest.

My lips curved bigger.

"You know Chen," Abel continued. "He's the youngest. He's the sensitive one. He's also the comedian. But that doesn't mean he isn't cocky and arrogant and a pain in the ass his own way."

I smiled outright to Chen as he shook his head and rolled his eyes.

"It's good you're here," Abel carried on. "You can drag Delilah's shit up to Jian-Li's so she can get cleaned up and changed. I'm gonna go out and see about finishing up the shower and toilet. I go, she stays up there and I want one of you on her at all times."

"You're actually gonna make this dump partially livable?" Chen asked.

"I'm gonna put a shower curtain up and a door on the toilet," Abel answered.

Chen looked at me. "Miracle."

I smiled at him again.

"It's gonna kill the mood of the dungeon," Wei noted.

"It's gonna make the place more comfortable for Lilah," Abel returned.

That made me feel nice.

"Finally. Been here a month and the place is still a shithole," Xun decreed, then looked at me. But when he went on, with what he'd said, I was only half-listening. "He doesn't even have cable and still has boxes of shit up in one of Ma's extra bedrooms, including his stereo and CDs. Don't know a man who can live without music, but it's impossible for a man to live without TV."

"A month?" I whispered.

"Yeah," Wei answered, moving further in and doing it in the direction of the fridge. "Usual drill. Ma and Chen came early, set up the restaurant, got shit sorted. Then I came out. Then Xun. Abel finalized things in Daytona and got here about a month ago."

If I wasn't freaked out, I would wonder about the "usual drill."

But I was freaked out.

I was freaked out because a month ago I woke up with a rabid desire to go to Serpentine Bay. A rabid desire that was not about communing with my biker brethren while on holiday in a cool coastal town. It was a rabid desire for something else. I just didn't know what it was (then).

I'd gone straight to work and asked my boss for vacation the minute I could get it.

Which meant I lived a month needing to be on the road to Serpentine Bay. A month where my mother gave me shit (as per usual), my father gave me understanding (also as per usual), and I practically counted down the minutes until I could get my ass on the road.

I'd arrived yesterday, unpacked my bags in the hotel, and went out.

Searching.

For what, I did not know.

But I'd found it.

"Lilah?"

Abel calling my name meant my eyes moved slowly to his.

He was studying me closely.

"What's up?" he asked.

We had an audience. It was clear he was tight with these guys. They were family the way I knew family, that meaning they didn't share blood but they were family all the same.

Still, at that moment, I didn't feel like sharing the latest bizarre nuance of all that was happening with anyone but Abel.

And maybe not even him.

Yet.

So I answered, "Nothin'."

Abel gave me a sharp look that would have been scary if he hadn't vowed never to harm me in a way I believed him, as in *believed him*. Then I felt relief when he didn't push it, just nodded his head and looked to his brothers.

"Grab her bags and get her upstairs so I can get my shit done," he ordered.

"Roundin' it out," Xun stated as he moved back to the bags he'd dumped, "Abel's the oldest. He's cocky and arrogant and badass and should be a general, not a biker, seein' as he likes givin' orders so fuckin' much."

"It's that big of a pain in your ass," Abel began. "I'll take her shit upstairs."

"I'll take it," Xun muttered, grabbing the handles.

"I'll escort the lovely to Ma's pad," Wei said from beside me. I looked to him and saw he'd purloined a hunk of cheese from Abel's fridge and was gnawing at it. He grabbed my hand, lifting it and curling my arm close to the side of his chest.

That was when it happened.

The room filled with something nasty and everyone went wired.

"Don't touch her."

This was snarled by Abel and my eyes flew to him.

Wei let me go.

"Brother," he murmured.

"You touch her only if I tell you to," Abel growled.

Holy fuck.

"You know you got nothin'—" Wei started.

"Wei." Abel cut him off. "No reply necessary. Yeah?"

"Right, yeah. Calm, man," Wei said.

Abel scowled at him, then I watched him take in a deep breath.

His eyes came to me. "No one touches you, Lilah. You got that?"

"I...uh..." I stared at him, noting his seriousness was *serious*, completely forgot about his vow never to harm me, then finished, "Yeah."

"Right," he muttered irately, looked through his brothers and ordered, "Go."

Apparently unperturbed by Abel's insanely protective behavior, Chen said, "Ma wants a family lunch in the private room upstairs."

"She'll get it, but seein' as it's near-on eleven o'clock, I don't get my ass out to pick up the shit, it might turn into dinner," Abel replied.

It was nearly eleven o'clock?

Well, I guessed after the last night's late night, I'd slept in.

"Hi-ho, off we go," Chen muttered, grinning at me and making me feel slightly better after the latest weirdness that had occurred.

I had never really considered what I wanted in a man. It was strange for a chick not to do this, but I didn't.

And I didn't for a number of reasons.

One being that my mom and dad had not had a good relationship, not when they were together in the time I remembered them together, and definitely not after. They fought. They hated each other. And they both let me know that in a way, in and of itself, it was enough to make a girl cautious about deciding to let a man in her life.

Two being that I had other concerns. Getting a job. Setting up an apartment. Buying shit for it. Having fun with my friends. And trying to forget there was something I was missing in my life that I feared I'd never find, and, further, that maybe my mom *was* right and I was whacked in the head.

The last being I was twenty-nine, and although I was getting to an age where I should think about sorting myself out (seeing as I wanted kids, I just wasn't sure I wanted a relationship to go with them), I was still young. Mom and Dad got together *really* early. Dad said straight up that was the biggest mistake of his life, and the only reason he didn't regret it in a way that would make him bitter forever, was that he got me out of it. He'd told me time and again to live my life, enjoy it, figure out who I was and what I wanted, and only then go out and find it. And when I did, not to settle for anything less.

But if I did consider what I wanted in a man, protectiveness would be one thing that would be high up on the necessary side. My dad was protective. His boys were protective. Even when Mom had custody of me, I had that when I was with my dad as well as when I wasn't. It was all I knew and that was definitely going to be a part of not settling for anything less.

Though, rabid protectiveness to the point a man wouldn't even let his brother take my hand was totally OTT.

I thought it best at that juncture to get my ass out of there, so I walked to the door. Chen moved aside as I came his way. I felt Wei and Xun moving in behind me.

Then I heard Abel speak.

"Lilah."

I stopped and looked his way.

"Later," he finished.

"Yeah. Later, Abel."

He held my eyes.

I swallowed and left the room.

The boys and I walked down the hall, up the stairs, and into the alley. This was not something I relished because none of this was welcoming—it was dark and damp, even in the daylight—and also because I was only wearing Abel's tee and had no shoes on.

I didn't complain. It was Abel's space. It suited him in a weird way, but I was glad to be out of the "dungeon."

We were in the back door of the restaurant, the kitchen bustling with activity, when Chen turned right.

He opened a door and I followed him through and up some stairs, feeling and hearing Wei and Xun behind me.

At the top, Chen dug in his track pants, pulled out a key ring, opened the door, and let us in.

I didn't have the chance to look around before Chen spoke.

"He's different."

I looked to him, knowing exactly what he meant. "I know."

"He can get intense," Chen went on.

Boy, was he not wrong about that.

"I've noticed," I replied.

Chen moved toward me, dipping his chin to keep my eyes, but stopping several feet away. "He loves with a love that's bigger than anything you'll know. He's loyal beyond reason. He'd die for any of us, endure the worst kind of torture and die. He'd kill for any of us. If we were hurt, he'd avenge us and he would make that painful and messy beyond anything you can imagine. He's the best kind of man you could know...the best son, the best brother...times about fifty thousand. Knowin' that, you understand his intensity. Knowin' that, you'll eventually understand everything."

When he finished his speech, I wasn't sure if I felt better or more weirded out.

So I just said, "Okay."

"I hope to God there will be a bunch of days in my life I'll never forget," Chen continued. "When I find the woman for me. When I make her mine. When she gives me kids. But I know one thing deep in my heart. I will never forget yesterday, when my brother found what he needed to take away his pain."

I swallowed again, feeling my eyes sting, and I nodded.

Now *that* made me feel better.

"He's protective of us. He's protective of Ma...to extremes," Chen went on. "It is not a surprise to any of us that that's ten notches higher with you."

"Okay," I repeated.

"So don't let that shit freak you," Chen finished.

I nodded again.

Chen held my eyes for a while before he nodded back and stepped away.

I looked to Xun and Wei and saw their eyes on me. They were watching me intently, their faces void.

And I knew they thought this was a test.

A test I had to pass.

I had to accept their brother as he was, cut him some slack, get to know him, get to understand him.

And I could do that, because, as my father had said, when I found what I needed, I'd win it no matter how I had to do that, including making these three loyal brothers believe I could.

"Yeesh, dudes, give me a break," I said. "Found the man I've been waiting for all my life and he's an overprotective werewolf vampire who drinks bagged blood for breakfast, has the strength of ten men, the speed of a superhero, not to mention we have people who want us dead. This is not something a girl takes in stride. At least give me to lunch."

This got me three smiles and a room with a lot less tension threading through it.

"I'll take your crap to the bathroom," Xun muttered.

"I'll go tell Ma you're up here," Wei stated before turning and using the door.

"I'll park my ass in front of the TV," Chen said, moving to the couch.

That was when I took in the space, and at the same time, took in a breath, for the apartment above a restaurant did not look like an apartment above a restaurant but an Asian décor showplace (and a posh one at that).

It was beautiful. Rich woods. Richer materials. Lacquer. Inlays. Intricate carvings. Strikingly formed hinges and handles. Amazing curios—jade, cloisonné, and polished wood statues of foo dogs, dragons, and elephants. Wall hangings, pictures, and a four-paneled freestanding screen in one corner, all of these last depicting delicate birds and flowers.

It was not cluttered, stuffy, and overdone. It was elegant and refined.

I loved it.

"Wowza, your mom could be an interior designer," I told Chen.

"Yeah, makes every place we go awesome," Chen answered, clicking on the TV. "But you haven't tasted her food yet." He looked over the couch that appeared to be covered in red silk Damask, with dark, woven material at the sides and back. It had carved wood for feet and ornamentation. It was a couch I would not park my ass on to kick back and watch TV. It was a couch I'd probably be afraid to eat on for fear of ruining it. "When you do, you'll know where her talents really lie."

That meant I was suddenly seriously looking forward to lunch.

"I'm gone," Xun stated, coming back into the room from the hall.

"North?" Chen asked mysteriously.

"Yeah. I'll send Wei south."

"Won't be south, brother," Chen told him. "A man comes out of the bay buck naked, a biker will give him a pair of jeans and a bottle of Jack and ask no questions. He does that shit down south, they'd call the police."

This was something I knew about Serpentine Bay. As much of a biker mecca as it was, it was also an old northwest coastal town, a beautiful one at that, so it had its ritzy side. But the ritzy side and the uppity folk who lived in it kept well to their areas of fancy restaurants, boutique shops, and cliffside mansions down south, while the bikers and their hangers-on did their thing in the bars, pool halls, and poker rooms up north.

"You're still going after him?" I asked, knowing from their words that they were going to keep searching for the werewolf.

"Could be he's gone by now," Chen said. "But we gotta try."

"That's cool," I murmured.

"That's brotherhood," Xun said, and I turned back to him.

"Thanks," I replied.

"You come with Abel. Anything for him, now anything for you," Xun told me. Then he walked out the door before I could express my further gratitude for the warmth that filled my heart at his words.

"Go, get in something other than my brother's tee," Chen told me, and my eyes went again to him to see him grinning. "You don't, I'll start havin' impure thoughts that may lead to me becoming a victim of fratricide."

"We wouldn't want that," I noted.

"No, we would not," Chen agreed.

I smiled at him.

He smiled back, then jerked his head toward the hall.

I took his direction and headed that way.

# 5
# The Miracle and The Monster

*Abel*

Abel heard him long before he got to the door and knew by the familiarity of the sound who was coming.

So he didn't stop drilling the screw into the hinge that would eventually be attached to a door to the toilet as the footsteps approached and the steel door opened.

"Yo!" Wei called over the drill. "Soup's on and Ma wants your ass upstairs."

Abel stopped drilling and looked to his brother. "Gonna get this done."

Wei looked to the hinge, then back to Abel. "You can finish it after. Food's on the table and Ma's getting shitty."

"I'll be up when this is done," Abel reiterated.

Wei's brows went up. "You gonna court the wrath of Jian-Li?"

Normally, he would not do this. He was older than her, helped raise her, was stronger than her by far, but the woman had a temper. She was also the matriarch, a matriarch with four sons, all of whom were unruly in one way or another (including him). So no matter that Abel had one hundred and forty years on her; when needed, Jian-Li had an iron fist, even with Abel.

Still, he was not dragging his ass up there.

Not until he had a handle on it.

And knowing Delilah was up there, he was not close to having a handle on it. Not after he woke up hearing her make noises in her sleep that told him exactly what she was dreaming. Not after hearing her say "Abel, baby" like she was just about ready to come.

It had nearly torn him out of his skin, staying seated in that chair and not going to the bed, positioning her and mounting her, even in her sleep.

But it was definitely more. Something in him he didn't understand was driving him to connect with Delilah in such a way, he was losing the struggle to fight it. In a way so powerful, he feared he'd harm her while doing it. But if he did, he knew at the very least he'd scare the shit out of her.

She told him she was hanging on by a thread and he got that. The shit she was learning, seeing, and experiencing—he was shocked as hell (and pleased as fuck) she was handling it as well as she was. And he was even more pleased that the destiny he knew was his, which included her in it, she clearly felt as well.

But he needed to make her feel safer, to guide her to trust him, trust his family, allow her time to get to know all of them, primarily him; not attack her, force himself on her, possibly hurt her, and, in doing any of that, destroy any chance of ever gaining her trust.

So he had to get his shit together before he saw her again.

He just didn't know how.

"She's cool with it," Wei stated, taking Abel out of his thoughts.

"What?"

"You goin' gonzo about me touching her. Chen explained you were intense. She told us she'd already noticed that, then made a joke. She's cool with it."

At least that was something.

"She's just cool," Wei said, getting closer. "She's up in the private room with Ma, Chen, and Xun, crackin' jokes about all that went down last night and tellin' us about her dad comin' tomorrow. A dad who sounds like a fuckin' lunatic." He stopped close to Abel, smiling his approval of Delilah's "fucking lunatic" father, but his smile died as he finished quietly. "She's settling in, man, a lot easier than any of us would have expected. You don't have to worry."

Even if all that was excellent news, Abel stared into his brother's eyes and laid it out.

"I need to fuck her."

Wei grinned. "I see that. Don't rip my head off, literally, when I say it's good to see your fated woman is seriously hot."

"No, Wei," Abel said slowly, "I *need* to fuck her."

Wei stared at him, the humor shifting out of his face.

"Consumed with it, brother," Abel whispered.

"Shit," Wei muttered.

"You touched her, honest to Christ, nearly did you harm. *You.* Almost couldn't control the urge," Abel admitted.

"Wolf," Wei stated, and Abel nodded.

"I'm thinkin'...yeah. Pack traits, alpha male on female. That connects."

"We'll all be careful," Wei promised.

"Know you will. But I gotta calm my shit before I'm with her again."

Wei tipped his head to the side. "That bad?"

Abel turned fully to him, keeping the drill in his hand even as he crossed his arms on his chest. "That bad. I do not want to make love with her. I don't wanna kiss her. I don't want my hands on her. I wanna *fuck* her, brother. Hard. Take her. Claim her. She's known me less than a day and shit has not been good, not by a long shot, so I cannot do that. I gotta give her time. I gotta give her me, and not in that way. And I don't know what this is...wolf, vampire, both...but I made breakfast with her, ate breakfast with her, talkin' about important shit, shit that matters, shit she had to know, shit she told me about her I wanted to know, and I did it the whole time struggling with the urge to bend her over my table."

"Fuck," Wei whispered.

"Yeah," Abel agreed.

"So you need to put up the door," Wei stated.

"Yeah, and find a way to be with her and give her what she needs without takin' from her what I need, takin' her away. Because I go in the way I need to go in, she'll be lost to me."

"You gotta get your mind off it," Wei advised.

He'd tried that, doing it by jacking off in the shower before taking off to get the shit he needed to make things more comfortable in his space for Delilah.

His self-induced orgasm was a piss-poor idea. He'd obviously done it visualizing her and it only made it worse.

Hanging the rod and curtain and installing the door wasn't helping either, mostly because all he could think about was her naked in the shower, him with her, and what he'd do if he was.

"Didn't find that wolf," Wei said, and Abel focused on him again.

"What?"

"Xun and me went around, did some asking, on the down low got folks on the lookout, and Chen made calls. So far nothing. He's vapor."

When they moved from one location to the next, there was a reason why they did it the way they did. Understandably, Jian-Li had to come first to find and set up the space she needed for her restaurant and where she wanted to live. She did this always of a mind that Abel would need his space close to her, and she found all of that with Chen helping.

Chen was friendly, social, and—even built and able to take care of himself in a serious way that anyone could see from just looking at him—he could come off nonthreatening. They never went anywhere without setting up their network, and it was Chen who started that job so they knew everything about their location. Looked into the local politicians and business owners, researched crime rates and who was committing them, and made connections on both sides of the law.

Xun and Wei came later, laying more groundwork. This was mostly making themselves available, offering services, providing favors, establishing trust, proving themselves capable at a variety of shit, and amassing a fuckload of markers.

Abel followed last, never the face of anything they did, connecting with humans very minimally. He received his briefings prior to coming but got fully briefed after he arrived.

But he did the quiet work. The work that needed to get done that no one could see.

And he did it well.

All of this was done because he knew that something would happen eventually and they needed to be prepared in any way they could when it did.

Something had happened, and luckily, they were prepared when it did.

"After lunch, we'll all go back out," Abel declared.

"You sure that's a good idea?" Wei asked. "You goin' with us, I mean. You said you sensed more vamps. If they got your skills, Abel, they can get a lock on you too."

"I'll be careful."

"Gets you away from Delilah," he guessed.

"And hopefully turns my mind."

Wei nodded just as his phone rang.

But his phone rang at the same time Abel's phone rang.

They both tensed, looking into each other's eyes while grabbing their phones.

Abel looked away first, to the screen, and saw it was Xun.

He took the call and put the phone to his ear.

"What?"

"Problem, brother. We're on it, but we need you upstairs in Ma's apartment. Like, now."

Wei was talking on his phone, but Abel was out the door and in Jian-Li's apartment within five seconds.

He got there and saw Delilah sitting on the couch, wide eyes to him, reacting to his speed and him coming into focus from a blur (something he was able to ignore, seeing as he'd had plenty of experience with that in his life). But one sight of her, his cock twitched, his jaw set, and he forced his gaze to Chen.

"*What?*" he barked.

"One of the waiters noticed them, told me. I looked. Two men outside. SUV like last night, according to Xun. And they are makin' no bones about the fact that they're casin' the place."

Chen was at the window, off to the side, peering around the sheers but doing it out of the way so no one could see him looking.

It was then he noticed that Jian-Li was busy lighting incense. A lot of it.

Masking his scent.

He moved with his natural speed to the window and stood behind Chen, who moved out of the way.

And he saw them.

Vampires. He knew it because he'd seen one of them last night. The one who was talking with the police officer, not the one talking on his phone who'd seen Abel. But today he had another one with him, big, built, but blond.

He couldn't believe he hadn't sensed them when he was downstairs. Up at Jian-Li's place with that incense interfering, he could see. But he had a finely honed ability to detect danger.

Fuck. His need for Delilah was totally fucking him up in a variety of ways.

He stared through the window.

They were both in nice suits and they both had eyes trained to the restaurant, the blond one leaning casually against the back of the SUV, the dark one standing on the sidewalk, his frame stiff like he was the kind of guy who had a stick up his ass.

"You think they caught your scent?" Chen asked quietly, and Abel looked to him.

"Yeah."

"Fuck," Chen whispered.

"Language," Jian-Li warned.

The door opened and Wei came in. "Covered the grate," he announced, shutting the door. "Far's I can tell, no eyes on the alley.

But figure they're here because they caught your scent, so they sniff it out, they'll find your lair."

"Fuck," Chen repeated.

"*Language,*" Jian-Li hissed.

"Where's Xun?" Abel asked.

"In the restaurant," Jian-Li answered.

"That's good, Ma, 'cause they're on the move," Chen said. "Headed toward the front door."

"Oh man," Delilah whispered.

"It'll be okay," Jian-Li murmured reassuringly.

"Chen, cover the hall. Wei, outside. Keep an eye on the alley. One of you tell Xun he just became a server and his only table is the one they're seated at."

"On it," Wei said and moved out.

Chen said nothing, he just moved out.

"Jian-Li?" Abel called, and she looked to him.

"I'll supervise in the restaurant," she stated.

He nodded.

She moved after her sons and disappeared behind the door.

"Abel?"

Fuck. Even her voice, low and sweet with a strange husky lilt in it, he felt in his cock.

He moved his eyes to her.

He could smell her, even smell the fragrant tang of her cunt, though he knew by her scent she'd taken another shower. She was in more biker bitch gear—sweet jeans, sweeter Harley tee that stretched tight across her tits—her long, dark hair down and wild. She had on maximum biker chick jewelry, lots of silver, leather, and studs, even if she was simply hanging at a Chinese restaurant and doing it so no one could see. Her face was made up, heavy around the eyes, making the light green of her irises stand out so it seemed like it was glowing.

First time he fucked her, he wouldn't be able to look in her eyes.

First time he fucked her, he'd take her on her hands and knees.

The *next* time he fucked her, he'd do it looking in her eyes.

"Uh," she started, ripping him from his thoughts. "Is there something I can do?"

"Sit and be quiet," he replied curtly, looking back to the window to see the SUV there but both vampires not, at the same time attempting to open his senses so he could detect further danger, or any at all.

"Well, I mean something else."

"No," he said shortly, not looking at her.

"You—" she began, and he knew through sound and smell she'd moved from the couch with the intent to come nearer.

He could not have her nearer.

"Don't get near me," he gritted through his teeth, sensing her stopping, also sensing her mood turning, and not to a good one. "Gotta focus," he finished on a lie for there was really fuck all he could do. He had to stay hidden. She had to stay hidden. And they had to hope like fuck those vampires couldn't smell him through the incense and make their play, because Jian-Li didn't need carnage in her restaurant and he didn't want to lose any of his family.

"Okay," she whispered, sounding confused, a sound that did not make his dick twitch. It made his heart hurt.

He moved from the window and started pacing like the caged dog he literally fucking was, thinking of his family, thinking he was hungry, thinking her blood probably tasted fucking *brilliant*.

He closed his eyes tight, opened them, kept pacing, and started thinking of puppies. To be precise, cute, wrinkly baby shar-peis.

The door opened, he stopped pacing, and watched Jian-Li walk through.

"They're leaving," she said in a voice he did not like after she shut the door.

He moved in a blur to the window and saw she spoke true.

"The boys are staying in position," she went on.

He looked back to her. "Why do you look frightened?" he asked.

"They asked to speak to the proprietor of the restaurant, and when I came to them, they asked for you directly," she answered.

He felt his throat get tight.

"By name?" he pushed.

"No." Jian-Li shook her head. "The blond one asked for the vampire."

"Fuck," Abel snarled. "To you?"

She nodded. "To me."

"And you said...?"

"I acted like he needed to see a doctor and told them I had no idea what he was talking about." She took another step into the room, her eyes going to Delilah, who she gave a soft smile, before they came back to him. "I don't know, but when the blond one asked this, the dark one appeared annoyed."

"This means...?" Abel prompted.

"I really don't know, *tian xin*," she said softly. "But I got the impression the dark one wished for this contact to be a little less aggressive."

"That's good, right?" Delilah asked.

Jian-Li looked to her. "I have no idea, but I hope so."

"And that was it?" Abel called her attention back to him. "They asked, you said you had no idea, and they left?"

"Yes, they left, but not before the dark one gave me this," Jian-Li told him, moving toward Abel, holding up what appeared to be a business card.

He took it and saw it was. Cream. Thick, expensive stock. Printed in bold, script letters was:

GREGOR
COUNCILMAN
DOMINION

This meant nothing to Abel. Then he looked to the back and sucked in breath.

On the back, written in pen, it said:

*We mean you and your mate no harm.*
*The Biltmore. Suite 1013.*

His mate.

*His mate.*

He looked to Delilah.

She was his *mate*. That was what his kind called them.

Something settled in his gut that Abel didn't trust because it felt good.

But even so, his throat tightened further because they knew he had a mate.

"What's it say?" Delilah asked.

He shoved the card in his back pocket. "Nothing that makes sense."

Having followed his movements, she looked from his hip to his eyes and he knew she didn't believe him. There was only a hint of hurt in her face, but it was a definite indication she didn't like shit kept from her.

He ignored this and looked to Jian-Li. "I gotta finish downstairs and then I gotta run."

"Of course," she said with soft understanding.

"Take care of Delilah," he continued.

"You don't have to ask," Jian-Li replied.

He knew he didn't.

"Sorry about lunch," he muttered, moved to her and leaned in, sliding his temple across hers before he headed to the door.

"Abel?" Delilah called.

"Later," Abel replied without looking back.

Then he shut the door.

Abel sat as wolf on the highest cliff at the south end of town, staring down at the lights spread narrow along the bay, his focus on one of the tallest, most attractive buildings in the city.

The Biltmore Hotel.

When he'd moved to the Bay a month ago, as a celebration of them all being together again, the entire family had gone to dinner at the restaurant there. Excellent steaks but filled with snobs.

Vampires stayed at swish hotels.

He snarled.

He snarled again, turned, and ran swiftly back toward where he'd leaped out of his clothes, thinking he in no way trusted those vampires did not mean harm to him or his *mate*. He'd met nine supernatural beings and every one of them had meant him or Delilah harm.

And he'd left her to put up a fucking door and go run.

He needed to, that couldn't be denied. He always needed to run, but when something was troubling him, he needed it more.

But even though he'd trained his brothers, their skill levels exceptionally high, their sparring partner *him* so they would in no way be intimidated by the kind of speed, strength, and agility his kind had—in fact, they'd all built defensive tactics that were highly successful, as demonstrated last night—it was his responsibility to look after Delilah.

And he'd left her hours ago to put up a door and then run as wolf.

It was late. Running had calmed the urge to claim his *mate*, so at least that was a positive.

But now it was time to get home to her.

He got to his clothes, leaped to man, put them on, forged through the woods to his bike, and jumped on.

He rode into the city and he did it with his senses open, taking in mostly human and animal, food, trash, and excrement, but no vampires or wolves.

He saw nor sensed eyes on him as he closed in on the restaurant. Not from cars. Not from buildings. Not from roofs.

They had to know he had the ability to do this, so he wondered if them retreating so completely was their way of making him trust them.

Trust them straight into an ambush.

He knew Chen was in the alley as he parked his bike. His brother moved out of the shadows as he swung off.

"All clear," Chen said softly.

"Yeah," Abel replied.

"You okay?" Chen asked.

"Yeah," Abel lied.

Chen stared at him through the dim lights of the alley before he nodded and asked, "You want vigilance?"

He was asking if Abel wanted Chen to keep his eye on the alley.

Abel shook his head. "We don't fight alone, brother. Go inside. Get some sleep."

Chen looked to the ground and headed to the back door of the restaurant.

Abel followed him.

Chen called, "'Night, Ma," as he headed up the stairs to her apartment.

"Goodnight, son," she called back from her office.

Abel headed directly there to see her exactly as she was the night before.

"It's late," she stated, not softly, her tone was sharp and annoyed.

"I have things on my mind," he explained.

"And Delilah is downstairs, watching a movie with Xun, having spent a confused and somewhat frightened afternoon and evening with your family."

Abel's jaw got hard.

"Is there a reason you've spent thirty years yearning for her and then you get her and leave her?" she pushed.

"There is, and these are reasons I'm not gonna share," Abel answered. "You're just gonna have to go with it and take my back."

She gave him a flinty look.

He accepted it and said nothing.

She then emitted a soft huff before she asked, "Are you going to The Biltmore?"

"No, I'm not."

Her head tipped to the side. "This is not wise, my Abel."

"You think I should walk into an ambush?"

"No. I think that I would like to feel the overwhelming gratification of understanding that my family's nurture is what created a good, kind, strong, wonderful werewolf vampire, suffocating his nature. However, rationally, I feel that cannot be so and there is a good possibility there are beings out there just like you, and by that, I mean the good, kind, strong parts."

"How about we know that before I waltz my ass into The Biltmore?" he suggested.

"How about you consider the possibility that centuries of questions will have answers if you waltz into The Biltmore?" she fired back.

This was not lost on him.

He knew one thing for certain about his kind: vampires called their partners *mates*.

That was all he knew.

And he had questions—questions about his behaviors, feelings, instincts, *everything*. All his life, he'd had questions.

In fact, it was a miracle he'd stumbled on how to numb his meal before he drew from them. It had taken him ages. He'd done it at what Mei had figured was when he was eight years old in human development, but he'd been alive for forty years. (Because, apparently, wolves, vampires, or both aged very slowly and then quit aging in their thirties in terms of human development—something else he knew, but only because he'd experienced it.)

Other than that, he knew nothing of the nature of his kind—either one.

So the impulse was strong, going to The Biltmore, finding answers. Especially now with what he was experiencing with Delilah.

It was also foolish.

"Do I have to remind you what happened last night, sweetheart?" he asked.

"No," she replied instantly. "But has it occurred to you that eight people were killed last night and no police officer has shown at our door?"

His mind consumed with Delilah (amongst other things), it actually hadn't.

He said nothing.

"This occurred on city streets," she reminded him. "It was in the dark of night, but that means nothing, especially here in Serpentine

Bay. Now, Abel, tell me, what could halt a police investigation?" she asked but didn't give him time to answer. She did it herself. "A powerful entity."

"That might not be a good thing," he noted quietly.

"It also might mean whatever is befalling you and Delilah, you'll have mighty allies," she retorted.

Shit. But he had to find a way to fuck Delilah so his mind wasn't consumed with it and shit this simple was not lost on him.

"I have to focus on Delilah," he told her, and she nodded.

"On that I would agree, my Abel. However, you haven't been doing that either."

"There are things you don't understand."

"I know you've waited lifetimes for her, and now that you have her, you're acting surly and impatient. So I assume I can guess quite accurately at what is causing your impatience."

Jian-Li, nor any of her line, were stupid. Usually this was good. Now it was aggravating.

"Do you have any advice on that?" he asked sarcastically.

"She's here," Jian-Li replied.

"I know that," he bit out impatiently.

"*She's here,*" Jian-Li repeated. "If she did not feel as you do, after the events of last night, would any sane female be anywhere near you?"

He shook his head. "She doesn't feel as I do."

"Are you certain?"

If she did, they'd be fucking right then.

So she didn't.

"I am."

"Guide her there, *tian xin,*" she advised quietly.

"She's human. She needs time."

"Yes," she stated, still talking quietly. "But I'll tell you this, she seemed very sure of herself when I saw her come out of my bathroom this morning. She was comfortable with me, Xun, Wei, Chen. Charming. Talkative. Amusing. She has hesitancy, which is understandable, but she was clearly embracing where she was in a way that's remarkable and gave me great relief. Until you left."

Abel's heart tightened.

"The longer you were gone, the more confused and unsure of herself and this situation she became," she continued. "And in the end, my Abel, she actually appeared in pain."

Abel felt his spine straighten. "Pain?"

She nodded. "As if your continued absence caused in her what you've been feeling for centuries."

"Fuck, I gotta get to her," he muttered, making a move to leave.

"Think on The Biltmore," she urged, and he looked back at her.

"I will."

She gave him one of her satisfied smiles, mostly because he was doing what she wished.

He shook his head, lifted his hand and called, "Sleep well," as he moved to the door.

"You too," she called back as the door closed.

He was in his room in a flash.

"Jesus, brother," Xun whispered when Abel came to a rocking stop next to the armchair where Xun was sitting. "Freak a guy out, why don't you."

Abel looked to the bed.

Delilah was asleep in it, not in his tee. She had on something pink and tee-like, but he hadn't owned a stitch of clothing in two hundred and five years that was pink.

His eyes scanned the space.

His boxes from Jian-Li's place were in the corner by the hutches where he and his brothers kept most of their weapons. His stereo had been set up on the floor, his CDs stacked by it. His books were piled along the back wall at the head of the bed. They'd also brought down his guitar.

A table from Jian-Li's place had been brought down, his flat screen and Blu-ray on it. The TV was on, volume down low. Some movie Abel didn't know was playing on the Blu-ray, since he had no cable and would never get clear reception down there.

His family had been busy.

"Am I off the clock?" Xun asked, still whispering in deference to Delilah sleeping, and Abel looked to him to see he'd taken his feet.

"Yeah, brother. Thanks," he muttered.

"Not a problem," Xun replied, then came to him, slapped him on the shoulder, and moved out of the room.

Abel went to the door and slid the steel shaft through the hinges that barred it.

He drew in a deep breath and moved to the bed, seeing Delilah in the same position as last night, except she didn't have a cheek to her palm—that arm was thrown out.

He drew in another breath, taking in her scent, using everything he had to ignore it, and moved a hand to shift the heavy fall of silken hair off her neck.

He shouldn't have done that either. Her hair was softer than he'd imagined, and the waft of fragrance that came from it went straight to his dick.

He pulled it together and ignored it as her eyes fluttered but stayed closed.

"I'm home, Lilah," he whispered.

"Good, baby," she muttered, her lips curving slightly before she moved, turning to her other side so her back was to him.

He'd been called "baby" by so many women, it would be impossible to count.

None of them felt like it felt when Delilah said it.

Having used up his reserves of control to keep his hands off Delilah, he went to the fridge and got out a bag of blood, seeing only two left in there. If he'd known a warm, delicious meal and its accompanying fuck was not in the cards for him for the foreseeable future, he would have stocked up.

He hadn't.

He'd have to see to that tomorrow.

He nuked the bag and sucked it back. He needed at least three a day, even if he was feeding and fucking. He'd taken one before he went running. But that one, as did the one he was currently consuming, left him hungry.

Definitely needed more.

He moved to the blue trash can, toed it open, and threw the bag in, his jaw clenching at seeing what was inside as he did.

He didn't like what he saw even though he needed it for sustenance. It was all he knew, all he'd ever known, but that didn't mean he didn't understand it was utterly repugnant on every level. He rarely fed in front of his family because they tried to bury it, but his senses were vastly superior to theirs and he felt it. He knew it disgusted them. And Delilah, not surprisingly, hadn't let her eyes wander to him even once while he was having his breakfast.

She'd get off on him drawing from her. He knew it, just as he knew he had to be careful with it. Due to his first and second mothers, Hui's and Mei's, efforts, he'd never once killed or even harmed a human being while feeding. And that shit was not going to happen with him drawing down Delilah's needed supply of blood. So he figured, when he got her there, he could give her that while fucking her maybe once a week.

That said, the bags sucked. They worked, but they sucked. There was nothing as good as a woman writhing under you, her pussy drenched, that smell in your nostrils, her blood in your mouth. It was revolting at the same time it was fucking true.

He'd had decades of bags. He'd have decades more.

Centuries.

Hui was his first mother; Mei was his second, raising him through human teen years after they'd lost Hui. Mei had told him during his second half century that he'd have many lots in life.

"But never forget, *bao bei*," she'd said, her hand curved around his jaw, her eyes tipped back to his height of towering over her. "You are a miracle. *A miracle*. A miracle brought to this family. A miracle upon this world. Never forget, and if you don't, you will endure."

*They* were a miracle, a family over six generations, accepting him as he was.

He was no miracle.

He was a monster.

He looked to the bed.

Another miracle, a dark-haired, green-eyed temptress coming to him in his dreams, then appearing in his life, accepting him and the insanity around her, ending her second night as a part of his life sleeping in his bed.

The miracle and the monster.

Abel winced at the thought.

But that thought was much easier to bury and he did so without effort.

And he did it without effort because he'd had a shitload of practice.

# 6
# You Okay Now?

*Delilah*

I opened my eyes and saw the light shining on Abel sitting back in his armchair, his eyes on me just like the morning before.

"Hey," I called sleepily.

"Hey," he replied, his tone strangely tight.

"You okay?" I asked, not moving, my head to the pillow, my eyes taking in his big frame, memories of the day before instantly available.

He'd been tensed and freaked, understandably so. Though, why he had to take off, I didn't know.

That said, when Xun brought me back down to his room late yesterday evening, I was touched to see the simple white shower curtain covering the stall and a door providing privacy for the toilet. It said a lot, like the purse. Primarily that he might be gone, but his thoughts were on me.

It was what I'd needed.

Perhaps not weirdly, but annoyingly, the longer he was gone and I didn't know where he was or *how* he was, the more that pit in my belly opened up again. And it opened, and opened, and opened. Then the pain came back.

In the end, it was so bad, I didn't know how I got to sleep. You would think I'd be used to it, but it being gone, then having it back again, it all seemed fresh.

And excruciating.

I just knew that when Abel touched my hair and told me he was home, I wasn't very awake, but I felt the pain was gone.

That was not something I relished, needing to be attached at the hip to some guy, and I hoped it was the situation that caused it, not his distance.

"Fine," Abel answered, taking my thoughts from yesterday-him back to the right-there him.

"Sure?" I asked quietly.

"Yeah, Lilah," he answered quietly.

"Thanks for the bathroom," I said.

He shook his head and his lips tipped up, but he didn't say anything or move any further.

"Dad called," I told him. "He and the boys are making good time, but they won't be here until around two today."

"You tell Jian-Li?" he asked.

I nodded my head on the pillow.

"She'll see to a welcome spread."

"She says she's closing the restaurant after lunch," I shared.

"Like I said, she'll see to a welcome spread."

I grinned at him.

His eyes dropped to my mouth and he frowned at me.

That was weird.

Then again, he seemed weird. Not that he was a normal guy, just that he seemed weirder than normal.

I pushed up to put my head in my hand, elbow in the pillow. "You sure you're okay?"

"No."

Oh man.

"What?" I asked. "Did you find something yesterday?"

"Nothin' happened yesterday, Lilah."

Well, at least that was good.

Still, I studied him, stretched out in his chair, ankles crossed, hands sitting loosely on his thick thighs, neck supported by the back of the chair, but head up, eyes on me.

There was something that wasn't right about that, a casualness that seemed false, and I didn't like it.

"Why are you not okay?" I asked.

"I lied yesterday."

Great.

I did not like this.

Lying sucked. I didn't do it. Dad taught me not to, and the lesson I'd had meant I'd only done it once, mostly because when he'd caught me in the lie I told (a lie I didn't remember, just his reaction to it), he was disappointed in me and that killed.

I could count on three fingers the times he'd been disappointed in me.

The first was when I'd dated a preppy who drove his parents' hand-me-down Mercedes. His family had a stable of thoroughbred horses, a huge house, and he wore pastel-colored sweaters draped over his shoulders (we'd only gone out five times, but that was five times too many for Dad).

The second was when I'd told him in a moment of weakness that I thought maybe Mom was right and I *was* whacked in the head.

And last, when I'd lied.

I'd never done it again. As far as I knew, Dad never did it with me either. He might not tell me everything, but that wasn't the same as lying to someone's face.

And if I made a list of what I'd want in a man, that would be in the necessary column.

Well, at least Abel was owning up to it. That was something.

"What did you lie about?" I asked, pushing up to sit cross-legged in the bed, the covers over my lap.

But when I did this, his body visibly tensed, his eyes dropped to my lap, and his jaw went hard.

I stared.

What was that?

"Abel?"

He sliced his eyes to mine and I saw a muscle jump in his cheek before he said, "That card the vampires gave me, it said something."

"I reckoned that," I replied.

He nodded once and continued, "It said they mean you and me no harm and invited me to The Biltmore."

"Oh my God," I whispered, not taking this as a good thing.

"Yeah," he agreed.

"Are you going?" I asked.

"I'm considering it."

My eyes got huge and my voice was two octaves higher when I cried, "*Why?*"

I did this because I knew one good supernatural being: Abel. The rest left a lot to be desired, considering they wanted us both dead. Therefore, I didn't want to have anything to do with them.

It was more, though. I didn't want Abel to have anything to do with them. He was strong, he had backup, but there were only so many times you could be outnumbered and come out the victor.

He drew in a breath and sat forward, putting his elbows on his knees but keeping hold of my eyes, just like he did the morning before.

Then, with no warning, he commenced in breaking my heart.

"I'm a monster, Lilah."

"What?" I whispered.

"I'm a werewolf vampire. I exist on human blood. I can tear a man's head off and I have. I'm a monster."

"You—"

"I am," he stated flatly. "And the first chance I've had in all my years to understand why I am as I am is to go to that fuckin' hotel."

I stared at him, then straightened my body so I was fully facing him. This caused his jaw to get hard again, but I ignored that and stated, "Okay, let's break this down."

"Nothin' to break down."

"Humor me," I snapped, his head jerked, and his lips curved up.

"Carry on," he muttered.

"Thanks," I bit out. "First, how many men's heads have you torn off?"

"Four, and two wolves."

"That's it?" I asked.

"Yeah."

"These being the night we met," I stated.

"Yeah," he repeated.

"The night some of them were trying to kill me and the others were trying to kill you."

To that he said nothing.

I kept going, "So you haven't torn off unsuspecting citizens' heads willy-nilly, for the fuck of it, or on a psychotic rampage?"

He pressed his lips together and I knew it was to hide his humor because his eyes lit with it before he unpressed them to say, "No."

"Right," I said sharply. "Have you ever *had* a psychotic rampage?"

He shook his head.

"So let's get to the human blood part," I suggested. "When you were," I paused, "*drawing* from one of your *ex*-bitches, did you ever kill one of them?"

"Fuck no."

"Take too much and make them sick?"

"No."

"Do it against anyone's will?"

His eyes went guarded, but he said, "No."

I threw up a hand. "Okay, so what's the problem?"

He blinked, straightening in his chair, but again said nothing.

"I mean, seriously," I went on, "I've seen lots of vampire movies and TV shows and even the good vamps screw up and overindulge. Hell, Jessica killed three fairies in a ravenous attack. She might have had her issues as a young vampire, but by that time, she was full-on good."

His brows shot together. "Fairies?"

"Fairies."

"What the fuck are you talking about?"

I threw up both hands and cried in exasperation, "*True Blood!*"

"Jesus, Lilah," he muttered.

"No, seriously, Jessica is very sweet."

"For fuck's sake," he growled, sounding like he was losing patience, which I didn't figure was a good thing.

"Okay, back on track," I began. "Tell me. Tell me one instance in your life where you actually behaved like a monster."

"I wanna fuck you," he snarled.

I stared.

"Yeah," he ground out. "I wanna fuck you, Delilah. Consumed with the need and I have no idea why, but I can guess, seein' as it's like you're a bitch in heat, I'm a dog that catches the scent and his mind is wiped...wiped of anything...but the need to mount you and," he leaned forward, "*rut*."

"Holy fuck," I breathed.

"Yeah," he said again. "That make you feel safe?"

"Abel—"

"I can smell your fear."

I swallowed.

"It turns me on," he kept going. "Makes me wanna tear into your throat and fuck you and feed from you. Now, does *that* make you feel safe?"

"No," I whispered, because it really fucking didn't.

"Right. No," he bit off. "So I'm not a monster?"

"It's...it's..." I stammered.

"Yeah? What is it?" he asked when I couldn't get it out.

"It's you," I said softly, because it was, even if it was scary as shit.

"You're absolutely correct," he clipped, then said with disgust, "It's me."

Then it hit me.

"You left yesterday because of that."

"I did," he confirmed. "I did, because if I spent another minute with you, I'd have you on your knees, takin' my dick, you wanted it or not."

"Abel," I breathed, suddenly understanding, and my heart started bleeding.

Yes, he was protective of me, overprotective, wanting me to feel safe, struggling against his nature to keep me that way.

"Your heart's beating so hard, it sounds like it's about to tear out of your chest. I did that to you. And I'm not a monster?"

"My heart is beating hard because I'm feeling a lot right now, and not all of it is fear, Abel," I told him.

"Then you aren't very smart because, even as I sit here, all I can think of is burying my cock inside you."

Oh shit.

Now *I* was getting turned on.

"Do you think other werewolves...do you think that they...?" I trailed off, but he got me.

"You're not a werewolf. Maybe there are female ones who get the way it is, but you are not one of them."

"But I'm yours," I pointed out.

"You ever transform into a wolf?"

I shook my head, giving him the answer he already knew.

"No," he said. "So how do I deal with this, Delilah? It's my nature, the monster in me for the only time in my life since I was a kid controlling me. I don't understand it and I don't know how to fight it except to keep away from you. Or go to The Biltmore and talk to these fucks and hope they aren't what I think they are and can give me some answers as to how I can deal and keep you safe."

"What if they're not nice vampires?"

"I got two choices...give into the urge and rape the woman destined for me or go to The Biltmore and find out."

"Or you could just fuck me," I blurted, and the room went wired.

*Shit.*

"Do not," he said simply, but both words were harsh and grating, hurting my ears.

Man, *oh man*, he *needed* to *fuck me.*

"You go and you get hurt or dead and Jian-Li loses you, Xun, Chen, Wei." *Me*, I thought but didn't say. "That's better than us having sex?"

"*Rutting*, Delilah."

I felt a rush of wet saturate the area between my legs.

God, again, strange, but that also turned me on.

"Okay, rutting," I whispered.

"I could hurt you," he stated.

"Try not to do that," I replied.

"What if I can't control it?" he asked.

"I...I don't know," I answered.

"And you're still willin' to take that chance?"

I widened my eyes at him but said nothing.

"I can smell you," he whispered.

Fuck.

"Abel."

"You want it."

"Um..." I started and stopped, finding that fact titillating, so much so, more wet hit between my legs.

"You cannot know, you'll never know, but I don't think you get what hanging on by a thread means, Delilah. I'm doin' that right now. And right now, you say one word, 'go,' and you won't see me again until I got it together. You don't say that word right now, it happens."

I should say "go."

I should.

But something deep in my heart knew I actually shouldn't.

So I didn't.

I stared at him, heart slamming in my chest, and said nothing.

"*Fuck,*" he snarled, surging from his chair, and in a flash, he was on me.

In another flash, I was whipped around, knees in the bed, nightshirt torn over my head, palm in my back, shoving me to my hands in the bed.

Oh God.

Then my hips jerked violently as he tore my panties away.

I bit my lip to bite back a moan because that was so...damned... *hot*.

Then he drove inside, filling me. Oh man, oh God, I was so fucking full. There was pain from stretching to accommodate him, but mostly it was pleasure since he was *huge*.

My head shot back and there was no holding back the deep moan that tore from my lips.

He rounded over me, hand in the bed, as his hips slammed into mine and I took the savage thrusts of his mammoth cock, fucking... *loving*...every...*fucking*...one.

"Abel," I whimpered.

"Tell me you can take it," he grunted, his hand not in the bed moving to my hair, gathering it in a fist at the back of my neck.

I arched my back, tipping my hips up, and got more.

It was *phenomenal*.

"*Yes*," I breathed. "I can *so* take it."

"Fuck, fuck, thank fuck," he groaned, twisting my hair, pulling my head back.

*Phenomenal*.

"Baby," I whispered, sliding my knees out, giving him better access.

"Jesus," he gritted, yanking my hair back hard enough I came off my hands and felt my pussy clutch at his cock that felt so fucking *good*.

He caught me around the chest, pulling me to him, still driving up inside. His hand shifted to my breast, cupping it. His other hand went between my legs, finger at my clit, pulsing, tight, hard, rough.

Holy *fuck*.

"Yes, Abel, don't stop," I urged.

His mouth went to my neck.

"Drink," I rasped.

"Lilah, *bao bei*," he whispered into my neck, still pounding inside.

"Take it all from me," I encouraged, lifting a hand to cover his where he held me at my breast, stretching my other arm out and behind me so I could clench my fingers into his ass, feeling the power of it flex as he pounded inside.

His hand at my breast squeezed hard. I arched my back again, driving my ass into his hips, and his finger at my clit pressed in harder as he groaned, *"Fuck yes."*

Then I felt his tongue at my neck, and again. Oh God, *nice*.

"God, your fuckin' pussy," he growled into my neck. "Ecstasy," he finished and licked my neck again, slamming his cock up and grinding inside.

My head fell back and hit his shoulder as his finger at my clit, thumb and finger now tugging hard at my nipple, cock grinding inside—all of it swept over me, fearful in its power, ready to engulf me, annihilate me. My body tensed, not to welcome it but to fight it off, because suddenly, it was terrifying.

"Abel," I gasped, gripping his wrists.

I didn't feel his teeth sink into my flesh, but I felt the blood gush.

And when I did, my orgasm came over me, my body bucking in his hold as he started moving again, my blood pumping and flooding his mouth with each thrust, the climax blistering through me on each drive, wave after wave of sheer heat. My mouth opened and a silent cry of rapture floated out, sweeping me away as I clasped him fast and deep inside me.

Still orgasming, I felt the blood stop flowing and his lips at my ear where he whispered, "Need you to take me on your hands and knees, pussycat."

He bent me forward. I put my hands out and settled into them as he continued to slam inside and my climax slowly drifted away from me.

I felt his hands at my hips slide up to my ribs to hold me steady as he kept driving deep, faster, rougher, oh God, so good.

"This what you need, baby?" I asked, my words hitching with his thrusts.

"Yeah," he grunted, one hand remaining at my ribs while his other moved up to curl around my shoulder, yanking me back as he pounded into me.

"Take it, honey," I purred.

"Fuck, Lilah."

Faster. Rougher.

Oh yeah.

"Take it," I urged.

"Fuck," he grunted.

His hand at my shoulder moved to grasp my hair. He tugged back. I let him, squeezing him tight inside me. He bucked, thrusting, groaning, his fingers digging into my ribs as he came hard, long, and violently inside me, jarring my body, laying claim to me.

I was a biker bitch. I was a biker's daughter. I'd grown up with pretty much anything goes with my father (though, he wasn't a loser, when I was younger, he shielded me from anything that might freak me, it was just that when I got older, that "anything" became a shorter list).

But I was not easy.

I'd once had a one-night stand and didn't much like how it made me feel, mostly because I hadn't actually thought it was a one-night stand until the guy left my bed with one word: "Gratitude." Then he left and didn't ask for my number.

I thought that made him a serious dick and it didn't feel great that I'd chosen to let him into my bed.

But it was safe to say, at that moment, Abel still buried deep, his hand gripping my hair, I had no remorse.

None.

Not even a little bit.

I was spent because I came harder than I had in my whole life. So I pulled at my hair to communicate I needed him to let me go so I could drop to my forearms.

His grip didn't lighten even as his voice was gruff but gentle when he said, "Need you up, baby."

"Okay."

"Bear with me," he murmured.

"Okay, honey."

"Fuck. Sweet," he whispered, then slid out.

The loss of his massive cock was like losing a part of me, a part I needed, and so I whimpered.

"*Fuck*," he groaned. "Sweet."

I stayed up on my hands even when he untangled his fingers from my hair.

Then I felt his hand between my legs. I was dripping—with him, with me—but not for long.

This was because he coated me with us, down the insides of my thighs, over my ass, between its cleft, up over my sex, to my belly, up, up, deep up, to between my breasts, his chest against my ass to give his long arm access.

I stayed on my hands and knees, thinking this was not weird, and not because there were men who got off on this kind of shit.

No, because the slow, sweet, gentle, reverential way Abel was doing it meant it was meaningful, meant it was profound, meant it was important in a way I didn't get, maybe he didn't get, but we felt it all the same.

Both of us.

His lips at the small of my back, he murmured, "Thank you, *bao bei*."

I had no idea what *bao bei* meant, I just knew it sounded very sweet.

"You're welcome," I whispered back.

Then I was not on my hands and knees but on my back, head to the pillows, Abel on me between my legs, yanking the covers up over us.

He was naked, which surprised me, but I guess with inhuman speed that meant a man could undress in the blink of an eye.

Good to know.

I focused on his face just as he finished with the covers and his hand came to the side of mine, middle finger trailing my hairline, his eyes watching it.

"You okay now?" I asked, then stilled completely, even my heart and breath, when his two-colored eyes looked into mine.

And I didn't still because I saw in the light blue one dark brown spikes gliding out from the iris, obliterating the blue, making them both a rich, warm chocolate, and that was weird and wonderful.

No, I did it because everything was in his eyes. The answer to the meaning of life. The truth about whether or not love was real (it was, very much so). Inalienable proof that nothing was more important than family. The knowledge that he would die for me. The understanding that he would kill for me (though, I already knew that).

Everything.

Before, I'd thought his eyes were enthralling.

Looking at them right then, I knew I could lose myself in them.

For eternity.

"Yeah, Lilah, I'm okay now," he whispered.

Oh man.

"Though, I'm gonna take this opportunity to be a lot more okay, doing it repeatedly from now until about two o'clock this afternoon," he went on.

I stopped being moved by what I saw in his eyes when they lit with humor.

I smiled before muttering "Give a werewolf vampire an inch, he takes a mile."

He grinned at me, and if he hadn't showed all his cards two seconds before, making what I gave him worth it (beyond the amazing orgasm he gave me), that would have done it.

His hand slid down to my neck and I sensed it moving there, but I didn't feel it.

"This okay?" he asked.

Shit, I forgot he fed from me.

But I didn't forget it was *awesome*.

"Yeah, do I...I mean, am I bleeding?"

He looked from my neck to me. "No, Lilah. Your wounds are already closed. By the time your dad gets here, they'll be gone."

I blinked. "What?"

He shrugged. "Yeah. Something else I can do. Odd, but useful."

"Whoa," I breathed, then I felt my eyes get big and I cried, "How cool!"

He looked into my eyes for some time, seeming strangely surprised and somewhat puzzled, before he replied in a way it sounded like he didn't quite mean his words, "Yeah. Cool."

I decided not to get into his reaction and instead noted, "Your eyes have both turned brown."

"Yeah," he replied.

"What is that?" I asked.

He dipped close and slid his temple along mine like he did when he'd first found me, like he did to Jian-Li the day before.

My belly melted and he whispered in my ear, "Magic."

He was full of it, but still, his answer was sweet so I let him have it.

He lifted away and was drawing random patterns on my neck that I could (unfortunately) only vaguely feel, seeming lost in thought, his eyes drifting from my neck to my lips, my jaw, my hair, so I took that opportunity to lift my hand in order to start tracing the wicked, but hot, scar on his face.

Before I even touched him, he jerked his head back and focused on me, his fingers at my neck stopping, and the moment was broken.

"Sorry," I murmured, feeling like an idiot, looking to his shoulder and dropping my hand.

"Happened a long time ago, Lilah," he said gently. "And still do not like shit near my face."

That made sense.

I still felt bereft. Like we'd shared something, come to an understanding, moved to a different level, and he'd taken it all away.

Suddenly I wanted him off me and I wanted to shower. Get some food. Go upstairs and be with Jian-Li and the boys, just so they could act as a buffer.

"I don't scar."

My gaze slid to his face when he said this.

"What?"

He dipped closer and his voice dipped lower. "I don't scar, pussycat."

"Okay," I whispered, knowing what pussycat meant and liking that he called me that.

"Don't scar, heal fast," he carried on. "Was out at a bar." He got even closer, putting his nose alongside mine, his eyes staring into mine. "To find a meal," he said super-quiet.

I rolled my eyes, and when I rolled them back, his were grinning and he pulled a bit away.

"And some bitch roofied me."

I stared.

He read my stare and said, "Yeah. Totally freaked me. Drugs don't do shit for me, not that I need them. Don't get headaches, muscle pain, colds, shit like that. But I haven't lived a choirboy's life. Tried some shit. Did nothin' for me. Whatever she gave me fucked me up."

"Oh my God," I breathed.

"Felt it," he went on. "Stumbled outta the place. In the parking lot, she was on me. Took me to my back." He shook his head, his expression turning preoccupied. "Saw her straddling me, the crazy-as-fuck look in her eyes, the weird-ass knife she had. Also saw and felt her carve into me. Couldn't move. Was totally at her mercy."

His jaw clenched as my stomach did.

"Abel," I forced out, and he came back to me.

"Last thing I knew, she was raising it over her head. Thought she was gonna embed it in my heart."

"She didn't?"

He shook his head. "Have no clue. I passed out."

My brows drew together. "Wouldn't you know?"

"Heal fast, Lilah. By the time I came to, was still lying close to that parking lot, but someone had dragged me into some grass away from the lot, the cars, the lights. Felt a sting in my face but knew it was healing. Felt nothing else. Got myself home, confused as fuck. I healed, but it left a scar. Had my share of dings and dents, nothin'. But whatever she used on me fucked me up."

"That's insane."

"It..." he started, but stopped and I felt every inch of his big body stringing tight.

But he said no more.

"Abel?"

He blinked and looked down at me. "It happened a week after Ming died."

"Ming?"

"Jian-Li's husband. We were in Dallas. He was stabbed during a mugging. They took his wallet. A week later, that shit happened to me and it was too much for Jian-Li. We moved. The boys were young so we were all gone in a day."

"Okay," I started hesitantly, "but you just had a moment."

He nodded. "Bad luck can come at any time. It doesn't discriminate. But Ming gets dead and some bitch at a bar knows how to roofie a werewolf vampire and uses a blade on him that scars, never thought about it. She did not smell like me. She was human. I just thought she was a cunt. But now..." he trailed off.

"Holy shitoly," I whispered, understanding what he was saying to me.

"She sunk that blade in me, I'd be gone."

I slid my arms around him and held tight. "Baby."

He looked over my head, muttering, "Why would they go after Ming?"

"Are you sure they did?"

He looked back at me. "Could be a coincidence. But I'm having some issues with coincidences, waiting for you for what feels like an eternity and then running into werewolves and vampires for the first time in my life when you hit town."

"So you think, for whatever reason they want us gone, someone tried back then?"

"That's what I think," he confirmed.

Marvelous.

"Why do you think she didn't do it?" I asked.

"Right now, I don't think she didn't do it. Right now, I'm thinking that someone stopped her from doing it. She took me down because she drugged me. But she was petite and slim. No way she could drag my ass thirty yards when I was dead weight. That said, the bar I was in was rough. I'm a werewolf vampire, but I'm a biker. That's the kind of place I hang. Could have been someone walked out, saw her, stopped her, dragged me to safety, but didn't want to get involved by phoning the police, or maybe they didn't want to bring trouble to the bar by doing it or having me found in the lot."

"I'm not liking this, Abel," I informed him.

"Not likin' it much either, Delilah, because I can't die. But with what it did to my face, I know that knife would have been the end of me."

My head jerked on the pillow. "You can't die?"

His eyes gentled as they looked into mine. "*Bao bei*, I'm a werewolf vampire. I'm immortal. Don't know for certain, but do know since Jian-Li's great-great-great-grandmother found me, I've lived two hundred years."

Was he serious?

"*What?*" I cried.

His head tipped to the side. "Thought I made that clear."

"You...did...*not*," I retorted.

"Delilah, I told you I waited three lifetimes for you, and that's only three because I was at one point a little kid, even being what I am, so I didn't know I had a hankering for green-eyed temptress, biker bitch pussy for a coupla lifetimes."

I ignored the *biker bitch pussy* part and snapped, "I didn't know you meant *literally*."

"Well, I did."

"That's also insane," I hissed.

"Any less insane than anything else you've learned the last coupla of days?" he shot back.

I clamped my mouth shut.

He grinned.

I unclamped my mouth. "Don't you grin at me, Abel. Remember that thread I was hanging by?"

He kept grinning as he answered. "Yeah."

"Well, you're supposed to keep it strong, not unravel it."

He dipped his face closer again and asked, "How do I keep it strong?"

I bucked up against his body in an annoyed way and answered, "I don't know. *You're* supposed to figure that out."

"Thinkin' I'm done drawing from you, I won't numb you with my mouth."

My head tilted sharply on the pillow again. "What?"

He didn't answer.

He slanted his head the other way and kissed me.

Our first kiss.

It had tongues. It was slow. It was long. It was sweet. It was gentle. Then it wasn't. Then it was rough and consuming and fucking *unbelievable* to the point that when he broke his mouth from mine, I was panting and clutching him to me with arms and legs.

"You okay now?" he asked, and at my words coming back to me like that, my stomach dipped.

"Better," I said snippily, but that was all for show and he knew it, since it was also breathy.

He gave me another grin.

Then he gave me another kiss.

While doing it, he rolled so I was on top.

That was when I started kissing him.

And I felt better.

Then I broke the kiss and looked down into his wild and beautiful eyes, more so right then because I could see they were lazy but turned on, the blue had partially seeped back, but the brown was again suffusing it.

And I went about making him feel better.

"I want this, whatever it is you're about to do to me, and I've spent twenty-nine years getting to know me, so I know I wouldn't give what I gave earlier and what I'm about to give to a monster. Monsters don't inspire loyalty like you've inspired in your family. And monsters don't think twice about giving into whatever urges they're feeling, even if it hurts somebody."

The look in his eyes changed, went gentle but intense, the blue totally gone.

However I wasn't done.

I curled my fingers around the side of his neck. "And it breaks my heart you've spent two hundred years getting to know yourself and all you've come up with is that you're a monster. You aren't, Abel. I've known you less than two days and I know that for certain. It might take twenty-nine more years of my life to convince you of it, but if this is what I think it is, I'll have that time and you have my vow I'll bust my ass to try."

When I was done with my speech, he lifted his hand to my neck, curled his fingers around and up into my hair, and he rolled me again. His eyes were no longer gentle but totally intense.

He didn't say anything.

He kissed me, not gentle or slow, all rough and consuming.

He continued to say nothing as he took my mouth, his hands moving on me, and it began again. Not the same as before. He was slow and gentle, taking his time, building it, his hands eventually getting the addition of his lips and tongue gliding on my neck, tracing a path to my nipple, then the other, down to my belly, only for his tongue to slide across the top of the triangle of hair between my legs and head back north.

All the time his hands still moved on me, heightening the sensations, so by the time he made it back to my mouth, I was ready for his cock.

This was good because he gave it to me, sliding in slowly, his eyes to mine, his face close, his breaths coming fast, mingling with my own.

He was halfway in when he dipped and kissed me. Angling his body to the side, one forearm in the bed so he could hitch his knee for leverage, he rammed the rest of the way inside and I whimpered against his tongue.

He commenced thrusting, deep and sweet, as he kissed me, his other hand smoothing down my neck, between my breasts, to my belly.

Still taking me, he lifted his head.

I opened my eyes, looked into his, and the instant I did, he asked, "Delilah, are you mine?"

I slid a hand up his chest and curled it around his neck, using it to pull my torso up to press against his. My lips to his, I whispered what I knew was utterly crazy, but I also knew to the depths of my heart was undeniably true.

"Yes, Abel, I'm yours."

His fierce, feral growl vibrated against my lips, along my skin, exploding between my legs as he drove a hand into my hair, shifted to covering me, knee still hitched, and he quit deep and sweet and started fucking me rough and wild.

I gasped against his tongue before I tangled mine with his.

Not long later, I whimpered my orgasm into his mouth.

Not long after that, Abel growled his against the skin of my neck.

And he kept us connected as we drifted out of our climaxes, his face in my neck, my body cushioning his, my limbs holding him tight to me.

And as everything that was him, everything that we'd done, everything that we were becoming began to settle inside me, I decided having a guy who was hyper-intense, ridiculously overprotective, and phenomenal in bed were all super-fucking-good things.

# 7
# Potential Bloodbath

*Abel*

Abel heard the rumble approach from outside. He looked to the bathroom sink where Delilah was aiming a hair dryer at a round brush that was wrapped around a thick lock of her dark, shining hair and called loudly to be heard over the sound, "They're here."

Hair dryer still on, her eyes slashed to him and she cried, "Shit, crap, shit, crap, shit, shit, *shit*! I still have to tease!"

She then turned back to the mirror and pulled out the brush, the lock falling soft with a smooth wave into her face. Abel felt his dick twitch even as his lips curved up.

His dick might be twitching again, but it wasn't the same. The consuming need he'd had for her was gone, or at least the dangerous part of it that he'd feared would harm her was.

He still wanted her, but now it was because she was fucking gorgeous, fantastic in the sack, had a spectacular body, and was intensely responsive, all on top of what he was getting was her natural sweet, generous, teasing, kind, funny, and accepting.

And he knew this because he had all of the first four times since they woke up that morning and he'd had all of the last since he'd met her.

He looked to the floor behind her and saw her two bags had exploded since they took a shower, after which she commenced getting ready.

He also saw Xun was not wrong. The bitch did not pack light, not by a long shot. He had no idea how long she planned to stay in Serpentine Bay. But by the clothes, shoes, toiletries, and cosmetics bags he'd noted as he saw her pawing through them, which contained makeup as well as jewelry, it looked like she was moving there.

Something unpleasant shifted through his gut, but he buried it, deciding instead to continue to feel amused that he'd get the only biker bitch he'd met who couldn't travel with a couple of clean tees and pairs of panties, an eyeliner pencil and mascara, and an extra pair of earrings to shake things up.

Not that he'd had a biker bitch. Losing Hui, then Mei, and after her Sying, and more before them and after, he'd learned not to form attachments to humans outside the family. Just being with his family, he knew gut-wrenching loss would eventually come, so he didn't court more of it.

That didn't mean he didn't have friends over the last fifty or so years who lived the life, their women on the backs of their bikes, wearing leather cuts, proudly proclaiming they were the "property" of their men. These women existing on what they could shove in a saddlebag.

This meant Abel had never had what he had right then—the smell of a woman, *his* woman, his *mate*, permeating his space. All of her smells, every nuance, from her shampoo to her body wash to her lotion, her perfume, the shit she slid through her hair before styling it, and the underlying scent that was all her, her skin, her cunt, her essence.

And he fucking loved it, every note, every trace. He loved that her bag had exploded behind her. He loved watching her frantically teasing her hair in the mirror, shifting from foot to foot in agitation and excitement to see her dad (both of these he could smell too, and both were fucking *brilliant*).

He also loved the fact that that night, he'd sleep beside her. He'd also wake up beside her tomorrow morning.

And repeat the next day.

And the next

He'd brought women to his space, slept with them, woke up with them, then took them home and erased their mind of where they were, giving them different memories. These being that he'd fucked them and slept with them in their beds, all so they wouldn't remember where he lived.

Delilah would be the first he didn't have to do that with. Delilah would be the first who that happened with day in and day out.

And he loved that too.

But Abel did not think beyond that. Did not think of the days passing into months, then years, all of it leading to an inevitable conclusion that would leave him again with that hole in his gut, the agonizing pain of not having what he needed, and worse, the hole she would eventually leave in his life when she left this world, her being *it*. The one. The only woman who could give him what he needed, leaving him with centuries of missing it with no shot at having it back.

For she was filling his life already, just days in, with her talk of vampire TV shows and her ready acceptance of her destiny and her bonding with his family.

And what she'd given him that morning.

Christ, what she'd given him.

He'd felt her fear, smelled it, but she sat on that bed knowing, since she'd seen his strength in action, that it was a very real threat he could harm her. And she didn't tell him to go.

Instead, when he drove his cock home, her cunt clenched around him, welcoming him deep, her head snapping back, her hair flying everywhere.

*Christ*. He'd never forget it, not how glorious it felt, not how colossal it was.

Then she'd given him her blood.

He'd had rat's blood, cow's blood, pig, chicken, goat, sheep, and finally, human woman. He'd never had a male's blood. It didn't smell good and the idea of taking it turned his stomach.

But he'd never had blood as warm and rich and sweet as Delilah's. Given to him freely, giving all of her in one go, giving him everything he needed the first time she took his cock...

*Fuck.*

He knew she was his destiny. He understood that would come with emotion.

He was still surprised at how quickly he was falling in love with her.

Her comb clattered to the cement.

She cursed and Abel again focused on her, thinking, if they were to stay there much longer (which they weren't), he'd put another sink in on the other side of the tub so he'd be able to get in to do the minimal prep he needed to take on the day. This was something he'd had trouble doing earlier, squeezing in at the side to brush his teeth while she leaned across the sink, swiping makeup on her face.

He'd also give her a vanity, a huge-ass one, where she could rest all her shit while she was getting ready.

She wouldn't have it here. But wherever they settled, he'd find that for her. For the rest of her life, he'd find her everything she needed.

She bent to retrieve the comb, giving him a full-on view of the ample curves of her sweet ass, the sight he again felt in his cock. Then she went back to her hair.

He finished pulling on his boots and moved from the milk cartons where he'd been dressing.

He approached her from behind, got close enough to touch, but reared his torso back when she snatched up a can of hairspray, aimed, and let loose.

"Fuck," he muttered.

She stopped spraying, her eyes went to his in the mirror, and she muttered, "Sorry."

"Everything about you smells good, pussycat. But that shit? No," he told her as she tossed the can back into the sink with a clatter and he moved in, putting his hands to her hips.

"I need hold," she shared, lifting her fingers to fluff and arrange her hair, her eyes back to herself in the mirror.

His eyes dropped to her tits where her tee was straining, his dick deciding it was time to yank down her jeans and panties and bend her over the sink. Fortunately, because of what Delilah gave him earlier, his mind had control over his dick again and he didn't do that while her father and his boys were right then parking their bikes in front of the restaurant.

"I got a lot of hair," she went on. "I don't spend thirty minutes getting it to look this good only for it to fall and look like garbage."

"I think your dad probably doesn't give a shit what your hair looks like," he pointed out, and her eyes flew to his in the mirror.

"I'm not doing this for my dad," she returned. "I have a long, tall drink of serious hot-guy werewolf vampire. I can't take his side and not be the best I can be."

Abel froze, staring at her in the mirror.

*Take his side and be the best I can be.*

"Abel, I need to spritz on more perfume," she told him.

He didn't move.

*Take his side and be the best I can be.*

"I don't want you to get a blast of it, honey," she stated.

He slid his hands to cross his arms over her belly, yanking her into his frame, bending his head and using his chin to shift her hair out of the way so he could bury his face in her neck.

There she didn't smell like hairspray.

There she smelled like Delilah, fresh and sweet and tangy.

"They're already inside, Lilah. You need to get the lead out," he said softly there, kissed her, and let her go.

"Okay, baby," she muttered before she spritzed, quickly turned, squatted, dug through bags, and put on jewelry. Then she sat on her ass and pulled on her socks and boots.

He moved close to her and offered a hand.

She lifted hers and he took it, hefting her up, way up, surprising her into giving a quiet cry as he took her clean off her feet. She automatically swung her legs around his hips, her female parts pressed to the side of his hip, his hand leaving hers so that he could wrap his arm around her back and hold her close.

She curved her arms around his shoulders. He turned his head and looked down at her, seeing her eyes were wide.

"Hold on, *bao bei*," he murmured.

She nodded.

He moved.

He heard her gasp as he went about taking her upstairs as fast as they could get there, including opening and closing the steel door and the back door to the restaurant.

All this took seconds.

As they came to a rocking halt in the kitchen, he smelled Jian-Li's lunch.

He also smelled biker. Five of them.

He gave Delilah a slight shake and she unwrapped her legs from his hips. He put her to her feet and looked down at her.

Her hair was slightly tousled and her eyes were huge and bright.

"That...was...*awesome*," she breathed.

He grinned.

She leaned deep into him, her hand hitting his stomach. Smiling up in his face, dazzling and gorgeous, she whispered, "Let's meet the parents."

*Meet the parents.*

He'd have that once. With her. Doing something natural for a human, something Abel couldn't ever have until her, knowing he found the woman for him and adding humans to his life, his family, giving him more.

More family, which was the only real joy he had in his long life.

Or, at least that joy would last for a while.

Abel wanted to kiss her for that reason and others besides.

He didn't. He shifted so she'd let him go, but he took her hand and led her into the restaurant.

When he did, he saw instantly that Jian-Li was in hostess mode, nodding, smiling, and greeting the bikers who were gathered inside. Xun, Wei, and Chen were close but off to the side, giving her space to do her thing.

He took in Delilah's family and saw instantly they were hardcore.

They weren't bikers.

They were live, breathe, eat, drink, fuck, bleed, and die for the life *bikers*.

And he knew the one to the front was Delilah's father. He knew it because she had his hair and his eyes and he had a tinge of her scent. It was masculine, but the tang was underlying it. She got her pale roses-and-cream skin from somewhere else, but she got serious goodness from her father.

He was maybe five foot eleven. He was stocky with a hint of a gut. And he was in leathers—chaps over jeans, jacket, even a suede shirt.

His dark but salted hair was long, as long as his daughter's, but just the back. The top was clipped and spiked. The mullet to beat all mullets that only a guy like him could pull off.

His face was weathered. It was clear he had no problem with sun and wind, drink and food, likely drugs. He lived his life, every fucking minute of it, and he enjoyed the fuck out of it, all of this written on his face.

Then something else was written on his face as he noticed Abel and Delilah coming into the room.

Love and joy. Pure. Absolute.

Delilah pulled her hand from his, raced across the room, and Abel forced himself to stop and freeze in that position, his jaw clenching, feeling a muscle dance in his cheek as she threw herself into her father's arms.

He knew from what she'd told him that they were very close. She adored the man, trusted him, her affection for him was extreme. Abel also knew from the look he'd just witnessed on her father's face that he returned all that.

Thus that man would never harm her.

Abel still felt the overwhelming urge to forge straight to them and tear his woman out of her father's arms.

"Daddy!" she cried as her father shook her in his hold, her feet off the floor, arms around his shoulders, face in his neck, his face wreathed in smiles.

"My little girl," he husked, his voice beyond gravelly, straight to shards.

Finally, he let her down but didn't let her go, just positioned her a foot away, his hands holding her at her forearms out in front of them.

That was when Abel moved, immediately getting close, wrapping his fingers around her upper arm, forcing himself to pull her away but doing it gently. He felt her eyes come to him, saw her father's eyes move to him. But when he got her where he wanted her, he did not hesitate to clamp an arm around her shoulders and tuck her tight, her front to his side.

"Things have been intense," he said quietly to her father. "I get who you are to Lilah. She told me. But the first time I had eyes on her, she was not in a good way. So I'm not good with men touching her. *Any* man. This might wear off. But until it does, I hope you get me."

He felt Delilah relax into his side as her arms snaked around his middle. Through this, her father held his eyes.

Then he hooted, "Fuck!" He turned and said to the men behind him, "Did I tell you I was gonna love this guy?" He turned back to Abel and Delilah and shouted, "I fuckin' love this guy!"

The tension that had sifted into the room at Abel's actions slid away as Delilah made the introductions. "Daddy, this is Abel."

"Yeah, little girl, I think I got that," he replied on a huge smile aimed at his daughter and then stuck a hand out to Abel.

Abel let her go, she did the same, and he moved to take the man's hand. But it was a surprise when he didn't shake and instead grasped Abel's forearm and gave it a powerful tug, forcing Abel forward so the side of his chest slammed into the side of Delilah's father's.

Both men leaned back, but Delilah's father lifted his other hand and pounded Abel's shoulder repeatedly, smiling up at him, before he lifted his hand again and slapped his cheek, again repeatedly, doing this lightly with fatherly affection.

At this, Abel tensed, feeling Delilah tense beside him, but the man stopped soon enough and let him go.

He looked to his daughter. "Trust you to find a warrior this good-lookin'. Fuck me, little girl, not a man I clapped eyes on in my life was a match for you, 'cept this motherfucker," he stated, jerking a thumb at Abel.

Delilah giggled and moved into Abel again, saying through her laughter, "Totally."

He let her wrap her arms around him and he returned the favor with one around her shoulders as her father turned his attention back to Abel.

"Hook," he declared. "Hooker Johnson. My parents named me David, but that's a stupid-ass name and if anyone ever called me that, I'd rip their throat out. So it's Hook."

"Hook," Abel replied, and Delilah forged in.

"Have you met Jian-Li and the guys?" she asked.

Hooker shifted and turned his gaze to Abel's family.

"We met this lovely lady. Hadn't gotten around to her boys."

"Right," Delilah replied. "That's Xun, Wei, and Chen. They're awesome, Dad."

"Yo," Hooker called.

"Yo," Xun said, and Abel looked to him to see his mouth twitching.

"Hey," Wei said, his eyes moving from Hooker to Abel and Delilah. He took in their positions, knew immediately what their comfortable closeness meant, and grinned a knowing grin at his brother, his eyebrows waggling, his lips mouthing, "Right on."

"Cool you're here," Chen said.

"And guys, this is my dad, Hook, and his boys, Poncho, Snake, Moose, and Jabber."

Abel looked at the men behind Hook and he didn't need to be informed which was which.

There was one who definitely had Hispanic in him and he was actually wearing a fringed, suede poncho, so he had to be Poncho.

Another was long and lean to the point of being coiled, thus the man had to be Snake.

Another had a mammoth gut, broad but sloped shoulders, was almost as tall as Abel, with shaggy brown-gray hair—in other words, Moose.

And the last was short, skinny, wiry, his eyes shifty and alert—clearly Jabber.

"I hope you gentlemen are hungry," Jian-Li said at this point.

"Fuckin' starved," Hook replied, then lifted his hand in an apologetic gesture and grinned. "'Scuse my French."

Jian-Li smiled and replied, "Don't mention it, I've raised all boys." This got an approving smile from Hook, but when Abel looked to his brothers, the older two were rolling their eyes and Chen was grinning at his feet. This because the only one of them she let get away with cursing (sometimes) was Abel. "Now, let's start with drinks," Jian-Li went on. "What can we get you?"

"Beer," Hook said.

"All around," Moose grunted from behind.

"Any preference?" Jian-Li asked.

"Knock us out," Hook stated. "You got something exciting that'll trip our triggers, we'll drink it. Just as long as it's wet and cold. Got a long length of road down my throat and that always tastes good, but it's time to wash it away."

"This we can do," Jian-Li murmured through grinning lips.

Her grin became a smile when she turned, her eyes lighting on Abel and Delilah before she bustled out.

Wei followed her.

Xun motioned to a big table in the middle of the room that was set for serving. The rest of the tables were minimally set in preparation for business when they opened again.

After Delilah gave hugs to all her father's men (something Abel didn't like very much, but he had no choice but to allow), everyone took their seats, Delilah next to him, her father across from them. Beers were brought in. Jian-Li's food was brought in. And conversation was free-flowing, not even close to stilted or awkward, which gave Abel a sense of why his mate so easily fitted into his family's fold.

These people did not judge. These people did not hold themselves back and wait for someone to earn their sociability. These people were who they were. You took them as they came, and if you didn't, they didn't give a fuck. If you did, they let you in right off the bat.

This didn't mean that if trust was broken or wrongs were done, that shit couldn't turn in a flash in a way that would be messy. It was just that they offered themselves up without any walls to tear down to get in there. If you built the wall, that was your issue.

They lived their lives free.

They were also big eaters.

The platters of food and bowls of rice were nearly decimated before Hooker turned his eyes to his daughter and stated, "Right. Good beer, great food, excellent company. Hate to do it, but," his gaze shifted to Abel, "we gotta get down to business."

Everyone came alert, including Hooker's boys, all their attention shifting to Abel.

But it was Delilah who spoke and Abel was surprised at how honestly she did it. She didn't hold back, even when she spoke of being attacked, and this was surprising because her father and all his men became visibly restless as she described the incident.

She also told them about Abel being the one she was searching for, including the unknown-to-him-at-that-point knowledge that she'd somehow felt his presence in Serpentine Bay the moment he'd moved there, this being why she came there on her vacation.

Abel liked this, but he was mildly pissed she hadn't shared it. After she said it, he knew it was what was on her mind the day before, when she learned he'd moved there and when, but she hadn't let him in on that.

Then again, he hadn't given her much opportunity. He'd been avoiding her and then he'd been fucking her.

So he settled in to simply liking it and listened to her explain about when Abel was attacked and his brothers' participation.

She was thorough yet succinct.

Except for the fact that she didn't share he was a werewolf vampire and their attackers were also supernatural.

He was not surprised that not only did her father and his boys take all she said in stride, including the lethal way Abel and his brothers dealt with it, he also wasn't surprised that natural camaraderie turned respectful to him, Xun, Wei, and Chen when they heard it. This meant they would have dealt with it the same way.

Finally, she stopped talking.

He didn't know if she intended to get into the supernatural shit. All he knew was that was hers to share when and if she was ready and he'd move with her flow.

When she quit speaking, Hooker looked to Abel and asked, "You got a clue?"

"Nope," he replied.

"Hate to ask this, son, but the question's gotta be asked, seein' as you got no problem takin' care of business in a way that makes you a bona fide outlaw. So, is any of your other business leakin' to my little girl, puttin' her in danger?"

"My family's business is a Chinese restaurant," Abel replied, and for the first time, he saw Hooker's mouth tighten with irritation, likely because he thought Abel was lying to him. However, Abel wasn't done. "Our other business we don't do messy," he continued. "We do favors, but we do not get involved. So the answer is no. We do what we do and we do it in a way where Jian-Li, her restaurant, and our lives are clean."

He knew what he said surprised Delilah and it occurred to him that even if a fuckload of shit had gone down since they met, they had not shared hardly anything.

But his answer made the tightness leave Hooker's mouth and he nodded.

"Though, I'll point out, they came after Delilah before I'd laid eyes on her. So no one could know who she was to me," Abel finished.

"This is a worry," Hooker muttered.

"We're connected, Abel and I, Daddy, in a way that's really awesome, but it's also not exactly..." Delilah paused. "*Normal.*"

"I get that, precious girl. Spent a lifetime worried you wouldn't fill that pit in your belly, so I'm glad you finally got what you need. But you both bein' targeted the way you have and *when* is makin' me all kinds of uneasy," Hooker replied.

"There's something we haven't shared," Delilah said softly, her hand moving out and curling around Abel's thigh.

*Here we go,* he thought.

His eyes pinned to Hooker, he moved his body closer to Delilah, draping an arm on the back of her chair, and he felt his family tense in preparation.

"What?" Hooker asked.

"Well, like I said, like you get, Abel and I are connected. While I was yearning for him my whole life, he was doing the same for me," Delilah stated. "And as I mentioned, it's not exactly normal. But what I've found out is that it's actually, um..." Another pause. "*Supernatural.*"

Hooker shocked the shit out of Abel when he returned easily, "I could get that too, Lilah."

"Well, the way it's supernatural is that the, um...*people* who attacked me were vampires and werewolves," she announced.

Abel and his family tensed further, and Jabber muttered, "What the fuck?"

Hooker just blinked.

Then he asked, "Uh...*what*?"

Delilah's fingers curled tighter into the muscles of his thigh when she leaned forward and gave it to them.

"And Abel is a werewolf vampire."

Hooker leaned back, the room going wired, his eyes slicing to Abel and narrowing.

His tone was a threat when he asked, "You playin' mind games with my little girl?"

In response, Abel bared his teeth and extended his fangs.

The second he did, Snake and Jabber shot back in their chairs and up to their feet, both men yanking the knives from the sheathes on their belts. Moose scraped his chair back and leaned forward like he was preparing to launch himself across the table. Wei, Chen, and Xun also gained their feet and positioned behind Abel and Delilah.

Abel didn't move, but Delilah tightened her hold on his thigh.

"Jesus, shit," Hooker murmured, staring at Abel's fangs.

Abel retracted them.

"We're takin' her and we're leavin' right fuckin' now," Snake clipped out.

"No!" Delilah cried.

"Let us all take a moment, gentleman," Jian-Li urged quietly.

"Don't need a moment. Need our girl. You try to stop us, don't give a fuck you got fangs, I'll take you the fuck *out*," Moose growled, his leg jerking up and down, his body strung tight, clearly itching to make a move.

"Please, everyone, calm down," Delilah begged.

Abel held Hooker's eyes.

"I would not harm her," Abel said low.

Hooker didn't twitch.

"There were those who would. They are no longer of this world. I made them that way and didn't give it a second fucking thought," Abel continued.

Hooker said nothing.

"It happens again, I'll do it again, my brothers at my side," Abel went on.

Hooker remained silent.

"I'd die for her. I'm two hundred and five years old and I've been raised with love. I've been blessed with family. I've shown and been gifted with loyalty. I've known joy. But I've never felt complete until I had Delilah."

Hooker stared into his eyes for some time before his gaze shifted to Abel's brothers at his back.

Finally, he turned his head and took in Jian-Li, who sat calmly amongst a bunch of twitchy bikers, the remains of her generosity scattered across the table, the depth of loyalty she'd created standing at Abel's back.

Hooker didn't miss it. Not any of it.

And he relaxed in his seat, murmuring, "Boys, stand down."

"Are you fuckin' kidding?" Jabber demanded.

Slowly, Hooker looked to his friend. "Look at her, brother. Look at our girl. Does she seem harmed to you?"

"That doesn't matter," Moose fired back, and Hooker looked to him.

"Drugged?" he asked.

"The fucker's a fuckin' *vampire*," Snake ground out.

Hooker turned to him. "Look around, man. You ever know an asshole who earned family like this?"

Snake glared at Hooker.

Poncho whispered, "*Magio*."

Everyone looked to him.

He was looking at Delilah.

"It's not surprising, *mi amor*, that you'd live a life filled with magic. Only the special ones live magic. I'm happy for you, Lilah."

Delilah relaxed by his side.

The rest of the room stayed tense.

"Jesus, Poncho, your mystical bullshit doesn't jibe here. The guy's a *vampire*," Moose reminded him.

Poncho looked to Moose. "He's a warrior. Destiny has brought Lilah to him and destiny can be fickle. Giving you bounty, but doing it at the same time tryin' to take it away. You can't have treasure, *amigo*, unless you endure the perilous journey to find it. Lilah had some weak-assed fuckwad at her side and shit went down in life, natural or supernatural, she'd hold him up, or fall trying. She didn't get that. She got magic. She got a warrior. You should be happy and you should be relieved. Because from the shit they just laid out, for whatever reason, she's a target, and we're all fucked without his fangs at our girl's back."

That was when Delilah said softly, "I love you, Poncho."

He turned instantly to her. "You got that back, Lilah. Know it."

Abel felt her head hit his chest as she collapsed into it. He looked down to see her gaze on her friend, her face soft, her lips curled up, but her eyes were bright and that look made his chest get tight.

He wrapped his arm around her and gave her a squeeze.

In return, she draped her arm over his stomach and gave him one back.

"Please, gentlemen, sit," Jian-Li urged. "We understand your hesitancy, and if trust needs to be established, we'll earn it. But for our Abel, for Delilah, you must give us the chance."

It took a while, but finally the men standing sheathed their knives and moved to their chairs, Moose dragged his chair back to the table, and Abel's brothers shifted back to their seats.

Hooker grabbed his fork, speared a fat shrimp from his plate, shoved it into his mouth, chewed twice, then said through a still-full mouth to Abel, "'Scuse them. They're partial to our girl, and seein' as that's the case, they're protective."

"Wouldn't have it any other way," Abel replied.

Hooker gave him a shrimp-toothed grin and scooped up some rice.

Delilah shifted away from him and went back to her plate.

Abel didn't. He stayed alert but again draped his arm on her chair.

"Brother, saw the fangs, but you turn wolf too?" Poncho asked, and Abel looked to him.

"Yep."

Poncho grinned. "Insane, man. *Fuck*. But also cool."

"Yep," Xun stated firmly, Abel's in-your-face brother clearly not feeling all that happy with what had just occurred.

"Calm, son, we're all friends here," Hooker said quietly.

"That remains to be seen," Xun returned. "If the threat we don't get comes back and you got your chance to shut up and put up, endin' your night covered in vamp blood so our man and his woman here can continue breathing," he jerked his head Abel and Delilah's way, "that's when I'll see it."

"Xun, cool it," Abel murmured. "In case it escaped you, it's all good now."

"It will be if no further disrespect hits my mother's table, a table covered in her food, her fuckin' beer, with her sons, *all* of them, sittin' around it," Xun shot back.

"Cool it," Abel clipped.

Xun scowled at him and kept doing it until Abel heard Wei thump his brother's boot with his own.

Angrily, Xun turned his attention to his beer, lifting it with two fingers hooked around the neck and sucking back a healthy pull.

Abel looked at Hooker. "You'll excuse Xun. He's partial to his brother, and since he is, he's protective."

That got Abel another grin from Hooker and a returned, "Wouldn't have it any other way."

Delilah again giggled.

And finally Abel relaxed.

"So, that started great, turned down the road to potential bloodbath scary-as-shit, but it ended up okay, don't you think?"

This was Delilah, standing at the sink, her ass moving as she leaned over it, rubbing some shit into her face that smelled like heaven, which was what her ass looked like wiggling like that.

He tore his eyes and thoughts off her ass, something he intended to have in his hands in a few minutes, and thought she was right.

Eventually, everyone calmed down. Jian-Li, Delilah, with Jian-Li roping in Xun—likely to give him a piece of her mind—cleared the table and did the dishes after Delilah brought out fresh beers. More shit was shot amongst the men as the beer kept coming. They had a getting to know you session that went relatively well, considering everyone was watchful and some guarded.

Finally, the night ended with Jian-Li offering Hooker her guest bedroom so he could be close to his daughter, Hooker accepting, and him bringing up his saddlebags.

The rest of the men decided on a schedule of vigilance, Abel's brothers and Hooker's boys taking turns keeping an eye on the restaurant and alley.

Abel was left out of this as Chen explained that he needed to keep out of sight, and smell, for both his and Delilah's protection.

Abel was down with this, not because he didn't want to do his part in taking care of his mate, but because he wanted time with her to get to know her better.

Those not on duty took off, Wei and Xun to their apartments, Hooker's boys to check in at The Chain. Chen and Poncho were first up.

Abel took one break from this to go down and heat up a bag of blood, making a call at the same time to replenish his supplies. After he drank it, he went up and had more beer, conversation, and Jian-Li's light dinner of loaded pu-pu platters after a heavy lunch. All this before they called it a night.

All in all, they'd spent eight hours together and that was about seven hours too many before he had Delilah to himself again.

"Yeah," he responded to her question.

She grabbed a towel, wiped her hands, tossed it on the sink, then walked in a way that was part walking, part skipping to the bed where he was lounging, back to pillows angled up against the headboard, body naked under the covers.

She jumped in, landing on her knees, undulated to bounce twice, all the while grinning at him as he struggled not to knife up and drag her on top of him so he could roll on top of her. Then she fell to her hands and knees, crawled up, and collapsed on top of him.

Fuck, she was fucking amazing.

He wrapped his arms around her and started to count down—five seconds to take in her grin, then he was going to fuck her.

This plan was thwarted when she tipped her head and asked, "You play guitar?"

"Yeah."

Her grin got bigger. "Right on! I love guitar."

"Good to know," he muttered, eyes dropping to her mouth.

"Though, I guess, you get as many years in as you have, you can learn a lot. Do you play any other instruments?" she asked.

He looked to her eyes, tightened his arms around her, and answered shortly, "No."

"Oh," she murmured.

He was about to take her mouth when she kept at him.

"What's *bao bei* mean?"

"Precious. Treasured."

Her eyes got soft, as did her body on top of him, and she whispered, "Sweet." Then she pushed further up him so she was closer to his face but leaned back, resting her arms on his chest, and she kept fucking going. "Do you speak Chinese?"

"Mandarin."

"No other dialects?" she pressed on.

"Nope."

"Did you live in China?"

"With Hui and Mei. It was Sying and her husband, Chang, who moved us to America."

"Hui, Mei, and Sying?"

"Hui found me. Mei was her daughter. Sying was Mei's daughter."

Her focus became acute on his eyes and her voice got quiet when she asked, "Do you think your eyes are cool and tilty like that because one of your parents is Chinese?"

"No clue."

"You have really beautiful eyes," she told him.

Fuck, he wanted to fuck her.

"Thanks."

"And great hair."

"Lilah—"

"What business do you have that you keep from being messy?"

Christ, she'd rounded him right into a corner in a way he couldn't get out.

He tried anyway, trailing a hand up her spine and into her hair, then pulling her face closer to his. "I'll answer, pussycat, but later. Right now, gotta fuck you."

Her eyes widened. "Is the urge back?"

"No. Just can smell your cunt. I've fucked it, haven't eaten it, and now I got a different kind of urge."

She squirmed on top of him and he smelled it, the surge between her legs.

She liked his urge.

"Take off your panties, Lilah," he ordered.

Without hesitation, she moved. Swinging her legs around, she pulled her panties down and tossed them away.

Abel clamped tight on her hips even as he shifted them both down the bed so his head was to the pillows, and as he did this, he heard her heart quicken.

"Climb on, baby," he whispered, and watched her eyes flare. Then she moved, knowing exactly what he wanted and not hesitating to give it to him. He liked that, but still, he squeezed in with his fingers before she got anywhere and muttered, "Kiss first."

Her body melted into his as her mouth descended to his. Her tongue sliding between his lips, Abel let her drink from him. Then he moved his hands to her ass, cupped it, and he drank from her.

He broke the kiss and said, "Now give me that cunt."

"Okay, Abel," she breathed, moved again, positioning and lowering her pussy on his face.

He grabbed her hips and pulled her down at the same time he lifted his head and drove his tongue inside.

Her hips bucked and her cunt coated his tongue with a rush of juices.

Yeah, responsive.

Fuck.

He ate her, he did it hard and mercilessly, holding her down as she panted, whimpered, ground in, rocked, tore her nightshirt off like she couldn't bear it anymore, then tried to shift away when he knew it was getting too much for her. But he kept at her, the sweet tang of her finally on his tongue outside a dream. It was the best thing he'd ever tasted. Better than her blood and her blood was sublime.

He made her come and she did it hard, slamming down on him and crying out, "*Abel, baby*," like she'd done in her dream.

*Definitely* better in reality.

She was still feeling it when he yanked her down his body and fisted a hand in her hair, looking at her face soft and languid with her orgasm, his cock aching to drive into her.

"You're gonna take my dick now," he said roughly.

"Okay, Abel," she breathed.

"Ride me or I ride you?"

Her head fell forward, her lips sliding across his cheek to his ear where she whispered, "Fuck me, baby."

He rolled her to her back, positioned, and drove in.

Her back arched clean off the bed, her knees jerking up, her head digging into the mattress, her moan driving straight to his dick.

Christ, she was unbelievable.

He let go and she took him. More than took him. He was not unaware he was generously endowed, but her pussy accommodated him, clutched him, gripped him, milked him, demanded more from him. All this even as Delilah did the same, clawing at his back, jerking up her knees to get more, panting and gasping. He held nothing back, ramming into her hot wet so hard, he drove her up the bed until her head was hanging off the side.

"Abel," she whispered.

"Yeah," he grunted.

She lifted her head, her eyes slits, the look on her face making him pound harder. She lifted her hands to grip his head on either side and she whimpered, "*Abel.*"

"Fuck yeah," he growled.

She held on as her head dropped back, her mouth opening, no sound coming out, but he knew she was there because her cunt seized his dick and immediately milked his orgasm right out of him. He buried himself deep, his ass clenching as he poured his seed inside her on a savage snarl.

The orgasm so big, unable to hold himself up, he dropped to her, his lips to her neck arched back over the mattress, her pulse pounding into his skin.

She slid her hands into his hair and held him there.

It took a while but eventually she spoke.

"You're kinda good at that."

He smiled against her skin.

"And by 'kinda,' I mean seriously fucking good at it."

He lifted his head, she lifted hers, and he kept his seat inside her even as he dragged her back down the bed so she could rest her head.

She glided her hands out of his hair to his neck, down his chest, and around, where she clamped them at his back, her thighs pressing into his sides.

He moved a hand to swing her calves in so she was all around him, then bent and touched his mouth to hers.

When he lifted away, he stilled when he saw uncertainty in her eyes.

"Lilah?"

"Is it as good for you as it is for me?"

Jesus.

She had to ask?

"Uh...yeah."

She studied him.

She didn't believe him.

"And by 'yeah,' I mean *fuck* yeah," he clarified.

Tentatively, she grinned.

"Tame the green-eyed temptress, pussycat," he started on an order, "so I can tell you what you already know but will get pissed at. I've been doin' this a long time, banged a lot of pussy, so I got practice to make it good for you. You don't have that and you're phenomenal."

"Really?"

"None better."

Her eyes got big before they went soft, as did her body under him. "Really?"

He slid his hands up her sides, one going in and to her face to cup the side of it.

"Really, Lilah."

"Two hundred years of competition, that's saying something."

He grinned down at her. "Only been fuckin' for just a hair over half that."

Her head jerked. "Whoa, you started late."

"Aged slow, *bao bei*, seriously slow. Took me fifty years to reach ten, eleven human years. So had a major long childhood."

Her hands drifted light over the skin of his back and she said softly, like she was seriously looking forward to eventually getting the words she was about to say.

"There's a lot to learn about you."

"Same with you."

"I don't have two hundred years of history, Abel."

"Doesn't mean the years you got won't be fascinating to me."

Her eyes went hooded and her voice went soft when she replied, "Yeesh, you're sweet when you aren't consumed with the need to fuck me."

He chuckled, liking that she thought that, liking the way her lips parted softly when she felt his humor. He dipped his head and touched his mouth to hers again but then lifted away and said nothing.

She slid the fingers of one hand in his hair and he should have known by the look on her face she was about to lay him to waste.

But he didn't.

So he couldn't guard against it before she wrecked him.

"Thank you for making a lifetime of longing worth every second, Abel."

Jesus.

*Jesus.*

She was unbelievable.

"Can you take more?" he growled.

Her pussy convulsed around his dick, but her eyes got huge.

"More?" she asked.

"More," he confirmed.

Her voice pitched higher. "Now?"

"Right now," he returned. "You can, we're gonna see how much you can take when I fuck your mouth. Then I'm gonna take your cunt again the way I like you, on your hands and knees in front of me."

He got another pulse from her pussy as she whispered, "I should probably be offended by that, but I'm absolutely not."

"Your cunt told me that before you did, pussycat."

"That particular part of me has a mind of its own when you're in a certain mood," she declared.

"Thank fuck," he muttered as reply.

She grinned.

He bent and slid his temple along hers, ending with his mouth to her ear where he asked quietly, "You gonna position for me?"

She turned her head and replied, "Absolutely."

Yeah.

Delilah.

Unbelievable.

He slid out, rolled off, and watched, his dick remaining hard and starting to throb as she gave him what he wanted and got to her hands and knees in his bed.

Once there, she turned her eyes to his.

They were hungry.

That was when Abel gave her what she needed, paying attention to her skin, her ass, her tits, her cunt, before he took her mouth with his cock.

She couldn't take all of him, but she definitely took enough to make it worthwhile and got off on it, nearly as much as he did.

Then he shifted and mounted her from behind, and she *seriously* got off on that.

So did he.

Then Abel bedded down with his mate, curling her into his arms, feeling her body soft just because it was, and softer due to sex, relaxing into his as sleep took her. He smelled her all around—her hair, her skin, the beautiful mixture of them between her legs.

And for the first time in his entire life, Abel's eyes closed and he drifted into a dreamless sleep.

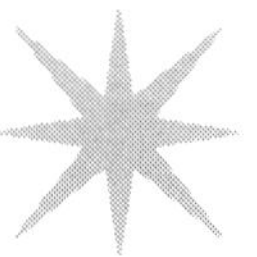

# 8
# I Got One Priority

*Delilah*

I opened my eyes, felt something, looked up, and saw Abel close, head resting on his hand, elbow in the pillow, eyes to me.

*Much* better than him across the room doing the same thing.

And he was there, right there, gazing down on me. Not a hole in my belly. Not talons clawing inside, making me bleed. Right there. Big and beautiful and mine, close enough for me to touch.

So I did.

Sleepily, I smiled and slid a hand to the hard wall of his smooth chest, feeling his warmth, his solidness, his *realness*.

And better, when I did, his face, which was warm and relaxed (also much different than the last two days when he was sitting across the room), shifted. It became warm, relaxed, and content.

Amazing.

"Hey," I whispered.

"Hey," he whispered back, the rough deepness of his voice gliding over my skin in a sweet way only to gather between my legs in a hot one.

"You sleep okay?" I asked.

"Fuck yeah," he answered. "You?"

"Yeah."

He moved in and I thought he was going to kiss me, but instead he slid his temple along mine and moved away.

I liked it when he did that. There was a tenderness to it that I'd never experienced and my dad could be very tender.

Even if I liked it, I still didn't get why he did it.

So I asked quietly, "What is that?"

"Don't know, but had to guess, wolf," he replied.

"Wolf?"

"Marking," he stated, and I got it because it made sense.

"It's sweet," I told him.

"Yeah," he agreed. "Sweeter for me, because when I do it, I can smell my scent on you. No one else can, but at least for me it claims you as mine."

God, I liked that.

I grinned and shifted closer.

Abel slid his arm around me and pulled me even closer.

I thought this might lead to something, but he said, "We should probably get up and go have breakfast with Jian-Li and your dad."

"What time is it?"

"Going on seven."

I shook my head. "Dad doesn't wake up until at least ten, even if he has a night that's early for him, like last night," I told him.

His expression changed and I felt that change trailing over my skin and gathering between my legs right before he rolled on me so he was covering me.

Oh yeah.

I slid my hands up the skin on either side of his spine as his hand lifted, sifting, then tangling in the side of my hair.

"We gotta talk," he announced.

I blinked.

"Talk?"

At my reaction, he grinned an arrogant grin that didn't glide over my skin but did gather between my legs before he muttered, "My pussycat wants my dick."

Well, yeah. He was good at what he did with it and it wasn't like I'd kept that knowledge from him.

I decided not to share what he already knew and only mumbled, "Uh..."

"I'll give it to you, *bao bei*, but we can't spend all our time fucking," he told me.

He was right, though we could try.

"What do you wanna talk about?" I asked.

"You. Me. Our future. The fact we have a future meaning we gotta talk about it."

He was right about that too.

I wrapped my arms around him and slid a leg out to curve it around the back of his thigh.

I did this to hold him, a gesture of affection, but his face darkened and he whispered, "She doesn't play fair."

"What?"

He studied me for a second before he spoke.

"Lilah." He dipped closer. "I smell you, *all* of you. Told you I can smell your cunt. Had that smell enough times when you wanted me to do somethin' with it to know when that is, which is what it smells like now. You opening your legs for me, call of the wild."

*Call of the wild.*

Nice.

"It might make me a freak, but that's totally hot," I shared.

"It is. So is your pussy right now. And I'll control myself 'cause we gotta have a get-to-know-you and discuss-our-future chat. But what I'm sayin' is, in future, you gotta have a mind to that."

"Okay, Abel," I agreed, then asked, "Do you want me to close my legs?"

"No, like it," he murmured.

Totally nice.

"Right," I said through a smile.

His eyes dropped to my mouth and he growled irritably, "Lilah."

Now I was confused.

"What?"

He looked to my eyes. "Baby, your smell coupled with that pleased-as-fuck, sexy little smile that says you know you got me wrapped around your finger and you like it is gonna get you fucked, in the good way. So cool it."

Holy shitoly.

"I have you wrapped around my finger?"

He looked to the headboard, which meant yes.

Oh man, I *so* liked that.

"Okay, I'll be a good girl," I told him.

To which he told the headboard, "Now all I can think is how good a girl she can be."

I slapped his arm. "Abel." He looked down at me. "It isn't me who has sex on the brain with *everything* I say."

"Bullshit, Lilah. Remember, *I can smell it.*"

"Then maybe we should just have sex," I suggested hopefully.

"And she gets her way," he groused.

I buried my grin at that.

"We'll be quick," I offered, and he rolled so I was on top.

"No," he replied, looking up at me. "*You* will."

Oh *yeah.*

I couldn't stop it that time. I grinned.

He frowned at my mouth.

I instantly commenced in doing something about that frown and I did it quick. I ended up riding him hard. Taking his big dick myself, stretching myself wide, filling myself full, fast and rough, again and again, my hands at my breasts, fingers at my nipples, eyes to my man, who had his fingers clamped deep in the flesh of my hips and was staring up at me with a face filled with hunger.

Fucking *ecstasy.*

I came and kept riding him until I gave Abel the same.

When we were done, I collapsed on top of him, got my breath under control, lifted my head, and looked into his sated, now-both-chocolate-brown eyes.

"Now we can talk."

One hand at the back of my neck, one at my ass, he squeezed both and his lips quirked, but he said nothing.

"I can't help it if you've got a big dick and I like it," I defended.

At that, he chuckled, his fingers sliding up in my hair and bringing my face down to get his kiss. It was long, slow, gentle, and sweet, perfect after we had quick, hard, and rough.

He broke it at the same time he tensed, his head turning sharply toward the door.

"What?" I whispered.

"Fuck. Wei," he replied and looked up at me. "Dress, pussycat. Nightshirt's okay. He won't be here long."

I nodded and we were out of bed in a flash, this including me losing him from inside me, which made me gasp for two reasons.

He set me on my feet, bent, retrieved my nightgown and panties, and handed them to me.

I took them and dashed to the bathroom while Abel moved to the chair where he'd thrown his jeans the night before, just as there was a knock at the door.

I got behind the closed door and dressed, deciding to take care of some other pertinent business while I was in there, doing this as I heard Abel open the door.

"Special delivery," Wei said as greeting.

"We're gonna hang tight outside, give Lilah some privacy," Abel returned, and I heard the door close, knowing from the silence they were on the other side of it and feeling that settle in my belly. There was a door to the toilet but no ceiling, and even though I didn't have a ton of hang-ups, taking care of business while two guys could hear it wasn't something I was hankering to do.

I got it done and left the bathroom, calling, "All clear," knowing at least Abel would hear me through the steel and cement (which meant he could probably hear the other parts, but...whatever).

The door opened.

I had a loaded toothbrush in my hand when it did and I moved back, shoving it in my mouth and lifting a hand to wave to Wei.

"Yo, Lilah," Wei greeted.

I waved harder and smiled through building foam.

The men walked in, both carrying coolers. I went to the sink but did it turned, watching them move to the kitchen.

Also listening.

"All's clear on the home front," Wei reported as he put his cooler on the floor. Abel went to the fridge and opened it, setting his cooler on the floor also, but he kept bent and slid the lid open.

He then commenced loading bags of blood into the fridge as I felt my eyes widen.

"Good," Abel replied.

"You think they got a load of us, then turned tail and ran, thinkin' whatever beef they have isn't worth it?" Wei suggested with what I figured was more hope than realism.

"I'm thinkin' they got a load of us and they're off for reinforcements and a strategy session," Abel replied, his eyes sliding to me.

I shrugged to show him that I wasn't freaked about his likely correct assessment of the situation and turned back to the sink.

"We need a get together, without Jian- Li. Can you call that?" Abel stated, and I turned back to them, surprised.

"Without Ma?" Wei also seemed surprised.

"Yeah," Abel said, moving the cooler out of the way with his foot just as Wei shoved the other one toward him with his.

"How do you think you're gonna get anything past Ma?"

"Have it at lunch when the restaurant is in full swing and she's too busy to come," Abel told him.

"Ma's a part of this, Abel," Wei said quietly.

"Yeah, and what I gotta talk to the men about I'll talk to her about, but privately."

I saw Wei's body tense, and due to it being imperative considering the amount of foam in my mouth, as well as to give them a hint of privacy, I turned back to the sink, spit, and turned on the faucet to rinse.

"I'll see what I can do," Wei replied.

"Thanks, brother," Abel muttered, now loading the blood bags from the other cooler into the fridge.

He finished this, snapped both coolers closed, and handed them to Wei, all while I watched through the mirror, rinsing the wash from my face.

"Later, Lilah," Wei called as he headed back to the door.

"Later, Wei," I called back as I dried my face with a towel.

Wei disappeared behind the door and I turned to Abel to see the microwave whirring, a bag of blood inside, but he was making coffee.

I tossed the towel to the sink, walked that way, and got close.

The microwave dinged.

"You know," I said softly, leaning my hip against the counter, "I liked it when you drew from me."

Abel's eyes, now back to brown and blue, making me wonder which way I liked them better, came to me. "Got that, pussycat," he replied quietly, turning to open the door on the microwave.

"So you can, you know, do it again," I told him.

He turned back to me, bag of blood in hand. "Want that, 'preciate you offering, and will take it, baby, if you ask for it. But you only got so much blood. I can enjoy it, get my fill, but gotta give it time for you to replenish it."

Of course.

"Right," I muttered.

"Have a look to see what you want for breakfast while I do this," he ordered, jerking his head to the fridge.

"Do what?" I asked.

"Drink," he answered.

I felt my brows draw together, thinking this was a little strange, as I replied slowly, "Oh...kay."

I moved to the fridge. Head in it, I called, "Well, in here, our choices are eggs and bacon or bacon and eggs."

"Got pancake mix," he replied. "Bread, milk, and eggs for French toast. Other shit on the shelves."

I looked beyond the door of the fridge to see him sucking back the last of the blood and toeing open the blue trash can.

"You could have told me that without my head in the fridge," I stated, and his eyes turned to me as he quickly finished with the bag and tossed it in the bin in a way that looked almost ashamed.

What the fuck?

"You pick, or I can ask one of the boys to go out and get donuts or some other shit you want," he said, dropping the lid on the bin and moving my way.

"What was that?" I asked.

"What was what?"

"The thing you just did."

He stopped and focused on me, eyes blank.

Carefully blank.

"Drink blood, Delilah."

"I know, Abel."

"Have to do it, but I'll do it quick so you don't have to watch."

I closed the fridge and faced off with him. "Honey, you've drawn from me."

"I know, I was there," he returned, his tone threaded with a sudden stiffness.

"And you left our beer and bullshitting fest upstairs yesterday to have your real lunch," I reminded him.

"Your point?" he asked.

"My point is you're you. That's what you do. What you need. Why would it matter if I saw you doing it or not?"

"It's not something humans do," he told me as if I didn't know.

"And?" I prompted.

"And, I saw your reaction the first time I did it. So I'll save you from bein' disgusted by it by not doin' it in front of you, or if I have to, doin' it quick."

Oh my God.

"Honey, I'm not disgusted by it," I said gently.

"Saw your reaction, Delilah," he returned, no thread now, his tone was full-on stiff.

I threw out a hand. "Well, you know, it was my first time. Cut me some slack for that. But now, things are different."

"How are they different?" he shot back. "I still drink blood."

"It's different because I know you better."

"Again, that makes it different how?" he asked.

"I don't know, it just does. It's a part of you. And I'm a part of you," I returned. "You've kissed me. You've held me. You've fucked me. You've made love to me. You've met my dad. You've met members of my family. You've slept beside me. You've come inside me, *repeatedly*. We're connected."

"Maybe we should quit talking about this," he suggested, and I did not like that.

I didn't because he clearly had some issue with this, an issue with something that might not be natural to me, but was not only natural but essential to him, he'd told me he thought he was a monster, and there was no way the things I was saying shouldn't be getting in.

Unless he'd built a wall to letting them in.

"Abel—"

"We're movin'," he declared.

"No, we need to talk about—"

"What I mean is, we're movin'. From Serpentine Bay. Just you and me. Not my family. Yours can escort us, act as guard close to wherever I find for us to settle that's out of the way and safe, but we're goin'. And I'm sorry, Lilah, but that means you gotta leave your life behind and you need to start doin' that while I look into finding us a place that's safe."

I stared at him, my throat getting tight.

It got tighter when he finished, "We'll also leave behind your dad and his boys when we get to a place we can do that. It won't be safe for them to know where we are either. But the way your dad is with you, he's gonna have to have a part in gettin' you where you're goin' and I gotta give him that. But he won't be goin' all the way."

"What are you talking about?" I asked on a horrified whisper.

"This shit that's goin' down, it isn't a surprise," he explained. "I've had decades of premonitions that something like this was gonna happen. Now it's happening. And the target isn't my family. It's you and it's me. As much as I love them, as much as I owe them, as much as they're a part of me, somethin' in me knows I got one priority. You. I gotta focus on keepin' you safe. I cannot focus on keepin' everyone safe. But I gotta find a way to make them safe, and turn my focus solely to you, which means getting them out of danger. And that means us out of their lives."

I couldn't believe this.

"But that...that..." I shook my head. "That will destroy them."

All of them. Jian-Li and my father especially.

His jaw got tight even as he replied, "Yeah, I know. Didn't say I liked it, but it has to happen. They may be destroyed, but they'll be it breathin'."

"Abel, I don't think—"

"Need you at my back with this, Lilah."

I threw out both hands. "But I'm not sure I agree with you."

"They'll be back," he whispered, his voice nearly a hiss, the sound crawling up my spine. "Not four of them. Not six. More. A lot more. My brothers, they can take care of themselves one-on-one. Two-on-one, that'll get dicey. More? No fuckin' way. These fuckers have power and speed, but they also got skill. I want my brothers to find women. I want them to make babies. I want them to live lives where they aren't movin' around every few years, protectin' me so no one will notice them age, but me not. I want them settled. I want them happy. I want them *alive*."

Oh God, I got him.

I *so* got him.

And what I got broke my heart because he was right.

We had to go to keep the people we loved safe.

"Okay, baby," I said quietly.

"You'll have my back?" he asked tersely.

I nodded.

"With your dad?"

I swallowed through the lump in my throat.

God, *Daddy*.

He'd hate it. He was going to lose it when it was suggested.

But he'd give into it. He'd give me anything.

I nodded again.

"I fuckin' hate this for us," Abel said low, his voice vibrating with the depth of that hate.

"Me too," I agreed, my voice shaking with the depth of my emotions, *all* of them.

"Found you, knew in my gut this is what we'd face. But wish like fuck I could give you somethin' else. Family. Laughter. Happiness. Peace. Us just settling in, gettin' to know each other, building a life together with your dad and all that comes with you, with my family and all that comes with me. But we can't have that unless I know the threat is gone."

"Okay," I agreed again.

Abel came to me and pulled me tight into his arms.

"I hate this for us," he murmured into the top of my hair.

I wrapped my arms around him and repeated, "Me too."

He held me close.

I did the same.

I felt him take in a deep breath before he muttered, "French toast."

I closed my eyes hard, opened them, forced lightness in my voice, suddenly not hungry in a way I didn't think I'd want to eat again for the rest of my life, and replied, "Works for me."

"That shit is *not* gonna happen," Xun declared fiercely.

In fact, his fierceness was clogging the room.

I curled my fingers tighter around Abel's thigh.

He'd just told his brothers, my father, and his boys what was going to happen. That being, Abel was going to search out a house somewhere far away and remote, Dad and his crew were going to take us almost there, then peel off, leaving us behind and leaving all of them without anyone knowing where we were.

"We'll come back when this shit gets sorted, Xun," Abel assured. "We'll find you." His eyes swept the round table in the private room in Jian-Li's restaurant where we were all having lunch, before he finished, "All of you when it's done."

"And what if it gets done in a way that there's no you to find us 'cause you got no one takin' your back?" Snake asked. "How will we know what happened to Lilah?"

"Sorry to say, man," Abel replied gently, his tone stating he *was* sorry, "you won't."

"That doesn't work for me, seein' as she's Lilah. A woman now, but she used to be a little girl I held in my arms and gave a bottle," Snake shot back.

My heart twisted.

"Then you need to make it work for you," Abel returned, "seein' as you fall in order to keep her alive, she's gotta live that life knowin' you did that shit for her."

"And she'll feel it. I know it," Snake retorted. "Then she'll settle in the knowledge she had that kind of love."

My heart twisted further and my lips whispered, "Snake."

He looked to me. "You are not takin' off."

"Please understand," I begged.

"Not gonna happen," he bit off.

I drew in breath then looked to my dad. "Daddy?"

Dad looked whipped and my heart endured another vicious twist.

"Always knew," he began, "one day I would no longer be the one whose job it was to shelter you from the storm. Hated havin' that knowledge, knowin' I'd have to give that over to the guy who'd claim you. Best job a man can have, bein' a father, lookin' after his little girl. Just had to hope like fuck the man that turned out to be was worthy." He looked to Abel, then back to me. "Don't know him all that well. I still feel in my gut that he is."

Gratitude and bitterness mingled in my soul at what I thought he was saying.

"But no way, little girl," Dad continued, "that storm turns into a fuckin' hurricane, I'm turnin' my back on you. Either of you."

"Dad—"

"It won't happen," he stated inflexibly, surprising me. "You leave, we follow. We gotta fight, we fall, shit happens. But I will not live the rest of my years knowin' my little girl lives a threat day to day and I didn't do what I could to keep her safe."

"It's important to us to know *you're* safe," I replied and threw out a hand to the table. "All of you."

"You known me your whole life?" Dad asked.

Shit.

"Yeah," I answered.

"Then you know this shit you're sayin' is not gonna happen."

Abel growled.

I squeezed his thigh and tried again.

"Please, Dad, see it from our perspective."

"I do," he stated. "But I'm seein' you don't see it from ours."

"Dad—"

"Lilah." He cut me off. "Give you anything, give you the world. I know you know that. But I will *not* give you this."

I clamped my mouth shut.

Chen, sitting beside me, stood, and when he did, I tilted my head back to look at him, seeing his gaze on Abel and his face twisted with anger.

"I did not start training when I was six years old to face a threat only to retreat when that threat came real," he declared. "Xun didn't. Wei didn't. Ma, knowin' this shit could go down for sixty-six years, fucking didn't. We're prepared. They can bring it on. We'll be here to face it."

"A smart warrior knows his opponent, when he can face him and when he should not," Abel replied.

"A brave warrior knows when it's worth it to face a lethal opponent anyway, even if the odds do not favor him," Chen fired back.

"*Fuck,*" Abel snarled, because Chen's comeback was a good one.

"Do not say this shit to Ma," Wei ordered, also rising. "Do not break her heart like this. Do not even *mention* this shit to her."

"It's her I'm lookin' after. She'll get it," Abel returned.

"It's her who will not survive a broken heart that never mended, which, if you do this, you'll shatter," Wei retorted. "And you fuckin' know that shit, brother. You fuckin' *know* it. She barely could live without Dad. You think she can end her days without you?"

"Wei—" Abel began.

Wei leaned across the table to his brother. "Every woman in our line for five generations has been born to you and has died with you. You can't take that away from Ma. She's lived knowin' one thing in this life is true—that she'll have you from the first breath she took to her last."

Oh...my...*God.*

I felt Abel's emotion roiling off him, but Wei wasn't done.

"This family gave you everything. You don't get to decide to take it away."

I felt Abel's emotion now beating into me and I leaned closer to him.

"You demand to have your dungeon close to Ma everywhere we go thinkin' it's you that needs to be near her so you can protect her. But you're wrong, Abel," Wei went on. "*She* does that shit. *She* finds these places so you can live close because *she* needs to protect *you.* Like her mother did. Like her grandmother did. I can go on and you know it. You're *ours*. Centuries of you in this family made you blood, even if we don't share it, and you don't turn your back on blood. We know that. We've lived it. Generations of our women have given that to you. Don't take that away."

On that, Wei did not wait for a reply, he stalked out.

Chen followed him.

Xun scraped his chair back and did the same.

Snake, Moose, and Jabber followed suit.

When they were gone, Dad turned his eyes from the door and looked to Abel. "Think on this, son, and do not make any rash decisions. I'll say it true...you take off anyway, I'll follow you. And from what I heard at this table, I will not be alone."

After delivering this, he pushed his chair back and walked out.

"Well, that didn't go real great," I muttered.

Abel growled again.

I started to look up at him but instead turned my gaze to Poncho when he spoke.

"Got an auntie who's a *bruja*."

"What?" I asked.

"Witch," he said. "She can see. She can protect." He looked to Abel. "Gotta have your permission, man, but wanna give her a call. Share. See if she can do anything for us. See if she can call up some visions."

After a moment's hesitation, Abel said, "Give me some time to consider that."

"Don't take too much," Poncho advised, then turned soft eyes to me, got up, and left the room.

I watched him do it, then turned to Abel.

"What now?"

"You mean after I successfully fight the urge to rip this room apart and then mind-control every one of those fucks into lettin' us do what we need to do?"

Oh man.

I leaned into him. "Don't do that, honey."

His jaw got hard and he gritted through his teeth, "I won't."

"I think we need to give this some thought. Give it a day or two for everyone to think about it," I shared.

"Yeah," he replied.

"We're loved. That's not a bad thing," I pointed out, and his eyes focused more fully on me.

"It isn't. It never is. Until that love turns to sacrifice. I've had a lot of humans sacrificing for me all my life, *bao bei*. The ultimate sacrifice..." He shook his head. "Fate saw it fit to grant me a long life, and that's a long time to live knowin' people who have a place in my heart gave it all up for you and me."

I understood him. It hurt what he was saying, the crushing significance of it, but I understood.

I also understood the men.

Impasse.

I lifted a hand and curled it around his neck, using my thumb to stroke the ridges of his throat. "A day or two, Abel, we'll all think on it."

I felt him swallow.

Then he said, "Yeah."

## *Jian-Li*

"Thank you for telling me that, Hook."

Jian-Li was standing in her office with Lilah's father. She was talking quietly. Hooker had also spoken quietly, since she'd shared with him over tea in her living room the night before (he'd had two more beers) all about Abel's abilities.

They didn't want him to hear.

"You're his ma, felt you should know. But it's more. We don't need to be facin' Armageddon inside the fold when we don't know what we're facin' outside it. Cohesion. This is what we need. You gotta work on your boy, woman," Hook advised.

He was correct.

But she had to do something else first.

She nodded.

Hook lifted his chin, gave her a small, worried smile, and walked out of her office.

Jian-Li watched him go, then moved out as well, up the stairs to her apartment. She got her purse and keys.

Then she walked downstairs, out the back door, and directly to her car.

She got in, started it up, and drove to The Biltmore.

# 9
# The Real Thing

*Lucien*

The vampire Lucien watched the petite, attractive, Chinese woman walk into Gregor's suite at The Biltmore.

She smelled of ylang-ylang, five spice, ginger, love, and fear.

"Mrs. Jin, we're delighted you've joined us," Gregor greeted, keeping a nonthreatening distance as he did so and her eyes darted about the room, taking them all in.

"Please, come in," Gregor invited, continuing to stay removed even as he swept an arm to indicate the living room of the suite. "Shall I order some tea to be brought up before I do the introductions?"

She tore her eyes from Callum, who was sitting on the arm of the couch next to his wife, Sonia, and looked up to Gregor.

"Please."

Her voice was strong and Lucien was impressed. It entirely masked her fear.

She still reeked of it.

"See to that," Gregor muttered to one of his lackeys, the only one in the room. A human—well-built, undoubtedly skilled, but still only human.

The man left and Mrs. Jin stopped well short of the seating area.

Gregor came to stand several feet from her side. "Allow me to introduce myself first. Although I did so at your restaurant, I did not do it fully. I'm Gregor. I'm a member of The Vampire Council, the working party which carries out the wishes of The Vampire Dominion."

She was looking up to him, and when he finished, she nodded.

"Now, may I present my son in a more formal way than how you received at your restaurant," Gregor continued. "This is Yuri." He swept an arm to Yuri, who was standing by the window.

"Mrs. Jin," Yuri murmured, then said in a way that made Gregor look sharply at him, which was to say in a way that was far from genuine, "Delighted to see you again."

The woman took Yuri in astutely but made no reply. She simply inclined her head.

She read his tone.

Lucien looked to Callum and saw Callum's eyes to him, his jaw hard, indicating they had the same thoughts.

Yuri was a pain in the ass.

Lucien returned his attention to Gregor when he again spoke.

"And also with us are Lucien." Gregor tipped his head Lucien's way, then gave her the information she needed in hopes of inciting trust. "Lucien is the mightiest of our vampires. By his side is Leah, his human bride."

She reacted to that, her body gave a small jolt, her eyes darting between Lucien and Leah. Lucien saw a note of sadness pass through her gaze, the origin of which he couldn't guess, before she dipped her chin to them.

"Mrs. Jin," Lucien murmured from his place standing beside the arm of the couch.

Leah, sitting in it, said, "Lovely to meet you."

"And this is Callum, King of the Werewolves, and his queen, Sonia," Gregor carried on.

"Pleasure," Callum said low.

"We're all very happy you've decided to come and meet us," Sonia stated.

Mrs. Jin remained silent even as she nodded to them.

"Please, if you'd like, take a seat," Gregor invited.

She hesitated, looking around the room, before she moved to take the armchair across from the couch where Leah and Sonia were sitting, Lucien and Callum flanking.

Gregor moved to one of the other four armchairs, his to the narrow end of the coffee table, the wide edge facing the couch and Mrs. Jin's chair.

"I hope you don't mind me sharing that we're most disappointed you have not brought your, erm...*ward*," Gregor noted cautiously.

Mrs. Jin watched him as he spoke, but she said nothing.

Lucien sighed.

She was exceptionally cautious, which meant this would take some time. Time they did not have.

Leah heard his sigh. He knew it when she reached out a hand and touched the back of his.

Leah's movements caught Mrs. Jin's attention and she watched this gesture, keeping her expression clear.

"Could I ask what your ward's name is?" Gregor requested.

She looked back to him and finally spoke, "I would prefer to be asking the questions, if you don't mind."

Gregor threw out a hand invitingly. "Please."

"Are there others like you right now in Serpentine Bay?" she asked.

Gregor answered immediately, "We have those with us to attend to necessary matters, but they're all human. The only immortal beings with our party are Yuri, who you may have guessed is a vampire, Lucien, Callum, and Sonia."

She looked swiftly to Sonia, then back to Gregor when he continued speaking.

"We are well aware your ward will be able to sense us and we didn't want to have a retinue of vampires in Serpentine Bay causing him alarm. Callum, who commands the wolves, has agreed with this and is also here without any of his people."

She nodded once and pressed, "No others?"

"I believe that the others discovered the hard way they were woefully unprepared to successfully complete their mission and they've retreated. Yuri, Lucien, Callum, and myself have moved extensively and frequently through Serpentine Bay since we arrived, including this morning, and we've sensed no others like us."

"And what precisely is their mission?" she asked.

"I'm afraid, Mrs. Jin, that what I'm sure you already know is the truth. They wish to see an..." Gregor paused, then finished, "end to your ward and/or his mate."

"Why?"

Gregor drew in breath through his nose and his tone gentled considerably when he replied, "It's your ward's right to know this, Mrs. Jin. I mean you no disrespect, but it's also his right to share it with you once he knows it. Or not, as he wishes."

"This is not going to happen that way," Mrs. Jin returned. "It will be me who decides if I wish to share what's happening with my..." She paused, as if struggling, before she said, "ward."

"If you allow him up from his underground cell long enough to learn," Yuri put in smoothly, the words said with no inflection, but they were still ugly.

"Yuri," Gregor spoke quietly but sharply.

"I know your play, Father, but you know I don't agree with it due to the fact that this woman keeps her vampire in a pit under a Dumpster, shameful and hidden away," Yuri bit back.

Lucien tensed in preparation to take care of Yuri so he couldn't fuck this up, and he felt Callum do the same.

However, they both looked back to Mrs. Jin when they heard her soft laughter.

"Yes," she said softly, mirth still in her expression. "My sons tease him often about his preference for space. Mostly my youngest.

However, that is what my eldest *son* prefers." Her gaze sharpened on Gregor. "And I'll correct you, albeit belatedly. He is not my *ward*. He is my *son*."

That morsel glided through the room and Lucien sensed both Leah's and Sonia's relief, not to mention Callum's and his own.

"And as his *mother*," Mrs. Jin continued, "it is my responsibility to keep him safe. Three nights ago, he was not safe. His *mate* was not safe. My sons rushed to their brother's side to offer him aid, and they were not safe. I am an old woman. I cannot do that. But *this*, meeting with you in an effort to understand what has befallen him, I *can* do."

"I understand, Mrs. Jin, and I will say it gives us great relief to hear your loyalty to one of our own," Gregor replied. "However, we must encourage you to ask your son to come here so we can speak to him personally."

"You don't understand, Mr..." She shook her head, appearing unfamiliar with her sudden uncertainty, proving she was a woman who wasn't often that way. "Gregor. My son is exceptionally protective of his family. He finds you a threat. I can only assume you're aware of his abilities, and him having these, he feels, even as my other sons are highly skilled and very strong, he's the only one who can protect us. He's keeping us safe by not putting himself in harm's way."

Lucien studied her, noting she didn't realize she'd given something away.

Her hybrid was not there, but she was, and they were far more a danger to her, a woman who could not defend herself, than to him, who had proven able to defend himself very well.

He didn't know she was there.

But Lucien knew, when he found out, he would not be happy.

"We do understand, Mrs. Jin," Callum put in quietly, cutting into Lucien's thoughts. "We understand intrinsically. For that is wolf."

"I'll ask you to explain," Mrs. Jin stated, and Lucien felt his stomach tighten.

She had no idea.

Which meant her son had no idea.

Lucien couldn't imagine not understanding his nature. The idea was abhorrent.

The third of The Three didn't. He'd lived however long his life was, and considering his maturation it had to be over a century, not knowing.

Fuck.

Callum had realized this too, thus he explained immediately, "The wolf is about his pack. *All* about his pack. There is nothing more important than their safety and nurture. The werewolf is the same. His," he dipped his head to his mate, "or her family is all-important. I don't know how long he's had his mate, but I can imagine you've noticed that this instinct is significantly heightened when it comes to her. This is because she represents the second half to the whole of the family unit. Protection of her is vital. To put it simply, a male wolf lives for that. He will eat, drink, sleep. But he exists for his mate."

She allowed her eyes to round with wonder for the barest of moments before she hid her reaction and said softly, "Thank you for that explanation."

"I'll be happy to share more with you, and your son, should he trust us enough to meet with us," Callum replied.

"And I'll be happy to share those traits he has that are vampiric," Lucien added.

Strangely, when her eyes came to Lucien as he spoke, they dropped to Leah briefly before coming back to Lucien.

This he read.

The third of The Three had a mate who was as The Prophesies foretold.

A human.

"There is much he needs to know," Lucien told her and held her eyes as he carried on, "And not simply about what occurred three nights ago."

She understood him and didn't wish for him to know that, this being why she looked to her lap.

Lucien felt Leah's fingers curl around his and hold fast.

She sensed it too.

"We don't wish to alarm you further than you and your family have already been alarmed, Mrs. Jin, but I'll tell you now, it's urgent we speak to your son *and* his mate," Gregor told her. "There are matters they must know, and the sooner they know them, the better."

Mrs. Jin looked to Gregor, allowing, "I'll speak with him again."

"Please," Gregor replied, "be convincing. As you know, the threat is very real. In an effort to establish trust, we have not approached again but kept our distance. However, we cannot leave. And we cannot because they will try again, Mrs. Jin. They will bring reinforcements and they'll try again. And even if we have the mightiest of vampires, with King Callum holding his position as sovereign of the wolves because he's by far the strongest of them all, we still fear without our own reinforcements, the threat they will bear when they return could be overwhelming. And if it is, that would be catastrophic."

Lucien sensed her escalating panic, even as she endeavored to hide it when she implored, "Then, *please*, share that with me."

"You've most assuredly earned our loyalty with what you've shown our brother," Gregor told her gently. "But I'm afraid it's his right to hear this and we cannot withdraw that right, even for you."

"Then I'm afraid I've had the bad manners to request tea when I cannot drink it, Mr. Gregor, since it's clear I should get home to my family," she returned.

"Of course," Gregor murmured, standing as she did the same. Callum came up off the arm of the couch out of respect and Mrs. Jin's eyes moved to him when he did so, taking that in. "I'll show you out," Gregor finished.

She looked back to him, then back to those on and around the couch, dipping her head in a small bow before she followed Gregor to the door.

"We hope we hear from your son and his mate soon, Mrs. Jin, and further, I have the opportunity actually to share tea with you on some occasion in the not-so-distant future," Gregor said as farewell at the door.

"We share this hope, Mr. Gregor," she replied. She looked to the room, nodded to Yuri, then moved out the door Gregor had opened.

He closed it behind her, and when he turned to the room, Sonia noted, "I think that went well."

"It did, mostly, outside my son needing to learn some diplomacy," Gregor returned, his eyes to Yuri.

"I do believe, Father, that my defense of one of my brethren was not taken negatively by that human," Yuri retorted.

"You couldn't know that when you opened your mouth," Callum put in with annoyance.

"No, but it's done and it caused no harm so there's no point in discussing it now," Yuri shot back.

"This is true, Cal," Sonia said quietly.

Callum's jaw got hard, which meant he kept his mouth shut.

Yuri turned to his father. "We know nothing about this hybrid. We don't even know his name. He's entirely off the grid to the point he's wind. We can trace that family to Daytona. To Dallas. To Pittsburgh. Through this, he doesn't exist, not in any of those places."

"You can well imagine, considering it's clear Mrs. Jin and her sons are loyal to him and wish him safe, why they would take precautions that his true nature not be discovered. We, ourselves, move frequently so that those around us will not come to realize that we don't age," Gregor replied.

"What I'm saying is, we do not know this hybrid. We don't know his mate. We don't *know* his nature. We don't know their strengths or weaknesses or what they're currently planning, including a possible attack *on us*, not to mention fleeing," Yuri returned. "We should send a human, at least, to keep an eye on that restaurant."

"Do you not think with the extreme care they're taking in protecting their son and brother that they wouldn't notice a human doing something like this?" Gregor asked. "The only reason you knew where he stayed was that you moved about that building and smelled him. In their state, with what befell them three nights ago, I do not wish to think what reaction they would have to *any* threat, vampire, wolf, or human, including us, which they've made clear they perceive as a threat. We need to establish trust, Yuri, not shed blood."

"Knowledge is power, Father," Yuri remarked.

"We need know nothing except they are the last of The Sacred Triumvirate," Gregor stated calmly.

Lucien tired of this back and forth and turned to Callum.

"Your wolves are close?" he asked, and Callum looked to him.

"Close but too far," he replied.

"The hybrid can't sense them, Callum," Gregor told Callum something he already knew as they'd had this discussion two days ago when he and Sonia arrived. "And the enemy can't know they're in wait. But in case we need them, we need them close."

"I have an excellent memory, Gregor, so there's no purpose in repeating yourself," Callum returned.

Gregor took no offense and looked to his son. "Our vampires?"

Yuri nodded curtly, visibly still impatient and annoyed. "They're amassing fifty miles south of town, to the wolves' north."

"I have hope Mrs. Jin will impress upon her son that he should meet with us, but there may be a need to prove we're trustworthy," Gregor murmured like he was talking to himself. "I just hope the losses are few should that occur."

"Me too," Leah muttered.

Sonia looked to her friend and gave her a reassuring smile.

"We should have sent in the women," Lucien noted. "Leah's human. She would be no threat and might be able to establish camaraderie with The Third's mate."

"Again, no use going over old ground," Yuri said.

"I'm not," Lucien replied. "I'm mentioning it again because it's still a play we can make."

"And you wish your bride and my sister to go into the den of a hybrid vampire werewolf who doesn't trust his own kind enough that he's dispatched every one he's encountered, save one who didn't meet that fate only because he ran away?" Yuri asked.

"I'd trust The Third with my wife because he did the same thing I would do if someone had touched her. He tore them apart. Even if he doesn't know who he is and all that means, he'd not harm Leah if she caused no threat. No one could say the same for those he slayed," Lucien retorted.

"Give them until tomorrow," Gregor cut in before things escalated as the look on Yuri's face said they would. Then again, Gregor had raised Sonia since she was a child, Yuri a part of that, so he too was protective of the woman Yuri called "sister." "Then we'll discuss Leah and Sonia being involved."

"I'll reiterate at this point," Leah said, "I'm all in."

"Me too," Sonia threw in.

Lucien sighed and looked down at his bride, who was looking at Sonia. "I have a taste for some Chinese food anyway."

"Me too," Sonia repeated on a grin.

Lucien moved his eyes to Callum, who had dropped his head back and was looking at the ceiling.

"He'll sense you as wolf, Sonny," Yuri reminded her.

"I know that, Yuri," Sonia returned. "And he's half wolf. He'd never harm a she-wolf that he senses as anything but a threat. And, it goes without saying, I'll be no threat."

"You can't know that," Yuri fired back.

"I live with wolves, Yuri, one in particular who is king because he's the shining example of all the rest," Sonia volleyed. "I *can* know that."

Yuri clamped his mouth shut when Gregor ordered, "Enough. Tomorrow we'll discuss this again. Today we hope that Mrs. Jin will talk sense into her..." His lips curled very slightly, then he said, "Son."

Lucien felt Callum's eyes and he looked that way.

What he saw was that Callum was hoping.

Lucien was too.

The time was nigh. The last of The Three had been found.

That meant they were all destined to save humanity from being enslaved by immortal beings.

Or they would die trying.

And they needed to get on with it.

One way or another.

*Abel*

"So, why don't you have an accent?"

This came from Delilah, who was lying naked on top of her naked werewolf vampire.

Suffice it to say, they had not gone down to their space to think on a change of mind of staying in Serpentine Bay and putting the lives of everyone they loved at stake. They also had not cuddled close and shared their histories.

They'd gone down to their space and fucked all afternoon.

And most of the evening.

Now, finally, Delilah had had enough and wanted to talk, this being only thirteen short hours after Abel suggested they do just that when they woke.

He wasn't complaining. He had a more than healthy sexual appetite and it would factor that the mate destiny chose for him would have the same.

Still, he was glad they were finally talking and not fucking. They needed to get to know one another.

She was also wearing him out, albeit pleasantly, and that had never happened in his life.

"Would you like something to eat before your interrogation?" he asked.

"You swiping that lemon chicken destined for someone else's table between round four and five was enough for me," she answered. "And by the way, your crazy-cool speed is awesome when it comes to theft, which is something we'll be talking about too...your non-messy '*business*.'"

She said the last word while pressing her tits deep into his chest since she'd lifted her hands to do air quotation marks.

He moved his hands from her ass to wrap his arms around her and replied, "Yeah, we'll talk about that. But as to your lead question, you're in a country for a century, pussycat, your accent tends to fade."

"Mm," she purred. "So do the boys speak Mandarin too?"

"They did. Ming, Jian-Li, and I all spoke it as well as English while they were growing up. As they got older though, they rebelled. Wanting to be like the kids around them, not wanting to be different, not understanding the importance of history and embracing your culture, even if your family decided years ago to leave the old world behind, they quit speaking it and stopped responding to it."

He tilted his head on the pillow, tightened his arms, and held her gaze before he shared the rest.

"I think they all regretted doing it when Ming died, but that made it worse for some reason. It was like they didn't want that reminder, the rebellion against the father they loved. Especially since Ming thought their understanding and respect for their heritage was important. I've no idea how much they take in now. They never use it."

"That's sad," she noted.

"It is," Abel agreed.

Since it was sad, and he was learning Delilah wasn't about sad, she changed the subject.

"So, you speak very, well...*contemporary*," she remarked.

He got her, so he explained, "You adapt, Lilah. I don't talk like I talked when I first learned English, or when we endured the sixties, or that valley girl bullshit, though I never talked like that." She grinned and he kept going. "You soak in what's around you. You probably don't talk like you did ten years ago either."

"This is true," she muttered, her eyes dropping to his shoulder.

It was Abel's turn for questions.

"Where did you live?"

Her gaze shot back to his and she let out a surprised giggle before her question shook with the same. "What?"

"Before we met, where did you live? Where is the life you're leaving behind?"

Her eyes went huge before she burst out laughing, her head falling so she could bury her face in his chest, her dark hair all around, her mirth vibrating through his skin, his flesh, straight into his heart.

Another dream come true, seriously so much better as the real thing.

Christ.

His arms tightened further.

She jerked her head back. "I can't..." She choked, giggled again, then made another attempt. "I can't believe you don't know that about me."

He grinned into her laughing face. "Well, I don't."

"New Mexico," she answered, gulped back more laughter, and went on, "Between Santa Fe and Taos, but I work in Santa Fe."

"What do you do, *bao bei*?"

"I'm PA to a lady who owns a string of boutiques," she replied immediately. "Two in Albuquerque, two in Santa Fe, one in Taos. They're pretty successful. She travels around a lot, dealing with things hands-on, going to buying shows, shit like that. I manage her travel schedules. Make reports of how the shops are doing. Stuff like that."

She drew in a breath, her face turned pensive, and she kept going.

"She's nice, but the job isn't that great. Kinda boring. The same thing over and over again. She pays me okay. I do better than some of my friends."

Her attention sharpened on him, and when she continued, she did it openly if still somewhat guardedly, as if needing to tell him what she was going to tell him but doing it concerned about his response.

"I didn't go to college. School just wasn't for me. Neither my mom nor my dad lived in a great part of town with a good school system. So Dad says it was because I was smarter than the system and I was bored." Suddenly, she grinned. "I like that he thinks that, but he knows better. So do I. It was mostly me being my father's daughter, hating authority, schedules, assignments, people telling me what to do." She shrugged. "That said, it wasn't a challenge and I got good grades. Just didn't want to buy into more even though Dad said he'd put me through college if I wanted to go."

Nothing about this surprised him, but two things about it troubled him.

He started with the hardest.

"You seem okay with leaving your life behind," he noted carefully.

She shrugged. "I am, but I'm not. I don't have a job I love, though I dig my apartment and will miss it. But it was just a place to live and I didn't suspect I'd live there forever. So I guess now's the time I'll be saying good-bye to it, though I hope there comes a time when I'll get my stuff back."

Abel decided that time would come soon, no matter how he had to manage it.

Her sadness filtered into her features and he braced before she went on.

"I'll miss my friends. That'll suck. And I hope we get to a place where they can be back in my life, even from a distance. But I've been waiting for you my whole life and I learned early that life is not a tiptoe through the tulips. Shit happens. Life changes. If it's important, you deal." Her eyes grew soft on him before she gave it all to him. "You're important. So I'll deal."

Her words meant he gave her another squeeze and he did it lifting his head to touch his mouth to hers, to show her just how much they meant.

Her eyes were softer when he dropped his head back to the pillow.

She knew what her words meant.

"Until just now, you haven't mentioned your mother," he remarked.

The grin left her face entirely.

Not a good sign.

He gave her yet another squeeze. "Lilah?"

"Mom and I aren't tight. She..." She shook her head. "She and Dad didn't get along and neither of them hid that from me, but she was bitter about it and she *really* didn't hide that from me, even knowing I totally adored him." She bit her lip, pausing before she carried on, "She also knew about the thing, that thing we share, that feeling of missing something. She thought I was crazy."

His brows drew together. "Crazy?"

"Bona fide take-me-to-three-shrinks crazy." She'd lifted up three fingers but dropped them when she finished, "I was in therapy for four years."

"Jesus," he muttered.

"Yeah," she agreed. "She also tried to have me medicated."

Her breath blew into his face in a *whoosh* when his arms contracted at her words.

He forced himself to loosen his hold, but his voice was dangerous when he asked, "Medicate you?"

"Yeah," she confirmed hesitantly. "She was convinced I had an eating disorder and other mental disorders besides." She curled her hand at his neck, her thumb sliding along the column of his throat in order to soothe him as she assured him quietly, "Dad stopped that part of my therapy before it ever happened, baby. I never was on meds. He totally got what was happening to me. I mean, not *totally*, but he didn't think I was crazy. Just missing something I'd eventually find."

Abel was beginning to understand her bond with her father.

"So you grew up with her and him?" Abel asked, and Delilah nodded.

"Yep. They had joint custody at first. But when Mom started the whole 'you're whacked in the head' thing, Dad stepped in. He was never a fan of having me only half the time. But when that happened, he fought for full custody. Even got a real job to pay for it."

Yes, he was beginning to understand their bond.

"I moved in with him when I was fifteen," she shared. "But I'd pretty much checked out on Mom way before then. If I wasn't at Dad's house for his week, I was with my friends. Mom and me never really recovered from that even though I didn't cut her out. I just keep..." Her head tipped to the side as she thought how to finish, then said, "Distant."

Abel said nothing, mostly because he didn't want to say what he had to say. That being that a mother not attempting to understand her daughter, instead sending her to others who would force asinine theories (he'd been with her for days and his woman had no eating disorder and certainly no mental ones) and unnecessary medications on her, was no mother at all.

She must have read this in his expression because she defended her mother by stating, "It isn't like what I felt was normal, Abel."

"Your dad seemed to get it," he pointed out.

"Dad loves me," she replied.

"As should your mother," he returned firmly. "No conditions, Delilah. I know. I turned from a puppy into a human who tried to sink my fangs in her flesh, and still had a mother who took me on, loved me, and accepted me, no conditions. In fact, I had two."

"I see your point," she muttered.

He was glad because he had another one to make which was almost as important.

"For your safety and everyone else's, she does not know about me or about us. When you start to break ties down there, she doesn't get the story and you share it with others in a way it won't get back to her."

"Okay, honey," she agreed.

Abel fell silent.

"Uh...speaking about that," Delilah started, "for everyone else's sake, what are we doing?"

"What are we doing?"

"About taking off," she clarified.

Abel drew in breath and let it out, noting, "Their reaction was violent."

"Yes," she agreed.

"Even more than I expected it to be."

"Yes again."

"And I haven't even mentioned it to Jian-Li."

Delilah made no response. She just pressed her lips together and widened her eyes, giving her unspoken opinion that Jian-Li's reaction would be what it was going to be—that being even more volatile than the rest—and his mate didn't even know Jian-Li very well

"Your father will follow us, his boys with him," he stated.

She kept stroking his throat. "He will, Abel. To be honest, I thought he'd give in. When he didn't, I was surprised. But even if I didn't guess his response, I know one thing for certain about my dad...when he digs in, he *digs in*."

Abel had that impression about Hooker Johnson too.

Not to mention his crew.

Abel looked from her to the ceiling, muttering, "Fuck."

Delilah said nothing, and when this lasted for some time as he contemplated the ceiling, it occurred to him there was something about that he liked.

They were talking about something, it was important to both of them, it weighed heavy on their minds, and even as she lay atop him, when he needed a moment in his head, she gave it to him.

He'd met many women in his life, not all he fucked, obviously, but both varieties, this trait was rare. Especially if what was being discussed was something important and she might have her point to drive home.

On that thought, he tipped his eyes back to her. "What's your vote?"

"Obviously my vote is not to have anyone I care about in danger, but that's been taken out of my hands by the evil supernaturals who want us dead. It's also been taken out of our hands by the people we care about, seeing as they've made it clear they won't accept a decision that they don't like. So I'm thinking we have no vote. Either of us. We have to give them what they need."

"Which means they may sacrifice their lives?" he asked, but he wished he hadn't when he caught her trying to fight a flinch.

His arms again grew tighter around her and he started stroking the skin of her sides with his fingers, something that worked and the flinch went away.

"That's our sacrifice, baby," she replied gently. "Our peace of mind for theirs. They need this to have peace of mind that they're doing what they can do. To have all the time they can have with us, even if it's short."

On these words, she dropped her head and rested her forehead against his jaw. She took her own moments in her thoughts and Abel returned the favor, being silent and letting her.

After a while, she kept going.

"No one likes this situation. But the one thing we'll all have as we go about navigating it is each other. So I guess that's not a bad thing."

She was not wrong.

And Abel had discovered something else about his destined mate.

Delilah Johnson was far from dumb.

*Very* far.

"Then we're decided," he muttered.

She lifted her head and looked into his eyes. "Are we?"

He slid his hands up to under her arms and clamped tight. "Not sure we have a choice."

"No," she agreed.

He rolled her to her back with him on top, murmuring, "Think I gotta fuck you again."

"Gotta?" she asked, her green eyes, which had been tinged with sadness, starting to light with humor, something he liked a fuckload better.

"Prefer to have my mind on your tight, wet cunt than this shit," he answered.

"With this I wholeheartedly agree. Though, for my part, I prefer you to have things *in* it, rather than your mind *on* it."

He dipped his head and grinned against her lips. "Goes hand in hand, pussycat."

"Uh...speaking of your hands..."

She let that hang.

He did as told.

And it worked. Being all about her and her body and her noises and her sweet, tight pussy while she was all about him and his body and making him growl with her growing devotion to his cock. It was much better than considering their future, which was clouded with an unknown threat.

And it worked so well it lasted even after they both came. It lasted while Delilah purred and Abel held her and she shared snippets of her life—her friends, her apartment, what she liked to do, stories of her father's and his friends' antics—doing it sleepier and sleepier until she trailed off and he lost her to her dreams.

When he did, Abel closed his eyes, and with his mate tucked close for the second night in a row, he became lost to a dreamless sleep, her sweet voice, lilted with its natural husk as well as love and sometimes laughter, still ringing in his ears.

# 10
# Small Successes

*Delilah*

They had him.

They had him.

*They had him.*

I had to get to him. I had to stop it. I had to save him.

They hit me in the back.

Paws.

The force immense, knocking my breath out of me, the weight tremendous, taking me down to my front so fast I didn't even lift my arms to cushion my fall.

He used his powerful head to nose me to my back.

Then he was on me.

The wolf.

And he didn't hesitate to bare his teeth and go for my throat.

I jerked violently awake to see Abel's face close to mine, illuminated only by the light from the lamp over the bed.

I felt his hand cupping my jaw.

My hand darted to his of its own accord, my fingers curling tight around his wrist.

"Lilah, *bao bei*," he murmured gently.

"Shit, I just had a nightmare," I breathed, realizing dazedly my entire body was hot and I was panting.

"You did, pussycat," Abel confirmed. "You were jerking around, got hot to the touch. Been tryin' to wake you for five minutes."

Seriously?

"Five minutes?" I asked.

"Maybe more," he told me. "You were beginning to freak me."

I focused on him and could only respond with "Ugh. Sorry."

"What were you dreaming?" he asked.

I blinked up at him as my mind went blank.

"I don't know," I answered.

"It just happened," he noted.

"I know, but..." I hesitated, trying to call it up but failing. "It's gone."

Abel studied me as his thumb started to stroke my cheek.

Then he asked, "Do you have nightmares a lot?"

I shook my head on the pillow. "No, I...I mean, I have them. But not a lot."

"When you do, do you remember them?"

I nodded. "Yes. Mostly."

"Do you dream a lot?" he pressed.

I shook my head again. "I dream, but I wouldn't say it's a lot. Why?"

"I do. Every night. Or, I did."

"Did?"

"First night you slept beside me was the first night I can remember for centuries that I didn't dream. This night the same."

Wow. Weird.

"Is that, um...good?" I asked.

"It is for me. Sometimes I don't dream good dreams. And all my premonitions came through my dreams." He kept stroking my cheek and gave me a small, sweet smile. "Tamed that in me, pussycat. Just by sleepin' at my side."

Wow. Weird.

And *awesome.*

"Cool," I whispered.

"Yeah," he whispered back.

I gave his wrist a squeeze. "Don't worry about my nightmare, honey. It happens and I've never premonitioned anything."

His sweet smile turned into an amused one. "Good to know."

"Is it morning?"

"No," he answered.

"Is there a reason, since you can walk in the day, why your windows are blacked out?" I asked.

"So no one can see inside," he answered.

"Oh," I mumbled.

"You gonna go back to sleep?"

"You gonna turn off the light so I can do that?"

"I turned it on, hoping it would wake you," he informed me.

"I'm awake, baby. Now I need more sleep."

He gave me a new look, one I hadn't seen before, one that I read as a my-Lilah-is-adorable-and-also-kind-of-a-pain-in-my-ass-but-I-still-like-it look.

It was a look I liked.

Then he twisted, reached his long arm out, giving me a lovely view of the bunched muscles of his defined biceps, and the light went out.

He settled in.

I snuggled close.

"Glad you're okay, *bao bei,*" he murmured.

It was safe to say I was *so totally* digging my werewolf vampire.

I cuddled closer. "I'm more than okay, honey."

He drew me even closer.

I grinned into his chest.

Then I fell back to sleep.

I opened my eyes to see the light by the chair dimly illuminating the space. Abel was not in the chair or in bed with me, but there was a note tacked to the back of the chair.

I got up on a forearm, throwing my hair back with my hand, and looked around in confusion.

The door to the toilet was opened, no one inside. The shower curtain was closed, but no shower noises. The rest of the room was empty.

Sleepily, I threw back the covers and padded to the chair.

I tore off the note that was pinned to it with a thumbtack, then lifted and read it.

*Bao Bei,*
*I'm out. You get up before I return and want company, just call one of the boys to take you upstairs. I'll be home as soon as I can.*
*Abel*

He ended this with a list of all of his brothers' cell phone numbers.

But...

He was out?

I thought he needed to stay in so none of the supernaturals could catch his scent.

This did not make me happy, and since I didn't have my werewolf vampire close to share that sentiment with, I went to my phone, programmed the guys' numbers in, and called Xun.

"Yo," he answered.

"Hey. It's Lilah. Abel's out and—"

Xun cut me off. "Uh, say what?"

"Abel's out."

"You're shittin' me."

Yeah, he didn't like it either.

Shit.

And I was beginning to feel that hole open up inside me again.

*Shit.*

"I wish I was," I told Xun. "I need to come upstairs. Can you come get me?"

"I'm not there, but Chen is. I'll call him."

"Thanks, Xun."

"Now, where's Abel?" he asked.

"No clue. Maybe donuts?" I suggested hopefully, trying to rein in the feelings of anger and fear that were battling for supremacy inside me as well as trying to ignore that hole that was opening wider.

"The man likes his sugar, but he is not gonna get his ass scented for donuts. He's doin' somethin' stupid."

This was my thought.

*Fucking shit.*

"I'll call Chen. Then I'm on my bike to find his stupid ass," he muttered.

"Thanks again, Xun."

"Don't mention it," he replied, still muttering, before he hung up.

I brushed, flossed, washed my face, and threw on some clothes, doing my morning routine breaking two cardinal rules.

One, I did not shower or do my hair and makeup even though I intended to be seen by someone that was not me (or, now, Abel).

And two, I did not make a pot of coffee so I could suck back some caffeine as a morning priority.

As I was tugging on my boots, I heard pounding on the door.

"Come in!" I shouted.

Chen opened the steel door. With one look at him I knew he wasn't happy, just like me.

"Please tell me there's coffee upstairs," I begged as I walked to him.

"Ma's got a war room filled with bikers. There's coffee," he replied.

This surprised me. My phone said it wasn't even nine yet. Bikers didn't do before nine.

I didn't take this as a good sign.

Then again, maybe The Chain didn't offer coffee, and bikers did coffee for certain.

"Have you heard from Abel?" I asked.

"Called him. Xun's called him. No answer. Xun's lookin' for him. Called Wei. He's gonna be lookin' for him too."

He closed the door and we walked down the murky hall made of cement (at our feet) and cinderblock (at our sides) toward the sun shining on the stairs at the end.

"Any idea where he'd be?" I asked as I hit the stairs.

"No clue," he answered.

But he had a clue.

I had a clue too.

The Biltmore.

And if he went there, when he got back (and I hoped to God he got back), I was going to kick his ass.

Chen escorted me through the back door of the restaurant and, thankfully, straight to the coffeepot. I poured Chen and me a cup. We were sipping, and I was doing it angrily in order to stop being scared out of my brain, when Jabber filled the door.

"Your boy's back and he wants his ma," Jabber announced.

My extreme relief that he was back, and the resulting closure of that fucking hole in my belly, was instantly replaced with extreme fury.

"Abel's back?" Chen asked before I could.

"In the war room. And warning, man, he's pissed," Jabber told Chen. "Like *werewolf* pissed, and this I'm seein' is *not* a good thing."

*He* was pissed?

I looked to Chen and saw he felt like me—that others should be pissed, not Abel. Then Chen moved to the stairs.

I moved to the war room with Jabber at my heels, prepared to go head to head with Abel for disappearing.

I stopped in the door when I saw him prowling the room like a caged animal.

One could say the sight of it was more than a little scary.

I ignored the scary and demanded, "Where were you?"

He stopped prowling and turned eyes to me that were even scarier than the prowling was.

They were both brown.

I was getting a lock on the "magic" of his eyes turning—they got brown when he felt something deeply, that being turned on or another good emotion.

Obviously, this also included bad emotions, like him being pissed off.

"Not now, Lilah," he growled.

"Now, Abel. You're not supposed to leave. It's dangerous," I shot back.

*"Not now!"* he roared. I jumped in surprise and Jabber got close to my back.

Moose and Snake, who were sitting in the war room sipping coffee while cautiously observing Abel, took their feet and inched my way.

"Calm down," I whispered.

"Where's Jian-Li?" he returned in a snarl, which I didn't like much, but at least it wasn't a roar.

"Chen's getting her," I told him. "But you need to calm down before she gets here."

"I'm not calming down," he replied.

"Take a breath, Abel," I advised.

"Delilah—" he started, just as Jian-Li said from behind me, "What's going on?"

Jabber and I turned to our sides and I saw Jian-Li with Dad trailing her, Chen trailing him.

My movement was the wrong one. This afforded her the opportunity to slide in front of me and into the room.

And when she did, Abel thundered, *"Have you lost your fuckin' mind?"*

Jian-Li came to a quick stop just inside the room. I slid in beside her and felt the others do the same.

"Abel, honey, calm *the fuck* down," I snapped.

"Went out, seein' as the boys can't smell what they're lookin' for and I can. Seein' as I can't be cooped up and everyone knows it. Smelled nothin' 'til I went to The Biltmore to see if I could get a sense of what we were dealin' with there. And when I did, I got hints *of you*," Abel informed Jian-Li, totally ignoring me for he was not calming down in the least.

But I was stuck back at The Biltmore.

"You went to The Biltmore?" I asked Abel.

His eyes sliced to me. "I went to The Biltmore."

"*Alone?*" I demanded to know on a near-shriek.

"This is not for now, Delilah," Abel bit out.

"It fucking is!" I shouted, moving further into the room, Jabber sticking close, Snake adjusting so he was closer. "They could have smelled you, set on you, *killed* you."

"They didn't. Didn't see them. Smelled them, didn't see them," Abel returned and looked to Jian-Li. "And, as I said, also smelled *you*."

"I went there yesterday," Jian-Li shared calmly, and my mouth dropped open as my eyes went to her. "I sat down and spoke with them," she went on, and that was when my eyes got big. "They were very gracious."

"You went to The Biltmore alone without tellin' anyone?" Abel asked, his voice quiet but frightening.

"I did, my Abel," Jian-Li confirmed.

"Then I'll repeat, have...you lost...your *fucking mind*?" Abel fired back.

"No," Jian-Li answered. "And I would have shared with you earlier, but you were with Delilah and you haven't had much quality time together. Even if their message seemed urgent, you connecting with Delilah was more urgent, so I decided this morning would be soon enough. Unfortunately, you found out before I could explain."

"Unfortunately I did," Abel clipped. "Now tell me, *tian xin*, how the fuck am I supposed to keep you safe if you walk your ass into a den of vampires and werewolves?"

"I took a chance for you, Abel, to keep *you* safe, and that risk bore fruit," Jian-Li replied. "They're not like the ones who attacked you and Delilah. They have urgent things to share with you. But they're good."

"They're good," Abel spat.

"They are," Jian-Li confirmed.

"And you know this," he threw out a long arm, "how? That they didn't kill you but obviously talked you into gettin' me to have a sit down with them. Is that how?" Abel asked.

"They wish to speak to both you and Delilah," Jian-Li told him.

"I bet they do. Two birds, one stone, and you deliverin' us up for that shit," Abel snarled.

Jian-Li's head moved like she'd been slapped.

I cut my eyes to my man. "Abel, *calm down*," I hissed through my teeth.

Abel again ignored me. "You are my daughter, my sister, my mother, and you put yourself out there for possible slaughter, then sat down with them and let them feed you bullshit."

"How do you know it's bullshit, Abel?" I asked, and he turned his angry eyes to me.

"Because I smelled them. Three vampires, one werewolf, all threats. I know. They smelled like me, but they also smelled like danger. The bad kind. The kind that'll get your head ripped off," he stated. "You do not mess with these guys. You do not look funny at these guys. Two of the scents nearly had me turnin' to wolf without control. I managed to fight that back, but my fangs came out and I *didn't* manage to fight that. That's how big of a threat they are."

Oh man. I didn't know much about his abilities or his control over them, but I got for certain none of that was good.

Dad moved from Jian-Li's other side to stand partially in front of her.

"You gotta be pissed, son, be pissed at me," he said. "I reckon Jian-Li did this because I told her that you and Lilah were thinkin' of takin' off."

"Then you're lucky you're Delilah's father or I'd rip your fuckin' throat out," Abel growled.

"*Abel!*" I yelled.

"Deserved that, Lilah. Keep cool," Dad muttered to me, his eyes on my man. Then he addressed Abel. "I hesitate to do this, considerin' your mood, but gotta point out, heard word you were gone. That means you're pissed at Jian-Li for doin' exactly what you did just this morning."

"I wanted to rip your throat out, Hook," Abel began, "I could. Before you could take a breath. Jian-Li cannot do that shit."

"My point still holds," Dad said quietly. "Now, we got a situation here where we got a lot of unknowns out there, but what we know is, some of 'em are not good. But we're fuckin' this shit up worse our own damned selves because we're reacting when we should be planning."

I *so* loved my dad, and in that instance, I did because he was *so* smart and he was *so* right.

I looked to Abel. "Please listen, baby."

Abel said nothing, didn't even look at me. His eyes were locked on Dad and a muscle was jumping in his cheek.

"You guys still thinking of takin' off?" Dad asked.

"We decided against that," Abel answered. I felt relief sweep the room, but his gaze moved to Jian-Li and he obliterated that relief. "Until I learned folks are doin' stupid shit that puts them in more danger than we already are, so now I'm considering it again."

"I hope, the man I need you to be to give a life of love and peace to my daughter, that you'll be the kind of man who reconsiders statements like that when you calm down," Dad replied.

"I wish to say something," Jian-Li cut in.

I kinda wished she wouldn't say anything. Dad was doing a good job and I sensed Abel pulling his shit together. We didn't need Jian-Li setting him off again.

"Your place, your son, your voice," Dad murmured, stepping back to her side.

Fabulous.

Jian-Li looked to Abel. "You know I'm no fool."

"Sweetheart—" Abel started.

"Those I spoke with yesterday shared openly that one of the vampires was the mightiest of their kind, and one of the wolves the same," she said. "Think for one moment, Abel, that the threat you sensed was just a threat, not to you, but instead it could be the threat at your side fighting your enemies."

"And what else did they tell you?" Abel asked. "Did they share what the fuck is going on?"

"No, they said they could only tell you and Delilah that," Jian-Li replied, and I looked to Dad but my eyes went quickly to Abel at hearing his nonverbal snarl.

Jian-Li kept speaking.

"They also shared with me precisely why you're behaving the way you're behaving right now. That you are wolf and the wolf is about his pack. A werewolf exists to protect his mate, his family. It was impressed upon me that he doesn't do this simply as instinct. It's his reason for existence."

My eyes got big at this total awesomeness. I looked to Abel to see him staring at Jian-Li with a weird look on his face that made my heart clutch at the same time I wanted to jump with glee.

"If we can perhaps arrange a meeting that you would be comfortable with, one of theirs alone but all of yours with you. Or perhaps one of their females—" Jian-Li started to suggest.

But I interrupted her. "Females?"

"One human who is bride to a vampire. One female werewolf who is queen to the werewolf king," Jian-Li explained.

"Holy shitoly," I breathed.

Vampire brides?

Girl werewolves?

Wow.

"The nonthreatening one," Abel whispered, and we all looked to him.

"What?" I called.

He focused on me. "I smelled another wolf who was nonthreatening. I didn't get it. Now I know it's female."

I wanted to roll my eyes before suggesting maybe it's the queen who kicks ass and takes names, but I decided that was probably not wise at that moment.

"Put your coffee down."

I focused when this order came to me from Abel and saw him heading my way.

Snake and Jabber didn't seem all fired up about this, but Abel clearly didn't care and I didn't have time to deal with it as I asked, "What? Why?"

He made it to me through the stiff bodies of my dad's friends and didn't answer. He also didn't wait for me to comply. He took the coffee out of my hand and set it on the table, doing this looking to Dad.

"Gather the troops. Strategy session here at noon," he decreed, then *zoom*. I was in his arms and my hair was flying out behind me as he took off like a bat out of hell. Then we were suddenly behind the closed steel door in his room downstairs.

My hair (and body) whooshed the other way as he stopped us, put me on my feet, and let me go.

I opened my mouth, probably to yell.

He got there before me.

"Your father is pissing me off."

I closed my mouth in order not to yell, because if I did, I'd probably say things I'd regret.

I took a deep breath.

"Fuck," Abel growled, dragging his hand through his hair. "He's like a biker guru."

Oh.

Well then.

Abel focused on me. "It's irritating as fuck when you're pissed to an extreme for someone to fight fire with logic."

I suddenly wanted to laugh.

Instead, with years of experience with my dad, I replied, "I feel your pain."

Abel stared at me. He did this a while.

Then, quietly, he said, "I did what I had to do."

All of a sudden not angry at all, I moved toward him, lifting a hand to touch him, starting, "Honey—"

"Apparently, it's beyond instinct. It's why I exist, Lilah. Yesterday was great. Fuckin' loved it, havin' time with you, gettin' to know you. But it's not in me to stay in bed fuckin' my woman while my brothers, her father, and his boys keep us safe. It just isn't." He shook his head and finished, "I did what I had to do."

I laid my hand on his chest and got close, murmuring, "Okay, baby."

The tightness of his chest relaxed (well, not all of it; it was safe to say my man was built so muscle like that stayed hard, thank God) and I got closer.

"You need to apologize to Jian-Li," I said gently.

His hands spanned my hips and he muttered, "Yeah."

*Yeah.*

I liked it that he agreed and did it so quickly.

Hell, I just liked my werewolf vampire.

I got up on tiptoe and touched my mouth to the skin under his chin.

When I rolled back, he dipped his chin deep and looked down at me.

The brown was seeping into his blue eye.

God, I loved that.

"You scared me," I blurted.

"I'm sorry, pussycat," he said softly.

"You gotta do what you gotta do, honey. I won't stop you. I promise. But I want you to tell me so I know where you are." I pressed into his chest. "I need to know where you are, like...*need*. It doesn't feel good not to, and when I say that, I mean physically."

He slid his arms around so he was holding me, his face getting soft with remorse, showing me he knew exactly what I was saying, as he replied, "You got it."

"Thank you," I whispered.

He bent his head and I rolled up on my toes to get his kiss. I thought he'd brush his mouth against mine. He didn't. He gave me a sweet, soft, wet kiss that was also long.

When he broke it, one of his hands slid up to cup the back of my head and he tucked my cheek to his chest.

"Gotta go talk with Jian-Li," he told me.

"Yeah," I agreed.

"You good down here by yourself, or you wanna come up with me?" he asked.

"I still gotta shower and do my hair and makeup so I'll stay down here." I put pressure on his hand and he let me tilt my head back to catch his eyes. "Give you both a little privacy."

"Thanks, *bao bei*."

I smiled.

He bent again but only to give me a lip brush this time.

When he lifted his head, he whispered, "Be back."

"'Kay," I replied.

Then, *whoosh*, he was gone.

"Rode Serpentine Bay north to south. No scent," Abel said to the men congregated around the round table in the war room.

I was sitting in his lap.

This was weird, seeing as there were a couple of chairs vacant (one for me, one for Jian-Li, who, after she'd forgiven Abel for being a horse's ass, had chosen to manage her restaurant and be briefed later about the session).

But when Abel and I walked in five minutes ago to a table filled with food, pitchers of water, and a variety of canned soft drinks and bottles of beer sticking out of a bucket filled with ice (Jian-Li knew how to throw a war party), Abel just kept dragging me to the far end of the table and then he pulled me right into his lap.

I didn't mind sitting in his lap, say, should we be having a quiet moment or he wanted a cuddle. In fact, I'd love it.

But this...

Weird.

I didn't protest, mostly because of the way he did it. Like it was natural. Like we'd done it a million times before.

It was not lost on me he'd had other women. But during a strategy session, I didn't need to get miffed and jealous, thinking about how he'd had practice yanking women in his lap and conversing like they were seated beside him, not *on* him.

We'd discuss that later.

Now, we had more important matters at hand.

"So none except the ones at that hotel," Dad replied.

"None except them," Abel confirmed.

"You think it's pertinent we move?" Dad asked.

"I think we should consider it," Abel answered. "They know where we are and we're an unmoving target."

Oh man.

"That said, we know the lay of the land here, we got a network, and they might expect us to move, gettin' us to a place where we lose that upper hand," Abel went on.

"Where are you leaning?" Dad pushed.

"Stay," Abel declared. "It's populated, and my guess is my kind are hidden. They attacked in the night, not broad daylight. They don't want attention. But we also can dig in. More cameras on the restaurant and alley, patrols with me to see if we can sniff any out, give a heads up to those in town who owe the Jin boys a favor to keep their eyes open for new players in the city and let us know who they are so we can take a look at them."

"Think that's smart, bubba," Dad grunted.

"I also think we make a meet with The Biltmore supernaturals," Abel continued, and my body went solid.

His arm around me got tight, his fingers digging into the flesh of my hip.

"Like Jian-Li said, one of them, all of us," Abel concluded.

"Agreed," Xun put in. "Ma isn't stupid. She trusted them. And if they agree to that kind of meet, that's more trust."

"Little girl?" Dad called, and I looked from Xun to him. "You don't look convinced."

"The only time I've been around supernaturals, they've been trying to kill us," I explained.

"See your worry," Dad muttered.

"We'll be safe, Lilah," Abel said, and I turned my head to catch his eyes. "Promise, *bao bei*. We'll take every precaution we can."

"We need to take Lilah out, teach her to shoot, if she doesn't already know," Chen announced and all eyes turned to him. "Teach her self-defense moves." He lifted his hand and shook it in a way that it was obvious someone was preparing to negate him. "I know a bullet doesn't stop vamp or wolf, but it might slow them down. And not much she can do without proper training, which would take years. But something is better than nothing."

I totally agreed with that.

And, luckily, my father had taught me to shoot.

Before I could share that, Dad did.

"You think I didn't teach my little girl her way around a firearm?" he asked with mild affront.

Chen might have responded, but I didn't hear him because, all of a sudden, I felt Abel's entire body tense.

Then, in a flash, he was out of his seat, me with him, his arms squeezing me so close it was like he wanted to absorb me. His head was turned sharply, ear to the back wall, beyond which was the front door.

He was sniffing.

"Wolf," he whispered.

The room went wired at the same time it filled with activity, everyone heading toward the door.

"Stop," Abel growled. Everyone stopped and turned to him. "It's the female."

"What?" I asked.

"Warn Jian-Li," Abel ordered, and Wei shot out of the room.

Abel sniffed the air again.

"Okay, crap, okay, *crap*!" I wasn't proud, but I started panicking. I mean, a wolf was descending! "Abel, are there more?"

"Only her," he murmured, then pushed me toward Dad. "Hold tight. I'm gonna check."

"What?" I asked. "No!" I cried when he was gone in a blur.

Dad grabbed hold of me.

"Cool it, little girl," he warned.

I stared at the door.

Thirty seconds later (I counted), we saw a blur, then we saw Abel, his eyes to my father.

I leaned against Dad in relief.

"No more. Just her," he declared. "You want different scenery for lunch?"

"Sit down with a female werewolf?" Dad asked, brows high, eyes dancing with the promise of adventure, the crazy biker. "Number one on my bucket list."

"I'm going," I stated.

Abel looked to Snake, Jabber, Moose, and Poncho. "She's in here with you. Xun will be at the door."

"What?" I snapped, and Abel looked to me. "I'm going."

"No, you're not," he returned.

"You said she wasn't a threat," I pointed out.

"Doesn't mean one isn't at her back," Abel retorted.

"You didn't smell him," I reminded him.

I could sense him digging in as he started, "Lilah—"

I sought compromise.

"Bring them back here. The men can stay. We won't hurt them, and if they want to establish trust, they'll accept that, sit, and break bread with us. They've come here for a reason, but this is our turf. We make the rules. They eat in the war room with you, with me, and with our family."

Abel narrowed his eyes. "Fuck, you're like a biker bitch guru."

I raised my brows.

Abel shook his head, giving me another new look, this one saying my-woman-is-adorable-but-also-a-pain-in-the-ass-and-a-big-one-at-that.

I didn't like it as much as the other, but I still liked it.

Then he looked to the door where Chen was standing and ordered, "Bring them in here."

Chen took off.

We all waited, and when they showed at the door, I was super glad I did the shower and primping thing.

The first one through was a classy, beautiful blonde with gorgeous blue eyes. The one who came after was a lush, sophisticated brunette with lovely green eyes. The blonde was in jeans, but the kind of jeans (with all the rest—fabulous blouse, kickass spike-heeled designer pumps, etc.) that they'd put in the pages of *Cosmopolitan*. The brunette also was in jeans and had on kickass high-heeled boots, but her thin sweater would be on the pages of *Cosmopolitan for the Outdoorsy Woman* (if they had that, which they didn't, but looking at her I was thinking they should).

"Yay, we're having a party," the blonde stated as her eyes fell on the table groaning with Jian-Li's food.

This was a surprising opener and I looked to Abel.

"Where should we sit?" the brunette asked like they were indeed at a party and had assigned seating.

"Show them their seats, Chen," Abel ordered, and Chen moved, showing the women the seats that Jian-Li and I never took.

They followed Chen like they hadn't a care in the world.

The other men drifted to their own seats, doing this cautious and alert.

Abel went to his and pulled me back in his lap.

The women watched this, and the minute my ass was settled, the brunette, smiling enormously, looked across the table at the blonde and declared, "Told you wolf traits would win out."

The blonde shrugged, grinning. "It seems you're right. Lucien will be disappointed."

"Perhaps you'll tell us who you are, then you can explain what the fuck you're talkin' about," Abel growled.

They looked to him, appearing not offended in the slightest by his less than stellar hosting skills. The blonde spoke first. "Sorry. Very rude. I'm Leah, Lucien's wife. He's a vampire. Like a superhero one."

"And I'm Sonia," the dark-haired one stated before I could process the idea of a superhero vampire. "Queen Sonia, but no one calls me that unless Callum is feeling kingly, which is a lot since he *is* king. That being King of the Werewolves." Her shoulders straightened and her eyes locked to Abel as she stated, "And I'm a she-wolf."

Holy shitoly, female werewolves were hot.

Leah followed this with a quiet request. "Are you going to tell us who you are?"

Abel apparently wasn't because next he demanded, "Explain what you meant about wolf traits winning out."

"The lap thing," Sonia shared, tipping her head to me. "Wolves hold their mates close in every way. To their hearts. In their minds. And when something like this is going down, even if it's just lunch, they hold them on their laps."

Wow.

Well, that explained that.

I looked to Abel, who I was surprised to see was looking at me and doing it like he didn't even know I was in his lap.

This I took as him putting me there but not really paying attention to the fact he did. He just did it.

Out of instinct.

"You've been raised as human," Sonia said softly, and both Abel and I looked to her.

"I have," Abel shared.

"I was too. It's a lot to take in when it all starts coming at you," she replied.

"You were raised as a human?" I asked.

She nodded, then shook her head, then lifted her hand and waved it in the air before dropping it and saying, "I was, but by vampires. Though, I didn't know they were vampires because I didn't know there *were* vampires, or werewolves for that matter. It was all quite a shock when I found out and I didn't handle it very well. But now it's all good."

Wild.

"Can you please give us your names?" Leah asked quietly, and Abel's hand at my hip tightened.

"I'm Abel and this is my mate, Delilah."

Both women smiled, but only Leah murmured, "Abel and Delilah."

Abel looked to Sonia. "Are there many like us?"

"You mean here in Serpentine Bay, or generally, throughout the world?" she queried.

"Both," Abel grunted.

"No to the first," she answered. "Callum, Lucien, Gregor, and Yuri have been going out to see if they can sense any, but none since the night you were, well...attacked."

"We're very sorry about that, by the way," Leah stated, leaning into the table, her head turned toward Abel and me. "It isn't very vampire unless, of course, it's provoked, and we know you didn't do the provoking."

"It isn't very wolf either," Sonia put in. "Unless someone is drunk or in a very foul mood or it's Christmas."

"Christmas?" I asked.

"That's just the she-wolves," she replied.

I stared.

"What we're saying is," Leah cut in, "this was an unprovoked attack. The King of the Werewolves and The Vampire Dominion know this, they condemn it, and they're very sorry it happened to you."

"We all are," Sonia added.

"And supernaturals throughout the world?" Abel prompted without indicating he accepted their apology, though he didn't throw it in their face.

"Thousands," Leah said.

"Tens of thousands," Sonia countered.

"*Loads*," Leah stressed.

I felt Abel's body, already tense, grow even tighter.

"You've never seen one," Sonia guessed.

"No," he grunted.

"I was raised by them but was having my wolf traits suppressed." My head jerked at this bizarreness, Abel's body grew even tighter, and she shook her head sharply as if physically pushing herself to get to the point. "Long story. That's all good now too. But what I'm saying is, I didn't know my kind even existed. You do. Can't you smell the difference?"

"I can. I just never smelled one other than those who attacked Delilah and me," Abel replied.

"Not in your life?" Sonia asked.

"No," Abel answered.

"Interesting," Sonia murmured.

"Why?" Abel rapped out.

This could go on for a while and the women were our guests.

Not to mention, I'd barely had a bite to eat and I was starved.

"Okay," I cut in semi-loudly. "How about this? We let these ladies fill up their plates. I get them some drinks. We let them eat. And then we can interrogate them some more." I looked down at Abel and asked gently, "Work for you, baby?"

He grunted but said no words.

I decided to take that as my go-ahead.

"Work for you, ladies?" I asked them.

"We're supposed to be here on a diplomatic mission, but I'd kill for some of that kung pao shrimp right about now," Leah declared.

I grinned and relaxed in Abel's lap. "Then let's not cause a supernatural incident. Just dig in."

Chen got them plates. I slid off Abel's lap, took orders, and brought them both beers.

I got a fresh one for my man too and climbed back on his lap.

They filled their plates and I went back to mine that I'd loaded earlier but had only been picking at.

"You know, me being a human and Sonia living nearly her whole life thinking she was one, explanations would be far more thorough if Lucien and Callum were here," Leah pointed out carefully.

Abel looked at her, then looked to Sonia. "Can you explain, if a wolf's mate is his reason for existing, why the fuck he'd let you walk in here with me, my brothers, and a fuckload of bikers?"

"Because you're half wolf," she said softly. "Because you would kill and die for your mate. Because he knows you know somewhere in your soul he would do the same. So he knows you'd never harm me, not only because it isn't the way you're made, but because you wouldn't take another's mate from him, nor would you unduly court the possibility that you would be taken from yours, leaving her unprotected."

Abel said nothing.

"That said, he wasn't a big fan of this plan even though he knows all of that," she finished on a murmur. "He's overprotective that way."

"Sister, do I get that," I shared.

Sonia grinned at me.

Abel growled.

"His growl is worse than his bite," I assured them.

"Too bad for you," Leah stated. "Mine bites and..." Her eyes got lazy as she said, "*Divine*."

"I hear that too, sister," I replied.

Abel shifted and I looked to him to see his jaw hard and his eyes on the ceiling.

I looked to my father to see his eyes to his plate, his lips smiling, his hand curled around his fork, shoveling in food.

In fact, I looked around the table and saw all the men doing this except Chen, who was staring at me and smiling huge.

So I looked back to the women and gave them big eyes.

A second later, we all burst out laughing.

I stood in the door of the restaurant watching Sonia and Leah leave, waving and then putting my hand to my ear with pinkie and thumb out, shouting, "Right! Call me! We'll sort these boys out!"

"You got it," Leah called back, waving behind her.

"Thanks for the delicious food, Mrs. Jin," Sonia yelled, folding into the back of a shiny, flash, black SUV at which a big brawny guy (their driver!—total class) was waiting at the door.

"My pleasure!" Jian-Li yelled back as she stood beside me.

She'd joined us not long after Sonia, Leah, and I bonded over being werewolf/vampire bitches and the meal descended into a girls' lunch at the Chinese restaurant.

Most of the guys drifted out, my dad and his boys going first. They didn't do bitch shit.

Chen, Wei, and Xun weren't far behind.

Abel had to stay because I was sitting on him.

As soon as the driver dude closed the door on Sonia, Abel yanked both Jian-Li and me in and slammed the front door.

I turned to him to see him opening his mouth to speak, but Jian-Li beat him to the punch.

"What did I say?"

He shut his mouth and scowled at her.

"I am no fool, Abel," she declared.

"Okay," I butted in, moving in between them and looking at Jian-Li. "Totally get your need for a nanny-nanny-foo-foo, Jian-Li, but all's well that ends well, right?"

She smiled a bit at my "nanny-nanny-foo-foo" comment and then agreed, "Right, Lilah."

I turned and looked up at a still-scowling Abel. "So, I'll chat with Leah and Sonia, we'll set up a meet with their men, find out officially what's going on, and move on from there. Yeah?"

"Yeah," he grunted.

I took a step to the side and pressed the air down with both hands. "Now everyone can relax. At least about the supernaturals at The Biltmore. Am I right?"

"You are, Lilah," Jian-Li replied.

Abel just jerked up his chin.

"I have a kitchen to supervise preparing for the dinner hour," Jian-Li murmured. "You two enjoy the rest of your afternoon."

"Will do," I assured her.

She grinned at me, moved to Abel, and even still annoyed, that didn't mean he didn't bend low so she could touch her cheek to his.

She bustled off.

I moved to stand in front of my man.

"Aren't you relieved?" I asked, taking in his continued displeasure.

"I'll be relieved when I have no threats against the ones I hold in my heart, not that one of them has turned out not to be a threat in the first place."

I understood that.

And it was sweet.

I got close and put my hands on his chest.

"Let's celebrate even small successes, yeah?"

His face got soft as he slid his hands from my waist to my back. "And how would you like to celebrate, *bao bei*?"

I tipped my head to the side and pressed in closer. "I have some ideas."

His eyes dropped to my mouth as his muttered, "I bet you do."

I slid both hands to his neck, lifted up on my toes, and whispered, "This time, I want you to bite me."

His eyes flared and the brown spikes started to obliterate the blue.

Then we weren't in the entryway of the restaurant. My hair was flying, I was holding on, and, *presto*, we were in Abel's room.

He tossed me to the bed.

I blinked, pulled in breath, and scrambled to my knees.

We looked into each other eyes.

Abel's were both brown.

Oh yeah.

He lunged.

I met him halfway.

*Sonia*

That evening, Sonia put her knee to the bed, her eyes to her husband who was lounging in it, chest bared, covers up to his hips.

She barely got in and settled back on her calves before Callum reached for her, muttering, "Why you persist in wearing nighties to bed, I will never know."

And then he tugged the tie on one side that held up the nightie at her shoulder.

Why she bought it knowing Callum would do just that, she did not know.

No, she did. Because she knew he'd do just that.

It was just that, right then, she needed his attention on other things.

She lifted a hand to hold the silk over her breast, saying, "Cal, we need to talk."

He stayed leaned toward her, weight now in his forearm in the bed, but his eyes came to her.

"We can talk after."

She knew what that meant, considering his voice was a rough growl and the tawny spikes were seeping into his blue eyes.

She also responded to it. Just hearing his voice, knowing what it meant he wanted from his eyes changing, but more, seeing the hunger on his face, the urge she used to try to fight but no longer bothered started to come over her.

"It's important," she said quietly.

He dropped his hand to her knee and replied, "It's important to me to get my *wife* out of that nightie and for her to lay on her belly and spread her legs so I can play."

The urge escalated significantly, but Sonia fought it back.

"I'm worried about Abel," she told him.

"We're all worried about Abel," he told her.

"No, my handsome wolf," she said gently, "I'm worried because he's somewhat like me. I'm worried because he knows nothing about his people." She covered his hand that was moving up her thigh and leaned his way. "I think before Gregor shares about The Prophesies tomorrow, you and Lucien should take Abel aside privately. Share about his nature. His people. Himself."

Callum's hand arrested, and not because Sonia's covered it.

"The Prophesies take precedent," he declared.

She shook her head. "No, Cal, I sense he's confused about who he is and what that means."

She watched her husband's brows snap together. "He has to be at least one hundred fifty years old, maybe older, Sonia. He couldn't have existed without learning about his nature. A pup has no control over turning wolf, and a vampire feeds on blood from the time they're weaned from their mother's breast."

"But there's so much more to it," she reminded him.

"Yes, there is, but none of it is more vital than sharing with him that he and his mate play a pivotal role in keeping humanity safe from enslavement, which includes the possibility one, the other, or both will die in the process."

"Cal—"

He leaned deeper toward her and his voice was firm when he said, "I know this. I know as wolf. You told me the wolf is winning out in him so I *know*, Sonia, that the most important thing to him is to know the extent of danger his mate is in and how he can do something to stop it."

She could not argue with this.

She still had a bad feeling.

"I'll talk to him. Later," Callum stated. His hand went back to moving up her thigh and his voice gentled but came thick when he said, "Now, baby doll, take off that fucking nightie and get on your belly for your wolf."

The blue in his eyes was gone and they shone with the hunger she felt gnawing through her. A hunger that had to be assuaged. An urge she could no longer deny.

So Sonia, Queen of the Werewolves, took off her nightie, slid off her panties, and moving on trembling limbs, she got on her belly for her wolf.

# II
# Dark Day

*Abel*

Abel stood at the basin, the light over it the only light that lit his space, his hands curled around the edge of the sink, his eyes to the mirror.

They were meeting the vampires and wolf that morning at nine at the restaurant.

He could not, for the life of him, sense anything other than genuineness from the human bride of the vampire and the queen of the werewolves, and his senses were keen. The women were open, honest, friendly, as well as slightly guarded, but only in a way that it was clear they wished to establish trust and not do anything that might harm that mission. They also bonded with Delilah swiftly and easily.

And he knew, being who he was and now understanding part of what he was, that it was a massive statement, their mates allowing them to come to the restaurant unprotected.

He was still worried.

That day was going to be a dark one; he knew it in his gut.

He'd left Delilah asleep in bed, but he sensed her stirring.

He didn't move. It was early and he hoped she'd go back to sleep, something he had problems doing after Leah phoned her to arrange the meeting. They'd gone back upstairs to make plans with the men as to how to handle it, then back downstairs to fuck yet again and go to sleep.

His hopes were thwarted when she didn't settle. After a few moments, he heard the covers thrown back, then he heard her pull on her nightshirt and panties, and finally he heard the fall of her bare feet moving across the floor his way.

When she came into view of the mirror, Abel watched her approach, her face sleepy, her eyes on him, her hair tangled and messy, the vision of her starting to make him hard.

She said nothing. Just disappeared behind his back at the same instant he felt her hands light on the sides of his waist right before he felt her lips brush the indent of his spine.

He closed his eyes to fight against the pull of how good that felt.

He'd hoped he'd have this. Just this. He'd hoped when he found her this was what they would be. What he saw with Jian-Li and Ming. What he saw with all the women who had been family to him, who had held him close to their hearts, and who he had watched with the men they eventually let in them. The casual affection. The quiet support. The catching of eyes where things were communicated perfectly with no words, things no one else would understand except the two communicating them.

But having it...

It was more than he could have imagined and he'd spent over a century imagining it, building it up, making it so beautiful that deep in his gut he'd worried the reality would never live up to it.

But it did.

And then some.

It got better when he felt Delilah press her cheek to his back and whisper, "It's early."

Abel opened his eyes. "Yeah."

"You didn't sleep well," she noted.

He thought she'd slept well, but apparently he was wrong. She'd felt his restlessness and he could tell by her tone and actions she was concerned.

Yes, she lived up to the dream and made it better.

"No," he confirmed.

She slid her hands around so her arms were wrapped around his stomach. He felt her shift her head so her nose and forehead were pressed to his spine. When she did that, the soft feathering of her breath drifted down his spine and he again had to fight against going hard at the same time he gave the tightness forming in his chest free rein.

After she did this, she gave him a squeeze and assured, "It'll be okay, honey."

"I hope so."

Another squeeze. "It will."

He didn't reply, just stared into his eyes in the mirror.

"Can I ask you a question?"

"Shoot," he invited.

He got another squeeze, this one seeming automatic, before she stated, "No recriminations. I don't know why I need to know, I just do, and it'll be okay because you've been around for a long time. You had a life. I get that. But have you, um...held another woman in your lap like you did with me yesterday?"

"Absolutely not," he replied immediately and felt her tense at his back.

"Really?"

Abel wrapped his fingers around one of her forearms and gave it a tug. She got him, let him go, and he shifted her to his front, moving in so she was pressed to the sink.

She tipped her head back, lifted her hands to rest them on his chest, and he caught her eyes.

"I honest to God didn't even know I was doin' it with you," he told her.

He saw relief in her face before she murmured, "I kinda sensed that, but I asked because I, well...had to be sure."

"It's only been you, Lilah."

Her peering into his eyes turned to staring.

She understood what he was saying.

Two hundred years and only one.

Her.

Still, she asked, "What?"

"Never lived with a woman," he informed her. "Never had a relationship. Never really even dated. Went out with women. Had drinks. Had fun. Did other shit," he added the last carefully. "Nothin' else. Especially not the lap thing."

"That's important," she guessed, still staring in his eyes.

"Only realized it when Sonia pointed it out. But yeah. The minute I became aware of where you were and that I put you there, I knew I couldn't handle you bein' anywhere but there." He dipped his face closer to hers. "Not another woman got that from me. Not another woman really got anything from me, save my dick. But I don't think in all my years I've even put one in my lap for any reason, pussycat. Not shittin' you. Musta sensed it was important so I didn't do it."

"That's cool," she whispered, the relief still there, but now it was heavier.

"Yeah."

"So many things about you are cool, Abel," she kept going and he felt her words deep in his gut. "The more you learn, the more awesome it all is."

Fuck, he fucking loved that she thought that way. And she was not handing him a line, saying words to make him feel better. It was written clear in her expression.

Awe.

And something else. Something warm and exquisite.

Something he felt in his gut, tightening further in his chest, and hardening his cock in a way he couldn't fight.

He gave in to the last, moved his hands to her nightshirt, and bunched it at the waist.

Her lips parted, her eyes went hooded, and he smelled the rush between her legs.

That did it. His cock stiffened and began to pulse.

He pulled her nightshirt up further, slid his hands in, then down. Hooking his thumbs in her panties, he pulled them down.

She bit her lip and leaned into him as they dropped to her ankles and she stepped out of them.

He gripped her hips and yanked her up, resting her bared ass on the edge of the sink.

She opened her legs, the lush rise of the scent of her cunt assaulting him, and he growled.

Her fingers went to the jeans he'd tugged on and gave a passable go at buttoning, leaving the last two undone. He dropped his mouth to hers and stared in her eyes, their breaths coming heavy, twining as she unbuttoned more, reached in, and wrapped her hand tight around his dick.

"Hard for me," she breathed.

"Yeah," he grunted as her hand got tighter.

She stroked and he braced, his fingertips digging into the flesh at the top of her ass, wanting to thrust into her hand but wanting more to give her what she wanted to take.

"Is this mine?" she whispered.

"Fuck yeah," he growled.

She stroked again, a groan stuck in his throat, and he slid his hand along the juncture of her thigh and in.

She gasped against his mouth, the rush of breath so sweet, he thrust into her hand as he slid two fingers deep into her wet.

"Is this mine?" he asked, voice rough.

"Oh yeah."

He thrust his dick into her hand again as he did the same with his fingers into her pussy.

Her breath hitched and wet flooded around his fingers.

Beautiful.

"You need me to fuck you, baby?" he asked.

"Yes, Abel," she whispered, then finished on a husk, "*Need.*"

He slid his fingers out, muttering, "Guide my dick home."

She didn't hesitate. She pulled him fully free of his jeans and straight to her cunt.

The instant his cockhead felt her wet, he plunged, her hand flying free, both going to his shoulders to hold on.

He tipped her ass on the basin so he had more of her, dipped his knees, and took her hard, back bowed, forehead to hers, their eyes locked, breaths cutting fast.

She slid her hands urgently up to the sides of his neck, slightly back, fingertips in his hair, and held tight.

"God, you fill me."

He knew she meant in more ways than one.

"Hold on, pussycat," he warned, and she held even tighter, jerking up her knees, taking more, loving it, showing him that by clutching hard with everything she had. Her thighs to his sides. Her hands to his neck. Her fingertips against his scalp. And her pussy around his cock, milking him deep.

"Fuck," he groaned, hammering hard.

"Faster," she begged on a breath.

He gave her faster.

"More," she gasped.

He wrapped his arms around her so he was supporting her weight—she was only balancing on the edge of the sink—and drove deeper.

Her head dropped back, her hair falling down, whispering against his arms.

"Drink," she breathed.

"Pussycat, no. Had you yesterday. Too soon," he forced out, wanting her blood, wanting it surging into his mouth every time he drove his cock home, but knowing he couldn't have it.

She lifted her head again, her eyes attempting focus but failing.

She was gone.

It was magnificent.

"Draw from me," she ordered, but her voice was vague.

"Can't, baby."

Her pussy gripped his dick so tight it was a miracle he didn't come instantly.

"Draw," she begged on a whimper.

Fuck.

He was powerless not to. She wanted it. He wanted it. And her cunt was demanding it.

He slid a hand up her back, tangled it in her hair, tugged, getting her throat, and he went in. Licking her, preparing her, her pussy rippled against his cock. Then he bared his fangs and tore through.

She cried out, her fingers driving up and fisting in his hair, her wet drenching both of them as she came hard.

He drove harder, her blood flooding his mouth with each thrust into her slick tightness, fucking, *fucking* ecstasy.

Abel felt it moving over him. He swept her wounds with his tongue, buried his face in her neck, his cock in her cunt, and groaned rough against her skin when he shot deep inside her.

When he came down, she was stroking his hair with one hand, had the other one stroking his lower spine, and had wrapped her calves around his ass.

"Don't do that again."

Her hands stopped moving and her body stiffened.

He lifted his head and looked in her eyes. "Love your blood, Lilah. But don't do that again."

"Abel—"

"You got me wrapped around your finger and it goes without saying, my dick is buried inside you, your cunt takes control. Give you anything to take you there. But it's not safe for me to draw from you too often."

She gripped his neck again and assured, "I'm not woozy from yesterday or anything."

He shook his head and pulled her closer in hopes of driving his point home. "Askin' you this 'cause it's important to me. I get you like it. You come the instant I tear through. You can want it. I'm fuckin' beside myself that you do. You can have it. But you gotta help me take care of you."

She held his gaze before she nodded.

He relaxed.

"Sorry," she whispered.

"Heat of the moment, *bao bei*," he replied gently. "Just need to be aware in future moments."

She grinned at him.

He grinned back, his eyes dropped to her mouth, then he put his lips there. He kissed her deep and wet and she kissed him back the same way.

In order of preference: cunt, blood, mouth—that's the way he liked the taste of Delilah.

When he lifted his head, he said, "Now, we're takin' a shower."

That didn't get him a grin.

That got him a smile.

Fuck, his Delilah.

Better than a dream.

At two to nine, Abel prowled the dining room of Jian-Li's restaurant.

Hooker and his boys were in the alley, prepared for the meeting (that being heavily armed with knives and guns) and chain-smoking.

Xun and Wei were in the kitchen, also heavily armed, with swords crossed on their backs.

Chen, also ready, was at the front door, keeping watch.

Delilah and Jian-Li were sitting at a round table in the middle of the room. Carafes of coffee, cups, jugs of cream, bowls of sugar, pastries Jian-Li had demanded Xun go out to get on platters, all of this was on the table, the women sipping coffee and gabbing like everything was A-OK.

He fought back the urge to snarl.

"Abel, eat a pastry," Delilah called.

"Not hungry," he replied, and he wasn't. He'd had her blood, which meant he'd had a gourmet breakfast. He didn't need a fucking pastry.

"Honey—" she started, but he turned his eyes to her and she snapped her mouth shut.

She then gave big eyes to Jian-Li, who replied by shaking her head and taking a sip of her tea.

Abel tensed.

Then he called to the back, "They're here."

"This is kinda exciting," Delilah whispered.

"I agree," Jian-Li replied.

Fuck.

"SUV's pullin' up," Chen confirmed from the front.

*Fuck.*

He heard and smelled the men coming in from the back.

Abel moved to position himself between the door and the table where his women were sitting.

He saw Chen standing at the front door, eyes to him.

Abel nodded.

Chen nodded back and turned to the door. He saw his brother take in a deep breath, then he opened it.

The scent of vampire and wolf drifted through.

Abel successfully fought his fangs extending and stood braced.

They came in: Vampire one, his human bride, male wolf, his she-wolf queen, and last, vampires two and three.

All the males' eyes were on him.

The females moved directly to the round table, Sonia greeting, "Hey! Good morning," with Leah's greeting being, "Oh thank *God*! Coffee and pastries."

Even as this happened and he heard chairs scraping, dishes clinking, his mate and Jian-Li returning greetings, Abel didn't take his eyes off the males.

They lined up in a semicircle ten feet from Abel.

He divided his attention between the first vampire and the wolf, not only because their threat was strongest, but because they were tense in a way that didn't sit well with Abel for this supposed we're-all-friendly meeting.

They didn't move when, as planned, Chen entered the room at their backs and Hook and his men entered from the kitchen, surrounding the women and the vampires and wolf in a circle around the room. Then again, they saw Chen and he knew they smelled the others.

"Precautions," one of the other vampires said, the one he knew to be Gregor. "I understand, Abel, but I do hope we can establish trust quickly as much is needed to get done this morning prior to our meeting and I haven't had my morning coffee."

As if Gregor didn't speak, the vampire he knew to be Lucien stated, "You feel it."

Abel looked to the tall, bulky, black-haired vampire and saw Lucien's black eyes sharp on him.

He didn't know how, but he got what the guy was saying.

They weren't edgy because of him.

They were edgy because they knew.

It was a dark day.

"I feel it," he confirmed.

"Fuck," the wolf called Callum growled.

Abel looked to him and saw the large, dark-haired man's light blue eyes were turning tawny.

And there it was. Another part to his wolf. But where Abel had two-colored eyes, one going brown when he felt extreme depth of emotion, this wolf had the same colored eyes and they both went tawny.

"We're fine," Gregor put in, his gaze to Lucien and Callum. Then he turned to Abel. "As much as I wish to discuss other things, as a priority, you need to be aware that it's come to our attention that our enemy has returned. They're outside the city limits, likely in an effort at keeping you, as well as ourselves, unaware they've returned."

This was not good.

"We have human scouts all over, however, so this intelligence has been reported to us. And I can assure you we have one who is currently watching them for signs of approach," Gregor went on.

"They're approaching," Abel told him.

Gregor shook his head. "Our scout is checking in every ten minutes. They're miles out." He drew in breath and finished cautiously, "You should also know we have a legion of wolves fifty miles to the north and a regiment of vampires fifty miles to the south. They're also aware that the enemy has returned, but their presence is still secret. They're set to advance at our call, which we will give them at any sign the enemy is on the move."

Abel was not a big fan of knowing Serpentine Bay was surrounded by supernaturals, but in that moment, he chose not to dwell.

He looked to Lucien and Callum. "You know this?"

"Yes," Lucien answered.

Callum only nodded.

"That make you feel any better?' Abel asked.

"No," Lucien answered.

Callum again growled.

"It's fine," Gregor stated impatiently. "And we have much to discuss. We should—"

Abel cut him off by looking to Xun and saying, "Be alert."

"Already am," Xun replied.

"*More* alert, brother," Abel said low.

Xun held his gaze steady and nodded.

Abel glanced around to all the men. "Threat not from within," he told them.

He got more nods and there was shifting of feet as they moved from facing the inner circle to facing out.

"Really, this is not—" Gregor began again but then stopped, tensed, bent slightly, and whipped his head around, baring his teeth, his fangs extending.

But Abel already sensed it, as did Lucien, Callum, and the other vampire, Yuri, all of them having the same reaction except Callum, who didn't have fangs to bare. Instead, he crouched in preparation to transform.

"Jesus, shit." Abel heard Jabber mutter.

"Sonia, get the women under the table," Callum growled. "*Now!*" he roared, crouched deeper and jumped, coming to wolf, snarling.

Abel heard chairs scraping, sensed Delilah and Jian-Li moving, smelled their fear, but he had to focus on fighting the transformation.

They were near and getting closer.

They had no time to run.

"Yuri, call Stephanie and Ryon," Gregor ordered.

Yuri pulled out his phone.

"Perimeter around the women," Lucien ordered. "No one breaches it."

"Got it," Hooker muttered, his back now to the center of the room, a gun in one hand, his knife in the other.

Xun, Chen, and Wei unsheathed their swords.

Jabber went to the table where the other weapons were hidden. He ducked beside it, Abel heard the steel scrape against the floor, then he emerged with Abel's sword and tossed it to him, point up.

"Got another one of those?" Lucien asked.

"Or three?" Yuri added, phone to his ear.

"Jabber, outfit them," Abel ordered.

Quickly, Jabber, going from table to table where the weapons were hidden, did as told.

Abel smelled it, felt it in his throat, and knew what was coming.

"We're outnumbered," he informed the room.

"Fuckin' great," Moose muttered.

"By a lot," Lucien shared. "Close ranks. They're almost here."

The men moved in to close ranks.

Lucien's tone had deteriorated a fuckload when he kept his eyes to a window but said to Gregor, "You'll explain how this happened when my bride and the rest of The Three are safe."

Callum was circling the outside of the group, growling low and snarling with his wolf lips curled high over his teeth, and Abel wondered briefly if he should turn wolf.

He had no time to wonder more.

They were there.

He lifted his sword as the doors flew off their hinges, front and back, and armed vampires and wolves burst through the windows, glass flying everywhere.

Abel knew in an instant, that instant being the next second when he was battling four-on-one, that he'd dreamed this. The location a blur because the action was too intense, but he'd dreamed it. And in the dream, he knew they were outnumbered and he knew they were all going to die.

He'd just never dreamed the end.

Now he knew how that dream would end.

But Delilah was there.

And she was breathing.

So he fought.

Viciously.

The room was a cyclone of activity. Grunts. Growls. Snarls. Gunshots. Steel clashing against steel. Wind wafting as bodies shot around the room. Flesh thumping against walls and floors. Blood spraying.

Within moments of the fight starting, he heard, sensed, and smelled Snake go down and knew the man was dead before he hit the floor.

The only other thing that could enter his mind was to fight until he died so they wouldn't get Delilah.

So he did that. Even when his flesh was torn away by wolves' teeth. Even when a blade sliced into his thigh, then his forearm and through his side, he didn't falter. He didn't tire. He took head after head because his mate's life depended on it.

"*No!*" He heard Leah shriek, sensed Lucien dart toward the table, and Abel knew all was lost.

But Delilah was still safe.

So he kept fighting.

"*Chen!*" Delilah shouted. Abel tensed to pounce, knowing he was going to her instead of his brother, his heart squeezing so tight he thought it'd explode.

And then the vampire and wolf he was fending off dropped, both headless at the hands of two women he'd never seen in his fucking life who'd materialized out of goddamned nothing and were floating in the air.

They didn't float long.

They, and dozens of others beside them, were darting around the room, unarmed but seriously fucking power-packed and in a motherfucking fury.

And they were on the good side.

What the fuck?

Abel didn't give it more time to process. He kept fighting with the others, pushing the enemy back. With their reinforcements joining the battle, they reestablished the perimeter around the center table and forced them back.

"*Withdraw!*" a vampire shouted, and as one, the enemy turned and shot through the windows and doors, the floating women charging after them.

Abel stood, breathing heavily, bleeding heavily, staring out the windows and listening to Delilah's rapid, but healthy, heartbeat.

Lucien didn't stand. He moved in a blur and ended another blur, slamming Gregor's body into the floor in front of Abel with his hand at the vampire's throat, Lucien kneeling over him, face an inch from Gregor's.

"Fucking *explain* how that fucking *happened* right...*fucking*... now," he snarled.

"Lucien—" Gregor choked.

"They touched *my bride*," Lucien bit out.

As Abel watched this, something cut through him, nearly bringing him to a knee. He twisted and saw Delilah on her knees on the floor bending over Snake, Hooker on Snake's other side, the rest of the bikers, his brothers, and Jian-Li gathered close.

"He's not dead. He's not dead. Tell me he's not dead," Delilah chanted, her hands moving over Snake's prone body frantically, her words and the rasping emotion behind them cutting Abel to the quick.

Abel bolted to her side.

"Fuck me, fuck, fuck me," Hook whispered, his fingers pressed tight around Snake's neck like he could stop the flow. But the blood rush was done. Abel knew it at a glance, seeing as Snake had no throat left, the entirety of it torn out by wolf teeth.

"We need a doctor, Abel," Jian-Li said softly beside him. "There are many injuries."

He crouched beside Delilah but tipped his head back as he did, his eyes to Xun.

His brother had cuts and bites, but he was relieved to see they were only flesh wounds.

"Call our guy," Abel ordered.

Xun nodded and moved quickly away.

Abel's eyes shot swiftly through the group.

Jabber was in trouble. He was down on a knee, his arm angled over his chest, his fingers curled into his shoulder, blood dribbling from his mouth, his wound hidden by his arm but bleeding profusely. His eyes were to Snake. Poncho was squatting close, hands on his friend to keep him steady, but Jabber was wheezing.

Wound to the lung. Or worse.

Abel kept looking and saw with a slice through his gut that Chen was also bleeding. An injury to his middle side. His brother was standing only because Moose was holding him up.

"Talk to me," he demanded to Chen.

"It doesn't feel great, but it won't kill me," Chen replied.

That was all Abel needed. He looked to Moose, who was bleeding profusely from a cut on his upper arm and had teeth marks on his neck, but they weren't deep.

"Put him down. Pressure to the wound," Abel ordered. Moose moved instantly and Abel looked to Jian-Li. "First aid."

She nodded and rushed away.

He looked to Wei. "Doc gets here, Jabber first, then Chen."

Wei jerked up his chin, then rushed after his mother.

Finally, he did what he needed to do most.

He put his hands to his mate, who was now quietly sobbing.

"Come here, pussycat," he murmured, trying to pull her away from Snake.

She tensed against his hands, then suddenly fought him, viciously, striking out at his arm, her other fist connecting with his jaw. Just as suddenly, before he could even move to contain her struggles, she collapsed into him, curling her hands in his tee and pushing in hard with all her strength.

And in another quick change, her head jerked back and she cried, "You're injured!"

"I'll heal quickly, pussycat," he assured her.

"But—"

He curved a hand around her jaw, getting closer. "Promise. I'll heal quickly."

She stared into his eyes, must have read the truth behind his promise, nodded, and again collapsed against him, burrowing her face deep in his chest.

He held her as she wept in his arms, his throat feeling thick, and watched as Hook finally moved away from his friend, his throat convulsing. Hooker grabbed a bloodied tablecloth from an upended table and draped it over Snake.

Abel's throat felt thicker.

"Abel, we must move."

He looked up and saw Yuri, covered in blood like the rest of them, looking down at him.

"We've suffered a loss," Abel told him, which he had to fucking know since the man was dead at his feet.

"We'll take the body with us," Yuri stated. Delilah bucked in his arms at his words and Abel felt his eyes narrow as the snarl ground up his throat.

"Careful," he growled.

A muscle jumped in Yuri's cheek and he nodded.

"We must move," he said, his voice quieter. "We have physicians who can see to your family's injuries. They're well-equipped. But it isn't safe here."

Abel glanced around at the carnage of headless vampires and wolves littering Jian-Li's restaurant, then back to Yuri. "No shit?"

"No shit," Yuri returned stiltedly. "So as you can see, we must move."

"Your physicians get here and say my family can safely move, we'll move. Until then, I got a doc comin' and we're stayin' put until I know they're good."

"This—" Yuri started.

"He says we're staying, we stay," Callum entered the conversation. He was back to man, dressed, and moving with Sonia clamped tight to his front.

"None of their injuries—" Yuri started but stopped when he reared back because Callum bared his teeth, snapped the air in Yuri's direction, then clipped, "*We stay.*"

"We stay, Yuri," Gregor said, getting close, his go 'round with Lucien obviously over. He was looking down with disheartened eyes to Snake before he took in Delilah and Abel's family and finally his attention came to Abel. "We have our people on the move. *All* of them. Including physicians who will be here imminently." His voice went soft. "And rest assured, we will care for your fallen."

He felt Delilah move in his arms and looked down at her to see her wet, grief-stricken face turned up toward Gregor. The sight of it, the heavy weight of her emotion he felt bearing down on him, forced another uncontrollable snarl to roll up his throat.

He had no idea what she would say, but when she whispered, "Thank you," that was a surprise. She then looked to him. "I'm okay now but need to go to Dad." She drew in breath and her fingers tightened in his shirt. "Please let me go to him, honey."

He nodded and didn't hesitate in giving her what she needed. He pulled her up to her feet, bent, and touched his lips to hers. Then he let her go.

She moved to her father.

Gregor got closer but stopped when Abel cut his eyes from his mate to the vampire.

"The Vampire Dominion has a compound about two hundred miles south of here," Gregor told him. "Considering what's been happening, it's been prepared for our occupation. It's very safe, already guarded, and where we'll be heading. Once your wounded have been seen to, you must pack what you need, including any weapons you wish to have, and do so in a way where you will be covered for a good deal of time as it's doubtful we'll be returning."

"You're serious, right?" Abel asked sarcastically, not about to go any-fucking-where with this fucking guy.

"Whatever happened that allowed this attack will not happen again," Gregor assured him, though Abel was far from assured. "But we must get you and the other couples that make The Three to a safe place and do it as soon as possible."

Before he could reply, including asking what this fucking Three business was, he heard ambulances and turned his head to the door.

"Our physicians," Gregor murmured, and Abel looked back to him. "You must trust us."

"And I do that how?" Abel asked. "One of my mate's family is dead on the fuckin' floor."

"Don't trust him, trust us," Callum stated from his side, and Abel looked that way to see Callum still holding Sonia close. Lucien was now there and was also holding a freaked-way-the-fuck-out-looking Leah just as close.

"It's where we need to be," Lucien added.

Callum leaned toward Abel. "Feel it," he said quietly. "Abel, you're fortunate. I know. You have many brothers, as do I. But now, you have two more."

He'd already felt it, when he knew they knew this day was going to be a dark one.

But he knew it more seeing how they held their women. There were men cut and bleeding, needing assistance, but those women, along with Abel's, had been under threat, a threat that almost took them all.

So they were not fucking letting go.

Yeah, he had two more brothers.

But he also had the ones he'd always had.

He looked down at the floor to Chen, who Wei was now bending over, putting pressure on his wound with a big square of gauze.

Chen read his gaze and nodded.

His eyes moved to Xun, who was in a squat, working with Poncho on Jabber. Xun felt his eyes, lifted his, and nodded.

"Wei," Abel called.

Wei looked up. "We go, brother."

Abel looked to Jian-Li, who was working on Moose's arm, and saw her already looking to him and nodding.

He finally turned to Hook, who looked uninjured but was still covered with blood and had both his arms wrapped tight around his daughter.

"We get stitched up, they take care of Snake, and we get...the fuck...outta here," Hook ground out.

Only then did Abel turn his eyes to Gregor and declare, "Right. We go."

Abel stood at the window watching the waves pound against the rock below the huge-fucking-ass fortress they'd brought them to.

On the journey, he rode his bike with Delilah at his back, wishing it was in better circumstances that he had her there for a long road trip, but liking her there all the same.

The others rode their bikes surrounding them. Chen's and Jabber's bikes were ridden by some humans Gregor had assigned to them, seeing as Chen and Jabber had been stabilized on the floor of Jian-Li's dining room, then transferred to ambulances for what Gregor referred to as their "relocation."

Gregor assured him that they were having rooms made up with everything needed so the doctors could continue to care for the men when they arrived.

Callum and Sonia, Lucien and Leah went back to the hotel to sort their shit, and his family sorted theirs. While they were doing this, a shitload of wolves descended, led by one who introduced himself to Abel as Ryon, cousin to Callum.

Ryon held his gaze steady and had a scent that was similar to Callum's, so Abel trusted him and allowed his family to move out while SUVs filled with a cleanup crew of wolves arrived to deal with the bodies.

He'd also left behind his doc, who he'd mind-controlled. The man was on retainer should they need him and part of that retainer paid for his silence. But what he saw when he charged in and helped Gregor's doctors with Jabber, no way he'd keep quiet.

So Abel had quieted him.

Once they moved out with their protective cavalcade of SUVs led by Ryon, they went to the hotel where they picked up the rest, then headed out to relocate.

After he was certain the wounded were settled, Abel had left Delilah with her father and Jabber (Jian-Li, Wei, and Xun were in with Chen) and he asked the first person he saw where he could find Gregor.

He'd been led to this room and told the vampire would "attend him shortly."

So he waited at the window, but not patiently.

The one good thing about this shit was that Gregor had not lied. They rode on a massive fucking compound, a building well back from the front gate and surrounded by a tall, brick fence you couldn't get through unless you spoke to someone at the gatehouse which held three men (all vampires). At either side were structures that Abel could smell were filled with the same.

There was also razor wire lining the upper inside of the fence so you couldn't see it from the outside looking in, but you sure as fuck would catch it if you tried to scale that wall.

The building itself was mammoth, a long, handsome, three-storied brick front with two wings jutting at wide angles back from its sides.

Each of them was to have their own room and, he reckoned, half an army could be put up there. Which was what was happening. He sensed it being filled with those arriving, mostly vampires, some wolves.

He was now in a room on the bottom floor at the far back of the north wing. It was the library, if the walls covered in shelved books was anything to go by.

Abel sensed Gregor's approach and turned from the view well before he walked through the door.

Abel watched the vampire close it behind him, but the instant he turned toward Abel, Abel spoke.

"You got a shitload of explaining to do."

Gregor lifted a hand, nodding and slowly moving into the room. "I understand, Abel. But I've requested Lucien and Callum come to us so we can finally share with you all that needs to be shared."

"My guess is they already know what those bitches were at the restaurant, so you can start with enlightening me on them while we wait," he demanded.

"Those...bitches?" Gregor asked, sounding confused.

"The ones who formed out of thin air," Abel explained.

"Ah," he murmured, moving further into the room, then stopping. "You mean the wraiths."

"The what?"

"Wraiths," Gregor repeated. "You see, there are more immortal beings beyond vampires and werewolves. There are wraiths, phantoms, golem, and The Wee."

Fabulous.

"You obviously don't know this," Gregor started as he moved to a chest that had a bunch of glasses and finely cut stoppered bottles on it. "But their appearance today was most welcome."

"I do know it, seein' as if they hadn't shown, we'd all be dead," Abel returned.

"No," Gregor said quietly, making the chest with the bottles but turning to Abel. "That's not the entire reason. You see, until recently, we did not have their allegiance. They've since explained to me that this was withheld for the purpose of them being able to intervene in the likes of what happened today. Knowing plans were being made, plans that were to be carried out, they were paying lip service to our foes. This meant there was a trust established that allowed them to be in the know of things we were not, including their plans to attack today, en masse, after they'd dispatched my scout. Something they did within seconds of his making his all-clear call, giving them the opportunity to be on the move swiftly and take us by surprise."

"And they found him how?" Abel asked.

Gregor shook his head, his expression turning profoundly unhappy. "I don't know. He was a human. Ex-Special Forces. Exceptionally well-trained at what he did, he was almost like a phantom, except not immortal, so I'm surprised they discovered him." The vampire turned to the chest, pulled out a stopper from one of the bottles, and poured himself a healthy dose of what Abel smelled was whiskey, doing this while talking. "He leaves behind a two-year-old son, a six-month-old daughter, and a wife he's been with since high school."

Abel's throat closed.

Fuck.

Gregor lifted the bottle Abel's way. When Abel shook his head, the vampire topped the bottle, grabbed his glass, and turned back to Abel. "He's a great loss," he said, sounding like he meant it, before he took a sip of whiskey.

"Your wraiths couldn't save him?"

"If they did, they would have exposed early where their allegiance lay and would not have been able to surprise our enemy, which allowed us to defeat them soundly and deliver to them a number of casualties. I haven't been able to tell you this, but none of them escaped. The wraiths dispatched them all."

Finally, good news.

"Right, so they couldn't have given that aid before Snake got his throat torn out?" Abel pushed.

Gregor's focus intensified on him. "I understand your anger."

"Sorry, you don't," Abel bit out. "See, my mate clung tight to my back on my bike, her cheek to my shoulder, and she cried the whole fuckin' way here. I felt it. I sensed it. I heard it. It's good my instinct to keep her safe is strong or I woulda crashed that bike, seein' as her grief cut me that deep. And I liked the guy. Didn't know him that well, but I liked him mostly because he loved my woman in a way he was willing to die for her. And then he did."

"Whatever burial your mate's people request, we will provide for him," Gregor replied quietly.

"That's appreciated, but my point is, we gotta have a fuckin' burial."

"Abel, we're at war," Gregor told him. "This happens. It's hateful. But it happens."

He was not wrong.

Abel let Snake go, since the man was dead and there was nothing he could do but help his woman and her people mourn him, and he asked, "You wanna explain this war?"

"Perhaps I should get you that drink you refused while we wait and get into that when Lucien and Callum arrive."

"Respect, you've held up everything you've promised, including getting my people medical attention and bringing us to your fortress." He threw out a hand. "But I got an injured brother. My woman has a member of her family down too, and she's fucked up with grief. I need to get to her and not do it after waitin' for Lucien and Callum to get here."

Abel was grateful Gregor immediately inclined his head.

"Then we'll begin."

And then the asshole began, spouting shit about mates destined not only for each other, but to save humanity from enslavement by the evil supernaturals, who had, for centuries, been wanting to make their play and were now preparing to do that.

The mates, known as The Sacred Triumvirate, or The Three, specifically three couples who have eloquent understanding of both supernatural and human existence, being prophesied to engage in what was called The Noble War and save the world.

Or die fucking trying.

It took a lot more words for the vampire to share this with Abel, but that was the gist.

When he was done, Abel snarled, "Are you fuckin' kidding me?"

"As I raised Sonia from a child, I love her as my own, and she is as vulnerable to these Prophesies as you and your mate, I wish I were. But I'm not," Gregor replied.

He knew both Lucien and Callum were approaching, but that didn't stop him from stating, "This is totally fucking whacked."

"That cannot be argued. But it's still true," Gregor told him.

Jesus.

"There's more you need to know," Gregor kept going. "such as the dreams." Abel's body got tight at that, but Gregor didn't stop. "And added abilities. For instance, today we were outnumbered, my guess, ten to one, and the reason we weren't bested swiftly is not only because you wisely trained your brothers to handle themselves against the additional speed and strength they'd be facing. Nor was it because Lucien and Callum are both experienced and exceptionally skilled. But because you, as Lucien is, as Callum is, are uncommonly gifted in battle."

Abel said nothing.

Gregor did, guessing, "You trained your brothers because you knew this day would come."

"Dreams," Abel grunted as the door opened and Lucien, followed by Callum, came through.

They said nothing, but Abel tilted his chin up to them as he caught their eyes.

They moved into the room, Lucien looking his way even as he went to an armchair and sat his ass in it, Callum dipping his chin as he moved toward the couch but didn't sit. Instead, he leaned against it.

As they settled in, Gregor asked, "Does Delilah dream?"

"Yeah," Abel answered.

"Yours are premonitory," Gregor noted.

"Dreamed today. Not the outcome, but dreamed it happened, felt we were gonna lose. Didn't dream about us getting help," Abel told him.

Gregor nodded and Abel had to give it to the guy. His expression shared he got that having that dream really wasn't all fun and games and living with sensing it might come real was worse.

Then he prompted, "Delilah's dreams?"

"Said she never dreamed anything that happened, but they've been frequent since we got together and they fuck her up."

"Fuck her up how?" Lucien asked sharply.

"Get hold of her. Know one was good from the noises she was making, *real* good," he said and knew Lucien got him from the vampire's lip twitch. "Another, not so good, took hold. I couldn't wake her. She eventually woke, but it was her comin' out of it, not me making her do it."

Lucien's lips quit twitching as his mouth got tight.

"Does she recall them?" Gregor asked.

"No," Abel answered and looked to Lucien. "Leah?"

"The same," he said on a curt nod. "Be vigilant, Abel. Leah's dreams took such hold, they nearly killed her."

"*Fuck,*" Abel hissed and turned his gaze to Callum. "Sonia?"

"She had dreams, but they were only the good kind," Callum told him.

"Lucky you," Abel muttered.

"Don't allow Delilah to sleep without you close," Lucien advised, and Abel turned his attention back to him. "My connection with her was the only thing that could keep Leah safe from her dreams."

"And you know that'll work for Delilah, if this same shit is happening to her?" Abel asked.

Lucien shook his head.

"With certainty, no. But I would strongly advise taking that precaution."

And Abel would strongly accept that precaution and not let Delilah sleep without him around.

"There's more to share," Gregor butted in, "and more to learn, most especially about you and your history."

"How crucial is that to know at this juncture?" Abel asked.

"Not more crucial than us learning what we all need to know, that being how our enemy was able to find you and Delilah before we did," Gregor returned.

"Yeah," Abel snarled. "That's somethin' I'd like to know too."

"We have people working on it," Gregor assured him.

"Like you had people keeping us safe today?" Abel asked derisively.

"I lost a good man I respected today too, Abel," Gregor reminded him quietly.

Abel clenched his teeth. His blow was low. He knew it and he had to cool it.

Gregor took a sip from his whiskey, giving Abel a moment to pull his shit together. Abel had to give that to him too. It was a cool thing to do.

Once he sensed Abel had sorted his shit, he went on.

"One of the many reasons I wished for Callum and Lucien to be here is that, unfortunately, I don't have more time right now as I have a great deal to do. Today's attack means things have escalated and I'm concerned how that escalation may be taking shape, not only here but elsewhere. The wraiths have information and I need to brief with them. I also need to contact The Vampire Council so they can make the world's governments aware of today's activities, giving them the information they need to continue with their own preparations."

"The world's governments?" Abel asked.

"Very few humans know of the existence of immortals," Callum explained, and Abel turned his attention to him. "But select trusted officials high up in every nation's government are aware. They've also been made aware that the enemy is uniting, planning, and we, all of us, must be prepared for attack. Not like today. On humans."

"This just keeps getting better," Abel muttered.

"It's a lot to take in, we know," Lucien said in a low, conciliatory voice. "But even so, you need to take it in, you need to prepare your mate and your family, and you need to move on from that to where we all need to be to fight this."

He didn't like it, but he was getting that this was the fucking truth.

Abel nodded to Lucien and looked back to Gregor. "Explain about the enemy uniting."

Probably because he had to get out of there, Gregor gave it to him quickly and without delay.

"As I mentioned earlier, we thought the wraiths had allied with those who would subjugate humans. Fortunately, they have not. Or, at least, not the vast majority of them who follow their empress, Serena. The Wee, who I also previously mentioned, have long since retreated under the earth. It's been centuries and no one has seen them or heard from them, thus there's no way to get a message to them. Regardless, they washed their hands of anything that happens topside a long time ago. They left the surface with some disgust as to how mortals and immortals were behaving, saying they would never get involved. Knowing this, it would be a waste of time and energy to attempt to communicate with them."

He paused, and when Abel nodded, Gregor continued.

"You must know there are factions of all immortals who side with the enemy. However, the bulk of vampires, werewolves, and, now we know, wraiths are with us. Phantoms, we don't know. They don't often get involved with immortal dealings so they could be neutral. They could also be foes. They're refusing to speak with us or Callum's emissaries. However, it's our understanding they're also refusing talks with our enemy. Unfortunately, golem have aligned with our adversary."

"And what the fuck are golem?" Abel asked.

"Human lore says they're creatures created of clay or mud, formed into human shapes and magically imbued with life, completely controlled by the human who created them, mindless besides," Lucien shared.

"And the real story?" Abel pushed.

"They're immortals whose procreation includes the female and male tearing away their own flesh and bones to form an infant. They cover the child in their blood, perform a ritual, and breathe life into their potential offspring from their own mouths," Callum finished the story.

"Fucking hell," Abel murmured.

"And they're not mindless," Gregor put in. "They're quite powerful, if clumsy in battle, their bulk, which is considerable, being to their advantage. They can also be beheaded and survive for some time, five, ten minutes, as long as they can find and reattach their heads."

"Jesus," Abel mumbled.

Gregor kept speaking.

"The only way to kill them is to dismember them into as many pieces as possible and set fire, again, to as many pieces as possible."

"They also don't procreate easily," Callum added. "The child formed by parts of their parents does not always take their breath and then breathe. Golem mates can try for decades, even centuries, before they create one child. This means they're particularly careful about losses so it's a surprise they've not stayed neutral. Then again, they don't look quite like humans, stay hidden almost completely, and have had a very difficult history, including much vilification at human hands that at many points some centuries ago was extreme."

Gregor sighed and Abel switched his gaze to the vampire. "I wish I had the entirety of the evening to share more, but I must prepare. Serena is en route and she and I have much to discuss."

"Right," Abel muttered.

"Lucien and Callum can fill in many blanks, Abel," Gregor told him. "But I'll leave you with this. I'm pleased you and Delilah are in the fold. But I'm more pleased with the immortal we've discovered you to be—a great warrior, loyal to his family, protective of his mate. As The Prophesies have foretold, you would be that kind of immortal. But in reality, you are that and more. I have always had hope, knowing Lucien and Callum were to lead our fight. Now, fighting at your side with the family you've created, the loyalty they showed, and the way they mourn their loss, my hope has increased greatly."

Abel didn't want to give a shit about what the guy thought, but he couldn't help but do it.

And since the vampire put it out there, Abel had to give it back, doing this by muttering his "Thanks."

Gregor smiled a small smile, downed his whiskey, set his glass aside, turned his head, and tipped his chin to Lucien and Callum.

He left the room, saying, "Until tomorrow."

The door closed on him and Callum remarked, "You want to get to your mate."

He gave the wolf his eyes. "And you want to get to yours."

Callum smiled and crossed his arms on his chest.

That meant yes.

Callum was also right. Abel wanted to get to Delilah.

But there were a few things to cover first.

"Can phantoms attack from the sky, and are there mermaids who can attack by sea?" Abel asked.

Callum's smile got bigger, but it was Lucien who answered.

"Phantoms can attack from the sky, but The Dominion has an invisible electronic net shielding that area. This net would not entirely stop them, but it would hold them back long enough for us to prepare." His lips quirked before he concluded, "There are no such things as mermaids."

"Well thank fuck for that," Abel murmured.

"My wolves are making camp on the grounds," Callum told him, and when Abel looked his way, he saw he was now deadly serious. "You undoubtedly sense the vampires filling the rooms of the compound. What you may not have noted was that The Dominion has soldiers in guardhouses lining the fences. They, and I, have wolves and vampires infiltrating the local towns. The wraiths are doing the same. This is for the humans' safety as well as ours. Our adversary would have to concentrate a foolish amount of their forces here in order to penetrate our current defenses and claim The Three."

"That makes me uneasy and easy at the same time," Abel told him.

"As you should be," Callum replied, "for that means they can concentrate elsewhere."

"And we have people out there concentrating on elsewhere?" Abel asked.

"We do," Lucien replied, "as well as the United States military being aware of the situation and on high alert for attack." He threw out a hand Abel's way, indicating his body which, since their earlier situation, had fully healed. "We immortals can sustain many injuries. But this doesn't mean modern weaponry is futile against our kind. Far from it."

"Will they fight fire with fire?" Abel went on.

"Likely," Callum grunted.

"So we're at war. We're just waiting to see what they do next," Abel surmised.

"We're also trying to discover what they'll do next in hopes of being in position to stop it," Lucien told him.

"And these Prophesies," Abel kept at them. "You know of them?"

Both men nodded, but Callum spoke.

"They're unfortunately vague. They're also unfortunately vaguely dire. There are no conclusions. We don't know what will happen definitively. We don't even know what will happen to lead up to the ultimate campaign. We just know the stories of The Three have all come true. So we know they are not just words written on paper by the Ancients."

Abel didn't even bother asking what the Ancients were, not that he didn't care, just that he was done with this shit.

For now.

"Further," Callum continued, "the wolves have Oracles. I've spoken with them, but they say the destiny of The Three has not yet been written in the stars."

"I'm sure you've impressed the importance of a phone call if that happens," Abel noted, and Callum grinned.

"Indeed, I have."

Jesus. The entirety of this shit was fucking *whacked.*

"This is a lot to take in," Lucien said quietly. "Go to Delilah. We'll talk more tomorrow."

That was the only good suggestion he'd heard all day.

He nodded to Lucien, gave a nod to Callum, and moved to the door.

"Take the whiskey," Callum called.

The second good suggestion of the day.

He gave the wolf a look, changed direction, and took the decanter of whiskey.

He had his hand on the knob when Callum declared, "I do not die in this war and my queen sure as fuck doesn't."

Abel turned to him, and if he was another man, say a human one, the look on the wolf's face would have him shaking in his boots.

Being who he was, what he was, and just learning what he and Delilah were facing, he did not.

He got Callum. He liked what he got. And he gave the wolf another nod.

"Leah and I the same," Lucien said with deceptive calmness, and Abel looked to him. "And we, none of us, will allow you or Delilah to fall."

"She likes people she cares about to call her Lilah," Abel said in reply.

Both men stared at him.

"She'll give you that go-ahead, my guess, tomorrow over breakfast," Abel finished.

Lucien's lips again twitched and Callum gave him another grin.

Abel didn't give them anything.

He turned back to the door, opened it, moved his ass through it, and went directly to his mate.

# 12
# It Felt Like Falling in Love

*Delilah*

My eyes opened in the dark.

I felt exceptionally soft sheets, the most heavenly mattress I'd ever experienced, as well as even more heaven.

Being tangled up with Abel.

Entirely tangled up. Our legs. His arms wrapped tight around me, mine around him, my face in his throat, my hair scattered over my neck and shoulder as well as his.

"Sleep, pussycat," he murmured into the top of my hair.

How he knew I was awake when I didn't move anything but my eyelids, I didn't know.

I just knew he wasn't sleeping, likely from worry for me.

"He taught me how to play checkers."

I meant Snake.

Abel knew what I meant and his arms gathered me even closer.

"When am I gonna settle in the knowledge I had that kind of love?" I asked, thinking of Snake's words days before.

"Baby," he whispered but gave me no answer. Probably because there wasn't one. It would happen when it happened and I just had to ride the wave of grief until it came to me.

"I see him when I close my eyes, Abel," I told his throat. "I fall asleep and wake, because in my dreams, I see him lying there in all that blood."

"Talk to me," he urged.

"I am."

"No, *bao bei,* about Snake. Talk to me. Tell me about him."

I didn't know if this was a good idea.

But still, I nestled closer, took a deep breath, and talked to my man about Snake. My father's friend. Someone I'd known my whole life. Someone I'd laughed with. Someone who'd also been disappointed I'd dated a preppy. Someone who'd come to my high school graduation, given me a hug and a present of a gold crucifix necklace, and told me he was proud of me.

Someone who'd taught me how to play checkers when I was seven.

Someone who'd died for me when I was twenty-nine.

I kept talking, held close in Abel's arms, tangled up in his powerful limbs, until my words drifted away and I went to sleep.

It wasn't until later that I'd realize, when I was hurting, my man gave me just what I needed.

The next morning, sitting in Abel's lap in the big chair by the window, still in my nightshirt, Abel having tugged on jeans, I listened to him talk as I stared at the sea.

I didn't say anything. Too much was in my head—what had happened the day before and all he was telling me.

I still didn't say anything when he was done.

He let me have my silence until he was finished letting me have my silence.

"Lilah?" he called, his arms giving me a squeeze.

"We're destined to save the world?" I asked.

"Apparently," he answered.

"Yeesh," I muttered.

"It's a lot to take in, pussycat."

He could say that again.

"It sucks. But one thing about it doesn't suck. It brought you to me," he stated, and I closed my eyes.

God, he liked me. He really, really liked me.

That was good since I felt the same.

I opened my eyes. "You're good at finding the silver lining."

He gave a soft, short chuckle.

It, too, was heavenly.

Then he said, "I gotta know you're processing this 'cause I gotta brief our families about that shit."

"I'll go with you," I told him and got another squeeze of his arms.

"No. Take your time. Have a bath. They say we can order up breakfast. I'll take care of that for you. Then I'm gonna go get some blood and, after that, talk to our people. You need to take care of you. Give Snake some of your headspace. Come to terms with what he gave you. I'll be back."

"I wanna check in on Chen and Jabber."

"You can do that after you take care of you."

"That *is* taking care of me."

"No, that's my Lilah takin' care of other people. But my job is to take care of you. This morning is yours. You don't need to think of destiny. Fuck, you don't even need to give your headspace to Snake. You just need to do what you need to do and have the space and time to do it."

One could say having a long hot bath in the huge, super-luxuriant bathroom that was all ours, hanging in the equally huge and super-luxuriant bedroom, taking time to get ready, have breakfast, get shit sorted in my head, all in a stronghold of The Vampire Dominion where no one could hurt us and I could stare out at the sea, was not a bad idea.

I cuddled closer even as I moved my head to catch his eyes.

He felt them, tipped his chin, and gave his to me.

"You get the sucky jobs," I said softly.

His eyes went hard. "Takin' care of you is *not* a sucky job."

Okay, I knew how he felt about that.

And I liked how he felt about that.

So much I felt my nose sting with oncoming tears and shoved my face in his throat so he wouldn't see me cry *again*.

He curled a hand around the back of my head and held me there.

"I like you," I sobbed into his throat.

I felt his body tense, then relax, and there was humor in his voice when he said, "Well, that's good."

"Like...*a lot*," I clarified.

"That's good too."

"You're very sweet," I told him.

Abel didn't reply to that.

My voice was croaky with tears when I went on, "You treat me right, and you're respectful of my family, and you've given me more by giving me yours, and you're great in bed."

"That's it?" he teased.

"You're hot."

He shoved my face in his throat reflexively when his entire body tensed again, but this time, because he burst out laughing.

Startled by the sound, I pulled my face out of his throat and watched him do it.

Yep, he was hot.

He kept doing it even as he focused on me, his hand sliding from the back of my head so he could use a thumb to rub the wet on my cheek away.

The laughter was gone when he said gently, "I like you too."

Fuck, that felt awesome.

"Well, that's good."

He grinned at me.

"I missed two," I told him.

He kept grinning when he asked, "Those are...?"

"You're a biker, and Dad likes you."

He continued to grin, but it died slowly as he said quietly, "Let me take care of you, *bao bei*. Later, you can face the world and all the shit that's goin' down. Now, you take time for you. Yeah?"

I nodded.

"What do you want for breakfast?" he asked.

"I'm not very hungry."

"How about fruit and toast, then?"

God, he was really good at this.

"That works. Plus coffee."

"Coffee," he murmured. Using his hand at my head to pull me to him, he dipped to me and touched his mouth to my lips. He moved away but not very far when he finished, "I'll give you a coupla hours, then I'll be back."

He moved as if he was going to bring us both to our feet, but I curled my fingers around his biceps where they were resting and he stopped.

"If Dad wants me, let him come to me, will you?"

"Absolutely."

I smiled at him.

He dipped to me again and touched his lips to my smile.

He brought us both to our feet and I watched him saunter to his tee and pull it on, followed by his socks and boots. Then he came back to me.

I got another lip brush before he left the room to get me breakfast, break the news to our family that he and I (with Lucien and Leah, Callum and Sonia) were fated to save the world or die trying, and give me space—all this taking care of me.

I'd had that from Dad all my life, part-time close, part-time distant, until he changed that last.

And if I'd made a list of what I wanted in a man, I'd have wanted to keep that. Having someone to take care of and love who gave the same back to me.

But I was glad I'd never made a list because it felt unbelievably cool whenever Abel ticked off an item on the nonexistent one, surprising me at the same time showing me what I needed that I didn't know I needed until he gave it to me.

It felt good.

No, it felt great.

Actually, it felt like falling in love.

"Dad, sit."

"Can't."

"Dad, please. For me?"

Dad didn't look from where he was standing, his gaze aimed out the window at the sea.

I was back in the armchair. I'd had a bath. A light breakfast. A shitload of coffee. I'd done myself up and got my head together.

I'd had exactly what I needed but didn't know I needed until Abel gave it to me.

That didn't mean I wasn't sad. Snake was gone and his loss weighed heavily on me. Chen and Jabber were hurt. Yesterday was extreme.

But I wasn't freaked.

Given the opportunity to think, none of this surprised me. What I'd felt my whole life was not natural. The bond I was building with Abel wasn't either, but it was strong and it was beautiful. The fact it was fate made sense.

And with who they were and what they could do, not to mention the fact that life was life, people were people, and evil existed, I could see some of the supernaturals thinking they should rule the world.

I didn't like it. I didn't particularly want to play a part in stopping them.

But I had no choice.

I'd gone to therapy when I had no choice, and I'd gotten through. I'd lived with Mom when I had no choice, and I'd gotten through. I'd existed with a hole in my soul until I met Abel, and I'd gotten through.

Now I had him and we faced this.

And we'd make it through.

"Will rest when Snake's at rest," Dad said, taking my thoughts back to him.

"Okay, Daddy," I said gently.

"After that, I'll worry about my little girl saving the world."

I sighed.

Abel had told him and we could just say Dad was not all fired up about that particular adventure.

I heard the door open.

I shifted to peer around the side of the chair and saw Abel walking in.

He looked to me, then to Dad, and back to me.

I shook my head.

An expression of sweet understanding moved over his features and I gave him a small smile.

Then I watched him walk to me, also taking in the room around him as I watched him move.

It wasn't very vampiric, which was kind of a letdown. No blood-red walls or black satin sheets or anything.

Actually, it looked like what I would guess a room in a mansion on the northwest coast would look like. Hunter-green walls. Lots of exposed wood. Accents of muted gold and burnished rust. Kickass paintings of seascapes. A headboard on the king-sized bed made of wood and scrolled iron. Attractive bed linens in greens, golds, and rusts. Lots of pillows. Furniture that was exceptionally attractive but bought and positioned around the room for ease and comfort.

I really didn't take in much of anything last night, including this room. But right then, I liked it a whole lot.

That said, I kinda missed Abel's dungeon, but only because that was the place where he and me became a we.

He stopped at the side of my chair and bent deep. Even though my head was tipped back for his kiss, he didn't give it to me. He rubbed his temple against mine, then lifted away.

I liked it when he did that so I didn't mind not getting a kiss.

He settled in, leaning against the side of my chair, his eyes moving to Dad.

"Hook, how you doin'?" he asked quietly.

I looked to Dad to see Dad taking Abel and I in.

Finally, he focused on Abel. "Be better once I put my man to rest."

"Gregor said they'd do whatever you wanted. Just tell me what you want and I'll get them to arrange it," Abel told him.

Dad held his eyes and stated, "Viking funeral."

"Come again?" Abel asked.

"Snake had shit parents, four shit wives, and mostly a shit life, unless he was with his brothers. Didn't get much of what he wanted outta life, that's just the way life rolled out for him. It sucked watching, but respect, Snake never let it get him down. Man always talked about wanting a Viking funeral. Thought he was nuts, picking the wrong women, not havin' great luck, and wanting an end he couldn't have, seein' as we lived landlocked and no one lets you do that shit. Reckon the vampires could do that shit though, so I like the idea of Snake gettin' one thing he wanted, even if he gets it after he's gone."

My chest depressed.

"Then he'll get that," Abel said.

"'Preciate it," Dad muttered, looking back to the sea.

Abel gave him time before he asked, "You process the other shit I told you?"

"One thing at a time, bubba," Dad kept muttering. "We put Snake to rest, then I'll deal with my little girl and her man savin' the world."

Abel looked down at me.

I again shook my head.

He nodded and looked back to Dad. "You had breakfast, Hook?"

"Not hungry."

"Gotta eat, man," Abel told him.

"Not somethin' I don't know," Dad replied.

"Hook—"

Dad cut his eyes to Abel. "Son, obliged for the concern, but you gotta know when to let an old man be."

"I never die," Abel returned. Dad blinked and I stared, not knowing where that came from.

Dad recovered first. "You bein' immortal, I got that."

"What I'm sayin' is, that means I have a long fuckin' time of remembering what Snake sacrificed for Lilah and me, a long fuckin' time to be grateful for it, and a long fuckin' time to honor that memory."

Yes, my Abel was good at this.

Dad's throat convulsed, but he said no words in reply, just nodded.

"You want time with your girl?" Abel asked.

Dad swallowed, cleared his throat, and answered, "If you mean alone, no. You don't have to leave. But I want time with my girl."

"You got it," Abel murmured, looked down at me and shared, "Gotta shower, *bao bei*."

"Okay, honey."

When he bent this time, he touched his mouth to mine.

Then he went to take a shower.

And I sat in my chair with my eyes to my dad, who was watching the sea, mourning his friend and doing it being with me.

"How's Jabber?" Chen asked.

I was sitting by the hospital bed they set up for him in one of the downstairs rooms, Abel standing behind me.

And I was worried. Chen looked pale and tired even though Abel told me he'd slept most of the day.

"Worse than you but bitchin' about not getting a cigarette even though he has a punctured lung, so I reckon he'll make it."

Chen gave a truncated chuckle that ended in a wince.

I reached out and grabbed his hand.

He stopped wincing and looked at me. He then looked at Abel.

Then he smiled a cheeky smile. "Destined to save the world, hunh?"

"That's what they're telling us," Abel confirmed.

"Action shot in my Wikipedia entry, once we take care of that shit," Chen declared.

I didn't know what Abel did because I burst out laughing.

It was surprising. I didn't think I could laugh. Not that day. Not the next. Not for a while.

But I did.

And I did because Chen was funny.

And I did because, with his words, I knew he was going to be okay.

"I need to find Abel," I murmured late that evening, rising from the couch in one of the downstairs living rooms (I'd peeked in a few, there seemed to be about ten of them), my eyes moving from Leah to Sonia.

We'd had a family dinner in Jabber's room, mostly to give him targets for his orneriness, to which he took aim and shot copiously.

Talk had drifted to biker so Jian-Li and I decided to leave them be. We found another space and Leah and Sonia found us. We shot the shit and I got the sense that the other two female parts of The Three found us just so they could take our pulse. Conversation was light but not lighthearted.

But now I needed my man.

"And I need to check in on Chen," Jian-Li added, rising with me.

"Okay, ladies. We'll see you tomorrow," Sonia said.

"'Night," I replied.

"'Night, Lilah. 'Night, Jian-Li," Leah returned.

"Good night," Jian-Li said.

We moved to the door, and as we did, Jian-Li tucked her hand in my elbow.

I brought it close to my side and covered it with my other hand.

Out in the hall, I asked, "You okay?"

"I've had days that were better," she answered.

"Mm-hmm," I murmured.

"Though, today was a great deal better than yesterday, so I'll take it."

"I hear you," I replied on a squeeze of her hand.

We kept walking toward Chen's room. We did this silently, but it was a long way so the silence didn't last.

"We're prepared, Lilah," she told me.

I looked down at her.

"You know about Abel's dreams?" she asked.

I nodded. I did. He'd mentioned them before, but he gave me the full briefing that morning about his dreams, the dreams I was having and not remembering, and Leah and Sonia dreaming.

"We're prepared," she said firmly.

"I think I got that yesterday when all your boys kicked ass."

She smiled. It was small, but it was proud.

"What you're saying is, all this new stuff, it's no surprise to you," I remarked.

"Oh, it's a surprise. My Abel and his fated partner saving the world, that's a surprise. But yes, in a way, you're right. We knew it would be something. I would have picked something less enormous, but there are a great number of things in life you can't choose."

"I hear that too," I muttered.

"But sometimes fate smiles down on us, giving us bounty instead of challenge." Her hand curled tighter on my arm. "That's what she gave us with you."

That felt so good, I stopped walking.

She had no choice but to do it with me, and when I looked down at her, she was looking up at me.

"You're making Abel very happy."

"God, I hope so," I whispered.

She gave me another smile, still small, but this one happy.

"You are."

"I like him," I told her, and her smile got less small.

"That's good, since he likes you too. A great deal."

I grinned. "I noticed that."

She looked forward and started us walking again.

Then she commenced in destroying my world.

"I cannot say what it means, my delight at what he's found in you, that he has what he's been yearning for, even in the short time you'll be with him as you live your mortal life. It will give him much to cherish as he continues his immortal one when you're gone."

I kept walking but said nothing, made no sound, carefully regulated my breathing.

Because I hadn't thought of that.

Not once.

I had no idea why, though obviously a lot was happening.

I still hadn't thought of that.

I was falling in love with him.

And evidence suggested he was doing the same with me.

But he couldn't die.

And I definitely would.

Oh my God.

"We're here," Jian-Li said, and I jerked in surprise, blinking at Chen's door. "Lilah, are you all right?"

I drew in a deep breath, pulling it together before I looked down at her. "Not really. Lots on my mind. But I figure I just need to find Abel and I'll be okay."

She studied me closely before she asked, "Are you sure?"

"Sure I'm sure," I said on a smile I didn't mean, but considering all that was happening, I hoped she didn't read it as what it really was.

"Yes," she agreed, squeezing my elbow before letting it go. "Find Abel. Then he'll be okay too."

*God.*

I bent to her and touched my cheek to hers, saying there, "Sleep well, Jian-Li."

"I will. You do the same, Lilah," she replied.

I moved away and she went into Chen's room. I stood at the door and waved when he looked to it, catching me there. He lifted his hand and waved back.

Then I took off.

I checked Jabber's room, but Abel was no longer there. So I hauled my ass to our bedroom.

Abel wasn't there either.

I left and went in search of him.

Although I knew there were tons of people around, they all had to be busy because they weren't bustling about the hallways. It took me a while of roaming the halls before I found someone to ask if they knew where Abel was.

I found her, a striking brunette with curling hair and fabulous blue eyes. She seemed on a mission, but I still flagged her to stop.

She did and I asked, "Uh, do you know where Abel is? Abel Jin. The—"

"I know who he is, Delilah, but I don't know where he is. I'll find out," she said, lifted the cell in her hand, hit some buttons with her thumb, and put it to her ear. She asked. She nodded. She hit the phone with her thumb again and looked to me. "He's in with Gregor. Bottom floor, south wing, three doors in on the outside from the main wing. You want me to take you there?"

"No, I think I got it," I replied.

"I'm Stephanie, by the way. A friend of Lucien's," she shared.

"Oh, hi," I said, sticking my hand out for her to take, which she did. "I'm, well, you know who I am."

"Yeah." She smiled, let me go, and her smile drifted away. "I'm very sorry for your loss."

"Thanks," I muttered.

"I'll let you go find your mate," she went on.

I nodded and repeated, "Thanks."

She said no more and kept walking.

I did too and found the third door on the outside on the first floor of the south wing.

It was slightly ajar and Abel's voice was floating out of it.

His irate voice.

"We talked about this earlier."

"Abel—"

I recognized that voice as Gregor's.

I stopped.

Abel cut him off. "You give my mate this. You give her family this. Just two days to put someone they love to rest. The day after tomorrow, we'll all sit down and make plans to save the world."

His words kinda made me want to laugh, but I choked it back.

"There's much to go over," Gregor told him.

"Yeah, I remember that from the other fifteen times you said it to me," Abel returned, and I leaned a shoulder against the wall, settling in for my man's show.

I didn't have my shoulder against the wall for long, because Gregor said, "Delilah is just outside."

"I know," Abel replied.

Of course. They smelled me. Or something.

Whatever.

I moved to the door and shoved it open.

"Hey, gents," I greeted, but I was looking at Gregor because, for some reason, I couldn't look at Abel.

"Delilah," Gregor returned.

I moved close to Abel and only then did I look up at him.

So very beautiful.

*It will give him much to cherish as he continues his immortal one when you're gone.*

He'd waited forever for me. Several forevers for a human.

I'd just waited one, and not a very long one.

Then I got him. And I'd have him until I died.

But he wouldn't have me.

On that thought, I stared into his two-colored eyes and the rest of it came crashing down on me.

Crushing me.

Because he also wouldn't have Jian-Li. Or Xun. Or Wei. Or Chen.

And he didn't have all the ones who had gone before. All of the ones who'd raised him, made him son, brother, father.

He'd lost it all.

Repeatedly.

My stomach clutched so much I thought I might throw up, and I reached out a hand to grasp his hard.

"You okay, *bao bei*?" he asked, his features now suffused with concern.

So very, *very* beautiful.

"It's just," that came out hoarse, so I cleared my throat, "been a sucky day."

"Yeah," he whispered, tugging my hand to draw me nearer. He looked to Gregor. "We done?"

"Yes, Abel," Gregor said on a sigh and turned his eyes to me. "I know it likely brings little relief to your sorrow, but we've made the arrangements as Abel instructed for your friend Snake. The boat will be in the bay tomorrow at sunset. If you can tell your family that's when the ceremony will begin, I'll leave you to them and see you tomorrow at the bay."

"Thank you, Gregor. That means a lot," I told him.

He shook his head and waved his hand. "The least we could do, Delilah. The very least."

That was nice.

"Good night," Gregor finished.

"'Night," I replied.

Abel said nothing, just pulled me out of the room. He dropped my hand but tucked me close, his arm around my shoulders, when we were in the hall.

I swallowed.

*It will give him much to cherish as he continues his immortal one when you're gone.*

Was he memorizing this moment, walking down a hall with me?

I knew I would if I were him.

I slid my arm around his waist and pressed close to his side.

"You want your dad?" he asked softly.

Yes, I wanted my dad. I wanted to wail in his arms and bitch about how unfair life was and get pissed and throw things because my man had to live an eternity without me, without *everybody*, and I had to live my time with my man, knowing he would.

But I didn't say that because I wasn't going to do that. I wasn't going to mention it at all. Because Abel didn't mention it at all. He didn't say that first fucking word. He didn't bitch or wail or throw things.

He carried on. He lived his life. He smiled. He laughed. He got pissed. He loved his family. He was falling in love with me.

So I was going to put all my time and energy in giving Abel much to cherish as he continued his immortal life without me.

"No, baby, I want you," I said to the floor as we walked on it.

He pulled me closer, bent in, and kissed the side of my head.

I closed my eyes and let him guide me to our room.

Naked, on my knees like he liked me, one hand to the bed, one arm stretched out, fingers curled around Abel's, which were curled around the ironwork of the headboard as he leaned over me, bracing himself in his arm, pounding inside me.

I dropped my head at the sheer beauty, the blazing heat.

"Touch yourself, pussycat," he ordered gruffly, sliding his other arm around my chest to keep me in position while I moved my hand from the bed to between my legs.

I touched myself, but I touched him, gliding my fingers back to feel his big cock stretch me, fill me, drive into me.

Yes.

This was it.

This was us.

This was what we'd be.

Wild and free.

Fucking wild. Living wild. Living free. Saving the world. Kicking ass. Packing it all in. Not missing a moment. Not wasting an instant.

I bent my neck back and twisted my head so I had lips to the skin on his neck.

"Love your cock," I whispered.

"Know that," he grunted, giving it to me, driving deep and grinding in.

I whimpered and then kept whispering, "Wanna sleep with you inside me."

"Give you that."

"Want you to wake me up, fucking me."

"Give you that too, baby."

"You'll give me anything."

"That's right," he growled, pulling out and starting to pound in again. "Anything, Lilah."

"That's what you'll get from me."

"Pussycat, fuckin' you hard on your knees. You think I don't know you'll give me anything?"

I closed my eyes.

"Up," he grunted, not giving me the choice and pulling my hand from the headboard, yanking me up with his arm at my chest as he sat back on his calves, taking me with him so I was sitting, impaled on his cock. "You give me anything, let me watch you take yourself there."

I'd give him anything.

So I fucked myself wild on his cock, rubbing my clit, my head resting back on his shoulder, one of his hands curled around my breast, the fingers of his other whispering through the hair between my legs, his mouth to my shoulder, his eyes watching me take myself there.

"Look at you, burying me deep," he murmured roughly.

I couldn't. I was coming.

Then I was coming harder when he pushed me forward, not to my knees, to my belly, cheek to the pillow, legs spread wide, his hands in the bed, his hips pistoning, his cock pounding into me.

"Abel, *baby*," I moaned, bucking with my orgasm, jolting each time I took his cock.

"Like that?" he growled.

"Yeah," I panted.

"Tell me you like it, Lilah."

"I like it, baby," I breathed, then it washed over me again, my lips parting with the force of my silent release.

Abel tangled a hand in my hair and yanked my head back and to the side so he could watch me come. And when he did, I gave him a show because one could say I seriously liked my man pulling my hair. But it was better because it felt like he was using it to drive me down harder on his big dick.

"I keep coming," I gasped as more burned through me, my body shaking with it.

"Yeah, fuck yeah, I feel it. Keep goin', baby. Milk me."

He had to shut up or I was going to die from orgasming.

"Abel," I cried, my body now spasming.

"Fuck..." He pulled out and rammed in. "*Yeah.*"

And finally he came, bucking over me, inside me, taking me along for his ride as he growled his climax. He released my hair but sank his teeth in my shoulder. Not the vamp ones. *His.*

Freaking *amazing.*

He brought us both down by continuing to fuck me, now slow and sweet but still deep.

I closed my eyes and took it, loving each stroke, listening to his breath even, feeling him shift his hips to guide his cock to hit a sweet spot, then back, giving it all to me.

Suddenly he pulled out and rolled off, but I was on my belly without him for only a millisecond before he tugged me over him again.

Sifting his fingers into my hair to pull it away at either side of my head, he moved it until I caught his eyes.

"Bring me back home, baby, so you can sleep."

Oh yes.

I grasped hold of his still-hard cock, bending my knees to straddling him, and took him, watching his teeth sink into his bottom lip and his now-brown eyes get lazy, then hearing the snarl roll up his throat when my pussy convulsed around his cock.

"Now, come here, pussycat," he muttered when he was seated deep.

I dropped over him, chest to chest, cheek to his shoulder.

He yanked the covers over us.

Once he had them settled and we were in our warm cocoon—connected, replete, his arms wrapped around me—he asked, "You'll sleep for me tonight?"

I took in a deep breath.

Yes, fuck yes, he was good at this.

"Yeah, baby."

"Right, give me a kiss before you do that for me."

I lifted my head and looked down at him through the moonlight coming from the windows. I looked down and I hoped with everything I had that he'd remember this. He'd remember falling asleep inside me. He'd remember me falling asleep on him, holding him inside. He'd remember how he was so good at taking care of me when I lost my friend. He'd remember it and know how important it was. He'd remember it for always and it would give him some peace.

Then I kissed him. I gave it to him soft and wet and long and I hoped he'd remembered that too.

When I was done, I whispered, "Thank you for taking care of me."

"My job, pussycat. One I like."

I sighed at Abel giving me more.

Then I settled in, pressing close, squeezing him inside, and whispered, "Sleep good, honey."

He tightened his arms around me. "Impossible not to, *bao bei*."

I smiled, giving myself that moment.

Another moment of feeling myself falling in love.

# 13
# Just Breathe

*Delilah*

The next evening, just prior to sunset, I walked down the steps behind the compound, steps that led to the bay, and I did it hand in hand with Abel on one side, my father on the other.

Behind us walked Moose and Poncho.

Behind them walked Jian-Li with Xun, Chen moving slowly with Wei two steps behind.

And behind them came Lucien and Leah, Sonia and Callum, Gregor and Yuri, Callum's cousin, Ryon, and Callum's brothers I'd met earlier that day, Calder and Caleb, as well as the woman I'd met the evening before, Stephanie.

Callum, Ryon, Calder, and Caleb were all carrying bows, each with one arrow.

I nearly lost it when we rounded the rock and I saw it, the flat boat with its rising bow and stern, the wood of the bow a carved bust of the torso and head of a proud, wild-haired lady. It had been dragged up so most of the hull was on the beach.

Along the small, pebbled shore that was encased with rising juts of rocks, lit torches were stuck in. Further up the shore, a big bonfire had been built, surrounded by logs with blankets over them.

Snake lay in the boat, all but his face shrouded in black, a large Harley-Davidson patch resting on his chest.

I took it all in, fighting tears, thinking when they said they would arrange things, they meant they'd *arrange* them.

Perfectly.

Jabber was already down there, having been brought down without an audience since he had to be carried. He was in a wheelchair on the rocks by the boat, five bottles of Jack Daniel's sitting on the rocks by his wheels.

We got to the bottom and everyone traversed the beach toward Jabber, but Abel let me go when I got close.

I looked up to him even as Dad kept pulling me.

Abel nodded toward the boat.

I nodded back and let Dad guide me to Jabber. Moose and Poncho followed.

The rest stayed behind, fanning out along the beach, silent.

I tried not to look at Snake, but I couldn't help it. His throat was covered, but I could see his face in the waning sunlight.

They should have covered him. He looked peaceful. He never looked peaceful. He always looked…*something*.

"Let's do this," Jabber grunted, flinching as he reached down to a bottle of Jack.

Moose and Poncho went to get theirs and Dad let me go to grab the last two. He handed one to me.

I looked around, not knowing what to do, then followed their lead as they busted open the caps, lifted them to their lips, and took a deep tug.

My throat was burning and my eyes were on fire when I was done, but I sucked back air and controlled the burn as Dad turned to me.

"Say good-bye, little girl," he murmured.

I knew what he meant by that, so I swallowed, nodded, and moved to the side of the boat.

I squatted down and stared at Snake.

"Thanks for teaching me checkers," I whispered. My throat started burning a different way as I croaked, "And thank you for dying for me."

The tears slid down my cheeks as I lifted my hand and touched my fingertips to the gold crucifix I'd clasped around my neck. I then moved my fingers to my lips and got out of my squat to lean over the side of the boat, reach out, and touch them to Snake's cold cheek.

I held them there until I felt hands on me. I looked behind me and saw Dad and Moose.

I moved away. Moose moved in. He did what he had to do. Then Poncho did. After Poncho, Moose wheeled Jabber close and he did. And finally, Dad did.

Then Poncho and Moose moved to the other side of the boat, Dad motioned for me to come to him, and Jabber stayed where he was, close to the stern of the boat.

"*Hup-ta*," Dad grunted the nonsensical words they always said before taking a shot. All the men lifted their bottles, grunted "*Hup-ta*," then poured and shook them all over the inside of the boat.

I did the same with mine.

They tossed their bottles in with Snake. I followed suit and did it knowing that either Abel arranged all this, understanding the kind of closure Dad and the boys would need, or he'd found out what they needed and made certain they had it.

And I loved the fact that, this time, my man gave my father, his friends, and, most especially, Snake, what they needed.

Moose went back to Jabber and wheeled him a few feet up the beach. After Dad jerked his head that I should go to Jabber, I did. And I stood next to Jabber as Dad, Moose, and Poncho bent to the boat and gave it a mighty heave, shoving it into the waves, going into them thigh-deep, pushing Snake to sea, the sun setting on the horizon.

I gulped back a sob as more wet hit my cheeks, and Jabber's hand came out and curled around mine.

Dad, Moose, and Poncho stood in the waves, watching the boat drift to sea before they turned and made their way out of the surf to Jabber and me.

Dad slid an arm around my shoulders and got close. I kept hold of Jabber's hand. We all stood and watched as Snake rode the waves, one last ride—not a wild one, a peaceful one.

As it should be.

Then I heard zinging and four flaming arrows arced through the violet of the overhead sky, falling and hitting the boat.

It burst into flames.

I couldn't hold back my sob. Jabber's hand tightened in mine as Dad lifted his hand and turned his body so he could tuck my cheek to his chest.

I didn't tear my eyes from the boat as it burned.

After some time, the silence that had been pierced only by the sound of the distant flames and the soft lapping of water against rock was interrupted with guitar strings.

I turned my head, Dad turned his body, and we saw that Abel had his guitar on a thigh that was up, his boot and ass balanced on a rock, his other leg straight. He was playing.

And then he was singing.

And that was when the tears poured out of me.

Because he was singing (and I didn't know he could sing) and doing it beautifully.

But mostly because he was singing Cat Stevens's "The Wind."

I listened to Abel's deep voice wrapping around the words as my eyes drifted back to Snake getting one thing he wanted in life and getting it after he died.

Abel finished the song, gave it a few moments, then I again looked to him when he kept going.

This time doing Pearl Jam's "Just Breathe."

When he started singing, his dark head was bent, watching his fingers move on the strings.

But on the first "stay with me," he lifted his head and looked right to me.

And my world stopped.

But my tears didn't.

My friend Snake burned, my life was turned upside down, and I stood on a pebbled beach with family, a bunch of vampires and werewolves, my man singing to me, and I fell in love.

Forever and completely.

But I'd already been in love.

Since the day I was born to be Abel's.

I stared into Abel's eyes as the words he sang poured into my soul, and I knew no matter what became of me, I'd live wild and free and full for the rest of my life.

Because he would give that to me.

And watching him pour those words into my soul, part of it died, knowing I couldn't give him the same thing.

As the song started to come to a close, I let Jabber go and pressed close to Dad for a second before I broke free and moved across the beach to Abel.

I stood right in front of him, his eyes soft on mine as he sang the final words, "meet you on the other side," and then the notes died away.

"That's a deal," I whispered.

Pain pierced the serenity of his expression because he knew I knew.

And that pain settled where the hole he'd filled had been in my belly. It settled permanently. I'd hold it with me until my last breath.

And I'd do it gladly. I'd take that pain because Abel gave it to me.

He swung the guitar by the strap until it was resting on a slant on his back and held his arms wide.

I didn't hesitate to move into them and press close, my cheek to his chest, my arms around him, his around me. I turned my eyes to Snake's burning boat.

"That's what I want," I said softly.

"Then that's what you'll get, *bao bei*," he replied softly, his voice thick.

We stayed there, me holding Abel, Abel holding me, and me trying not to think of the time that would come, whenever it might be, where he'd be just like he is now—strong, handsome, and amazing—but he'd also be somewhere on a beach, watching me burn.

"I was born to be yours, you know," I told him.

"I know," he told me.

I nestled deep and whispered, "I'm sorry I took so long."

Abel said nothing, just held me tighter.

"We'll live wild and free," I promised.

"You got it," he agreed, now his voice was rough.

"After we save the world, that is."

A deep, startled laugh surged up his throat and he pulled me even closer.

"Born to be yours, baby," I kept whispering.

He again said nothing, just turned his head so I felt his lips at my hair.

"Born to love you, Abel."

That was when his arms squeezed the breath out of me.

When he loosened his hold, I said, "Thank you for giving this to Snake."

"My mate has me wrapped around her finger. I'd give her anything. But the man who died to make sure I could still hold her in my arms, I made sure he went home exactly how that needed to be."

Yeah, I was born to love this man.

I snuggled close. Abel shifted his bent leg so his thigh and body trapped me precisely where I needed to be.

And the breeze blew our hair as we held each other on a pebbled beach with our family, a bunch of vampires and werewolves, and we watched Snake burn.

# 14 Awesome

*Abel*

Abel and Delilah walked into the breakfast room the first fucking thing the next fucking morning. They'd been summoned there by a loud knock on the door an hour ago, one of Gregor's minions calling to them that this was what Gregor was expecting.

Regardless of this, Abel was in a mellow mood.

This had a lot to with last night, feeling the centuries of pain inside him swept away with Delilah's quiet understanding.

And her love.

Christ.

He'd never forget it.

It got better after their moment, which was whacked because they were at a funeral.

But after the sun had set and the flames died, they all wandered to the bonfire and sat around it. Gregor's minions had brought bottles of whiskey, chilled vodka, premium tequila, bags of marshmallows, bars of chocolate, and boxes of graham crackers, and some good-looking human guy came to sit with Lucien's friend, Stephanie.

Poncho, Moose, Hook, and Jabber told stories of Snake. Conversation flowed, shifted, turned, and did it naturally. The melancholy stole out and goodness drifted in on a wave of memories, booze, sweets, and good people sharing time.

They drank. They made s'mores. They smiled. They even laughed.

And Stephanie turned out to be one seriously hilarious bitch.

She also was the first who started making out with her guy.

This prompted Moose to grumble, "We shoulda ordered bitches," which made Delilah, Leah, and Sonia giggle and the men exchange smiles.

Things got heavy with Stephanie and her human around the time Sonia and Callum started going at it. Stephanie left with her man. Wei and Xun took Chen back up, Jian-Li following them. Sonia and Callum left not long after. Gregor and Yuri drifted away. So did Ryon, Caleb, and Calder. Leah and Lucien started whispering and kissing, then they took off. And finally, with Moose carrying his friend, Jabber bitching about it, Hook lugging up the wheelchair, and Poncho handing Jabber shit, they went up.

Leaving Abel and Delilah on the beach with a roaring bonfire and blankets.

So he'd made love to her there with Snake's ashes floating up the pebbles at the edge of the sea.

He'd never forget it, not a second of it, not in his life. Even the part with Snake being there when he sank his cock in Delilah for the first time after she'd shared her love.

Snake belonged there. He'd died so they could have that and Abel thought it was fitting.

So he was good the next morning when he pulled Delilah in the bright breakfast room, which was one of several conservatories at the compound, this one jutting from the end of the south wing.

And he was good with who was there: Gregor, Leah, Lucien, Sonia, and Callum.

That was it.

The Three.

And, of course, Gregor.

"Sit. Let's get you some coffee," Gregor greeted expansively as they hit the room, throwing out an arm to two empty chairs to his left.

More greetings were exchanged and Abel sat only after he'd shoved Delilah's chair with her in it under the table.

Delilah looked at Gregor. "Last night was exactly what we needed, Gregor, so I need to thank you again."

"No thanks necessary, Delilah," Gregor replied.

"Lilah," she corrected.

He smiled.

Abel looked to Lucien and Callum, who were both grinning at him.

"Right." Delilah shook off the mood and reached for the coffeepot. "Saving the world."

"We'll get to that, Delilah—" Callum started.

"Lilah to you too," she cut him off to say.

Callum's glance darted to Abel, his lips twitched, then he said, "Lilah. But first we need to understand something."

"That is...?" Abel asked.

"Your scar," Lucien stated.

He felt Delilah tense at his side, but he looked to Lucien. "What about it?"

"We don't scar," Lucien informed him. "We're wondering if you do because you're the only known hybrid in the world. So we'd—"

He stopped speaking when he sensed Abel's and Delilah's moods swing, that being to complete fucking shock.

"Uh...*what*?" Abel forced out.

"Fuck. He didn't know," Callum muttered.

"Of course he didn't know," Sonia whispered with more than mild irritation.

"Know...what, exactly? The only known hybrid? What the fuck does that mean?" Abel demanded.

"Werewolves and vampires can't procreate, Abel," Gregor shared, and Abel swung his gaze to the vampire. "Not until...well, you."

"Oh my God," Delilah breathed.

"Are you kidding me?" Abel asked.

"I'm afraid not," Gregor said carefully. "You had no idea?"

"No fuckin' clue," Abel grunted.

"Your parents didn't share that with you?" Gregor went on.

"My parents didn't share dick," Abel told him.

"Do you know where they are?" Gregor asked.

"I know they left me in an alley two hundred years ago. Other than that, like I said, I don't know dick. Don't remember dick about them either," Abel answered.

"Interesting," Gregor murmured.

"Not interesting. Abusive," Delilah suddenly snapped, her back shooting straight. "He was left in an *alley* as a *pup*. It's a miracle Hui found him, took him in, and kept him, even after he transformed. Others might have done him harm, or *worse*."

"I meant no offense, Lilah," Gregor said pacifyingly. "It is, of course, unspeakable for a parent to leave their child in an alley."

"It absolutely is," Delilah agreed sharply, and Abel reached out a hand to cover hers on the table.

When he did, her head jerked around and she caught his gaze.

He shook his head.

She narrowed her eyes.

He shook his head again.

She sighed a sigh that sounded like a grumble, pulled her hand from under his, and reached for the jug of cream.

"Was this in China or here, in America?" Callum asked.

"China," Abel muttered distractedly, watching Delilah finish with the cream, put it down, and again commandeer the coffeepot.

She lifted it his way and tipped her head to the side.

He nodded.

She poured him coffee.

"Do you have registers of wolves in China two hundred years ago, Callum?" Gregor asked, and Abel sliced his eyes from his cup to the vampire.

"Wolves check in with governors if they move to a territory, and governors pay attention to wolf activity, but only if there's a need, such as insurrection or activities that might lead to humans discovering the existence of werewolves. Outside that, we let wolves roam without keeping records, so no," Callum returned, then asked, "What about vampires?"

"We tend to keep tabs," Gregor murmured. "I'll ask The Dominion. But it's not very helpful if we have no wolf."

"Are you talkin' about finding my folks?" Abel asked.

Gregor shook his head like he was clearing it. "Sorry, yes. Sorry," he repeated. "Very rude. Much is on my mind. " He took in a deep breath and focused closely on Abel. "But I'll repeat my apology for not being sensitive, something we'll be in future. But I'll do that now by warning you I'm about to speak bluntly. I'm concerned that perhaps you were not left in an alley. Perhaps you were saved in one, purposefully, for your parents might have been hunted due to The Prophesies. The Prophesies were not widely known. However, we've recently learned that a once-trusted member of The Council, Marcello, was an insurrectionist. He shared them. And it's our understanding he shared them some time ago."

"Great," Abel muttered.

"He's since been dispatched," Gregor told him. "But if your parents were under threat, or felt that you were, there's a possibility they would find the kind of human who would do no harm to an immortal once they discovered that. A human who would keep you hidden in the mortal world due to your abilities. A human they could leave you with to do just that." His voice lowered as he finished, "It might have been their only choice to keep you safe."

"Jesus Christ," he snarled and felt Delilah's hand curl around his thigh.

"Yes, terrible, if it happened that way. Tragic," Gregor said. "But if we can trace this, we may be able to trace whoever found you and Delilah in Serpentine Bay."

"And who scarred me," Abel added.

"Sorry?" Gregor asked.

"Who scarred me, seein' as I don't scar either. But some bitch in a roadhouse in Texas slipped me a mickey, somethin' else that doesn't work on me, 'cept hers did. Then she used some weird-ass knife to carve into my face. She was goin' for my heart, but I passed out. She didn't finish me off, and considering what that knife did to my face, that would have finished me off."

Gregor looked to Lucien, so Abel looked to Lucien and saw his jaw get hard.

"Did she..." Leah began, then paused before asking, "get cold feet or something?"

"No, he was saved by somebody," Delilah answered.

"What's got you tweaked?" Abel cut in, asking this to Lucien.

Lucien looked his way, then replied, "Witches."

"Oh shit," Delilah muttered. "More supernaturals. Fabulous."

"There are witches?" Sonia asked, surprising Abel. Then again, she was new to this supernatural business too.

"Yes, baby doll, and some have power, but not much," Callum answered. "I never mentioned them, because, by not much power, I mean they're no longer of consequence."

"Those who held long lines of power, and thus were very strong, were annihilated centuries ago," Gregor explained.

"By who?" Leah asked.

Gregor shifted in his seat, suddenly looking uncomfortable, his eyes going to Lucien.

So everyone's eyes went to Lucien.

"Unfortunately," he began, "I've learned only recently, as I've also learned only recently that true magic exists on this earth, it was vampires."

"Perhaps not one of our more shining moments," Gregor murmured.

"You think?" Delilah asked sarcastically. "Now they've gotta be pissed too, pissed enough to roofie a vampire werewolf and carve into his face when they meet one at the local roadhouse!"

Her voice was rising so Abel pulled her hand from his thigh, curved his around it, and dropped it back, holding it there.

She took in a calming breath.

"Or, perhaps she was sent on a mission to take care of one of The Three," Gregor said in a carefully even voice.

Watching Gregor, Abel knew he, too, was tweaked.

Abel broke it down. "So what you're sayin' is, vampires knocked off all these witches, the witches who remained are probably seriously shitty about that, so they're probably workin' for the dark side."

"This could be," Gregor allowed.

"Great," Delilah muttered.

"And they came after me, which means they know of The Prophesies," Abel kept at him.

"Oh, they know about The Prophesies. The witches have seers among them, even now. We may have kept The Prophesies secret, but as witches have that power, they've known about them for centuries," Gregor confirmed. "But we have yet to discover if they knew who you were."

"Why did vampires kill off all the witches?" Leah asked, and Gregor looked to her.

"There was a bit of a power struggle."

"I'll say," she muttered.

"It was a different time," Gregor murmured his lame explanation.

"It was fucked up," Lucien put in.

"You will remember when I shared with you our history with witches that I did not support The Dominion's decision," Gregor reminded him.

"You didn't," Lucien returned. "But you enforced it."

"It was my duty," Gregor shot back, beginning to sound impatient. "And I'm sure I don't need to remind you that when Callum's father...and I, I'll add...finally talked members of The Dominion into seeing sense, those vampires who'd championed that unfortunate situation were dealt with harshly."

"After hundreds of years of persecution and thousands of witches extinguished, executions that were quick and for the most part painless was hardly a proper punishment, as the lasting chasm between vampires and witches will attest," Lucien retorted.

"Whoa, the supernaturals certainly have a dark and checkered past," Lilah muttered and Abel looked to his mate to see her giving big eyes to Leah, who gave them back to her.

"Enough," Callum cut in. "It's been done for hundreds of years. There's no undoing it." He looked to Abel and changed the subject. "Who saved you? Any clue?"

"I was passed out, man, so I have no idea."

The door opened while he was answering and Yuri walked in, eyes to his father, his face strange.

"A word," he called.

"Yuri," Gregor began, "we finally have The Three assembled and—"

"A *word*, Father." His eyes shifted to Abel, something Abel didn't like much, then they went back to his father. "It's urgent."

Gregor sighed, threw his napkin on the table, and pushed away, murmuring, "One moment."

He took off.

Abel let Delilah's hand go and reached to a platter of bacon, hoping like fuck that wasn't about Chen or Jabber taking a turn for the worse.

As if reading his mind, Leah asked, "How are Chen and Jabber this morning?"

"We don't know," Delilah answered. "We came up late last night and got the knock on the door this morning. I hardly had enough time to hop in the shower and not to scare you by coming down here without doing my hair." Leah grinned and Delilah continued, "We'll go see after we're done here."

She took the platter of bacon from Abel and was picking her strips when the door opened and Gregor called, "Lucien, a word."

"Fucking hell," Lucien groused, shifting his seat back and stalking to the door.

"Never boring when you're saving the world," Leah noted, her eyes to where her husband disappeared.

Delilah laughed softly, as did Sonia.

Abel shared a look with Callum, who looked about as happy as he was with their interruption, then Abel reached to the eggs.

He'd handed them off to Delilah when the door opened again.

"Abel, will you join us out here, please?" Gregor called.

Abel looked from his plate to the door. "Is this a big deal?"

"We believe it is," Gregor answered.

"A big deal in a way that everyone in this room can't know what the fuck you're all talkin' about in the hall?" Abel asked.

"This was my question," Callum put in.

"It's private," Gregor explained.

"To who?" Abel asked.

"To *you*," Gregor answered.

Abel's chin jerked back. "What?"

"Please join us in the hall," Gregor said as Yuri moved into the room from behind Gregor, who was standing in the door, Lucien following him.

"We need to have a chat elsewhere," Lucien said carefully.

What the fuck?

"A chat?" Abel asked.

"What's going on, Lucien?" Callum demanded to know.

"Yuri, Gregor, and I need to speak with Abel. It may take some time. Eat your breakfast. We'll return as quickly as we can," Lucien replied.

"Not hip on secrets," Abel declared.

"You may be...*hip* on this," Gregor replied.

He felt and smelled Delilah's anxiety and his patience slipped. "What the fuck is goin' on?"

"Oh for fuck's sake," Yuri clipped. "You're drinking bagged blood."

Abel's brows snapped together. "Yeah, so?"

"The kitchen told us you requested they place a large supply you brought with you from Serpentine Bay in their refrigerators," Yuri told him something else he knew.

"Yeah..." Abel said slowly. "So?"

"And you requested they heat it...*in a microwave*," he said with disgust, "for your meals."

"Man, you're tellin' me shit I know. What's the big fuckin' deal?"

"Why aren't you feeding from your mate?" Gregor asked cautiously.

"Not that it's any of your business," Abel bit out, "but I am. Though, seein' as she was destined for me, I waited a couple of centuries for her, and I kinda like having her around, draining her, or drawing her down so she's got no energy, isn't somethin' I'm big on doing."

The mood in the room changed completely in a way that Abel had to concentrate on his fangs not snapping out. Delilah felt it too. He sensed it and knew it when her fingers curled around his forearm.

But the expressions on their faces didn't match the mood.

Yuri looked incredulous. Gregor and Lucien looked remorseful.

"*What?*" Abel clipped.

"He doesn't know," Leah breathed, and Abel glanced at her to see she'd grown pale.

"*What?*" he snarled.

Gregor, Yuri, and Lucien advanced into the room, closing the door behind them.

It was Lucien who spoke.

"Do you know you can numb skin?" he asked.

"Figured that out," Abel answered.

There was some relief in his expression before he went on, "Abel, vampire saliva is healing."

"Figured that out too," Abel told him. "Numb, bite, draw, heal."

"No." Lucien shook his head before lifting a hand and dropping it. "Of course, you're partially correct. Numb, bite, draw, heal, but when I say vampire saliva is healing, I mean miraculously so. I feed from Leah three times a day, sometimes more."

Delilah's fingers curled tight on his arm as Abel grunted with revulsion, "What the fuck?"

"My saliva in her bloodstream means her blood regenerates faster. It takes time to build it up, but only weeks until she can withstand feeding regularly," Lucien shared.

"Oh my *God. Awesome,*" Delilah whispered.

"It's more," Lucien went on. "The longer you feed, the more healing properties she gets. You immunize her from disease, and by that, I mean *any* disease, like we vampires cannot suffer. Including diabetes, cancer, neurological disorders, all of them."

"Christ," Abel whispered.

"And more," Lucien continued. "She'll begin to heal more rapidly. Cuts, scrapes, bruises will disappear within hours, then within minutes. And the longer you feed from her, things such as broken bones will heal in days."

"Oh...my...*God*! *Awesome*!" Delilah exclaimed on a muted cry.

It was then Lucien gave it to them.

Everything.

In a variety of really fucking good ways.

"And feeding regularly will halt aging. Meaning as long as you continue to do so, she will never die," Lucien finished.

Delilah's nails sank into his flesh, but he didn't feel it.

He didn't feel anything.

*She will never die.*

"You must feed from her regularly, Abel, starting once a day for several days. Then twice a day for perhaps another week. Then you can likely feed from her whenever you wish, doing her great good while you do," Gregor said.

He heard it. He understood it.

He still didn't move or speak.

*She will never die.*

"Honey," Delilah called.

*She will never die.*

"Baby," Delilah called again.

He felt her leaning into him, her hand on his neck, squeezing.

*She will never die.*

"Abel, baby, this is good," she whispered into his ear.

That was when he moved. In a blur, he had her in his arms, and in seconds, he was tossing her on the bed in their bedroom.

She bounced, blinked, and looked up to him.

"You'll never die."

She stared at him before her face went soft, her eyes shining bright and her lips started curving.

"Told you you were awesome," she whispered.

Fuck, she was right.

She was fucking *right*.

He *was* awesome.

Because he could keep his Delilah alive.

Forever.

He lunged.

He'd had a bag of blood brought up while she was doing her hair, thinking the other vampires in residence were probably doing the same thing.

But he still drew from her as he fucked her, hard, fast, rough, quick, making her cry out when she came, his cock driving deep, her blood flooding his mouth.

*She will never die.*

He'd have that, all of it (or countless varieties of it, they had centuries to get creative), for a lifetime.

*His* lifetime.

*She will never die.*

Fucking *finally*.

Abel lay on his back, naked, Delilah on top of him, also naked, with his cock still inside her since he rolled her there after he rode her.

Her head and shoulders were up. She was looking down at him, the fingertips of one hand stroking lazy on his chest, his hands were curled on her ass.

"What's in that awesome head of yours?" she asked softly.

"Coulda saved Hui," he told the ceiling.

"Abel—"

"Mei."

"Honey—"

"Sying."

She slid her hand to his neck. "Baby, stop."

He tipped just his eyes to her. "Coulda saved 'em all."

"That wasn't meant to be," she told him gently.

"Obviously not," he replied caustically.

"Okay, I'm trying to go easy here, so cut me some slack, but I'll point out that feeding is sexual."

He looked back to the ceiling, his gut roiling at the idea of drawing from any of them.

Obviously, in the beginning, when he was a kid, feeding was feeding.

But she was right. When his body started changing and the world became all about his dick and how he could get off, he'd never drawn from anything but a human female, giving it to her as he took.

Doing that to Hui, Mei, Sying—it would be like having sex with your sister. Or your mother.

"You wouldn't do that so maybe it's good they never knew you could," she suggested. "And that you never knew either."

He couldn't argue that, but it didn't make him move out of his current dark mood.

"Since I knew I'd have you, lived knowin' I'd lose you," he told the ceiling.

"I know, baby, but you won't lose me now."

"No," he stated, again giving her his eyes. "Now I gotta worry about losin' you to these fuckin' Prophesies. Had a whole twenty minutes to celebrate. Now I know I can have you forever with me, and that hangs over our heads. So somehow that makes the thought of losin' you worse."

She stiffened on top of him. "We're not gonna let the evil supernaturals beat us."

"Yeah? You're sure? 'Cause they probably got witches on their side, *pissed* witches, who got knifes that can fuck an immortal up."

"That wasn't the best news of the day," she muttered, her eyes drifting to his shoulder.

Too much was flooding his mind, he couldn't sort it all. He needed space, so he dug his fingers into the flesh of her ass and ordered, "Off me, pussycat."

He saw the hurt shift through her eyes, but before he could do anything about it, she rolled off. He moved to catch her, doing it with human speed, which was a mistake. She kept rolling and was off the bed, nabbing her panties and pulling them up.

"*Bao bei,* just need some room to think and breathe," he explained.

"You got it," she said, her voice forced to light. "You gave that to me yesterday. I'll give it to you now. I'll go downstairs. Check on Chen and Jabber. Go and tell the others you need a few hours and we can start again."

She said all this while struggling to put on her bra. When she finally got it on, he moved, grabbing her hips and yanking her back into the bed, settling them on their sides, her back to his front, their bodies curved to each other.

"By 'room to think and breathe,' I just meant you off my cock. I still want you at my side," he said in her ear.

She took in a deep breath, but it was ragged.

What the fuck?

"Lilah," he growled.

"You have this...thing where you turn off on me, pull away from me," she explained, but did it facing the pillows. "It's just seconds, but I lose you and I don't mean your dick. I mean whatever is going on in your head."

"I don't do that."

She twisted her neck to catch his gaze. "Yeah, you do."

"Tell me when I did that," he demanded.

"Just now," she replied.

"I explained that."

"You didn't see your face when you told me to get off you."

Fuck.

"When else did I do it?" he asked.

She averted her eyes and started to scoot away, muttering, "It doesn't matter."

He hooked her with an arm at her belly and yanked her back. "Answer me."

She twisted to look at him again. "You know, I'm going to be essentially immortal too. So all that gut-wrenching despair I felt for you and with you and for me when I got my head out of my ass and realized how shitty your life had to be and how awesome and tragic it was you finally got me, that was for nothing. We should be celebrating. Not edging toward a fight."

"I agree, except about the part you're using not to answer me."

She turned in his arms to face him. "We have a world to save, Abel."

"And now you're using *that* not to answer me."

"I don't touch your face," she declared suddenly.

"What?" he asked.

"I don't touch your face," she repeated.

He shook his head in confusion. "Why not?"

"Because the first time I tried, you pulled away from me."

Fuck, he did.

And she was right, she'd touched his neck, she'd kissed him, she'd touched his hair, but she'd not once touched his face or even tried since that night.

And she'd given him total access from the first time he fucked her. Nothing was off limits, not when they were fucking, not when they weren't.

He'd waited lifetimes for her. He had her. He touched her all the time, held her all the time. But more, she shared liberally and he always had her attention. Fuck, as she was walking to her friend's burial, the burial of a man Abel had known for days, when he let her hand go, she looked to him to include him in something that wasn't his to have.

"I explained that then too," he reminded her, beginning to feel uneasy.

"Yeah, and the first day we met, you calmly discussed banging other women. The first morning I woke up in your bed, before you even kissed me, before I even realized to its fullest what you were to me, I still lost it just thinking of you with other women in that bed. What we have isn't natural. What it does to *me* isn't natural. Fuck, you can't leave with me not knowing where you are without me eventually getting the pain back that I'd had for years. You pulling away from me doesn't affect me like it would some normal biker bitch. It guts me."

"Jesus," he muttered.

"Yeah, Jesus," she agreed. "And trust me, this does not make me happy. I'm not clingy. I don't want *to be* clingy. Not one guy I've been with have I been—" She stopped on a sharp cry because he was squeezing her side uncontrollably with all of his strength.

*All of it.*

He forced his hand to relax and did it miraculously before he snapped her ribs.

"Fuck," he whispered.

"What was that?" she whispered back, her entire body stiff.

"Sorry, pussycat," he muttered.

"What was *that*?" she bit out.

He stroked the skin he'd no doubt just marked, saying, "You shouldn't talk about bein' with other guys."

Her eyes got big.

Then she whispered, "You feel it too."

"Just don't do that again."

"Oh my God, we're so fucked," she kept whispering. "We're *both* gonna be clingy."

"This has to be something else," he kept muttering.

"What?" she cried, no longer whispering at all.

But it came to him.

"Added abilities."

"What?" she repeated.

Abel focused on her. "I told you about my dreams. When I told you about all this saving the world shit, I told you that your dreams might be like ones Leah had and we had to be careful. I told you Sonia dreamed too."

"I remember."

"What I forgot to tell you is that Gregor said The Three had added abilities, like me being gifted in battle. But that was a for instance. As in, there were others. We just haven't gotten around to hearing them yet."

"Keep going," she urged.

"So, you came to Serpentine Bay because you sensed me there. I sensed you in danger. You sensed the same with me. I don't know, maybe we're attuned to each other somehow. We lose that, like you not knowin' where I am, and it causes pain. If I'm not with you and you know where I am, do you feel it come back?"

She shook her head.

"So we just need to be careful about letting each other know where we're going."

"That doesn't explain the hyper-jealousy and how I feel when you pull away from me, mentally or emotionally," she pointed out.

"The hyper-jealousy, yeah. Though, if we're connected as in *connected*, it wouldn't be a stretch to think that even the consideration of us connecting with someone else might strain that. But when I drift away in my thoughts, shutting you out, that jibes with you not knowing where I am."

"That *is* actually a stretch, Abel," she remarked dubiously.

"I'm not sure it is," he returned.

She continued to look dubious so he explained.

"When you and me were talkin' about whether we should leave our families behind or not, you had your quiet moment, I had mine. You gave me mine, I gave you yours. You knew where my head was at, I knew where yours was at. Did you get that feelin' of me pullin' away then?"

The dubiousness started lifting when she answered, "No."

He nodded. "Right. No. Because you knew where my head was at, which makes sense with the rest."

"It kinda does," she whispered.

"So maybe this shit is more and it'll develop as we're together," Abel continued. "We'll get a lock on it, figure it out, maybe even learn to control it. But dreams that tell the future, me bein' good at fighting, it seems whatever the fates have chosen to give us, if we figure out how to use them, they're weapons. And if this shit gets any more extreme, me knowing you're in danger and the same with me for you is a good thing."

"That's the damned truth," she mumbled.

"So we tell each other where we're gonna be if we're gonna be apart, I have a care with not shutting you out of my thoughts, and you don't *ever* mention bein' with other guys again."

"Same with you with women," she shot back, and he grinned.

"Learned that lesson already, pussycat. Think that toothbrush marked me."

"Bullshit," she retorted but did it fighting a smile.

The mood shifting, he curved both arms around her and rolled to his back, pulling her on top of him.

"Now we can get back to celebrating," he announced.

"Or we can check in on Chen and Jabber, then go back to planning our efforts to save the world," she offered an alternate, not near as tempting suggestion.

It was also one they weren't doing.

"We haven't even been gone an hour."

"And I haven't had but two sips of coffee and no breakfast."

"I've had two breakfasts and you didn't have to do any work the last time." He slid his hand into her hair and pulled her face closer to his. "Just gotta lay on your back for me to eat you."

She squirmed but said, "Saving the world is kinda important."

"And just lay on your back when I fuck you," he continued like she didn't speak.

"Abel," she snapped, but it was breathy.

"Though, thinkin' of bangin' you against the headboard...not sure about that. That iron might hurt."

"Oh, just shut up and fuck me so we can get on with saving the world."

He grinned.

She shook her head like he was a naughty boy she didn't know what to do with.

So he rolled her and played the naughty boy who knew exactly what to do with her.

But he didn't bang her against the headboard.

Because the iron might hurt and he had years of drawing from her before he could make her heal.

*Years.*

## *Callum*

Late that evening, Callum walked into the bedroom he shared with Sonia and saw his queen sitting in bed wearing another fucking nightgown and rubbing lotion in her hands.

Her eyes were on him and he kept his on her as he closed the door behind him and watched her start to open her mouth.

He beat her to it.

"You tell me I told you so, I'll turn you over my knee."

She shut her mouth in order to smile but then opened it again to speak.

"Not sure that's a deterrent, my handsome wolf." He moved toward her as she kept going, "How was your run?"

He sat down, his hip to hers in the bed, and answered as he leaned toward her to rest his weight in his hand at her other side. "It was an honor to be the first wolf to run with Abel Jin."

Her eyes got soft and she gave him another smile, this one sweet.

"And his first run was with his king," she said softly.

"Yes," Callum agreed. "He didn't hide that he liked it either." His mood shifted as his gaze went unfocused, thinking on this. "I can't imagine a lifetime as a lone wolf. Running alone by choice, yes. Running alone because you knew no other like you, no."

"That part of his life is over," she replied, still speaking softly and placing a hand on his chest, so his focus returned to her. "He has brothers now."

"Yes," he repeated.

"Did you and Lucien fill him in on all the rest?" she asked, and he nodded.

"With Gregor and Yuri. Believe it or not, Yuri was best with him. He's a proud vampire. Lucien's confidence is a part of him. Gregor's as well, in his way." He shook his head and gave her the grave news. "I got the sense, little one, that Abel's lived his whole life not thinking he's simply an anomaly but that he was some kind of unnatural, loathsome beast."

"Oh no," she whispered.

"Yes," he told her. "So Yuri's pride in who he is and all that comes with that was welcome."

"Yuri can be callous, but he isn't entirely unfeeling," she told him, and she would know. She'd lived with the vampire as her brother most of her life.

That said, there came a time when Yuri didn't want to be her brother but something else entirely. Unfortunately for Yuri but exceptionally fortunate for Callum, she was destined to be his queen.

He nodded and went on, "There's a great deal more for Abel to learn. While we were running, he was like you on your first run. Unable to communicate. He can control the transformation but can't converse as wolf, though he was picking it up by the end. He's a fast learner."

"Also like me."

He grinned at her and lifted his hand to curl around hers at his chest. "Like you, my queen." She returned his grin and he kept going. "He's excellent with a sword, but he still needs training. He should learn how to fight with his claws and teeth."

"Hopefully you'll have time to teach him."

"We spoke of it and we're starting tomorrow," he shared.

She tipped her head to the side. "And the rest?"

"After we finished with Abel, he called Lilah in and they both now know it all—Leah's absorption of Lucien's abilities, sensing danger, being able to track and mark, speaking to his mind as he's able to do with her. Your affinity with wildlife. All of our dreams. We'll be sitting down with Serena, Avery, Stephanie, Cristiano, Ryon, and

Caleb tomorrow to discuss what we know about our adversaries and how to proceed."

"And does Lilah have any special abilities?" Sonia asked.

Callum shook his head but said, "Abel does. He can control minds."

"Like Lucien?" she asked.

"No," he answered. "Not exactly. It's more powerful. He doesn't have to be in the same room or even the same building as his target to achieve his purpose. They also don't remember it or know they're being controlled. When Lucien uses his skill, his voice can be heard in their head and they know he's doing it. Abel leaves barely a trace."

"Wow," Sonia breathed, and he smiled.

Then he shared, "So far Lilah's only having dreams she can't remember. However, their connection seems even stronger than ours or Leah and Lucien's, but not all in good ways."

"What does that mean?"

"The good part is they can sense if one or the other is in danger, even know where they are or are able to get to where they are without actually knowing where they are," he explained.

"That *is* good," she noted.

"The bad part is that Lilah feels pain, quite significant pain, if Abel is away from her and she doesn't know where he is. They also both experience what Lilah refers to as 'hyper-jealousy' if they even think of one with another that is not their mate."

"I would say we would experience that too, if it was in a wolf to be with another outside his mate," she pointed out.

"Well, it's not. However, you had others before me, and I did too. We both knew this and it was far from welcome, but for them, their responses are more extreme. Abel explained he'd not even known Lilah a day when she flew into a rage at his mention of ones before her."

"Strange," Sonia murmured.

"Indeed," Callum agreed.

"Do you know what that might mean?" she asked.

He shook his head. "I've no idea, baby doll. We can just hope we have time as Leah's abilities increase and you practice with yours, so that Lilah will come to understand hers and they'll be useful."

"Mm," she murmured, and when she did, Callum lost interest in their conversation.

"Time for bed," he declared.

Her head gave a slight jerk. "I'm *in* bed, wolf."

"Then time for me to get in it with you and turn you over my knee."

Her eyes said one thing, her lips said another. "You'll not be spanking me."

"No, I won't," he confirmed. "But I *will* be doing other things to you."

The message in her eyes deepened as he saw the tip of her tongue slide out to wet her upper lip.

"Get rid of your nightie," he ordered.

"Yes, my king," she said on a breathy false grumble.

He straightened from the bed to take off his clothes.

She got to her knees and he watched as she pulled off her nightie.

It was then Callum wasted no time joining her and turning his queen over his knee.

## *Abel*

Lilah was lying naked on top of him after he'd made her come for the fifth time that day.

And she was bitching.

"Why can't I have something cool, like being able to speak in your head?"

"Maybe you'll get somethin' like that," he responded in an effort to get her to quit bitching.

It was like he didn't speak.

"Or talking to animals?"

Abel decided this time to say nothing.

"All I've got is the ability to give good sass."

"And you got that down," Abel muttered, and she focused on him in order to narrow her eyes.

"And be *clingy*," she hissed. "What's the good of that?"

"You cool it and be patient, we might find out."

She glared at him.

He had shit to do and he needed her asleep so he could do it. Therefore, he had to deal with her mood to get on with it.

He also had to give her something, something she needed, something he had no idea he'd withheld until she told him.

And he was hoping, in giving it to her, he'd kill two birds with one stone.

So he set about attempting that, taking one of her hands from where it rested on his chest and lifting it.

"Abel—" she started and he had no clue what she was going to say but she snapped her mouth shut when he kept lifting her hand until he touched her middle finger to where he knew the scar began on his forehead.

"She started here," he murmured then slowly slid her finger across his forehead, down through his broken eyebrow, and picked up the scar on his cheek. He kept going, trailing her finger to his jaw where he stopped but held her finger there. "She ended here."

She didn't look pissed anymore, thank fuck. She looked something he wasn't sure he liked much more, but it was better than pissed.

She looked sad with a hint of angry.

He lost her look when she leaned up and put her lips to the start of the scar on his forehead. Her hand cupped his jaw and his cupped hers as a thrill chased down his spine while she traced the scar with her lips until she had to move their hands away to get to the end.

Delilah's touch, how it made him feel, he wouldn't have been surprised if he went to the mirror, looked, and saw the scar was gone.

He didn't reckon that actually happened, but in his gut, the touch of her lips had a different kind of healing power that meant almost the same thing.

Finally, she slid her lips to his and looked in his eyes.

"You're awesome," she whispered.

"So I've been told," he whispered back.

"You beginning to believe it?" she asked.

"Maybe," he answered.

He watched her eyes smile.

Then he asked, "You good to go to sleep, or do I need to fuck you again?"

The smile in her eyes got brighter before she closed them to press her mouth to his. Then she broke away to settle over him, snuggling close, her face in his throat.

"I think I'm all fucked out," she replied.

Abel grinned at the ceiling as he wound his arms around her.

"For today," she finished.

That was when Abel tightened his hold and started chuckling.

"It's been a good day," she said softly.

"Yeah," he agreed.

"Best part, outside the *bestest* best part, was telling your family and my dad about the bestest best part. That we can be together, literally forever."

That *had* been the best part, outside the part where they learned they could be together forever.

After they told them, Jian-Li had excused herself, but Abel knew she'd begun crying. Fuck, even Hook had lifted a hand to squeeze the bridge of his nose before sweeping his thumb and a finger under his eyes to hide the wet gathering there.

Delilah's dad got it. He'd sorted it out way before Delilah did and his relief was extreme, for the both of them.

Delilah cuddled closer. "So Snake died for forever love. It was beautiful before. But now..." She sighed. "Now maybe I can start to understand the gift he gave me. Gave us. And settle into it."

Thank Christ.

Abel kept her held close as he replied, "Yeah, baby."

"We're gonna be happy," she told him, sounding like she was getting sleepy but still sounding convinced.

He hoped she was right.

"Yeah," he agreed.

"Wild and free and happy," she kept talking.

"Yeah," he repeated.

"For eternity."

He rolled them to their sides but kept her close as he whispered his final, "Yeah, pussycat."

She drew in breath and let it go.

In five minutes, she'd relaxed, asleep in his arms.

Abel waited fifteen more to make sure that sleep was deep.

Then he carefully extricated himself from her, rolled off the bed, tugged on his jeans, and moved silently to and through the door.

He walked five doors up the hall, stopped at one, and knocked.

It was opened in thirty seconds by Poncho, who was like Abel, wearing nothing but faded jeans, his hair a mess, his eyes alert.

"Everything okay?"

"Not really, but there's nothing new that isn't okay. Just need a chat," Abel replied.

Poncho kept his eyes sharp on Abel and guessed, "My auntie."

"Yes, and no," Abel told him. "See, found out today that the vampires killed off a bunch of witches a long time ago."

"Fuck," Poncho mumbled.

"Right. So it's likely they're not hip on helpin'. The thing is, it wouldn't hurt to have one on our side. So yeah, I need you to get in touch with your aunt. But I need you to be cool about that. I need you to see where she's at with this supernatural shit before you tell her you're neck-deep in it. Only when you know she isn't gonna fuck us will I talk to the others and see if we can make an approach."

"Consider it done," Poncho stated instantly.

"Poncho—" Abel started.

"No." He shook his head. "Don't need to say more. I dig this has to be handled. You got my word I'll handle it."

Abel looked into his eyes and nodded.

Poncho jutted his chin down the hall. "Get back to our girl."

"Right, later."

Poncho gave a short salute and a "Later, *amigo*."

He was closing the door before Abel turned down the hall.

As silently as he'd left their room, he returned, carefully gathering Delilah in his arms after he pulled the covers back over his body.

Unconsciously, she snuggled deep and relaxed in his hold.

That was when Abel took a breath and let it go. He did this hoping Poncho could handle it and hoping Delilah would get some ability, and not only so she'd quit bitching. He also did it letting the sheer brilliance of all he'd learned that day wash through him (and there was a fuckload he'd learned that day about who he was and the fact it was far from monstrous).

Then he closed his eyes and went to sleep, doing it further hoping a dream would come.

Not like the dream come true he held in his arms.

Any dream they could use to help them stop evil so he and Delilah could live wild, free, happy...

And *forever*.

*Gregor*

Gregor sat at the desk in the compound's study, tapping his fingers, his eyes to edge of the desk, his mind filled.

"It's impossible," Yuri said from his seat in a chair across from him.

"I know," Gregor murmured.

"His senses are acute, wolf and vampire. It's impossible he hasn't run across at least one of our kind in two hundred years."

Gregor lifted his eyes to his son and stopped tapping. "I know, Yuri."

"He's been protected, and not by a family of loyal Chinese," Yuri declared.

Gregor sighed.

"He was saved from that witch," Yuri said quietly.

"He was," Gregor agreed.

"We can trace her. We have a date and a place. We can find out who she is. We might also find her."

Gregor kept his eyes to his son. "Do you think another immortal would happen upon a witch attempting to dispatch the only known hybrid and she'd survive?"

"No," Yuri replied. "Especially since it wasn't just another immortal. It was his mother, or his father, or both. There's no chance they allowed her to survive. But that doesn't mean we shouldn't look for her. She might have people. People who may know things. People who I can make talk."

Gregor's attention on his son became acute.

Yuri was hotheaded. He was also passionate. It was uncanny since it was not vampiric nor was it inherited from his father or his mother, who showed less emotion than even Gregor.

He was almost like a wolf.

But he was not wolf. He was vampire, a vampire with a variety of skills he'd honed over his centuries so that he was uniquely gifted in using them.

"Find who you can find," Gregor said quietly. "And make them talk."

He watched his son's slow smile.

Then he watched his son straighten from the chair and move to the door.

Only when he had it opened did Gregor call, "Yuri?"

Yuri turned back and lifted a brow.

"Be careful," Gregor whispered.

Yuri nodded once.

Then he disappeared.

# 15
# Destiny Fuckin' Loves Me

*Delilah*

I walked down the street cautiously, my stomach roiling with nausea, blood and bodies everywhere. On the streets. In the doorways to the shops. Necks gashed open. Throats ripped out. Limbs ripped away.

They were all gone. Every last human.

Save me.

This couldn't be right. This couldn't be what they wanted. This was worse than we'd expected.

They needed humans to survive.

So why were they killing them all?

"This is a warning."

I whipped around at the voice and saw him standing in the middle of the street.

A vampire. Handsome. Proud.

Evil.

"This is what we can do. This is why they will submit," he went on.

"Where's Abel?" I asked.

"He will sacrifice himself for you."

I felt my insides freeze and it was agony.

The vampire smiled like he knew he'd caused me pain and liked it. "You won't have forever. You won't even have tomorrow. You will only have a lifetime of mourning." His head cocked to the side. "Don't worry, it won't last long. It'll only be a human lifetime."

"*No!*" I screamed.

"*Bao bei,*" Abel called, gently shaking me.

My eyes opened and I saw him leaning over me. Instantly, I latched on, holding tight, pressing deep.

Abel rolled to his back, keeping me close.

"You had another dream," he murmured.

"Yeah," I agreed.

"You remember it?" he asked.

I searched for it.

Nothing.

"No," I whispered.

"Try, pussycat. It might be important."

I tried but still got nothing.

"It's gone," I told him.

"That's okay," he replied softly.

"Did I say anything?" I asked.

"Just screamed 'no,'" he shared.

I lifted my head to look at him. "Screamed?"

"Yeah, you sounded scared and I don't like that for you, Lilah. But still, part of me wishes you'd say more so I might be able to get a lock on what's happening."

I didn't like me screaming in my sleep either, not for me and not for Abel, but I agreed.

"Maybe I can get hypnotized or something so I'll remember," I suggested. Abel said nothing so I asked, "You don't think that's a good idea?"

"The situation we're in, not sure I want anyone controlling your mind."

At his words, it hit me.

"Do you think you can get in there?"

His brows drew together. "What?"

"When I'm dreaming. Do you think you can get in my head before I wake up? Use your mind-control abilities, see what's happening?"

He shook his head. "Never tried that. Not sure I can even do that."

"Maybe you should try it."

He studied me for a second before muttering, "We'll see, next time you dream."

"Okay."

"We got a big meeting today, baby. Best get up."

I sighed and repeated, "Okay."

But Abel didn't let me go.

He rolled me to my back, him on me, his eyes to my neck where he also put his finger, trailing it like a whisper along my pulse point.

"First, I wanna feed."

I felt my body relax and my lips smile.

He looked to my mouth, then to my eyes, and his got lazy.

"You wanna take care of me," he said quietly.

I so did.

"Yeah," I agreed.

"My Lilah's sweet, warm blood...for eternity."

My head tilted on the pillow and I lifted a hand to his neck and stroked his jaw, feeling the ridge of his scar against the pad of my thumb, loving how he gave that to me.

But still, his words made a thought occur to me, so I asked, "Will it get boring?"

"No."

I didn't believe that.

"You sure?"

"You taste like you every time, but you also taste different. Sometimes it's richer. Sometimes it's thicker. Sometimes it's more tangy. Sometimes sharp. Sometimes sweet. Don't know what's happening in you to make it that way, but it isn't like I'm eatin' steak for every meal. It's a variety, depending on the time of day, where your mood is at, whatever."

"Wow. That's cool."

"Yeah," he grinned. "Cool." Then he dipped his head and ran his tongue along my neck. I shivered while he whispered there, "Sometimes I get Lilah cotton candy."

I felt his tongue again and slid my hand from the side of his neck into his hair.

"Sometimes I get Lilah nectarine."

I felt his tongue again at my neck, but the numbness was invading.

I wasn't numb at my ear where he whispered, "Sometimes I get creamy Lilah."

"Abel," I breathed, squirming beneath him, thinking he was about to get seriously creamy Lilah.

He slid a hand low on my belly, almost there but not there enough.

"What're you gonna give me today, pussycat?" he asked.

"Don't know," I answered.

He slid his hand an inch lower. "Want me to find out?"

"Yes," I panted, clutching his hair and lifting my hips as best I could.

"Whatever you want, baby," he murmured, sliding his nose down my jaw as he slid his hand lower.

Then he found out.

And whatever it was for him, for me, it was *awesome*.

"You nervous?"

We were walking down the hall toward the dining room where we were going to have a breakfast meeting with our Save the World Posse.

I looked up at Abel and answered, "No, are you?"

"No," he replied. "You just seem...not right."

My head jerked. "Not right?"

"You were right when I was drawing from you and doin' the other things to you," he said, and I grinned. He was not grinning. "Before that and since, you've been off."

I stopped outside the door to the dining room, stopping him with me. "Off how?"

"Can't get a lock on it, but it's like you're tweaked."

"Lots of shit is going down, Abel," I reminded him.

"Yeah," he muttered. "Probably just tweaked myself and reading too much into it."

He started us moving toward the door but stopped instantly, shoving me behind him as the air shimmered and a woman suddenly formed in front of the door.

Peering around Abel, I stared at her.

Back at the restaurant, I'd seen bits and pieces of what Abel told me were wraiths, but considering I was hiding under a table when all that went down, and they took off after the bad supernaturals before I got a good look, I didn't get a whole eye view.

Now I was getting it and it was freaking phenomenal.

She seemed mostly solid, you could only partly see through her. She had white hair, elegant features, and a pastel dress with lots of ripped edges (but also lots of cleavage). She looked like she was in a music video that had the wind machine set to low, except she was also floating.

And smiling at us.

"Abel and Delilah," she said, her voice very real too, but still somehow dreamy.

"Serena," Abel replied, but it was also a question.

"Indeed," she confirmed.

Serena. Empress of the wraiths.

Awesome!

"Uh..." I pressed into Abel's back and got up on my toes to whisper toward his ear, "Are we supposed to curtsy or something?"

"Only if you're in a ceremonial chamber, and this is not one of those," she answered.

I caught her eyes. "Oh, okay."

"I rule my wraiths, but that doesn't mean I am not equal to them, and them me. I'm also equal to you," she continued. "The curtsy in a ceremonial chamber is just tradition. And tedious. But ceremonies wouldn't be ceremonies if there wasn't tradition." She paused and grinned. "And tedium."

"True enough," I murmured.

"I'll say now, it's lovely to meet you both," she told us.

"Same," Abel grunted.

"Yeah," I said on a return smile.

Motioning to the door, she invited, "After you."

Abel hesitated before he reached out and opened the door. We went through and I did it wondering if she could float through it if it was still closed.

At that time, she didn't. She floated but did it through the open door.

"Excellent, we're all here," Gregor said as Abel and I were confronted with much the same as yesterday, except the table wasn't covered in platters of food. Instead, a buffet had been set up to the side (and I was happy to see pancakes were on offer, seeing as I was getting tired of eggs).

There were also more people. This meant Serena wasn't the only new person we met. We met a handsome, dark-haired vampire with an accent named Cristiano, who was also on The Council. We also met a tall, large, strange-looking man with big hands, which were bizarrely knobbly, and kind eyes. His name was Avery, and although he was strange-looking, he was also strangely attractive, though I couldn't put my finger on exactly how. He just was.

What he wasn't was explained in the sense that he didn't share if he was vampire, wolf, or what, though he didn't look like any that I'd met. Since it wasn't offered and it would be rude, Abel and I didn't ask.

Stephanie, Caleb, and Ryon were also there.

We were invited to load up plates and we did. After everyone was seated, Gregor began.

"Since Serena does not eat as the rest of us do, and she has information we need to know, while we partake, she'll give us her briefing."

Serena was doing her music video thing by the window and I wondered if she sat, seeing as she could float apparently effortlessly.

Obviously, I didn't ask this for more reasons than the fact that she started talking and I started eating.

"Although fortunate that we were on the inside with the traitors, which meant we could intervene when they attacked The Sacred Triumvirate some days ago, this also means that we are no longer on the inside."

I looked to Abel who felt my eyes and looked to me.

I mouthed, "Traitors?" since I hadn't heard them referred to that way.

He gave a slight shrug and we both looked to Serena when she kept talking.

"By the time we exposed our true allegiance, we'd learned that, while planning to do damage to The Three—and they were looking at this a variety of ways, such as total annihilation or simply dispensing with one which, according to The Prophesies, would make the rest ineffectual—they're also planning to expose the existence of immortals to humans. And they were not planning on doing that diplomatically."

Leah, Sonia, and I gave each other looks even as we ate and Serena carried on.

"However, the one wraith we have left in position, who infiltrated our sisters who have long since sided with the traitors, has shared with us that the plans we were once privy to have been changed. Unfortunately, due to my sisters intervening to save The Three, they're being far more careful with all wraiths, including the ones who actually share their ideology. Therefore, she hasn't been able to ascertain any of their new plans."

I swallowed pancake and butted in quietly, "Thank you for that, by the way. Your, um, sisters, coming to the rescue. We wouldn't have made it or would have..." I shook my head, swallowing for another reason, thinking of Snake, Chen, and Jabber, before I finished, "Things would have gone far worse if your sisters hadn't been there."

"We're committed to equality amongst ourselves and all beings, so it was an honor to come to the aid of The Three who'll keep all beings allied and free," she replied.

"But if that's your philosophy," Leah put in, "how did you get the others to think that you might be on their side?"

Serena looked to Leah. "Our mates are phantoms."

"Sorry?" Leah asked.

"Wraiths are ethereal, for the most part," she stated, drifting a hand in front of her. "For those humans who have seen us who we did not let know what we truly are, we're known as ghosts. All wraiths are female. Phantoms are the same, but they're male."

She looked to Abel and me and had clearly been informed we were new to this supernatural business, because she kept explaining.

"We aren't actually ghosts. We're born in this form and have always lived in it. We are much like all other beings. We live. We sleep. We love. We make babies." She smiled. "And for us to make babies, we need phantoms."

"All right," I said when she stopped.

"The problem with this is, we and our phantom mates had a falling out some time ago. There was..." She hesitated before continuing, "A situation and we didn't agree on how it would be handled. Our mates are quite protective and felt we should stay safe and they should deal with it. We wraiths felt we should fight at our mates' sides. They'd demanded we stay behind and they do the fighting. We did what we felt was necessary and had joined the fight against their wishes. They thought that was disobedience. We found that concept repugnant as we're not children, we're simply a different gender. The situation we were engaged in was sorted, however, our mates are quite stubborn. Rather than being grateful for our assistance, they punished us by disconnecting."

"When did this happen?" Sonia asked.

"Twelve hundred years ago," Serena answered.

My eyes got wide. "Whoa, phantoms can hold a grudge."

Serena smiled at me. "They can indeed, as can wraiths. The longer they stayed away, the more the grudge switched from one side to the other, turning us away from them should one try to approach for reconciliation. As you can imagine, this has gone back and forth for over a millennia. There were, of course, some..." Another hesitation before she went on with a not-hard-to-read-grin, "*Connections* as we all have needs."

I got her so I grinned back.

She kept going.

"But this struggle started over equality. The sisters who have not turned traitor still wish for nothing but a lasting reconciliation with our mates when they accept us at their sides, not at their hearths. However, we were able to convince the traitors that we were tired of our disconnection with our lovers, and could deliver the phantoms to the other side through our subjugation to our mates. As the traitors are being led by males, it's not surprising they would believe this, as even vampires, who well know that females of their kind have the capacity to be exceptional warriors, can be chauvinistic. Therefore, it didn't take much convincing."

"And the sisters who have turned traitor?" Sonia asked, and Serena's expression became anything but serene.

"To survive, we feed off mortal energy," she stated.

I tensed and felt Abel tense beside me.

She must have felt it too for she looked to us. "This does not harm mortals. It does not take from you. It emits from you all the time. It's natural. We don't need to control you to absorb it. You just need to exist so we can do the same." Her tone changed to dire when she continued, "This doesn't mean that all beings don't have those amongst them who thrive on negativity. The majority of wraiths and phantoms absorb positive energy. They crave joy. Or contentment. Or success. Or humor. A variety of these things. But there are those who feed off despair, anger, fear, jealousy, prejudice, hate. In our case, quite literally, you are what you eat."

"Yikes," I muttered.

"Yes," she agreed. "And those who have sided with the traitors would thrive if humans were enslaved. A world of unhappy humans would mean they'd have even more of what they crave."

"Not good," I kept muttering.

"No, and worse, it's gluttony. For there is already much anger, jealousy, prejudice, and fear for them to feed from." She shook her head and, along with it, her music-video-drifting hair. "It makes no sense to the sisterhood. The more you consume, you just become more of what you consume. It doesn't make you more powerful. It just makes you angrier, uglier, more hateful."

"Just like humans," Leah stated.

"Exactly," Serena replied.

"The good news is," Gregor butted in, "although Serena and her sisters have lost their foothold amongst our enemy, she's managed to make a meeting with Gastineau."

"Who's Gastineau?" Abel asked.

"My lifemate," Serena answered. "He's also emperor of the phantoms. We were reconciled seventy-five years ago, but this lasted under a decade. However, we made a child during that time, our third daughter, and since he dotes on her, but I'm raising her, we've had to stay in close contact. As his brothers wish after the last situation they involved themselves in, which segregated our kind, Gastineau prefers to keep to the shadows and allow other immortals, and humans, to do what they will. Including making their mistakes. I hope to impress on him during our meeting that this time he must take a stand, with his brothers, alongside their sisters, uniting us all once again in order to keep peace."

"And how is he leaning?" Abel asked.

"We, like wolves, once we find our mates, never stray. Imagine you were separated from your mate for decades, a mate you love who you're simply angry with, a mate who's raising your child." She tipped her head. "I think you know how he's leaning."

"In other words, you got leverage," Abel remarked, and her smile came back.

"Indeed, I do. But also, most phantoms, like most wraiths, prefer positive energy. Even if I didn't have that leverage, I know my Gastineau. He would never side with the traitors. He may not wish to get involved, but he would not ally himself with them. Therefore, in order to keep the state of the world as it needs to be, I believe inside he understands that he must lead his brothers to maintain that. I just have to point out that this situation has become dangerous. Instead of pockets of rebellions breaking out, this is a real threat."

"Why do you call them traitors?" I asked, and her attention turned to me.

"They know we'll not feed on negativity and therefore will perish. To ally with those who would wipe all goodness from humanity would mean vast amounts of wraiths and phantoms would cease to be. And this is the same for vampires. There are those who don't like fear and desolation to sour the blood of humans, but they're resigning their brothers and sisters to that fate. In the end, we are all of this world. We all must find a way to live together in harmony, and anyone who doesn't agree is a traitor to the way things need to be."

"Amen to that, sister," I said.

"Yes, amen to that...sister," she agreed on another smile.

"Something else you need to know," Lucien began, and I looked to him. "Abel, you saw it back in Serpentine Bay, but Lilah, it's doubtful you did. Wraiths can appear and disappear. When they're invisible, they have less ability to manipulate their surroundings. They can move things...adjust a chair, knock a vase off a table. But this is limited. When they appear, their power increases exponentially."

"Uh, yeah. Ripping a head off with your bare hands is pretty powerful," Abel murmured.

I pressed my lips together and gave Leah big eyes.

She mouthed, "I know," in return.

"Our ability to be invisible, although it weakens us in the earthly world, allows us to appear unannounced. As we can move through solid things both in our invisible bodies as well as our visible ones, this is an added strategic advantage," Serena went on.

"Not if we're dealing with your sisters who are against us," Abel replied.

"Yes, this is why you need to know that there are physical manifestations even when we're invisible. An unusual coolness to the air in a room could mean a wraith or phantom is close. A chill could mean they're *very* close. A shiver could mean they're sliding through your actual person," she explained.

"Whoa," I whispered, not liking the idea of a ghost sliding through my body.

She nodded to me but kept explaining.

"We can't overtake your bodies. We can't possess you. And prior to transformation into a visible being, the air will shimmer. As our attack was completely a surprise, the vampires and wolves you were fighting with didn't have the attention to sense our presence or see the shimmer. However, in the future, just in case, you need to know all of that."

Abel nodded to her and Callum spoke, asking Abel and me, "Do you have any questions for Serena?"

Abel looked back to the wraith. "Not to put too fine a point on it, but still gotta know. How do you die?"

She tipped her head to the side again and answered, "An extreme blast of electricity can sap us of all of our energy and we'll blink out of existence immediately."

"That's it?" Abel asked.

"Well, no." She shook her head. "When we're visible, not only do we have the power to navigate the world like a human or other immortals...touch things, move them, do battle...we can also be touched. And harmed. It's difficult and requires a great deal of strength, but if any of our limbs were removed forcibly or by a weapon, unless we receive attention from a fellow wraith or phantom or absorb a large amount of mortal energy, all the energy we have will escape and we'll eventually die. This, obviously, hastens if our heads are removed from our bodies."

Ugh.

"'Thanks' seems like a fucked-up thing to say, but thanks," Abel said quietly.

She inclined her head.

"Uh," I butted in, "if you guys can float through walls, or float at all, doesn't that make us vulnerable here, even in this compound?"

Serena didn't answer. Gregor did.

"There's an invisible electric net over the entirety of the land the compound is on, Lilah," he told me. "And the walls surrounding the compound have a slim chamber the length of them situated between the inner and outer walls which contains an electrical charge. Another net runs from the beach up the cliffside. If a wraith or phantom were to try to breach any of these, a surge of electricity would occur. A surge that would be noted by our security and we'd be aware that an attempt was being made. In other words, wraiths and phantoms must enter the compound like any other being...through the front gate."

Well, that was good.

"Any other questions?" Callum asked.

Abel shook his head at Callum. So did I.

Callum dipped his chin sharply in response and turned to Gregor.

"Right, that's out there. Now where's your Council with the president?"

"The president?" I asked, and Callum looked to me.

"Of the United States."

I blinked.

Gregor spoke. "It would be good if you sent Ryon or one of your brothers as an emissary to our delegation."

"I'm happy to go," Ryon stated immediately and I had to stop myself from shrinking back in my chair when Callum's expression changed at his words.

"Regan is en route to the compound. She'll be here today," Callum replied. "And no member of my family will be sent to join the delegation since any of them, if captured, could be used against me. All of them will be safe from that here, with Sonia and me. So this is where you all will be."

"Regan is Callum's mother," Sonia told Abel and me quietly.

"Cal, wolves don't hide," Ryon stated at this point and did it impatiently. I got the feeling they'd had this conversation before.

"I've lost a brother and a father to this shit, Ryon. I'll not lose more, which means I'll not lose you. Until we know more about what they're planning, who's with us and who's against us, you're all staying safe," Callum fired back.

"Which blows," Caleb muttered, then rolled his eyes at Ryon when Callum's expression turned downright ferocious.

"Safe does not blow, Caleb," Callum clipped. "Safe means our mother, who lost her mate and her son to these rebels, will not lose more."

Caleb appeared like he didn't much enjoy being told off, but he said nothing else. Ryon said nothing else mostly because his jaw was clenched so hard, I wasn't sure he could speak.

So Gregor took this opportunity to butt into the family argument. "Callum, we must impress upon the president the gravity of the situation, and the king sending one of his governors—"

Callum cut him off. "Saint is a skilled diplomat. He has a direct line to me. And if the president doesn't understand that my number one priority is my family, I don't give a shit if the gravity of the situation is impressed upon him or not. He makes a fucked-up decision based on the fact that he doesn't have the attention he thinks he deserves, then he pays for that through his legacy."

"You wanna fill us in on what you're talking about?" Abel suggested.

Gregor looked to Abel. "We're attempting to talk a variety of world leaders into devising a plan to expose the existence of immortals in a way that will not be alarming, at the same time sharing that there is some cause for concern due to those who wish to cause harm and explaining how they could take precautions."

"And you're gonna manage that how?" Abel asked but didn't allow an answer. "First off, humans are gonna totally freak. Then they're gonna totally *fucking* freak when you share that there're evil supernaturals who want to enslave them, are pretty much impossible to kill, can get in their homes without invitation, and are impervious to silver, garlic, shit like that, which means humans are essentially completely unsafe."

"I'll admit, it's a diplomatic challenge," Gregor conceded, and I swallowed back my snort.

"Yeah, a challenge," Abel muttered sarcastically, obviously feeling the same as me.

"It's your destiny not only to ensure humans live freely but also to create harmony between humans and immortals," Serena pointed out, and I was glad she seemed so positive and didn't mention it could go the other way.

"Which brings us to you and Lilah, Abel," Gregor stated, and I looked to him. "We've consulted with experts in the field and they believe that, of The Three, with your manner and the fact you're a hybrid, as well as Lilah's vivacity and, well," he flicked a hand out to me, "her attractive every-girl characteristics, you two would be the best poster couple to show how not only are immortals nonthreatening, but that humans and immortals can live in harmony."

I felt Abel's tenseness and reached out a hand to curl it around his thigh as he asked, "Poster couple?"

"We'd like to place carefully crafted articles in a variety of reputable media outlets about you and Lilah, sharing that you're an immortal and she is your human mate. This would include photo spreads," Gregor explained, and unfortunately he wasn't done. "And due to our need to prove this is not nonsense, we must utilize television in order that people can see you transform."

That was when I got tense.

Abel performing for the masses?

I did not like that.

"Are you fuckin' *crazy*?" Abel barked.

He didn't like it either.

Gregor ignored Abel's question and assured, "This would all occur behind these walls so you both would remain safe. And we'd have approval over what was written or broadcast. It would help enormously if Jian-Li and your brothers would agree to participate too. Our experts feel your close connection with a family of humans would hold much sway with humanity."

"You are crazy," Abel whispered dangerously, and I gave his thigh a squeeze.

Gregor again ignored him.

"After this is shared, we'd strategically release Leah and Lucien's story. And after that, we would share about Callum and Sonia, they being last as both are wolves," Gregor continued. "However, Sonia's lifetime as a human would be carefully communicated. We also have other wolves who have taken human mates, not to mention vampires who have recently coupled with humans. We would ask they tell their stories as well. And the concubines have agreed to come out about what they do for vampires and share our own version of..." He paused, "Humanity."

I knew about concubines, or the women (and dudes) who, for centuries, provided their blood to vampires so that vampires didn't have to go out and find their meals, freaking out humans in the process. There had been a lot of rules around selecting them and keeping them. Some of those rules ended when Leah, who had been Lucien's concubine, fell in love with her vampire and he did the same in return, this being forbidden. Until them.

"The Council is crafting a media plan that will eventually expose wolves and vampires within society," Gregor kept going. "Doctors. Nurses. Businessmen and women who provide jobs. It will be explained we already live harmoniously with humans. We own property. We pay taxes. We purchase goods and services. We provide employment opportunities. We're involved in our communities."

"Did you live amongst humans all your centuries?' Abel asked when Gregor quit speaking.

"I have, indeed, Abel," Gregor confirmed.

"Right, so you know all that's shit and they...are gonna...*freak*," Abel returned. "It doesn't matter that I'm a biker who has a Chinese American family and Lilah's the shit. They're just gonna freak."

I was feeling warm inside about Abel describing me as the shit when Gregor kept at him.

"This would be you doing what you need to do as a member of The Three to convince the American people, the people of the world, that your people mean no harm."

I felt Abel preparing to reply so I squeezed his thigh and quickly leaned into him.

"He's right. It is," I said quietly.

"He's right. It is," Abel agreed. "It's also not gonna work."

"That doesn't mean we shouldn't try," I pointed out.

"And put your face out there for people to think shit about you? You with a werewolf vampire? So even when we do sort out those assholes, everyone everywhere knows you and me and can give us shit...for eternity?"

"Uh, babe, you're hot. Women the world over are totally gonna get it," I shared, and he stared.

Then he stated, "Lilah, this is not about me bein' hot."

"People forgive a lot if you're hot, believe me. That means Lucien is gonna kill and so is Callum, and I mean kill in a good way. Everyone will want their own vamp or wolf." I turned to Gregor. "Actually, that's more of a problem than the other stuff. Especially if it gets out that vamps can make their mates live for eternity."

"Specifics about certain things will be shared carefully, Lilah, or not at all, until that knowledge is needed," Gregor told me.

"Good call," I muttered.

"Seriously, are you thinkin' of goin' for this shit?" Abel asked, and I looked back to him.

"Do you have another idea?" I asked.

"Find those fuckers who wanna turn the world upside down, obliterate them, then go back to normal," Abel answered instantly.

"This idea holds more merit for me as well," Lucien put in.

"We're working on that too," Gregor shared.

"That's good since an eternity of fame is far from tedious. It's often frustrating and can be aggravating and I'd rather not expose Leah to enduring it," Lucien shot back. "Therefore, I can obviously understand why Abel feels the same."

"Lucien can seriously kick ass, as you know," Leah said as explanation to me. "What you might not know is that the immortal world knows it too and thinks it's awesome, and that's not always good."

"Ah," I murmured.

"Find another way," Lucien ordered Gregor.

"We are all destined to live in harmony," Gregor returned, then finished on a dire note. "Or not."

"We can accomplish that without all of us being poster couples in the press," Lucien retorted. "So find that way."

"Do you have another idea?" Gregor asked calmly.

"That's not my job," Lucien bit out, not calmly. "My job is to save humanity while keeping my bride and the rest of The Three alive. You're the politician. Do your job."

"I had concerns our plan would meet with negative reactions, so this isn't surprising," Gregor replied. "However, I'd still request that all of you consider it."

"You've explained that you're concerned about your family's safety." Cristiano spoke for the first time, his attention on Callum, "That being the case, I would further request that you consider utilizing Calder. He has a vast worldwide network and is able to find out a good many things. If The Three don't wish to come out publically, then we must intensify our efforts privately to understand what the enemy is planning."

"And Calder has activated his network," Callum told Cristiano. "He's just organizing those efforts from here."

"He has a way with them," Cristiano pointed out carefully.

"And he'll use that way over the fucking phone," Callum returned.

Cristiano drew in a breath before he nodded.

"Avery?" Leah called softly. "What do you think?"

The strange-looking man turned kind eyes to Leah and didn't hesitate with his response. "Although I understand why it was suggested we utilize the media in our efforts, I'll share with you what I shared with Gregor, that being I don't think it's an exceptionally good idea to have any of The Three identifiable by anybody around the globe. I believe this creates unnecessary vulnerability."

To that, Gregor's only response was for his lips to thin.

"There might be desperate times that call for desperate measures," Avery went on. "Fortunately, we have not yet hit that time." He took in a breath and finished, "Unfortunately, if we do not do something, I'm afraid that time is fast approaching."

"And your idea would be...?" Callum prompted.

"My idea, I'm afraid, will be even less popular," Avery told him.

"Share it anyway," Callum ordered, and Avery nodded.

"I believe we should allow our adversaries to make their first move."

Something about this made my body string tight.

Abel felt it and his hand curled around mine at his thigh.

"This way," Avery continued, "our immortals, and there are many, including The Three, would swoop in to protect humanity. This would offer a very powerful message. Obviously, losses would be had on both sides. But humanity would see that there are immortals who are guardians, not vanquishers. The Three would be able to go about whatever they're required to do anonymously so that, when we all taste victory, they can enjoy their eternities without celebrity."

"I'm not all fired up about that plan," I said quietly.

"I'm not either, Delilah," Avery replied. "And we can hope we receive some intelligence that will allow us to make much the same statement without any human losses. Thwarting such a plan by immortals and doing it publicly, sharing in that way that immortals exist, the bad being in the minority, the good willing to put their lives on the line for harmony, would also be a powerful message."

"I hear you. I'm not super hip on the idea, but I'll deal with people knowing who I am if it means saving lives," I shared, and Abel's hand tightened around mine. "Though, I'm not big on Abel transforming. I haven't even seen that. He could just extend his fangs or something."

"That says a great deal about you, my dear," Avery returned but did it shaking his head. "But even if you and Abel, Lucien and Leah, and Callum and Sonia made the public aware of who you are, that doesn't ensure that an attack will not be forthcoming."

He had me there so I could do nothing but nod.

"There's much to think about and much to do," Gregor put in. "So I suggest we go about that and reconvene this evening for further discussion." He looked to the wraith. "Serena, you're away to Gastineau shortly?"

"Indeed," she confirmed.

"Let's brief," he murmured, throwing his napkin down and pushing his chair back.

He rose and gave Cristiano and Avery meaningful looks.

Cristiano took a sip of coffee before he rose.

Avery said, "You'll excuse me," and he got up as well.

Stephanie muttered, "I haven't had a real breakfast yet so I'm going to Kyle." She got up and looked around, finishing, "Later."

Caleb threw his napkin on the table and rose from his seat too, saying irritably, "I got twiddling of my thumbs to do."

Callum sighed.

Sonia smiled at me.

"We'll talk further after we have our session with Abel," Ryon stated, also moving to leave.

It was then I remembered that Abel was going to train as wolf with his wolf brothers. It was also then I hoped I got to watch.

My thoughts came back into the room when it hit me that the only ones left were The Three.

"Gotta admit, sittin' on our hands and waitin' for shit doesn't sit good with me either," Abel told the table.

"It's smart and it's safe," Callum replied.

"It's still irritating," Lucien murmured.

"Your last battle was five hundred years ago, Lucien. Mine was last Christmas," Callum said quietly. "We should be smart and we should remain safe."

"I don't disagree with you, Cal," Lucien returned. "However, this..." He swept a hand across the fine china and silver littering the table. "It isn't our nature. Especially when that's going on out there." He pointed a finger at the window. "Therefore, we need to remember precisely what our nature is so we don't end up doing something stupid due to impatience or frustration."

"Agreed," Callum said. "So we prepare. I train Abel to fight as wolf and you work with Abel's brothers to further improve their abilities."

"Agreed," Lucien repeated Callum's word.

"That's good with me," Abel added.

"Uh, what do we girls do?" I asked.

Lucien, Callum, and Abel (yep, all three) looked at me, baffled.

Yeesh.

Men.

"We *are* in on this destiny of saving the world too," I reminded them and turned to Abel. "Xun, Wei, and Chen offered to train me in some of their kung fu magic."

"I want them going two-, three-, four-on-one with Lucien and Callum's wolves so they can improve their 'kung fu magic,'" Abel said the last three words like they amused him, then added, "And so they can stay alive again if more shit goes down."

"Okay, so I'll get in on that. Leah and Sonia can do it with me if they want," I returned.

"Sonia's practicing with her abilities, attempting to increase her affinity with wildlife by communicating with them," Callum shared. "Perhaps you can go out with her."

"And miss my opportunity at throwing a ninja star?" I asked.

Callum's lips quirked and his eyes slid to Abel.

Abel's arm slid along the back of my chair and I looked to him. "Pussycat—" he began, and I knew what was coming. I didn't know how, but I did.

And all I could think about what was coming was, *Oh no he didn't.*

"I get your protective instinct, baby, but I have one too," I reminded him.

"The boys need to be prepared," he reminded me.

"So do the girls," I returned.

"True, but it's doubtful any of you will see actual fighting," Abel retorted.

"You don't know that," I pointed out, and his face got hard.

"I fuckin' do," he growled.

Oh man.

"Abel—"

"Let us do what we gotta do."

"Abel!"

His face suddenly was in mine. "Lilah, let us *do* what we gotta *do*."

I narrowed my eyes. "And what about what *we* gotta do?"

He leaned a bit back and threw up a hand. "I don't know. Go try to zap some shit. See if you got some ability like Leah and Sonia."

I blinked.

Then I glared.

Then I fought back slapping him upside the head.

When I got that under control, I hissed, "You didn't just say that."

"Right," he clipped, his patience gone. "A day, Lilah, for me to work with Callum and see what I gotta do to get my shit sorted, fighting as wolf. A day where Lucien works with Xun and Wei to see where they're at and what they need. After that, we take you on."

Compromise. And a good one.

It was also an annoying one precisely because it was good.

"A day," I snapped, and he grinned.

More annoying.

Then he leaned into me and ran his temple along mine.

That was not annoying, but I decided to pretend it was by turning away in a huff when he was done.

"Good call, not weighing in on that," Sonia noted, and I looked to her and Callum.

Callum just grinned at his empty plate and murmured, "Mm."

"Next time I'll let one of you go a few rounds with your bitches so I can avoid gettin' shit from mine," Abel remarked, and my angry eyes shot back to him.

"What you did was avoid the doghouse. Don't court a permanent stay," I warned.

"Like you'd send me there for eternity," he retorted.

"Don't try me."

Abel burst out laughing.

I again fought back the urge to slap him upside the head.

I did this by pushing my chair back, throwing my napkin on the table, and announcing, "Time for me to go and try zapping something. Any of you girls with me?"

"I'm in," Leah stated immediately.

"After you're done zapping things, we'll all go out so I can talk to bunnies," Sonia added.

"We've got a plan," I decreed and turned to go but didn't get very far when Abel caught my hand.

I looked down at him.

"Thanks, *bao bei*," he said softly.

"Just so you know, you being sweet totally works. I'm still gonna pretend it doesn't and bust your chops," I informed him and got another grin.

"Have a feeling I draw from you again later, I'll get tangy Lilah, seein' as you're in the mood to be sassy," he replied.

"And just so you know, you being hot totally works too. I'm still gonna bust your chops."

That got me a full-blown smile.

It also got me a tug on my hand that forced me to bend to him. When I got close, his other hand shot up in a blur and caught me at the back of the head so he could pull me to him and give me a short, but hot and wet, kiss.

When he broke it, he whispered, "Good luck zapping something."

To which I replied, "Whatever."

To which he delivered his kill shot, giving him the win.

He did it with his eyes to my mouth, still whispering. "Regardless of the extraneous shit and the centuries I had to wait to get what was mine, destiny fuckin' loves me."

As completely awesome as that was, still, I was me, so I shared, "That's the sweet part I'm pretending doesn't work."

His eyes came to mine. "Keep it up, pussycat. I like tangy Lilah."

"Let go of me so I can be annoyed somewhere else," I ordered, though what I meant was so he'd stop turning me on.

"So full of shit," he replied.

He knew what I meant, but of course he would. He could smell it.

I pretended that wasn't the case too and told him, "I'm almost at my quota of bickering for the day so you need to let me go so I can save some up for later, seeing as I'm gonna need it."

Abel kept smiling, this time doing it giving my hand and head a squeeze. Then he let me go.

Without looking at the other men, I stomped out, Leah and Sonia on my heels, so I could try to see if I could zap something.

I couldn't. But I knew this already.

I still tried, though not for very long, since it was a lot more fun to go out and watch Sonia talk to bunnies.

# 16
# Let the Day Begin

*Abel*

Abel woke and did it because he felt Delilah getting agitated.

He opened his eyes, feeling her body tucked to his, back to front, his arm draped around her waist.

He tightened his hold and opened his mouth to say something to wake her when her words of three days before came to him about trying to get in her head during a dream.

He closed his mouth and his eyes, tipping his head forward to rest his forehead against her crown. He made his attempt, using his abilities to control her mind by telling her to let him in her dream.

He got nothing. She simply shifted in his arms as she normally did when she was having a dream.

He'd never tried to control anyone's mind while they were sleeping, so he tried a different tack.

As a test, he ordered her to find his hand and hold it.

Instantly, she did, but she did this still asleep.

And still dreaming.

That meant he could get to her. He just needed to keep trying.

*"Bao bei,* let me in," he whispered, curling his fingers around hers and repeating his words to her mind.

Nothing.

*Let me in your dream,* he again ordered.

Her movements became more agitated but whatever was going on in her head was not his to have.

He tightened his hold on her hand and tried again, shouting, *Lilah, let me in!*

Instantly, he saw it in his head. A street. Blood. Bodies. Delilah there, several feet in front of him, her back to him. A man down the street from Delilah. Classy, haughty, a look on his face that was an amused sneer. A vampire.

The man looked beyond Delilah, saw Abel, and gave a start as his chin jerked back in shock.

Delilah turned and Abel's eyes went to her, his body growing taut at the fear etched on her face. Fear so extreme, even in a dream, he could taste it.

She saw him, lifted her hand his way, and screamed, *"No!"*

A bright blue flash obliterated everything and he was out of her mind, back in bed, gripping Delilah to him in a hold that he forced himself to relax or he'd break her fingers.

"What the fuck, what the fuck, what the fuck?" she chanted, moving in a way he knew she wanted to turn, so he let her go and she did so, facing him, eyes open and scared.

"I was there," he told her.

"Where?" she asked on a soft pant, her breath coming fast, the fear still clinging, making the air around them heavy, sticking in his throat.

"Your dream," he answered.

"Shit, I dreamed again?"

Fuck, she didn't remember.

"Yeah."

She shook her head on the pillow, but it wasn't in the negative. She was just doing it, probably to clear the fear that still had a hold on her.

"A street. Bodies. Blood. You standing there. A vampire with you," he explained her dream.

"You got in?" she asked, her eyes growing wide, and he held her gaze.

"You don't remember?" he asked back even though he knew the answer.

She shook her head again.

"Nothing?" he pressed.

Her eyes went unfocused as her body stayed tense and he waited. He was used to this whenever he'd ask her to try to remember her dreams.

She refocused and relaxed against him. "No, baby, nothing." She pushed closer, her hand on his chest between them. "But you got in?"

"Yeah," he nodded. "Saw what I said I saw."

"Blood. Bodies. A vamp?" she asked.

"Yeah," he confirmed.

"A good vamp?"

"Not even close."

He felt her shiver and gathered her closer.

"Was Leah there? Sonia? Callum? Lucien?" she went on.

He shook his head.

Her brows drew together. "Just me?"

Just her. Just her, an evil vampire, and a street full of dead humans.

Abel did not like this.

"Just you," he said quietly.

"Why would I be alone?" she asked.

"No clue," he answered.

"I wouldn't," she told him, pressing even closer and pulling up so her face was near his. "I wouldn't, honey. No way would I be alone. You wouldn't let that happen. None of The Three would. So this dream can't be premonitory."

He hoped like fuck she was right.

He didn't reply.

"It's just me freaking out about all the shit that's going down," she assured him.

It could be.

Though, no shit was going down.

They'd been at the compound now for a week and dick was happening.

Not dick, precisely.

He was training with Callum and his family.

Lucien and Stephanie were working with Xun and Wei.

Chen and Jabber were getting better.

Hook had caught the eye of some female vampire two days earlier. They'd then disappeared behind her door in the south wing and no one had seen them since. All they knew was that four bottles of Jack had been delivered to that room, as well as sandwiches, steak dinners, made-to-order omelet breakfasts, and a bottle of caramel syrup.

So they actually did know what was going on between those two. Abel just refused to think about it even though Delilah thought it was hilarious and shared with him that she was glad her father had found someone with whom he could "pass his time."

Poncho had left days earlier, saying he had an errand to run, but Abel knew it was to go back to New Mexico to meet with his aunt. Abel had gotten progress reports, including the fact Poncho made it home safely. He had to pass some test that involved a goat and a snake (he didn't give specifics and Abel didn't ask), and once he did, Abel would hear from him again.

With Hook hooking up and Poncho gone, Moose had lost it the day before, unable to be cooped up, even on a twenty-five-acre compound, not without his crew there to help pass the time. Jabber didn't do it for him considering Moose was not a man prone to bedside vigils at all, but definitely not when they included listening to a biker bitch about how he wasn't allowed to move around, have a smoke, or down a bottle of Jim Beam.

Moose had roared off on his Harley, saying he'd be back after he found himself some bourbon, a brawl, and a bitch.

Other than that, and the fact that they'd heard nothing from Serena and Yuri had disappeared, according to Gregor "to see to something important," zero was happening and Abel was feeling like Moose.

He was restless.

If it wasn't for Delilah's insatiable need for orgasms, Abel's need to give them to her, and Callum's training, he'd be going out his mind.

He sensed the same with Delilah.

What they had was not the wild and free she wanted.

She was wild, that was certain. She took his dick and gave back all she could any way he wanted. She was up for adventure. She was up for *anything*.

And he loved that.

But outside of her getting off in another way, that being watching him transform to wolf and train—something she didn't hide seriously turned her on—and the minimal training in basic moves that Xun and Wei were giving her, Leah, and Sonia, there was nothing wild and free about eating off fine china and fucking in a bed that some human servant made for them after they left it.

"Abel?" she called, bringing him back to her.

He gave her his attention, rolling to his back and pulling her on top of him.

"Yeah. Maybe it's nothin'," he muttered.

She slid her hand up to curl it around his neck and dipped her face close.

"Something's gotta give for my man," she said softly.

She sensed he was restless too.

"Big place. Still feel caged," he admitted.

"Maybe they'll let us out to do some day-tripping," she suggested.

"Rather feel caged than have you an open target."

Her face got soft at his words and she muttered, "I hear that. Still sucks."

"Yeah," he agreed.

She shifted her hand so her thumb ran the edge of his lower lip, and not surprisingly, his cock responded to her touch.

"Take your mind off it by sucking your big, beautiful dick," she offered, her gaze heating, her lips curled up.

She was good with her mouth. She was good with everything. So he was not going to refuse.

"Like that, pussycat," he murmured and watched her green eyes flare.

His mate. His temptress. Abel had known a lot of women in his life, including some who could go a few rounds and not lose the mood or their energy, but he'd never had anyone like Delilah. A woman who matched his appetite. A woman who wanted it all the time, with no boundaries.

Wild and free.

She dropped her head and kissed him, her sweet tongue sliding between his lips to play with his. A tease. A dare.

Abel let her have the first before he took the second. He tensed one arm around her and drove his other hand in her hair, slanting his head and taking over, demanding it all.

She gave it to him.

When he let her break it, she gave him a sexy smile that made his balls draw up before her face disappeared in his neck.

He shifted the pillows behind his head and shoulders so he could watch as she moved her mouth down his chest, making her way to the target. He spread his legs, cocking his knees to give her all access.

She didn't disappoint. She never did. She fucking loved his cock. Worshipped it. Lavished it with attention, tongue, suction, hand, taking him as deep as she could. So deep, when he was inside, he could feel the back of her throat with the tip.

He watched her blow him, gritting his teeth and gripping the inside of his thigh with one hand, balling the sheets in the other, doing both in order not to move his hands to her head, hold her steady, and thrust into her mouth.

When she replaced her mouth with her hand, started jacking him, and moved to gently draw his sac into her warm, wet mouth, he was done.

"You want my cum on my stomach, keep that shit up, pussycat," he growled and watched her lift her head.

She'd released his balls, but her hand kept jacking him.

"You wild, Abel?" she whispered.

"Close," he gritted, and she grinned, eyes languid, lips wet and swollen from his kiss and her blowjob.

Fuck.

"I want you wild, baby," she kept whispering.

"Might lose control," he warned, ending on a groan when she guided his dick to her mouth and sucked hard at just the tip.

"I like it like that," she told him after she released him and before she blew on his sensitive head.

He gripped his thigh harder, his entire body tensing.

She sensed it, he knew it when she turned her head and sank her teeth into the flesh of his inner thigh.

At the sting, a nonverbal snarl ground up his throat.

Her eyes came back to him and he almost lost it at the greed and power shining bright in them, searing his skin with the intensity.

Then she lifted up to her knees in the bed and slid them wide, still jacking him. Her gaze locked to his, she stroked hard, tugging from the root, as she slid her hand down her belly and between her legs.

He knew she found the right spot when her head dropped back, her hair swaying all the way down to her waist, her lips parting.

"Jesus," he grunted, no longer able to hold it back, surging his hips up, thrusting into her hand.

Her head dipped forward, her gaze unfocused and hot as fuck, only just managing to catch his.

She whispered, "Wild," then worked him hard as she worked herself and he watched it all, her hips moving with her fingers, riding them, fucking *fuck*. It was so magnificent he shifted to his knees, hooked her behind her neck, and drove into her tight fist. "Yes," she breathed.

He bent his neck so his forehead was to hers.

"In a minute, gonna fuck you so hard, you're gonna taste me."

"Yes," she panted.

He gripped the back of her neck harder and took her mouth, fucking her fist, feeling her move as she rocked her hips into her fingers, whimpering down his throat.

That was all he could take. He grasped her hair and heard her gentle cry as he used it to whirl her around and shove her face in the bed. Her ass up, he mounted her and commenced rutting, just as he liked it, just as his mate fucking loved it.

She came in about three seconds.

He came three minutes later but only after he took her there again.

He gave himself a few beats before he dragged her up, impaled on his cock, and sat back on his calves, his arms around her.

She turned her head and pressed her forehead into his neck, wrapping her arms around his, her fingers curling around his wrists.

"Now we can let the day begin," she said quietly.

He felt his lips curl into a smile and twisted his neck until he found her mouth.

"Now we can let the day begin," he agreed.

Then he kissed her before pulling her off his cock, out of bed, and into the shower.

"You're a fast learner," Ryon said after they transformed to human behind a hedge.

The hedge was where they'd leaped out of their clothes three hours earlier in order to begin training.

Before he bent to retrieve his jeans, Abel's eyes slid to the balcony where Delilah, Sonia, and Leah were sitting and watching. The reason for the hedge. His woman was intimately acquainted with his dick, but he wasn't real hip on the other two being even a modicum of the same. Further, the other men, particularly Callum, had a lot to write home about in regards to their manhood. Delilah liked big dicks so he wasn't fired up about her seeing the others'. He was relatively sure the rest of the wolves felt the same.

When she caught his gaze, Delilah gave him a finger wave.

Fuck, she was cute.

He grinned at the ground, shaking his head.

"Thanks," he muttered in response to Ryon as he nabbed his jeans and pulled them on.

"You're favoring your claws to your teeth," Callum noted quietly. Abel looked to him, now buttoning his jeans. "I know your instinct is to use your hands," he went on, "but wolves deliver the kill with their teeth. Remember, incapacitate with your claws, Abel. Go for the kill with your jaw."

Abel nodded before he bent to grab his tee. He yanked it over his head as he sensed Lucien's approach. He twisted his torso, catching Wei and Xun moving to the women on the balcony as he did so.

Obviously Lucien was done with them and it was time for his brothers to train the women.

He twisted further and watched Lucien walk toward the pack of wolves.

"I'm off," Ryon murmured, clapping Abel on the shoulder. "Good session," he finished and sauntered away.

"Later," Caleb said before he bent to grab his boots and socks and walk away.

Calder just gave them a jerk of his chin before he followed his brother.

Lucien nodded to them as they passed him and Abel looked back to the balcony to see the door closing on Sonia. Leah and Delilah had already disappeared inside. Lucien had stopped close to him and Callum by the time the door shut behind the queen of the werewolves.

Abel focused on Lucien as he said, "I just had a conversation with Gregor in the hall on the way here."

"And...?" Callum prompted.

"Nothing," Lucien reported.

"What, is Serena engaging in a reconciliation fuck-a-thon with her phantom while the world hangs in the balance?" Abel asked impatiently. "Jesus."

Callum's lips twitched.

Lucien's did not.

"Asked him where the fuck Yuri is," Lucien told them and doing so got their undivided attention.

"Did he share?" Abel asked.

"Said Yuri had an idea on where to get some information, but so far, Gregor's heard nothing from him," Lucien replied. "He said if nothing comes of it, nothing comes of it. If something does, he'll report it to us as soon as he knows."

"That's vague," Callum muttered suspiciously.

"That and annoying," Lucien agreed.

"That vampire has both those down to an art," Abel noted, bending to grab his socks and yank them on.

"He does," Lucien stated and waited until Abel had his socks and boots on and had straightened before he continued, "Is Lilah dreaming?"

Abel nodded. "Had one this morning. She suggested a few days ago I try to get in her head while she does it since she isn't remembering. It was a good suggestion. Took a couple of tries, but I got in."

It was then Abel had both their attention, but it was Callum who asked, "You got in her dream?"

"Yeah, couple of seconds of it," Abel confirmed and shook his head. "Not thinkin' she's even got that dream shit happening to her like the rest of us."

"So the dream had nothing to do with our situation?" Lucien asked.

"It did, but it doesn't make sense, seein' as in it, she's on a street littered with dead human bodies, but she's alone. She pointed out no way that could come true since she'd never be alone, and she's right. Not only wouldn't I let that happen, neither of you would either, not to mention Gregor, her father, and a dozen other people."

"Just a bad dream," Callum muttered.

"A street with dead human bodies?" Lucien asked.

Abel nodded. "That and some vampire. They seemed to be facing off. He saw me, but she forced me out of her dream before I could catch anything."

Lucien stared at him, his stare acute, and stated, "The vampire saw you in her dream."

Abel tensed at what he was feeling coming off Lucien and replied slowly, "Yeah."

"And she forced you out?" Lucien asked.

"Yeah," Abel repeated.

"How did she do that?" Lucien pressed.

"Turned, saw me, lifted her hand, shouted 'no,' then we were both awake," Abel told him.

"The vampire, did you know him?" Callum queried, and Abel looked to him.

"Don't know any of them except the good kind and the dead kind, but the last I don't actually know since they got dead before I could get to know them," Abel answered.

Callum looked to Lucien speculatively so Abel did too.

"What?" he asked.

"What did this vampire look like?" Lucien questioned, and Abel shrugged.

"Blond. Lean. Tall. Think he had blue eyes. Know he had asshole written all over him," Abel told him and then tensed at what he now sensed coming from Lucien. "*What?*" he snarled.

"I need you to come with me," Lucien declared.

"Why?" Abel asked.

"Please, just come with me," Lucien said, his voice going low.

Abel looked to Callum, who was watching Lucien. "You know what this is?"

Callum turned his gaze to Abel. "Perhaps."

"Either of you gonna share?" Abel asked.

"My father is blond, tall, and lean," Lucien stated, and Abel looked back to him.

"So?" Abel prompted.

"So, he's also the leader of the rebellion," Lucien shared, and Abel's entire body strung tight.

He had to be fucking kidding.

"You consider sharin' that sooner?" he bit out.

"Actually, I have," Lucien returned calmly. "However, telling someone who you need to trust you implicitly that the immortal behind a faction of others like him, who wish to obliterate the world as we know it and execute unspeakable acts, is your father is not something that engenders trust."

Abel scowled at him but made no comment, seeing as he spoke truth, so Lucien drew in a breath and continued.

"Trust like that has to be earned. Unfortunately, I was in a difficult position for I'd hoped to make inroads with you, but I also had to do it making a decision that had no right answers. Keep from you something that would mean you wouldn't trust me not only because of what that something was, but that I was keeping it from you. Or share something dire with you upon first meeting that would make it difficult for you even to begin to trust me."

"I hope, brother, that you can see Lucien's dilemma," Callum put in quietly.

Abel didn't take his eyes from Lucien.

The fuck of it was he *could* see Lucien's dilemma.

He didn't respond so Lucien kept talking.

"I have a photo of my father on my iPad inside. I'd like you to look at it and tell me if that's the man you saw in Lilah's dream."

Abel didn't move.

He stated, "I'm taking it the apple fell far from that tree."

"I'm eight hundred and twenty-three years old and not one day in all those years was a day where I felt even a modicum of warmth for my father," Lucien returned.

Abel felt his body relax and his lips curl up. "So you hate him."

"He's despicable and this is only the latest in a very long history of him proving just that," Lucien replied.

"In other words, you hate him," Abel said again, and finally, Lucien smiled.

"Yes, Abel. In other words, I hate him."

"Right, then let's go see this picture," Abel muttered.

Lucien nodded and turned, Callum and Abel following him into the house. Abel and Callum waited in one of the dozen living rooms the place had while Lucien went up to his and Leah's bedroom to get his iPad. He did this with vampire speed, which meant they waited about five seconds.

Abel was feeling no humor when he looked at the photo of the man on Lucien's tablet.

This was because it was the man in Delilah's dream.

"What the fuck?" he whispered.

"Fuck," Callum also whispered.

Lucien just drew in an annoyed breath.

Abel focused on Lucien. "She's dreaming of someone she doesn't know."

"Yes," Lucien agreed.

The seconds of the dream he saw and felt, the slaughter, Delilah's terror, raked through him.

"This means whatever the fuck that was might happen," he bit out.

"None of the dreams have come true, Abel," Callum reminded him. "Except the good kind that Sonia and I or Lucien and Leah have had."

This did not make Abel feel better.

"She was terrified in that dream," Abel told him. "She reeked of it so much, I tasted it and I was only in that dream for a coupla seconds."

Callum's jaw tightened, but he said nothing.

"He saw you," Lucien said, taking Abel's attention back to him.

"Yeah," he confirmed.

"Be careful, Abel," Lucien warned, his voice low and heavy. "In war, anything can happen. I cannot imagine a scenario where anyone, especially you, would allow Lilah to be in that situation by herself. That said, there are many forces at work here and anything we do, as frustrating as it is, we must proceed with caution."

"What you're sayin' is, I should let her have her dreams and not try to get in again," Abel deduced, and Lucien nodded.

"We've learned that our dreams can cause harm. If Lilah's aren't harming her, and she isn't remembering them, then there's no reason for you to try to get in," Lucien said.

"Because some bitch of a witch somewhere has got the power, or some other supernatural shit might be goin' on, and they're usin' Lilah and her connection to me as a channel to lure me in and maybe do me or both of us harm in her dream," Abel guessed.

"I don't know," Lucien replied. "But as I said, I would be careful."

"So what if they get frustrated that they aren't gettin' to me and they step things up with her and her dreams *do* do her harm?" Abel asked curtly.

"Then you go in, but you do it with me close so I can mark you and pull you back," Lucien returned.

"You can do that?" Abel asked.

"I've no idea," Lucien answered. "But I can attune myself to you, or her, so I'm relatively certain I could pull one or the other of you out of a dream state."

Abel's eyes narrowed. "Relatively certain?"

"It's all we have," Lucien said quietly.

"*Fuck*," Abel clipped.

"We need to move," Callum growled, and Abel and Lucien looked to him.

"What?" Lucien asked.

"We need to move. We need to *do something*," Callum ground out. "We need to take the offensive to them. We need to hunt them, inactivate their soldiers, dismantle their infrastructure. We can't have them manipulating dreams. We can't give them any in to get to somebody. And we can't sit around on our asses for eternity."

Obviously, Callum was feeling restless too.

"With due respect, Cal, it was you three days ago who advised caution," Lucien noted carefully.

"That was three days ago," Callum shot back. "Now there's a possibility one of The Three can be murdered in their beds without the enemy even penetrating the outer wall. So my advice has changed."

"And how do we start doing that?" Abel asked.

"We begin to gather intel, doing it aggressively by giving them a target," Callum answered.

Abel's entire frame went wired. "Delilah's in enough danger. I won't have her in more."

"The women stay here. *We'll* be the targets," Callum told him. "Whoever comes after us, we take them down but not out. If we have a prisoner, he or she can be interrogated."

Finally. A plan. Not a great one, but it was something.

"I'm in," Abel stated immediately, and Callum grinned.

"Wolf," he whispered.

"Whatever we do must be meticulously planned," Lucien added.

"And vampire," Callum said on a smile.

Lucien settled in, crossing his arms on his chest, but he didn't contradict the king of the werewolves.

"I'll go extract Hook from his vampire," Abel said.

"I'll find Stephanie," Lucien stated.

"I'll get Ryon and my brothers," Callum put in.

"We wait until Xun and Wei are done with our mates to fill those men in," Lucien declared. "Our decision will not be popular with the females. My sense is that it would be far easier to deal with all three after the fact, not before."

"Agreed," Callum replied.

"Got a problem with that," Abel muttered, and Lucien looked to him.

"I know Lilah has issues with you leaving without her knowing where you're going. Of course, I hesitate to advise you to lie to your mate. Destiny has chosen certain types of women for all of us, and when we return from this, not one of them will make it easy. But prior to going, if you share with Lilah you're training on the grounds but away from the house, perhaps that will eradicate any pain she might feel because she'll *think* she knows where you are."

Abel didn't like it, but he also didn't like hanging around waiting for shit to happen. He knew himself and he was quickly getting to know his mate. Wild and free. They both wanted it. Wanted it in a way that their current situation couldn't last long before something had to give.

And maybe Lucien was right. If she thought she knew where he was, she'd have peace of mind and the men could get out and *do something*.

Therefore, he said, "It's worth a shot."

Lucien nodded and murmured, "Then let's go."

Without hesitating a moment, that was what they did.

*Yuri*

Of course, she had to be beautiful.

Yuri disliked using his skills on females who were beautiful.

Even so, he held her by her throat, suspended several feet up from the floor against the wall. He put enough pressure on for her to fear the oxygen depletion so she couldn't focus on magic.

And she felt the fear. He smelled it. It permeated the air all around them. And staring in her blue eyes, with her dark hair framing her heart-shaped face, he wanted to rip into her throat and taste it.

When those eyes clouded over and her nails clawing at his hand fell away, he dropped her. She slumped to her side at his feet, drawing in weak, ragged breaths.

"You try me further, I'll drain you and find another witch," he warned, tipping his chin only slightly to stare down his nose at her.

Feebly, she lifted her hand to her throat but moved no further, outside of sliding her eyes up to catch his gaze.

Her voice was rasping when she whispered, "You are as they say you are. Ruthless."

"I am as I need to be to save my sister, my people, *your* people," he retorted.

"Right, your sister," she spat weakly. "Another vampire who no doubt stood by, smiling, during The Burning Times."

"My sister is a wolf," he informed her coolly.

She blinked.

"If memory serves, The Burning Times ended when the werewolf king, McDonagh, intervened with The Dominion on behalf of your sisters," Yuri went on. "And my sister is married to McDonagh's son and was born a mere thirty-seven years ago. She doesn't even know what The Burning Times are."

She pushed up to a hand, her voice stronger and completely disbelieving when she noted, "It's impossible your sister is a wolf."

"Much has happened in the last several hundred years," he returned. "But factually, you're correct. My sister cannot be wolf. Essentially, she was adopted, which might not make her blood, but she's still my sister."

It was then that Yuri had to admit to a mild sense of admiration when, even in her current situation, she didn't let it go and snapped, "You nearly annihilated my species."

"I did nothing of the sort," he returned. "At the beginning, I was busy feeding and fucking. At the end, I was listening to my father petition The Dominion on the witches' behalf in support of McDonagh's intervention. I've never touched a witch in my life until tonight, and further, I've never had an issue with a single one of your kind."

"Even so, we endured four hundred years of persecution and genocide at the hands of *your* kind," she hissed.

"And the members of The Dominion who championed that were removed and executed," Yuri shot back. When she opened her mouth to again speak, he continued, "Now, as enjoyable as it is debating history with you, as I shared with you earlier, matters are quite urgent."

"I remember," she stated sarcastically. "The end of the world as we know it."

"You're aware of The Prophesies," he reiterated, which he'd mentioned before their *tête-à-tête* degenerated.

Though, their *tête-à-tête* didn't start on a good note. The second she got out of her car, she saw him as vampire and fled, necessitating him pursuing her, which was an immensely easy task even if she did throw magic his way as he did it. He was still twenty times her speed and strength, and she was young, nowhere near the height of her powers.

Nevertheless, even though he chased her only from her car to her home, this taking approximately ten seconds, it was irritating and shaved away a minute edge of his patience, something that was paper-thin on the best of days.

With all that, there wasn't much conversation to degenerate.

However, when he cornered her in the living room of her home, she again tried to conjure magic rather than listen, which eradicated any patience he had left.

"Of course. And apparently, in order to explain your unwarranted attack, you wish me to believe that they're coming true," she replied as if she didn't believe him in the slightest.

"They are."

"Right," she muttered, pushing up further, and Yuri regarded her.

Long, dark hair with a lustrous sheen and attractive wave, the mass of it curling over her shoulders and down her chest. Big eyes that were a startling blue with a midnight edge to the iris. More than ample breasts from which he would very much enjoy feeding. The same with her thighs and ass. A musky scent that would not normally be his preference, but mingled with her residual fear, as well as her courage, he couldn't help but find it alluring.

With the restrictions on vampire feeding finally lifted, if this was any other time, and indeed if he were not vampire and she were not witch, he'd take her, making her enjoy it. He'd start with her inner thigh, close to her sex, so he could feed at the same time he watched his fingers thrust deep and listened as excitement overcame her fear.

"Uh, I don't have to read minds to see you're looking at me like I'm your next meal," she pointed out, taking his attention from where it had fixated on the pulse in her neck and bringing it back to her eyes.

"I'm hungry," he warned. "And you're immensely beautiful," he went on, seeing her blink again at his words. "And you smell magnificent, like blood and earth and wind, fear and bravery. I want that taste on my tongue," he told her with blunt honesty and watched as her eyes grew round. "So perhaps we can hurry this along so my control doesn't snap along with my patience."

"You're hungry?" she asked, the fear edging back, but he couldn't help but notice there was a hint of curiosity.

"This mission is important and dangerous, so I left my concubine behind." He ignored her wrinkling her nose, not only because he didn't like the indication she found his use of a concubine distasteful, but also because it was annoyingly adorable. "This means I haven't fed in three days."

It also meant he hadn't fucked in three days. Since the restrictions were lifted, he, like all other vampires, took advantage. And after five hundred years of having the sweetest blood to be tasted in his mouth, blood that came from attractive women who very much enjoyed his feeding to its fullest (when he could not), he took everything a concubine could offer, not only her blood.

But he wasn't doing this now.

Which was yet another reason he was in a foul mood.

At his words, her eyes got huge and she pushed against the wall, whispering, "Oh my God."

Yuri sighed and forced them back on track. "A witch. In this town. Twenty years ago. With a blessed athame that can scar an immortal. A name and address would be useful."

He watched her head twitch and he knew she knew of whom he spoke, something that wasn't surprising. Since he began hunting witches, when he sensed this one, he knew she was the one he'd approach—the only one he'd found who was young enough to be malleable and old enough to know what he needed to know.

So he crouched and she pressed deeper into the wall. He could hear her heart thumping hard and fast in her chest.

"A name," he pushed.

"Scar an immortal?" she asked.

"A hybrid vampire wolf."

That time, she jerked her head side to side in a sharp negative. "There are no such things."

"There are. I've seen him. Spoken to him. Fought at his side when someone tried to kill him and his mate along with the others who make The Three."

"You've got to be lying."

Bloody hell.

He threw out an exasperated hand. "Why would I be lying?"

"Because if he exists, The Prophesies actually *are* coming true."

Yuri clenched his teeth.

She stared at him. Then she did it harder. Finally, she squinted at him so hard he thought she'd have an aneurysm.

Watching this, it caused Yuri to have the contradicting desire to shake her because she was being aggravating, smile at her because, regardless of how maddening it was, it was still adorable, and kiss her, mostly because it wasn't just adorable, it was damnably adorable.

Suddenly, her face went slack and she breathed, "Holy crap, The Prophesies are coming true."

He had no time for this.

"Stop being charming and tell me what you know," he ordered.

Another blink and a breathed, "Charming?"

He bent closer so his face was in hers. However, she simply stared into his eyes, no longer pressing back.

"You know of the athame I spoke of," he bit out. "Now, you can choose to tell me who possesses it, or possessed it twenty years ago. Or you can choose to force me to extract that information from you. What you can't do is take time to make your choice since I don't have time. So choose now."

"Extract it from me?"

He shrugged. "Waterboarding, flaying, skinning, tearing your fingernails out by their roots, pulling your teeth out one by one, burning, pressing, choking, or I could feed from you while I play with you, denying you your climax until you tell me what I wish to know," he shared.

"Climax?"

"Orgasm," he clipped.

Another blink.

Bloody fucking hell.

"Witch—" he started to warn.

"You didn't get them all," she declared, and he pulled back an inch.

"Pardon?"

"There were witches who held power that you didn't burn or drown. You didn't get them all. None of the ones who'd survived held the power of those your kind swept from the earth, and they have been using the powers they have left to hide for centuries. But that isn't it. The important thing the vampires missed is that you didn't destroy the implements."

Fuck.

"The athame," he murmured.

She nodded. "I know who has it. I know who used it on the hybrid. I didn't know he was a hybrid, but the story went viral after she'd messed it up. She's a little, well...out of it because she didn't succeed in her mission and they were pissed and didn't hide they were pissed. They went loco and didn't care who knew it. But they have it. They actually have several blessed instruments that it isn't real great they have. They sent her on that mission. They're a coven. A powerful one. You're fast and strong, but they have protections no way you'll get through. You could bring a hundred vampires and you'd all burn."

He drew in breath through his nose as he stood.

While he contemplated this new dilemma, she pushed to her feet and he noted what he hadn't had the opportunity to note before: she was petite. She couldn't be taller than five foot three. As he was six-one, he towered over her.

Another contradiction for he usually preferred statuesque women who met his height, or close to it, in heels. However, there was something immensely attractive about her stature and he was beginning to understand the escalation in the already-rabid protection that was his nature that Callum had toward Sonia. Sonia was small for a wolf, shorter, and when Callum met her, slimmer (though, Callum had seen to the last without delay, filling out his sister's curves as was wolf).

Yuri had never felt protective of a female in his entire life, but regardless of the fact that he'd just been choking her, right then, he couldn't deny he felt it with this witch.

He also couldn't deny that he enjoyed the feeling.

He kept her pinned close to the wall simply by not moving as he buried these feelings that, at that time, he didn't have the luxury to explore.

"You wanna save the world?" she asked softly, and he focused on her.

"I'm not hunting witches for the fuck of it in the middle of a global crisis," he returned.

She nodded, then asked another question. "It was really the hybrid?"

Yuri scowled at her for he'd already given her that information.

She studied him and she took her time doing it.

"Time is of the essence," he drawled. "By my calculations, you have approximately three seconds to contemplate your desire to assist me before I make the decision for you and force you to do so."

She straightened her shoulders and held his gaze. "You'll need me to get to that coven."

"And have you lead me to my burning?" he asked and shook his head. "I don't fancy that."

"Okay," she said, throwing out a hand. "I'm not a big fan of vampires, and my mom would be, like, *super* pissed if she knew I was even *thinking* this, but for some messed up reason, I believe you."

"That reason might be because I'm telling the truth."

At his words, she smiled and he wished she hadn't done that. It lit her eyes and made her smell like nothing but blood and sunshine and happiness, and he wanted that taste on his tongue so much, he felt it in his cock in a way it was not a desire, it was a need.

He made a warning noise in his throat.

She kept smiling. "And Mom would lose her *mind* if she knew I was gonna help you."

"And you'll be doing that by giving me the names of the witches in this coven and their location," he prompted.

"Nope." She shook her head. "I'll be doing that by taking you to the witch who attacked the hybrid and helping you talk to her so you can get her story. Then I'll be taking you to the coven and getting you in so they don't burn you to oblivion."

He opened his mouth to tell her she'd be doing nothing of the sort, but she kept going, lifting her hand to point her finger at him and assuming a severe expression that was far from severe and a lot closer to adorably amusing.

"No waterboarding," she warned.

"Witch—"

"Or flaying, fingernail tearing, tooth pulling, or any of that other stuff you said. We talk, I do some hocus pocus, we get her story. But I'll warn you now, she's cuckoo." She lifted her hand higher and circled her finger at the side of her head. "They did a number on her when she failed. But rumor on the witch vine is that she wasn't all there before she went on that mission. So it might take some doing. We just have to do it without waterboarding."

Yuri took a step back but didn't retreat further. He simply did it so he could more comfortably cross his arms on his chest.

"And how am I supposed to trust you?"

"I don't know. Isn't that what trust is? You just give it and, *abracadabra*, it's there."

His brows snapped together. "That's the most ridiculous thing I've ever heard."

"It's still true."

"I'll repeat, that's the most ridiculous thing I've ever heard, but this time I'll share that's the case and I'm bloody six hundred and ninety-seven years old."

Another blink, this one coming along with her full lips parting.

"Witch—" he tried again.

She stuck out her hand, interrupting him. "I'm Aurora."

For fuck's sake.

"Please tell me your witch mother did not name her witch daughter Aurora," he clipped.

Her hand dropped and her expression betrayed hurt when she said quietly, "She did."

He looked to the ceiling, partly due to exasperation but also irritatingly due to the fact he didn't like to witness that expression, especially with the knowledge he gave it to her.

Once his eyes were to the ceiling, he muttered, "Bloody hell."

"They'll kill you," she said softly, and he looked back to her to see she'd rearranged her features, hiding them behind a vacant mask, and Yuri found that even more difficult to witness. "They're witches. And since they are, has it occurred to you that if they're conniving to trip The Prophesies one way or another, they would never, *not ever*, ally themselves with vampires?"

It hadn't.

It should have.

Yuri said nothing.

"They're planning something else," she continued.

Brilliant. They did not need to contend with angry, conniving witches along with everything else.

Yuri again clenched his teeth.

She wasn't done and she straightened her shoulders when she continued, "So, you need me. I'm young, but I come from a long line so I've got juice. I also know people and they have juice. I can speak for you and get you what you need without anyone dying, most especially *you*."

He examined her. She was still wearing her mask, but she couldn't hide it all from him. There was a hint of fear but a stronger hint of excitement. And, again, courage. Her heart was beating steady and strong, if fast.

Her gaze was unwavering.

Fuck it.

"I'm not one to be trifled with," he warned at the same time he capitulated.

She lifted her hand to her neck, which was marked with the red welts he'd given her, and fuck him, he had to fight back a flinch.

"I got that."

He tilted his head to the side. "This is dangerous for you."

"In a variety of ways, least of which is teaming up with a vampire, and since my kind seriously hate your kind, that's saying something."

"Then explain why you're doing it," he demanded.

That got him yet another blink. "Um, well, I guess to save the world. I know a fair number of humans. It'd suck if they were enslaved and forced to exist for the whim of demented immortals. And Lord knows what that coven has in mind. They've been chewing on centuries of rage and that's never a good thing."

At least with that she unquestionably spoke the truth.

"So you're assisting me as well as giving me your protection," he stated.

"Yes," she confirmed.

"If that's the truth, I also give you mine, to the death," he returned, and her head jerked.

"Is that a vow?" she asked.

"It is," he answered firmly.

Her eyes again grew wide and she breathed, "A *vampire vow*?"

She clearly knew that no vampire would break a vow, not for any reason. They'd kill to keep it, or die for the same reason.

"I am vampire and I just verified it was a vow, so yes, obviously, it was a *vampire vow*," he answered unnecessarily.

"Well then." The mask slipped as a smile dawned and her hand came out again. "We just became a team."

Heaven help him.

He stared at her beautiful face, then he stared at her small, lovely hand.

Slowly, he lifted his and curled his fingers around hers, engulfing her hand in his.

She didn't let him go as she asked, "What's your name?"

"Yuri."

"Promise me something, Yuri," she said, still holding his hand.

"What?" he asked.

"When you meet my mother, be cool. No choking or the like. She's already gonna flip. I'll talk her around, but there's no talking around choking, and...erm, the like. Not with my mom. She's awesome, but

I'm sure it won't surprise you that vampires are not her thing, like *at all*. She'll be big on helping to save the world, but she won't pretend to like doing it with a vampire."

Yuri did not like where this was going. "And why would I meet your mother?"

She continued to hold his hand but lifted her other one and his tightened around hers when she flicked out her fingers.

A profuse scattering of pink and blue particles flew from her hand and twinkled for but a moment before they exploded into hundreds of butterflies that drifted about the room, lighting it with a glow from their shimmering gossamer wings. Then they exploded in miniature fireworks and disappeared.

Yuri was six hundred and ninety-seven years old and it was one of the most beautiful things he'd seen in all his history.

Slowly, he turned his head back to her when she tugged his hand.

He found her grinning even as she leaned in, her mouth moving.

"Because I have juice, but my mom..." Her grin turned into a smile he definitely felt in his cock. "She *rocks*."

Bloody...fucking...*hell*.

# 17
# Brother

*Abel*

Abel sat in the passenger seat of the SUV beside Callum in the early morning dark before dawn.

And he did it feeling shit.

He'd lied to Delilah.

He'd left her half-asleep in bed after he kissed her and he did this with her thinking what he'd told her the day before: that he was training with all the men somewhere on the property and he wouldn't be back until noon.

Delilah wasn't big on early mornings, and seeing as he left their bed before four, this meant she didn't haul her ass out to watch him train. She also didn't ask what was up and why the training had changed.

She trusted him.

Completely.

Which was part of the reason why he felt shit.

But he'd been feeling shit for a while, the entire lead-up to having to tell the lie, knowing he'd eventually have to do it.

So he felt more shit now having done it.

The only good thing that came from the last four days of planning this mission was Abel coming to the understanding that Lucien and Callum knew their shit.

With Callum, this wasn't a surprise.

With nothing to do but fuck, train, and sit around chatting, Callum and Lucien had explained a great deal of supernatural history to him. And although vampires kept a choke hold on their kind after the last insurrection burned down half of London, wolves didn't. Seeing as Callum explained wolves were passionate, lusty, and prone to quick tempers, this meant they skirmished often.

And that meant Callum had experience, including experience with the rebel wolves who wanted world dominance for supernaturals. The good news with that was he'd been successful in bringing them low during a recent battle.

The results of this were that even Gregor's intelligence reported that the wolf part of the current rebel faction was few. This was because Callum and his army had recently kicked their asses in a way that any who might be leaning toward that would think twice. Losing a brother and his father to it, not to mention Sonia being targeted by the rebels, it wasn't surprising he didn't leave a lot of them breathing.

Lucien's last experience was five hundred years ago as a general in the last vampire-on-vampire war, but he'd not grown rusty.

Abel had none of their strategic or battle experience, but even so, they were cool with him, explaining everything, sharing it all, asking for his input and opinions.

He didn't have much to give them, and although it sucked not having anything to offer, so they'd get on with shit, Abel made it clear he was down with that. He wasn't happy to be a soldier in this mess, but he'd do anything to ensure his future with Delilah, his mate, the one he'd waited lifetimes for, the only human who would be at his side for eternity.

So they had it all covered, including letting Gregor in on what they were planning and utilizing his resources.

Gregor had not done cartwheels after learning their plans. He even went head to head with both Callum and Lucien in an effort to put a stop to it. But the vampire was not on his game and gave in surprisingly quickly.

Abel got this, seeing as he'd finally shared what his son was up to, this being looking for the witch who'd cut Abel in order to find out who'd sent her.

Abel was mildly pissed about this as he'd have liked to have gone with Yuri mostly because he wouldn't mind seeing that bitch again. That being so he'd have the opportunity to return the favor and give her a scar she'd have for a lifetime. One you could see, or one you couldn't, he didn't give a fuck.

But he hadn't been given a choice, and even if Gregor wasn't exactly a vampire prone to great displays of warmth and kindness, it was obvious he gave a shit about his son and was worried.

So they were off, all of them, on their mission. Free from their elaborate cage. Abel in the SUV with Callum, Hook in the backseat. Lucien driving the SUV they were following, Ryon, Calder, and Caleb with him. And last, there was a detail of security around them that included Wei and Xun on their bikes.

Moose had not reported back, another thing that prayed on his mind, as it did Delilah's. Hook assured them his bud could win a medal at squeezing all he could get out of a bender. But that was before anyone who meant anything to one of The Three was in danger.

Poncho had reported in that he'd bested the goat and snake test, but apparently, that wasn't enough for his aunt, so something involving cactus juice and a visit with his ancestors was up next. Again, Poncho didn't go into specifics and Abel didn't ask.

His cell went, taking his mind off all that shit, and he leaned forward to pull it out of his back pocket.

He checked the screen and took the call.

"Yo."

"Reporting in. All in place. We're a go," a man said, then disconnected.

Abel took the phone from his ear and told the windshield, "They're in place. It's a go."

"Good," Callum muttered.

"Fuck," Hook also muttered.

Abel looked to the backseat. "You all right?"

It was a pertinent question. Hook looked wiped, hungover, and worn way the fuck out.

Then again, Hook had decided to spend last night with his vampire and it was written all over him they both gave it all they could give.

"Can't complain," Hook answered. "Fucking with that bitch feeding, meetin' a woman who can hold her liquor as good as I can and go all night, finally hit the foot of the stairway to heaven. So yeah, I'm all right. *More* than all right. But that doesn't mean I'm not fucked out, my balls shot dry, and I don't got bourbon instead of blood in my veins. Even so, if things go south for me this mornin', least you know I ended my days on this earth just like I wanted."

Abel faced forward, murmuring, "Way too fuckin' much information," then heard Hook's chuckle.

Callum must have felt his mood because he didn't chuckle.

Instead, he assured quietly, "All is in place and we've planned well, brother."

Abel said nothing because Callum was right. They'd planned well. No matter what happened that morning, they'd get something out of it. Hopefully it would be one of the enemy, alive and breathing, who they could break for information. But even if no one showed, they had human scouts everywhere surrounding the meeting place—fishermen, campers, hunters, and just men who were driving the roads like they had somewhere to go but were on the lookout.

This mission, on the face of it, was Lucien meeting with his friend Cosmo.

Cosmo was in charge of the vamps, wolves, and wraiths in the surrounding areas who were keeping an eye out for the enemy, something the supernaturals reporting to Cosmo shared were nonexistent.

That didn't mean the enemy didn't have human eyes.

But Cosmo couldn't approach the compound, because if he did, the enemy, if they were watching, would know he was the one leading that effort. And according to Lucien, Cosmo was a force to be reckoned with and his involvement and proximity to The Three at that juncture was something advantageous to keep secret. Lucien, and Gregor, wanted their enemies to guess what Cosmo was up to, not know.

Now they were outing Cosmo themselves, with a purpose.

Their road trip was early, the meeting place clandestine, the route they were taking to it was circuitous, all of this to show anyone who might be watching that they were taking precautions to hide the fact this was a trap.

And if they found themselves with a fight on their hands, they'd know they were being watched. Even if no one showed, the scouts they had in place were trained to spot who they were supposed to be spotting. So if Cosmo was followed but not approached, or their convoy was, they'd still know that they had enemy eyes on them, active ones.

That didn't seem much to Abel, but he was cool with it because it was doing something. But Callum and Lucien said any intel was good to have in order to analyze and then strategize.

And this, they said, was only the beginning. This wasn't a for-the-fuck-of-it mission so they didn't climb the walls of the compound.

Callum and Lucien had planned beyond this mission.

No more sitting on their hands.

Thank fuck.

This was something else Gregor wasn't fired up about, and Abel knew, when they found out, all three of their women were going to lose their minds.

But again, it was doing something and he'd take Delilah's sass just to breathe different air. He also had a feeling she'd get that. He'd just have to put up with her bitching before she got to that place.

Callum followed Lucien off the road to a narrower one, and not long after, they all turned onto a dirt lane. They drove into the forest and the trip wasn't short. Eventually, they stopped, parked, got out, and hiked a short distance where they found the ATVs.

They loaded up and trekked deeper into the forest.

They were at it for five minutes before some of the ATVs pulled off, their security detail riding through the trees to set up watch.

They were at it another five minutes before, out of nowhere, the wolves joined them, running at the sides of the ATVs.

Callum, ahead of Abel, looked back and jerked up his chin.

The wolves were good.

By the time they hit the small clearing, all that was left were those close to The Three, the rest of the detail having moved to their positions. The remainder of their party drove their ATVs around it, circling it before they stopped, all the ATVs facing in, their lights illuminating the clearing.

In the clearing was a big, blond vampire, his only company being the wolves that had followed them, patrolling beyond the ATVs.

Hook, Wei, Xun, Calder, and Caleb took positions outside the ATVs, keeping watch.

Lucien, Callum, Ryon, and Abel approached the vampire.

"Cosmo," Lucien murmured, offering his hand which Cosmo took.

Greetings were given, as well as an introduction for Abel, who Cosmo took in head to toe in a sharp way that gave the impression he missed nothing. This was something that made Abel feel more at ease. The vampire was obviously not a moron. Then again, he had yet to meet one who was.

"Were you followed?" Lucien asked once the preliminaries were done.

"No," Cosmo answered, shaking his head. "Nothing. Not a hint."

"We've had men in these woods for two days. They've seen nothing either," Lucien shared.

"They either have human allies, which I can credit, your father's skilled with charming his victims before he goes in for the kill," Cosmo replied. "Or they're concentrating their efforts elsewhere. Planning something that will draw you out."

"We're getting nothing," Lucien told him.

"The calm before the storm," Cosmo muttered.

"A calm they may have manipulated, forcing The Three into a high security compound in the middle of fucking nowhere in Oregon while they carry out an attack in Spain," Lucien clipped impatiently.

Abel looked questioningly to Callum.

Callum felt his eyes and said, "They weren't unaware of the compound's existence. Which means the attack at Jian-Li's restaurant may have been a play to get us there."

"Which would also mean, if we moved, now that The Three are together, they can assume we'd do it as one, they'd know where we're moving from, can manipulate where we're moving to, and they'd be in position to pick us off," Abel returned.

Callum's jaw got tight which meant Abel's guess might be right.

"Fuck," he whispered.

"I'm more use to you elsewhere, Lucien," Cosmo stated.

"You are," Lucien agreed. "Move out all vampires and wolves, but leave the wraiths."

Abel watched Cosmo nod right before a blinding pain shot through his head.

He tensed, his head jerking automatically as if the pain was a physical blow, and he lifted his hands so he could press his palms to his eyes, where the pain kept burning.

"Abel," Callum called.

The pain shot through again, so severe, nausea tore up his throat and he had to swallow against vomiting as the agony bent him double.

"Abel!" Callum bit out, and Abel felt hands on him.

He shirked them off, the pain in his head so bad he was unable to bear touch.

Still bent double, he snarled, "Don't touch me, man."

"This ever happen before?" he heard Lucien ask, to which Xun answered, "Never."

"Smell anything?" Callum asked, and Ryon answered, "Nothing."

"Wolf," Callum ordered, and Abel sensed them transforming to wolf as the pain shot back, worse this time, taking him down to his knee.

*"Fuck,"* he spat, digging his palms into his eyes in an effort to quell the pain.

"Talk to us, Abel," Lucien demanded from close.

"Jesus, fuck, pain, fuck, *bad,*" was all Abel could force out before it happened.

The pain vanished, and the instant it did, the clearing and beyond was lit with a blue flash that illuminated the space, straight to the heavens.

Everyone tensed and Abel's head shot back as he watched sparks fly in the trees and heard things crashing through them.

"Prepare," Lucien growled as Abel got to his feet, ready to jump to wolf.

But Hook was running into the trees.

"Careful, Hook!" Abel shouted.

"Fuck!" Hook shouted back. He bent, straightened, and turned to the clearing holding something up in his hand. "Camera! Fried now, but fuck!"

"Go, now," Lucien ordered, turning and sprinting to his ATV, still calling out commands. "Gather the cameras. Cosmo, compound. You've been made."

Everyone was running. Then everyone was on ATVs. A fuckuva lot faster, they got to the SUVs, hauled ass climbing in, and took off.

Cosmo was with them, in the backseat with Hook, and they were barely on their way before he stated the obvious: "They've a man inside."

"No shit?" Abel bit out.

"Abel, on the line with Gregor. Have him lock that place down," Callum ordered, and Abel dug his phone out.

"Tell him to get Yuri on the job," Cosmo added.

"Yuri's out on a mission," Callum told him.

"Fuck, no one's better at extracting information. But Stephanie's no slouch." Cosmo leaned forward as Abel connected to Gregor and demanded, "Tell him Stephanie's up."

"Since you're phoning me, I can only assume that this is not going to be a cheerful conversation," Gregor said as greeting.

"They had cameras at the meeting place. Lock the compound down. They've got an inside man," Abel told him.

"It's done," Gregor stated.

"Place may be bugged," Abel noted.

"Impossible. Random sweeps are done at least three times a day," Gregor informed him.

"Then start Stephanie with the guy in charge of the sweeps," Abel ordered and hung up.

Callum had turned from the dirt road to the narrow one when Hook asked, "Anyone know what the fuck that blue shit was?"

No one said a word.

But Abel knew.

He'd seen it before.

In a dream.

Delilah.

He had no clue how, he just knew however it was, it was her.

He didn't share this with Hook. Instead, he looked to his left at Callum's profile, keeping his gaze steady on the wolf until Callum glanced his way, looked back at the road, and dipped his chin sharply.

He got him.

"I'm gonna take that as that shit is need to know," Hook said into the cab.

"Good call," Callum told him.

They had silence until they reached the compound. Security was tightened, but they didn't fuck around letting them in.

They drove the long drive, rounded the front, and exited the vehicles.

Callum peeled off at a call from Ryon, Calder and Caleb sticking with him. Lucien waited for Cosmo and they strolled up the steps to the front door slowly, heads bent, talking. Hook lagged behind, likely still freaking out. Wei and Xun drove on to put their bikes in the garages that were detached from the main house.

So unfortunately, it was Abel who went through the door first.

He saw her just inside and she looked sweet. Red Harley tank, tight, some rhinestones, the letters stretched out across her tits. Shorts, ragged hem and cut short as in *short*, affording a nice view of lots of leg. Hair wild, like it was when she just woke up.

And eyes flashing in a way-the-fuck-pissed-off kind of way.

That was all he took in before he had to duck, seeing as she threw something at him.

He didn't know what it was. He just knew whatever it was was fragile since it exploded with a crash against the doorjamb behind him.

"*Early morning training session?*" Delilah shrieked, turned, and that was when he saw she had allies. He saw this because Sonia and Leah were lined up beside her, Leah handing her a vase.

A vase she threw.

"Jesus! What the fuck?" Hook shouted after he jumped out of the way and the vase flew out the door, smashing on the flagstone outside.

"*You!*" Delilah screeched, jabbing a finger her father's way as Abel felt the rest of the crew flood through the door behind him. "You were in on this too?"

"Now, little girl—" her father started, hands up in a placating gesture.

But he should have known better. He had years where Abel only had weeks, and still, Abel knew there was no placating this Delilah.

"Don't you fucking '*little girl*' me, Dad. I cannot believe you!" she yelled, then moved her finger between the two of them. "Either of you!"

"And, might I add at this juncture, I cannot either, and that includes you, Mighty Vampire Lucien," Leah drawled dangerously, her eyes slits and aimed at her husband.

"I would think of something clever to say, my king," Sonia put in. "But I'm having difficulty not ripping someone's throat out with," she lost it and leaned forward, eyes narrowed and locked on her husband, *"my teeth."*

"Perhaps we can move this out of the foyer," Lucien suggested.

"Fuck that!" Delilah shouted, her gaze glued to Abel. Then she asked in a saccharine-sweet voice, "You know how I woke up, baby?"

*"Bao bei—"* he started but did it knowing it was futile.

And it was futile.

"With pain so fucking bad, so fucking *hideous*, I thought my insides were melting," she hissed, and Abel flinched. "I couldn't even crawl out of the bed, it was that fucking bad."

"Lilah—" he began in a gentle voice, no longer feeling like shit but missing that feeling because the pain of guilt was a far sight worse.

"Excruciating," she cut him off to hiss. "Paralyzing. And worse, I thought it was that bad, could only be that bad, because you were *dead*."

Fuck.

"Baby," he whispered, moving toward her, but she stepped back.

"And even *worse*," she kept going, "was that I was powerless. Drained. I couldn't even move to find someone to tell them they had to find you."

She hit wall and Abel kept moving toward her.

"Don't get near me," she warned, a warning he didn't heed.

She tried to fight him. But in half a second, she lost and Abel had her over his shoulder and behind closed doors in one of the living rooms.

He put her on her feet and she quickly stepped back. "That's a ride I'm unwilling to take again for at least half a century, Abel Jin. You pick me up again *only* when I expressly allow that shit."

"You need to calm down and listen to me," he said quietly.

"Fuck calm, Abel. Did you miss the part about me being in so much pain I thought my insides were melting?" she asked sarcastically.

"Right, then don't calm down. Just listen," he kept at her and continued to do it quietly.

"So you've got something to say? Something that explains you lying to me and causing me that kind of pain when you *know* that shit happens when you leave me and I don't know where you are?" she demanded.

"I thought if you thought you knew where I was, even if it wasn't where I actually was, you wouldn't experience the pain," he explained.

"Wrong!" she yelled. "Very, very," she leaned toward him, "*wrong!*"

"I get that now and it won't happen again," he promised.

She crossed her arms on her chest. "Yeah? You sure? You can say that for certain?"

"I can," he confirmed.

"Right, you can. Now, next question. How the fuck am I supposed to believe you when you're totally okay with," another lean, "*lying to me?*"

Fuck, he'd screwed this up, and huge.

Now he had to see if he could find a way to fix it.

He started with conceding, "I deserved that."

Her eyebrows shot up. "No fucking shit?"

He stared at her, deciding not to share that she was cute when she was pissed.

"No fucking shit," he replied.

Her face changed and Abel braced because he didn't like the change even a little bit.

Her voice changed too and he liked that even less.

"You can't be sweet and you can't be hot and you can't be reassuring," she stated, soft and low but firm and full of hurt. "Not after you lied. After you lie, Abel, it takes a fuckuva lot more than that to earn back what you lost."

"I had to get out of here, *bao bei*. I had to do something and I wasn't alone," he told her.

"You knew I knew you were going stir-crazy," she reminded him.

He nodded and replied, "I knew you knew. I also knew you wouldn't be fired up about what we were planning and it was something we had to do, all of us."

"I actually don't even know what you were planning to do, but if it was taking you out of safety and into harm's way, you're right.

I wouldn't be fired up about it. But I wouldn't hand you shit about it either."

Suddenly, she threw an arm straight up in the air, apparently indicating herself by what she said next.

"Clue in, Abel, I am not your normal bitch. I grew up with *bikers*. Bikers do what they want when they want because they got something inside them that makes them have to do that. And nothing can stand in their way. Not a job. Not a law. Not a woman. So if you love them, you don't stand in their way. *Ever*. I've also learned if you give them that, it'll be worth it. It'll come around with them giving you what *you* need because they get it."

She shook her head, sucked a huge breath, and kept at him.

"But even with that, I'm of a mind that a woman should never stand in her man's way when there's something he *has* to do. Doing something to end what's eating at him, crushing him, suffocating him, stopping him from being who he is, or whatever the fuck. So regardless if I didn't like it, if I was a biker bitch or just a normal one, I *still* wouldn't stand in your way."

He stared at her, unblinking, her words coursing through him in a way that far from sucked.

"Uh, me bein' this pissed, baby, is not the time for you to lapse into silent brooding," she warned, slamming a hand on her hip.

"I have nothing to say," he told her and watched the hurt slice through her face. "Except that I'm sorry."

Her expression blanked as she blinked.

"Really, fucking, seriously sorry," he went on. "If I thought that you'd feel that kind of pain, no way in fuck I would have gone without telling you where I was going. And this doesn't help, but I felt shit just knowin' I was gonna lie to you and that got worse when I did it. Doesn't make it better, I get that, but you gotta know I didn't do it easy and I didn't like doin' it. And I can tell you now, how I felt thinking of doin' it, then doin' it and what it caused, that shit won't ever happen again. You have my word. You believe in that or not, it's still solid, Lilah. As a rock."

She studied him for a few beats before she looked to the fireplace, took a deep breath, and looked back at him.

"I thought you were dead," she whispered.

Fuck, he wanted to go to her, but her body language was screaming for him to keep a distance, so he controlled that impulse.

"Wish I could take that back," he whispered in return. "Wish like fuck I could turn back time and make it so that didn't happen. I can't. The only thing I can do is tell you I hate that you felt that, I hate it more that I did somethin' to make you feel it, and repeat how fuckin' sorry I am."

She held his eyes before she again looked at the fireplace. He watched her and he sensed her. She was pissed, there was fear, and last, there was hurt.

His jaw tightened.

Her throat convulsed and he put all his energy into fighting the urge to go to her and, instead, gave her time.

He won the fight not to go to her, but he had shit to share and he was forced to stop giving her time.

"You seem okay now," he observed, and she gave him back her gaze.

"The pain went away," she shared. The words were hard but at least they were relatively calm.

"When I was out of danger," he surmised.

She stared at him in a new unhappy way at getting the knowledge he was in danger, then she shook her head.

But she said nothing.

"We had a meeting with one of Lucien's men," he informed her. "Callum and Lucien planned the whole thing. Gregor got his people involved, so we were actually safe the whole time. The goal was to draw them out or ascertain if they're watching. They are. They had cameras at the meeting place, which is way the fuck in the middle of nowhere so no way they could know where we were to meet unless someone on the inside told them."

"Fabulous," she hissed. "More shit to worry about."

She was right, but he couldn't get into that just yet.

"You gotta know all that because you deserve me comin' clean, but it's more important you know something else," he continued.

She took her hand from her hip to flick it out. "That would be...?"

"We didn't know about the cameras until a flash of blue light fried 'em."

She stared again, this time not angry, astonished.

"Say what?' she asked.

"I got a pain in my head that was so bad it took me down to a knee. Then a flash of blue light lit up the place and fried the cameras. If that hadn't happened, we wouldn't have known they were there. We were being watched and probably listened to."

"What the fuck?" she whispered, her brows inching together. "You were in pain?"

"Yep." He nodded, not dwelling on that. "And, pussycat, I've seen that blue light before."

"Where?" she asked.

"When you forced me out of your dream."

Her mouth dropped open.

"Don't know for certain," he kept going. "But I figure that pain in my head was you locating me. What I do know for certain, that light was you. You got an ability, Lilah. A fuckin' powerful one. Spans miles as long as it's connected to me."

"Holy shitoly," she breathed, and he allowed himself to smile.

"Could do without feeling my head was gonna explode, but yeah, that shit rocked."

"So, what you're saying is, I'm not clingy. I'm so hyper-attuned to you, I can locate you in my subconscious from miles away, unknowingly sense you're in danger, and actually do something about it?" she asked.

"That's my take," he answered.

Slowly, she grinned and whispered, "Right on."

Abel relaxed.

Then he asked, "You gonna let me put my arms around you and show you how sorry I am that I pulled an asshole stunt, or you wanna throw more shit at me?"

"Don't piss me off, Abel, or I'll blast you with my blue light," she shot back, and it wasn't entirely a joke.

He smiled at her and said quietly, "Baby, wanna hold you."

"Then do it," she returned.

He moved instantly and took her in his arms.

She didn't wrap hers around him. She lifted her hands and laid them on his chest. He sensed it was to keep distance but, being Delilah, doing it still gave him what he needed.

"Still pissed at you," she told his throat.

"I'd still be pissed at me too," he told the hair on the top of her head.

She took in a breath that was rough, exposing she was still feeling emotion and doing it deep.

"Hate a lot of what went down this morning. Figure Lucien and Callum are right now dealing with shit of their own making too," he said, still speaking to her hair because she wasn't giving him her face and he wasn't going to force her to. "But we got shit happening within these walls so there's shit to be done."

"Right," she mumbled. "Go."

"Before I go, don't need you to assure me we're good," he told her. "Just need you to tell me we're inching that way."

At that, she tipped her head back and caught his eyes.

"Abel." She slid a hand up to curl it around the side of his neck. "You did something you had to do. You fucked up doing it. You apologized. A lot has gone down, but that doesn't mean we aren't still getting to know one another. Not to mention all this supernatural shit we don't have a lock on. I know you didn't have any clue your fuckup would be that huge. It was. It's over. You promised it won't happen again." She took in breath and finished, "What I'm saying is, let it go. I am. Which means we're not inching toward good. We're there."

Simple as that. She blasts it out, says it like it is, he takes his licks, then she's done. Over it. Moving on.

Jesus, he loved her.

She wasn't a dream come true.

She was a fucking fantasy come to life.

"Abel?" she called, and when she did, he realized he'd been staring at her for longer than he thought.

"Can't say how much it means to me, you bein' this cool," he told her quietly, and she grinned a feisty grin.

"You don't have to. I know I'm totally awesome."

She was.

His Delilah.

Totally awesome.

He grinned back.

Then he dipped his head and kissed his mate. He did it hard and as thorough as he could when shit needed to get done.

And when he was finished, he didn't leave the room alone to get shit done.

He took her hand and pulled her with him so they both could see to it.

Together.

## *Yuri*

"Told you," Aurora stated after lifting her eyes to him. "Cuckoo."

Yuri stood back from the women, arms crossed on his chest.

He did this because he was allowing Aurora to work. He also did this because it meant her mother, with the shockingly unworthy witch name of Barb, was at his front.

Not at his back.

To say his meeting with Aurora's mother was thorny was a vast understatement.

Luckily, she was well aware of The Prophesies and trusted her daughter wasn't an idiot.

She would know. She'd raised her.

And after spending the last several days with the both of them, Yuri now knew that neither of them were.

Barb Lenox was sharp, no-nonsense, blunt-speaking, affectionate with her daughter through actions, not words, and she utterly detested vampires.

Aurora Lenox was intelligent, humorous, talented, energetic, openhearted, quick to smile, and unconsciously appealing, which made her infuriatingly alluring. Thus, with all this being her, along with her body and beauty, she was damnably fuckable.

In other words, the last four days had been torture, and not simply because Barb eyed him like he was manure on her shoe at the same time she did things, like sharpen a wooden stake, something she knew didn't work on him, but that was not her point, even if she was making one.

And also not simply because he was forced to procure bagged blood, which was hideous, but he couldn't feed nor take the time to find a Feast where there were hundreds of mortals with The Dominion's stamp of approval he could partake from.

It was because he wanted his errand to be done since the information he sought was important to the cause, and also because it would mean Aurora would be out of danger *and* he was free to turn his mind to other things.

Like how to get her in his bed.

But right then, after exhaustive efforts, which were exhausting because they needed to be clandestine and because no one had seen her in years, they'd found the witch who'd scarred Abel.

And when they did, Yuri found further proof that Aurora Lenox didn't have a deceitful bone in her delicious body because she was right. The witch, known as Sula, was a recluse, a hoarder, existing in a vile, cramped, putrid pit so far removed from civilization she was unintentionally (or subconsciously) and very effectively hidden.

And she was completely mad in a way that was not natural.

"Brother brother brother brother brother," Sula chanted, this being all she'd said since they'd arrived and Aurora started her gentle work.

Except her first communication, which was a shotgun blast. This meant Barb had to do her not-gentle work, magically disarming her and doing it cursing under her breath and sticking a finger in her ear and wiggling it, since the blast was loud.

Sula didn't like visitors. She'd made that plain. And her panic at being confronted with witches was difficult to witness, even if Yuri gave not that first fuck about a witch who had, when she had a minute level of sanity, readily carved into a vampire.

She was tormented and had been for years. Demons in her head that had had enough time to eat away anything that was healthy left nothing but a walking, breathing, but only existing shell behind.

"Brother brother brother brother brother," Sula chanted again.

"Shh, sweetheart," Aurora cooed. "Shh. Feel my hand. Feel it, Sula. Look into my eyes. You've got dark in there, honey. Look into my eyes. It's okay. You're safe. I just want to show you light."

"Devils," Barb muttered as Aurora kept trying to coax Sula's vacant stare to meet her gaze.

Yuri looked at Aurora's mother. "Pardon?"

She kept her gaze steady on her daughter's work but answered, "Knew of Sula. Never met her. Reckon you're as old as Aurora says you are, you know witches. So you know, just like anyone, they can be born good, bad, or crazy. Even before all this, word was Sula was born crazy."

He had no doubt about that. Strong magic was working behind the insanity of the wild-haired, wild-eyed, unwashed woman Aurora was crouched beside, but that took root and bloomed outrageously because the ground was fertile.

"Pretty thing," Barb went on, talking like she was speaking to herself. "Never saw it. Heard it. Exceptionally pretty, they said. It was a waste, they said. That's all gone now."

Yuri looked to Sula.

She was right. It was all gone. But it had to have been there at one point for her to get close to Abel at a bar in order to drug him.

"But they're devils," Barb continued, and Yuri turned his gaze back to her only to see, to his surprise, she was looking over her shoulder at him. "You protect those who are vulnerable. You don't use them. And you absolutely do not ever punish them when your plans go awry because you've manipulated a human instrument to do your bidding when they're not equipped to handle it. They sent her to kill a hybrid vampire werewolf knowing full well he could have cottoned on and torn out her throat. Then, when she only half succeeded with their scheme, which was a miracle in itself, they took the mind she had left away."

She looked back to Sula, as did Yuri.

"Devils," she whispered, and he was again surprised by Barb. This time it was hearing the sorrow mingle with anger in her tone.

But hearing it, Yuri felt one side of his lips hitch up, knowing fortune favored him, guiding him to allies who might be uneasy (in Barb's case) or tempting (in Aurora's) but were true to the cause all the same.

"Brother brother brother brother brother," Sula droned.

"Okay, bear with me," Aurora urged, lifting a hand to Sula's chin.

This made Barb tense and start to move to her daughter.

Which made Yuri shoot forward to hover over her back, making it there in a millisecond.

Aurora glanced up at him, smiled, then whispered, "It's okay," and turned back to Sula.

Yuri looked to Sula as well and then went completely still.

Because she was looking up at him, right in his eyes.

"Blue-brown, blue-brown, blue-brown," she intoned.

"Dear goddess," Barb breathed from his side.

"Blue-brown, blue-brown, blue-brown," Sula kept at it.

"What?" Aurora asked Sula. "What does that mean?"

Sula looked to Aurora and regressed. "Brother brother brother brother brother."

"Sula, honey, look back up to Yuri. He's okay. He's not going to hurt you. Look to him," Aurora urged.

Surprisingly, Sula looked back to him and switched again. "Blue-brown, blue-brown."

Aurora snapped her fingers low between them and a delicate rise of gold and silver glimmers drifted up before it rained down over Aurora and Sula.

"Give us more," Aurora coaxed.

Sula's chant changed but only slightly. "Brown-blue, brown-blue."

"More, Aurora. Gently," Barb advised, and Aurora snapped again. The glimmers rose and fell.

Still holding Yuri's gaze, Sula went back to, "Brother brother brother brother brother."

"You're telling us something. We just don't know what it is," Aurora whispered.

"Blue-brown, blue-brown, blue-brown...brown-blue, brown-blue, brown-blue."

"What does that mean?" Aurora asked.

When she did, with a suddenness that had Yuri tensing and fighting back baring his fangs, Sula snapped her mouth shut and focused acutely on Aurora as if she wasn't mad but as sharp as a blade.

She then lifted her finger and touched the cheek under her right eye. "Blue." She moved it to the cheek under her left eye. "Brown."

Yuri watched, understanding hitting him, so he did it murmuring, "Bloody hell."

Sula touched under her right eye again. "Brown." To the left. "Blue." She blinked, jerked her chin back, then chanted, "Brother brother brother brother brother."

Bloody *fucking* hell.

Abel wasn't looked after by his mother. Or his father.

But his brother.

"We have what we need," Yuri told Aurora.

"We do?" Barb asked, and he looked to her.

"Abel, the hybrid, has one brown eye, one blue."

"Sweet goddess," Aurora whispered as she straightened, which brought her very close to Yuri's side.

Without hesitation, Yuri took her hand and moved them away from the mad witch.

Barb watched this and Yuri knew what she saw.

He also didn't give a fuck.

"Mom, can you give her some relief?" Aurora asked, her gaze pointed to Sula.

Barb tore her eyes off their still-clasped hands and nodded her head once, sharply. "Take the vampire to the car. I'll be out in ten minutes."

"Just ease, Mom, and peace," Aurora pushed.

"I'll take care of her, girl. Take the vamp to the car."

"As you know, my name is Yuri," he reminded Barb, something he was staggered he had not tired of doing considering he'd done it approximately five hundred times since they'd met.

"You're all the same to me. *Vamps*," Barb returned. "So I don't really need to know your name, seeing as we get this done, we're done with you."

She was right, except the part where there was a "we."

"Now, you got hold of her, take my daughter to the car," she finished.

Yuri didn't make her ask again. He pulled Aurora out of the house, enjoying the fresh air so much, he took as much of it in as he could get.

"It stunk in there," Aurora mumbled.

"That, my sweet, is an understatement," Yuri muttered in reply.

He felt her eyes and looked down to her as he stopped them beside the car.

"We should, you know, call one of those hoarder programs so they'll come and sort her out. Mom will get her so she's functioning, if still not all there, but that's serious magic and even Mom doesn't have the juice to undo it all. Still, they'll probably see the state of this place, and her, and commit her or something."

"You can likely do that a lot quicker if you didn't call the producers of a television program and instead called someone who works for the state," he noted, and she grinned.

"Yeah, that's probably a better plan."

Yuri's gaze dropped to the pulse in her neck before he looked away as he released her hand.

"You know, Mom's pissed," she remarked.

"I sensed that," Yuri replied.

"We heard Sula was messed up, but we had no idea it was that bad."

Yuri said nothing.

"She's not going to let that stand," Aurora announced.

Yuri looked down at her but still didn't speak.

"What are you going to do now?" she asked.

"Assist you and your mother and likely the bevy of witches you'll need to accumulate to take on that coven in order to deal with the retribution your mother feels appropriate to unleash on her sisters who perpetrated that anguish on one of their own."

Her eyes lit, and the instant he saw it, Yuri wanted that light when he was covering her, his cock still buried deep after he'd made her come and given it to himself and they were laying connected, a time when he'd allow her again to be charming.

"A vampire acting out of the kindness of his heart," she teased.

"Hardly. That coven guards implements that are dangerous to immortals. I'll be doing it in order to get those weapons out of the hands of witches who intend harm and into the hands of a witch I slightly trust. Namely your mother. And I'll note an emphasis on *slightly*."

"Mom wouldn't hurt a fly," Aurora assured.

"She would if that fly hurt you," Yuri returned.

"Well, yes, there's that," she murmured, grinning at her shoes, which were ridiculous since they were high-heeled boots and the last thing anyone should wear in an uncertain situation.

They were, however, attractive.

"Or one of your kind," he went on.

She looked up at him. "That too."

He moved his gaze to the house.

"What are you gonna do after Mom and her posse exact retribution and you make sure the blessed implements are held by a witch you can *slightly* trust?" she asked.

He looked again to her. "I'll be finding the brother of Abel Jin."

She cocked her head to the side. "You know, I can help with that."

"Then I'll be finding the brother of Abel Jin with your help," he amended, and she grinned at him again.

"All I need is a little bit of his blood," she told him.

"That can be arranged," he replied.

"It'll be quicker and require a lot less paraphernalia, chanting, and fiddle if I could see him in person and touch him. I mean, it's not like it'll happen in a snap, but it won't take as long."

Yuri tensed. "That'll not happen."

Her brows knit together. "Why not?"

"He's a member of The Three, Aurora, currently hunted and residing in a safe house, an extravagant one, but one that's guarded by hundreds of vampires, wolves, and state-of-the-art security. Regardless of how safe it is, it doesn't negate the fact that being around him is dangerous."

Her lips parted.

"I'll send for his blood," he continued. "They'll deliver it while we deal with that coven. Then you can help me find the brother."

"You like me," she whispered, and he focused more closely on her.

"You're likeable."

The light came back into her eyes before she shared, "I like you too, you know, though you're altogether too smug and dry as a bone, but that last isn't so bad when you're being funny."

"Your flowery compliments warm my heart, my sweet, in a way I'm sure never to forget."

She laughed softly even as she said, "Like that. Dry as a bone but funny."

"I do know what dry means, Aurora," he informed her.

"You're also cute," she shared.

Fuck.

She called him cute.

He looked to the house not knowing whether to laugh or show her how not-cute he actually was.

"In a hot way," she added.

It was at that boldness when it suddenly became clear she was not unconsciously appealing. She was extremely conscious of just how appealing she was.

She was also a consummate game player.

And a tease.

And both made him want her all the more.

"Perhaps we should cease talking," he suggested to the house.

"Okeydoke," she replied agreeably but did it not acquiescing to his suggestion. "Though, I'll point out, when someone tells you you're cute and hot, the done thing is to return the compliment."

That was when he looked down at her, right in her eyes, and returned the compliment.

And he did it like the vampire he was.

"You know you're beautiful. You can't not know, you're that beautiful. I want to taste you in a variety of ways. And I want very badly to fuck you, doing it slow and gentle to the point it drives you mad and you beg for more, which, of course, I'll give to you, as much as you want. Then I'll take from you, as much as *I* want. You know that too. You're far from stupid, which is another reason why I want to fuck you. What you might not know is that it will happen. It'll happen after taking down a coven and before finding Abel's brother. So in the meantime, I'd appreciate if you'd stop playing your games. I'm all for a tease. But I also decide when the teasing ends. And I'm not sure you're ready right now for how I'll do that."

"Uh, okay," she breathed, staring up at him, and he was wrong even if he was right.

He wanted that light in her eyes while he was buried inside her after he'd made them both come.

But he wanted that light that was in her eyes right then while he was fucking her and she was begging him to make her come.

"I kinda want you to kiss me, like, right now," she whispered.

"That would be foolish since I absolutely want to kiss you, like, *right now*, but I want it in a way that it won't stop at kissing and I'm not keen on finding out what your mother will do if she walks out of that house and sees me fucking her daughter who I mounted on the hood of a car."

"Okay, maybe kissing right now isn't a great idea," she replied, still whispering.

"Agreed."

"Though, if you'd find the time, you know, sometime," she made her eyes big, "*soon*, I'd appreciate it."

"You're being charming again," he noted.

"I'm not sure how to stop that," she returned.

"This is part of what makes you charming," he murmured, again looking to the house.

"Yuri?" she called.

He sighed and turned his eyes back to her.

"I have a feeling I'm gonna be super glad you chased me into my house and started choking me," she declared.

That was when it happened.

That was when Yuri stood outside a hoarder's hovel, staring down at a beautiful witch in the middle of nowhere in Texas, threw back his head, and burst out laughing.

With fortunate but disastrous timing—because when he was almost done, instead of pulling Aurora in his arms and giving her the kiss they both wanted—Barb made her presence known by demanding, "What on earth in these circumstances could possibly be funny?"

Without hesitation, Yuri looked to her approaching and answered, "Your daughter."

She shrugged a shoulder and muttered, "Right, I get that." She stopped three feet away and declared, "I'm driving."

"Barb, we had this discussion on the way here. You aren't driving. If I'm in a car, I drive. And further, it's my car," Yuri said.

"I'm still driving," she retorted.

"You absolutely are not," he returned.

"You got to drive here," she pointed out.

"Indeed, as it's *my car*," he replied.

"This car kicks butt," she stated, swinging a hand out to the Jaguar he'd rented upon arrival in Dallas. "I wanna drive."

Yuri looked to Aurora.

When he did, he saw that Aurora was having trouble not laughing. But even fighting her humor, she caught his hint.

"Mom, Yuri's driving. It's his car."

"Aurora—" Barb began.

"But," she said quickly, interrupting her mother, "maybe he'll let you drive out to get us some Kentucky Fried Chicken when we get home."

Suddenly, for the first time in nearly seven hundred years, he wanted someone to kill him.

"Kentucky Fried Chicken?" he asked, and Aurora turned bullshit, guileless, big blue eyes up to him.

"I've got a craving."

Looking at her, he understood craving.

Also looking at her, he understood he was not only eating fast-food fried chicken that evening, he was letting her mother use his car to go and get it.

"Fuck," he muttered.

"You have a vampire wrapped around your little pixie-dusted finger, is what you have," Barb muttered over him, then shouted, "Shotgun!"

Yuri looked to the sky.

"No way! You get to drive to KFC!" Aurora shouted back.

Perhaps he was demented, having run across a witch he did not detect had spelled him insane, which meant he'd found an adorable, petite, but lushly beautiful witch attractive enough to put up with her annoying mother and her own frustrating, but effective, games.

"Battle it out amongst yourselves, but when the car is in gear, it's moving. So whoever isn't in it gets to spend the night with Sula," Yuri declared as he moved around the hood of the car.

He was about to open his door when he heard one shut and looked across the roof.

Barb was gone, presumably in the front seat.

He presumed this because Aurora was standing at the door to the back, her eyes on him.

"You have a beautiful laugh," she called softly.

What he had was the hope she liked getting a spanking.

Because she'd earned one.

And she was going to get one.

He didn't share that.

Instead, he said, "Thank you, my sweet."

She sent him a soft smile, then folded in the back of his car.

He folded in the front and reluctantly headed them toward what would eventually be a dinner of Kentucky Fried Chicken.

# 18
# I Got Skills

*Delilah*

"Everyone in the compound has been quarantined," Gregor stated as all the members of The Three sat around the table in the conservatory, listening to him. "Stephanie has begun her interrogations with the human staff." He turned his eyes to Lucien, then to Callum. "Rooms have been set up for the both of you, Ryon, Cosmo, Calder, and Caleb, so you all, as well, can start working to find the traitor, or traitors, as the case may be."

"Uh," I cut in hesitantly, having zero experience with interrogation tactics but still thinking they had a sure thing and should use him. "Wouldn't it go a lot faster if Abel just mind-controlled everyone to spill their secrets until he found the bad guys, or gals, as, erm, the case may be?"

Gregor blinked at me.

"I mean," I cautiously went on, "he could get them to 'fess up, then he could get them to keep doing their dastardly deeds, except we'd control what they're doing and saying."

"Seems a good plan to me," Abel muttered.

I looked to him to see him grinning at the table, but I felt his hand come out and curl around mine.

"I apologize," Gregor said, and I turned my eyes to him. "I'm unused to having someone with Abel's extraordinary skills available for such tasks. You're correct, Lilah, that would likely make things go a great deal faster, not to mention put us in an advantageous position."

I smiled at Gregor and gave Abel's hand a squeeze.

He squeezed mine back even as he looked to the vampire. "How about I get started now?"

"Capital idea," Gregor murmured, his lips twitching as he pushed back his seat.

Everyone was on the move then, including Abel and me. But when I got to my feet, I tugged his hand.

When his gaze caught mine, I said, "I wanna watch your awesomeness in action."

He gave me a grin that lit his eyes, the grin beginning to turn the blue one brown. "You got it, pussycat."

That was when I gave him a smile.

"You're done," Abel stated, then looked at me and said softly, "Next, Lilah."

I nodded to him as I switched off the video camera on its tripod, which was pointed at a woman who was sitting in the lone chair in the room. She got up and started walking to the door. I opened it for her but stuck my torso out before she got to it and looked to Caleb, who was waiting in the hall.

"It's not her. Next," I told him.

He jerked up his chin and I got out of the woman's way.

I closed the door after her and looked to Abel. "You okay?"

"Been at this three hours, lost count of how many people been in that chair, and we've got nothing," he answered, looking and sounding frustrated.

I moved to him and put a hand on his chest. "This is a lot of work, baby," I noted. "Does it drain you to do it?"

"Outside of bein' hungry, I'm good," he answered.

"Maybe we can take five minutes for you to draw from me."

His distracted eyes focused sharply on me and he stated, "You are not a meal, Lilah."

"I know, but—"

"We do that, every time we do that, you get somethin' out of it, same as me. It never becomes me takin' what I need from you. It's always something for the both of us."

God, I loved my werewolf vampire.

Still, I leaned in closer and said quietly, "I love that you want that, honey, but just so you know, I always *will* get something from it even if it's just knowing I'm giving something to you. But just saying, the more you take from me, the more goodness I get from your superpowered saliva."

His intensity cleared and he lifted a hand to cup my jaw. Then he dipped his head and took my mouth in a light, sweet kiss.

When he lifted his head, he murmured, "Couple more. Then we'll take a twenty-minute break so I can get what I need and give you *all* you need."

That *way* worked for me so I smiled, got up on my toes, and gave him my own light, sweet kiss.

When I was pulling away, a knock came at the door.

Abel's hand dropped and I turned to the door, calling, "Bring them in."

Caleb opened the door and escorted a man inside while Stephanie stood in the frame. The man looked unconcerned. Then again, they all did, seeing as we were currently working our way through the vampires and I'd noted that vampires tended to be pretty cool customers.

On the other hand, the staff had been freaked. Then again, you wouldn't want a bunch of vampires and werewolves to think you were up to no good. Further, the bad guys had no way of knowing what Abel was capable of (unless there were bugs, something we couldn't know for certain there weren't until Abel found the inside man, or woman, as the case may be) and could exonerate them, or not, pretty quickly.

I moved to the wall and settled in for the quick show that, even though I'd seen it often over three hours, I still thought it was cool as shit.

Abel didn't waste time. Caleb began escorting the vamp in, Stephanie standing at the door, but Caleb moved away from him because the vampire was woodenly walking to the chair and seating himself in it.

This was because Abel told him to do it.

Stephanie shut the door.

The vampire tipped his eyes to Abel.

Abel looked to me.

I reached out a hand and switched on the video camera. Abel could mind-control them into telling the truth, but the questioning was verbal, taped, and there were witnesses, at least one (me) and sometimes more (Caleb and/or Stephanie).

Abel started questioning, "Are you a traitor to The Three?"

"No," the vampire answered.

"Have you given any information to anyone about anything you've learned inside the compound's walls?"

"No," the vampire repeated.

"Do you believe humans should be slave to immortals?"

"No," the vampire said again.

"Are you aware of anyone who wishes to see the end of The Three or has given information to anyone who you suspect should not have that information?" Abel asked.

"No," the vampire replied.

"Have you seen anyone acting suspiciously?" Abel went on.

"No," the vampire stated.

"If you become aware of anyone who's conspiring against The Three or those who are allied with them to keep mortals free from enslavement, what are you gonna do?" Abel began to finish it.

"Report this directly to the inner circle," the vampire said.

"That being...?"

"You, King Callum, Lucien, the king's brothers, the werewolf Ryon, or the vampires Stephanie, Cosmo, Gregor, or Yuri," the vampire responded.

Abel looked to me, then to Caleb. "He's clear."

I turned off the video camera and Caleb nodded, moved to the vampire, and walked at his side as he escorted him out of the room.

The door closed on Caleb.

We repeated this three more times, one of them being with Dad's female vampire buddy, Ursula (who was clean, thank God), before it happened.

Caleb escorted the vampire in. Abel mind-controlled him to his seat. He got his eyes. I turned on the video camera.

And Abel started his questions.

"Are you a traitor to The Three?"

"Yes," the vampire said, and my body went solid as my eyes shot to the man in the chair.

He was handsome, all lean muscle, tall like all vampires, and he had thick brown hair that was two shades down from dark but not light. I'd look twice at him, but then again, I hadn't seen a vampire I wouldn't look at twice. On the vamp scale of hot, hotter, hottest (the last being Abel and Lucien, and maybe Yuri), he was in the "hotter" zone.

I felt Abel's tension, as well as Caleb's, as Abel repeated, "You're a traitor to The Three?"

"Yes," the vampire said again.

"Did you provide information to the enemy of The Three about our meeting with the vampire Cosmo this morning?" Abel asked.

"Yes," the vampire said.

Abel looked to Caleb and Caleb moved to the door. He went out. Stephanie came in and closed the door behind her.

Her eyes never left the vampire in the chair as her mouth hissed, "Is it him?"

"Yep," Abel answered, his word casual, his tone and stance not.

I tried to decide whether to edge toward my man, which would mean passing an obviously pissed-off Stephanie, but didn't come to a decision before Stephanie pinned me to the spot by looking at me.

"Are you taping?" she asked.

I quickly looked to the camera, ascertained all was well, turned back to her, and nodded.

"How did you become aware of the meeting this morning?" Abel asked the vampire.

"My room is next to Ursula's," the vampire answered, and Abel's eyes shot to me.

Dad's vampire. He heard them talking during their festivities.

Shit.

I gave Abel big eyes.

Abel looked back to the vampire. "You listened."

"Yes."

"Did you use any electronic devices to do this?" Abel continued.

"I don't need to," the vamp told Abel something he knew.

"At any time did you use any devices of any kind to learn anything about The Three?" Abel pushed.

"No."

"Were you placed here by the enemy?" Abel went on.

"We aren't the enemy, we're true immortals," the vampire stated. "True immortals know it's against our nature to follow rules, be lorded by laws, forced to hide ourselves, our power, our dominance. We are all rulers. Kings and queens. Lesser beings are meals. Playthings. Drones. They exist to serve us and the time has finally come for the true immortals to take their rightful place as overlords of humanity."

This speech gave me a shiver, but Abel didn't hesitate. He just amended his question. "Were you placed here?"

"Yes."

"Are there others like you?"

"One, a vampire soldier."

"What's his name?"

"Bjorn."

Abel looked to Stephanie. She nodded and took off.

Abel kept going.

"Do you know of my abilities?"

"Abilities?" the vampire asked as an answer.

Abel didn't answer him. He kept going.

"Do you know of any abilities The Three have?"

The vampire's brow knit before he repeated, "No."

"Have you been listening to The Three?" Abel asked.

"It's difficult to get close to the quarters of The Three without being noticed. The brothers and cousin of the false king of the wolves are untrusting and annoyingly watchful."

Well, thank God for that.

"So you've been trying to listen," Abel remarked.

"Unsuccessfully."

There was a sharp knock on the door, but before I could go to it, it was opened by Lucien.

He came in followed by Stephanie. Lucien glanced at Abel and me before Stephanie closed the door behind them. Then turned his attention fully to the man in the hot seat.

Abel continued without hesitation. "Who do you believe the true king of the werewolves is?"

"The true king of the werewolves will be the true immortal wolf who takes the head of the false king or any of his family who try to oppose him."

I swallowed at that, but Abel kept at him.

"Are you aware of any of the plans of those who call themselves the true immortals?"

"Only that the golem attack this compound tomorrow evening by sea."

I pulled in breath and looked to the side, taking in Abel, Stephanie, and Lucien. Lucien's jaw was hard. Abel's eyes were narrowed. Stephanie looked ready to pounce.

"And how will the golem attack by sea with the compound's security in place?" Abel pushed.

"The vampire soldier, Bjorn, will be on shift at that time and he supervises the cliffside security."

Abel kept at him. "You're aware of no other plans those who call themselves the true immortals have against this compound, the members of The Three, or humanity?"

"I am a spy for The True. I gather information and communicate it to those who will use it. I'm not privy to strategy. However, I'm expected to keep watch for Bjorn tomorrow night."

Abel carried on, "Who put the cameras in the trees?"

"Humans working on the security detail for The Vampire Dominion. Being human, they are easily swayed by payments of large sums of money."

I watched Abel's eyes narrow further and knew why when he stated, "I'd asked if there were others and you spoke of no humans. Only this vampire, Bjorn."

The mind-controlled drone of his voice held a hint of sneer when he replied, "You asked if there were others *'like me.'* No human is *like me.*"

"Then we need the names of all the humans, and any other beings you know of, who are working for these true immortals," Abel returned.

The vampire listed five names.

"Did those cameras have feeds or were they static?" Abel asked.

"The tapes were to be collected by the humans who were on our payroll after the meeting was over. There were too many of the detail not on payroll to have time to establish a feed."

"Well, at least there's that," I muttered.

"Lilah, would you please go and get Gregor?" Lucien asked, and my eyes went to him to see him looking at me. "Tell Gregor we need to gather immediately."

"Abel is hungry," I told him.

Lucien nodded and looked to Abel. "Put him in a trance. I'll have him watched and gather the others. Half an hour?"

"That'll work," Abel murmured, looked to the vampire in the seat and I did too.

His face went slack.

Yeesh, my man so rocked.

"There's another," I shared with Lucien.

"We'll handle him until Abel gets back," Lucien replied.

I nodded and Abel moved to me, saying to Lucien as he did, "Half an hour."

"Half an hour," Lucien agreed.

Abel got close and slid an arm around my waist. "Hang on, *bao bei*."

I curved my arms around his shoulders and then...*whoosh*...we were out of the room, up the stairs, and behind the closed door in our bedroom.

I caught my breath as Abel set me down and held me steady with both hands at my hips. When I had it together, I tipped my head back to catch his eyes.

"Word with your father, be smart about what he says to who and where," Abel said gently.

I nodded, whispering, "He's gonna feel shit he screwed the pooch."

Abel shook his head. "He didn't do wrong. He couldn't know. None of us knew. And his vampire is true to the cause. He's not responsible for the actions of assholes."

This was true.

I thought this as I caught the look on Abel's face. A look I couldn't get a lock on, but it was a look I felt like a shot to the heart.

"What?" I asked.

"I got skills," he answered confusingly.

"Well...yeah," I confirmed unnecessarily.

"No, Lilah." His fingers dug into my hips. "I...got...*skills*. Skills that can help. Skills that are vital. Skills that help make you safe. Sonia, Leah, all of us."

"Well..." I started. "Yeah," I repeated to finish, still confused.

"I'm not a soldier."

I shook my head. "Abel, I'm not following."

"I'm powerful. I'm *necessary*."

My heart clutched as what he was saying finally dawned on me.

I got close and shifted my hands to the sides of his neck. "Of course you are."

"I'm not a freak," he said like I didn't speak. "What I can do is what we need."

I leaned my weight into him and held on to his neck. "You were never a freak," I said softly.

His eyes went unfocused, so I squeezed his neck until I got his attention.

"Never, baby," I stressed. "You've always been necessary. But, just saying, even soldiers are necessary. Important and necessary."

He shook his head as if not quite believing me and stated, "Three hours and we got them. Three hours and only I could get us what we needed."

"Yeah," I whispered on a grin. "You totally rock. Then again, you always did. You just didn't know it."

He stared at my face like he wasn't seeing me, then suddenly, his eyes closed and he bent his neck so his forehead was resting on mine.

"I'll take the craziness," I kept whispering, and his eyes opened. "The danger. The uncertainty. I'll take it all if this leads to you understanding how *totally*," I squeezed his neck, "and *completely*," I squeezed again, "*awesome* you are."

Abel's hands drifted up my sides and his eyes went from vague and incredulous to something I liked much better.

"Hungry," he murmured, his hands stopping at the sides of my breasts, his thumbs gliding in.

"Hope you get Lilah champagne," I told him. "The occasion merits it."

"Don't care what I get, just as long as it's Lilah something, which, lucky me, is what it's gonna be."

Yeah, my man *so* rocked.

I smiled into his eyes.

His eyes smiled back.

His hands slid to under my arms and I was up.

Then I was down, on the bed, Abel on top of me, and seconds later, my man was feeding.

Minutes after that, Abel's hand down my shorts, I was coming.

"Okay, this shit I do not like," I declared irately the minute Abel closed the soundproofed door to our bedroom.

"Lilah."

I turned to him and saw that was all he was going to say.

I, on the other hand, had a whole lot more to say.

It was late in the evening. Bjorn had been handled. The bad spy vampire, who was named Patricio, had been handled. The greedy, turncoat humans had been handled.

And due to Abel's kickass ability, neither of the immortals remembered anything that had happened that day and Patricio was providing the report Abel gave him to give to the bad guys. That being, the excursion that morning was a training exercise for Abel, Xun, and Wei. Cosmo—Lucien's friend and a vamp I met, who was tall, blond, hot (to the point he was at the "hottest" end of the scale), and nice—was still "in the wind" as far as the bad guys knew.

And last, the golem attack was to commence as planned.

This being the shit I did not like.

"They're gonna attack us!" I snapped.

"They are and they're gonna lose since we know they're comin'," Abel replied calmly.

"You hope," I returned.

"I know," he stated firmly.

"Neither Bjorn nor Patricio knew how many were coming," I pointed out.

"Won't matter. They had the element of surprise. Now they don't."

I shook my head. "I don't have a good feeling about this."

Then again, who would? My man was fighting *golem* tomorrow. Hell, he'd never even seen one!

And my friends were too.

Abel took the two strides that separated us and curved his arms loosely around me, tipping his head to keep hold of my eyes.

"It's a solid plan, Lilah," he said quietly. "We can defeat them and do it with them not knowing we had the knowledge in order to do that soundly."

"What if they send a shitload of golem?"

"We'll defeat them."

"What if people get hurt?"

His arms got a lot less loose when he replied, "We're at war, pussycat."

I shut my mouth.

"You, Sonia, and Leah will be safe," he declared.

"And you, Cal, and Lucien?" I asked.

"Nothing will happen to us."

God, I hoped he was right.

"And you're down with those who might fall tomorrow night?" I pressed.

"No," he clipped, his voice suddenly curt. "I'm not down with that. I'll never be down with it. I'm not down with Snake bein' dead. Chen and Jabber are gettin' better, but I'm not down with them havin' that need. I'm not down with *any* of this shit," he said, squeezing his arms on the *any*. "But I got no choice. You heard that guy. Overlords of humanity? That shit is whacked. And that shit can't come about. Not a single person on this compound disagrees and they all know what's at stake, including their lives."

I looked to his throat, hating that he was right.

Abel kept speaking. "We got inside men, Lilah. Men who don't know they're inside men, but we got 'em. Today was good. Tomorrow will suck, but we'll come out all right. Good shit happened today. Good shit that might help us make everything come out all right in the end. We should rejoice, then prepare for the next thing that will suck until we get past all the shit that will suck so we can get to a life that will *not* suck."

He was again right.

I sighed.

Abel read my sigh and gathered me closer. When he did, I gave him my eyes.

"Your talk go okay with your dad?" he asked.

He'd been busy mind-controlling traitors while I had a word with Dad.

"He's pissed at himself. I tried to explain no one blames him and nothing bad happened so he shouldn't be so hard on himself, but I'm not sure how much of that he took in."

"Gregor told me that Ursula has requested her room be soundproofed."

At that, I finally smiled.

"Thinkin' she likes the taste of my old man," I muttered.

Abel made a face that clearly said we should stop talking about this just as there was a knock on the door.

He turned his head to look at it while I leaned to the side to look at it.

"Abel, Lilah, I'm sorry to interrupt, but can I have a moment?" Gregor called through the door.

"Part of the life that's not gonna suck is not havin' that guy up in our shit day in and day out," Abel muttered as he let me go and moved to the door.

I walked to one of the chairs and leaned against it.

Abel opened the door and there were murmurs as Gregor came in.

His eyes came to me. "Lilah, my apologies for the intrusion. I know it's been a long day."

I threw out a hand and gave him a small smile to tell him it was all right.

Abel shut the door, saying, "Whatever this is, can we make it fast, seein' as it actually *has* been a long day?"

Gregor's gaze was to Abel when he nodded, then announced, "Yuri phoned. He found the witch who scarred you."

I felt my body go solid as I watched Abel's do the same.

It took a few seconds but finally Abel demanded, "Say again?"

"He found the witch who scarred you," Gregor repeated. "Her name is Sula. She lives in a hovel in rural Texas and is completely insane. This might be a layman's diagnosis, but from how Yuri described her, it's not incorrect."

I stared.

Gregor went on, "He was quite prepared to exact retribution for you or detain her so that you could enjoy that opportunity. However, he explained that she's already been punished by the witches who sent her after you. Punished because she failed in her mission, that being, we believe, to bring about your end. Therefore, even if retribution were to occur, she wouldn't process it."

"Wouldn't process it?" Abel asked.

"According to Yuri, she's entirely lost her mind. There's nothing you or anyone could do to harm her. The harm has been done. She's been living an agony for twenty years."

"Can't say I'm real bothered to hear that news," Abel muttered, matching my thoughts.

Gregor nodded and spoke again, "She used a blessed athame to cut you. An athame is a witch's knife imbued with magic. As we suspected, this is why you scarred. Yuri reported that he's allied himself with two witches who are keen not to see The Prophesies unfold. They're also going to assist him in retrieving the knife and perhaps a number of other blessed implements, which could cause harm if in the wrong hands."

"If he needs help with that, we're kinda tied up up here," Abel noted.

"He assured me he has all the help he needs," Gregor stated, but I didn't get a good feeling about how he stated it, mostly because he was Gregor. He didn't give a lot away. But even if it wasn't written all over him, I could still tell that he was worried about his son.

"Right, then I'm obliged you took your time to come up here and share all that," Abel replied in a leading way, that leading to Gregor taking off.

"I'm not done, Abel," Gregor said, and I again tensed at the change in his tone of voice.

Abel heard it too. I knew by the intensity of his focus on the vampire.

"Perhaps you should sit down," Gregor suggested, which didn't make me any less tense.

What it did was make me move Abel's way.

"I'm good standing," Abel told him, not taking his eyes from the vampire.

Gregor nodded, but I didn't think it boded well that he waited until I made it to Abel's side and slid my arms around his middle. He also waited until Abel slid his arm around my shoulders.

Only when we had each other did Gregor again speak.

"Yuri and I feel it's rather strange that you've not encountered one of our kind in all your time on this earth."

"You're not alone in that feeling," Abel replied with a guarded voice.

"My son and I both feel that perhaps someone has been looking out for you."

Abel and I, both still tense, got more so.

Gregor kept going, "This was only a theory, however, it would stand to reason that one of our own would be able to sense one of our own and, thus, keep them away from you. Not to mention, that night, it's clear someone intervened."

"Yeah, it is," Abel agreed.

Gregor took in a deep breath, then holding Abel's eyes, he rocked my man's world.

"The witch Sula reported to the witches Yuri is working with that you were saved that night by a man with one brown eye, one blue."

I gasped and did it hearing Abel's swift, hissed intake of breath.

"You have a brother, Abel," Gregor said gently.

"Holy shitoly," I breathed.

Abel said nothing so Gregor carried on.

"One of the witches Yuri is working with, her name is Aurora, says she can assist us in locating him. Their priority mission is getting that athame and the other implements, which are being guarded by a coven in Texas. After that, they'll be finding your brother. And to do so, they'll need your blood."

"He's close."

My head jerked back to look at Abel's profile when he said these words.

"You feel him?" Gregor asked.

Abel shook his head. "No. But it stands to reason that if he's looking out for me, then he would be, right?"

"Well, yes," Gregor agreed.

"Why is he hidden?" Abel asked.

"We won't know until we can speak to him."

"If he's a brother, then he's either vampire or werewolf or both. So if he's close, why can't I sense him?" Abel went on.

"That we also won't know until we can speak to him," Gregor answered.

"Right, then do you need my blood now, or can I give it to you tomorrow?" Abel asked, and I stopped watching his profile and started staring at it because he was taking this in stride and this was pretty fucking huge news.

"As Yuri and his witches need some time to prepare to approach this coven, tomorrow will do. I'll dispatch it by courier to Yuri as soon as it's drawn," Gregor said.

"Great. Now, can these witches be trusted?" Abel asked.

I heard the stiffness of mild affront in Gregor's tone, so I looked back to him as he answered, "If they could not, Yuri wouldn't be working with them."

"Right. Then good. 'Preciate you comin' up to tell me this. I'll get one of the nurses to draw my blood tomorrow," Abel replied, and when he did, I saw Gregor was just as surprised by his non-reaction as I was.

"Uh..." I started but didn't get any further because Abel kept talking.

"Or is there something else?"

"No, Abel," Gregor said quietly. "That's all we have for now."

At that, Abel disengaged from me and moved to the door. He opened it and turned back to Gregor.

"Then again, appreciate you tellin' me this. Now, we all got a big day tomorrow so we all should rest up."

I pressed my lips together and turned my head to give big eyes to Gregor.

He took in my big eyes and his face got slightly soft before he looked to Abel and nodded. "You're right. We all should rest." He looked back to me. "Good night, Lilah."

"Uh, 'night, Gregor."

He tipped his head to the side, then walked to the door. "Good night, Abel."

"Later," Abel muttered.

Gregor's gaze came to me once more before he walked through the door.

Abel closed it on him and turned to me. "You need the bathroom?"

I stared.

"Lilah?" Abel prompted.

"You have a brother," I blurted.

"Yep," he agreed, then started striding toward the bathroom.

I watched him do this. When he disappeared in it and I saw the light come on, but he didn't close the door, I moved that way.

When I was in the door, I saw him bent over the sink, splashing water on his face.

"Baby, twenty years ago, he saved your life," I said gently.

Abel turned off the taps and muttered, "Apparently."

I watched him reach for the hand towel, nab it, and use it to dry his face.

"This is kinda huge news," I pointed out.

He kept his eyes to the mirror as he said, "Kinda."

"Okay, no," I stated. "It's not 'kinda' huge news, honey. *You have a brother* and *he saved your life*." My voice had risen and it, or my words, finally got me his eyes.

"Went over that, Lilah. Now a coupla times."

What was going on?

"You have no reaction?" I asked.

"What reaction do you want?" he asked back.

I threw out a hand. "I don't know. Something."

"He saved my life," Abel declared.

"Yes, honey."

"And they think he's been lookin' after me."

"Yes," I repeated.

Abel held my eyes and decreed, "He sucks at it."

My head jerked. "I—"

Suddenly, he twisted his torso. Bunching up the hand towel, he threw it violently across the long vanity. It flew, opened, and fluttered, landing on the far edge of the other sink.

Just as suddenly, he twisted back to me and bit out, "All my life, thought I was a monster."

There it was.

I started to move into the room.

Abel's voice kept biting. "All my life, thought I was the only one, alone in who I was. Deviant. Abnormal. *Wrong*. Wondering where I came from. Wondering how I could even *be*."

"Honey," I whispered, getting close but stopping when his long legs took him a long step back.

"Watched people I love die. Not one. Not three. *Generations* of them. When I found the woman for me, didn't know I could keep her alive."

"Maybe your brother doesn't know that either," I suggested carefully.

"And maybe he does. At least if he's lookin' after me like they think, he saved my life, he knows what I am, what we both are, he knew *he* wasn't alone."

"Perhaps you should wait to be this angry after you hear what he has to say," I offered, keeping up with my suggestions.

"And perhaps you know me enough to know that if *I* had a brother, I would *not ever* leave him hanging," Abel shot back, and he was right. I knew him enough to know that for certain.

I lifted a hand toward him and said, "I don't know what to say to make it better."

"Bury my cock in your cunt. That'd work," he clipped, and I didn't like that, what he said or how he said it.

Therefore, I told him, "That part of what we have is not about you being angry and spewing asshole remarks."

"Okay then, Lilah, how 'bout you give me a minute to wrap my head around that shit Gregor just shared without you up in my face about it," he fired back instantly, his aim true and hurtful.

I took a step back. "You need a minute, you only have to ask."

He stared at me before he inquired, "You got any siblings?"

"You know I don't," I answered.

"I didn't either, until five minutes ago."

"That isn't true. You've had generations of them. I know it hasn't occurred to you because you're too busy being pissed, but do you think your brother, in looking out for you, maybe didn't have even that?"

His jaw got hard.

He didn't think of that.

"You can be pissed at him," I stated. "You have a right because you're correct. He left you hanging. He left you alone. He left you to come to the conclusion that you were a monster. And even if he doesn't know much about who he is, at least you could have had each other. But as for me, he saved my man's life. So I'm not going to be pissed at him. When they find him and bring him to us, I'm going to give him a big hug and thank him and maybe make him cookies. And you're gonna have to put up with that and not go wolf on me, or, honestly, burying your cock in my cunt will only be a memory for you for at least a decade."

His eyebrows shot up, and when they did, they did it scarily. "You'd deny me?"

I ignored his scary eyebrows.

"Fuck yes, if you don't let me hug anyone who saves your life. *And* make them cookies. Though, just saying, I kinda hope your brother is the only one who gets that distinction. But with the way things are rolling for us, I might be handing hugs and cookies around to entire armies."

"This is not the time to be a smartass, Lilah," he growled.

"You're right. So, for future reference, you need time in your head and away from me, *ask for it*. You don't want to talk things out, *tell me*. You need to be a dick, just saying, there is never a time when that's okay to do with me."

"You laid that out, believe this, I took it in. But Delilah, there is no way in fuck you couldn't have taken it in that I didn't wanna process that shit with you at the precise moment *you* wanted to process it, and you pushed it. You don't want the dick, then maybe you should learn to read me and back off when I need you to, not makin' me ask you to."

Fuck, he had a point.

"Okay, Abel, you're right. I read that and pushed it. I'll try not to do it again."

"Brilliant. Now, do you mind I take a piss?"

My head tipped to the side, shocked at this request because we hadn't been together for weeks without that happening and he always did it with the door open. Not to mention, I'd grown up around men who did it wherever, whenever, no matter who was around or even watching.

Therefore, I queried, "You need privacy for that?"

He blew out an annoyed breath, then declared, "You're my world, my reason for existing, but I got a brother I didn't know I had, who saved my life, and I gotta take a piss. So no. I don't give a shit you see that. Just right now, I wanna take a piss and be with my own thoughts. That work for you, or you want me to drag a chair in here so you can watch?"

"Now you're being an amusing dick," I told him.

"Baby, I gotta piss," he ground out impatiently.

I tried not to smile as I flicked out a hand and muttered, "Carry on," before I walked out of the room, closing the door behind me.

I went to the window and stared out at a sea that was undulating calmly. A sea that supernatural beings, who created their offspring by tearing away their own flesh and bone, were going to use to attack tomorrow night with the intent to kill people I cared about, including me.

Since that was not the greatest train of thought, I thought about Abel's brother, wondering what was up with that.

Since I would get no answers until we met him (I won't lie: I could dig Abel being pissed, but I couldn't wait to meet him), there was no use thinking about that.

That was when Abel's words rang in my head.

*You're my world, my reason for existing.*

Now *that* was worth thinking about.

I leaned forward, pressing my forehead against the cold glass and seeing from my reflection closeup that I was smiling and doing it big.

After the day we'd had, I couldn't believe I was doing it. But knowing I was Abel Jin's world, his reason for existing, I couldn't help it.

I heard the bathroom door open and kept my forehead to the glass. I only took it from the glass when Abel wrapped his arms around me, one at my upper chest, one at my ribs, and pulled my back tight to his front.

"For future reference," he said softly in my ear, "don't give a shit you see that with me, but you gotta take care of business, you close the door."

I stared at us in the glass—Abel holding me close, his head bent, his lips to my ear—and it was an awesome picture, but I didn't really process it because I was stunned at his words.

"For a biker, your preference is surprising."

"You wanna be open about that shit, have at it. Just stating my preference."

"I prefer privacy," I shared.

"Kinda noticed that."

"Why is it that men taking care of business seems completely natural to me and I feel the need for privacy?"

"Probably because you grew up with bikers who had no problem marking their territory wherever it might be, and being around men, you valued you privacy. And I grew up with women who were like you so it's what I know."

"That makes sense," I muttered.

He pulled me closer and shoved his face deeper into my neck before he said, "Thanks for talking about pissing and not my brother."

I smiled at the glass. "Anything for you, baby."

That was when he gave it to me.

"I'm sorry I was a dick."

God, I loved it how he did that. Just put it out there. So easy. Never making me work for it.

I drew in breath and let it out. "It was understandable. I'm sorry I didn't back off and forced you to be a dick."

"You were dealing with the news too."

"I was, but it was your news, so I should have had a mind to how you needed to deal with it, not how I wanted you to."

He slid his lips up my neck, back to my ear, and whispered, "Right. That's done. Can I bury my cock in your cunt now?"

I melted against him but replied, "Immediately?"

"No, I'll get you there."

I knew he would.

"Then yes."

I thought he'd move, either breathtakingly fast or nice and slow.

He didn't.

"Abel?"

"Tomorrow night, it's all gonna be okay."

I closed my eyes.

I opened them, whispering, "Okay, baby," and I put a lot of effort into making it sound like I believed him.

And I did.

I just worried he was wrong.

He tightened his arms around me, slid his lips back down to my neck, and I'd find it would be a while before we made it to the bed because Abel was in the mood to take his time.

And he did, going slow, being sweet, not fucking but making love to me. Again giving me what I needed but didn't know I'd need. A long, intense orgasm that left me sated and languid and meant, once he'd tangled himself up in me, on the eve of a day that would end with fighting, I didn't have to search for it.

I fell fast asleep.

"I can't believe fuckin' *vampires* have a fuckin' *non-smoking policy*."

It was the next night and this was Jabber complaining about the state of affairs not only in the compound but also in the safe room in the bunker below the compound where we were all hunkered down, waiting out the fight that was either happening above or imminently going to happen.

That "we" included Leah, Sonia, Jian-Li, and me. With us was Regan, a beautiful, dark-haired woman who looked like Callum's sister but was actually his mother. Under Callum's orders, she'd arrived at the compound several days earlier. She was sweet and nice and openly adored her family, so, obviously, I dug her big time.

The "we" in the bunker also included a seriously ticked off Chen (who was better but not better enough that Abel would let him fight, which was not a decision Chen agreed with, but his other two brothers and mother did, hence, he was there). And lastly, an also better-but-still-not-great Jabber, who never liked being cooped up, and doing it knowing my dad was somewhere close and in a hairy situation, he liked it less.

Moose had yet to return and this freaked me out, but I couldn't think on that.

I couldn't because I was freaked out about whatever was happening above us. We'd been there hours. They'd been reporting in that all was clear but way too infrequently to my way of thinking.

Now they were not.

We had guards in the room, guards outside the room, guards stationed in the hall, and guards securing all the routes to the bunker. These guards were being led by Caleb, who surprisingly didn't bitch about this assignment but, instead, took it seriously.

That was nice and even flattering. Callum's brothers were definitely action wolves so that said a lot.

But I was not thinking about how flattering Caleb taking his assignment without bitching was.

I was worried about what was happening that meant they were no longer reporting in.

The good news: I was not reacting physically to whatever it was and I was hoping this meant Abel was not in danger.

I didn't get agony in my gut when Callum or Lucien were in danger so I couldn't help Leah or Sonia with their own worries. Sonia was actually being very cool, acting calm and collected, and her being this way helped me not to totally lose it.

But she'd had experience waiting out Callum in battle. It was Leah and I who were the newbies. Neither of us liked this much and neither of us bothered to expend the effort not to show that.

Therefore, I wasn't totally losing it. I was *close* to totally losing it.

"It's not like they can die from secondhand smoke," Jabber went on.

"I believe," Jian-Li began, "even if we don't share your habit, at this juncture, we can all appreciate your need, Jabber. However, voicing your objections will not change their policy at this time, seeing as they're all rather busy with something else."

Jabber glared at Jian-Li.

"I could actually use a cigarette and I've never smoked," Leah muttered to me, but her eyes were on the door.

I had, though only while acting out against my mother, but I knew having a smoke now wouldn't help.

Only our men walking through the door would help.

"I'm thinking we need tequila shots," I muttered back.

She looked to me. "Lucien isn't a big fan of secondhand drinking, that being feeding from me after I've become inebriated." She shook her head. "Actually, that isn't true. If I drink champagne or vodka, he quite likes that. Tequila..." She trailed off and made a face before carrying on. "When this is all over, we're celebrating and I want him to enjoy that to its fullest. So no tequila for me, even if we did have it."

I was with her.

I was also interested in what she'd said about drinking.

So I asked, "Really? He doesn't like it when you drink?"

She shook her head.

My eyes wandered to the door as I mumbled, "I wonder how Abel feels about it."

"Everyone is different," Leah noted, and I hoped she was right because Abel and I hadn't tried drunk sex. I figured drunk sex with Abel would absolutely rock, and therefore, that was something we'd be rectifying immediately.

Namely, when he showed, healthy and intact, in the door I was staring at.

"Have you seen a golem?" I asked the door.

"No," Leah answered.

"Abel said they're large and hard to kill," I said softly.

"Lucien told me the same thing."

We went silent, both staring at the door. We stayed silent for a while and our silence was only broken when Jian-Li moved from the couch where she was sitting with Sonia and Regan to the couch kitty-corner to where I was sitting with Leah.

She perched on the arm of the sofa next to me and patted my shoulder.

"It will all be well."

I looked up at her. She was seemingly cool and collected too, and she had three boys up there doing whatever they were doing, only one of them immortal.

"Yes, it will," I agreed, lifting my hand to her leg and patting her back.

She smiled down at me and patted my shoulder again before her eyes drifted to the door.

Chen approached and threw himself in an armchair close to his mother and me. I winced, thinking he should take more care, seeing as he was still recovering, but the look on his face did not invite sisterly concern or advice.

"It'd be better if we could at least *hear* something," he griped.

"We will," Jian-Li told her son. "Soon."

Chen looked to his mother. "You know this how?"

I watched as she looked to her son. "I know this because I'm a mother."

"Motherly clairvoyance?" he asked. "Did you just get this, or is it something you've had for years but never told us about?"

I gave wide eyes to Leah because Jian-Li's boys could be abrasive and even give lip to their mother (not that she took it, but that didn't mean they didn't give it occasionally), but his tone was derisive and I didn't think Jian-Li was going to stand for that.

She wasn't and she didn't waste time sharing that with her son.

"I've always had it, Chen," she said with patience, though that patience was strained. "From the moment each of you was born. That happens with mothers. However, in this case, it isn't clairvoyance. It's hope. And being here not knowing anything, not seeing anything, not even hearing anything, that's what we have. It's all we have. And we have to hold strong to it."

That was a good comeback and Chen knew it because he gave her a scowl, then looked to the door.

And when he did, it opened and Caleb walked through.

The room went wired and everyone jumped to their feet.

"All's clear," he announced, and the tension immediately evaporated as relief flooded the space. "You're all to stay here while they see to some cleanup."

I watched Sonia scrunch her nose and had a feeling I knew what that meant, and what that meant was gross.

I didn't care. I'd take gross. I wanted to see Abel.

Before I could relay this desire to Caleb, Jabber piped up.

"Can someone bring me a pack of smokes and a lighter?"

Caleb looked to him. "That's not our number one priority right now, Jabber."

"Can someone make it their number *two* priority?" Jabber returned.

"Uh, hate to cut in, but can someone at least tell the guys to come down?" I asked. "All of the male Three, but also Wei and Xun. Just, you know...because," I finished lamely.

Caleb looked to me. "I'll talk to them, Lilah. But Callum reported directly to me and said they're all unharmed."

"That's good to know. Thanks," I replied, still wanting to see my man.

"My smokes?" Jabber butted in.

"Jab—" Caleb started.

Jabber cut him off. "I can see the boys not wantin' the women to see dead shit, blood, and body parts, but I don't got a problem with that, so at least can I get outta this fuckin' room?"

"Me too," Chen put in.

"Fine," Caleb agreed shortly, stepping aside to let them pass. Both men moved quickly to the door.

"So the men can leave, but the women can't?" Leah asked, and Caleb turned his eyes to her.

"Callum ordered you all stay here. So you all stay here," Caleb returned.

"I'm not fond of blood and body parts, therefore, I'll stay and have another cup of tea," Jian-Li murmured as she sat in the armchair that Chen vacated, leaning forward to the teapot and cups that were on the coffee table in front of her.

"I'll ask them to come down as soon as they can," Caleb said and wasted no time backing out and closing the door.

Leah flopped on the couch, grumbling, "Maybe I *will* do tequila shots. It'll serve Lucien right for sticking me in a bunker and leaving me here."

I sat next to her and asked, "Do you want to see blood and body parts?"

I asked this because I really didn't. I could be a tough cookie, but I was okay with not seeing that, just as long as Abel showed (and soon).

She looked to me. "I want to see my *husband*."

Obviously, I got that and nodded, then pointed out, "Sorry to say, there's no tequila. Just coffee and tea. I probably shouldn't have mentioned it. We'll be certain that they equip our bunker better next time."

She huffed out a breath but said no more.

Jian-Li lifted the pot my way in a nonverbal offer of tea. I shook my head. So did Sonia and Leah when Jian-Li offered it to them. Regan accepted.

The waiting before seemed to take back to back eternities.

The waiting right then thankfully didn't last that long.

The door opened and the men walked in.

Lucien whisked Leah out in a *whoosh*. Callum went directly to Sonia.

Abel came to me as Wei and Xun went to Jian-Li.

He looked fine. Tired but fine. Both Wei and Xun looked the same (though, Xun had a bandaged hand).

When Abel got close, he lifted both hands to cup my jaw, dipped in, ran his temple along mine, caught my eyes, and whispered, "It's all good."

I nodded, clutching his tee at its sides, staring into his eyes, and believing him.

It was all good. Everyone was alive, breathing, and fine.

Thank God, it was all good.

For now.

And this was great at the same time it sucked, because I knew as for tomorrow being good, we would have to wait and see.

# 19
# At All Costs

*Abel*

"I don't know how it happened," Abel watched Patricio say to his phone, which he had held up in front of him and on speaker. "It's like they knew the golem were to attack."

Abel was in his room with him, though he'd mind-controlled Patricio into not seeing him, as well as putting the call to his superiors on speaker so Abel could listen.

It was the morning after the attack.

They'd sent a shit-ton of golem. And golem were huge, strange-looking, lethal motherfuckers that Abel hoped he never encountered again. They'd sent so many because it was clear they meant business. It wasn't an exercise. They meant to annihilate The Three, or as many of them as they could get.

And the golem who showed absolutely meant business. It was lucky they'd found the traitors, or Abel didn't know what the outcome would have been.

It could have been ugly.

It could have been the end.

But it wasn't and that was where they were now.

Still alive.

Still breathing.

Now they had to move the fuck on.

They just didn't know to where.

"Bjorn?" the voice on the other end asked.

"I can't ask him, seeing as he was killed in the fight," Patricio answered.

This was true. Bjorn lost his head and he'd done it to Wei's sword. Abel had been close. It was unavoidable. It was Wei or Bjorn and Abel thanked God it came out the way it did.

"As far as I know, he was faithful to The True until the end," Patricio finished.

"He was killed by golem?" the voice asked.

"I wasn't there, but as our orders were to remain covert, which meant he had to at least pretend to fight them, I can only assume that's the case," Patricio told him.

That wasn't the case. When they'd met the surprise attack with prepared force, things turned pretty quickly for the golem, which meant Bjorn switched sides pretty quickly, to his detriment.

*Press for details of what they're doing next,* Abel ordered.

"What are your plans?" Patricio asked into the speaker.

"None of your concern," the voice replied. "Find out if they knew about the attack, and if they did, how."

*Keep pushing but be smart about it,* Abel commanded.

"I could be of further help if I knew what Etienne was planning for his next move," Patricio said.

"I'm not certain how that would be or why you're requesting this information, Patricio, when you know it isn't yours to have unless we feel it pertinent to share it with you," the voice returned.

*Back off,* Abel demanded.

"You weren't here," Patricio snapped. "They were merciless. You sent two hundred and fifty golem and only seven survived the fight."

Those seven didn't know either. They'd had their mission and that was all they had. Abel had gotten that information out of them the night before.

Though, there were more golem allied with The True, and what they were up to was anyone's guess.

"Do you fear for your safety?" the voice asked.

"They have no idea I'm True," Patricio replied.

"Then do your job," the voice ordered. "Watch. Listen. Report. If we have anything for you, we'll be in contact."

"Right," Patricio said into the phone, but he was talking to no one. The voice on the other line was gone.

*You're needed, Abel, immediately. In the hall. Keep Patricio in his room as you leave.*

This came into his head in Lucien's voice, the first time he'd done that to Abel, and Abel tensed when it started. Then he gave his orders to Patricio and walked out of the room, seeing Lucien just outside the door.

Lucien caught his eyes and immediately moved down the hall, doing it quickly, his body language communicating urgency.

Abel followed in the same way.

Lucien only stopped when they were all the way down the hall and had descended half a flight of stairs.

"What?" Abel asked before Lucien could say anything.

"Moose has returned," Lucien told him.

"Shit," Abel clipped, his stomach tightening. "Is he okay?"

"He's perfectly fine. The three humans he brought with him, however, are not."

Abel stared at the vampire.

"Come," Lucien murmured and again began to descend the stairs.

Abel followed all the way to the front door, out it, down the steps, and to an SUV that had a wolf behind the wheel.

Lucien got in the backseat and Abel angled in beside him.

They barely closed their doors before the wolf hit the gas.

He turned to Lucien. "Wanna tell me what's goin' on?"

"I don't know," Lucien replied. "This was called in. They didn't give details, just asked for us to come to where Moose is and where they're holding the humans. Callum was out with his wolves and he's on his way. We'll be at the barracks where they're holding them shortly."

Abel nodded.

"Did you get anything from Patricio?" Lucien asked.

Abel shook his head. "Nothin'. Worse, tried to get him to press for info, but the minute he did, they shut him down. Patricio reported it was like we knew there was an attack coming, and with the other one out of the picture, they can't know which one gave it up. But if Patricio pushes when that's not his normal gig, they might turn to thinkin' it's him. We gotta be cool with that."

"Annoying," Lucien murmured, his eyes drifting to the windshield.

"Any word from Serena?" Abel asked, and Lucien gaze returned to him.

"Not that I know of."

"Annoying," Abel muttered.

Lucien's lips turned up just as the SUV started to slow. Abel looked out the window and saw they were at a barrack at the far northwest part of the property. There was a lot of activity outside, and Abel had never been there to know for certain, but it seemed more than what would be normal late-morning activity at a vampire barrack.

They got out and Abel followed Lucien into the barrack.

Ryon met them inside the doors and said instantly, "This way."

They moved behind Ryon down a hall to the end and into a room that was guarded outside by two wolves.

The door closed behind them.

In the room were Callum, Moose, and three young men who looked like they were in their midtwenties.

They were also fucked right the hell up. Eyes nearly swollen shut. Noses twice their size, one of the kids' looked broken. Fat and split lips. Serious bruising. Cuts seeping blood. All of them holding their bodies gingerly like the visual damage was not all they'd sustained.

They were also warily surveying the vampires and wolves in the room and looking scared out of their minds.

They looked something else too. Something that creeped Abel right the fuck out. That being, when he and Lucien walked in and the men's attention turned to them, they looked less scared and more hungry.

And not for food.

For whatever Abel would give them.

"Right, you're here. I can get this out all in one go, then get back and get some shut-eye," Moose proclaimed the moment the door shut behind them, and Abel tore his attention from the guys and turned it to Moose.

He motioned to the kids with a swing of his arm and Abel saw his knuckles were split and bloodied, but otherwise, he looked fine.

"Was at a bar coupla days back, doin' my thing. Heard these fuckers talkin'," he began. "They were hammered. The kind of drunk that makes you messy and they got all kinds of messy."

"And how's that?" Callum prompted when Moose quit talking.

Moose jabbed a finger at one of the kids. "That one was off on one, braggin' about how good it felt to get fed from while takin' it up the ass."

Abel looked to the kid Moose indicated. Blond, slight, his was the nose that looked broken.

Moose kept going, "The other two, they didn't like that shit, seein' as they didn't get their asses fucked, but they did get fed from and wanted the other with it. Now, I don't give a shit what a body's gotta do to get off. I just got tweaked when they were talkin' about bein' fed from. So I paid attention. They didn't say much more, seein' as they got into a bitch slappin' fight. Middle of this, some big dude walks in and gives them a look. They all immediately go docile and follow him out."

"Vampire?" Lucien asked.

"I didn't know, but I guessed and followed them," Moose replied. "Since vamps can sense things, didn't get close enough to watch, not that I'd wanna see that shit. But between me kickin' the snot outta them and bringin' them here, they spilled the dude was vamp."

"Shit, Moose," Abel clipped. "You followed a vampire without backup?"

"Yeah," Moose retorted curtly. "And it's good I did, seein' as he had three boy toys to take his concentration so he didn't make me, even if I stayed distant, because now I know where the motherfucker is stayin'. It's far enough to be off compound radar, but it's still close. I been watchin' and followin' for days now so I also know that these assholes," he swung an arm out to the men again, "are his human eyes and ears on the compound. Not only that, they pass some shit to some dude named Bjorn *in* the compound."

"This is all very good information, Moose," Callum stated. "But that doesn't explain why they aren't in very good condition and are here instead of simply you being here reporting this to us so we could utilize this intelligence and they could stay in play."

"They made me," Moose explained. "Tried to jump me." He shrugged. "That didn't work out too good for them."

Abel looked back to the kids, thinking Moose was not wrong.

"Did you get the vampire's name?" Callum asked.

"They called him Miko," Moose answered.

"You have an address on where he's staying?" Lucien asked.

"Already gave that to Stephanie. She's been and gone, took off with it," Moose told him.

Lucien stepped back, pulling his phone out of his pocket, and murmured, "I'll give her a call."

Callum turned to Abel. "We need them back in play."

"Say what?" Moose asked, and Callum turned back to him.

"We'll brief you later," he said and again gave his attention to Abel. "Make up a story as to why they're in the shape they're in, erase all memory of Moose and their visit to the compound, and get them back in play. Once they're set loose, they need to get the vampire away from where he's staying so we can set up electronic surveillance."

Abel lifted his chin to Callum and moved to the young men. They shrunk from him, but he got that under control, thought fast, and sorted out the rest.

When he was done, he stepped back and looked to Callum. "They're good to go."

Callum nodded and turned to Ryon. "Get them out of here, let them loose, but put a human on them. The minute Miko's clear, get eyes and ears on him."

"Got it," Ryon muttered, opened the door, motioned to some wolves beyond it, and they moved in.

Callum got close to Abel and they watched the men being moved out.

Once they were gone, Lucien finished his phone call and joined their huddle.

"Stephanie knows of this vampire. She's never met him, but she's not surprised he's part of The True," Lucien shared.

"They're everywhere," Abel muttered.

"This isn't surprising," Callum noted and held Abel's eyes. "Lucky we have you so they don't know that we *do* know."

Shit had been extreme with the golem, but they'd made it through...because of Abel.

And now there was this, but they were turning the tables... because of Abel.

He could not say that this didn't feel fucking great, but he didn't share that with Lucien and Callum. All he did was again lift his chin.

"We'll let that take its course, see what we can glean from it," Callum continued. "You brief Moose on what's been happening. Then we have an appointment to train."

In other words, carry on as normal.

Abel could see going that way, not making a big deal out of what little they just gained so no one would get any hint they'd gained it, so he nodded.

"Once we know more, you're likely up again," Lucien warned him.

Abel didn't have a problem with that. He'd had centuries of being able to do something that was huge, but it had no purpose except to make him feel like a freak.

Now it had purpose.

No, he had no problem with that.

"Whatever needs to get done," he replied, before he asked, "Where's Gregor?"

"Gregor's distracted," Callum told him. "Yuri moves on the coven this evening."

Abel could see this too. Gregor and Yuri looked like brothers, but they were father and son. And since Yuri had been gone, Gregor had been like a man who was worried about his son. He had serious shit going on that he had to have a lock on, but most of his mind was in Texas with his boy.

If Abel had any doubts about Gregor, this would have satisfied them.

"Right," Abel muttered, then stated, "I'll talk to Moose. Then we'll get on with shit."

"Yes, then we'll get on with shit," Callum said on a smile.

"But first, gotta get Moose back to my mate. She's worried. She'll wanna know he's back and safe."

"Take the SUV we came in," Lucien offered. "I'll ride back with Callum."

Abel gave Lucien a nod and looked to Moose. "Let's go, big man."

Moose didn't hesitate, obviously ready for soft sheets. Abel did the best he could to get him up-to-date on the way back to the compound and left him in a living room when they got back, deciding to find Delilah himself, give her the news, and get her to her friend.

He found her three living rooms down. He also found her alone, not with Jian-Li or any of the other women. She was standing at a window, staring out, completely oblivious to anything, including him walking into the room.

"*Bao bei,*" he called when he was close.

He watched her jump in surprise and turn to him.

"You okay?" he asked.

She kept her face aimed at him, but her eyes slid back to the window.

When he made it to her, he looked out and saw three dark gray columns of smoke heading straight up to the sky through windless air from beyond the dense woods that surrounded the sides of the compound.

He knew what those were. Those were the ultimate end to the dead golem. An end that included certain body parts that had been hacked to shit and then far removed from their mates, especially the heads, all this being burned to ash.

"They might have had women," Delilah said softly, and Abel looked back to her to see her head again turned to the window. "They might have had kids."

"And if they'd succeeded, there is no 'might' about what they were gonna do, which was something we couldn't let them do. At all costs."

"At all costs," Delilah whispered to the window.

"Pussycat—" he started, lifting his hand to curl it where her neck met her shoulder.

This again got him her eyes. "Are you okay with all costs?"

He didn't understand the question.

"What?"

She turned fully to him and rested her hands on his abs. "You took lives, honey."

Now he got her. More than got her.

She was reflective and looking out the window because the bodies of men who likely multiple someones had loved were being reduced to ash. She was also reflective and looking out the window because she was worried about his state of mind.

"I'm good," he assured her.

She wasn't assured and he knew this when she tipped her head to the side and asked, "You sure?"

He slid his hand to the back of her neck, pulled her closer, and bent to her.

"I'm sure," he said, soft and firm. "And you're going to be good too, seein' as Moose returned, he's fine, and he's waiting in living room three for you."

Her eyes lit in a way he liked at the news Moose was back and they started dancing in a way he liked even more at his comment about living room three.

"Which one is that, then?" she asked.

"I'll take you there," he offered.

"Awesome," she said softly, and he used his hand at her neck to pull her around until she was at his side. Then he wrapped his arm around her shoulders and started guiding her to the door. "We should officially number them so there's no confusion, you know, seeing as it seems we're gonna be here awhile," she went on as she slid her arm along his waist.

"We'll do that after you welcome home Moose and I get your dad and Jabber so they can do the same."

She looked up at him and said, "Right on."

Even as they walked out the door, he bent and touched his mouth to hers.

Her arm curled around his waist gave him a squeeze and her eyes gave him a smile when he lifted his head.

Then he took her to her friend and found her father and Jabber and took them to Moose too.

It ended up being after training when they officially numbered the living rooms.

There were twelve.

## *Yuri*

Yuri was annoyed, and thus, he didn't speak.

"Yuri?" his father on the other end of the phone called. "Did you hear me? I want you to report in the minute you secure the implements."

But Gregor didn't want Yuri to report in the minute the implements were secured. He simply wanted him to report in.

"I'm not one hundred anymore, Father," he replied drily.

"I'm aware of that," his father returned even more drily.

"I've got a coven of thirteen witches who Aurora has shared are quite powerful at my back," Yuri reminded him of something he'd told him but moments before. "However, as per their plan, which they're quite adamant I follow, they are the ones who are in the most danger."

And this was true, as Barb had told him, and he believed her.

Which meant Yuri was concerned.

He might not be Barb's favorite being, but he had to admit, he held some regard for her if only for the fact she adored her daughter.

Though, it was more.

She might not like him, but he couldn't help but have some affinity for her, considering she was not only Aurora's mother, she was also taking her life in her hands to assist with this mission. Not to mention the fact she could be quite amusing when she wasn't being irritating.

But the truth of the matter was, Yuri was mostly concerned about Aurora.

He'd learned she was only twenty-seven years old. She was brave. She had what she referred to as "juice," something he'd witnessed repeatedly, and she was far from stupid. However, if something happened, this would affect Yuri's future plans of fucking her, which he was very much looking forward to.

But it wasn't only that.

If something happened, it would mean a world without the witch Aurora living in it, and Yuri didn't like the thought of that at all.

It was Gregor's turn to be silent.

"It'll all be fine," Yuri told him.

"After this is over, I'd like to meet this Aurora," Gregor stated, and Yuri sighed.

It was rare when he envied humans. However, this was a time when he did.

His father had had centuries to get to know him and could likely correctly predict any move Yuri made before he made it. More, Gregor could read into subtleties no human parent had enough time or experience to read.

This meant that Yuri had not shared Aurora's pull on him, but his father had read it.

"There's a great deal to do before such a meeting can occur, not only securing the implements, but also in locating Abel's brother," Yuri reminded him.

"Of course," Gregor muttered just as a knock came at the door.

Yuri moved that way, speaking. "I'm to leave shortly to meet the coven. I should let you go."

"Fine, Yuri. I'll expect a call in a few hours," his father replied.

Yuri didn't reply this time because he smelled her before he made it to the door. He looked through the peephole, regardless, and saw her standing outside, her head turned, eyes aimed down the corridor, her mass of dark hair arranged in soft plaits leading to a loose bun at her nape.

She looked as if she was prepared to go on a date, not approach a volatile coven in a battle of magic that might have dire consequences.

Furthermore, he was meeting her and her sister witches. Why she was at the door to his hotel suite, he had no idea.

Except she was Aurora, vexing in a way he liked.

"Good-bye, Father," he murmured into the phone.

"Until later, Yuri," his father replied.

Yuri ended the call, then unlocked and opened the door.

Her little, curvaceous body jolted when he did, as if she wasn't expecting him to answer.

"You're here, my sweet...why?" he asked as greeting.

"Hey, Yuri," she returned.

"Hello, Aurora," he replied, then ordered, "Now, answer my question."

She looked beyond him and asked, "Aren't you going to ask me in?"

He had no desire to ask her in. They had important tasks to see to that night. They had no business being in a suite of rooms that included a king-sized bed and two double beds, not to mention two couches.

Nevertheless, it was Aurora, and he had less desire to leave her standing out in the hall. Therefore, he shifted to the side to allow her entry.

She took his invitation and moved in, graceful on another pair of attractive, but ludicrous in the circumstances, high-heeled boots. She wore them with enchanting light gray slacks that hugged her generous heart-shaped ass and a very un-witch-like, stylish periwinkle sweater that did lovely things to her eyes and was woven so loosely, he could see the skintight matching camisole underneath.

He cast aside his reaction to her garments, shut the door, and inquired, "Do you have an assignation after our business tonight?"

She turned to him to give him startled but amused eyes. "An assignation?"

He moved into the suite while flicking his hand her way. "You're quite fetching, Aurora." He stopped several feet away from her and crossed his arms on his chest. "More fetching than normal. More, indeed, than need-be considering our business this evening."

She lifted a hand and lightly touched a tendril of hair he had no doubt was not tucked in her attractive coiffure for the very purpose that it was more appealing curling around the skin in front of her ear. Appealing enough to make him want to touch it, curl his finger around it, and maybe tug it lightly just to see her response.

He tore his attention off the tendril and gave it back to her, prompting, "Aurora?"

She started before she wet her bottom lip, peering at him under the thick fan of her lashes, and whispered, "You haven't kissed me yet."

Bloody hell.

He sighed before he began, "Aurora—"

"It's important you kiss me," she stated on a rush, and he felt his eyes narrow.

"Pray, why?" he asked.

"We need that connection," she explained.

"I beg your pardon?"

She made to take a step toward him, stopped, lifted her hands to her sides in a helpless gesture, and dropped them.

But she spoke.

"I need to be connected to you. The more connected to you I am, the better I can protect you."

He needed to be connected with her as well, but not for that reason, nor would that be happening now.

"From what Barb has explained about tonight's proceedings, it would seem you need to focus on protecting yourself," he stated.

"You'll still be there and you'll still be in danger," she returned.

"This is true, but you're there to take care of me, as are your witch sisters, and beyond that, I can assure you, I'm quite adept at taking care of myself."

"And I can take better care of you if we..." She trailed off, moved a step toward him, and began again. "Something's happening between us," she said quietly.

"No, my sweet," he disagreed. "Something *will* happen between us after we finish tonight's business. Before that, neither of us needs distractions."

"But I—" she started.

"Want me to kiss you," he finished for her. "Because you're young, you desire me and tonight frightens you, so you came here hoping I'd give you something to see you through. And if the fates frown on us, the unspeakable happens and you don't get through, at least you'd have something you wished to have before you die."

"Okay, to put a very fine point on it...yeah," she muttered, casting her eyes to the floor.

"Aurora, come here," he ordered, and her gaze instantly came back to him.

She hesitated nary a second before she moved to him.

When she got close, for the first time, Yuri gathered her in his arms and brought her closer.

And he very much liked the feel of her there.

"Put your arms around me, my sweet," he murmured when she seemed not to know what to do with herself.

She did as told, and when she did, he slid a hand up her spine to the back of her neck and around to the side where he stayed it, curled there.

"No harm will come to you tonight," he told her quietly.

"Yuri—"

"No," he stated, still quiet but now also firm, underlining his word by pressing the pads of his fingers into her flesh. "I will not allow it, your mother will not allow it. We will prevail tonight."

"Okay, I believe you," she replied in a tone that said she didn't exactly, but she was trying. "Still, I don't understand why you won't kiss me."

Yuri pressed the pads of his fingers deeper, bent his neck, and took her mouth, demanding and receiving access inside by gliding the tip of his tongue along the crease.

When he had her, she tasted better than he imagined—of honey, moonlight, and fear.

He ended the kiss moments after he started it, his cock already beginning to harden, opening his eyes to see hers closed, her lovely face dreamy, her breaths escalated, feeling her fingers clenched into his sweater at his back and her breasts pressed tight to his chest.

And his cock continued to harden.

"That, my sweet," he whispered, "is why I didn't kiss you."

Slowly, her eyes opened and the dreamy was still there, as was the moonlight and fear.

Enchanting.

She didn't move away and he knew why when she breathed, "That was the best kiss I've ever had."

Unfortunately, in their current situation and as short as it was, he could say the same and he'd had vast amounts more experience than her.

"Do you want more?" he asked, knowing the answer. He could see it, feel it, and smell it.

"Absolutely," she answered.

"Again, Aurora, that's why I didn't kiss you."

Confusion glided into her features as she peered up at him. "I don't understand."

"A kiss like that leads to other things. We need to focus our minds elsewhere. Now, you need to be very good, leave me and go back to your mother. As arranged, I'll join you in half an hour."

"Why can't you just take me to go get Mom and the others when it's time to leave?"

He dipped closer and slid his hand at her jaw back into her hair, against her scalp, under her soft, thick bun.

He also pressed his now-swollen shaft into her belly.

"Because," he whispered, watching her eyes widen, knowing he need say no more. "Now, go," he ordered.

She studied his face for long moments before she nodded and said, "Okay, Yuri."

As he loosened his arms, she pulled from them, and he felt a curious sensation of loss when she did. He ignored it and turned to watch her walk to the door.

When she had her hand on the knob, he called, "Aurora."

She turned back to him, and finally, Yuri addressed the real reason she came to him.

"I die before you," he vowed, but he wasn't done. "And I do not die tonight."

Her entire demeanor calmed right before his eyes, and as he watched it, he felt another curious sensation, this being an odd mixture of pleasure and relief.

He felt something else curious (and wonderful) when she replied, "Right back at you," before she disappeared behind the door.

Thirty minutes later, Yuri walked into Aurora's charming bungalow and stopped dead.

"Bloody hell," he muttered at what he saw.

Primarily, Aurora standing amongst a bevy of women, and gone was the delightful chignon at the nape of her neck. Gone also were the lovely garments she'd been wearing.

In their place were black jeans, a black turtleneck, her hair shoved under a black knit cap, and she even had black smudges marring the rose and cream of her face.

Her witch sisters were similarly attired.

Yuri, too, had on much the same outfit—a black V-neck sweater and black slacks—however, he'd donned them that morning as a matter of course.

"Are we approaching a coven or a terrorist cell?" he drawled, shutting the door behind him.

Aurora giggled, a sound that had a pleasant effect in two very different places in his body.

"This operation is covert," one of the witches hissed at him. Yuri vaguely recalled her name was Jane.

"Indeed," he murmured but decided to say no more.

"Right, let's start this," another witch, named Jordana, stated and looked to Yuri. "Remember, we get the protections down before you approach. We may need your speed and strength and we don't need you going up in a ball of flame before that."

Yuri wholeheartedly agreed with any plan that included him not going up in a ball of flame.

"As we finalized plans not twenty-four hours ago, I do recall them," he assured her.

She sniffed and did it with her eyes on him as if she smelled something foul and it was emanating from him.

He sighed, walked further in, and pinpointed Barb with his gaze.

It was time to share what he'd decided between Aurora's visit to his suite and his arrival at the bungalow.

"Aurora stays with me and doesn't approach until it's safe."

"Yuri!" Aurora cried.

"Agreed," Barb stated over her daughter's cry.

Aurora turned sharply to her mother. "Mom!"

Barb turned calm eyes to her daughter. "Leave this to your elders."

"I've got juice," Aurora snapped. "I can help. I *want* to help."

Barb completely ignored her and looked to Yuri. "If something happens to me, you'll see to her."

Yuri gave one short nod. "Until she dies."

Barb immediately looked relieved and this was an expression Yuri didn't much care for considering it told the tale of how uncertain she was about the outcome of that evening's events.

"Yuri," Aurora whispered, taking his mind off Barb and onto her.

She didn't look peeved anymore. Under her black smudges, her face was soft, and around the delicate makeup still adorning her eyes, her gaze was warm.

"It wouldn't be a hardship, my sweet, considering I'm a billionaire."

Those warm eyes got wide and her lips parted.

Taking her in...*fuck*.

He was looking forward to fucking her.

"Centuries and nothing changes. Put a vampire in close proximity to a comely witch, shit happens," an elderly witch, her name Yuri believed was Ruby, muttered. "I just hope this isn't the beginnings of history repeating itself."

"Considering I have a few centuries on you and I was actually alive during said history, incidents my father kept me privy to while they were happening, I'll share that the dispute began when a witch accrued a vast amount of debt, found herself in dire circumstances, and spelled her vampire lover to dispatch those who held her debts. Alas, one of those had a wife who was also a witch. She cast a different spell on the vampire and this unfathomably ended with five vampires being burned at the stake," Yuri noted.

"One bad apple," Ruby mumbled.

"In that story, there were two," Yuri pointed out wryly. "However, upon hearing it, quite a number of other witches cast their lot, spelling their vampire lovers, or simply vampires they were aware of, to do their nefarious bidding, which saw one hundred and fifteen vampires burned or beheaded at the hands of witches and their partners."

Ruby's eyes narrowed on him. "And this excuses centuries of persecution?"

"Do not ever test a vampire," Yuri whispered, and the room went still. "Your kind tested mine, exerting power over them, forcing vampires to bend to their will and do their bidding. Your ancestors knew that was playing with fire. They got burned. I disagree with how and just how long that fire raged. But it's been centuries. Tonight, we have a common mission, therefore, at least for this evening, shall we call bygones?"

"Whatever," she muttered and looked away.

"Let's prepare," Barb called, thankfully putting an end to that discussion.

Yuri sighed and moved further into the room as he'd been instructed to do the night before.

The women surrounded him and his eyes sought Aurora's. Her hands were up and white-hot and burnt-orange sparks were glittering between them. All the witches started muttering, chanting, so mote it being and then the sparks burst forth around him, glinting on his clothes and against his skin before they were gone.

"Right, that's done. Let's roll," Barb ordered, and everyone moved to the door. Barb looked to Yuri. "You're in van two, driving. Aurora is with you."

He said nothing. Only when he felt and smelled Aurora coming to his side, did he murmur, "Why the lot of them consistently remind me of things I know, I cannot imagine."

"They're nervous," Aurora murmured back.

Excellent. Nervous witches.

They were fucked.

A vampire never got nervous. Or at least Yuri never knew one to do so, including himself.

Therefore, he calmly climbed behind the wheel of one of the three black vans parked at the front of Aurora's house. Aurora climbed in beside him as four witches climbed in the back.

Their convoy was on their way before Aurora remarked, "I'm prepared to go in with them. Do my bit."

"You'll wait until you're cleared to do so," Yuri replied.

He knew she'd turned to face him when she stated, "I know what they're up against and I'm not afraid."

She was lying. He could smell it.

However, she was brave. He could smell that too. And in that moment, facing whatever they were to face that night, he wanted to stop the van, gather her in his arms, and absorb both until he knew he'd never forget either, even if he lived until the sun fell from the sky.

He gave no indication these were his thoughts. He kept his eyes on the road as he returned, "That may be so, but you'll wait until you're cleared."

Her voice held a soft snap when she shot back, "Yuri, I'm not a child."

That was when he looked at her. "No, you're not." He returned his gaze to the road but kept speaking. "However, you're young. You have much life ahead of you and that life, God willing, will be beautiful. Your mother loves you, she wants that for you, she's worried about you, and she does not need to face that coven with her mind on you. So you'll wait until you're cleared."

She made an adorable exasperated sound but said no more.

Yuri joined her in silence, and within an hour, they arrived at the designated stopping place. All alighted from the vehicles and Barb and Jane approached Yuri as Aurora made it around the van and stopped at his side.

"Hopefully, they'll only have three or four guarding the implements," Barb said to him. "But word on the witch vine is that they hang here so we'll undoubtedly be facing more. You need to get close so you can sense us. If things turn, that spell we cast on you will deflect two, at most three direct hits from them. You take them running and get my daughter out of here."

Yuri nodded.

Barb turned to her sisters and called quietly, "We ready?"

She got a lot of "Yeps," "Yeahs," and "Readys," and they moved.

Yuri took hold of Aurora's elbow and trailed up the rear.

After some trudging, the witches stopped at a bank of trees and looked back at them, which was when Yuri knew that was where he and Aurora were to stop. He tugged gently at Aurora's arm and she came to a halt beside him.

"Careful, Mom," she called.

"Always, sweetheart," Barb called back.

"Love you," Aurora went on.

"Same," Barb finished.

The witches moved into the shadows.

Yuri looked through those shadows and saw the house. Not a hovel, not a mansion. It was nondescript, old, established, comfortable-looking, alone in the middle of nowhere, and not something that would catch attention.

Not that it would, having a lane off a narrow rural road that meandered half a mile to the house.

It was several minutes after the witches disappeared when Aurora whispered, "Okay, I'm a little freaked."

He'd known this since she'd visited his suite, but he was pleased she had the courage to admit it.

He slid his hand down her forearm to catch hers and murmured soothingly, "Calm, button."

Her hand spasmed in his, and still whispering, she asked, "Button?"

He looked to her. "You. As cute as."

There was no spasm of the hand at that. Her fingers simply tightened their grip and didn't let go.

Yuri returned the gesture even as he returned his attention to the shadows, listening, feeling.

"Anything?" Aurora asked after more minutes passed.

"No." He squeezed her hand.

More minutes passed.

"Anything?" she repeated.

"No, my sweet," he murmured.

More minutes passed.

"Any—" Aurora began just as a shaft of violet light shot from a window of the house and pierced the dark sky, straight to the heavens.

And that was when it hit him in a wave so violent, it knocked him back on a foot.

Fear.

And agony.

"No no no no no," Aurora chanted, and he knew it was strong enough, she'd felt it too. Then came a terrified, tormented, "*Mom.*"

"Fuck," Yuri bit out, took the van key from his pocket and turned to her. "Back to the van. Get in, start it. You get a bad feeling, go."

"Yur—"

He caught her at the back of the neck with his vampire speed, bending and yanking her to within an inch of his face.

"*Go,*" he growled.

He let her loose, and maddeningly, as she was wont to be, she didn't run as he instructed, and this time, he didn't find it charming.

Her voice dripping with fear, the rest of her reeking of it, she asked, "What if they haven't gotten the protections down?"

"There's little time, Aurora," he warned.

She latched onto his arm. "What if they haven't gotten the protections down? You'll burn, Yuri."

"Then be prepared to stop me from doing that if I make it to the van and I'm on fire," he replied. "Now, go."

"But—"

"*Go!*" he thundered.

She wasted a precious second, then turned and ran.

Yuri ran the other way.

Toward the clashing covens.

He was far faster.

Within an instant, he was at the door, and without hesitation, he burst through.

What he didn't do was burst into a ball of flame.

What he did do was take in the state of play which, unfortunately, was grimmer than he'd suspected.

The coven that guarded the implements was not formidable.

It appeared they were invincible.

He dashed over Jane's dead body, sensing and speeding toward Barb, who was hanging upside down at the top of the stairs, her frame contorted in unnatural ways, her face twisted in agony, her mouth opened in a silent scream.

He located the witch spelling her, made it to her in a millisecond, snapped her neck in less time than that, and Barb was falling.

Before she hit the stairs and broke her neck, Yuri caught her, raced out of the house, and dropped her to the grass by the side of the van.

"Mom!" He heard Aurora shout from inside the van.

He also heard her moving.

And last, he heard Barb beg, "Help them."

Yuri caught her anguished eyes, jerked up his chin, and sprinted back.

When he arrived, in short order he found Jane was lost. Jordana was as well. Ruby was still fighting, and apparently losing, until Yuri dispatched the witch she was battling, then grabbed hold of her and deposited her back at the van before he went back to the house.

He then dispatched six of the opposing coven, and while doing it, saw that eight of Barb's coven were gone.

He vaguely felt the blast of a spell and knew he was under attack. He slayed the witch who'd spelled him only to feel the blast of another spell. He dealt with her too before he heard something that made his blood turn to ice.

"Yuri, watch out!"

He was hit with another spell that deflected as he turned to see a witch with her hand up, a ball of red and blue fire floating in her palm, her aim: Aurora.

In a flash, the warm gush of blood spraying his torso, the witch's body was at his feet, but her head was in his hands.

Then Aurora screamed and shoved both hands forward. A shimmering wall of undulating white and glittering vermillion and silver burst forth, moving through him, and Yuri looked over his shoulder to see a ball of deep blue slam against it and ricochet back, hitting the witch who threw it, making her immediately burst into flame.

"Fuck," he clipped, sprinted to the witch and shoved a hand through the fire and into her chest with such force, she flew backward through a wall and outside, where he heard her short scream as she fell.

He also heard her scream die when she landed.

He raced back, hooked Aurora at the waist, and felt her body move like a ragdoll as he bolted through the house, locating the last of the enemy coven and eliminating them, all with Aurora held close to his side, her arms locked around him.

He stopped, dragged in a deep breath, and opened his senses.

There were humans alive in that house, not many, but they were all from Barb's coven.

The rest were dead.

He put Aurora to her feet, whispering, "It's clear."

"Thank the goddess," she whispered back.

At the sound of her voice, Yuri let her go and took a step from her as he took in another breath.

A breath that didn't work.

Therefore, he bent toward her and roared, *"Are you out of your mind?"*

Her body gave a jerk before her expression turned placating and she said softly, "Yuri, I was just—"

"Living out a death wish?" he finished for her irately.

"No, I wanted to—"

"See the end of your days?"

"Let me—"

His voice turned deathly cold when he informed her, "You'd already earned a spanking, my sweet. This fucking stunt," he threw out a hand to indicate the house they were in, "means writhing."

She blinked and asked, "What?"

He bent closer. *"Writhing,"* he hissed. "What you'll be doing, along with begging, before I allow release."

Her eyes rounded as he heard her pulse spike. "I—"

"Nearly got us both killed."

She straightened her shoulders. "I saved your life."

"Something that would not have occurred if I hadn't first saved yours," he retorted.

Her eyes shifted side to side before they fell to his throat and she admitted, "That's kinda true."

"There's nothing '*kinda*' about it," he clipped.

She lifted her gaze. "I was worried about you."

"And this, my sweet, is the only reason you'll be writhing and begging for hours rather than days."

"Yur—"

"Is the coast clear?" They heard Barb call from downstairs, and Yuri clasped Aurora about the waist again, dragging her to him, and took her with vampire speed to the bottom of the stairs.

There, Barb, Ruby, and one of the other remaining members of their sisterhood stood. The other witch was bent to the last survivor, who was unconscious on the floor of the foyer.

"Okay, that didn't go too good," Ruby muttered.

Yuri kept Aurora clamped tight to his side as he took in Ruby, then slowly turned his infuriated gaze to Aurora's mother.

"Were you aware they were that formidable?" he asked.

She had the good grace to look abashed before she answered, "I had an inkling."

He let that go and noted with false calm, "According to the intelligence you reported to me last night regarding their numbers, the entire coven was here."

"Apparently, they were having a party," Barb shared.

Yuri gritted his teeth.

"That was good," Barb noted. "They were involved in that, which meant we could get their protections down so you could get in and help."

"Indeed. You achieved that, leading your daughter to it and your sisters to slaughter," he grated.

"And our other option was what?" she snapped back.

"Gather more intelligence and hit them when their numbers were fewer," Yuri returned.

"We can't sit on this house. They'd know," she retorted. "We had to go with what we had and hope for the element of surprise. The Sacred Triumvirate has been united. There was no time to waste and we both know that."

He couldn't argue that, but that didn't mean he was done.

"Regardless of popular culture saying otherwise, I do not relish taking the lives of twelve living beings," he bit off. "And you lost eight."

"I'm standing," she shot back. "That doesn't mean my heart isn't bleeding."

Yuri snapped his mouth shut.

Tense moments passed before Aurora asked quietly, "What do we do now?"

Yuri took in Barb and Ruby and noted the other one was helping her now-conscious sister to her feet.

"You four, find the implements and secure them," he ordered. "I'll call The Vampire Council and have them send someone to deal with the carnage."

"Witches require a pyre," Ruby told him.

"That will be arranged," Yuri replied, "for all of them." He looked back to Barb. "How is this going to read on your witch vine?"

"The quieter we can keep it, the better it will be," she answered.

Yuri pulled in a breath before deducing, "They have allies."

"Pretty much everyone is scared of them, but a vampire taking out a coven isn't gonna go over too great, even if the true story is told and nobody much liked this coven," Barb shared.

"Fuck," he murmured and felt Aurora's small hand curl around his.

"We should finish the mission," she said gently. "Get this done. Cover our sisters, do a blessing over them, get the implements safe, and get home."

Finally, she said something smart.

Yuri gently pulled his hand from hers and shoved it in his pocket to retrieve his phone. "Go. See to the implements. I'll call The Council."

A call he did not relish making. His father would be pleased the implements were secured. He would not be the same about the bloodbath.

He'd engaged his phone but had not pushed any buttons when he felt a light hand on his arm.

He looked down at Aurora even as he sensed her mother and the others moving to search for the implements.

"Thank you for saving Mom," she whispered. "And me. And well..." She squeezed his arm. "All the rest." Her voice turned melancholy. "What's left of us, that is."

He regarded her and took his time doing it, before he lifted a hand and trailed the tip of his middle finger from her temple, along the apple of her cheek, to the side of her lip. Once he made that destination, he dropped his hand but dipped his face close to hers.

"You should be aware, Aurora, that when I'm angry at you, being sweet will do much to tame that emotion," he told her quietly.

She nodded, drawing in breath through her nose, and he easily read she was relieved.

"However, when I'm furious at you," he continued, "being sweet will only fan that flame."

She bit her lip and he watched her do it, therefore, he had more to say.

"And being adorable will make it worse," he carried on.

"Maybe I should leave you to your phone call," she suggested.

"I would run with that," he agreed.

She nodded, removed her hand from his arm, and swiftly moved away from him.

With iron control, Yuri didn't watch her go but turned his attention to his phone.

This didn't last a second before he heard Aurora call, "Yuri?"

He lifted his eyes to see her—her black clothing, her ridiculous knit cap, and her utterly preposterous black smudges—standing halfway up the steps, looking down at him.

"I know you're mad, but my thank-you still stands. If it wasn't for you, I don't...I mean, it doesn't bear..." She trailed off and he sensed the sorrow saturating her soul because he could smell it in his nostrils and taste it down his throat.

Therefore, within half a second, he was one step below her. As she gasped at his sudden proximity, he laid his hands gentle on her cheeks and pulled her to him. He bent and kissed one glistening eye, then moved and kissed the next.

He kept hold of her face as he urged, "I'll comfort you when we've finished our mission. Now, you must go. Help your sisters."

She held his eyes, hers brimming with tears, before she nodded, pulled free, turned, and continued to walk up the stairs.

Yuri watched until she disappeared.

Then he again pulled out the phone he'd put back into his pocket, engaged it, moved his thumb across the screen, and put it to his ear.

Her body jolted against his and Yuri opened his eyes to the dark.

He folded her closer.

"Sleep, button," he murmured.

"Mom," she breathed.

"Your mother is safe in the other room."

And this she was, slumbering in the other bedroom attached to his suite, with Ruby and the other two in another suite on that floor. In the hall stood a guard of vampire soldiers, complements of The Vampire Council.

Aurora, however, was in his bed with him. Somewhere she'd gone without demur (not a surprise) and somewhere her mother had allowed her to go without a fight (a definite surprise).

Another surprise was that she'd slid between the sheets—her little frame enveloped in one of his shirts—and promptly passed out.

"I'm dreaming that feeling," she whispered.

He knew what she meant and wished he could wash it away from her.

He couldn't.

All he could do was remind her, saying, "Your mother is safe in the other room."

She pressed closer. "Jane. Marianne. Jordana—"

Yuri cupped her cheek with his hand, pressing it to his chest as he tightened his other arm around her, and murmured, "Shh, sweet. It's done and there's no undoing it. You have work ahead of you, and what little I knew of those women, forging in to face what they knew they might face, they'd want you to rest so you can focus on that and quickly get to where your memories of them are comforting, not solemn."

"Yeah," she mumbled. "They would."

"So close your eyes, Aurora." He slid his hand into her hair and through it, then back. "Sleep," he finished, continuing to run his fingers through her long, silken hair.

She pressed closer, winding an arm around his middle, before she relaxed into him.

Yuri continued to run his fingers soothingly through her hair.

"You feel good." Her voice was muffled against his chest, sounding mostly asleep. "All warm and hard and soft and nice."

Yuri kept his gaze to the ceiling, continuing his ministrations with her glorious hair, and fought getting hard in the way she was not describing.

Her weight pressed into him as sleep claimed her.

Only then did he succeed.

# 20
# You Want That, Don't You?

*Delilah*

I wandered naked out of the bathroom and saw my man in bed, his back against some pillows shoved up against the headboard, one leg straight, one leg bent, also naked, totally hot, eyes on me.

I went to the bed, put a knee in and then the other, and walked on them to him as he watched. When I got close, I swung a leg around him, straddling him, and rested against him, tucking my face in the side of his neck, wrapping one arm around him, laying the other hand on his chest.

Abel curled both arms around me.

Post-morning-sex snuggling.

The best.

"I think Moose wants his own vampire," I told his throat.

I felt his body move with his amusement and I gloried in the feel.

"Your dad's been sharin'," he guessed.

"Yeah," I confirmed.

"Hook caught the eye of one and there're tons of 'em around. Probably won't be hard for Moose to get his own."

Using my index finger, I drew mindless patterns on the warm silk of his skin, muttering, “That’d be good. Might keep him around and out of trouble.”

He gave me a squeeze and whispered, “You worried.”

Absolutely, I worried. We’d lost Snake. I didn’t even want to imagine losing someone else I loved.

I thought this.

I said, “Yeah.”

“He’s home now,” Abel pointed out.

“Yeah,” I repeated.

Abel started drawing his own mindless patterns on the skin at the small of my back.

I had no idea, but I’d put up a good argument that he did it better.

“What’d you do before me?” I blurted, not knowing where it came from, just knowing it came out.

His fingers stopped. “What?”

I pressed my hand flat on his pec, lifted my head, and looked down at him.

“Before me, before this,” I began to explain. “What did you do to make your way in life? You know, your business that wasn’t messy.”

His eyes shuttered as his mouth muttered, “Cuddled close, sneak attack.”

That didn’t sound good.

“Abel?” I prompted.

He looked at me as he slid a hand over my hip to my belly, up between my breasts, and up where he curled it around the side of my neck.

“Did whatever I could do,” he stated cautiously. “Someone needed somethin’, I got it for them. Someone needed somethin’ delivered, I delivered it. Someone needed information, I got it.”

“I...” I shook my head. “For money?”

“Depending on what it was and who it was for, money or markers,” Abel explained, still watching my face closely. “Xun, Wei, and Chen did their bit, getting a lock on the lay of the land, so by the time I showed, we knew who was who and how they fit. If it was a big player who it would be good they owed markers, that's what we asked for. If it was somethin' else or dangerous for a mortal, but it wouldn't be dangerous for me, we asked for money, and not a small amount of it."

"Oh," I mumbled, not knowing what else to say.

"You gotta have it all, *bao bei,* so I'll tell you that, outside the information which I couldn't help but knowing, I didn't get involved. I didn't know what I was delivering. I didn't pay attention to what I was finding. I did the job. I didn't take sides. We were free agents. We worked for anyone. We kept out of it. And if needed, I made a statement when someone would try to drag us in."

"What does that mean?" I asked.

"They needed the hurt put on them to make the point, I did that too."

"Oh," I mumbled again, that syllable a lot more tentative.

Using his hand at my neck, Abel gave me a squeeze and a shake.

"It's the only thing I could do to take care of my family," he declared fiercely. "We moved around a lot. Jian-Li could cook, as could her mother before her, but it takes time to establish a restaurant. By the time things would be rolling with that, we couldn't enjoy it long before we had to leave. It's not easy to set up house and a restaurant every decade or so. And I don't die. I couldn't be on the grid in any way. I have no social security number. No birth certificate. I couldn't go to college, be a doctor, a lawyer. You live out in the open like that, people could cotton on. I could take money under the table. Be a day laborer. But they make shit. We needed more. So I did what I had to do to take care of my family."

I had no reply mostly because there wasn't one. I could see this. I could even understand it.

Abel took my non-response the wrong way.

"I knew the information I found and shared. I knew the men who asked me to deliver shit were not good citizens so I could guess what I was delivering wasn't food for the needy. But I did what I had to do."

"Became an outlaw," I said.

"Yeah," he grunted.

"We all do what we have to do, Abel," I remarked, and his head twitched. "I mean, my mom isn't the greatest mom in the history of momkind, but she's my mom. And to be healthy, I don't see her much. I know she doesn't like this. She isn't the greatest mom and it isn't good that she wants me around mostly to bitch about Dad and make me feel like I'm nuts. But in her way, she also loves me, likes my company, so she feels our break. It isn't healthy to be with her so I struggle with that being the wrong choice, but I feel in my heart it's the only one."

"It isn't the wrong choice," he told me.

I grinned. "It isn't to you because you kinda like me, and all that's in your head is looking after me. But it is because she's my mom. The only one I'll ever have. She might not take me as I come without giving me shit about who I am, but that doesn't make it right that I don't take her as she comes. Two wrongs, no right."

"Seein' with your mom, you're too sweet for your own good," he muttered.

I decided to let it go. Dad felt the same. He didn't think I should hold any guilt for cutting Mom out of my life (for the most part).

Dad was wrong too.

I didn't discuss it with him either.

"My point is, you shouldn't worry about what you did," I advised. "I could tell you didn't want to give that to me, but that only means you're a good person and you know it's what you had to do, not what you wanted to do or got off on doing. So don't worry about it."

It was then he declared, "That shit ends when all this other shit ends and I got you to look after too."

I gave him another grin and snuggled closer, whispering, "I kinda like bein' hooked up with an outlaw."

He let his eyes drift away, muttering, "Says the biker's daughter."

I gave him a squeeze and got his gaze back, happy to see it was smiling.

That done, I kept at it, thinking I might as well get it all out in one fell swoop.

"Taking us out of the heavy and into more heavy, you gotta know we're covered, birth control-wise, since I'm on the Pill. You take me ungloved, you've never done anything but, so I'm assuming since you can't get sick or catch disease, you can't give anything to me. But the time was ripe about two weeks ago for me to make certain of that, so obviously, now, I need to make certain of it."

He slid his hand up into my hair, tucking my forehead back into the side of his neck as he shared, "You're safe with that and you're right. I don't catch anything. I don't carry anything." He paused and his voice was quiet, his hold strong, when he finished, "And sucks, baby, hate to share this with you, but you gotta know, if you want, you can go off the Pill. I can't get you pregnant either."

I blinked at his throat. "Yes, you can."

"*Bao bei*," he said gently, giving my head a squeeze, "I can't. Won't go into specifics of how I know, but trust me, I know."

I pushed against his hand to look at him. "Werewolves can get humans pregnant. Sonia told me so."

"Vampires can't get them pregnant and I'm half vampire."

"Then why are Lucien and Leah prophesied to have a brood of kids?"

His big, hard body stilled under mine.

Completely.

And when he spoke, I actually felt the effort it took for him to force out the word.

"What?"

"Uh...you didn't know?"

"Fuck no," he snarled.

"Abel—"

He cut me off by knifing up, forcing me to right myself in his lap, and his fingers clamped around my hips.

"Are we prophesied to have kids?" he asked.

"Um...when Leah told me that, she said we weren't mentioned. I mean, obviously, they're only going to be able to do that if they both survive this mess, which they will. And she also told me that normally vampires have trouble procreating, and never with humans. But things are changing and—"

"You and me bein' special, we might be able to have kids," he finished for me.

"Maybe," I whispered.

Staring into his eyes, both of them brown, I was warmed to my soul by the light shining there.

"A family. My own family, my own blood. Sons and daughters who could be that for eternity."

I stared at him.

God, how he'd suffered.

*God.*

I lifted my hands to his jaw and whispered, "Not a definite, honey, but maybe."

"Go off the Pill now."

I felt my eyes get huge.

"Uh...what?"

"Now," he clipped, then declared, "We got a shot, we're takin' every shot we can get."

"Just a reminder, the state of the world is kinda shaky," I told him.

"It's gonna get un-shaky and I'm gonna plant my babies inside you and we're gonna have a family."

Wouldn't that be *awesome*?

I slid my thumb under his cheekbone and asked softly, "You want that, don't you?"

His eyes narrowed in a way that was kind of frightening even as his fingers clenched the flesh of my hips.

"Don't you?"

"Fuck yeah, you're hot. Your kids'll be gorgeous."

His hands relaxed, his gaze softened and grew warm, and his tone gentled when he said, "Make little girls who look like you, spoil 'em rotten."

Oh God.

*Wouldn't that be awesome?*

I melted into him. Abel felt it and twisted us so I was on my back, sideways on the bed, and Abel was covering me.

"You want that, don't you?" he whispered.

"Yeah," I whispered back.

"Off the Pill," he ordered again, gentler this time.

"But—"

"Off. The. Pill," he repeated, not quite as gentle, so I knew I had to proceed with caution.

"Okay, according to Sonia, werewolves are prolific," I started quietly. "Vampires are not, but you have two halves to you. I see both traits in you. Anything can win out."

"And...?" he pushed when I quit speaking.

"We make a deal," I proposed. "I go off the Pill when we finish saving the world."

"Lilah—" he started but stopped when I suddenly lifted both hands to the sides of his head and lifted mine off the bed so my face was closer to his.

"If something happened to you, I'd want that. I'd want that piece of you inside me, knowing I had a bit of you to hold with me for the rest of my life. But I have to think of him, or her, and what I think is, my man watched mother after mother die and I would not want that for my kid, not once, not ever."

His expression softened, but I wasn't done.

"I'm also thinking of you, baby. If this goes on for a while and you get me knocked up and something happens to me, you lose me and you lose that life we created. You've lost enough. I don't want you to court losing more."

His expression got a lot less soft.

"Nothing's gonna happen to you," he growled.

"Maybe not. But give me this, let's prepare for the maybe, because if it did, I couldn't bear knowing you endured more than you had to."

"And what about you with me? What if you lose me?" he asked, and pain sliced through my insides, white-hot, boiling them until they felt liquefied.

"Don't say that again," I wheezed through the pain.

I watched his expression register understanding before he pressed his body into mine. "Right here, pussycat. All me, right here. Feel me and let the pain go."

"Yeah." I pushed out, feeling him, letting his weight bear into me, and also feeling the pain lessen.

Abel shoved a hand under me and up so he could stroke the side of my neck with his thumb.

He gave it time, then asked, "Better?"

I nodded.

"Wrapped around your finger," he said bafflingly.

"Uh...what?"

"You want that, what you asked for? Wrapped around your finger. In other words, *bao bei*, you have a deal."

I closed my eyes tight and slid my hands from his head to wrap my arms around him.

I opened them and whispered, "Thank you, Abel honey."

"The minute we save the world," he stated firmly and I smiled, the pain gone, and squeezed him with my arms.

"Pills in the toilet the minute we save the world."

He grinned before he dropped his head to kiss me.

He was in the middle of doing it, and I was in the middle of liking it a lot, when his phone sounded. It wasn't his ringer. It was something else.

He lifted his head, his eyes going to the nightstand, his lips muttering, "Fuck."

"What?"

He looked to me. "Those kids Moose found?"

"Yeah."

"Told them what to do. They did it. Now we got eyes and ears in that vampire's house. Since we found Patricio and Bjorn, I went through every vampire, every wolf, every human at the compound to make sure we got them all. We did, but still, Callum wants only the inner circle to have eyes on that house. That alarm means I'm up. I'm supposed to take a shift, watch and listen. That alarm means I got half an hour to get down there."

Crap, just when we were out of the heavy and into the good stuff.

"I'll keep you company," I offered.

"Probably gonna be boring," he warned.

"Will you be there?" I asked and saw his eyes again warm. "So it won't be boring," I finished.

"You know what else isn't gonna be boring?" he asked, and I shook my head. "The shower we're about to take."

"Right on," I breathed right before I was out of bed and in the shower.

My man.

So.

*Awesome.*

"Uh...what'd you say about boring?" I asked.

Abel, whose lap I was perched on, murmured in disgust, "Jesus."

I stared at the television screen that was transmitting what was right then occurring in the vampire Miko's house, this being him bending a young man, who had his jeans around his thighs, over a table and taking him hard up the ass.

Miko was the enemy, but he was a vampire so he was gorgeous, built, and endowed.

Thus, that was *hot*.

I squirmed in Abel's lap.

"Fuck, is that shit turning you on?" he asked.

I didn't tear my eyes away from the screen as I answered, "It doesn't you?"

"Take you any way you want me to fuck you, baby, but guy-on-guy..." Abel paused. "Not my scene."

Obviously, I was down with that.

But still.

"You don't have to do it to get off on it," I shared.

"Uh, thinkin' you do," he mumbled.

I decided not to respond because he had a dick. He would know.

"Christ, least he could do is give the kid a coupla days to recover before he went at him," Abel kept mumbling.

I fought another squirm as I watched Miko bend over the guy he was doing, latch onto his hair with a fist, and yank his head back. The guy had two black eyes and a cut lip, but this didn't disguise the fact that he was feeling no pain, except maybe the kind he liked a whole lot.

"You wanted my cock. Rear back, fuck yourself as I fuck you," Miko ordered.

"I'm not sure Miko is the soul of kindness and consideration," I murmured, struggling against the squirm as his fucktoy did as ordered and that shit got hotter.

"Christ," Abel grumbled.

When he got what he wanted, Miko gave him his reward. Bending deeper, yanking his hair so his neck was arched unnaturally, he bared his fangs and sunk them in to feed.

His toy came immediately, bucking violently on the table even as Miko kept thrusting.

I bit my lip and lost the fight against the squirm.

"See I might have to take the hit of askin' one of the staff to get us some lube," Abel griped.

I tore my eyes from the screen and smiled down at my man.

"Don't act like you don't want that."

"Told you, I'll fuck you however you want. I try to take your ass though, baby, might have that shit in my head and I'm thinkin' you might not like the results of that."

I dipped closer. "I'll see what I can do to keep your mind on me."

"Fuck yeah! Fuck yeah! Fuck! Fuck! Give me that! Fuck yeah!" We heard coming from the direction of the screen. It wasn't Miko's voice, seeing as Miko was groaning an unmistakable groan that his partner made clear he liked giving to him.

I watched Abel's eyes frown even as I knew my eyes kept smiling.

Abel shook his head.

I bent deeper and touched my mouth to his before I turned in his lap to look back at the screen. I caught Miko pulling out none too gently and shoving the guy off the table. With his jeans around his thighs and after what just happened, he didn't have it in him to do much but throw a hand out to break his fall.

It was then I stopped enjoying what I was seeing.

Because the guy didn't go for his jeans. He rolled to his ass, lifting his eyes to Miko, and the look on his face was chilling.

Worship.

Sycophantic adoration that was not healthy in the slightest.

That guy would die for Miko. That guy had taken a beating from Moose, and even though Abel had wiped that memory from his mind, he was still battered and bruised and had taken what he'd just taken, then was tossed aside perfunctorily, not even being given a kiss.

And now, standing with his eyes pinned to a spot in the room we couldn't see with our cameras, stroking his own cock, keeping it hard, Miko said, "You. Next. Jeans to thighs, but I'm going to fuck your face."

Another young man came on screen and stood meekly in front of the vampire, pulling his jeans down to his thighs. Even though he did this without hesitation, Miko must have lost patience because he shoved the guy to his knees.

Then without any ado, gentleness, or even a hint he gave a shit, fisting his hand in the guy's hair, he commenced.

They were playthings, servicing him.

And they didn't care.

They loved it.

Worshiped it.

Would do anything for it.

"We shouldn't have let those guys loose," I whispered, not getting off on watching it now.

"You think?" Abel muttered.

"They need help." I looked to Abel. "If this is who they are, they should find a healthy relationship, settle down, adopt a baby."

"That's not what they want," Abel replied, a perpetual flinch on his face since he was still staring at the screen.

"What?"

He looked to me. "They're hangers."

"Hangers?"

"Those guys gave me a bad feeling so I talked to Lucien about it and he told me about them," Abel explained. "Hangers are humans who somehow sense the existence of vampires. They live on the edge of the vampire world, not being let in but wanting it, not understanding who we really are or *how* we really are."

He tipped his head to the screen and kept sharing.

"They want that. They want the gothic novel. They want to be used, abused, discarded. They want a vampire to treat them how they think vampires should act. Not just guys. Girls. And before you ask," he said the last quickly because I'd opened my mouth to speak, "Etienne knows this and he's recruited nearly all of them. The rest have gone to ground, understanding somewhere in their minds when their kind started disappearing that shit was going to get extreme. So they're lost to us because the ones Etienne has are getting exactly what they want, something none of the good guys—Lucien, Stephanie, Cosmo, Gregor, Yuri, me—would give them."

"Oh my God," I whispered.

"Yeah," he agreed. "Sucks."

"Those guys will do anything for that Miko vampire," I told him, which he probably already knew.

His eyes drifted back to the screen from which muffled moans were coming. "I got that."

I didn't look back to the screen. I looked out the window.

Well, one thing I could say, regardless that it took a nasty turn, the surveillance shift was not boring.

On that thought, the door opened and we heard Callum say, "Abel. Lilah. You're needed. Immediately."

I looked over Abel's shoulder and Abel twisted in his chair to do the same, so we both saw Callum standing in the door, Calder coming into the room.

"Calder will take the rest of your shift. We need you," Callum went on. "Now."

"What the fuck?" Calder muttered, his eyes to the monitors as Abel got out of the chair, taking me with him and putting me to my feet.

"Yeah, brother, not pretty," Abel muttered back as he grabbed my hand and started us toward the door.

Calder looked to Abel. "What you got is less pretty."

"Shit," Abel whispered as my body got tight.

We got through the door and Abel closed it behind us. But Callum wasn't waiting. He was already walking down the hall.

"Cal, what's goin' on?" Abel called after him as he pulled me with him, walking with long, swift strides to catch up.

"The True have made a move," Callum told the hall, then looked back to us, still moving. "And it's not a good one."

"What is it?" Abel snarled impatiently.

"It's not something to be discussed in the hall," Callum replied, again facing the hall.

"Cal—"

Callum looked back over his shoulder. "Hurry," he clipped.

We hurried. He took us to living room six, and when we entered, he closed the door and I glanced around, taking in all who'd gathered.

Chen was there, as were Wei and Xun. Lucien was there, as was Sonia. Ryon was there. Gregor was there. Stephanie was there.

Leah was not.

My eyes flew to Lucien. "Where's Leah?"

"She's indisposed," he grated harshly, and my heart stuttered. He looked to Callum. "And I must go to her. Let's get this done."

"Maybe Lilah shouldn't be here," Chen suggested quietly.

Oh no.

"Why?' I asked.

Chen didn't look at me, keeping his eyes to his brother. "Seriously, man, maybe Lilah should wait this out. You hear it, you decide."

Abel looked down to me, opening his mouth to speak.

I shook my head. "No. No way. I can't wait to know what's going on."

"It's gone viral," Wei stated, obviously losing patience, and Abel and I looked to him. "A video. All over the Internet. A site will take it down, another one will put it up. Chen was surfing, keeping his eyes on things, and found it."

"A concubine being drained," Stephanie spat, and I felt Abel's hand tense so tightly around mine, I thought he'd crush it. But I didn't do anything about it because I'd frozen solid. Stephanie kept going, "He raped her while he drained her. The 'her' being Myrna, Leah's cousin."

"Oh God, no," I whispered, falling back in horror until Abel jerked my hand and clamped an arm around my shoulders, holding me tight to his side.

"Almost the moment Chen found it, calls started coming in," Gregor said, and I looked to him. "Concubines are missing worldwide, including three other members of Leah's family."

"But, why them?" I asked, my voice pitched high. "They know about vampires. They *like* them."

"Those who call themselves The True think concubines are parasites, and I'm sorry, Lilah, as evidenced in that video, they do *not* like concubines," Gregor explained.

"Gregor has people working with the media," Callum put in. "They're trying to convince them this is a hoax in order to curtail mass hysteria."

"I'm annoyed our hand has been forced for we obviously don't wish to push the message that vampires don't exist while we're trying to decide how to share they do. But there's little time to consider it and The Council have all agreed," Gregor added.

"I really don't give a fuck what people think," Abel snarled, his eyes locked to Gregor. "What I wanna know is what you're doin' to get the concubines outta those vampires' hands."

"Everything we can," Gregor replied in a calming voice.

"Well, do more," Abel ground out and didn't wait for a response. He turned to me and declared, "You've had enough video viewing for today."

I nodded. I was not fired up to watch a woman murdered and raped at the same time, not ever, but absolutely not Leah's cousin.

I looked to Lucien. "While you deal here, can I go to Leah?"

"No," he bit off, then looked between Abel and Callum. "Brief me later. I need to see to my bride."

On that, with a gust of wind, he was gone.

I looked at the door that had slammed behind him, then to Sonia.

She felt my eyes, gave me hers, and they were bright.

I was right there with her.

Then suddenly, I wasn't.

Suddenly, I was enraged.

So enraged, I tore from Abel's hold and shrieked, "*Why are we standing around? We gotta stop this shit!*"

Iron arms clamped around me and I fought them even as I heard Abel order, "Go get Hook. Now."

"Let me go," I hissed, struggling against his hold. "We have to go get Miko. Mind-control him. Torture him. I don't care." I stilled and screeched, "*Make him tell us everything he knows!*"

"Your mate is quite the strategist," Callum murmured. "Fancy a drive?"

I whipped around in Abel's hold to see Callum looking at my man.

"Fuck yeah," Abel said.

"What?" I asked.

Callum looked to Wei, Xun, and Chen. "Play backup?"

"I'm in," Xun said immediately.

"In," Wei grunted.

Chen looked to Abel. "You leave me outta this, I'll never forgive you. No fucking joke."

"You're in," Abel declared.

I whipped back around to Abel.

"You're gonna go get him?" I asked.

"Keeping him in play and mining information would be preferable," Callum answered, and I twisted to look at him. "We court The True realizing we've turned Patricio with some of the things we ask him to do. Miko is free to do what he wishes, but we would see it all. However, when things change, you change with them."

"Let's go," Xun said impatiently.

"I'll round up Hook and Moose," Wei offered and didn't wait for anyone to accept. He took off, Chen following him.

"I'll pull together a team," Stephanie stated and looked to Gregor. "Coming?"

Gregor nodded and they moved out.

"She does not watch that video," Abel stated, and my attention went to him to see his on Sonia.

"She won't, Abel," Sonia replied.

Abel looked down at me. "I won't be long."

I nodded.

"Kiss," he ordered.

I rolled up on my toes and kissed him hard.

When I was done, he lifted and pressed his lips to my forehead before he looked over it and asked, "Ready?"

"Absolutely," Callum answered.

Abel smoothed the pad of his thumb over my jaw before he completely let me go.

Callum kissed Sonia's nose before he let her go.

Then they were gone.

*Yuri*

Yuri sat on the couch in his suite and watched Aurora, who was sitting on the couch opposite, leaning forward toward a wide, flat bowl in front of her on the coffee table. Strewn around the bowl were a large variety of bottles, vials, and tools, all of which she'd used.

She took up the vile of Abel's blood, unstoppered it, and poured it in the bowl.

A soft poof of gray, green, and red smoke wafted from it.

She put down the vial and looked to Yuri.

"Okay, that has to marinate for at least twenty-four hours, but thirty-six would make it stronger, which means we'd get a reading faster," she told him.

His reply was, "Come here."

Her head twitched before indecision marred her beautiful face. This didn't last long and she rose, slowly making her way to him.

Her hair was in a side ponytail, the curling, waving length of it falling down the front of her becoming blouse, which fit tight to her ribs and breasts. She was also wearing a circle skirt and high-heeled, platform pumps. She'd taken off the light cardigan she'd put on after he'd taken her home to pack and get the things she needed to start the procedure for finding Abel's brother.

He'd also taken Barb home. She was packing and moving into the other room in the suite in order for him to keep her safe as well. However, right then, she was with her witch sisters and a detail of vampire guards, taking the implements to a safe place and casting protection spells around them so no one could find them, and in the unlikely event they did, they couldn't get to them.

Gregor did not agree with this plan. He'd wanted Yuri to be in possession of the implements so that he could hand them off to a member of The Vampire Council Gregor sent in order that The Council could secure them.

It took some doing, but Yuri impressed on his father that it would not be diplomatically prudent to take witch implements from witches the day after a vampire had massacred an entire longstanding, powerful coven.

So Barb and her colleagues were sorting that, something she'd explained would take some time in order to find the right hiding place and make the protections strong.

She didn't expect to be back at the hotel until the next day.

Which gave Yuri plenty of time.

He tipped his head back to keep Aurora's gaze as she approached and stopped in front of him. Only then did he lean forward and wrap his hand around hers.

"If you need thirty-six hours, my sweet," he started quietly, "this means we have thirty-six hours to kill."

He took in her excitement mingled with nerves with all his senses. His favorites: seeing the pulse quicken in her neck, hearing her heart beating strong but fast, and smelling the scent that was uniquely hers gather between her legs.

The last told him all he needed to know.

"You have much to be punished for," he whispered, and her hand convulsed in his as her eyes grew alarmed. But the scent between her legs grew stronger, muskier, so he carried on, "You've played me."

"I haven't," she whispered back, and he tilted his head.

"No?"

Her teeth came out to bite her lower lip and his hardening cock went stiff.

"You have," he said softly. "And last night, you went against your mother's orders, my orders, and put yourself in danger."

"You were in danger too," she replied, her voice breathy.

"That's not the point," he returned, holding her eyes and tightening his fingers around hers. "You obey a vampire."

"Yuri," she whispered.

"Perhaps others don't expect that, but you must know I do."

"I..." She trailed off and he listened to her heartbeat escalate as she finished, "Okay."

"And if you don't, there are consequences," he continued.

She swallowed and the thrum of her pulse quickened.

"We have not begun," he said gently. "Not like this. Therefore, on this occasion, I'll give you a choice. One, your punishment will be me withholding myself from you. You shall wait here, order room service, watch television, read a book, and I'll leave, returning after your potion has matured. Only later, after we've located Abel's brother, will we move forward the way we both want."

"And my other choice?" she prompted huskily when he stopped speaking.

"You take your punishment as you would if we'd already begun," he answered instantly.

"That being...?" she pressed, and Yuri shook his head.

"No, my sweet," he said softly. "You don't know until you choose. That's part of the punishment. In future, when you will have no choice, not knowing the punishment until you earn it, and get it, will *always* be part of it."

Her blue eyes held his and he took her in—her agitation, her anticipation, her excitement—and he enjoyed every part of it.

Finally, she wet her lower lip and asked, "Will you be gentle with me?"

His sweet, little witch feared it, but she was up for it, wanted it, and that was *perfect*.

Yuri wanted to shout his elation.

Instead, he shared, "I will always be gentle with you, Aurora. You will not ever receive more than you can take."

She studied him.

Then she whispered, "Okay, then I pick option number two."

Staring into her eyes, slowly, Yuri smiled.

Aurora's heart skipped a beat.

"Lift your skirt and pull down your panties."

Aurora's heart tripped over itself.

"Now, my sweet," he ordered when she didn't move, and he released her hand.

He heard the soft pants blowing from her lips as she lifted her skirt at the sides. His eyes dropped there, but the folds were enough that he saw nothing as she hooked her thumbs in her panties and pulled them down.

His Aurora, always the tease.

One side of his lips hitched up.

The panties dropped to her ankles and his cock started throbbing.

"Step out of them," he commanded.

With less hesitation, she did as told.

He opened his thighs. "Closer, Aurora."

Rubbing her lips together, she moved between his legs.

Yuri bent forward and wrapped his hands around the backs of her knees, his head tipped far back to hold her gaze captive. Then he watched, he listened, he smelled, he heard her anticipation heighten as he slid his hands slowly up the backs of her thighs until he cupped her bare ass.

Her lips parted.

She liked his touch and he very much liked touching her.

He smoothed his thumbs against the soft skin at the sides of her cheeks. "This will be sore, Aurora," he noted, carefully taking in her response in order to ascertain if there was fear that was not the good kind, aversion, or anything to indicate she didn't desire that.

Instead, he got a waft of musk from between her legs that nearly had him lifting up her skirt and burying his tongue there.

Abruptly, he let her go and sat back.

"Over my knees," he demanded.

He again saw indecision before she watched him closely as she moved to his side. When she positioned to put a knee in the couch beside him, he gave her a short nod. He heard her breath catch as she looked away in order to finish arranging herself precisely as he wanted her over his thighs.

He reached out an arm, grabbed a toss pillow, and gently tucked it under her head, which was resting on the couch, her face turned away. This would not be his choice, but he allowed it. The next time, he'd demand she face him so he could watch her reaction to what he gave her.

"You may wish to hold on, sweet," he murmured.

Instantly, her hands came up and gripped the pillow at its sides.

When she had her hold, slowly, excruciatingly slowly, he slid a hand up the back of her thigh and up, until he'd bared her ass.

Perfection. So much so, he'd sink his fangs there.

Eventually.

But now, she'd earned different.

And he gave it to her, his hand landing on her cheek, filling the room with a sharp crack.

She jumped.

He drove his hand between her legs and found her, already wet.

Ready for it.

She moaned.

He gave her that until she was lifting her ass and grinding into his fingers that were drenched with her moisture, all this whimpering uncontrollably.

Only then did he go back to her ass.

She cried out, a sound that scored a path straight to his shaft, but she kept her ass lifted.

She was there, exactly where he wanted her.

Yuri smiled and he kept her there, taking her further until he did as he'd promised he'd do, her ass pink, her body writhing, her lips begging for release. It took some time. She'd held out beautifully.

But it was so spectacular, he needed more.

And it was time to give his little witch what she needed.

With his natural speed, he had her up, his cock out, and had her straddling him before he stopped her, her soaked cunt barely a hint against the tip of his cock.

She was blinking, recovering from the swiftness of her change in position, and only when he had her focus did he use his hands on her hips to slowly lower her down on his cock, filling her.

Taking her.

Bloody hell.

Finally, she was *his*.

He watched her head drop back and the pulse pound in her neck, that same pulse throbbing around his cock.

Fucking *divine*.

"Now, sweet," he murmured, his voice rough. The velvet feel of her was driving him mad, and it took a great deal for him to finish. "You take what you want."

She lifted her head and found his eyes. Hers were vague and heated. She placed her hands on his shoulders and whispered, "You feel good, Yuri. I want more."

"Then take it," he ordered.

"Okay," she breathed and moved.

Bliss.

Bloody fucking hell.

Digging his fingers into her hips, scraping them back to her ass, he coaxed her to go faster.

She didn't need a great deal of coaxing. She rode him, fast and hard, gliding her hands from his shoulders to his neck and up into his hair, fisting them there.

"Sweet goddess," she whimpered, pleasure suffusing her face, making the rose of her cheeks rosier, her fresh musk all he could smell, and it was beyond brilliant, so much so, she was fucking him and his mind was filled with that as well as the myriad ways he intended to fuck her.

"I want your mouth," he demanded.

She bent forward and gave him her mouth. He took it, thrusting his tongue inside to taste peaches and rain and Aurora just as she cried out with her orgasm, bucking against him, grinding onto his cock, her cunt gripping him and thrumming with the rapid beat of her heart.

He lifted, flipped her to her back on the couch, and powered hard and deep into her slick tightness until he groaned his release against her wet lips.

When the sensations moved through him, he slid his cheek along hers, down, until he could glide his lips along her jaw. He went up and captured her mouth, finally kissing her as he'd wanted from near the moment he met her, thoroughly and for a long time.

When he lifted his head, her eyes were still vague but replete, the light in them dimmed to an indolent glow.

It wasn't what he'd wanted to see.

It was better.

Yuri lifted a hand and stroked her jaw with his knuckles, feeling her body melt even further under his, before he dropped his hand to the tail of her hair and wrapped its softness around his fist.

"Are you going to be good for me from now on?" he asked.

"Uh...well, probably not," she whispered.

Again, very slowly, Yuri smiled.

Her eyes dropped to his mouth and watched. When he was done, they lifted back to his.

"You're not cute," she declared.

"No." He continued to smile. "I'm not."

"But you're hotter than I expected."

Excellent.

Yuri said nothing.

"No one's ever done that to me before," she admitted quietly, and again, Yuri had to bury his howl of elation.

"If that's the case, my sweet, there are a great number of things I intend to do to you that no one's ever done before."

"Sweet goddess," she breathed.

He bent and slid his nose down hers, holding her gaze.

"Shall we get started?" he asked.

"Now?" she asked back, her eyes widening.

"We have thirty-five and a quarter hours to kill," he answered.

"Then, yes," she breathed.

And again, very slowly, Yuri smiled.

Yuri shifted to his back in the bed, keeping his cock buried deep inside Aurora's wet sheath and settling her on top of him.

She snuggled closer and sighed.

He stroked her spine and listened to her heartbeat quiet.

After long moments, she murmured, "You're staying hard."

"That's because I'm not done fucking you."

She lifted her head and gave him big, blue eyes.

"Wow, vampires have stamina."

He lost count of how many times he'd done it that day, more than any in recent memory, he was certain, but he did it again.

He smiled.

She watched him do it and melted into him.

However, after she did that, she said, "I hate to say this, sweetheart, but that bowl needs to be checked and stirred occasionally. We've been busy. I should see to that."

He nodded, adding, "I should also probably feed you."

Not to mention, he needed to feed. Her pulse had been calling to him for hours.

He'd been introducing her to a variety of things she very much enjoyed. But she was young and obviously had little experience, so he would take his time introducing her to that.

He did not savor the idea of bagged blood.

But for Aurora, he'd endure it.

"I'll get the room service menu while I'm out there," she told him.

"Do that," he replied, lifted his head and brushed his mouth to hers.

Then he moved his hands to her waist and watched her face as he slid her off his shaft.

He'd learned in the past few hours that she liked him inside her and missed him when she lost him, and she didn't hide either.

All of which he relished.

"Hurry," he whispered.

She nodded and slid off him, but when she got to the end of the bed, she hesitated, curling the end of the sheet around her breasts.

More of what he relished. He could make her abandon all thought with what he was doing to her when he was pleasuring her, but now, she became Aurora. A hint uncertain and definitely shy, both utterly charming.

"My shirt," he said, and she looked his way. "Use my shirt, button."

"Right," she murmured, then slid from between the sheets and hurried to his shirt.

She shrugged it on and threw him a timid grin as she left the room.

He watched her doing this, deciding he was going to keep her. As soon as he could, he would release his concubine so it was only Aurora.

How long he'd keep her, he had no idea.

However, he knew it would take some time to lose his taste for her.

Perhaps eternity.

This was not a thought Yuri had ever had. He'd never been tied to a vampire or human. His longest relationship had lasted eleven years, and at his age, that was not very long.

But he remembered his father's agony when, in order to save her life when The Dominion outlawed vampire/human partners in a way they meant it, and if defied, they killed both, Gregor had denounced his human mate.

Thus, he was the sole vampire in recent history (that being five hundred years) who broke a vow.

But he did it for the best reason there was.

Love.

His father had not shown his torment to anyone but his son. And his suffering held Gregor in such a grip that Yuri worried he'd end his own immortality. It didn't help that Gregor kept tabs on the mate he'd saved from the noose. Even watched her himself on occasion.

And thus, he saw her marry another human, give him children, and find her brand of happiness.

But Yuri also watched her. He'd liked her. He'd liked that she'd made his father happy. But in the life she built without him, she had not been truly happy. Not as she was with Gregor. Not the happiness of a woman who knew she was with the precise being on this earth who the fates had destined for her.

Yuri rarely thought of it as it brought back unpleasant memories, but he knew then, as he knew now, that his father had found his life-mate—the one being who would exist throughout eternity who was meant for him.

She died at ninety-two years of age, a long life for that time. However, Gregor had been giving her his saliva for decades so he'd given her one last gift: an elongated life. A gift Yuri had no doubt she didn't want, living those extra years without Gregor.

Experiencing this through his father, living under the edicts that vampires were not allowed to take human lovers unless at a Feast, he'd not thought of eternity. Not with vampire. Not with wolf. Definitely not with human.

He found it freeing to be able to do so now.

And thinking of it at the same time thinking of Aurora, it was not only freeing, it was pleasant.

His phone rang, and considering all that was happening, Yuri didn't have the luxury of ignoring it. Therefore, he moved to the end of the bed and reached out an arm to his slacks. He got his phone, looked at the screen, and saw it was his father calling.

He gritted his teeth but took the call.

"Father," he greeted.

"I've sent you an email," his father said as reply. "In it is a video that's gone viral on social media. A video that shows Myrna Buchanan being raped by a vampire while he drained her...*completely*."

Yuri knifed to sitting and bit out, "Pardon?"

"We've received reports," Gregor carried on. "Currently, the number stands at two hundred and seventeen concubines, either currently in service or retired, who have been taken."

"Fuck," Yuri growled, throwing the covers off, angling out of bed, and bending to gather his clothes.

"You're needed back here."

He dumped his clothes on the bed as he reminded Gregor, "Five witches survived the slaughter last night, Father. The rest of the witch world gets wind of that, they might be in danger."

"We'll leave a detail for them."

"No," he clipped.

"Yuri, after this is sorted, you can go back to play with your new toy."

Fire burned through him and it took effort not to throw his phone across the room with his natural strength, which would reduce it to dust.

"I'll say this once, knowing you'll understand me and I'll not have to repeat. That was the last time you speak of Aurora in that manner. Now, she comes with me. As do her witch sisters."

Gregor's tone was conciliatory even when he said, "We have enough on our plate up here."

"And when we get there, you'll have more."

"We can't host five hostile witches," Gregor's voice nearly snapped.

"What you mean is you don't want to. But you can."

Gregor was silent but only for a moment.

"I'm hiring a private jet. Bring them, but don't delay. I'll text you the location of the airstrip. You have two hours."

"We'll be there."

Gregor hung up and Yuri didn't turn to his clothes.

He called his concubine.

Once he ascertained she was still safely in the compound where he'd left her, he called his friend Jordan and arranged for him to see to her. That being, see she was safe but not in the compound where he would soon be taking Aurora.

Only when that was sorted did he turn to his clothes.

He was zipping his slacks when Aurora walked in looking adorable in his shirt, hair tousled, leather-bound room service menu tucked under her arm.

At one look at him, she halted two feet into the room.

"Is everything okay?"

"No, my sweet," he answered, pulling on his sweater, then pinning her with his gaze. "Does that bowl travel?"

Her eyes widened, but she answered, "Uh...probably."

He nodded once before ordering, "Dress, Aurora, and phone your mother. We're going to Oregon."

"But they won't be able to finish their work," she protested. "The implements won't be safe."

"She can bring them with her."

"She won't—"

He was standing in front of her in a nanosecond.

"Dress, button, we have no time to waste."

She stared up into his eyes and whispered, "Oh boy."

Oh boy was right.

His Aurora, her mother, and three other witches, all in a building that was crawling with vampires.

Not to mention The Three.

Bloody *fucking* hell.

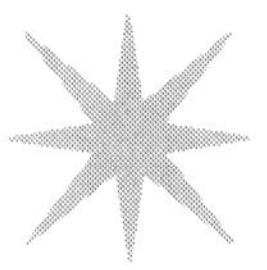

# 21
# Blocked

*Abel*

"Can I kick him?"

This question came from Hook, who was in the room they were using to interrogate Miko. Though, "interrogation" wasn't exactly the word since Abel had controlled his mind and he'd spilled all he knew.

And he knew a lot. Enough that vampire, wolf, and wraith rescue teams worldwide were preparing to extract a number of concubines from the vampires who were holding them.

But for some, it was too late. Six more videos had appeared on social media sites. Six more concubines losing their lives while being violated. The last one posted had included a vampire walking onscreen after the event and relaying a message:

*Give up The Three, or there will be more. And worse.*

If that wasn't enough, Miko also shared the not-great news that the reason they hadn't heard from Serena was because The True had captured her en route to her mate, Gastineau. They'd tortured the good wraiths still deep cover in their ranks and got the details on where to find her and how to capture her.

They were holding her on charges of being traitor to her race as well as traitor to the rightful governing body of immortals, The True. They intended to put her on trial, a case she'd lose, and then they were going to execute her as another message to immortals who did not fall in with their plans.

Seeing as nothing was coming from the phantoms at all since Serena left (as it hadn't before she took off), even though Gregor frequently attempted to contact them, Gregor sent yet another message to Gastineau. This one to see if he knew his mate had been taken. Gastineau had a policy of being incommunicado with any supernaturals outside of phantoms so Gregor also sent a crew of wraiths to see if they could access him, share and get his allegiance and support in locating then rescuing his mate.

Hook knew all this, seeing as he'd been in the interrogation room since Abel started, so Hook, like all of them, wasn't a big fan of Miko's.

Abel looked from the vampire, who sat blank-faced in his chair, to Hook, but it was Gregor who answered Hook's question.

"As we'll be holding tribunals for war crimes after we quell the rebellion, which would not play well on videotape," he explained as he floated an arm toward the camera filming the interrogation, "I think not."

Hook didn't take his eyes off Miko as Gregor answered, but when Gregor was done, Hook bared his teeth at the vampire almost like Hook was wolf.

"Maybe it's time you take a break," Abel suggested.

Hook tore his eyes off Miko and gave them to Abel.

They were burning with angry, badass biker hellfire.

Fuck.

"You don't do that to a woman," he growled low.

"I know, Hook," Abel said low too, and hopefully calming.

"You sure as fuck don't do it to six of them. And I'm not talkin' about takin' their lives, which everyone knows is not fuckin' cool. I'm talkin' about makin' their last memory on this earth—"

Abel cut him off. "I *know*, Hook."

Hook looked to Miko. "He's lower than a piece of shit."

"You need to take a break, man," Abel repeated.

Hook moved his gaze to Gregor. "You execute traitors too?"

"Absolutely," Gregor answered.

Hook scowled at him.

Then he jerked up his chin, muttering, "Time for me to take a break," and he walked out of the room.

Abel gave his attention to Gregor. "He's given us all he's got."

Gregor nodded his head, his eyes cold and on Miko. "Indeed."

"You want him back in play?" Abel asked, and Gregor looked to him.

When he did, Abel felt a chill glide down his spine.

"I want to build a great fire and have you control his mind so he walks into it himself and burns to ash, all while we record that and send it to Etienne."

"I hear you," Abel said quietly.

"Alas, we cannot do that," Gregor continued. "So I believe our best course of action right now is to return him to his home and continue to monitor him, with you programming him to report to us should there be communiqués he receives while not in his house. If those who call themselves The True believe we're scrambling or inactive, and still don't know we've turned their own against them, we build our upper hand."

"Right," Abel agreed. "But he's got three kids that he's..." Abel trailed off when Gregor shook his head.

"They're hangers, Abel."

"He's abusing them. They think they like it but—"

Gregor interrupted, "They *do* like it."

Abel turned fully to the vampire. "It isn't healthy."

"No, agreed, it's not to your understanding of what's healthy, as well as mine, as well as anyone who has a fit mind. However, hangers do not have healthy minds and they cannot be rehabilitated. This has been tried. It would serve no purpose to keep them away from Miko. They'd only find the next closest vampire and hope for more of the same."

"Isn't there anything we can do to get them help?" Abel asked.

Gregor again shook his head. "There have been vampires who have studied hangers quite thoroughly. The agreed theory is that they're descendants of those who offered the same services to our kind in times when vampires were not ruled by any governing body, likely against their will. However, there was no Council, no Dominion. They were free to do as they wish, treat humans as they wish. The ancestors of hangers endured what we consider abuse for centuries to the point, perhaps so they could retain a modicum of sanity, that they convinced themselves they enjoyed it. To the point it became part of their psyche. It's who they are. It's what they crave. There is no way to help them. It would be as impossible as making you not vampire, not wolf. They are, Abel, what all of humanity will likely become if The True succeed in their aim."

Abel tasted the thought of that in his mouth and it was foul.

"It would be interesting to see if you could use your ability to change this," Gregor commented. "But I predict that would fail."

Abel crossed his arms on his chest. "Right, then I was responsible for letting those kids loose for this asshole," he jerked his head to Miko, "to treat them like shit once. Gotta tell you, not hip on being responsible for doing it again. If I can't adjust what they crave, at least I can wipe all memory of this guy from their heads, and them from his. They'll be cast adrift, but they'll also be safe for a while."

"If that's what you wish to do, then do it."

"That's what I wish to do," Abel told him.

"Fine," Gregor replied, now sounding distracted. "Then I'll ask you to finalize things. I need to be upstairs to see if our media specialists have managed damage control. You're good to finish here?"

"I'm good."

"I'm sure I'll see you later," Gregor finished, giving Abel a dip of his chin, Miko a cold glance, and walking out of the room.

Abel looked back to Miko. He dealt with wiping all memory of the compound, interrogation, and the three young men from his head. He continued with giving him orders to become their informant. And he finished with commanding him not to take another hanger, ever.

"Now you get to go home, asshole," he muttered to the slack-faced vampire, then turned to the door, opened it, and gave orders to the soldiers out there to find someone to take the fuckwad home.

Abel stood with his shoulders leaned against the back wall of living room eight, his eyes on the TV.

The newscaster was talking.

"All across social media sites today, disturbing videos depicting the apparent rape and murder of several women were posted. As the murders appeared to be actual vampires draining their victims dry of blood, this alarming multitudes of people, experts examined these videos and found them to be an elaborate hoax, seemingly perpetuated for no purpose but to shock the masses and titillate the few who might find this depravity appealing. A task force of federal law enforcement has been created to track and arrest the individuals responsible. And the large social media sites have sent widespread messages to their users that if any of these videos were again shared, the user would face lifetime bans from their site."

And there it was—Gregor's media specialists had done their jobs.

"You agree with that play?" Abel asked Callum, who was standing beside him in the same stance.

Jian-Li and Regan were sitting on the couch in front of them, their attention to the TV.

Sonia and Delilah were up in Lucien and Leah's bedroom, giving Leah whatever they had to give and checking on her state of mind.

"No good play after that," Callum answered. "The Dominion and my kingdom come out saying there actually are immortals, but we're not all murdering rapists, it'd cause mass panic."

He wasn't wrong.

"After that shit, how we gonna lead humans and supernaturals into living together harmoniously?" Abel asked.

"No fucking clue," Callum replied.

Jian-Li turned her head and looked over the couch at Abel. He forced a smile her way. She forced one back.

While that was happening, Regan looked over the couch at her son. When Abel caught her smile, he figured they were doing the same thing.

"Want my mate," he muttered, pushing away from the wall.

"Same. I'll go with you," Callum said.

Abel moved to Jian-Li first, reached out a hand, and touched his finger to her chin.

"I'm gonna call it a night, *tian xin*," he told her as he heard Callum murmuring to Regan.

"All right, my Abel," she replied.

"You okay?" he asked.

"It has not been a good day."

He shook his head. "No."

He said it, it was more than true, but he hated looking into her face, seeing her worried eyes, unable to do shit about it.

"We'll have good luck soon," she said softly.

He hoped like fuck she was right.

"Sleep well," he said.

"And you," she replied.

He moved away, waited briefly at the door for Callum to follow him, and they walked silently together to Lucien and Leah's room.

Callum glanced at him before rapping his knuckles on the door once.

In moments, it was opened and Delilah was poking out her head.

"Time for bed, *bao bei*," he told her quietly.

She nodded to him and looked to Callum. "You want Sonia?"

"Yes, unless Leah needs her."

"I think Leah needs a sleeping pill chased by bourbon," she mumbled, her expression turning unfocused. She shook her head as if to clear it and refocused. "I'll get her." She looked to Abel and said, "Hang on."

The door closed, but it wasn't long before it was again opened and both Sonia and Delilah appeared.

They gave the king and queen their good-nights and headed to their room, Delilah leaning heavily on Abel as they walked.

"She's not good," he pointed out the obvious.

"None of the other ones killed were her family, but she's terrified," Delilah said. "She and Myrna weren't real close, but Myrna was still her cousin. The other members of Leah's family that they have, she's close to."

"Extractions are probably happening while we speak, baby," he told her. "Maybe some of the ones rescued will be Leah's kin."

"I hope so."

He tightened the arm he had around her shoulders to give her a squeeze.

They entered their room and mutely got ready for bed, brushing their teeth side by side, taking off their clothes standing close, Abel waiting for Delilah to pull on a nightgown. Then they slid into bed together.

He turned out the lights. She snuggled into him, and the way she did, he knew it would be the first night since their relationship became intimate that they didn't make love.

He was down with that. If she needed to cuddle her man, he'd give that to her.

Abel stared at the dark ceiling and waited, holding her, stroking her, letting her call it. Either she'd talk, he'd listen and do what he could to soothe, or she'd go to sleep.

She talked.

"If they'll do that, what else will they do?"

"I don't know, baby. Try not to think about it, okay?"

He felt her nod against his chest.

"Leah said Myrna was a good concubine. The best. She adored her vampire—"

"Stop," he ordered gently.

She stopped.

Then she started again. "I guess her vamp is out of his mind."

He would be. Vampires took protecting their concubines seriously. Gregor had told him that every one of the hundreds who'd had concubines taken, even inactive ones, were out of their minds. Some had to be restrained so they'd do the cause, and themselves, no harm in their need to rescue.

And their thirst for vengeance.

"He would be. Of course he would be, pussycat."

She pressed her face into his skin and whispered, "I want this to end."

He tightened his hold, bent his head, and said into the top of her hair, "I do too."

He kept her close and waited for her to lose it, either yelling or crying, however she needed to do that, or get a lock on it.

He felt the tension build in her body before it released and she took her face out of his skin and rested her cheek on it.

She got a lock on it.

"Sleep," he urged.

"Okay, baby. 'Night."

"'Night, *bao bei*."

It took her time, but she found it.

Abel didn't.

Then again, she hadn't seen the videos.

He had.

They played in his head and he let them. Used them as kindle to feed the flame in his gut. A flame that had been burning hot with desire to see to it that Delilah was safe, to make certain they had a life together. But now that flame also burned to wreak vengeance for Leah's people.

He was no nearer to falling asleep when he heard the muffled tone of his phone ringing in his jeans' pocket.

Carefully extricating himself from Delilah, he left their bed, grabbed his phone, and, when he saw who was calling, engaged it and put it to his ear.

"Yeah?"

"Miko was assassinated tonight," Callum shared.

Abel sucked in breath.

"They knew he was taken," Callum continued. "They found all the cameras but one. We didn't have eyes, but we did have ears. Your control held—he told them nothing about what he gave up at the compound—but they knew we'd had him, took him to the compound, and then turned him loose. After they took his head, they talked about autopsying him. They think we have a drug."

"Patricio?" Abel asked.

"His name was mentioned. They're gonna demand a meet."

"How'd they know he'd been taken?"

"Got him chipped. They knew he was at the compound and how long. From what Ryon heard, they have them all chipped, including Patricio, so in case they get caught, they know where to send a rescue team, or an assassination squad." Callum's voice turned into a disgusted mutter. "Chipping vampires. Unbelievable. We wouldn't even think to expect something that vile."

Fuck.

"You got any good news for me?" Abel requested.

"Miko gave us twenty-seven names. So far, fifteen concubines have been successfully extracted. One of them is Leah's cousin, Natalie."

"Thank fuck," he muttered.

"Yes," Callum agreed.

"Maybe now I can get some sleep,"

"Yes," Callum repeated. "Do it well."

"Back at you."

They disconnected and Abel put his phone on the nightstand before again joining Delilah in bed.

Then, finally, he slept.

He just didn't do it well.

Abel's phone sounded with a text the next morning as he and Delilah were walking down the hall toward Lucien and Leah's room. She wanted to check on her friend. He wanted to let her do that and then find Gregor.

He felt her gaze as he dug his phone out and looked at the screen.

*You're needed in the library.*

Gregor.

"I can get there myself," Delilah told him, and he knew she'd read the text.

"Right, pussycat," he replied, stopping them, curling her close, and dropping a kiss on her lips. "Later," he said when he was done.

"Later."

He grinned at her.

She grinned back.

He let her go and watched her continue down the hall for a few seconds before he used his vampire speed to take him to the library.

But he stopped outside it when he heard a woman's raised voice and sensed she wasn't the only woman in that room.

"Was dog-tired when I got here last night, so I took a bed. But I am *not* spending another *night* in a den of vamps."

He felt his brows draw together as he opened the door and walked into the room.

All eyes turned to him and two pairs of those were in faces he knew, Gregor's and Yuri's, who had apparently returned. The rest were five women he didn't know.

"Yo," he greeted.

"Holy goddess and all her great sisters," one of the women breathed. "It's the hybrid."

He looked to her and confirmed, "Yeah." Then he looked to Yuri. "Welcome back, man."

"Abel," Yuri greeted.

That was when he looked to the pretty, petite, dark-haired woman at his side who was dressed like a sex kitten schoolgirl who'd graduated two days ago and knew just how hot that was, even though she didn't want you to know she knew it.

In other words, she was something.

Something a man liked looking at and something to Yuri, seeing as she was standing very close to him, and even though they weren't touching, there was no mistaking that fact.

"Found a friend," he muttered to Yuri, feeling his lips twitch.

It was then Yuri touched her. Putting a hand to the small of her back, he moved even closer to her, saying, "I'd like you to meet Aurora Lenox. She's assisting us with finding your brother."

Abel's lips stopped twitching and his eyes went back to the woman.

"Hi, Abel," she said. "So cool to meet you."

He jerked up his chin, but with what Yuri said, that was all the good manners he had in him.

Therefore, he asked, "You find him?"

She looked to a wide, flat bowl filled with dark liquid sitting on a table between two armchairs, then back to him.

"It's not quite ready yet. A few more hours," she answered.

He turned his gaze to Yuri and rearranged his expression to read, *What the fuck?*

Yuri read him.

"The potion somehow guides us to him," Yuri explained.

Jesus. So far, he'd fought side by side with what were essentially ghosts. He'd torn apart men who were close to giants, hairless, and scary motherfuckers. He'd watched videos of terrified women enduring violation while their blood was drained from their bodies.

Now, obviously, he was in the presence of bona fide witches who made potions.

Yeah, he was with his mate. He was ready for this shit to end.

"Be obliged you tell me when the potion is ready," he said with little enthusiasm.

He was curious to meet his brother.

But he wasn't looking forward to it.

"I've not asked you here for that, Abel," Gregor butted in. "These ladies are witches. This is Barb, Aurora's mother." He motioned to a woman who looked somewhat like an older version of Aurora. "Ruby." He gestured to the oldest one of the lot. She carried some weight and had thick, long gray hair, but it was obvious she'd had it in her younger years because she'd retained it in her older ones. "And last, Jezza and Flo."

He gave them all chin jerks, then immediately turned his attention back to Gregor.

"And I'm here...?"Abel trailed off on a prompt.

"They wish to leave," Gregor told him.

Abel shook his head in confusion and reiterated, "And I'm here...?"

"We don't want them to leave," Gregor explained.

Abel gave him a hard look, then looked to the women.

"You don't like vampires," he stated.

"How old are you?" Ruby rapped out her question.

"Two hundred and five," Abel calmly gave her his answer.

"Right, then you weren't alive at the time, and you're likely too young to know, that vampires—"

"Did a bunch of bad shit to witches and you're pissed," Abel finished for her. Ignoring her eyes lighting with fury, he went on, "I get that. I'd be pissed too. That was whacked. So whacked, I'd hang on to it for centuries just like you're obviously doing. But, just sayin', it's not real safe out there for anyone supernatural or even remotely involved in the supernatural life. It's safe in here. You wanna take your chances out there, all I got to say to that is...your funeral."

"Ruby, Jezza, Flo...Yuri's vowed to keep you safe," Aurora added at that juncture.

"I believe, my sweet, I vowed to keep *you* safe," Yuri drawled, and she jerked her head around and back to look up at him.

"And, by extension, my sisters," she declared.

"It doesn't work like that, Aurora," he explained.

She turned fully to him. "Well, vow you'll keep them safe."

His tone didn't change when he replied, "I will not."

"Yuri!" she cried. "You've vowed to keep me safe. I don't know why you can't do the same for them."

He bent slightly toward her. "I like *you*."

He left it there. Then again, him leaving it there said it all.

Abel's lips were again twitching.

She leaned into him and hissed, "I can't believe you!"

"All right, all right," Gregor broke in, and Abel looked to him to see his gaze on the other witches. "*I'll* vow to keep you safe. Does that work?"

"Works for me," Barb said instantly. "Now, when's breakfast? I'm starved."

"Barb!" Flo exclaimed.

Barb turned gentle eyes to her sister and said softly, "Video."

All the witches suddenly started looking at anything that wasn't breathing and shuffled their feet.

They'd seen the videos.

This surprised Abel. He cut his eyes to Aurora, who was still glaring up at Yuri, then to Yuri, who was looking at Abel.

"Barb saw it before I could stop her. Aurora has not seen it, nor will she," he declared.

"Keep that oath, brother," Abel muttered.

Yuri dipped his chin.

Abel looked to the other witches. "Stay. You'd be fools to go out there. These assholes we're dealin' with are cold as ice. Don't know you and still know you're a lot better people than they are, seein' as it would be hard not to be. So it'd suck you not bein' on this earth." His looked to Gregor. "That's it. I said my bit. Now, if you'll let me know when that potion's done, I'd appreciate it."

On that, seeing as he didn't have time for that shit considering the fact he had to prepare to find out where his brother was, he walked out.

Abel was training as wolf with Callum, Ryon, Calder, and Caleb when he saw Xun heading their way.

He communicated this to his brothers, turned, jogged to his clothes, and jumped to man.

He had his jeans on, the others around him having turned into man and also dressing, when Xun made it to them.

"Patricio took a day-trip this morning," Xun said as an opener. "Gregor put a human on him. He drove about a hundred miles out, had his meet, they took his head."

"Jesus Christ," Abel snarled.

"Guess they're not taking any chances," Calder muttered.

"That's it?" Callum asked.

"The guy we sent after him couldn't get close enough to hear what they were saying. He just reported the conversation didn't last long before things got bloody. Figure they weren't real big on the rest of those concubines gettin' rescued last night and decided cleanup crews were necessary."

All the missions had been successful the night before and a further twelve had been rescued utilizing local intel on turncoat vampires.

That still left hundreds in the hands of the enemy, though they'd had no more videos or any other communication, such as threats or ransom demands.

"'Nother bit of news," Xun went on. "That Gastineau phantom has been in touch."

"And he said...?" Abel asked.

"Said he's on it," Xun answered.

"Nothing more?" Callum pressed.

"Nope, just that he's on it," Xun told him.

Abel looked to Callum. "You got any clue what that means?"

"My read, the phantoms don't like their queen held captive, but they aren't asking for allies to assist in rescuing her," Callum replied.

"They got what it takes to be successful on their own?" Abel asked.

"Phantoms and wraiths are like brothers and sisters," Callum said. "You watch them, you'd think they hated each other. But you are not one of their own and say one word against them, they'll rip your head off. So I would assume he's very determined to be successful. Whether his determination will bear fruit..." He shrugged.

Abel broke it down. "So now we got no inside men, a bunch of concubines who are in mortal danger, a rogue phantom determined to rescue his mate and the outcome of that is iffy, a gaggle of witches in the compound who don't want to be here because they hate vampires, and they got magic. And last, we got fuck-all knowledge of what our enemies are planning next, but the last shit they pulled was fucked way the hell up. Did I get it all?"

Callum grinned a grin that was more a grimace and confirmed, "You got it all."

"So we're again sitting on our hands," Abel concluded.

"Unfortunately, yes," Callum replied.

Abel made a nonverbal snarl.

Callum looked to Calder. "Perhaps you should go back to your network."

Calder shook his head. "Told you, brother, this True identified, recruited, and closed ranks. There's no getting in. And the only way out is to give up your head. The single shot we had was the wraiths and they had to give it up to save The Three. Other than that, no one has heard anything and it'd be impossible to infiltrate."

"I need to get my hands on another one," Abel declared, and all eyes came to him. "The ones who met Patricio, did our guy follow them?"

"Not his orders," Xun answered. "Stay safe. Report back. We all know it's not safe gettin' near these guys. He did his job, finished it breathing, and is on his way back."

Dead end.

Abel kept at it.

"During the rescues, were any vampires detained?"

Callum shook his head. "To my knowledge, so far, the need for termination was utilized."

"Then we need to tell the teams who locate the next concubines to bring a vampire in breathing," Abel returned.

"Even if we found one, they're chipped," Ryon pointed out. "They'd know that he, or she, has been to the compound."

"Then I go to them," Abel returned.

"Brother," Xun said quietly.

Abel looked to him. "Saved twenty-seven women with what I got outta Miko."

"You did, within the safety of the compound," Callum noted.

"Yeah," Abel shot back. "Now we don't got that choice. So we locate one, or twelve or a hundred of those motherfuckers, and go to them."

Callum held his eyes.

Then he turned to Ryon. "We're tracking the three men who Miko was entertaining, yes?"

"Yes," Ryon confirmed.

Callum turned back to Abel. "Lucien's in constant contact with Cosmo. We'll watch those three men. They might lead us to someone. We'll notify all those on the hunt for concubines to attempt to bring the vampire captors in alive. And we'll ask Lucien to tell Cosmo to put together a team to aggressively hunt The True, find a vulnerable one, or several of them, then we go in."

"Puts Cosmo out there, man," Xun pointed out.

"He's already out there as he's already trying to sniff them out. But we'll send Stephanie to him. Teffie will have his back," Callum replied. "And Cosmo will be setting up a team. Won't be difficult to find vampires willing to undertake a dangerous mission. We just have to approach ones who had their concubines taken."

"Brother, those vampires will be hostile *and* unstable," Ryon warned.

"They'll also be determined," Callum returned.

"The vampires don't want escalation," Ryon told him. "They want to end this as quietly as possible."

"Rape and murder were videotaped and posted to share with the masses, Ryon," Callum noted. "I think quiet is becoming an impossibility."

Ryon studied his cousin a moment before jerking up his chin.

"Let's get on this," Abel growled, bending to snatch up his thermal.

"Right," Callum agreed.

They finished dressing. They went back to the compound. They did their thing.

Then, fuck them all, they had nothing else to do but wait.

"You got any more of these macadamia nuts, Yuri?" Ruby asked, lounging in an armchair by a window in the library, one leg thrown over an arm, popping macadamia nuts into her mouth after plucking them from a huge-ass silver bowl that lay on her round stomach.

Abel, sitting on a couch next to Delilah and opposite Aurora, who was staring at her bowl on the table between them, her eyebrows pulled together, looked to the witch.

Yuri, standing behind Aurora, looked to *his* witch.

Aurora twisted her neck and looked up at her vampire.

Then she aimed her eyes back at the bowl on the table and said, "Ruby, can you please be cool? We're doing something important here."

"What's not cool about wanting more macadamia nuts?" Ruby asked. "It's not like anything is happening."

"I'd like to know that too," Jabber said, wandering over to Ruby. "You mind?" he asked her.

"Got no problem sharing the wealth," Ruby answered, lifting the bowl to Jabber. He took a massive handful, several of them dropping to the carpet.

At that, Abel's eyes shifted through the room.

All the witches were there, as were Jian-Li, Xun, Wei, and Chen. Hook was there too.

Yuri was there because Abel reckoned he didn't let Aurora too far out of his sight. And with them were Jabber, Moose, and Gregor.

His family being there, Abel could get. Aurora had told him the potion was ready and a reading was due any second. His family would want to be close to him when he found out where his brother was. And Hook was now family.

He had no fucking clue why the rest were there.

He turned his eyes to Delilah and she gave him big ones before she shrugged.

Not getting the answer he wanted, he decided to communicate verbally.

"You wanna help me out, pussycat?"

"They're here for moral support," she explained.

"You wanna help me out, pussycat?" he repeated and watched her fight her grin.

"Jesus! What's takin' so fuckin' long?" Hook suddenly exploded.

"Hook, calm. It'll happen when it happens," Jian-Li said. "Patience."

"It's not like we're waitin' for cookies to bake, for Christ's sake," Hook fired back. "A man's waiting to find his long-lost brother." He pinned Aurora with his gaze. "Girl, I get this is probably a delicate procedure, but you said you were close and we been in this room for forty-five minutes."

"I'm sorry, sir, I don't understand," Aurora replied, shaking her head. "It should be ready." She looked back to the bowl with confusion. "It's given every indication it's ready."

"It's magic and magic is done when magic is done," Barb put in from her spot next to her daughter on the couch.

"Which means it could take some time so we need more macadamia nuts," Ruby added.

Abel growled.

"And some beer," Moose threw in, prowling toward the window, which meant prowling toward the bowl of nuts.

Abel caught Delilah's eyes and growled again.

"Yuri, son, can't she zap it with a wand or somethin'?" Hook asked.

"I've no idea," Yuri returned. "I'm a vampire, not a witch. And no offense intended, Hook, but I'm six hundred and fifty years older than you so I'm far from your son."

Aurora let out a nervous giggle.

"You get me though, yeah?" Hook asked.

"I do, indeed, *get you*," Yuri replied, and Aurora let out another nervous giggle, this one she stifled.

"Honey," Delilah said softly, and Abel watched her lean toward Aurora. "My man is two hundred years old. He's lived his entire life around humans. Humans he watched being born and fell in love with. Then he watched them grow until they grew old and died. He only found out he had an immortal brother a few days ago. A brother who's been looking out for him. A brother who could be in his life for the rest of it, which is a very long time. This is tough on him. If that stuff isn't ready yet, maybe we should go so he could turn his mind to other things."

Abel wanted to kiss her, but instead, for some reason, he looked to Jian-Li, who was sitting in a chair positioned at the end of the couches.

She was watching Delilah, her face soft, her eyes a mixture of warm, happy, and melancholy. But finally, since Delilah showed in their lives, the warm and happy were winning out.

"I—" Aurora started, then cried, "Oh! It's happening!"

Abel tensed and Delilah shot back and leaned into his side, her hand coming out to grip his knee.

A poof of gray, green, and red smoke exploded out of the bowl with some green and red sparks. It lifted up, floating straight into the air before it disbursed at the ceiling.

Aurora leaned over the bowl.

"I...wait...but...oh no!" she cried and looked to her mother. "He's blocked us!"

"Fuck," Abel snarled.

"Goddammit!" Hook burst out.

"Let me see," Barb said, leaning forward too. Attention never leaving the bowl, she lifted her hand her daughter's way, palm up. "Athame, sweetheart."

Immediately, Aurora reached for a knife on the table and handed it to her mother. Barb used the tip of the blade to stir the liquid in the bowl and they both mumbled over it.

Then Abel saw it happening and knew Delilah did too because he heard her gasp.

The image of a compass formed, undulating with the liquid but looking like it was spinning.

Barb pulled the knife out.

"There it is, there it is," she whispered. "There!" she exclaimed.

He leaned forward, Delilah leaned with him, he felt everyone gather around them and lean in too, and in the bowl they saw a street map.

"Drat! He's cloaked," Aurora snapped.

"What's that in the bowl?" Delilah asked.

Aurora sat back and lifted her eyes to Delilah. "A street map. Where he is. It should pinpoint him with some kind of beacon, but it isn't. We just have that street map and nothing further. And that map could be anywhere."

Abel heard a camera click and looked up to see Chen had taken a picture of the map with his phone.

He wandered away, head bent to his phone, muttering, "Let me see what I can do with this."

"Use Abel."

Abel's head jerked back to look at Yuri, who said these words.

"I'm sorry?" Jian-Li asked.

Yuri looked to her. "Aurora said if she touched Abel, she could find his brother." He cast his eyes down to Aurora. "Use Abel, my sweet."

"He's so digging on her," Delilah whispered to no one, her lips tipped up, her gaze on Yuri.

"Use me," Abel said, and Delilah turned her attention to him.

"I...well, I already did. I used your blood," she told him.

"Try again," he replied.

"Um...are you sure?" Aurora asked.

"Would it harm him?" Jian-Li asked.

"No, but it could take even more time," Aurora answered. "I only didn't suggest it before because the potion had been marinating and, as you know, should have produced results a while ago."

Abel stood. "Use me."

Aurora pressed her lips together, straightened from the couch, and moved to him.

"If we're lucky, this will go fast. But if he's blocked us, it may take a while," she shared.

"Whatever," he muttered. "Just do it."

"Ladies, let's help her out," Barb called, moving from the couch to come close to where Aurora joined Abel.

Delilah stood and backed away to give them room as Aurora took his hand and led him to an open area. The other witches circled them.

"Ready?" Aurora asked.

"Yep," he answered.

She nodded.

Then they started. Lifting their hands, all of them, they began chanting. It was disjointed at first, then they got it together and chanted as one.

It turned out Aurora was right.

It did not go fast. Green and red sparkling motes drifted up from their hands and floated all around Abel, but nothing happened.

They kept chanting and the motes kept coming, floating, blinking out, and disappearing.

More chanting. More motes. More nothing.

This went on for what felt like fucking ever and Abel trained his eyes on Delilah.

"Keep with it, baby," she called her encouragement.

He stood, crossed his arms on his chest, and kept with it.

Barb's voice started rising and the rest of the witches' voices rose with hers. They weren't shouting, but they were loud and more motes formed. Tons of them. They lit the space to the point Abel could see nothing but them.

More chanting (a lot more) and they stopped floating and started swirling.

"What the fuck?" He heard Hook ask.

But he couldn't see him. He was enveloped in red and green sparks that were spinning around him, now so fast, they were streaks.

"Shh, Hook," Jian-Li shushed him.

More chanting. More motes. And now the things were blowing like a breeze in his hair and against his clothes and skin.

The witches got louder.

"I am *not* liking this," Delilah said.

Then Abel growled and crouched as if to turn to wolf, his fangs descending when he felt it, the threat, right before the swirls exploded in a firework of white sparks and all five of the witches flew back, right to their asses, Aurora doing it and landing on the edge of the table.

Yuri was at her side in a flash, down on a knee, bending over her.

But the threat was gone.

Abel retracted his fangs.

The motes were also gone. The sparks were gone. The room was clear.

"She good?" Abel asked.

Not taking his attention from Aurora, Yuri answered, "Banged up but okay."

"Yeah, I'm okay," Aurora said, pulling her hair out of her face.

"He's blocked," Ruby decreed.

"Crazy, stupid blocked," Jezza added.

"Abel, he's with a witch," Barb announced, and Abel looked to her. "A powerful one."

"Come again?" he asked.

"There's no way to block a witch finding you," Barb explained, "except by using a witch."

"We got some mojo," Ruby declared. "The five of us against one cloaking spell?" She shook her head. "He didn't find some random witch to give him a bit of invisibility that'd see him through. He's got an active witch *with* him who's keeping him hidden. And whoever she is, she's got more mojo than us. By *a lot*."

"I'm sorry, Abel," Aurora said softly, and his gaze turned to her to see her on her feet.

"Not a problem. You tried." He grinned at her. "Even wounded in the battle. I appreciate it."

She grinned back.

Yuri put an arm around her and tucked her close.

Abel grinned at him, but it was different this time, seeing as the guy was *seriously* digging his little witch.

He felt Delilah take his hand and he looked down at her.

"Bummer," she whispered.

He wasn't sure he agreed, but he could see she felt that word intensely, so he lifted his hand to cup her jaw, running his thumb along her cheek.

She pressed into his hand and he slid it back into her hair and tugged her face into his chest.

She wound her arms around his waist.

He looked to Jian-Li.

The second she saw his eyes on her, she wiped the concern from her expression and gave him a small smile he knew she didn't feel.

He returned it.

"Sorry, son," Hook said from close, and Abel turned in that direction just as the man patted him on the arm.

"We'll try some other things," Aurora offered.

"That'd be good," Abel replied, not sure he meant it. His brother wanted to stay hidden? He'd done a brilliant job with that for maybe centuries. Abel wasn't sure he was real fired up to make him stop. Still, he finished with, "Thanks."

She tipped her head to the side and grinned at him.

"Fuck, that was some crazy shit. Need bourbon," Moose grumbled. "Like, immediately."

That, Abel agreed with.

Delilah pulled away, letting him go. "I'll go get it."

"I'll help," Aurora said.

"Don't forget the nuts," Ruby called as they made their way to the door.

They took off and Abel moved to Jian-Li. He sat on the arm of her chair, bent deep, and touched his lips to the top of her hair.

When he lifted up, she tilted her head back to catch his eyes.

"I'm good," he said quietly.

She studied him.

Then she reached out, grabbed his hand, and gave it a squeeze.

"Our luck will turn," she promised.

He squeezed her hand back, hoping she was right.

# 22
# Visitors

*Delilah*

I crouched my body low to avoid a karate chop from Wei, dropped into a squat, swung out my leg, and caught him at the ankles.

He went down to his ass.

The first time I took him out.

I jumped up, throwing my arms up in the air, shouted, "*Woo hoo!*" and immediately was tackled in the back by Xun. I fell to my stomach with an "*Oof!*" and then was incapacitated with a knee between my shoulder blades and one arm twisted back, my wrist imprisoned in his fist.

It was two days after Aurora and her witch sisters had tried to help Abel locate his brother. Leah and I were out with the guys, learning self-defense (and then some).

Sonia was with the wolves since she was one and asked Callum if she could start to train with them so she had both human and wolf defense at her disposal.

Leah had sat everything out the last couple of days, but I'd talked her into starting up again because she needed to take her mind off things. She'd understandably been moping. Although two of her cousins had been rescued, one had been killed and another was still captive, still....she couldn't mope forever. There was a world that needed to be saved.

The good news about this was that we'd had no word other concubines had been harmed. The bad news was that there were still tons of them whose whereabouts were unknown.

So now, at the compound, we were back to business as usual.

Xun let me go and I rolled to my back to see him extending a hand to me.

I took it as he said, "Don't ever let your guard down."

He pulled me to my feet and I grinned at him. "I still took Wei out."

"You did." Wei got close. "You're learning fast."

I turned my grin to him.

"Aside from the part where you were flat on your face with your arm twisted around your back, that was *awesome*," Leah decreed, hitting our huddle with her hand up in high five position.

I didn't leave her hanging.

"Incoming," Wei muttered.

I looked to him to see his eyes aimed over his shoulder, so I looked in that direction and saw Moose lumbering toward us in an ungainly jog, something which put me on edge for two reasons. First, because Moose didn't jog so his news had to be big. And second, because Moose didn't jog and I didn't want him to have a heart attack.

"Yo!" he called through a wheeze when he got close. "Poncho's back."

Thank God. It was good news.

I clapped my hands and shouted, "Yay!"

Moose halted when he got to us, took in a deep breath, and shared, "Got the *bruja*."

"Say what?" Xun asked.

"He brought his aunt. The *bruja*. A witch," Moose explained.

"Cool," I whispered. Abel had told me what Poncho was up to, including all the "tests" he had to go through to win her trust to the cause.

He'd obviously won it.

I hoped.

"Another witch," Wei sighed.

"Is she with us?" I asked Moose. "You know, on our side?"

"Don't reckon he'd bring her ass here if she wasn't."

That was a good point.

"Chen went off to get your man. Poncho wants you both at the house," Moose went on.

"Right, I'm off," I said.

"Coming with. Not gonna miss this shit," Xun stated, moving with me.

Moose moved with me too.

"You could continue to kick my ass, but I think I'd rather meet a *bruja*." I heard Leah say to Wei, and Wei must have agreed because I felt them joining us.

We hit the steps to the front of the house, and as we did, we saw Abel, Callum, Sonia, Chen, and the rest in the not-too-distant distance so I stopped to wait for them.

"You figure we're in for more hilariousness, another witch in the mix who has no problem givin' lip to a vamp at any occasion?" Xun called when Abel and his crew got close.

This had been our last couple of days. Aurora's witch sisters were ornery and clearly felt it was their mission to make every vampire pay for their rocky history by being surly, demanding, grouchy, and insulting at every turn.

The vampires, on the other hand, had a lot of making up to do, so they pretty much had to take it. They didn't like it. They showed they didn't like it. But they still had to take it.

It was pretty funny, though obviously, the vampires didn't think so.

Neither did Aurora, who was often forced to play peacemaker because it was definitely clear she liked vampires.

Or at least one of them.

"Don't give a shit what she gives to a vampire as long as she's willing to throw her magic on our side," Abel answered his brother, doing it coming straight to me, grabbing my hand, and tugging me up the stairs.

He was in a bad mood. Then again, he'd been in a bad mood since the videos came out.

I got this. I got it not only because I got it, but because Abel might be a badass werewolf vampire, but he was one who communicated so he'd told me this.

He wanted us safe. He wanted us free to live our lives. He didn't want anyone else harmed.

And he wanted that yesterday.

The problem was that it was imperative The Three were kept safe. Which meant action men such as Abel, as well as Callum and Lucien, had their hands tied.

None of them liked that.

Lucien had been in a worse mood than Abel, so much so, he kinda scared me.

I got this too. His woman suffered a loss, but he was a vampire who'd had a great number of concubines in his life. They were important to him. They remained important to him. And knowing their kind was targeted did not sit real great with him.

Currently, Leah's entire family was in a safe house somewhere, guarded by Leah's sister's vampire, Rafe, Lucien's daughter, Isobel, and Orlando, another vampire friend of Lucien's.

In other words, according to Abel, Lucien had pulled out all the stops, seeing as these vampires weren't ones you would trifle with.

We entered the house just as a human woman was walking through the foyer.

"Find the other witches and bring them to us," Callum ordered her.

She nodded and scurried off.

"What's that about?" I asked Abel as Moose led the way to wherever Poncho and his aunt were and the rest of us followed.

"Those women are eatin' macadamia nuts and drinkin' wine and doin' whatever shit they're doin' to find my brother...unsuccessfully," Abel answered. "But finding my brother is not a priority. Stopping this shit is. They got magic. We gotta know what that means and they gotta use it to help us. Including Poncho's aunt."

Moose turned into living room eleven and we all followed. I saw Dad was there, as was Lucien and, of course, Poncho. There was also an elderly Hispanic woman with lots of wiry gray hair she'd pulled back into a bun at the base of her neck.

And, I wanted to laugh, but she was wearing a female-type poncho.

I guess that ran in the family.

I didn't laugh.

Instead, I smiled big at Poncho and called, "Hey! Welcome back!"

My body jerked when the woman shouted, "*Basta!*"

I looked to her but only got a quick look in because Abel yanked my hand so he could haul me behind his back.

This was likely because the old woman had her hand up, palm out toward me, eyes narrowed, fear etched into the wrinkles of her face, and she was now chanting in Spanish.

Poncho had his brows drawn and was moving to her, but as the others fanned around us, her head jerked from side to side as she took them in.

She stopped chanting and started shouting, "No! *Basta! Basta! Déjame!*"

Then she grasped the edge of her poncho, twisted it around her, whirled where she stood, and as she would have come back to facing us, she disappeared.

My mouth dropped open.

"What the fuck?" Abel clipped.

"Shee-it," Poncho hissed, staring at the empty space where his aunt had just been.

"Uh, brother, you wanna clue us in to what just happened?" Dad asked, and Poncho looked to him.

"Sounded like she was chanting for protection," Poncho told him.

"Against what?" Dad asked.

Poncho's gaze came to me. "Against Lilah."

"Me?" I asked, lifting a hand to my chest. "For goodness sake, why?"

He shook his head. "Don't know. But when the other two came in, that's when she lost it."

"The other two?" Callum queried.

"Her," Poncho pointed at Sonia. "And her," he pointed at Leah. "Your bitches."

"I don't get it," Sonia said quietly just as I felt activity at the door.

I turned that way to see Barb and Ruby walking in.

Barb stopped and lifted up both hands, her eyes getting big.

Ruby stopped and planted both hands on her hips, snapping, "Crap. Hoodoo. The place stinks of it. You got a *bruja* in here?"

"Who are you?" Poncho demanded to know.

"White witches," Ruby shot back.

"*Mi tía* don't practice no *brujeria magia negra*, woman. So, what gives?" Poncho returned.

"There's great power in this room," Barb stated.

"So?" Poncho asked.

"Does that mean she's still here?" I asked at the same time.

"Our practice and the practice of *magia blanca* are quite different," Barb answered Poncho.

"Again, so?" Poncho repeated.

"So, we have some professional differences," Barb replied.

"Is she...still here?" Abel asked tersely.

"Yes," Barb answered.

Abel turned to Poncho. "Talk to her, man. See what the fuck is up."

Poncho nodded, then looked uncertain for a second before he cast his eyes upward and started talking in Spanish.

Watching him do that might have been funny, but I was weirded out.

I didn't have a lot of time to process that before there was more activity at the door. I looked that direction and saw Ruby getting out of the way in order for a male vampire to stand in the doorway.

"Lucien, there's someone at the gatehouse. Human. Hanger. He's asking for you," the vampire said, and the room got tense.

"A hanger is at the gatehouse and he knows I'm here?" Lucien asked, his voice scary.

"Yes. Says his name is Breed," the vampire replied.

Lucien looked to Callum, then Abel, and finally Leah before he nodded and moved to the door, saying, "I'll return."

Lucien left just as Aurora and Yuri showed at the door. Aurora, probably sensing the *bruja*, halted before going through it, which meant Yuri almost bumped into her. Instead, at her quick stop, he wrapped an arm around her chest from behind in a protective way, narrowed his eyes, and scanned the room.

Totally cute together.

"*Magia*," Aurora whispered.

"Yeah, they got a disapparated *bruja* clinging to the ceiling," Ruby informed her.

Aurora grinned, her face lighting with excitement, and walked into the room, bringing Yuri with her, exclaiming, "Cool!" Then she waved at the ceiling and called, "Hey there!"

One side of Yuri's mouth hitched up.

Totally cute.

"We're standin' around 'cause we got plenty of time to stand around, seein' as fuck all is happening," Abel shared with the room. "But we actually *don't* have time to stand around, seeing as people's lives are in danger. Around about a few billion of them. So something has to give with that. Now, while we wait for Poncho's auntie to reappear, maybe you all can tell us how you can use what you got to do something to help save the world," he suggested, lifting a hand and pointing a finger toward Barb, but he turned it side to side to indicate Ruby and Aurora too.

"What do you want us to do?" Barb asked instantly, easy as that, and I blinked.

"Whatever you can do," Abel shot back. "But seein' as I don't know what that is, maybe you can tell us so we can get you started."

"It'd be helpful if we had more witches and the *bruja* would work with us," Barb told him.

"Poncho's currently workin' on that," Abel returned. "As for more witches, that's up to you to recruit. But you still haven't answered what you can do, with others or with what you got."

"Well, we can cast protection spells," Aurora shared. "And we can do location spells, as you know. Though, we need blood from the person you want to locate, and if not blood, then hair."

"The first might help. The second, as we have no blood of our enemies, or anything else, no," Callum said. "What else?"

Aurora lifted her hands up to her sides. "It really kinda depends on the situation."

"The situation is saving the world," Abel clipped, clearly losing patience.

I got close to him, grabbed his hand, and murmured, "Baby."

"Auntie says she'll come back if the women leave the room," Poncho announced, and we all turned to him. "Not the witches." He dipped his head my way and said, "You three."

"Why?" I asked.

"She said you're dangerous," Poncho answered.

"What? How?" I pressed.

He looked to the ceiling, nodded, muttered, "Unh-hunh, unh-hunh," then he looked to me. "Lilah, darlin', auntie says you got lethal energy. Says that one," he jerked his head to Leah, "is a human vampire and that shit's not right, though she didn't say 'shit.'" He finished by indicating Sonia with another jerk of his head. "And she says that one is every animal all in one and that shit's not right either."

"Whoa," Leah breathed.

"Sounds like you might not need witch help," Ruby noted.

I ignored her and lifted my hand to wave it around, saying to Poncho, "We have abilities. We're The Three. But we're cool. We wouldn't hurt her."

Poncho looked to the ceiling, did some nodding, and returned to me. "Auntie says you three have enough power to take over the world."

My voice rose. "What?"

"Whoa!" Leah exclaimed.

"Interesting," Sonia whispered.

"I don't sense that," Ruby sniffed.

Poncho looked to her. "Auntie says you would, if you used the blood of the goat."

Ruby curled her lip.

"Lilah, leave," Abel ordered.

I turned my head to him. "Leave?"

He gave a short nod. "Leave. We need to talk to the witches and we can't do that with you and the others here."

"But—"

"*Bao bei.*" He leaned to me. "Take Leah and Sonia and *go.*"

I stared at him.

Then I muttered, "Oh, all right," and let his hand go. "Sonia, Leah, let's get outta here."

We left the room and saw Jezza and Flo wandering down the hall toward it, taking their time, as if there wasn't a world to save.

"In there," Sonia told them.

They passed us and the door closed behind them.

"We have enough power to take over the world?"

That came from Leah.

"That's what she said, but I don't know what to do with that."

That came from me.

"This is so *frustrating,*" Sonia snapped. "It's like we have it all, we just don't know what it is so we can use it."

"Maybe we should stop karate chopping and I should test out my blue light," I suggested. "You should work on talking to the animals," I said to Sonia. "And you..." I turned to Leah. "Well, I don't know about you. A vampire human?"

"I'm getting Lucien's abilities," Leah reminded me.

"Well, maybe you should try them out," I replied. "Maybe there's something there."

"It's a plan, a nebulous one, but it's something," Sonia said.

"Leah."

We all turned to look down the hall and saw Lucien approaching.

He didn't look happy.

"Darling," she called, moving his way. "Is everything okay?"

"Breed was with the enemy," he declared curtly, stopping close to her and putting a hand to her waist. "Are the men in there?"

"Uh...yes, but what did—?" she started but stopped when he bent in, touched his mouth to hers, and then walked straight to the door and through it, closing it behind him.

"You know, for three women who can take over the world, we don't seem to get a lot of respect," Leah grumbled.

"Then let's earn it," I replied and looked to Sonia. "Let's go talk to bunnies."

She grinned and hooked her arm through my elbow.

I hooked mine through Leah's elbow.

And we went to go talk to bunnies.

I stood in living room two, thinking bad thoughts.

Thoughts of losing Abel.

Thoughts of him leaving me, whereabouts unknown.

Thoughts that made my stomach hollow, the emptiness edged in a dull pain.

Then I swung my arm out, finger pointing at the red Solo cup I put on the table there, and...

Nothing.

"Shit," I muttered.

I tried something else, thinking of Abel with another woman.

When the pain became sharper, I lifted up both my hands and pushed them out toward the cup.

Nothing.

"Shit!" I fairly shouted.

"Little girl," Dad started, "give it a rest. You been tryin' that crap for an hour now and getting nothing. You're doin' your own head in."

Frustrated, I glared at him.

"Yo, Lilah," Moose called, lazing on a sofa with his head to the arm, hands linked behind his head, ankles crossed, and eyes closed. "When you take over the world, get me a mansion big enough I can ride my Harley in the front door," he requested.

"Moose, I'm not taking over the world," I told him.

"Shame," he murmured. "Figure you'd do a better job runnin' it than the assholes who got it now."

That probably wasn't a bad guess, considering the world was on the brink of disaster.

"If you're takin' orders," Jabber, sitting in an armchair with an open bag of potato chips in his lap, an open bottle of Bud at his side, put in. "I want one of those sisters, the ones in that reality show about bein' famous for bein' famous. I don't care which, but the tall one is far from hard on the eyes."

"Jabber, I'm *not* taking over the world," I snapped.

"Okay, say you get famous," he kept at it. "You might meet her at a party. You could put in a good word for me."

"Jabber, open your senses and read my mood," I hissed.

"Girl, known you since you was three," he replied. "I can read your mood. But if I learned I got it in me to take over the world, I wouldn't be staring at a red Solo cup and gettin' pissy. I'd be layin' *plans*."

"Well, I'm not you," I pointed out.

"Pity," he muttered.

I turned to Dad.

He shrugged.

"Perhaps, Lilah, this ability cannot be honed," Jian-Li suggested, sipping tea in the chair opposite Jabber. "Perhaps it only comes naturally. Abel has said it's powerful and it was so when you didn't even know you were using it." She tipped her head to the side and her voice went gentle. "There's much to be frustrated about, *qĐn ài de*, therefore there's no purpose to making yourself more frustrated."

She had a point.

I moved to a vacant armchair and slumped into it.

"All that starin' and throwin' your arm out and shit, it's gotta take it out of a girl. You want me to get you a beer?" Jabber offered.

I'd learned from years of him being around that Jabber was annoying.

He was also sweet.

So I grinned at him and said, "No, Jabber, I'm good."

He nodded and reached for his own beer.

The door behind me opened.

I twisted to look around my chair and saw Abel striding in with his brothers, those being the brothers Jin.

Instantly, I decided I was pissed at him, and I decided this because I hadn't seen him since he'd asked us to leave the room when we were talking to Poncho's auntie.

So I turned right back around, crossed my arms and legs, and started bouncing my foot.

I felt Abel stop at the side of my chair.

"*Bao bei,*" he greeted.

"*Bao bei* yourself," I muttered irately, not looking at him.

"Lilah?" he called.

"What?" I answered, still not looking at him.

"Baby, what's up?" he asked.

"I don't know," I answered and finally tipped my head back, my slitted eyes catching his. "I was asked to *leave the room.*"

"Lilah—" he started.

"Feel a domestic comin' on," Dad said over Abel, his voice sounding like he was on the move. "Recommend we vacate the premises."

"I'm all over that," Jabber said.

"I'm comfortable," Moose grunted.

I looked his way to see Dad punch Moose lightly in the gut, to which Moose opened his eyes and knifed up a couple of inches, head and feet, scowling at Dad. But he did not get up.

"Bud, give my little girl and her man some space," Dad ordered.

"No one has to leave," I declared. "Since I've decided I'm not talking to Abel for the next three hours, there actually isn't going to be a domestic."

I felt Abel's hand curl around the back of my neck even as I felt the room empty of people. Dad jerked his thumb toward the door at Moose, then grabbed his hand and yanked him out of the couch.

"Good luck to you, bubba," Dad muttered to Abel on his way out.

I heard the door close, then I was out of the chair but back in it, sitting in Abel's lap.

"Uh, dude," I said low. "Think I made it clear how I felt about you hauling me around when I'm pissed."

"How about when I'm pissed?" he asked, and it was then I felt his vibe and took in the look on his face.

My back went straight. "Why are *you* pissed?"

"I don't know, maybe 'cause we had a powerful witch who finally came to us after Poncho jumped through hoops for her, but she wouldn't talk unless you were gone and we need her to help us and the only way to get her to do that was actually *speak* with her. So the best thing my mate could do to help with that situation was move her ass out of the room, trust I'd tell her everything when I got to her, and not get shitty about it."

He was being annoying because he was right.

"How would you feel if you had to leave the room when important shit is happening?" I asked instead of giving in.

"I wouldn't like it. But if it had to be done, if *anything* in this situation has to be done, I'd do it."

He was right again, thus, even more annoying.

"Just an FYI, but sometimes it feels like you big, powerful vampires and wolves don't think we girls have anything to offer," I shared.

"Bullshit," he returned, and I blinked.

"Uh...say what?" I asked.

"That's bullshit, because that's not it," he told me. "You're frustrated. I get that. I am too. Nothing is happening with the potential of everything happening, it's all bad, and we're hangin' around doin' fuck all. It's puttin' you in a bad mood. I get that because I'm in a shitty mood too. I also get that I'm the safe one you got to lay your shit on when it gets too heavy." His arms around me gave me a squeeze. "I'll shoulder that burden but that offer doesn't include me not holdin' that mirror up to your face. You got no reason to be pissed, Lilah. You lashed out, now rein it in."

And he was right again.

I looked to my knees.

"She's gonna help," he said, and my eyes went back to him. "Poncho's aunt. Her name is Josefa."

I wanted to hug him. He'd called me on it. He was right. He knew it and he knew I knew it.

But he didn't push it. He didn't rub my face in it. He didn't drive it into the dirt. He said his bit and now we were moving on.

I didn't hug him. I didn't say anything about that.

I moved on with him.

I did this by relaxing into him and asking, "She is?"

"It took time for us to get her to agree, but she's gonna try to get her some visions. Tell the future," he said.

Sudden fear gripped my throat. "Oh God, that might not be good."

He shook his head. "Future is elastic, according to her. She could say it like it is now, that doesn't mean that's the way it has to be."

Well, thank God for that.

"How long are her visions going to take?" I asked.

"Don't know. Apparently, magic isn't exact," Abel told me. "But first we got to get her some weird shit so she can perform a bunch of rituals and get in the zone."

"What weird shit?"

He shook his head. "I stopped takin' it in at ingredient three. Poncho's got the list and Yuri's assured us they'll get everything we need."

"Well, that's good," I noted.

"Yeah. More good, the other five are gonna keep on my brother, but they also think they may be able to locate Lucien's father using Lucien's blood, seein' as they're connected, father and son. They said it's a long shot, it might work better with more witches, but since their coven was almost wiped out a few days ago, they're not thinkin' it's a good bet they can recruit more and time is something we don't have. But they're gonna give it a shot with what they got."

I felt my eyes get big. "That would be great!"

He grinned. "Yeah." Then his grin died.

"What?" I asked.

"The good part of the rest I've gotta tell you is, we know it's happening. The bad part is, it's happening."

My body got tight again, but I didn't repeat my *what*.

"That hanger who came to see Lucien?" he started, and I nodded. "He was recruited by The True. He stayed with them while they were doin' what they were doin' with hangers. And when it was safe, he hauled ass to find Lucien to tell him what that is."

"What is it?" I whispered.

"Buildin' an army. Training. For battle to help with this Noble War, whenever that's gonna start, and for other duties."

"Like what other duties?"

"Like guarding the camps where they're gonna intern humans."

I felt bile glide up my throat.

"Uh...*what*?" I breathed, my voice sounding strangled.

"They got lots of plans," Abel went on. "Obviously, they gotta leave some humans to do their thing. Need food to keep humans alive so they'll need farmers, shit like that. And they'll be able to take what they want when they want. The *delectable morsels*," he said the last two words like they tasted funny, "that's what they call them, they're gonna breed and they want them available to feed. So they're gonna build camps, corral those kinds of humans into them, and see to that shit. But there will be more."

"This keeps getting worse and worse," I muttered.

"Yep," he agreed.

I let that go because I had to.

"How did this hanger know where to find Lucien?" I asked.

"Apparently, Lucien had showed him kindness. The guy hung around at places Lucien would go, did Lucien favors. Lucien didn't accept these favors for free, gave the guy money which kept him clothed, fed. Lucien guesses that somehow, that built a bond. That's a guess, though. He doesn't exactly know how and he's not exactly comfortable that the guy *did* know."

"At least he did us a favor," I said. "Kindness always pays off."

"Yeah."

"What now with that?" I asked.

"More good, this guy gave us the location of this training camp and told us there were others. Obviously, they're covert, but they're big operations, according to this Breed. Not easy to move, say, should one hanger go AWOL. We know where one is, not the others, but we now know to look for them. Gregor's set some of his higher-up vampire soldiers on making a plan to take this base out. At the same time, they're calling the president to access intelligence satellites to see if they can locate any other camps so they can hit them."

"Wouldn't the US government have a lock on any such activity, seeing as they *do* have spy satellites?"

"They can't attack every compound that they reckon bad shit is happening in, and until today, we didn't know they were up to this crap. Now that we know what that bad shit is, they can pay closer attention, get men on the ground to pay closer attention, and maybe weed out The True's bases so that they can be targeted."

Something unknit inside me as I said softly, "So we actually have a plan."

Abel nodded, also looking a shade less stressed out. "Finally, we got somethin' solid to go on and we're able to do something."

I took in a long breath and let it out, dropping my head to his shoulder. He cuddled me closer and laid his cheek against the top of my head.

I gave it some time to let the goodness of being tucked close to Abel penetrate completely before I said, "Sorry I was a bitch earlier."

"Can't guarantee you, this situation continues like it does much longer, that I'm not gonna be a dick. It's gonna get to us. All of us. We just gotta be aware and not turn on each other."

I snuggled closer. "Seems like two hundred years on the earth makes a guy pretty smart."

There was a smile in his voice when he muttered, "Whatever."

He barely got out the *er* in *whatever* before he was standing, me held in his arms so tight, I feared he'd break my bones.

"Abel, wh—?"

Suddenly, I was on my feet but pushed back.

Abel crouched in front of me like he did when he was going to leap to wolf.

"Abel! What's going on?" I yelled.

He turned only his head to me. He was baring his teeth and I saw his fangs extended.

"*Run!*" he roared.

I started to turn to run even as he leaped to wolf, so beautiful, so big, so proud. I loved him as wolf, all his dark mixed with silvery fur, his intense brown eyes, his intelligent face.

But right then, I couldn't do what I usually did when my man was wolf, which was to admire him and think he was awesome.

I couldn't do this because he'd landed on all fours, but he immediately bent low over his two forepaws, snarling at what appeared to be nothing.

Until it was something.

Something that made me freeze.

Abel barked a canine bark at me, circled around until he was in front of me, and backed me up using his hindquarters.

But I was mesmerized by the sparks that were swirling in the space Abel as wolf had been snarling at.

Green, violet, and red ones, sparkling and streaming, like they were in a centrifuge, round and round, going fast.

So cool, so beautiful, it was mesmerizing.

Abel kept backing me up, barking constantly and very loudly, as the sparks kept going.

And on a turn, they disappeared, but in their place were two people.

One was a tall, very slender, unbelievably beautiful African American woman with a full, longish Afro of soft black curls, big, dark brown eyes, and incredible cheekbones. She was wearing a choker made of three lines of oblong bone, feathers hanging down at the bottom. She also had on a brown suede halter vest and seriously low-rider suede pants with fringe down the sides. Last, she had large, gold hoops in her ears—the insides of which had dangling spikes—as well as kickass leather bands wrapped around each wrist and rings on every finger, including some that fit snug between the top and middle knuckle and one that covered her whole finger, from the nail bed over the bottom of her last knuckle.

She was fabulous and her outfit was *amazing*.

I took her in and then I looked to the big man at her side.

And every inch of me turned solid.

Because it was Abel.

Boots. Jeans. Thermal. Tall. Dark hair. Lean but powerful body.

Top to toe.

Except he had no scar and his brown eye was where the blue one should be and vice versa.

"Holy shitoly," I whispered.

His eyes went from Abel, as wolf, to me.

"You called?" he asked, lazily lifting his brows.

And he asked this just as the door burst open and the room filled with snarling, snapping wolves.

# 23
# Beauty and Pain

*Abel*

*Do not attack!* Abel ordered Callum, his brothers, and Ryon even as he leaped to man.

But he figured they weren't going to attack anyway.

Because he was standing before them.

Even though it wasn't him.

Keeping his eyes pinned to what could be none other than his brother, Abel prowled to his jeans and bent to snatch them up.

"We're lucky girls." He heard murmured and looked to the woman with his brother.

Her eyes were on his cock and she was smiling.

She was also addressing Delilah.

Abel ignored the woman checking him out and looked back to his brother as he jerked on his jeans. He barely had them over his ass when he felt Delilah's hands on him, one at his lower back, one at the side of his waist. Then she had the side of her front pressed to the side of his back, pressed deep, as close as she could get.

It should have made him feel better. In any other circumstance, his mate's silent support would have made him feel better.

Staring at his blood brother, he didn't feel better.

The others prowled the room, keeping a distance, remaining wolves.

He felt Delilah move, staying close, which was the only way he'd let her move, and he knew she'd nabbed his thermal Henley when she pressed it into his hand.

He kept eye contact with his brother, losing it only when he pulled the shirt over his head.

Even when he tugged it down his stomach, he still said nothing.

"You wanna start?" the vison of him asked. "Or you want me to do it?"

"You," he grunted, and Delilah pressed even closer.

"This is Teona," he stated, curling the woman in the curve of his arm closer. "My mate. My witch."

He saw in his peripheral vision that she waved a hand in a half circle in front of her. "Hey."

Abel didn't take his eyes off his brother. "You?"

He watched the man tense.

"I'm Cain."

Abel stared.

"Seriously?" Delilah whispered.

"Abel, is everything all right?" Lucien asked from behind them. He knew the vampire had been standing in the door since the wolves came in, but Delilah jumped against him when she heard Lucien speak.

"Meet my brother, Luce," Abel invited. "This is fuckin' *Cain*."

He felt Lucien approach and stop at his side, though he did it partially to Abel's back.

Not aggressive.

This was Abel's play.

"It would appear your parents have an unusual sense of humor," Lucien remarked.

Abel didn't reply.

"You wanna call off your wolves?" Teona requested.

He felt Callum's canine eyes on him.

"Go," Abel said and finished, "But come back."

The wolves whirled and exited the room.

He watched his brother's gaze move to Abel's mate.

"Delilah," he said softly.

*"Eyes to me,"* Abel barked, and his brother cut his gaze back to him.

"I have a mate, Abel. I know you two are new, but you've got to know that I'm no threat," he stated.

"So you know," Abel returned, and Cain shook his head with apparent confusion.

"I know?" he asked.

"You know that wolves are protective of their mates. Fiercely protective," Abel explained.

Teona shifted uncomfortably, doing this pressing closer to her man.

Cain held his brother's eyes.

"I know," he said softly.

"How?" Abel asked.

That was when his brother, who he'd known for less than five minutes, gutted him.

"Pop taught me."

They'd left Abel in an alley.

But they'd kept Cain.

Instantly, Delilah slid to his front, doing it keeping herself plastered to him along the way. When she got there, she put her hands to his abs and started pushing at him gently.

She did this speaking.

"Lucien, can you see to it Cain and Teona are made comfortable? Abel and I have to have a chat."

"Of course," Lucien agreed.

"We'll be back," she went on, but seeing as he didn't take his eyes from his brother, he only assumed she was speaking to Cain and his woman.

She kept pushing.

He didn't budge.

"Baby, in the hall," she urged softly.

"You knew our parents?" Abel asked his brother.

She pushed harder and was louder when she said, "Please, Abel honey, in the hall." He opened his mouth to say something else to his brother, but Delilah fisted her hands in his shirt and her voice was ragged when she begged, "*Please.*"

It was her tone that got to him. He tore his eyes from his brother and looked down at his mate and saw it immediately.

This wasn't about her pushing him to do something she wanted him to do when he wasn't ready to do it.

This was something else.

She was suffering.

For him.

Therefore, without hesitation, he clamped an arm around her and pulled her into the hall and down to living room five. There, he walked them in and shut the door.

The instant he did, she wrapped her arms around him, pressed close, and held on tight.

"Just hold on," she whispered into his chest.

He folded his arms around her, dropped his mouth to the top of her head, and did as told.

It took a while, but the feel of her, the smell of her, what he knew she wished desperately to give to him penetrated, and the numbness, which had invaded in order to control the fury, slid away to a stillness that he knew was fighting the fury.

"I love you," she whispered, and the stillness became warmth that wasn't the blaze of anger but a soothing balm so beautiful, in centuries, he'd never experienced anything like it.

He knew she loved him. She'd mostly said it.

But not straight out.

Not like that.

But she wasn't done.

"I love the way you love your family. I love how protective you are, of me and of everyone you love. I love how into me you are. I love how you seem to be able to give me everything I need before I even know I need it. I love that you say you're sorry straight up when you feel those words. I love that you're beautiful to look at. I love that that beauty runs so deep, even when I have it for eternity, I know I'll never find the end. I love the way you touch me. I love the way you smell. I love the way you dress. I love the feel of your hair. I love the sound of your laugh. I love that you're smart. I love that you're fierce. I love that I know I have thousands of more things I love about you, and I love that you'd stand there, holding me and listening to me, even if it took a year for me to say them."

"Yeah, 'cause you're tellin' me how awesome I am," he replied, his voice gruff, and lifted his head when hers tipped back. He caught her eyes. "Any guy would stand here for a year and listen to that."

She kept whispering, her heart in her eyes, her love for him etched in her expression, and it was the most beautiful thing he'd seen in two hundred years.

And he knew right to his gut that it would be the most beautiful thing he'd see for eternity.

"And I love it when you're a smartass."

He'd had enough. More than he could take. He'd never known beauty needed limits, but he now knew that if you took in too much, like all Delilah was giving him, you might explode.

So he had to stop her.

He did that by slanting his head and dropping his mouth to hers, drinking deep, taking all he could get.

And as usual, Delilah, his temptress, his mate, his woman, the love of his life, the only love he'd had, the only love he'd ever have, held on tight and gave him everything she had.

When he broke the kiss, he didn't move away.

He stayed close, looking in her milky-green eyes, eyes he hoped like fuck he'd be able to look into for eternity, and it was him who was whispering.

"I love you too, *bao bei,* with everything I am, and I'll do it until the sun falls from the sky."

He saw tears glisten in her eyes so he slid a hand up her spine, curled it around the back of her head, and shoved her face in his chest.

They held on to each other and they did it a long time.

And as they did it, it hit Abel that, with what had just happened, like she said he gave to her, before he knew what he needed, she'd given him exactly that.

An anchor.

A safe harbor.

A sense of belonging.

The certainties of his world, love and life, all this inextricably mingled with loss, took new meaning.

It became nothing but a journey, a journey filled with beauty and pain.

A journey that led to her.

A journey that would never end, but now one thing would remain constant.

She'd be at his side.

He closed his eyes against the stinging he felt in them and bent his neck, pressing his lips to the top of her head.

He took in a deep breath, taking in more of her scent, letting the feel of her in his arms, the feel of being in hers, soak in deep.

Then he said into her hair, "I'm good to go back now."

He again lifted his head when she tipped hers back. "You sure?"

He nodded.

She studied him for a moment before he felt her hands fist in his shirt at his back.

"He's your twin," she noted quietly.

"Yep," he replied.

Her lips tipped up. "You're hotter."

That was when it happened. Something he couldn't imagine happening so soon after he came face to face with the brother who, for centuries, he hadn't known he'd had. Something he *could* imagine happening so soon after Delilah shared the depths of her love.

He threw his head back and burst out laughing.

"It's true," she said through his laughter, giving his shirt a tug.

His body was shaking and he was still laughing when he dipped his chin to again catch her eyes, and when he did, he caught her grinning.

"He looks just like me."

"A mate can tell the difference. And anyway, every girl knows that scars are hot."

"Right," he said through his continuing chuckles.

"Though, I'd bet the farm she's a biker bitch. That outfit, which, by the way, when this is done, I'm getting one just like that, screams biker." She pressed into him. "She's something."

"You're hotter."

Her grin remained in place, but her eyes warmed, and seeing as they were already warm, the affection in them now was amazing to behold.

But she didn't reply to what he said. She rolled up on her toes and kissed his throat.

When she rolled back, the warmth was still there, but the grin was only lingering.

"We should go back."

He nodded.

She gave him a squeeze before she let him go with one arm, keeping the other around his waist. He did the same but with an arm around her shoulders.

Holding each other, they walked back to where they'd been.

When they arrived in the room, everyone was there. Callum and Sonia. Lucien and Leah. Jian-Li, Xun, Wei, and Chen. Hook, Poncho, Moose, and Jabber. Yuri and Aurora. Barb, Ruby, Jezza, and Flo. And Gregor.

All eyes came to him and he immediately felt overwhelmed. Overwhelmed by the wave of loyalty and tenderness that swept over him, nearly taking him back on a foot, definitely settling firm in his soul in a way that felt like it'd be there forever.

He gladly took that feeling and turned his attention to his brother and his woman.

Cain didn't look comfortable.

Teona didn't look happy.

It was Teona who spoke.

"You think we could do this a bit more private?"

"This is my family," Abel declared. "And when something important is happening, I keep my family close."

He felt Delilah move and looked down at her to see her exchanging glances with Jian-Li. And if Delilah's look mirrored Jian-Li's, it was filled with pride.

Abel felt his back get straighter and he threw out an arm.

"You wanna take a seat?" he offered.

"Good standing," Cain muttered.

Abel nodded and then got right down to it.

"You grew up with our parents."

Cain watched him warily and nodded.

"Why didn't I?"

"We're twins," Cain stated.

"Got that," Abel returned.

"We're anomalies," Cain told him.

"Got that too, though, found out when I was two hundred and five when you were lucky enough to have your parents share that info with you," Abel replied.

Cain took that hit with a subtle wince but powered through it.

"They knew of The Prophesies."

"And how's that?" Abel asked.

"Pop knew King McDonagh," Cain answered. "When we were born, the king explained."

Abel said nothing, but he felt Callum become even more alert.

"Through The Prophesies, they knew it would be you," Cain went on.

"There were two of us. How'd they know that?" Abel asked.

Cain shook his head. "I've no idea. But I've not fathered a child. I have no idea what parents know and what they don't. They just knew, and turns out they were right."

Abel couldn't argue that.

"I'm your keeper," Cain said quietly and with total seriousness, regardless of his words. "What our parents did was necessary."

They'd get into that in a second.

"Are they alive?" Abel asked and braced when he felt what was coming from Cain and Teona.

"No. Pop died when we were attacked when I was forty-seven human years, about nine wolf. But he gave Ma and me time to run. We got away. She was killed fifty-two years ago. She died protecting me. They took her head, but she succeeded in her goal. I got away."

His words were terse and he didn't hide the burn in his eyes.

Abel got that.

The first, their father, with Cain that young, he'd had no choice but to run.

The second had to kill.

"I'm sorry," Abel murmured and felt Delilah put her hand, light and soothing, on his abs.

Cain lifted his chin. "Pop was wolf. Ma was vampire."

"They found Hui for me, didn't they?" Abel guessed and got a short nod.

"Ma told me she was always feeding stray dogs and cats. Giving them scraps," Cain confirmed. "A puppy, she'd take in. She took you in. Ma told me Pop watched and waited. Made sure she looked after you. Tagged you as a puppy with your name so they could give you at least that, looked like a collar, but it was a necklace, only thing they felt safe to leave you with. They stayed close as long as they could. Then they were after us so we couldn't."

Somehow, from somewhere he didn't get, Abel understood.

And he whispered, not bothering to hide his shock, "They used you as a decoy."

Cain's mouth tightened. "The immortals after us didn't know there was another."

"Oh my God," Delilah breathed even as he felt the spike of tension hit the room.

"Ma found Teona for me," Cain went on. "Teona masked me so you'd never scent me. That way, I could get close, keep watch, you wouldn't know. She also cloaked me so no one else could find me. Took Teona and me about a minute after we met to realize we were lifemates. She's been at my side for decades."

"You were always close," Abel said. "To me," he finished.

Cain nodded again. "So was Ma, as close as she could get without you feeling her when you were old enough to understand what you might be sensing. Best day of her life was when I could go out on my own. Look after you. And by then, cameras had been invented. Made me take any shot I could get. In the end, she must have had thousands of pictures of you."

Delilah's hand pressed deep as everything about Abel strung tight to fight the feelings his brother's words caused.

His mother had had pictures of him. His family stuck close. They'd had to let him go to keep him safe, but they'd stuck close.

For centuries.

He knew that had to kill too.

It was almost too much to fight, but in an effort to do that, he said, "You saved me in Dallas."

Cain's eyes slid to Jian-Li before looking back to Abel. "That witch located you. Don't know how. Only one who did until you hit Serpentine Bay. With the Bay, my guess is, you and I were so far off the grid, they'd had no shot at finding either of us. So they somehow sniffed out Delilah. Followed her. Put her in danger to draw you out. Figure this since the witches did that before."

Abel's body got tighter at the glance to Jian-Li, which kept happening as his brother spoke.

But he knew that glance meant they'd also taken out Jian-Li's husband, his brothers' father, Ming. He also knew when Cain said the witches had done that before, they'd made the attack on Ming in a failed effort to do the same thing.

Ming had died for Abel. Senselessly.

He fought the burn as he fought looking at Jian-Li, at Xun or Wei or Chen. He wasn't going to explain about Ming to them. Not now.

"Any clue why the witches got mixed up in this?" Abel asked.

Cain shook his head. "No, just know they weren't working with immortals. Their activities in Texas were theirs alone. You took off after what happened to you, they lost you. But whatever they were up to, that witch wasn't going to kill you. It was about capture, not kill. Witches have a hybrid at their command, they got power. At least that's what Teona believes. History bears this to be true. Not the first time witches tried to leash immortals. But if they got one of the three immortals who are noted in The Prophesies, it'd put them at the upper hand with *all* immortals. Something they'd want after all they went through. Especially that coven. They'd been harboring ill will for a very long time."

This made sense. It was clear that the witches held great amounts of anger. Vengeance wasn't a far path to stray when you held that kind of anger for that long. Witches with one of The Three at their command would have both sides of the immortals at their mercy.

Since that made sense, Abel let it go and pointed out, "It was vampires and wolves who went after Delilah in Serpentine Bay."

"Yes." Cain nodded.

"Any idea about that?" Abel pressed.

"No clue, except it was clear the other two of The Sacred Triumvirate had been identified," Cain told him. "Which meant The Prophesies were unfolding and the Noble War almost upon us. The existence of magic has been hidden for centuries, but obviously, it's out there. Witches. Seers. These rebels, they'll do anything, as they've proved, including finding someone to force into guiding their way."

That made sense too.

"So you, our mother, and our father lived your lives hunted because they thought you were me, but at the same time you stuck close to make certain they couldn't actually find me," Abel summed it up.

Cain nodded and confirmed, "Yep."

It sucked, but Delilah was right.

He should have waited to get pissed until after he got his brother's story.

"And you're here now...?" Abel asked.

"I'm here now for the same reason I've been anywhere since almost the time I started breathing. Because Teona and I have been staying close to make sure no threat can get to you. But I'm *here* now," he pointed at the floor when he said *here*, "because you seem to be finding any threat before we do and you either neutralize it or it's neutralized for you."

The wary intensity Abel's blood brother had worn on his face since he appeared in the room cracked as his lips quirked.

"And last, I'm here now because you got a bunch of witches on my ass and it's annoying my mate. She's not big on being annoyed, but she *is* big on telling me when she is and I'm sick of hearing that shit."

He felt Delilah relax against him, but he was stuck back on something Cain had said.

*I'm here now for the same reason I've been anywhere since almost the time I started breathing.*

*Almost the time I started breathing...*

He stared at the vision of himself that was not himself. He stared at the only other living vampire werewolf on the planet. He stared at the man who'd been hunted, whose father died protecting him, whose mother died the same, whose family he'd lost, and didn't have any to take their place, until he found his mate.

He stared at the man who had a different story than Abel's, but it wasn't any prettier.

Then he looked to that man's mate.

"Thank you for keeping my brother safe."

He heard a telling noise come from Delilah as she pushed super close. He also saw a telling sheen at the edge of Teona's eyes and he was glad for it.

This meant she felt deep too.

For his brother.

And then Abel didn't waste another moment.

Carefully guiding his silently crying mate to his brother, he stopped two feet in front of him, left Delilah leaning on him as he moved his arm from around her, and stuck his hand out to his brother.

Delilah straightened away as Cain took his hand.

Cain's grip was strong, warm, and sure.

Feeling it, Abel's throat got tight.

Then he jerked his brother's hand until both were caught against their chests and he wound his other arm around Cain's shoulders.

It felt fucking good when Cain returned the gesture.

It was then he heard more than one sob. He knew one was Delilah's, the other he reckoned was Leah, and the third he figured was Aurora. He thought this because Sonia was queen, she kept her shit sharp. And Jian-Li would do that in private.

"Fuck! This means party!" Hook shouted, and Abel pushed back but not far. He kept his hand on Cain's shoulder. Cain did the same. "Gregor, you vampire motherfuckers are cool customers, but please, God, tell me in this huge-ass house you got the makin's of a low-down, tits-up, ball-bustin', howl-at-the-moon *shindig*."

"Essentially, my father-in-law," Abel explained quietly.

"Ah," Cain murmured, lips again quirking.

"If they don't, a wolf can make a party out of anything," Sonia announced. "Hook, let's go see what we've got to work with."

Abel stepped back, dropping his hand from his brother's shoulder but keeping hold of their grip, and looked toward Hook only to see Hook headed his way.

When he got close, he pounded Abel on the back, the man's eyes locked to his.

"Glad for you, bubba," he muttered. "Beside myself, son." He pounded him once more, dropped his hand, and looked to Cain. "And fuckin' pleased to meet you, brother. Know it."

Cain gave him a chin dip and Hook whirled away.

"Now, little queenie, let's get this party rollin'!" he yelled at Sonia.

"Right on!" Jabber yelled after him.

That was when Abel was forced to let his brother go. Everyone moved toward them to get introductions and give greetings. After that, many moved out to help Hook and Sonia make a party.

It was only Gregor who dampened the mood.

"It's always important to celebrate when a celebration is in order," he said low. "But Cain, there's a great deal you need to be briefed on."

"How about you give the family an hour to get to know each other and then we can give my brother his briefing?" Abel suggested in a tone that stated plainly Gregor had only one choice of response.

Not a stupid man, he gave that response, but he shocked the shit out of Abel when he did it with a smile that said the vampire was happy for him.

"Of course."

Gregor moved away.

Delilah took over, gaze aimed at Teona.

"Babe, seriously, if you don't tell me where you got your outfit, we're starting our relationship with a catfight."

"No need, sister, I'm a bitch who likes to share the wealth," Teona replied.

"Right on," Delilah returned.

Abel looked to Cain.

"From the look of your woman, not to mention you." Abel tipped his head to the familiar uniform Cain was wearing. "I take it you got a bike."

"Fuck yes," Cain said firmly. "Harley. Vintage. Got my first about a week after you got yours."

It was a hit, knowing this and learning it so far after the fact.

But it still felt good just knowing it.

"Pop would have loved motorcycles," Cain said quietly. "Ma said the minute you got one, then I did, she wasn't surprised because she knew if he had the chance he'd get one too and his boys were both just like him."

That was a hit too.

But this time, it felt fucking *great* knowing it.

"How about we share over bourbon?" Delilah suggested.

"My baby likes Kentucky's finest, but you got vodka, this sister will be grateful," Teona said.

Delilah gave her a huge smile, moving around and tucking her arm through Teona's.

"We've got everything. Let's get you *set up*!"

Then she led Teona out, and as she did, Teona threw a sexy, happy grin over her shoulder.

Delilah threw just a happy grin over hers.

Abel tossed out an arm and muttered, "Let's get set up."

His blood brother jerked up his chin and moved forward.

Abel followed.

And he did it knowing he, too, was wearing a happy grin.

"It no longer matters," Jian-Li whispered to the window.

"Sweetheart," Abel whispered to her profile.

"It no longer matters," she repeated, not looking to him.

Abel had just told her about Ming.

"Ma—" Chen, close to her other side, started.

But he stopped when she suddenly turned her head and tipped it back to look up at Abel.

"He would die for you."

Abel clenched his teeth to beat back the emotion her words caused, emotion that was threatening to bring him low.

"He would, *tian xin*, for all of you boys," she told him gently. "He's at peace having died for you, Abel. And you know this is true."

He knew it was true.

Wei and Xun, who were at their mother's back, close to their huddle, got closer.

They knew it was true too.

Abel lifted his hand and touched her chin with his finger. When he did, it was the first time in a long time sadness didn't sift into her eyes. Her gaze simply held his steady.

"I'm sorry," he said quietly.

"You had no control over it," she replied.

"It was senseless," he told her cautiously.

"Nothing is senseless," Jian-Li returned. "We may not be able to make sense of it, my Abel, but that doesn't mean it was senseless. We moved soon after that. We moved to a place we were all much safer for we were all possible targets. If that's the only purpose of my husband's death, and he knew it, he would die a million times to make that so."

That was true too.

Knowing it, Abel swallowed and slid his finger along her jaw to curl his hand around the back of her neck, pulling her into his chest.

She wrapped her arms around him.

Her other sons drew closer. Chen lifted his hand to rest it on the small of his mother's back. Wei drifted a finger through her hair, over her ear, to the bun at the base of her neck. Xun pulled one of her hands from around Abel so he could hold it.

Jian-Li allowed this affection for a few beats before she pulled away from all of them and looked through them, saying, "Enough sorrow. There's a celebration happening. Sorrow has it's time. That sorrow has had its time. Now, we celebrate."

As ever (well, mostly), when Jian-Li spoke, her sons listened.

This time, she made them do it by promptly walking out of the room on a trajectory to rejoin the party, which was in full swing.

After exchanging looks, her sons followed.

"Can you believe Teona is *ninety-eight years old*?" Delilah asked, leaning heavily on Abel as he opened the door to their bedroom.

His woman was sloshed.

Suffice it to say, a biker and the queen of werewolves could throw together a fuckuva party. It was three in the morning and Ryon, Moose, Jabber, Poncho, Calder, Caleb, Regan, Jian-Li and the boys, Hook and his vampire, Ursula, Barb, Ruby, Jezza, and Flo were still at it.

The rest, having mates, decided to take their parties elsewhere.

Cain and Teona had taken off five minutes before Abel and Delilah.

Abel knew why he stayed as long as he could. He wouldn't have guessed it, but getting to know his brother and hearing about his parents far from sucked.

What also didn't suck was the fact that Cain, even while getting cues from Teona like Delilah was giving him that they were in the mood for a different kind of celebration, stayed as long as he could.

This meant Cain thought sharing with his brother far from sucked.

Abel liked that.

But a brother was a brother, long lost or not, and a mate was a mate.

Eventually, you couldn't ignore the call of the wild.

"Yeah, pussycat, I was there when she shared that tidbit," Abel murmured, a smile on his face as he guided his mate into their room and shut the door behind them.

He watched Delilah take two unsteady steps in front of him before she turned, whirled (his hands flew out when she started teetering, but she got herself sorted), then planted her fists on her hips and tipped her head saucily to the side.

"I'm *so* gonna love being young *forever*," she declared, and his smile got bigger.

There were many times in his life he'd thought that sucked.

Being the same, young forever, but doing it with her, finally, he was looking forward to it.

"Yeah," he agreed, getting close.

When he got close enough, she put her hands on his chest and leaned into him.

"In case you're keeping track, that's something else I love about you. That you can give me that."

Her words were kind of slurred, but they were still beautiful.

"Me too, *bao bei*."

She tipped her head to the side again and asked, "You know, there's something else I left off my list."

He rested his hands on either side of her neck. "What's that?"

She slid one hand down his chest, his stomach, to cup his crotch.

He pulled in a hissed breath, but his breath snagged when she gave him a squeeze.

"This," she whispered.

"Baby," he groaned.

Her other hand slid down and she undid his zipper.

"Mama feels like sucking cock," she shared, her voice hot, her eyes bothered, all of it telling him she *really* wanted that.

"Not me gonna stop you," he told her.

She grinned, cute and inebriated.

Then she dropped to her knees, pulled him out, and hesitated not a second before she commenced going down on him.

His head dropped back and he slid his fingers into her hair.

"Fuck, you're good at that," he growled.

She took that encouragement and did amazing things with it. She did them for a while and she gave them her all.

And she did it until he could take no more.

"You wanna swallow or you want me in you?"

She pulled him out, rolled his head with her tongue, and tipped her eyes to him. When she did, it was a wonder he didn't come all over her lips. Her eyes were drunk. Drunk with booze and life and sex and love, wild and alive and carefree.

It was a close second, but it was nearly as good as the beauty she'd given him that afternoon in living room five.

"Your choice," she whispered.

He took his choice, fast, so she only had time to gasp before he had her jeans over her ass, her torso bent over the back of a chair, and she was taking his cock.

She didn't take it long before he leaned over her, prepared her neck, and sank his fangs in.

Her blood gushed into his mouth and she came instantly.

He kept at her, pounding hard, jolting her, forcing the chair forward, pushing her orgasm to the limit, his hand finding her tit, pinching and twisting.

She cried out, arching her neck, rearing her ass into his hips as he gave more, she took more, and she gave it all to him.

He swept her wounds with his tongue, drove a hand into the curls between her legs, and found her, still pinching and twisting her nipple, still driving deep.

"Keep coming," he ordered roughly into her ear.

"'Kay, baby," she whimpered, the words ending on a moan, her head still back, her mouth opened as the moan continued but went silent.

Her cunt gripped him and he kept working her, reaching for it, getting close.

"Keep coming, pussycat," he groaned.

"Yeah," she panted, clutching him with her pussy, her breaths hitching as she rode the wave of a long orgasm, or the span of several.

He loved that.

Fucking loved it.

Giving it to her and knowing she had it in her to take it.

Now it was his turn.

He shoved his face in her neck and pulled hard on her nipple.

"I'm there," he snarled as he drove himself in to the root and exploded.

It was raw, it was wild, it was phenomenal, so it took him time before his head cleared. After it did, he cupped her breast, lapping gently at the fast fading marks on her neck.

"Knew drunk sex with you would be the bomb," she said quietly, her voice still breathy.

"Any sex with you is the bomb," he told her and got silence for long moments.

She broke it, saying, "Yet another thing I love about you. That you think that."

He shoved his face further into her neck and he actually felt the roughness in his voice when he asked, "Anything you don't love about me?"

"Not yet."

Christ.

"You have an eternity to find something," he told her.

"Figure it'll take that long."

*Christ.*

His temptress, his mate, his woman.

The fates fucking loved him.

"You sleepy or you got more in you?" he asked.

"I can go all night," she answered.

"Not hard, since it'll be morning in about two hours," he teased.

She twisted her neck to look at him. "Then I can definitely go that long."

Slowly, he slid out, and when she lost him, he bent in to touch his mouth to hers.

When he lifted his head, he whispered, "Then get naked for me, pussycat. Wanna see how long you can go."

"A challenge," she noted.

"Yeah."

"Accepted," she declared, then pushed him back, shuffled two steps, and stood in front him, getting naked.

He watched, loving what he saw.

Abel was immortal. He had super strength, super senses, and super stamina.

Delilah was not. She didn't have any of that shit.

But his bitch *still* wore him out.

Fuck yeah.

The fates fucking loved him.

## *Yuri*

Lazing on an elbow in the pillow, his other hand toying in her wetness, Yuri watched, smelled, and listened to what he was doing as it took hold of Aurora.

She was on her knees in the pillows, those knees spread wide at his command, hands to the headboard, back arched, ass tipped to the ceiling, and she'd been that way for a long time as Yuri toyed with her.

She was gripping hard, panting, her heart tripping over itself, the musk of her sex strong. Her body had long since grown taut, searching for it, wanting it, desperate for it, but he withheld.

"Yuri," she gasped, twitching her hips to find his fingers after he took off the pressure and made them merely a whisper. Vague and magnificent, her eyes found his. "*Please.*"

"Have you had enough, my sweet?" he asked calmly, a calm belying the pounding throb in his cock.

"Yes," she panted.

"All right, my love," he murmured and drove two fingers deep into her drenched pussy as his thumb manipulated her hard nub.

Her spine arched forward even further, her head fell back, her hair swaying against the smooth, creamy skin of her back, and her hands clutched the headboard as the sweet little noises of her climax poured from her throat and she ground into his hand.

When it began to leave her, he stroked her deeply but gently, pushing high inside but taking his thumb from her clit, and he watched her head fall forward as she kept her ass tipped to the ceiling, enjoying what she was getting as he enjoyed giving it to her.

"All right, button?" he asked.

"Yeah, sweetheart," she breathed.

He slid his fingers out, running his hand over her ass, murmuring, "Relax."

She did as he lifted from his elbow, wrapped an arm around her waist, and pulled her to him. Sliding them down in bed, he twitched the covers over them and settled her snug to his side.

She rested her cheek to his chest and whispered, "What about you?"

The answer to her question was, by giving her that but not giving himself release, when he had her next, his orgasm would be extraordinary.

Or more extraordinary than what his little witch always gave to him.

Sometimes it was good to give so that what you took later could be so much better.

He didn't explain that.

He gave her an alternate explanation that was nonetheless true.

"You'll learn, sweet, that I take pleasure in pleasuring you."

She pushed closer and snaked an arm around his middle. "I've already learned that."

He smiled at the ceiling.

"Are you...eventually are you..." She lifted up and caught his eyes. "Are you ever going to, you know, um...feed from me?"

His heart thumped and his still-hard cock jumped.

"Do you think you're ready for that?" he asked.

"I've heard that it's...well, nice."

"It is," he confirmed.

"You've given me a lot of nice things, Yuri."

He was delighted she thought so.

He gathered her closer, pulling her up his chest, and lowered his voice when he said, "I intend to continue giving you a variety of nice things, Aurora, for a very long time."

Her face warmed, those big, blue eyes telling him how she felt about that idea.

"So, will you...soon?" She didn't spell it out, but Yuri understood.

"Tomorrow morning," he told her, and she relaxed into him.

"Good. I like the idea of getting something nice." Her hand slid up his stomach, his chest, to the base of his throat. "And I like it more that I finally get to give something nice to you."

"My sweet, if you don't think that watching you take pleasure from me, which means you're allowing me to give you pleasure, isn't giving me something nice, you're very wrong."

She bit her lip and dipped her face closer.

Letting her lip go, she whispered, "Good."

"Now kiss me, Aurora, and let's get some sleep."

A smile hit her eyes before she bent to him and pressed her mouth to his. Her timid tongue touched his lips and he gave her access, allowing her to taste him before he tightened his arms on her and gave her the good-night kiss she deserved.

Her heart was slamming in her chest when he released her mouth and pulled her back down his body.

"Settle in, my sweet," he murmured as he reached to turn out the light.

When the room was swept with darkness, she did as told.

But she didn't sleep.

He allowed this for some time before he called, "Aurora?"

"I'm not a seer," she said strangely.

"Pardon?"

Her arm around his stomach went tight.

"I'm not a seer, Yuri, but I still can't get it out of my head that something is gonna happen soon. I've never had this feeling before." She took in an unsteady breath. "And it kind of scares me."

He turned into her, keeping her close, and when he settled on his side, he tucked her closer.

"This is just a feeling?" he asked.

"Yes."

"No visions with it?"

She shook her head on the pillow and said, "No."

"It isn't a stretch, button, to have anxiety about what's happening."

She was silent, thinking on this, before she said, "I hope that's it."

Yuri hoped the same.

"Try to set it from your mind so you can sleep."

"Okay, sweetheart."

He gathered her closer at the same time she snuggled deep into him.

Having given her concerns to him, she found sleep quickly.

Smelling her, feeling her tiny softness pressed close, her warmth, listening to the steady thrum of her heart, even with all this, Yuri did not do the same.

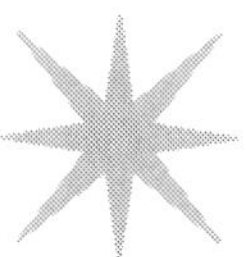

# 24
# Hope Is Powerful

*Delilah*

"Let me get this straight," Cain started over breakfast three days later. "You've got some crazy Mexican witch in the back forty sacrificing a yak, or some shit, in order to get visions of what might happen, doing this either to put your minds at ease or so she can tell you what you've got to stop. You've got six other witches, my mate included, chanting over a bowl you hope will guide you to the leader of this mess. You've got a lock on one, and maybe five other, training camps that, right now, teams of immortals and mortals are setting up to go in and take down. And if any of this is successful, it's going to seriously anger the enemy. You've also got a vampire you trust who's cornered an enemy vampire, rescuing the concubine he was set to rape and murder but detaining him. Because of that, even though the security in this place is so tight it's a wonder anyone can breathe, you're planning to put The Three in danger to take all of them over two thousand miles just so Abel can interrogate this guy. A guy, mind you, who might not know anything or anything you can use."

He took in a breath, his eyes scanning the people at the table, which included all of The Three, the rest of the family, Gregor, and Yuri, but none of the witches.

Then he finished, "Do I have that right?"

"You do," Abel, sitting beside me, confirmed.

Cain's eyes narrowed on his brother. "Are you *insane*?"

I felt Abel get tense so I put my hand on his knee and squeezed.

"No," my man clipped.

"You are, brother. You've totally lost it," Cain returned, and I squeezed harder.

We'd learned, not surprisingly, that Cain was born first.

And we were now learning, also not surprisingly, that even though he was about fifteen minutes older than Abel, he definitely had big brother tendencies.

"What do you suggest we do?" Abel shot back.

"I don't know," Cain retorted. "But not that." He shook his head in frustration. "Dammit, you got all of me, why didn't I get all of you so I could go instead?"

I understood this.

Cain didn't have Abel's mind-control abilities.

That was just for the last of The Three.

"I wouldn't want you in danger either, brother," Abel bit out.

"Yes, well, I didn't spend a century keeping you safe, and the century before that watching our parents do it, for you to go on a suicide mission," Cain bit back.

It was me who got tense at that.

Needless to say, when Abel shared this plan with me, I wasn't gung ho on it either.

But he was my man, my mate, the one destined for me.

I had to have his back.

This meant at the current juncture, I had to keep my mouth shut.

Abel felt my tenseness. I knew it when I heard his voice get tight as he said, "It's not even close to a suicide, man. We'll be covered."

"You sure about that?" Cain returned.

Abel's voice was still tight when he answered, "Nothing's sure in war. That doesn't mean you sit back and wait for devastation to occur before you do shit about it. We need as much information as we can get, considering we don't have that much of it, and even if this guy doesn't have much either, what we get will be more."

"I understand that, so have the people who've got him work him," Cain suggested.

"They are," Gregor butted in. "Cosmo and Stephanie are both skilled in interrogation. They just aren't succeeding."

"So bring him here," Cain said to Gregor.

"They're chipped," Callum told him something that Cain, having been fully briefed on the situation, already knew.

"So?" Cain asked. "A chip is not going to erase what he knows on his way across the country."

"If we move him to this location, they'll know we have him. Currently, he's being kept in his home, which won't arouse suspicion," Lucien pointed out.

"And I'll repeat, a chip is not going to erase his memory," Cain stated.

"Yes, but if he is, indeed, important, whatever he knows and can share they'll also know, and they might make moves to change plans if they believe he's been compromised," Yuri put in. "We must know what they're planning, not what they planned and aborted because we captured one of their men."

Cain sat back in his chair and I watched his jaw get hard.

It was a little freaky seeing the spitting image of my man, who was sitting beside me, also sitting across the breakfast table from me. I knew I'd get used to it. It didn't make it any less freaky.

There was a sharp rap on the door and all eyes went there. But before anyone could call the invitation to come in, the door opened and a vampire stood there.

He was looking at Gregor.

"Sir, if I can have a word," he called.

"Nothing you say cannot be heard by those in this room," Gregor called back, circling a hand in front of him. "Come in, Terrance."

The vampire stepped in and started to close the door, but he also started talking before he accomplished that feat.

"We've had a communication from Gastineau," he declared.

I pulled in a breath and leaned closer to Abel, who, in return, draped an arm on the back of my chair.

"His rescue attempt of Serena was unsuccessful," the vampire Terrance went on.

"Oh no," Sonia whispered.

"Phantom losses were significant," Terrance stated. "He's requesting reinforcements."

"So he found her," Gregor noted, tossing his napkin on the table and pushing his chair back.

"Indeed," Terrance agreed.

"Did he report that Etienne was at that location?" Gregor asked, moving along the table to the door.

"No, sir, he didn't report that. He didn't report anything except their failure and his desire to make another attempt. He's on Skype right now. He wishes to speak directly to you."

Gregor nodded, not looking back to the room as he said, "I'll return with news."

He walked out the door, followed by Terrance, and Terrance closed it behind them.

"Not good news," Leah murmured.

"Phantom losses were significant," Cain stated in a way that got everyone's attention.

But his attention was solely on his brother.

"Do me a favor," he went on quietly. "Wait. A day. You want to give me a gift, wait two. See if that witch gets a vision. See if the others can locate the leader. Just wait, give it a little time, so maybe we'll know what we're facing, or when you go in, you'll have a target that's worth the risk."

"The Three have to agree," Abel replied, and I felt something loosen inside me.

Maybe he was giving in.

Cain pushed back his chair, his gaze moving around the table, before he said, "Then you'll all be doing me a favor. I finally have my brother. I don't want to lose him."

On that, he tossed his napkin on the table and stalked out.

"Shit, I need a cigarette," Jabber muttered, pushing his chair back.

"I'm with you, brother. It's time for a smoke break," Hook stated, getting up to follow Jabber.

Moose did the same.

Poncho stayed seated.

"Any way you can get your auntie to speed things up?" Abel asked him.

"Not good to interrupt her when she's working," Poncho answered.

I sighed.

Abel's jaw got hard.

"Is she really sacrificing a yak?" Leah asked.

"Ox," Poncho told her.

Her eyes got big and they turned to me.

I gave her a lip curl but shrugged.

"I would agree with Cain," Lucien interrupted his bride's and my nonverbal communication. "A day, two, we can wait. Cosmo is working that vampire. Perhaps he'll break him."

"Abel?" Callum called after Lucien finished giving his vote.

And when Abel gave his, I knew it not only came from the fact that he wanted to give his brother this, but he also wanted to give it to me.

"Two days. Then we go," he said.

"Agreed," Callum finished it.

It didn't escape me that they didn't ask for Sonia's, Leah's, or my opinion, but since the vote went the way I wanted it to, I kept my mouth shut.

"We should train," Abel announced.

"There's little else to teach you, brother," Callum told him. "By the fates, you're a natural."

"Then we should attack each other to blow off some steam," Abel returned.

Callum held his eyes and nodded slowly. "All right, Abel."

The men pushed back, including Lucien, his eyes to Xun, which meant they were training too.

Considering I didn't think I was destined to karate chop my way to saving the world, I stayed where I was and reached for the silver coffeepot.

I had it by the handle held up in the air when I felt Abel's hand curl around my neck.

I tipped my head back, he bent in to give me a short, soft kiss, then he was gone.

With similar gestures for their mates, Callum and Lucien were gone with him. Without bitches to kiss, the rest just filed out.

Leaving Leah, Sonia, and me with Poncho.

"Don't you smoke?" Sonia asked him, and he grinned wickedly at her.

"I do, beautiful, but I do not when I got a shot at sittin' at a fancy-ass table with three gorgeous women, drinkin' coffee, and shootin' the shit."

That was Poncho. He was a flirt.

I gave him a smile.

He returned it.

Then I poured my coffee, sat back with mug in hand, and while the world continued to hang in the balance, I shot the shit with my friends.

I moved through the grass toward the wolves doing what they'd been doing for days and days.

And I did it enjoying what I saw.

Callum was an incredibly handsome wolf, Ryon, Calder, and Caleb weren't slouches either, but Abel was glorious. Big. Beautiful. And his fur was amazing. I'd touched it and it was thick and soft.

Seeing him as wolf, I hoped one day I'd have a chance (or many of them) to go out with my mate while he roamed.

Abel sensed me, separated from the pack, and leaped to man.

Okay, more glorious.

I turned, walking backward, giving them all time to do the same and get decent before I made it to them.

"We're good, Lilah," Abel called, and I turned back.

"Sorry to interrupt," I said loudly since I still wasn't that close, "but Gregor's chat with Gastineau is done. He reported to us girls and I'm here to report to you."

"Leah go to Lucien?" Callum asked.

"Yes. And Sonia's with the witches," I told him, now close enough to stop so I did. "We decided to ask them if they could give Gastineau and the immortals that Gregor is sending to him a protection spell."

"So Gregor is giving him reinforcements," Ryon said, and I nodded.

"Etienne wasn't where they're holding Serena," I shared. "It's in a bunker, three stories down under a vampire-owned skyscraper, apparently where an old Feast used to be held. Hard to breach. They're gonna try again anyway."

The men had no response to this.

"Gastineau is, um...antsy," I told them. "The second attempt is gonna happen soon."

"He should wait," Ryon muttered.

"Maybe, but a second attempt done quickly after so many losses were sustained would be unexpected," Callum replied. "Perhaps that will aid their cause."

Abel got close and curled a hand around my neck.

I looked up to him.

"You good?" he asked softly.

Two days of him safe, The Three safe, my friends and family safe, before we started to take risks in order to save the world?

I knew it made me chicken, but I was good.

"Yeah, honey," I replied.

He studied me like he was attempting to see if I was fibbing, must have got the correct answer (since I wasn't), and slid his arm along my shoulders.

"Think I'm done," he told Callum.

Callum lifted his chin.

Abel looked down at me. "Let's go see what the witches had to say."

It was an unnecessary errand. They'd do whatever we asked. They might hate vampires, but they dug us. Not to mention, they kinda liked the world as it was.

Even knowing this, and knowing Abel knew it too, I replied, "Yeah, let's go see."

With waves to the others (from me, Abel did a chin lift), we walked to the house.

And when we got to the witches, we found we were right.

Late that night, everyone was crowded in Gregor's office. Most people were lounging in the copious seating available (he had a serious big office), including me. I was sitting in Abel's lap.

Aurora was up and pacing.

Although she was the only one pacing, the air in the room was thick with tension.

Suddenly, Aurora stopped pacing, looked to her mother, and asked, "Did we do all we could do?"

"Yes, sweetheart," Barb answered. "With the time given and the distance between us, we did all we could do."

"Teona ain't no newbie," Ruby put in. "She's got serious mojo. We gave it to them good."

This loosened a bit of the tightness I felt in my chest and I looked to Teona. When she felt my eyes and looked to me, I smiled.

She winked.

I totally liked Abel's sister-in-law.

"The operation began three hours ago," Abel declared, eyes to Callum before they moved to Lucien. "Your gut, what does it mean that we haven't heard anything?"

Callum looked to Lucien before both men scanned the room, their gaze stopping with meaning on any woman it touched.

There you had it. Protective vampires and wolves.

I rolled my eyes.

"Give it to us straight, darling," Leah encouraged Lucien. "We can take it."

"As you wish, my pet," he replied, then looked to Abel. "It could mean they were successful, but just barely, and are currently securing a safe place in which to hide and see to Serena if, and this is a good possibility, she's been harmed."

That wasn't great, the good possibility of Serena being harmed, but the possible outcome was, so I relaxed against my man.

"Or, it could mean The True decimated them and there's no one to report back," Lucien finished.

"Fuck," I whispered, not relaxed anymore at all.

"We cannot know until we know," Jian-Li pointed out the obvious. "So there is no need to waste negative energy on lamenting loss when we aren't certain we've sustained one. And as positive energy sustains these beings, gives them their light, their lives, it's crucial we honor them by staying as positive as we can."

Yeesh, if all her ancestors were as wise as her, it was no wonder Abel was so smart.

On this thought, I felt something funny so I looked to Abel to see his gaze aimed across the room. There was a small smile playing at his mouth.

I looked where his eyes were aimed, but I knew what I'd see.

The mirror image of my man, including the smile playing at his mouth.

Cain.

He knew his parents had chosen well as to who would raise Abel.

But I bet it didn't suck to have that confirmed.

We all fell silent and I held Abel and his brother's nonverbal communication close, using that to send positive energy out there to Serena and her mate and all those who were trying to save her.

Our silence lasted awhile before Dad broke it, muttering, "Christ, I could use a doobie." I looked to him to see his eyes on Gregor. "You got any pot around this joint? My stash ran out three days ago."

I felt Abel shaking with laughter and I turned to grin at him just when an unmistakable *boop, boop, boop*-ing sound came from Gregor's computer.

His eyes sliced to it as his hand went with vampire speed to his mouse.

He clicked.

The *boop, boop, boop*-ing stopped and the room filled with a deep, smooth voice.

"Serena has been secured."

I slumped against Abel as relief swept the room.

"However, the losses were again great," the voice went on.

The relief vanished.

"We're safe. My mate is weak, but she's being seen to," the voice kept going.

That meant it was Gastineau.

"The news of losses is distressing, Gastineau," Gregor replied to the computer. "But I'm very pleased to hear of Serena's rescue."

"You have the phantoms," Gastineau declared, and I stopped slumping against Abel. "A delegation is en route to your compound now. I'll send missives to the rest. And you're already aware that my queen has committed her wraiths to the side of The Real True."

"We're most grateful," Gregor told him. "I await your delegation and word of Serena's successful recovery."

"Right," Gastineau returned, then there was a different *boop* sound and I knew he had disconnected.

"Not a surprise. Positive energy works," Teona stated, and I saw her smiling at Jian-Li. "Not our asses on the line, and probably just hopeful we did anything to help, but hope is powerful. We can never forget that."

She was not wrong.

"No truer words spoken," Barb voiced my thoughts (kinda).

"I'd suggest another jamboree, but all I got in me is to fuck my vamp and crash in preparation of whatever shit we're gonna face tomorrow," Dad declared. "So I'm off to hit the hay."

I grinned and looked at Abel, who was looking at Dad and shaking his head.

It didn't take long for us to disburse, which we did on quiet, relieved, but edgy good-nights and tight hugs.

Abel and I were silent all the way to our room. We remained silent as we got ready for bed.

I continued the silence when we slipped between the sheets and he pulled me in his arms, front to front, and tucked my face into his throat.

I was guessing this meant no nookie.

I was disappointed, but I got that. He had a lot on his mind and I had to give him space to sort through it.

After a while, Abel ended the silence, giving me what was on his mind.

"They're gonna be pissed that we got Serena."

I closed my eyes.

"Yeah," I whispered, pushing closer and holding him tight.

"They're gonna retaliate."

"Yeah," I repeated, moving in to press my lips to the column of his throat.

"A lotta them still got concubines."

I gave him a squeeze.

"This shit is gonna explode, Lilah, and soon," he said.

"Probably," I agreed.

"I hope like fuck we're ready," he muttered.

I did too.

But I did it to myself.

Out loud, I stated firmly, "We're ready."

"And I hope like fuck you're right."

"Shh, baby, clear your head. Sleep."

"Need your hands and mouth on me." He pulled me up so we were facing each other and dropped his voice low. "Need your wild. Need your brand of alive. Need to feel free the way only you can give to me even when we're cooped up."

"Whatever you need, honey," I whispered, moving my hands on him.

"Love you, Lilah," he whispered back, moving his hands on me.

"Love you too, Abel," I replied before he dipped his head and kissed me.

Then I gave him my hands. My mouth. My wild. My brand of alive. And I did the best I could to make him feel free.

I guess I did all right, because after the third round, he cuddled us close again and fell asleep.

But I lay awake, hoping. Doing lots and lots of hoping. Sending my positivity into the universe with more hope that it would reach the fates that tied me to Abel, handing me beauty, making them decide on the side of right.

Only after I'd tired myself out hoping, I fell asleep.

They were dead.

All of them.

Every one.

Blood dripped in the gutters as I stood in the street amongst the results of pure evil, staring at the blond vampire. Taking in his arrogant grin. But also taking in the malevolence in his eyes.

Yes.

Pure evil.

And also fury.

My body was locked, frozen, but I still felt the chill race up my spine as terror took hold of my heart.

"Tell them," he hissed. "Tell them to give us The Three. Tell them there will be more of this," he snarled as he swung out an arm, "if they do not capitulate."

His chin came up an inch and he stared down his nose at me.

"We're prepared to face a death of hunger and completely annihilate the weaker species, if they do not yield. We will lose our lives and they will lose theirs—an end to the earth as we know it, opening the chance for a new beginning. Tell them. Tell them we're prepared to wipe the earth clean. Tell them to give us The Three."

"Goddamn it, Lilah, baby, *wake up!*" Abel roared, and I jerked awake.

The instant I did, a sharp knock came at the door.

Abel, looming over me and looking freaked out, whipped his head that way.

"Downstairs!" a voice I didn't recognize shouted. "Immediately! Library!"

"Fuck," Abel snarled, rolling over me and taking me with him when he exited the bed.

I wasn't exactly awake so he guided me to my clothes, bent, nabbed my panties, and handed them to me.

I had them on, and he had his jeans on, when I asked, "Was I dreaming?"

"Yep," he replied, bending to snag my jeans.

"Do you know what's going on?" I asked.

He handed me my jeans, and when I took them, he cupped my jaw in his hands, leaning in close.

"No clue, pussycat. Now, do me a favor and dress. Quick."

I nodded and did the best I could, shaking off sleep as I did it.

The minute I was dressed, though both of us were still barefoot, Abel grabbed my upper arm, pulled me into his hold, and *whoosh*, we were out of the room and in the library.

Gregor was there, his hand to his ear on the phone. Lucien and Leah were there. No one else had arrived yet.

They all had their eyes glued to one location in the room.

I looked that way as Abel put me to my feet and I saw that the media cabinet, which usually shut the large, flat-screen TV from sight, was open. It was playing the news, a newscaster reporting, a scrolling bulletin going across the bottom of the screen, pictures inset to the top left.

"...carnage today. Current reports state a small town in northeast Iowa, a village in the highlands of Scotland, another village just outside Sofia in Bulgaria, and a hamlet in eastern China were all decimated. In each instance, only one survivor, a witness, was left alive. The attacks were timed, occurring precisely across the globe. When the first reports came in of the slaughter, this video was sent to the press."

The newscaster disappeared and the head of a handsome, clearly uppity, blond man came on. Just his head. A black background.

Etienne.

"Today, The True successfully carried out our first mission. It was important to do so to make our intentions clear. However, now, we wish no further bloodshed. Therefore, we urge the leaders of the world to submit their populations to us without delay. The True immortals, the vampires, werewolves, and golem amongst you, demand your capitulation."

I felt Callum and Sonia join us, but I didn't move my eyes from the screen as the blond vampire continued talking.

"We will no longer hide our supremacy. We will no longer live in the shadows. We will no longer tolerate the efforts of our brethren to protect our human slaves from their rightful bondage."

His eyes went scary and I felt my throat get tight.

"We will not be denied," he warned. "Yield. Or you will fall."

After that, he bared his teeth, extended his fangs on a snap, and the screen went back to the newscaster, who wore a troubled look.

"I can imagine our viewers believe this is another hoax. It distresses me to report that it is not. The thousands of victims of this senseless slaughter have been reported to be torn apart and drained of blood. Not a one has been found to sustain an injury by any weapon. The witnesses, all of them, thousands of miles apart, report that men and women with extreme speed and strength, as well as a number of wolves and what they describe as 'hairless giants,' invaded their towns, their homes, and wrought their butchery, leaving nothing but death in their wake and thousands of losses." He leaned slightly toward the camera and lowered his voice as he finished, "And these attacks lasted *moments*."

"This can't be happening," Sonia whispered.

Lucien, holding the remote, lifted it and clicked.

The next channel was news of the slaughter.

He hit another button.

More news of the attacks.

And another.

Every channel had been taken over by the news.

He left it on one with a female newscaster who was stating, "The videos seen several days ago all over social media sites were apparently exactly what they seemed to be. There are vampires amongst us. With the most recent heinous attacks perpetrated by these creatures, we have yet to receive explanations as to why the media received false information to relay to our viewers."

"Get off the fucking phone," Abel growled in a way my eyes went directly to him.

He was looking at Gregor.

"*Off the fucking phone!*" he roared.

"Honey," I whispered.

"Yes, good. I'll phone you back," Gregor said and dropped his phone from his ear.

"Thousands dead. Us sitting on our hands and thousands dead," Abel snarled.

"Avery is on his way. He'll be here—" Gregor began.

Abel was in Gregor's face in the flash of an eye.

"I do not give *one fuck* where fuckin' *Avery* is." He kept his face in Gregor's but threw an arm toward the TV. "Thousands. *Slaughtered!*"

"Brother, stand down," Callum called quietly.

Abel turned swiftly away from Gregor and narrowed his eyes at Callum.

"You down with that?" he bit out.

"You know I am not," Callum retorted curtly. "Do not turn on me, Abel. Do not turn on your own. Get a *fucking* lock on it."

Abel drew in a deep breath and stepped away from Gregor.

But the fury still burned in his eyes.

"Do we have any idea, whatsoever, where they plan to strike next?" Lucien asked Gregor.

"We don't," Gregor answered. "The President of the United States is about to make a statement, one he's worked on with The Council and we approve."

"And what's that going to say?" Leah asked sharply. "Yes, there are immortals, and yes, some of them are evil, but, rest assured, most of them aren't. We have no idea what the bad ones are up to and only a few more million of you are going to die...we hope...before we sort this. But hang tight."

It was kinda funny.

It was also totally not.

"We must move," Abel declared.

"To where?" Gregor asked.

"I don't know," Abel clipped. "*Somewhere.*"

"I know you're frustrated, Abel—" Gregor started, but Abel cut him off.

"Yeah? You know that?" he asked sarcastically.

"*As am I!*" Gregor thundered, and the room went completely still at his uncharacteristic loss of control.

But he wasn't done.

"I have eaten and slept and breathed these *fucking* Prophesies for decades, knowing one of the few beings I love on this earth was vulnerable to them." He swung his arm to Sonia. "Knowing that though we could prevail, we could also *not* and all would be lost. *All. All would be lost.* And I've been working every moment to see that this does *not* happen. Yes, Abel, I know you're frustrated. As...am...*I*."

Abel drew breath in through his nose and his voice was a lot calmer when he said, "I hear you. I was out of line. I'm pissed. And you got my apologies."

"I'm grateful for that," Gregor returned, also sounding calmer, but his voice was still terse. "And I hope you understand that since we became aware that The Prophesies were about to come true, I have lived nothing but being certain The Three were safe. I hope you understand my caution. You are our *only* hope. And it has been my duty to my people, to the immortals, to all who inhabit this planet, to do just that. So I did."

"I get you," Abel said quietly, perhaps not calm, but now wanting to calm Gregor.

"Now," Gregor kept going. "I've ordered all the teams that were preparing to take the hanger training camps to move as soon as they're ready. They've been ordered to capture as many immortals as they can. Once that's done, my suggestion is that we move from here to the nearest camp in order that Abel can work his way through the captives. We'll be certain to have a very tight security detail on you as you travel. The phantoms and wraiths have already been contacted and are at the ready for our command. Although The True will be on alert that we may use them and their invisibility to attempt to get close and gather intelligence, we have no choice but to send them in. This will make these missions extremely dangerous, but we must do all we can. And last, The Council is currently speaking with leaders across the globe to procure their allegiance in military matters and in attempting to calm the fears of their people. That's all I have. Now tell me, are you ready to move?"

"Yes," Lucien stated immediately.

"Absolutely," Callum agreed.

"I'm with this all the way," Sonia added.

"Me too," Leah said.

I just nodded.

Abel grunted, "You know what I think."

"I'll arrange the detail," Gregor muttered.

"No," Abel said. "We got mouths, we'll deal with that shit. You got enough on your plate. Deal with that, and just sayin', any of that we can take on, give it to us."

Gregor looked to him and nodded.

Then, in a blur, he was gone.

My eyes drifted back to the TV.

"It's begun," Sonia said.

"It's begun," Leah repeated.

A chill slid up my spine that was highly unpleasant and weirdly familiar.

"It's begun," I whispered.

"My fellow Americans," the president said on TV.

We all were sitting together in the library. All of us save Aurora, Teona, and the other witches. They were off somewhere trying to find Etienne as well as working like crazy casting protection spells on The Three, on our loved ones, who had since declared they were going with us, and on the teams that were right then invading the training camps.

Gregor also wasn't there. He had shit to do.

If our morning wasn't bad enough, through an email communication direct to The Vampire Dominion, as well as one to Callum, we learned that the rest of the concubines being held were murdered, the proof of this further atrocity irrefutable as they'd videotaped each life being blinked out.

One hundred and seven concubines gone, including another member of Leah's family.

Now our bags were packed. We were ready to roll the minute we got the word.

"As you can see," the president went on, "there are immortals in this world." He gestured beside him to a handsome, blond vampire named Rudolf, a Council member, who had just extended and retracted his fangs. Also beside him was a wolf named Saint, who the cameras had caught transforming but now sat docilely, being pet by a beautiful, dark-haired she-wolf in human form, his mate, named Juliana. And last, there was a stunning, ethereal wraith hovering, seated over another chair.

The president drew in breath and locked eyes with the camera, but it didn't pan in, keeping the immortals sitting beside him, who seemed normal and, more importantly, not aggressive, in the frame.

"They have lived among us as long as there have been humans roaming this planet," the president went on gravely. "They are your colleagues. Your neighbors. They are productive, involved citizens. They pay taxes. They create jobs. There are some who are doctors who save lives. Nurses. Scientists who help to eradicate disease. Our existence with theirs has been harmonious for millennia. They have kept themselves hidden only for the purpose of our safety, however, there are many among us who know of them. Work with them. Take them as husbands and wives. Indeed, they are *of* us, human, just a different race. But as with any race, there are those who desire to destroy harmony."

At this point, the camera panned in, broadcasting only the president's face, which he'd arranged into a mask of concern and determination.

"I know it's asking a great deal of the citizens of this great nation, but I urge calm. This faction...who attacked our own in Iowa and others around the world...is few. We, as well as the immortals, are aware of their existence. We are prepared to retaliate. We have more than hope that we will quash any further barbarisms perpetrated by this small, rogue offshoot before they happen. We have weapons to defeat it. And I promise, as your president, as your commander in chief, as a man who knows these races and trusts them, we, with our immortal brothers and sisters, will prevail."

The president disappeared and we saw the newscaster.

Callum, who had the remote, turned the volume down.

"You think that worked?" Xun asked.

"Nope," Moose answered.

I sighed.

"Is that true, you guys human?" Wei asked.

"Propaganda," Lucien answered. "We were born of magic. However, that likely won't be accepted very well at this juncture."

"I hear that," I muttered.

Lucien got up from the arm of the chair that Leah was sitting in, saying, "I'm going to find Gregor, see how things are—"

He didn't finish.

Abel's head turned to look over the back of the sofa where we were sitting, so mine did too.

A second later, I saw a blur materialize as Gregor.

He didn't waste a second.

"The mission to take the training camp in Pennsylvania was successful. They've detained a goodly number of The True. Our jet is on standby."

Everyone was on the move as he spoke.

And everyone stopped being on the move when, suddenly, Poncho's auntie materialized beside him.

Her hair was wild, her face was caked in mud, as were her clothes, she smelled really, *super* bad, and she was in a serious state, arms waving, mouth moving a mile a minute to spit out words.

Unfortunately, all of them were Spanish.

Fortunately, Poncho was with us.

*"Tía, despacio, por favor,"* he said.

She nailed him with a look that I reckoned could pulverize rock, literally, seeing as she was a *bruja*, then she went on talking.

It seemed just as fast to me, but apparently it was slower because Poncho was catching it and he started translating.

"She says you can't go," he told us, then listened before telling us more. "She says you must remain here."

"Fuck, seriously?" Abel bit off.

Poncho ignored him and kept translating.

"She says your work will be done here. She says the fates haven't decided the outcome. She says the human race will decide the outcome. She says if you leave the security of this compound, which will keep you safe, The True will triumph."

Poncho's auntie quit talking.

"Our work will be done here?" Leah asked.

"That's what she says," Poncho answered.

"How can the human race decide the outcome?" I asked. "It would be nearly impossible for them to win against immortals."

Poncho turned to his aunt, she said something to him, then he turned to me. "She said this is a test. She said they must pass or they'll suffer for their failure."

"Great, now we got hazy predictions to deal with," Dad muttered, then said louder, "No offense, *tía de* Poncho."

She shrugged at Dad.

"There are people in danger if we don't move," Callum noted. "Did Josefa see harm come to any others?"

Poncho again talked to his aunt.

Then he spoke to Callum. "The next fight, we'll be there."

I shook my head. "How, if we're here?"

"No clue. Auntie just said we would," Poncho told me.

"Brother," Jabber began, "a lot's riding on this. Is the old broad that good at tellin' the future?" he asked, then looked to Poncho's aunt and added, "No offense."

She skewered him with her eyes.

"My first wife, she told me the bitch would cheat on me. My second, she told me the bitch would steal from me. My third, she told me the bitch would try to cut me," Poncho said.

"Whoa," Jabber breathed, his eyes getting big. "She's *good*."

"Yeah, she's good," Poncho returned. "Any other questions?"

"So we sit and wait...*more*?" Abel asked, pure frustration naked in his tone.

Poncho's aunt started talking again.

Then Poncho started translating again.

"For you, yes. For her, she has to get started with her protection spells. She says the *gringa* witches do good work, but what you're gonna face, you need to pack a punch and she's gonna give that to you."

"Well, tell her to get started," Dad stated immediately.

"Uh...does she speak English?" I asked before Poncho could give the order for her to begin.

"She understands it, doesn't speak it. Says it fucks with the purity of her magic," Poncho answered.

That was interesting.

"She can get started now, Poncho," Lucien growled.

"Right," Poncho muttered and turned to his aunt.

"Are you going to take the advice of this witch?" Gregor asked.

"Well, just to say," I began, "Poncho's first wife cheated on him, the second stole from him, and the third totally tried to cut him."

"Fabulous," Abel muttered, dropping his head to study his boots, so I found his hand with mine and held tight.

"I..." Leah started, and when I looked at her, she was shaking her head. "Well, I feel this is magic, what's happening, what unites us, what made some of us, what gives us what we have to fight it. So, I figure, someone who knows magic, we should listen to."

"I'm concerned about further delays, but I must say, I agree," Sonia put in.

Everyone looked to me.

I kept my eyes on the *bruja*.

She had her eyes on me.

"Keep us safe," I whispered.

She nodded and disappeared.

And again, Abel muttered, "Fabulous."

## *Gregor*

Later that night, Gregor sat in his office with Callum's mother, Regan.

"We're agreed?" he asked.

She held his eyes and nodded once.

"Yes, Gregor. We're agreed."

He grabbed his phone and hit the button, which made the call.

He put it to his ear.

The call was answered with, "Is it time?"

"It's time. Release them."

"It will be done," the voice said.

He listened for the disconnect before he drew in a long breath and let it out.

"They won't be happy," he told the desk blotter.

"They slaughtered entire villages."

Regan's voice was so harsh, coming from a gentle she-wolf such as she, Gregor's eyes cut to her in surprise.

"We have no choice," she finished.

She was right.

They had no choice.

He just hoped, if they survived whatever was to come, The Three would agree.

*Barb*

"We're all in?"

Barb looked around.

Flo was nodding.

Jezza looked worried, but she was nodding too.

Ruby was just staring at her.

"Ruby?" Barb prompted.

"Could mean the death of us, our entire coven wiped out, all of this in less than two weeks," Ruby replied.

"Could also mean, we don't do what we can, we don't help, next month our coven is hiding our magic, serving tea to an immortal, and doing that crap until the day we die," Barb replied.

"See your point," Ruby muttered.

"So, you're in?" Barb pressed.

Ruby hesitated.

Then she nodded.

"Good," Barb said and turned to the vials filled with fizzing pink liquid that were on the dresser in her bedroom. She passed them around, saying, "I'll get Aurora's to her." Her eyes slid through Flo and Jezza. "You'll take care of the wolves and the brothers Jin?"

At their nods, she gave them more vials.

When she gave Ruby hers, she asked, "You'll speak to Teona?"

"Yup," Ruby answered.

Barb gave her a second vial.

In their thoughts, preparing for what was to come, they all went to the blessed instruments sitting on Barb's bed, chose one, and moved toward the door.

"See you in your dreams," Barb called to their departing backs.

Ruby, the last one out, caught her gaze.

"See you in your dreams, my beloved sister," she whispered.

Then she closed the door.

The minute she did, Barb went to the bed, made her choice and slipped the blade under her pillow. She would sleep with her hand around the handle.

Then she did what she very much as a mother did not want to do but had to.

She left her room to find her daughter.

# 25
# Pray with Me

*Leah*

Lucien moved his lips and tongue at my neck where I knew the wounds he'd given me but moments before were gone.

He lay atop me, one arm curved around my back, the fingers of his other hand laced in mine and pressed to the bed at our sides.

He was still buried deep inside me, unmoving, keeping us connected, giving me much of his weight, his warmth. His fingers tangled in mine, holding so fast that the rings he'd given me as a symbol of everything that was us dug into the base of my fingers.

He'd also marked me so our hearts were beating as one.

Beauty.

As for me, with the one arm I had free and both my legs, I held him tight to me.

"We're going to be okay," I whispered in his ear.

He lifted his head to look down at me.

He was troubled.

I hated to see his face that way. In fact, I wasn't certain, even with all that had happened, that I'd ever actually *seen* his face that way.

The Mighty Vampire Lucien, who was the strongest, fastest, and smartest of his kind, didn't get troubled.

I knew he was worried about the fate of humanity.

I knew he was more worried about the fate of me.

"We're going to be okay, darling," I repeated.

"I'm almost a millennium old and I've only known true happiness since the moment I laid eyes on you at your Selection, doing it knowing you would finally be mine."

I felt my eyes start burning and swallowed.

He dipped his face closer. "I cannot lose you, sweetling."

"You won't lose me," I promised.

He pulled his arm from around me to lift his hand to my face. Using his thumb, he traced around my temple, my cheekbone, along the side of my nose, across my lips, his eyes watching, his other hand continuing to hold mine tight.

Then his gaze caught mine, and at the fire in his, I held my breath.

"If you are lost to me, I vow to you, I will go down fighting."

"Darling," I breathed.

"But I will go down," he continued. "I cannot live without you, Leah. And I will not."

"Don't say that," I urged quietly but fiercely. "Your children. Isobel. Julian. Your mother—"

"They'll understand."

I lifted my free hand to his face too, cupping the side, digging the pads of my fingers in.

"And if I lose you, do you think I shouldn't go on?"

"You won't," he stated. "Eventually, this world will be deprived of your beauty. Your spirit. Your humor. It's natural for you to find your end. So you will carry on until that time comes. But I would be sentenced to an eternity without any of that. And I know in my soul I cannot face it."

That was beautiful (most of it).

I still hated it.

"You made a vow to me," I reminded him. "Until the sun falls from the sky."

"Leah—" he groaned, my name sounding torn from him.

"You are vampire," I hissed. "You cannot break your vow."

"You're right, I cannot," he agreed. Then he devastated me. "Unless I'm forced to do so."

Suddenly, I couldn't abide this conversation.

"It's a waste of time to talk about this," I declared. "We'll survive. We'll prevail. We'll have a family and we'll live happily ever after."

"I do hope you're correct, sweetheart."

I lifted my head off the pillow. "Hope hard, Lucien darling, because that's what we have. And hope is beautiful. It's also strong. It will guide us to victory."

His eyes burned into mine before he bent his head and took my mouth in a searing kiss.

When he was done making both our hearts beat faster, he gently slid out. He rolled me to rest on top of him as he reached to turn out the light. Then he moved us to our sides, facing each other, and gathered me close.

"Sleep, my pet," he murmured.

"Only if you do too," I replied.

There was a smile in his voice when he said, "I will."

I cuddled closer, wrapping my arms tight around him. "Good."

"I love you, Leah."

I closed my eyes and pressed a kiss to his chest.

Then I whispered, "I love you too, Mighty Vampire Lucien."

It would turn out to be a boon from the fates that the last thing I heard before I fell asleep was my mate chuckling.

## *Sonia*

After they'd finished making love, Sonia sat astride her handsome wolf, his cock still planted inside her, his knees angled, cocooning her, his torso up, his arms around her, big hands moving soothingly along the skin of her back, his face buried in her chest, his chin resting at the vee of her breasts.

Sonia slid her hand through his hair, her neck bent, lips to the hair on top of his head, allowing him his thoughts even though she knew they were not pleasant.

He proved her right when he spoke.

"I lost you once."

She pressed her lips to his hair as she cupped the back of his head in both hands.

"You didn't," she whispered.

"I thought I did. And it was agony."

Sonia flinched at the pain behind the truth buried in his words.

"I know, wolf," she replied, lifted her head and fisted her hands in his hair, gently tugging it back. As she wanted, his head tilted so she could catch his eyes. "That won't happen again."

"If that witch is right, I understand now why the Oracles have not seen our future. Because it hasn't been written yet. And our fates are in the hands of humanity. I don't understand that. I also don't like it."

"Humans have the capacity for a great deal of love. Generosity. Kindness. Hope," she told him.

"They also have the capacity for a great deal of hate. Judgment. Envy. Prejudice. And they've proven over centuries that they do not handle fear very well," he returned.

She slid her hand to his jaw. "This is true, husband, but that's the stuff that gets all the attention. You've lived long but not often close to humans. Trust me, the good stuff happens far more often, but it doesn't make headlines."

"I hope you're right," Callum murmured, dipping his chin and kissing her chest.

Sonia again rested her lips to the top of his head. "I do too. But you've lost so much already to the cause of keeping humans safe. I cannot believe that the fates, and more importantly God, would make you lose more."

He pulled his face out of her chest and she lifted her head again when he tipped it back.

"We have babies to make," she whispered when she caught his eyes, normally an amazing clear blue, but now, with the emotion her king was feeling, a brilliant, breathtaking gold. "Pups to raise." His hands stopped soothing so he could wrap his arms around her. She dropped her lips to his, moving both her hands to his neck before she stroked his jaw with her thumbs. "An eternity to live and love, my king. That future will not be taken from us."

"No," he growled.

"I will not lose you," she declared. "And you will not lose me. Not again."

"No," he repeated his growl.

"No," she whispered, tilted her head and slid the tip of her tongue across his generous bottom lip.

Her husband, her handsome wolf, her king, as ever, accepted the invitation and he kissed her with a ferocity that was both man and beast.

When he broke the kiss, he lay back, reaching to the light. He turned it off as she pulled the covers up over them.

As was their wont, they stayed connected.

Sonia cuddled deep, pressing her forehead into the side of his neck.

"You know I love you?" he asked into the dark, and Sonia closed her eyes.

"I do," she whispered into his skin. "And I love you too, my handsome wolf. With everything I am and everything I'm meant to be. And I know, *know*," she said the last fiercely, pressing close, "I'm meant to be *a lot*."

Callum's arms around her gave her a squeeze. "And I love you the same, baby doll, with everything I am and everything I'm meant to be."

She tilted her chin to touch his skin with her lips and then she settled in.

Callum ran a hand gently up and down her spine.

Connected, as close as they could get, just as she liked it, as did he, Sonia, Queen of the Werewolves, fell asleep on top of her king.

## *Hook*

Standing outside his daughter's door, Hooker Johnson hesitated before he lifted his hand and knocked.

After a few seconds, the door opened a crack and Lilah's man stood there wearing nothing but jeans.

Fuck, but the kid was built.

"Sorry to interrupt, bubba," he muttered. "But wanna say good night to my little girl."

Abel studied Hook's face, his own holding an expression of understanding, and seeing that, yet again, Hook was relieved that this was the one she'd been yearning for all her life.

"You got it, Hook. Just a second," Abel said quietly. He left the door slightly ajar and disappeared.

It didn't take long before Lilah filled it, opening it further, doing this wearing her man's thermal.

"Daddy?"

He forced a smile, his heart heavy, his gut gnawed raw with unease, his beautiful little girl, who now had it all—finally—standing in front of him.

"Just wanted to say good night, Lilah."

Her expression softened and she moved into him, wrapping her arms around his back and pressing her cheek to his chest.

"I'm glad," she said softly, giving him a squeeze.

He'd curved his arms around her and he took her in, felt her solidness, her softness, her warmth, smelled the sweet scent of her hair, felt her love for him burrowing deep. He did this remembering the first time she was put in his arms. She was naked. Goo all over her barely wiped off. Arms and legs pumping. Eyes squeezed shut. Mouth open, bawling.

She had been the most beautiful thing he'd ever seen and that was the most precious moment in his life.

Until she gave him more.

And more.

And more.

His arms got tighter.

As did his throat.

He coughed shortly to clear it before he said, "You sleep good."

"I will, Daddy. You too."

He gave her a squeeze and let her go.

She didn't let go until she gave him a squeeze back.

He didn't prolong it. He couldn't. He was a tough guy, but that... that he couldn't take.

He just gave her a smile, turned, and began to walk away.

"Daddy," she called.

He turned back.

"Love you," she said quietly.

A lump hit his throat, threatening to suffocate him.

"Love you more, little girl," he replied gruffly.

She smiled and he saw the wet hit her eyes.

He tipped his head to the side, forced a return smile, turned, and walked away from his baby, hoping like all fuck that whatever was going to happen within these walls, it wouldn't be the last time.

*Aurora*

"Oh goddess, *sweet goddess*," she moaned as Yuri, behind her and under her, his cock driving deep and hard, his arms around her, the fingers of one hand toying with a nipple, the fingers of the other toying with her clit, had his face buried in her neck.

He'd just torn through and she felt her blood flow.

She also felt her climax devour her, violently bucking her against his hold as it laid her to waste.

The first time her vampire fed.

Unbelievable.

Vaguely, due to her orgasm and the numbness Yuri had explained she'd feel, she felt him lap at the skin of her neck before he pushed her gently down, cheek to the covers. He held her there with a hand between her shoulder blades, keeping her steady against the beautiful brutality of his lovemaking with his other hand clasped at her hip, as he continued to power between her legs.

The climax was receding, but Aurora kept moaning as she took him.

She loved what Yuri could give her. She loved the way he played with her. She loved his tender dominance. She loved the velvet violence she received once he was inside. She especially loved that every time he gave her something exquisite: an orgasm that was always better than the ones he'd gifted her with before.

But she also loved this, when she was done and he was not. She could come again, easily, but she tried to hold it back. (This failed when he wished for her to orgasm. Yuri tended to get what he wanted and Aurora always liked giving it to him.)

She tried to hold it back because she wanted to be all about him after he'd been all about her. She loved the sound of his grunts and groans. She loved the feel of him losing control and rearing inside her before he found his own climax. She loved the power it made her feel, knowing their play seemed as if she handed it all to him, but in these moments, she knew she held it all along.

She gloried in it.

Power over a vampire.

Power over *her* vampire, Yuri.

She *gloried* in it.

She was, of course, a witch.

So she would.

And right then, he gave it to her. Sliding the hand between her shoulder blades to the side of her waist, he clamped on and lost control, thrusting wildly, his grunts filling the room, his groan of release thrilling through her with enough power to make her whole body quiver, inside and out.

He made love to her gently as his climax descended, and she knew it had left him when his hands slid high on her hips so he could stroke her bottom with his thumbs.

Finally, he slid himself in to the root and asked gently, "All right, button?"

"Yes, sweetheart," she replied.

"Mm," he murmured, the purr of it making her clit twitch.

Oh yes, she gloried in her power over her vampire.

Slowly, he slid out and she bit her lip at the disappointment of losing him.

Then she felt his tongue lapping the swell of one of the cheeks of her bottom.

Another lap and she made a soft mew when she felt the dull bite of his fangs sinking through.

She tipped her bottom up, deeper into his mouth.

He growled against her skin, gripping his fingers high on the inside of her thigh before she felt his tongue again. Then with his natural speed, she was on her back with her vampire on top.

She looked to his face, which could be cold, or remote, or bland, and it was often this way when he looked at her.

So she didn't look at his face.

She looked in his eyes, eyes that always told her what she wanted to know.

That he gloried in his witch just as much, if not more than she gloried in him.

More power and he gave that freely.

She loved that, maybe most of all.

No. Aurora Lenox knew what she loved best.

She loved the fact that she was falling in love with a vampire.

She smoothed her hands over his shoulders, lifted up, and kissed the underside of his chin.

When she settled back down to the pillows, it wasn't only his eyes that told her everything. It was his whole face.

"When this is done, my sweet, I wish for you to consider moving in with me."

She blinked as her heart skipped over itself with glee.

He smiled.

He'd heard her heart.

"Really?" she asked.

He moved his hand to caress her side.

"Really," he confirmed.

She felt her brows draw together. "Do you live in Texas?"

He shook his head. "No, I have homes in Napa, Tuscany, and Miami, as well as apartments in New York, Paris, Sydney, and Barcelona, and last, a villa on Crete. Once this is done, we'll need some time to recuperate. You can pick where you'd like to visit first."

She knew her eyes were big when she asked, "You have all that?"

"Yes, and before this started, I was in negotiations to purchase a residence in Japan." He bent closer. "The garden is extraordinary."

"I've always wanted to see a Japanese garden," she breathed. "A real one, like, in Japan."

"Then you shall," he told her.

"I, well..." She hesitated. "I have a job. A house. I gave my boss an excuse when all this started and they gave me a leave of absence. But I—"

"You don't understand," Yuri interrupted.

"I...okay, then maybe you should explain it to me."

"If you wish to work, but also wish to spend time in one of my homes, we'll find you a job. If you enjoy your current employment, I'll purchase a home for us in Dallas. However, if you wish to enjoy the opportunity I can afford you and explore what my world has to offer, I'll take care of you. You can also do any combination of the above. Whatever you wish, Aurora, you will receive."

"Wow, that's a lot," she breathed.

"Perhaps," he murmured.

Aurora gave him a squeeze. "It's a lot, Yuri."

"To you, absolutely. To me, not quite."

"Seeing that it's that to me, then—"

"My sweet," he whispered, then touched his mouth to hers before he lifted his head half an inch. "I'm not done explaining."

"Okay," she whispered back.

"I've lived a long life," he told her.

"I know," she replied.

"And I have never, in all those centuries, found someone like you."

Her breath stuck.

Yuri stopped caressing her side and trailed his fingers down her arm until he found her hand. He curled his big one around her small one and pulled it up, pressing their hands to his heart.

Aurora kept not breathing.

"I wish to keep you with me," he said gently. "And my further, most fervent wish is that you wish to keep me."

She forced her breath out, saying, "I do."

She felt him relax and hadn't realized he was tense.

And when she did, she thought that was unbearably sweet.

"After the world is saved, we'll work it out," he declared.

"Yes, Yuri. After the world is saved, we'll work it out."

His eyes warmed and he bent again to give her a deep, lavish kiss.

Only after he broke it did he reach to the light to extinguish it.

Then, as he always did, he positioned her as he wanted her. This night, spooning, his arms around her, pressing her smaller body deep into the warm, hard curve of his bigger one.

She found his hand and laced her fingers through.

When she did, his tightened.

Again, unbearably sweet.

"Good night, sweetheart," she whispered into the dark.

"Good night, button," he murmured into her hair.

*As cute as*, he'd said.

Her vampire.

Unbearably sweet.

On that thought, she tried to relax, tried to calm her heart, knowing he'd know exactly when she went to sleep.

She couldn't do either.

Now that it was quiet and he wasn't touching her, making love to her, coloring her world by offering her his, in the silence, Aurora fretted.

She didn't want to take him on the journey she knew she would make that night. It was dangerous. Too dangerous. And she was falling in love. She didn't want to risk the chance of losing him.

But when she came back, he'd be so very angry that she went alone without him to protect her.

She had not known him long, and although they spent a lot of time together, he was centuries old. There was much to discover about him so she still did not know him well. Though, she was learning.

The one thing she did know was that he would indeed be very angry with her in a way that it wouldn't earn her an enjoyable spanking ending in an outrageously fantastic orgasm.

He might never forgive her.

And she couldn't have that.

Because, she couldn't be sure, but she was beginning to believe, she wouldn't be able to live without him.

So she had to take him.

And she hated that.

Even so, she prepared, keeping her hand tight with his and shifting her leg so he had no choice but to hook his thigh over her hip.

Tangling them up together, so that in sleep, they were connected.

So that when she dreamed, she would take her sweet vampire with her.

*Abel*

"Oh yeah, fuck yeah, Abel, baby, *yes!*" Delilah cried as she reared back into him on all fours and came.

He reached out, grasped her hair, and drove her back on his dick, listening to her pants and whimpers as she kept taking him, kept coming, the smell of her cunt in his nostrils, until all that and her sweet pussy drove him over the edge and he exploded, embedding himself inside her and shooting his cum deep.

As he came back to himself, he felt her fucking herself gently on his cock. He let her hair go and bent over her to kiss her shoulder blade.

"Love you, baby," she whispered.

"Love you too, pussycat," he whispered back and pulled out. "I get to clean you tonight."

"Whatever you want," she murmured, dropping to her side, curling up, and giving him her eyes.

Fuck, so goddamned beautiful, it hurt looking at her.

But he couldn't stop himself. The hurt felt too good.

He slid a hand over her hip before he got out of bed, went to the bathroom, wet a washcloth with warm water, came back, and gently cleaned her while it sounded like she purred, letting him.

He didn't bother going into the bathroom when he left her to return the cloth. He just tossed it into the sink from the doorway, then with his vampire speed, he was in bed with his mate, pulling her close, yanking the covers over them, and finally nestling deep.

"You good?" she asked.

"Real good," he answered.

There was a pause before she went on, "You ready?"

"More than ready," he told her. "Whatever happens, after it's done, finally, we get wild and free."

"Wild and free," she whispered, burrowing closer.

"Wild and free, baby. You and me for eternity."

She kissed his chest, settled in, and held him tight.

It shocked the shit out of him, but his Delilah had no trouble finding sleep.

Abel did not have the same.

Staring at the ceiling, holding her tight, he did it hoping he hadn't lied. Hoping he was ready. Hoping all of them were ready. Hoping that whatever was going to happen, he and his mate got wild and free.

After doing that for a long fucking time, finally, Abel fell asleep.

## *Gregor*

Having not slept a wink, at six o'clock the next morning, Gregor moved into the room, which was already bustling with people and filled with equipment, including a large television camera aimed at an armchair set close to a fireplace, a warm fire blazing in its grate.

"We're ready, sir," a man wearing big headphones and sitting at a bank of monitors said to him.

Gregor nodded but kept his eyes on the woman standing by the chair.

He approached her, taking her in.

She wore a lovely frock, red satin embroidered with delicate wisps of green and blue flowers. Mandarin collar. Her graying black hair was smoothed into an elegant knot at the nape of her neck. Her makeup was dramatic, highlighting her exotic eyes.

She appeared calm.

The red was chosen as it was a power color, but the deepness of its hue and the delicacy of the embroidery, they were assured, would also communicate tranquility along with its strength.

"Are you ready?" he asked quietly.

"I am," Jian-Li replied.

He nodded.

"They're starting," someone announced, and he turned his head to the bank of television screens.

"Volume, please," he called.

The volume came up and Gregor watched a black woman with soft curls in her long bob of hair, who was wearing a smart and stylish but casual outfit all in taupe—woven cashmere turtleneck, ribbed cardigan with long lapels, expertly tailored wool slacks. With this, she wore understated gold jewelry but exquisitely elegant, spike-heeled pumps.

They'd been assured, with her history of demanding frank, in-depth interviews, prompting surprising candor and emotion from her subjects, that she was by far the most trusted member of the media, not only in the United States, but in all of English-speaking North America.

On screen, she was walking up a wide, sweeping set of stairs at the base of a castle. She moved toward the balustrade that led up from its end, which had a statue of a proud wolf carved in stone.

She did this speaking.

"I stand on the steps of Canis, the home of the king of werewolves, a man known as Callum. And I do it with the unprecedented honor of sharing with you the tales of the warriors who are on the brink of saving humanity from the shocking threat we learned we were under at the hands of a rebel faction of vampires, werewolves, and a race known as golem."

She stopped and laid a taupe, leather-gloved hand on the balustrade.

"I am at Canis," she went on, "but I'll begin my report not with King Callum and his queen, Sonia. I begin my report with Lucien, a vampire whose strength is said to be unparalleled. A vampire who was the general in the last battle the immortal vampires fought alongside humans against a foe who wished the freedom to hunt, feed from, and kill members of the human race. This was a secret battle that was deadly, and great losses were suffered on both sides, but the vampires and their human allies prevailed."

Her expression became grave before she carried on.

"But during it, Lucien lost his human partner, a woman he loved implicitly. She was captured by his enemies, tortured, and put to death. I tell his tale first, along with that of his human wife, Leah. A concubine, these being not what you might think they are when I say that word. They are a centuries-long line of strong women who swore duty to vampires, giving them their allegiance, and their blood, in order that vampires could sustain without hunting humans. Protecting us. Keeping us safe. Strong women who many saw brutally violated and murdered in recent videotapes streaming online."

Pictures of Lucien and Leah, with Leah's photos starting from birth, came on with the presenter's voice telling stories of them, moving onward to photos of their Claiming Ceremony. Both of them smiling. Both of them clearly outrageously happy.

This moved on to the presenter introducing Sonia and Callum's story, with more pictures as their tale was told.

And this continued with the presenter introducing Abel and Delilah's story, a montage of photos of them also helped to tell their tale.

The stories were powerful and presented beautifully, but Gregor felt Abel and Delilah's played the best. Although both of them were extraordinarily good-looking, each had led very humble lives and he believed theirs would be the one that would resonate the strongest.

By this time, the presenter was inside Canis, seated in a chair in what looked like a warm and welcoming (because it was) library.

She had an attractive earthenware mug sitting on the table at her side. Nothing extravagant, the power behind the throne was depicted by her walk up the steps to the castle. Now she was metaphorically seated in the lap of the werewolves—unpretentious, openhearted, relaxed, gracious.

In the meantime, in the room Gregor was in, they'd seated Jian-Li in her chair.

"And today," the presenter stated, "I have the pleasure of speaking with one in a long line of Chinese American women who opened her heart and home to the hybrid werewolf vampire, Abel. Generations of her family kept him safe and hidden, with the immortal Abel doing the former for her family. Keeping them safe. Providing for them. I'm pleased to introduce you to Jian-Li Jin, a restaurant owner and mother of four sons, one of whom she counts as Abel." She tipped her head to the side. "Jian-Li, it's lovely to meet you."

"And it's lovely to meet you as well, Susannah," Jian-Li said on a soft smile.

Gregor watched as the presenter asked gentle, then more and more probing questions and Jian-Li answered them unwaveringly, frankly, and proudly.

He watched knowing this was being broadcast on every network, including cable. He watched knowing that after it was over, it would be rebroadcast, repeatedly. He watched knowing that after it was done, it would take but moments for it to be available to stream on every online outlet offered to the masses.

And Gregor watched hoping that the stories of The Three, humans and immortals inexorably connected together in love and loyalty, would win the hearts of billions.

"Thank you, Jian-Li, for your time and your honesty. But mostly, thank you for sharing the private matters of your family in hopes of giving peace of mind to the many who understandably fear what might come next after the events of yesterday," the presenter finished the interview.

"It was my pleasure, and my honor, to speak of my son, his lovely mate, and the others who I have met, grown to know, and grown to care about deeply," Jian-Li replied.

The presenter smiled.

The red light on the camera blinked out.

"Excellent!" the production manager exclaimed, rushing up to Jian-Li.

But Gregor watched the television as the presenter finalized things, summing up, injecting humanity into every word she spoke about The Three, and finally concluding.

"We are not privy to what awaits these couples, husbands and wives, kings and queens, partners, or as they refer to themselves, as do we, *mates*. We have only been told that they have selflessly agreed to undertake a very dangerous mission to see to it that the human, vampire, werewolf, wraith, and phantom races can live peacefully, harmoniously, and safely."

Her gaze intensified as the camera panned in subtly.

"And I, for one, with all my heart, thank them for their service and hope each one of them, Lucien, Leah, Callum, Sonia, Abel, and Delilah, emerge unscathed. To this end, I will pray for them. I do hope for these brave souls that you pray with me."

She drew in breath and dipped her chin.

"Thank you for watching. Stay calm. Stay safe. And stay hopeful," she finished.

The program ended and a newscaster came on.

The volume was muted and Gregor felt Jian-Li touch his arm.

"That went very well," she stated.

"It did, indeed," he agreed, moving his hand to cover hers on his arm. "You did beautifully."

"I hope so."

He gave her a small smile.

"What the hell?"

This came from the man with headphones and Gregor's attention moved to him immediately.

Then his body locked.

"What's that?" a woman carrying a clipboard and standing behind him asked, her eyes glued to the bank of monitors.

"Don't know. What...? I...Fuck!" the man with headphones cursed. "The feed has been taken over. I don't...Shit!" he exclaimed, rising from his seat.

Jian-Li's hand had become a claw on his arm as he felt her body strain against the tightness in it, doing all it could to survive the unhealthy speed of the beat of her heart.

And Gregor knew why.

Because on every screen was Etienne, standing in the middle of a street somewhere.

And with her back to the camera, facing him, stood Delilah.

# 26
# We Are The Three

*Delilah*

I walked down the street cautiously, my stomach knotted with panic. I saw faces in windows peeking out from behind curtains. I felt eyes on me from everywhere. I felt fear choking the air.

I had no idea where I was. I had no memory of putting on my tee, my jeans, my motorcycle boots.

I had no idea how I got there.

This couldn't be right. I couldn't be here.

Why was I here?

Alone.

No one with me.

Not a single one of The Three.

Not my mate, who I knew would protect me.

"This is a warning."

I whipped around at the voice and saw him standing in the middle of the street.

A vampire. Handsome. Proud.

Evil.

Etienne.

"You know what we can do. You know what we *will* do. We showed you yesterday," he went on. "This is why they will submit."

Okay, maybe it was good that I'd learned a few karate chops.

But me, alone against a vampire? Those wouldn't keep me alive very long.

So.

Again.

*How did I get here and where was everybody?*

I thought these thoughts.

But facing off against Etienne, I stood my ground, back straight, head held high, and I kept my eyes locked with his.

I was a member of The Three. I had mojo.

I just hoped I could figure out how to use it to help me.

Holding on to that hope deep in my heart, I said firmly, pleased as fuck my voice came out steady, "We will prevail."

Etienne shook his head. "Today, we destroy The Three and finalize our mission to assert our dominance over humanity."

"Impossible," I hissed.

"Your mate will come for you."

If he could find me, wherever the hell I was, he would.

I didn't confirm this.

Etienne didn't need confirmation.

"He will sacrifice himself for you."

I felt my insides freeze and it was agony.

The vampire smiled like he knew he caused me pain.

And liked it.

"As for you, you won't have forever. You won't even have tomorrow. You will only have a lifetime of mourning." His head cocked to the side. "Don't worry, it won't last long. It'll only be a human lifetime. But during that lifetime, you, Delilah, will be *my* personal slave."

Then, in a blur, shapes formed behind him.

An army of vampires.

And lumbering up the rear, the vampires were backed by huge, hairless, scary-as-shit giants.

Slowly, even by human standards, they started moving toward me.

I lifted my hand, hoping like fuck my blue light would come out.

Then I screamed, "*No!*"

## *Gregor*

Gregor, Jian-Li, and those around them watched the interplay between Etienne and Delilah.

Somehow, they also heard it.

"I talked to Control," the man with the headphones said. "They don't understand how this is happening. But they say their satellites have been hacked and they can't stop it."

Gregor said nothing, because the instant Etienne announced that Abel would sacrifice himself for Delilah, Jian-Li ran from the room.

Gregor turned to one of The Council's humans.

"Alert The Three. Contact Gastineau. Bring weapons to this room, as many as you can. Find out where the fuck that is." He pointed to the screens. "And bring me Josefa." He leaned forward and finished on a roar, "*Now!*"

On a quick nod, the human female dashed out the door.

## *Abel*

"Delilah, baby, wake up," Abel called, hand to his mate's hip, shaking hard.

She continued moaning and moving with agitation.

"Lilah, *bao bei*, wake the fuck up." He shook her harder.

"*No!*" she screamed, but she did it in her sleep.

And after she did it, she didn't wake up.

"Goddammit," he growled, rolling her to her back and looming over her before he curled his hand under her jaw. "Delilah, wake up." He bent close, digging his fingers in as hard as he could without harming her as she stopped shifting and started writhing. "Wake up," he repeated. When she didn't, he barked, "*Wake up!*"

The door to the bedroom flew open and he looked over his shoulder to see Jian-Li rushing in.

"My Abel—" she began.

"They got her," he cut her off. "I can't get her out. I have to go in."

She skidded to a halt by the bed. "But—"

"Go get Lucien," Abel ordered.

"Abel, you don't—"

"*Go get him!*" he bellowed, turned back to Delilah and concentrated solely on his mate. *Let me in,* he ordered. *Let me in, Delilah.* He dipped his face so close that his nose brushed hers. *Fucking let me in!*

With that, he collapsed on top of her, his chest to hers, his forehead sliding down her cheek, his eyes closed, for all appearances asleep.

Jian-Li hesitated not a second before she turned and rushed from the room.

*In a Pub Somewhere in London*

"What's that?" the bartender asked, his eyes to the telly.

The football game was gone.

Instead, they had some bird standing in a street, facing a ton of tall men and women and...

He peered closer.

"What are those things?" he asked the screen.

Doing so, as well as when they heard the scream, the attention of a couple of blokes sitting at the bar went to the TV.

## *Delilah*

At my scream, no blue light.

Shit.

I started backing up as they kept advancing.

Okay, this was not good.

I kept backing up as they kept coming and Etienne started talking to me.

"No mate?" he smirked. "Why doesn't he come for you, Delilah?" He threw out a hand. "Perhaps he understands one human is just like the next. He can easily find another. He can find hundreds, *thousands*, and enjoy them after you're gone."

"You've obviously never been in love, asshole," I muttered.

*Let me in.*

I heard Abel's voice in my head and I blinked.

"I tire of this," Etienne stated, suddenly stopping, and when he did, his army did the same.

*Let me in, Delilah.*

Uh-oh.

I was in a dream.

But I wasn't in a dream. I was *in a dream.*

I stared at the sea of supernaturals before me.

With only one of Abel and my puny efforts, against all of them, neither of us would survive.

I did what I could (not knowing what the hell I was doing but still hoping) to hold him back.

"We need to give them incentive," Etienne said to a vampire at his side. "Bring me a human."

*Fucking let me in!*

In a flash, a vamp was gone.

Then he was right back, shoving a young woman who cried out in terror toward Etienne.

A teenager.

She was in her pajamas. A tight pink cami and cute pink bottoms with white and blue polka-dots on them.

She was sobbing, struggling, her fear reaching out, clawing at my flesh.

Etienne yanked her in front of him and put his hands on either side of her head.

He was going to break her neck or tear her head clean off. He was moving with a human's speed and doing it so I could watch.

I knew it.

*I knew.*

I prepared to rush him, hoping Xun, Wei, and Chen gave me *something* that would allow me to stop this. To save one.

Just one.

Before they ended me.

Etienne's lips curved in a sick smile.

But in the blink of an eye, faster than the girl could scream, she was no longer in his hands.

I felt a presence behind me, chanced turning, and stared at Abel, who was pushing the girl.

"*Run!*" he roared.

She ran.

*In a Home Somewhere in Idaho*

"Good God, honey, what is this?"

"Shh."

"Oh my God, is that the man we saw earlier on Susannah—?"

"*Shh!*"

The woman sank down on the arm of the chair her husband was sitting in.

And together, they watched.

*Gregor*

"Shit, one of the dudes is there," headphone man stated, and Gregor's mouth got tight.

Her dreams.

Abel had gone to his mate in her dream.

"Have you located where the signal is coming from?" he asked.

"I got Control on it," the man answered.

"Get them to move faster," Gregor ordered.

"They're doin' the best—"

"Get them. To move. *Faster*," Gregor hissed.

The guy nodded his head.

Gregor turned his eyes back to the monitors.

*Delilah*

"Retrieve her," Etienne ordered.

"I wouldn't do that," Abel warned.

"Now," Etienne snapped.

A vampire flew forward in a blur, but he dropped headless to the ground very visibly right beside me with Abel standing over him, the dead vampire's head in his hands.

My man.

Awesome.

Even if that was serious gross.

Etienne turned to his other side.

"You, both of you, go," Etienne commanded.

"We gonna do this?" Abel asked tauntingly before they did as Etienne demanded, tossing the head he held underarm like it was a soccer ball being thrown in for play. "Or are you gonna get smart real fast, get on your knees, and wait for The Council to get here and take you in so you can answer for all your fucked-up shit?"

"I have two hundred and fifty immortals at my back, young Abel. Do you honestly think you can take us all?" Etienne returned, brows lifting.

"Man, wise up," Abel shot back derisively. "I'm a destined member of The Three for a reason. So is my mate. Trust me, you do *not* wanna learn those reasons."

"Honey," I said, sidling toward him, not taking my eyes off Etienne, "don't give away the good stuff."

Abel's hand shot out in a wink, capturing mine and tugging me behind his back.

"Don't worry. She will not die. I have uses for her." Etienne's eyes slid down me in a way that made my stomach turn over nauseatingly and caused fury to start beating from my man. "You, we'll take your head. But she will watch."

"Done with this. You're not gonna get on your knees, quit talkin'," Abel demanded. "Time to play."

Etienne shook his head like Abel was all kinds of stupid.

Then he said, "As you wish." He turned to his right and nodded. "The both of you." He turned to his left. "And both of you." He twisted his torso and nodded three times. "You, you, and you." He pointed beyond the supernaturals to an extra-large, extra-scary golem. "And you."

He turned back to us and smiled, not quite finished, showing clear as day he was enjoying this.

Immensely.

"Secure the mate. Bring the hybrid to me alive."

Eight-on-one and Abel had no weapons.

My stomach dropped.

"Now," Etienne whispered.

*In an Apartment Somewhere in Washington DC*

"Thank God, he saved the girl," a woman whispered, her coffee cup forgotten on the counter beside her, her eyes glued to the TV hanging from underneath her cabinets. "Now, I hope those two know what they're doing."

It kept going.

She kept watching.

And hoping.

*Gregor*

"Oh God, I can't watch!" the woman with the clipboard cried, her board crashing to the ground as she turned, lifting her hands to her ears, her eyes shut tight.

Gregor turned his face to the ceiling.

"*Where are The Three?*" he boomed.

*Delilah*

The supernaturals shot forward.

I heard grunts.

All Abel's.

I felt wind whipping around me.

I saw blood splatter on the Tarmac of the street.

And I knew it was the end.

*Wild and free.*

Wild, okay.

But not free.

Never free.

Suddenly, I heard other grunts and saw action that I could actually focus on.

My heart slid up, lodging in my throat.

Xun, Wei, and Chen were there.

Weaponless.

But also fearless.

I saw an opportunity, bent low, whipped my leg out, and hit hard. The pain spiraled from ankle to hip as I connected with what felt like a tree trunk, but I'd caught him unawares.

The golem teetered, and with ungainly swings of his arms, he fell.

He was barely on the ground for a moment before his limbs and head were torn free in a haze of motion, the parts of him tossed haphazardly but powerfully, landing houses away.

It didn't take three minutes before all eight were headless (and one limbless), their remains scattered around me.

Xun, Wei, and Chen stood, surrounding me close, breathing heavily, their clothes bloodied, their eyes pinned to the army in front of them as Abel sauntered to the golem, picked up his torso, tore it in half, and tossed each half away from him, one at either side.

More awesome and more gross.

Whatever.

Not taking a moment even to glance at his brothers to get a lock on how they were there, he faced Etienne.

"We done now?" he asked. "Or do you want more?"

Etienne apparently was unconcerned with the loss of his followers, their headless corpses littering the street.

He was still smiling.

Man, this guy was *whacked*.

Suddenly, he shouted, "Humans!"

Abel, the boys, and I all braced. Abel was crouching, obviously to prepare to turn wolf. Xun, Wei, and Chen were lifting their hands and shifting their legs, bending just at the knees as if they were track stars at the starting line. But before any of us could take a breath, a line of vampires in front of us held humans in front of them.

I stopped counting at thirty.

No, I stopped counting when I saw one had a little boy. He couldn't be more than five, also in his jammies—a crumpled blue tee, bottoms with turtles on them.

His little, pale face was a mask of fear.

Sick rolled up my throat. Sick with a chaser of panic.

Etienne's head tipped to the side as he challenged, "Do you think you can save them all?"

I knew by the tightness of his body that Abel was freaked.

And worried.

So was I.

"Yep," Abel replied carelessly.

"Good luck," Etienne whispered, lifting his hand.

"*No!*" I again screamed.

*At a Convenience Store Somewhere in Florida*

"They got no shot," one of the throng of people standing around the counter, watching the small television on the shelf behind the cash register, said.

"Holy cow, that's the guy and girl Susannah River was talking about this morning!" a woman who just walked up exclaimed. "What's happening?"

"Shh," another woman shushed her.

"Those Chinese guys can fight, and that big guy's got speed, but those poor people are goin' down," another man muttered. "And they're takin' the good guys with them."

"Pray God they don't," a woman up close to the counter whispered. "Pray God. Pray God. Pray God they save them all."

*Gregor*

A vampire whirred into the room and stopped.

"Sir, The Three," he stated.

"This is not good, this is not good, this is not good," headphone man chanted, gaze to the monitors.

"What?" Gregor clipped to the vampire.

"We tried to get them but—"

"*What?*" Gregor barked.

"We can't wake them." He drew in a deep breath. "And we just received word. The compound is under attack."

*Delilah*

I didn't see it.

Until it was done and all the humans were rushing by me, a big man carrying the boy with his turtle jammies, running for their lives.

But in front of me stood Abel, with Xun, Wei, and Chen at his back.

And at his sides...

Lucien and Callum.

At my sides....

Leah and Sonia.

*At the Convenience Store Somewhere in Florida*

"Yes! They did it!" a man shouted, turning, lifting his hands, and he got high fives from the man and woman closest to him.

"Good Lord, it *is*!" the woman who came late cried. "It's all of them. All the ones Susannah River was talking about this morning." She turned to the man beside her. "Did you see it?"

He didn't answer.

Eyes to the screen, he whispered, "It's not done." He swallowed and stared. "Those assholes are far from done."

## *Delilah*

Finally, Etienne was rattled.

"How—?" he began.

"Hello, Father," Lucien greeted drolly.

"You—" Etienne tried again.

"We *all* dream," Lucien informed him. "You didn't know that, I'm certain, when you found a witch to invade Delilah's dreams. And apparently, you weren't aware we have our own witches."

Etienne didn't reply.

He squared his chin, his eyes fixed on his son. "I did not wish to take your head."

"Really?" Lucien asked. "That's interesting. I'll have no trouble taking yours."

Lucien.

Awesome.

I chanced taking my eyes off the action to grin at Leah, feeling a whole lot better that we were all here.

Together.

The Three.

Finally.

She took her own chance and grinned back at me.

We both looked ahead of us.

Callum glanced at the bodies littered around him, then back at Etienne. "One of us, and his human brothers," he stated, meaning that was what Abel and the boys had wrought. "Do you yield?"

"We will never yield," Etienne returned coolly.

"Shame," Callum muttered.

"I don't think so," Abel put in. "I'll enjoy takin' more of these motherfuckers out."

Etienne looked back to Lucien. "As my son, you have my vow. Your death will be quick."

"As your son, you have my vow. Yours will not," Lucien replied.

"So be it," Etienne said softly, then called loudly. "Bring in the wolves!"

And then, from everywhere, all around, streaming past houses, through yards, down the street behind the legion of supernaturals in front of us, waves of wolves came running.

*Waves.*

Hundreds.

Callum and Abel leapt to wolf.

In a blink, Lucien was tossing what appeared to be the bottoms of mailboxes and the posts of street signs at Xun, Wei, and Chen.

"Guard them...your lives," he ordered shortly.

"You got it," Xun replied good-naturedly.

Lucien turned just in time for the wolves to close in.

*Jian-Li*

Jian-Li sat on the bed beside Delilah, her eyes to the two twitching, unconscious bodies lying in it.

She reached for Delilah's hand. Keeping hold, she reached for Abel's. Firmly, she curled their fingers around each other and held them tight in both her hands.

She closed her eyes and bent her head.

"You will be safe," she whispered. "You will be safe," she repeated. "You will live so you can be happy."

She didn't open her eyes and she didn't let go of their hands.

She held them tight in hers.

And she hoped.

*In a Café Somewhere in Nevada*

"Those must be werewolves," a man said, crowding close to the long counter where every stool was taken, behind them a huddle of bodies. The patrons and the waitresses were all gathered, their heads tipped back, their eyes on a TV suspended from the ceiling. "And fuck, there are a lot of 'em."

"You see that thing this mornin'? Those cats were on that program, and their women," another man said, lifting his coffee cup to the screen. "That shit...that many of those immortal fuckers...they're gonna be torn to pieces. Then we're all gonna be screwed."

"They aren't backing down," a waitress whispered.

"What, Naomi?" her colleague asked.

"They're outnumbered. But they haven't run. They haven't given up," Naomi said.

"Crazy," one man said.

"Stupid," another one said.

"Brave," Naomi said quietly, her eyes never leaving the screen.

*Delilah*

One of the wolves took down Xun, opening a path to Leah, Sonia, and me.

As he went for Xun's throat, I kicked out, hitting him in the jaw as Sonia transformed and attacked another beast that would breach us.

My kick offered Xun just enough time to scuttle back on his elbows, but the wolf found another target, baring his teeth and going for Xun's thigh.

He didn't latch on.

Another wolf, not Sonia, Abel, or Callum, attacked him from the side and, without hesitation, tore his throat out.

I recognized that wolf. I'd watched them training enough and done it with rapt attention.

Calder.

"Yes, yes, oh yes," Leah breathed, her back pressed to mine as I jerked my head side to side.

They were all there.

Calder.

Caleb.

Ryon.

Maybe we had a chance.

We were seriously outnumbered, but please, God, let us have a chance.

I sent out my prayer, but it didn't look good. Wolf bodies were strewn everywhere, not one I recognized, but the fighting was ferocious, bloody, *relentless*.

Sonia attacked anything that got close to besting Wei, Chen, and a Xun who was back on his feet, fighting. Then she emitted a high whine, her wolf eyes directed to the fray and I looked that way.

Ryon was going down.

"No, God, no!" Leah cried.

The wolf went for Ryon's throat, but he was butted to the side viciously by the head of a wolf I'd never seen but who was very familiar. The new wolf skirmished with the one who nearly took Ryon and then Ryon joined the fight and the enemy lost his throat.

The new wolf turned and attacked one of the two Chen was holding back with sure swings of a sign post pole, and I knew when I saw his brown eyes, he was Cain.

*Thank you, God.*

There were high-pitched whines and strange-sounding barks and, suddenly, Callum leaped to man and bellowed, "*Retreat and I'll be merciful!*"

Half the wolves that were left in the fight turned tail and bolted away.

The rest, in short order, at the teeth of our wolves, fell dead to the Tarmac.

As the last one went down, ours leaped back to man.

## *In a Pub Somewhere in London*

"All right!" a man shouted, tossing his fist in the air.

"Did you see that, mate?" another man asked, slapping the man sitting on a stool on the shoulder. *"Retreat and I'll be merciful!"* he shouted, then whooped, "The man is naked and outnumbered, and still, half those beasts tucked tail and ran. Bad-fuckin'-*ass*."

"The one with the two-colored eyes is hot," a girl said.

"Which one?" another girl said.

"Both of them." The first girl smiled, not looking away from the telly.

"I like the good vampire. He's *lush*," a third girl said.

"Shut it, it isn't done," a man snapped.

"Testy," the second girl mouthed, giving big eyes to the third.

The third smiled.

Then they both looked back to the TV.

## *Delilah*

Callum pulled on his jeans. Abel pulled on his jeans.

Sonia circled around, stayed as wolf, and sat next to her king.

And Teona, appearing out of nowhere, grinned appreciatively as she handed out more jeans to her mate, Ryon, Caleb, and Calder.

"Jesus, you're cock mad," Cain muttered as he tugged his on, giving her a look that said he was close to laughing.

Or growling.

"Maybe," she replied saucily. "But you know, baby, there's only one cock for me."

He rolled his eyes and turned, joining the line of The Real True who faced the posers.

Etienne took in Cain.

"A twin?" he asked quietly.

"Surprise," Cain replied.

I tried not to giggle.

They kept bringing it; we kept giving it.

Hope bloomed inside me.

Etienne ignored Cain and looked beyond him.

"And there is your witch," he noted.

"Dude, you are *not* cluing in," Abel spat with frustration. "You've no idea what we've got, and I told you, you don't wanna know." He threw out both arms, indicating the dismembered bodies. "This enough evidence for you?"

"You also have no idea what I've got, young Abel," Etienne returned.

"Maybe not, but I know it's not enough," Abel replied.

"Are you sure?" Etienne asked.

"Christ, what's wrong with you?" Abel asked. "These jacked comebacks, like you're the bad guy from a movie. Seriously, this is real, and if you don't stand down, you're not gonna be breathing much longer."

"Let's put that to the test, shall we?" Etienne asked.

I watched from behind him as Abel shook his head and muttered, "Whatever."

In a trice, we were surrounded by vampires.

Not a couple hundred of them.

A *lot* more.

And they were all armed with lethal-edged swords.

I sucked in breath as the blooming hope inside stalled.

"Fuck," Xun whispered, slowly turning his head side to side, taking them in while backing into Leah and me, Wei and Chen doing the same, surrounding us.

"Now would be a good time for whatever we got to come out," Leah murmured.

"I hear you," I murmured back.

"Now how sure are you, young Abel?" Etienne sneered.

"Bring it on," Abel snarled.

Great.

My man was awesome and The Three and our families had it going on.

But right then, we were in trouble.

Big-time trouble.

I needed my blue light, however that could help.

But Abel was in danger, serious danger, and it wasn't coming to me.

"Take their heads!" Etienne yelled.

Abel was right.

Earlier, they'd been playing.

Right then, it began.

*In a Home Somewhere in Idaho*

The man reached out and took hold of his wife's hand.

She leaned into him, her body resting against his shoulder, as she held on tight.

"Please, God, please," she whispered, her gaze unwavering on the screen. "Help them. *Please.*"

*Gregor*

"Got a lock on it!" headphone man cried loudly. "The signal's coming from a suburb in Missouri."

Gregor tore his eyes off the screens, long since noting they had cameras everywhere, microphones everywhere, and someone was switching them to get the best angles.

This right now being a blur that, with his vampiric eyesight, Gregor could see was Lucien battling eight vampires.

And losing.

He whipped his head to the line of vampires awaiting orders.

He looked to the first. “Get the exact location. Send everything we have close there.”

He looked to the second. “Phone Gastineau. Give him the location. Have him send everyone he can.”

He looked to the third. “Find out what’s happening with Josefa.”

As the third shot out, another vampire shot in.

“Status,” he said immediately. “We’re holding them at the wall. We have help—phantoms and wraiths are attacking them from their rear.” He drew in breath. “But there are a lot of them, sir. We need to throw at them everything we’ve got.”

“Round up as many as you can and go,” Gregor ordered, and the vampire shot out.

Gregor knew their play. He knew Etienne somehow understood that he could get at least Delilah in her dreams. And perhaps draw Abel.

Which would make The Three vulnerable and the time ripe for an attack on the compound.

“Thank God!” the production manager exclaimed, and Gregor looked back to see Teona had spelled those around Lucien. They’d been thrown back and Lucien again had a fighting chance.

And he was taking it.

“Where’s my baby? Where’s my little girl? Where’s my baby?” Hook whispered.

The man and his brothers had joined them five minutes ago.

Now Hook was leaned into the screens, his hands braced on the console, his eyes inches away.

“Step back, brother. She’ll be good. She’s tough. She’s smart. She’ll be good. Calm down,” Moose urged gently, his hand on Hook’s back.

But Hook didn’t have it in him to hear his friend.

He was focused.

“Where is she? Where’s my baby?”

“There!” Jabber yelled. “I saw her, standing. She’s good, man. She’s still standing!”

"Shit, okay, shit, *awesome*!" Moose bellowed. "The rest of them witches are there!"

And Gregor saw they were. Barb, Ruby, Jezza, and Flo lifted their hands, tossing what Gregor knew had to be spells at the enemy, magic that interestingly didn't translate to the screen. It looked like they were simply throwing out their arms.

But they were also using weapons that could easily be seen.

Short, sharp blades, long, curved knives, and thin daggers.

The blessed instruments.

With each slash and jab, the immortals, wounded, fell back.

But he knew those witches and Poncho's aunt had given them more too. There was no way The Three and their families could hold back the onslaught from that many foes.

Unless they had the powerful protection of magic.

But watching it, Gregor tensed.

Because he saw his son close to Aurora, fending off three vampires and a golem, with no weapon.

His son.

There.

In her dream.

Keeping his witch safe.

It had been the girl who became his daughter, Sonia.

Now it was both his daughter *and* son.

"Fucking where...is...that—?" he began.

"She's here, brother. She's here, *amigo*." He heard Poncho huff and looked to the door to see the nephew escorting his aunt in hurriedly.

Her eyes went immediately to the screens and her lips thinned.

"I need her to send me, and those," Gregor pointed to a collection of swords resting against the armchair Jian-Li had sat in what felt like centuries ago, "there." He pointed to the screen.

She turned her head to her nephew and said something.

Poncho nodded and looked to him.

"She says you shouldn't go."

"My son and daughter are there," Gregor returned curtly.

Poncho looked to his aunt who spoke, then back to Gregor. "Man, she says—"

"Oh fuck, one of those Chinese guys is down," headphone man said.

"Wei," Jabber whispered, the sound of his friend's name coming out rough.

"Send me and *those weapons* to…*my children*!" Gregor shouted.

Ursula suddenly was at his side. "I go too."

Poncho spoke to his aunt as Moose bellowed, "*Fuck!* Why are we *fuckin'* here and they're *fuckin'* there?"

"Time is wasting," Gregor bit off.

Poncho looked to him. "Grab the swords."

With their vampire speed, Gregor and Ursula had the swords and were standing in front of the witch.

"Do not go and do not send Delilah's family," he ordered. When Poncho looked ready to argue and he heard a gruff noise from Moose, Gregor swiftly carried on, "It will be too distracting. They need focus. And the compound needs to be defended at all costs, so do not send any immortals either. Josefa must look after The Three from here. Their minds are there, but their bodies are here and vulnerable."

"Got it, man," Poncho agreed.

"Hook," Ursula called, and Hook must have looked to her because she kept going. "You gave me happiness. I vow to fall before your daughter does."

"Babe," Hook whispered and said no more.

The witch was reaching up toward their heads, muttering under her breath.

"Good luck," Poncho said softly.

Gregor slid his eyes to the man and nodded.

The next instant, he was in hell.

*Somewhere in a Café in Nevada*

"Not good, not good, not good," one man chanted.

"Get 'im! Fuck 'im up! Yes!" another one shouted.

"*To your back!*" Naomi screamed, then moaned, "Thank God."

"No! Yes! No! *Yes*!" a woman cried.

"Get up, guy, get up, guy, get up," a waitress whispered, eyes on the fallen Wei, his body lifeless amongst the carnage on-screen.

"*Shit!*" a man boomed. "They got that female wolf!"

*Delilah*

With a frightening yelp, Sonia as wolf slid on her side across the Tarmac, and every inch of my skin prickled to see her coat matted in blood, claw and teeth marks everywhere.

The next second, the wolf that pounced on her was grabbed by the throat and thrown through the air.

But he left something behind.

The gore of his gullet in Callum's jowls.

Callum tossed it aside with a shake of his head and nosed her. She shook her head and got to her paws.

Then he nosed her firmly in our circle and turned toward an attacker.

I caught all this before I felt movement close beside me.

After thinking how I could ever see the whip of action to make my play, somehow, the action around me had come into focus.

Vivid focus.

Using it, I jumped on the back of a vampire who was all over Xun. He twisted to throw me off. With experience with Abel hauling me around, I held on with everything I had. Calling for more, I curved my hand around his jaw and yanked back.

I didn't get him very far, but I got him far enough for Xun to shove the jagged end of the mailbox pole straight into his throat. He twisted and slashed it to the side, opening a gaping wound, blood spurting.

The vampire fell to his knees.

I jumped off and kicked him in the head so he fell to his side.

Xun lifted the pole over his head and bore it down, hacking into his neck.

"Back!" Xun grunted, still hacking. "Now, Lilah!"

I backed into Leah.

"Babe, Gregor's here," she told me, grasping my hand.

I didn't see him.

What I saw was that our guys now had weapons.

Gregor must have brought them.

It didn't matter.

Wei was down. By the looks of him, I was sure he was dead.

I'd seen Cain appear and he was sliced to shit, looking like he was barely standing.

I'd lost track of Jezza and Flo.

Ruby was down, like Wei, unmoving.

We were losing.

All was going to be lost.

Standing in a sea of bodies, drenched in blood, we were going down.

*In a Convenience Store Somewhere in Florida*

The crowd was larger.

They didn't realize it, not a one of them, but they were all holding hands.

They were silent.

All their gazes were locked to the screen.

## *Delilah*

"No," I whispered. "*No!*" I screamed.

Sonia barked. It sounded like she was trying to say something, but I didn't speak wolf.

"Fuck this," Leah hissed.

Bending down, she pulled a sword from a fallen, headless vampire's hand and I blinked when, fast as lightning, she entered the fight.

It was then I heard an indistinct roar of fury and I looked that way to see Lucien had appeared.

The sound was coming from him.

Then he moved, hacking his way to where his bride was fighting.

I heard a whiz and a clash and I whipped around.

Shit! I was nearly taken out by a vampire sword.

That vampire was now headless, and Ursula, who saved my ass, turned and winked at me before she shot away.

I had no time to watch. Chen was fighting a golem.

Head down, I charged, barreling into the giant headfirst, agony shooting down my back but catching him off guard, allowing Chen to hack off his hand.

"Come on, blue light, come on, blue light, come on!" I cried, lifting, twisting, and hauling up my knee hard, catching him right in the golem family jewels I couldn't understand why he had, considering he tore off flesh to make babies.

Apparently, it was a good target.

He grunted, his remaining hand going between his legs.

Chen hacked off his head.

I stepped back, looking for what I could do to help next, seeing Leah, shit-hot, moving at almost a blur of speed, using all Xun, Wei, and Chen had taught us (and then some), kicking major bad guy ass side by side with her husband. They were working as a team, weirdly in tandem like they were synced.

Then Chen took off the golem's leg at his knee and he teetered before crashing to the ground.

That was when I saw we had new allies.

Surprising ones.

Dogs.

And cats.

And rats.

And snakes.

And fucking *bunnies*.

They were everywhere.

They couldn't do much.

But considering there were hundreds of them, and they all were straight up pissed and attacking the bad guys, they sure as hell were distracting.

Creating opening after opening for the small army of The Three to deliver devastation.

*In an Apartment Somewhere in Washington DC*

The woman smiled a very small smile, a weak stream of hope filling her heart where fear had taken hold.

"They even have the bunnies," she whispered.

*Delilah*

"Holy shitoly," I breathed, staring at a vampire who was trying to shake a dog off his leg as a cat was clawing his face.

"Down!" I heard Abel shout, and instinctively, I hit the deck, landing on bodies (and body parts).

I felt something whiz over me.

Then Abel whizzed over me. I lifted my head right when a body dropped in front of my eyes, neck first.

Blood gushing.

I didn't even have time to gag before I was hauled up and twisted so I was front to Abel's back.

"Jump on," he ordered.

"Baby, you can't fight with me—"

*"Hold the fuck on!"* he thundered.

I wrapped my arms around him and held tight, swaying, jerking, jolting, as he kept fighting.

"Can you use mind-control?" I asked into his ear, keeping my hold tight.

"Too many," he grunted, swinging. "Gotta focus."

Shit.

A sword slashed through my shoulder, the pain so immense I almost dropped my arms.

But I held back my whimper. I didn't want Abel to have to think about me.

It was then I heard a strangled, terrified, tortured, *"Mom!"*

Aurora.

This meant Barb.

Abel whirled and leaped over bodies, me looking around him, seeing Barb on her ass, one hand behind her holding her up, the other one outstretched. She was bloodied and cut, a weak ray of vermillion light sparking from her palm, a vampire over her, arm with a sword swung out to the side to take her head.

As he swung and Abel raced to him, the sword clashed against another one.

Gregor was there.

Abel had to stop to fight someone, whipping this way and that, taking me with him.

But he'd whipped back when it happened.

Even if it was a vampire blur, I saw it with total clarity.

In fact, it went in slow motion.

So I had every second. Every *fucking* second of Gregor losing his head burned in my brain.

Burned in my memory.

For eternity.

*In a Pub Somewhere in London*

"No!" a girl cried out, her voice hoarse with despair.

But after the sound faded away, the room went silent.

And everyone kept their eyes to the screen.

Each one holding hope to their hearts.

By a thread.

*Delilah*

I let go of Abel, my feet hitting the ground, and the world stopped.

All action around me suspended.

Completely.

There was only Gregor's headless body, slowly, so *damned* slowly, sinking to the ground.

Like the sound was muted, distorted, drawn out, and slowed down, I heard Yuri's desolate, enraged howl.

My breath stopped, my heart stopped, my frame electrified as Gregor finally crashed to the Tarmac.

And it was then I tipped my head back, drove my arms straight down, and balled my fists.

I opened my mouth and cried my despair to the heavens.

The sound was foul.

It was wreathed in anguish.

And while I made it, unbeknownst to me, from the middle of my body, a ring of blue light flashed, sweeping out in a circle, growing wider, wider, wider, *wider*, cutting through the combatants, the houses, and beyond.

I dropped my head, saw my bloodied boots. Next to one, the arm of a golem; at the tip of the other, the head of a vampire.

I closed my eyes.

"Gregor," I whispered, his name torn from me, and I felt every letter as they passed my lips ripping me to shreds.

*In Front of an Electronics Store in New York City*

On every screen in the window, dozens of them, was a shot of the mortal, bloodied, injured Delilah Johnson, head bowed, grief for a fallen vampire she liked and respected etched along every centimeter of her frame.

Scores of people stood on the sidewalk, the crowd arcing out into the street, having stopped traffic.

But the drivers honked no horns. Car doors were left open so they could get out, approach, and watch.

And from the throng who gazed at the television screens, there was nothing.

Nothing but silence united in heartache.

*Delilah*

"*Bao bei*," Abel whispered, and I felt his hand on my back.

I stood unmoving.

"Lilah," Abel said from closer, his lips to my ear, his hand pressing into my back.

I remained still.

"Baby, you did it."

I opened my eyes to blink and lifted my head.

I looked around.

Standing were ours, the few of them we were, except Xun and Chen were bent over an immobile Wei.

Scattered in endless heaps were the bodies of the dead enemy.

Wandering around, aimless, sniffing, slithering, hopping, were the animals.

And on their knees, weirdly motionless, was our enemy.

"Told you, pussycat, whatever you got, that shit is *the shit*," Abel told me.

"Wh-what?" I stammered, my eyes drifting to him.

"That blue light?" he asked, and I nodded. "Went through them. All of a sudden, they quit fighting. It took them down to their knees. Left 'em there."

"I...you're joking," I whispered.

"Look around," he threw out an arm then grabbed my hand and pulled me to the nearest one. Keeping me close, he asked the female vampire. "Feel like moving?"

Her eyes fired and her body jerked.

Only slightly.

But she stayed on her knees.

"Holy shitoly," I breathed, then stopped doing it altogether when it crashed into me.

My head shot to Wei.

"Already checked, pussycat," Abel whispered to me. "He's still with us."

Xun was looking at us. "He's breathin', brother, but we gotta get him home."

"I'll see to that," Teona said, prowling to them. She crouched, then carefully lifted Wei's body between her legs and into her arms, pressing his back to her torso.

I squeezed Abel's hand tight as Wei's dead weight swayed lifelessly when Teona took him into her hold.

"Touch me if you're going back with me," she said to Xun and Chen.

"You go back. I'll stay," Chen said to his brother.

Xun nodded, touched his hand to Teona's shoulder, and Teona looked to Cain.

"Later, baby," she said softly and disappeared.

I let that impossibility filter through me before, mindlessly, I turned and slowly started walking, my hand in Abel's, taking him with me.

As Abel and I stepped over bodies, I saw Yuri crouched over his father, his head down, his gaze to Gregor, his frame blocking our view of the man who kept us safe so we could fight the good fight.

And whose death, apparently, led us to victory.

"Allow me to take him home, sweetheart," Barb said quietly, bending and touching Yuri's shoulder.

"Take Aurora with you," Yuri replied, his always-smooth, cool voice gruff with unconcealed emotion.

Hearing it, my throat clogged.

"Okay, honey," Barb whispered and bent over Gregor.

Aurora got close.

"Yuri, sweetie—" She touched the back of his hair but got no further speaking.

"Go, button," he ordered gently.

God, they were *so* freaking cute together.

"As you wish," she whispered, bent, kissed his hair, and moved to her mother.

They clasped hands, and after both of them turned sorrowful eyes to Yuri, they disappeared, taking Gregor with them.

Abel and I got close to Yuri's back as the rest of us gathered around him.

He lifted his head but didn't come out of his crouch.

His eyes turned to the vampire who took his father's life.

"You will not die so mercifully," he whispered, and at his tone now, goose bumps rose all over my skin.

We heard sirens in the distance and I suddenly felt cold.

There was a reason for that as three phantoms, with a bevy more behind them, as well as some wraiths floated in front of us.

"We've taken out the cameras. You're free to do as you wish with the others," the phantom in the middle of the three at the front stated.

"Cameras?" Leah asked.

"This was televised around the world. Everyone saw it. Now the cameras and microphones have been disabled," the phantom to the left said.

"Brilliant," Lucien clipped.

"Yuri, let's go home."

I looked down to Yuri to see Sonia on her knees in front of him, Callum standing close behind her. She was bloodied but clothed. There were claw marks slashing across her upper chest, more across her hip, if the blood seeping through her jeans was any indication, and bite marks on her neck and arms, but she looked strong.

"Yuri, honey." She lifted her hands to his cheeks when he made no reply. "Let's go home."

"You survived," Yuri said, his voice freaking me out because it was not cold, it was not rough. It was nothing. "The Three survived. He fell."

A tear tracked down Sonia's cheek as she said nothing but kept holding Yuri's face.

"He fell," Yuri whispered, and there was no longer nothing in his voice.

It was full.

Full to the brim with pain.

My eyes got wet.

"Please, come home with me. We need to be with Gregor," Sonia begged, her voice edged with a sob.

Suddenly, Yuri stood.

"Yes, Sonny. Home," he stated shortly.

She nodded, straightening, but I moved fast.

Getting in front of Yuri, I got close and wrapped my arms around his middle, pressing my cheek to his chest as I hugged him tight to me. And only when I had him close did I say, "Your dad was the total bomb, Yuri. The absolute bomb. The vampire Gregor was *awesome*."

Yuri stood motionless in my hold for a long time and I was going to give him that. In that moment, I'd give him anything.

But finally, I felt his hand curl light on the back of my neck.

"Yes, Lilah," he said quietly. "He was."

"We're fading, honey. Grab hold," Sonia called.

I let go and Abel wrapped his arm around my chest, pulling me back just as Yuri lifted his hand, Sonia took it, and she and her brother faded away.

"King of the Wolves, what do you wish for the rest of them?" one of the phantoms called on a prompt.

That was when I looked around and took everything in.

It was gruesome.

But we'd been joined by others, and not just the phantoms.

The humans had left their houses. Some were sticking close to their doors, standing on their stoops. Some had wandered into their yards, though not far. All of them held weapons, guns, baseball bats, knives.

I didn't know if they were worried about us or if they got it together to come and help.

It didn't matter.

It was done.

I kept looking and saw at each end of the block, cop cars were angled in, their lights flashing, the cops out, bracing their weapons against hoods and roofs, using the cars as shields.

"Are we sure how long Lilah's light will hold?" Callum asked.

"We're not sure of anything," Abel replied.

"Then incapacitate them and contact The Council," Callum ordered the phantoms.

They nodded and most floated off.

One remained behind and shared, "The Council is aware of your location. Reinforcements will be here within five minutes."

"Little late," Cain muttered.

I sighed.

The phantom drifted away.

"How can they incapacitate them?" Leah asked while leaning heavily against Lucien.

"They feed on energy and sometimes they can be...greedy," Callum answered. "In this instance, it might make them ill." He jerked his head to the scene behind us as phantoms swooped down on the motionless supernaturals who then dropped to their sides or backs like they were narcoleptics. "All that negative energy. But they can purge it when they get to somewhere safe where it will dissipate and not infect another being."

"Ah," Leah murmured.

Suddenly, Lucien transferred her weight to Callum and stalked off.

We all watched.

Then, noting his destination, we all quickly followed.

He stopped, looking down at his father, who was on his knees.

"Yield," he whispered.

His father stared up at him, mute.

I gasped as my next vision was Lucien holding Etienne aloft by his throat.

"*Yield!*" he thundered.

"Neh...ver," Etienne forced out.

Lucien hauled him to within an inch of his face.

"Then you will burn," he growled and, with no further ado, tossed his father aside.

Etienne barely landed before I felt Abel's body jolt.

I whipped around, panic instantly having a stranglehold on me that we had new aggressors.

Then I gawked.

The girl in the pink camisole and polka-dotted pajama pants was hugging my man around the middle.

My heart squeezed.

"*Come here, Amelia!*" a woman standing on the sidewalk shrieked.

The girl tipped her head way back.

"I'll never forget you," she whispered. "Never. I'll never *ever* forget you."

Abel lifted a hand and dropped it to the top of her head.

She grinned. It was weak, it was shaky, but she managed it.

Then she let him go and ran to her mother, leaping over bodies, sliding on blood and gore.

We heard vehicles. Some of us looked one way, others looked the other, and we saw army green Jeeps and sparkling black SUVs angling in behind the cop cars.

"Let's go home," Leah said, getting close to her man and hugging him from the side.

He slid an arm around her shoulders.

She reached out and grabbed Callum's hand.

Callum lifted his other hand and dropped it on Cain's shoulder.

Xun shouldered in and wrapped his arms around Leah and Callum. Ryon, Calder, and Caleb pushed in and connected. Ursula did the same. Jezza and Flo, helping a hobbling Ruby, joined us.

Abel pulled me close and took Cain's hand, lifting them up and moving their bodies close so their hands were tucked to their sides.

Even though Abel gave me a tug, I stayed removed.

And I did this to look up and down the street.

Finally, I shifted forward, reaching out to clasp hands with Lucien, and I did it with my head thrown back, shouting, *"We are The Three!"*

And on a radiating circle of blue light, our huddle disappeared.

So we missed the cacophony of human cheers.

In a home somewhere in Idaho, a husband and wife embraced, his eyes rimmed with red, hers wet with tears.

In a pub somewhere in London, a bartender called to the unruly crowd, "Pints! All around! On the house!"

In a convenience store somewhere in Florida and on a street in New York City, perfect strangers embraced, smiles quivered, and tears flowed as all experienced sweet relief.

And in an apartment somewhere in Washington DC, a woman listened to a newscaster, quietly sobbing.

But she did it smiling.

## *In a Café Somewhere in Nevada*

The cheers deafening behind her, Naomi kept her eyes to the screen.

Then she lifted them to the ceiling.

Her prayer was short and silent.

*I never doubted, but even so, thank you.*

Once done, she turned around and shouted, "Lemon meringue pie all around!"

The cheer of jubilation split her ears.

But they didn't care about pie.

Knowing this, Naomi smiled.

## *Abel*

Abel opened his eyes and lifted his head.

He felt his mate stirring beside him, but he saw Jian-Li sitting on the bed and felt her hands clamped tight around his and Delilah's.

A tear dropped down her cheek as she caught his gaze, and her lips were trembling when she spoke.

"Welcome back, *tian xin*."

He grinned at her, and when he felt Delilah lifting up, he helped her, sweeping her in one arm at the same time he caught Jian-Li in his other.

He tucked his women close.

He held them tight.

And he did this for a long fucking time.

# Epilogue
# All That We Can Be

*Delilah*

As the sun snuck beneath the horizon, the sound of Abel's guitar strings bounced against the rocks of the bay.

A bay that was crowded shoulder to shoulder with vampires, wolves, wraiths, phantoms, and humans.

Up front, his khaki pants rolled up his ankles, the breeze blowing at his white linen shirt, the sea lapping against his bare feet, stood Yuri.

To one side, leaning in, her hand in his, her head on his shoulder, stood Aurora.

On his other, her arm around him, her head also on his shoulder, stood Sonia.

And at Aurora's side, also holding hands with her daughter, stood Barb.

A few feet behind them, arms wrapped around each other, stood Callum and Regan.

And we stood behind Callum and Regan. Me. Leah and Lucien. Jian-Li, Xun, and Chen, the boys holding up Wei who, even with his injuries, refused not to come. Dad, Ursula, Moose, Poncho, his auntie, Josefa, and Jabber. Aurora's witch buddies. Ryon, Calder, and Caleb.

All of us held hands (except one of my hands was unavailable since my arm was in a sling, so Leah held me about the waist at my other side).

The rest, there to pay respects, stood to our backs.

Our eyes were on the Viking ship drifting peacefully on the waves.

Abel's guitar was joined with another, the power of the strums reverberating through our bodies.

And as Abel's voice rang out, the strings of an orchestra joined him.

In his baritone, he sang John Denver's "The Eagle and the Hawk."

The words tore through me as tears raced down my cheeks.

But I listened.

I listened to every beautiful word.

As the final notes drifted through the still air, hundreds of flaming arrows arced their buttercream light through the dark lavender blanket of sky.

Some hit the water.

Most hit the boat, and it and its precious cargo, taking its final journey, burst into flames.

I failed at swallowing back my sob and Jian-Li's hand in mine tightened.

The boat burned.

No one moved.

I felt Abel push in beside me and take my hand from Jian-Li's to hold in his.

"All that we can be," Leah whispered.

At her words, more tears slid down my cheeks. The burning boat was blurry, but I kept my eyes to it.

*Soar, Gregor,* I prayed. *You've done your job. We're safe now. The whole world is safe now, because of you.*

Sparks shot to the heavens on my thought.

I tasted salt as I smiled.

Aurora lifted her head from Yuri's shoulder and we all heard her say quietly, "I'm glad I got the chance to know him, Yuri."

With his gaze straight to the sea, Yuri dropped her hand and curled an arm around her shoulders.

But he made no reply.

Callum did.

"You will never meet a stronger man in your life," the king of wolves declared, his eyes on the burning ship. "With eternity lying before us, not one of us will."

Sonia looked back at her husband and smiled through her tears.

I dropped my head to Abel's shoulder and gave him my weight.

And Abel, my mate, he stood strong and let me.

## *Lucien*

"Where were you?" Lucien demanded.

"We were there," Avery replied.

"You were? You were *where*?" Lucien clipped.

"We were there. The Ancients are everywhere. Do you think the insurrectionists had the ability to hack satellites?' Avery shook his head and his eyes claimed Lucien's in an unbreakable hold. "The humans, Lucien, they had *to see*."

"*You* televised it?" Lucien hissed.

"They had to see."

"You've said that," Lucien bit out.

"The magic, Lucien, the magic that makes us, the magic that binds us, the magic that gives us immortality, links our races, flows through all of our veins only exists because of hope. Hope and love. Etienne and his minions represented the death of that. The Three was its salvation."

"If you knew what they had planned, why didn't you help us?" Lucien asked.

"We did," Avery told him.

"And how's that?" It was a scoff.

"For the last several decades, we gave you Gregor."

Lucien's jaw went hard.

He changed subjects. "After he attacked Leah, I could have dealt with my father. You wouldn't allow it. I could have done something before he violated concubines, slaughtered villages—"

"Yes, but if you had, they would not have *seen*."

Lucien blew out an infuriated breath. "I don't understand your logic. In love and hope, you accept innocent collateral damage?"

"If you don't understand, then I'll tell you this," Avery returned. "If I'd told Gregor he would lose his life to this fight, he would not have changed one thing he did, including going to aid his son, his daughter, *you*. That's love, Lucien. That's hope. That's beauty." He leaned forward. "That's *magic*."

Fuck, but Lucien couldn't argue that.

"They saw," Avery continued. "All around the globe, they saw you fight. They saw you bleed. They saw you sacrifice. They saw you face an undefeatable foe. And they saw you beat it. They saw the power of hope. They saw the might of love. And now, what do we have?"

Lucien didn't answer.

"Harmony," Avery whispered. "Immortals and mortals, after millennia, living together in harmony."

He wasn't wrong.

In the five days since the battle, there had been incidents.

But immortals were outing themselves around the world and none of the incidents had been violent. None of them alarming.

What Avery said was true.

The acceptance was astonishing.

Lucien let that go and asked, "Did you know we would lose Gregor?"

Avery shook his head. "I am millennia old, I have skills and strengths, but I'm no seer. Neither are the others. We knew what the enemy had planned because we had the skills to find out. But we had no idea of the outcome. Only hope."

Lucien held his gaze and said, "Lilah's light."

"She's the best of you."

It was then that Lucien stared. "Pardon?"

"She was the key all along, Lucien. Her light. Lilah's light made her the most powerful of all of The Three."

"Love," Lucien guessed, and Avery nodded. "But we all had that," he pointed out.

"Acceptance is a word not in Delilah Johnson's vocabulary," Avery announced. "I'm sure you've noted why."

It was dawning on him. "Because she sees no difference. She doesn't have to accept, because she doesn't even begin to judge."

Avery nodded again. "She takes everyone just as they are. Even under frightening circumstances and even more frightening explanations, she took Abel's side almost immediately. The power of that, Lucien, coupled with her capacity for love, loyalty, hope...There is nothing more powerful than that on the planet. Delilah is not all that we are. Delilah represents all that we *can* be."

Lucien knew down to his bones that Avery was right.

There was no more to be said.

Therefore, he rose from his seat, murmuring, "I wish to get back to my bride."

"Give her my love."

Standing, looking down at Avery sitting in Gregor's chair at Gregor's desk, he felt his throat constrict.

He liked Avery. Respected him. As angry as he was, that would never change how he felt about him.

But he detested seeing him in Gregor's chair.

"We often do not know what we have until it's lost," Avery said gently. "You've been on this earth a long time, but that's a lesson we all seem consistently to forget." Avery regarded him warmly. "I hope that this time, you won't forget, Lucien."

Lucien lifted his chin.

He wouldn't forget.

None of them would.

Then he walked out of the room to find his bride.

*Yuri*

"Douse," Yuri called.

When he did, the witches lounging on blankets and in lawn chairs on the grass around him, sipping wine, popping cashews or grapes or crackers slathered with brie in their mouths, lifted lazy hands and the fire consuming the vampire chained to the stake went out.

It was the vampire who'd killed his father.

His screams of agony faded to whimpers.

Yuri, with his back against a tree, legs out in front of him, laptop on his thighs, continued to catch up on email.

It had taken some time, but when he hit send, he saw he was finally done.

"Fire," he said, and Barb, Ruby, Jezza, and Flo lifted their hands again.

The fire blazed and the screams returned.

Yuri snapped his laptop shut and rolled to his feet.

"You know," Ruby stated casually over the shrieks, staring at the roaring fire like it was a campfire and not a vampire burning at the stake, "this is doing wonders helping me work out my feelings for vampires."

Yuri felt one side of his lips hitch up.

"He's at your mercy," he announced, and the witches looked to him. "However, when you're finished, so is he."

Barb nodded.

"I go to Aurora," he said to Barb. "We're dining at a seafood restaurant in town tonight. You'll join us for dinner?"

"Of course," she replied.

"Be there with bells on," Ruby called, shoving another cheese-smeared cracker in her mouth.

She wasn't exactly invited.

Then again, she would be amusing company.

He dipped his chin Ruby's way.

Then he walked away to find his little witch.

## *Callum*

"We don't do things that way in the United States," the president, on the large screen in front of him, snapped.

"We've had our governments alongside yours for centuries, Darren," Callum replied. "We dispense justice our way and you do not interfere. You do it your way and we return the favor."

"That was before. Now the immortals are out—"

"We've already spoken of this," Callum cut him off, allowing his impatience to show. "The nation of wolves will continue to be governed by me, the vampires by The Dominion," he went on, gesturing to Rudolf and Cristiano who were sitting at his side. "And the wraiths and phantoms by Serena and Gastineau," he finished, gesturing to the pair who floated at his other side. "This is as it was and as it always will be."

"He and his army attacked *two* American towns," the president shot back.

"And he and his army will pay for their crimes," Callum returned. "We've already rounded up the golem and all the others. They have fallen."

"The vampire Etienne must stand trial," the president declared.

"He has and has been found guilty. Which is why we're speaking," Callum reminded him.

"You can't simply execute him without—" the president began but stopped when Callum leaned forward in his seat and his expression changed.

"Humans do what they do and much of it I don't understand. I know what you wish. I know you wish for his trial to be televised. And, in a small way, I understand that would provide closure, not to mention the understanding of justice being done...and vengeance. But mostly, the only purpose it would serve would be to provide titillation and an opportunity for voyeurism. Immortals don't do things that way. We will make the transcripts of the trial available to the ruling bodies of all nations and you can decide to do with them what you will. But Lucien takes Etienne's head tonight. And then it is done."

"We cannot—" the president tried again.

"This call was a courtesy," Callum bit out. "It was our people who committed the atrocities. It was also our people who bled and fell to put a stop to it. *We* will have justice. You will only be assured of it. And now, we're done."

"If this is how you intend to conduct our affairs for the future, Callum, I have grave concerns," the president sniffed.

"And if you haven't learned from our sacrifice that we wish harmony but autonomy, not dominance or interference, I fear for your nation's future as that would prove you're not a very astute leader," Callum retorted.

The president reared back in his baronial chair.

"As you are very aware, this threat was not new. We have lost much in order to contain it for a very long time. And further, in all matters, we have kept order amongst our people for an equally long time," Callum shared something the President knew. "We know how to govern our own. You have no idea. But regardless, at no time during the negotiations to conceive a plan to share the knowledge of immortal existence with humans was such meddling discussed. I've carefully gone over the minutes and Gregor's copious notes on all of your meetings. After we, and we alone, secured a safe transition into society for our people, changing your tactics now would be foolhardy."

The president's brows shot up. "Is that a threat?"

"If you wish to take it as one, I've no control over that," Callum replied. "However, it wasn't one. It was simply a statement of fact."

The president glared.

Callum finished it, "We'll share with you when we've concluded the matter with Etienne before we release a statement to the press. Now, I wish you a good day."

With that, he leaned forward, moved the mouse, and clicked, disconnecting the call.

"In the upcoming election, the candidate campaigning against him and favored to win is a much more open-minded human," Cristiano noted.

"This is because his daughter is dating a wolf," Callum muttered, rising from his seat. "I must go to Lucien."

"When you speak to him, if you would, mention our invitation to join The Council," Rudolf called as Callum moved to the door. "He's refused, but he would be an excellent addition to our fold and your recommendation would hold great sway with him."

Callum stopped and cut his eyes to the vampire. "Don't you think he's earned at least a small time of peace?"

"He's revered, Callum, and we're all going through colossal adjustments," Cristiano replied. "He could be very helpful."

He understood their concerns.

They'd lost Gregor.

They needed to fill that hole.

A hole that couldn't be filled. Not even by Lucien. Hell, *especially* not by Lucien, who was absolutely no politician.

"Give him his time of peace, time with his mate, a year, five, then try again," Callum suggested, even though he knew no matter how much time elapsed, they would fail.

The vampires nodded.

Callum looked to the queen of wraiths and the king of phantoms.

"You'll attend?" he asked.

"Absolutely," Gastineau replied, curling his arm around his mate to pull her close to his side.

The wraiths and phantoms had reunited.

An additional gift to Gregor's legacy.

Callum jerked up his chin.

Then he left to tell Lucien the execution would commence as planned.

After that, he would find his queen.

## *The Three*

In Speranza, Italy, at the headquarters of The Vampire Dominion, where the trial took place, they stood side by side along with Yuri but save Lucien, who stood in front of them, the shining, long, thin, lethal blade of a sword with its ornate gold grip that curled in swirls around his hand.

Serena, Gastineau, and a delegation of wraith and phantom witnesses floated behind them, off to the right.

Standing amongst them were Julian and Isobel, Lucien's children, and Magdalene, his mother. They did not come as representatives of Etienne's family. They came as the blood of Lucien and were there, as it was their due, to witness Lucien's vengeance.

Beyond the phantoms and wraiths stood a five-person delegation of humans.

Regan, Ryon, Calder, Caleb, Saint, and a delegation of wolf and she-wolf witnesses stood to their back left.

Right behind them, Leah's mother, her aunts, and a delegation of concubine witnesses stood.

Etienne, diminished of much of his strength due to the efforts of the phantoms, looking haggard and wearing an unattractive khaki jumpsuit, was on his knees in front of Lucien, his hands manacled behind his back.

Rudolf was off to the side, Cristiano just behind him. Rudolf had a tablet in hand and was reading out the charges.

And the verdicts.

The Dominion didn't waste time. It had been only two weeks since the battle had taken Gregor's life.

However, regardless, the evidence was irrefutable.

And unfortunately, there was a great deal of it.

When Rudolf finished, his gaze went to Lucien before he moved to him.

"Are you sure you wish it to be you?" he asked quietly. "This is unprecedented. His crimes are against all immortals and a member of The Council normally would carry out such a sentence." He got closer and finished, "Cristiano has volunteered to take up the sword."

"It will be me," Lucien bit out.

"Lucien—"

Lucien turned his eyes to Rudolf and Rudolf fell silent.

"As discussed, I call this as my marker," Lucien growled. "The Dominion's debt to me is paid."

Rudolf slowly nodded before he moved back to his earlier position.

He looked to Etienne. "You understand the charges. You understand the verdict. And now we carry out our ruling. Do you have any final words?"

Etienne's face twisted with malevolence and he opened his mouth.

But no sound came out except a gurgle because Lucien had sunk the tip of the blade into his throat and twisted.

"I think we've all heard enough from him," Lucien declared.

"Hear, hear," Kate, one of Leah's aunts, called.

"You feel the point of my blade through your throat for touching my mate," Lucien said softly, eyes to his father's.

Hate beamed from Etienne's straight to his son's.

Lucien was impervious to it.

"You've lived long, Father," Lucien said to Etienne. "You've had much time to read, I know. It was something you enjoyed."

He twisted the tip the other way and another gurgle discharged from Etienne's mouth as his eyes got wide in hatred mixed with pain.

"You encouraged that with me when I was a child," Lucien continued. "Mother did as well. She gave me a book once, which was excellent. Since she gave it to me, I've read it several times. It taught me a great deal. She told me you dismissed it as fantasy and unworthy of your attention. But it had an important lesson. One that clearly escaped you."

Lucien twisted the blade again, pushing it in deeper as he leaned toward his father.

"Might does not equal right," he whispered, his eyes locked with Etienne's. "Right equals might. It's a shame, so soon after you learned that lesson, you will die. But at least you learned it."

Etienne's eyes narrowed.

Lucien pulled the blade out, and with a human's speed, he took his father's head.

Without hesitation, he tossed the bloodied sword on Etienne's body and moved to his bride.

With no one saying a word or even giving the remains of a monster a passing glance, they all filed out.

And an hour later, on televisions around the globe, news agencies broke into regular programming to report that the vampire Etienne had been executed by the Allied Protectorate of Wolves, Vampires, Wraiths, and Phantoms.

There were a variety of responses.

But mostly, the response was relief.

And the next day, everyone went to work as usual.

Except some of them did it alongside vampires and wolves they'd had no idea were such.

Until now.

*Abel*

His bike in the distance, parked on the road, Abel had been roaming as wolf, his mate at his side.

Now he was man and he had her on her back in the leaves, the stars overhead, his hands curved around her ribs, yanking her down on his face between her legs.

He was sucking, deep and hungry, at her clit.

*Phenomenal.*

He stopped and buried his tongue inside.

He felt her back arch. He tightened his fingers and drove her down harder on his mouth.

He heard her moan.

Fuck yes.

His mouth opened on her clit again, tongue lapping, then he went back to the suction.

She dug her heels in his back. He knew it was coming.

So he stopped, surged over her, and bathed her neck with his tongue as he rammed his cock inside the hot wet of her cunt.

He tore through, her blood pouring into his mouth, and he knew it was on her.

"*Abel, baby,*" she moaned.

Abel heard it, kept thrusting, kept feeding, but did it smiling.

Wild.

As usual.

But now...

Free.

"Brother, take that back," Hook warned.

"Nothin' to take back, it's the damned truth," Moose retorted.

Abel turned his head, not knowing why the mood in the room shifted so quickly. Also not having heard anything since he'd been listening to Sonia talk about Calder's (enforced by Callum) reluctant but adventurous search for his mate.

"Then I'll make you take it back." Hook, at the head of the table, Delilah to one side, Aurora to his other, with Abel next to Delilah, shot out of his chair.

He then leaped over the table, arms extended, and as he did it, he took plates and platters filled with food, as well as much of the tablecloth, with him.

He hit Moose, who was sitting beside Yuri, the vampire next to Aurora, and Moose's chair fell back.

They started grappling immediately on the floor, rolling around, grunting, and cursing.

Delilah leaned forward in her chair toward a wide-eyed Aurora and said, "Don't worry. This happens a lot."

She was speaking truth.

It was Thanksgiving at the Johnson compound and it was far from surprising that all hell broke loose.

Ursula, who had been sitting down the table between Moose and Jabber, leaped to the seat of her chair and shouted, "That's it, my darling. Show him how it is!"

Abel looked down to the foot of the table to see Jian-Li watching the biker wrestling match with amusement settled firm on her features.

"Bummer, man, the hoisin sauce is all over the floor and I needed some," Xun muttered.

Aurora started giggling.

Delilah burst out laughing.

Sonia and Leah grinned at each other.

Lucien raised a brow to Callum, who just shrugged.

Chen asked for the eggrolls, which were one of the only things left on the table.

Barb handed them to him.

Cain held Teona in his lap, where he'd pulled her five minutes ago, and he shoved the last of his pancake filled with crispy shredded duck in his mouth as his mate craned her neck to watch the action.

Wei took a sip from his beer bottle, doing it eyes to the floor behind him where the men were fighting, his lips grinning.

And Abel sat back in his chair, staring at one of what he'd discovered was his mate's myriad brands of wild, and he did it with a smile, feeling free.

The wrestling match turned out to be a draw.

And then the table was cleared and Jian-Li and Delilah served four types of pie.

Abel lay on his back in their bed, eyes to the ceiling, his woman curled close, her finger moving in a whisper of touch, drawing patterns on his chest.

"Everyone leaves tomorrow," Delilah said quietly.

"Yeah," Abel replied.

"We'll be back together for Yuri and Aurora's Claiming Ceremony in December," she told him something he knew.

"Yeah," Abel repeated.

"That'll be fun," she muttered.

"Yeah," Abel agreed yet again.

"Hope Dad and Moose behave," she kept muttering. "Barb might spell them bald and impotent if they don't."

Abel's body started shaking with laughter.

Delilah snuggled closer, resting her cheek to his chest and stopping her hand in order to wrap her arm around his stomach.

"You wanna ride out the next day?" she asked.

He did.

Absolutely.

For months, they'd rode.

They did it from place to place. To visit Lucien and Leah. Jian-Li and his brothers. Cain and Teona. Or just places one or the other of them wanted to see.

And in that time, Abel had stood at the back of a roadhouse outside Austin, sipping beer, watching his mate scream and shout and dance with abandon to live music.

They'd also stood on the top of a cliff in northern California, holding hands, jumping off together, and falling straight into the salty, warm waters of the sea.

And she'd sat on his lap while trying to break the record of eating forty Coney dogs (she lost, she only could hold down fifteen) at some place outside Philly.

They'd fucked on the beach in the moonlight in South Carolina.

They'd sat in a speedboat Lucien drove fast on Dragon Lake next to the house he shared with Leah, Abel holding Delilah close, Delilah having both arms in the air most of the time, screaming in glee.

They'd sat at table after table with those they loved, eating, talking, sharing, laughing, dream after dream coming true as he'd seen his mate sitting back, chopsticks in her hand, boots on the table, teasing Jian-Li.

They were going to Scotland after Yuri and Aurora's Claiming Ceremony to spend Christmas with Sonia and Callum and their family.

While doing all of this, they were often recognized practically everywhere they went.

But they'd found, surprisingly, and gratefully, that this was always respectful.

Always.

Someone might approach but only to say "thank you" or ask to shake Abel's hand or give Delilah a hug.

Mostly, they just got nods or smiles.

The others reported they experienced the same.

So nothing marred their eternity of adventure.

Nothing marred their wild and free.

"Baby?" Delilah called into his contented thoughts.

"Yeah?"

"Wolf traits won out."

His brows drew together as he dipped his chin.

She slid her cheek on his chest to look up at him.

"What?"

"They're prolific," she whispered, and his entire frame strung taut.

"What?" This word came out on a sharp breath.

"I'm sure you want a girl you can spoil rotten. But I want a boy with two-colored eyes and—"

She didn't finish because she was on her back, bearing his weight, taking his tongue in her mouth.

When he broke their kiss, his voice was hoarse when he asked, "You havin' my baby?"

She nodded.

Abel stared into her green eyes that were filled with love and joy.

His mate.

His woman.

His temptress.

His Delilah, who would soon be the mother of his children.

Then he tipped his head back and did something he'd never done in his life.

And he'd never done it because he'd never had a reason to.

To the ceiling, Abel Jin howled his exaltation to the moon.

Those in the Johnson compound who heard and understood it, smiled happily at each other.

Those who didn't understand it still couldn't mistake it.

And they smiled happily too.

## *Retired Warriors*

As the onlookers stood silent after the new president of the United States turned from the podium where he'd just made a stirring speech of gratitude and remembrance, they watched him move to the towering, veiled mass behind him.

Then they watched him tug on the red velvet cord.

The dark shroud fell away, revealing the statue of a woman set hauntingly in bronze, the wound in her shoulder gaping, her neck bent, each line of her body the picture of sorrow.

On a plaque at the base, it read:

"We are The Three!"

Delilah

Of The Three

In Memoriam of Gregor

Fallen

In the Battle of Goodwill, Missouri

The Beginning and End of the Noble War

"So that we all can be free."

The First Lady set a large wreath of red roses at the base of the statue, then moved to her husband and held his hand, their heads bent to take in the plaque as silence kept the large crowd in its hold.

Eight figures stood looking down from the swell of a hill well beyond the onlookers.

They said not a word.

Until one of them did.

"I need a drink."

That was Abel.

"Aurora's and my suite?" Yuri suggested.

"See you there," Lucien muttered, taking Leah's hand and guiding her to the gleaming black Porsche parked on the street.

Callum lifted his chin in assent and slung his arm around Sonia, moving her to the green Range Rover parked behind the Jag.

"Hope you got Jack," Abel said.

Aurora laughed.

Yuri replied, "We have everything."

Abel nodded and hooked Delilah around the neck. "We'll be there after we check on Jian-Li and Greg," he said to Yuri before heading with his woman toward his bike.

"You ready, my sweet?" Yuri asked, looking down at his mate.

"Always, Yuri," she replied, gazing up at him, her lips twitching.

He took her hand, and as was his habit whenever he did this (and he did it often), when he had her small hand in his, he rubbed his thumb over the large diamond nestled between bands of gold on her left ring finger.

It was a reminder that she was his.

It was a reminder of his love for her and the gift of her returning the same.

And it was a reminder of his father, who did much in his long life, including helping to make their union possible.

Then, as one, he and his little witch strolled to their Jaguar.

*This concludes The Three Series.*
*Thank you for reading.*

Printed in Great Britain
by Amazon

43359570R00359